— AN ASSASSIN'S CREED SERIES —

LAST DESCENDANTS

P9-DBY-796

— AN ASSASSIN'S CREED SERIES —

LAST DESCENDANTS

FATE OF THE GODS

BY

MATTHEW J. KIRBY

SCHOLASTIC INC.

In bringing this trilogy to a close, I feel grateful for the continued support of this project by an amazing team of fellow storytellers and bookmakers. At Scholastic, Michael Petranek, Samantha Schutz, Debra Dorfman, Charisse Meloto, Monica Palenzuela, Lynn Smith, Jane Ashley, Ed Masessa, and Rick DeMonico have all worked tirelessly to bring readers the best story possible. At Ubisoft, Aymar Azaïzia, Anouk Bachman, Richard Farrese, Caroline Lamache, and Andrew Heitz continue to make me feel at home in the world of Assassin's Creed. Finally, my family and friends, especially Jaime, remain at my side, cheering me on as I begin each new project, and each new adventure. Thank you, all.

© 2018 Ubisoft Entertainment. All Rights Reserved. Assassin's Creed, Ubisoft, and the Ubisoft logo are trademarks of Ubisoft Entertainment in the U.S. and/or other countries.

All rights reserved. Published by Scholastic Inc., *Publishers since 1920.* SCHOLASTIC and associated logos are trademarks and/or registered trademarks of Scholastic Inc.

The publisher does not have any control over and does not assume any responsibility for author or third-party websites or their content.

No part of this publication may be reproduced, stored in a retrieval system, or transmitted in any form or by any means, electronic, mechanical, photocopying, recording, or otherwise, without written permission of the publisher. For information regarding permission, write to Scholastic Inc., Attention: Permissions Department, 557 Broadway, New York, NY 10012.

This book is a work of fiction. Names, characters, places, and incidents are either the product of the author's imagination or are used fictitiously, and any resemblance to actual persons, living or dead, business establishments, events, or locales is entirely coincidental.

ISBN 978-1-338-26702-0

10 9 8 7 6 5 4 3 2 1   18 19 20 21 22

Printed in the U.S.A.   40
First printing 2018

Book design by Rick DeMonico
Map created by Matthew Kirby and Joshua Kirby

To my nephew, Will, a fellow adventurer.

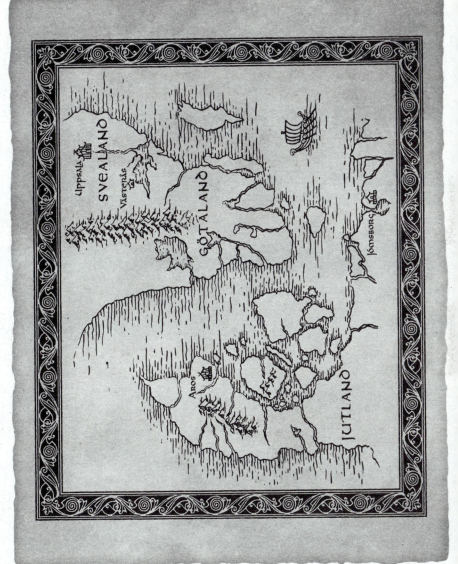

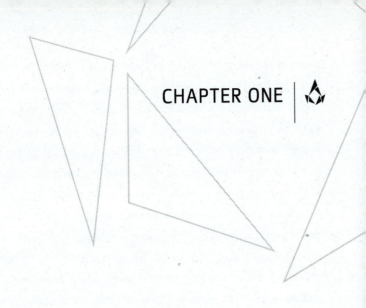

CHAPTER ONE

Sean had grown accustomed to violence, but he didn't yet enjoy it the way his Viking ancestor did. Styrbjörn gloried in the sights, sounds, and smells of battle: the feel of a shield shattering under a blow from his bearded axe, Randgríð; the cleaving of limbs by his Ingelrii sword; the cackle of ravens flocking over corpses.

In fact, Styrbjörn privately felt glad that the Danish king, Harald Bluetooth, had rejected the terms of peace. It meant the battle could begin at last. Even though Sean did not look forward to the violence of the memory, he could admit to himself that he did enjoy the strength and power he felt in his ancestor's body.

Styrbjörn's fleet waited off the coast of Jutland, at Aros, as Harald's longships rowed out to meet him. The Dane-king's fortress would never hold against a land assault by Styrbjörn's force of Jomsvikings, and he no doubt believed his larger fleet could easily win an engagement at sea. It was also possible that Harald suspected that Gyrid, his wife—and Styrbjörn's sister—would commit some treachery unless she was kept far from the battle. Regardless of the reason, Styrbjörn smiled at the oncoming ships.

Sean could taste salt in the air as cormorants and pelicans dove into the sunlit waters around him. The journey to this moment had taken him weeks in the Animus, traversing years of Styrbjörn's life, seeking the moment when his ancestor would finally gain possession of Harald Bluetooth's dagger, the third prong of the separated Trident of Eden. But to find its modern resting place, Sean still had to learn what Styrbjörn had done with it before his death.

The simulation is holding very well, Isaiah said in Sean's ear. *It appears another battle is imminent. Are you ready?*

"I'm ready," Sean said.

Isaiah had removed Sean from the Aerie facility ten days ago, after it was compromised. Sean still hadn't heard from Grace or David or Natalya, or even learned what happened to them. Isaiah said they had gone rogue, and that Victoria was helping them, possibly even working with the Assassin Brotherhood. It was up to Sean to find the Piece of Eden before it fell into the wrong hands.

Your fortitude continues to impress me, Isaiah said.

"Thank you, sir."

The world owes you a debt of gratitude.

Sean smiled within the current of Styrbjörn's mind. "I'm glad I can help."

Let's get to it.

Sean returned his attention to the simulation, focusing on the flexing of the ship's timbers beneath his feet, and the shouts rolling toward Styrbjörn across the water from Harald's advancing ships. He turned toward his own men, his dreaded Jomsvikings. At the heart of his fleet, he'd ordered two dozen ships lashed together into a floating fortress from which his men could cast spears and arrows. His other ships would engage the enemy in close battle, ramming, grappling, and boarding. Styrbjörn planned to find Harald's ship so that he might engage the Danish king in single combat and end the battle quickly. It wouldn't help Styrbjörn's cause for his men to kill off the very warriors he hoped to command.

"I count at least two hundred ships," Palnatoke said beside him, hardened and gray. In the years since Styrbjörn had defeated the chieftain and assumed leadership of the Jomsvikings, the two men had arrived at a grudging respect for each other. "No, more than two hundred ships. Are you sure about this?"

"I am. But if it comforts you, last night several of the men made an offering to Thor. One claimed he was shown a vision in which I reached the coast of my home country with Harald Bluetooth tied to the mast of my ship like a dog." Styrbjörn removed his outer fur, then pulled his axe, Randgríð, free of his belt. "Harald's fleet will be mine."

Palnatoke grunted. "I wonder if the Bluetooth has made offerings to his White Christ."

Styrbjörn gestured across the water toward the oncoming ships. "And if he has, does that worry you?"

"No," Palnatoke said. "The Christ is not a god of war."

Styrbjörn scoffed. "Then what good is he?"

out of the sea onto the deck of the ship, where he rolled to his feet, heavy with water.

Harald's ship still lay within reach, but Styrbjörn would have to cross the decks of two Danish vessels to reach him. He had lost his shield in the water, but had his axe and pulled his dagger from its sheath just as the first two Danes rushed him.

He ducked and parried, throwing them both off-balance, and managed to stab one of them in the back as he stumbled past. In a different battle, on a different day, he would have stayed to finish them, but he could not waste the time. He rushed down the deck of the ship, shouldering men aside, blocking and dodging their blows, letting Randgríð taste their blood when he could.

As he reached the stern, he slashed the man at the rudder with his knife and vaulted over several yards of ocean to the deck of the next ship. The Danes there were ready for him, and a mass of them blocked his path. Beyond them, Harald's vessel had already started to retreat. Styrbjörn sheathed his weapons. Then he wrenched a heavy oar from its spur and, holding it across his chest, he charged at his enemies, using the oar as a bull uses its horns.

He smashed into their line, dug his heels into the deck, and drove the enemy backward. Some went overboard, and some fell and were trampled by Styrbjörn and their own kinsmen. Those that managed to stay on their feet tried to strike at him with their weapons, but he kept them in retreat and none of their blows landed. His back and arms and legs strained, the heat of his muscles turning the seawater in his clothing to steam, until he'd pressed the enemy line all the way to the bow.

Within the power of Styrbjörn's memory, Sean found

the feat he was experiencing almost unbelievable, and if he'd read about it he would have dismissed it as an exaggerated legend. But the strength he experienced in his ancestor's body was very real.

Styrbjörn now stood at the bow and realized Harald's ship had already rowed too far away to make the leap. But he couldn't let the king escape. This battle had to end with Harald's defeat at Styrbjörn's hand, and no other way.

Styrbjörn tossed the oar aside, and before any of the Danes he had plowed under could rouse themselves, he dove into the sea. The cold snapped at him, and the waves shoved him, and the depths reached for him, but he surged through the water toward Harald's vessel, and soon arrows and spears split the water around him. Before he had reached the king's ship, an arrow bit deep into the back of his thigh.

Sean and Styrbjörn let out a roar of pain, but the Viking kept swimming. Moments later, he pulled Randgríð free and used her once again to pull himself onto the ship.

He landed hard on the deck, exhausted, soaked, and bleeding, but still he towered over the shocked Danes. They gaped as Styrbjörn wrenched the arrow from his leg and tossed it into the sea, but after the shock of that moment had passed, two of them attacked. Styrbjörn felled them both before he charged at Harald.

"You are neither man nor king!" he roared.

The intent of those words could not be mistaken. Harald, shorter than Styrbjörn by two hands, flinched and faltered, giving ground before combat had even begun, and in that moment Styrbjörn knew he had won. But Harald had to know it, too. The Danes had to know it.

Styrbjörn did not wait for his opponent to recover his footing before attacking. The first blow from Randgríð cracked Harald's shield, and the second shattered it. Harald raised his sword in a meager posture of defense, but his arm had no strength, and fear filled his eyes.

Styrbjörn laughed so that it filled the ship. "Do you yield?"

"I yield!" Harald said. His sword clanged against the deck. "I yield to you, Bjorn, son of Olof."

Styrbjörn nodded. "Then give the signal before any more of your Danes die."

Harald stared up at him for a moment before nodding to one of his men, who raised a large horn, and then the order of surrender sounded across the waves, picked up, and carried to the edge of the fleet. Several minutes later, the clamor of battle had ceased, Dane and Jomsviking ships rising and falling with the waves.

"It didn't have to come to this," Harald said.

Styrbjörn let out a heavy sigh. "You would prefer I go on raiding your villages?"

"We could have reached an agreement."

"I tried to reach an agreement with you. My sister, your wife, tried to persuade you—"

"You asked for too much, Styrbjörn."

"But now I have everything," he said.

"You want my crown? Is that it?"

"My sister already has your crown. I came for your fleet."

"To attack your uncle? You would take my men to Svealand?"

"Yes," Styrbjörn said. "And you will come with them."

Sean felt the rush of his ancestor's victory, in spite of the pain in his thigh, but he also noticed the dagger at Harald

Bluetooth's belt. It had an odd curve to it, and it obviously wasn't an ordinary blade, but Harald clearly had no idea what it was, or how to use it. That dagger was the entire reason for this simulation, and at some point, it would come into Styrbjörn's possession. A part of Sean wanted to simply reach out and grab the Piece of Eden now, but doing so would desynchronize him from the memory and throw him violently out of the Animus. Instead, he had to wait, as patiently as he could, and let the memory unfold just as it had happened. There wasn't anything Sean could do to change the past.

But the past could change the present. And the future.

CHAPTER TWO

O wen leaned against the third-floor glass railing, over-
looking the open atrium below. The Aerie's glass walls
admitted a pale green light from the mountain forest
that engulfed the facility. Griffin stood next to him,
and together they watched three Templars in dark suits, two
men and a woman, as they marched across the atrium floor
toward the elevator, their footsteps echoing up the vaulted space.

"Who are they?" Owen asked the Assassin.

"I don't know," Griffin said. "But I assume at least one of
them is a member of the Inner Sanctum."

"Inner Sanctum?"

"The Templar governing body." Griffin's posture had tensed
up, and Owen knew what that meant. It was how Griffin looked

in the moment before he struck, hidden blade no longer hidden.

"This bothers you, doesn't it?" Owen nodded toward the elevators right as one of them dinged, and the Templars stepped inside. "Just watching them come and go."

"Templars have killed friends of mine. People I thought of as brothers and sisters. So, yeah, it bothers me." Griffin flexed one of his hands in and out of a fist. "Doesn't matter. The only thing that matters is stopping Isaiah. That means letting them come and go."

"Are you worried Victoria might turn you in?"

"Yes. But I've decided to trust her."

"I wonder what the Templars would do to you if they knew you were here."

"What they would *try* and do, you mean."

Owen shrugged. "Sure."

"Victoria has it under control. And my alliance is with her, not the Order."

"What would they do to her if they knew?" Owen asked.

Back in Mongolia, Victoria had seen that it was necessary to join with Griffin against a common enemy. Now that Isaiah possessed two of the three daggers, the prongs of the Trident of Eden, he had already become too powerful for either the Assassins or the Templars to stop on their own. If he found the third, he would be all-powerful. A conqueror and god-king unlike any the world had seen since Alexander the Great. Humanity didn't have time for ancient rivalries and politics. Victoria and Griffin had kept their alliance a secret from their masters because they couldn't risk any interference in their plan.

"Victoria has already betrayed the Order once before," Griffin said. "They forgave her then. I don't think they'd forgive her a second time. Of course, if we don't stop Isaiah, none of that will matter."

"What about after we stop Isaiah?"

"I hope for her sake the Templars recognize that all of this was necessary."

"What about you?" Owen asked. "What will the Brotherhood do to you?"

"Me?" Griffin looked up at the ceiling of the atrium, a glass dome filled with blue sky and two crisscrossing contrails. "There's no going back for me."

Owen balked. "Never?"

Griffin shook his head.

"Why?"

Griffin said nothing and Owen frowned. This was his first moment alone with the Assassin since they'd left Mongolia, and he still had serious questions about the Brotherhood.

"The last time I was in the Animus," Owen said, "my ancestor killed Möngke Khan. After that, the Mongol army retreated and never recovered. My ancestor literally changed the history of the world, all on her own, but because of an injury to her knee, the Brotherhood just abandoned her. They even took away her father's hidden blade." Owen still shook a little with the pain and confusion of that memory. He raged against the cold and ruthless calculation to leave someone behind. "Her mentor said she wasn't 'useful' anymore."

"She *wasn't* useful anymore. Her knee would never be the same. She couldn't—"

"So? It isn't fair. She was a hero."

"No one said she wasn't."

"But you're saying the Brotherhood would do the same thing to you just for working with Victoria?"

"The last time a Templar spy infiltrated the Brotherhood, we were almost wiped out. So, yes, I'm saying that working with a Templar means that my life as an Assassin is over. I don't regret my choice, and I don't blame anyone else for it."

Owen found that difficult to believe. "You're telling me that you're really okay with them kicking you out?"

Griffin's posture softened. His shoulders relaxed. "Yes," he said.

"But that's not right. It's not fair—"

"Or maybe you're just a kid and you don't get it," Griffin said, his voice harsh. "To serve humanity and the Creed, you have to let go of what you think is true. You have to let go of your ideas of fairness. Even your ideas of right and wrong. One day, you may have to do things that you can't imagine yourself doing right now. You have to realize that in any given moment, what is best for the world may not fit neatly inside your comfortable box."

Owen looked away from him, back toward the floor of the atrium. "I don't know if I want to be a part of something like that."

"No one is forcing you."

Owen turned his back to the open atrium and leaned against the railing. No matter what Griffin said, right and wrong were important. Fairness was important. They had to be, or else it didn't matter whether Owen's father was guilty of robbing a bank and shooting a security guard or not. It didn't matter that he had died in prison for a crime he didn't commit. Owen couldn't accept that, because those things mattered to him more than anything else.

"Isaiah showed me a memory in the Animus," Owen said. "My dad's memory."

Griffin nodded. "Monroe mentioned that."

"Did he tell you about the Assassin? The Brotherhood forced my dad to rob that bank, and then they framed him for that murder."

"He told me that's what Isaiah showed you."

"Are you going to deny it?"

Griffin gestured his arm in a wide circle. "Look where you are. Look what Isaiah has done. And you need me to deny that?"

"Yes," Owen said. "If it's not true, deny it."

"What if I don't?" Griffin said. "What if I refuse to, because it offends me that you would even think about taking Isaiah's word for anything. What would you do then?"

Owen looked away, scowling, and the two of them stood there until the three Templar suits came back down the elevator, crossed the atrium floor, and left the Aerie.

"When we first met," Owen said, "you told me that my dad wasn't an Assassin. But you said he might be involved somehow. You have never explained that. So, no. I'm not taking Isaiah's word for anything, but I'm also not taking yours."

Griffin sighed. "Look, the bank your dad robbed—sorry, was accused of robbing—was a Malta bank. They're a financial arm of Abstergo. That's all I meant." He went quiet. "We'd better go check in with Victoria."

So they walked to the elevator and rode it the rest of the way to the top floor, to the office that had belonged to Isaiah before his defection. The setup reminded Owen of a chapel, with rows of benches, and a large desk-like altar at the front. The others had come, too, and Owen took a seat next to his best friend, Javier. Nearby, Natalya looked exhausted, with dark circles under her eyes, and a somewhat vacant stare. She still blamed herself for the death of the Assassin Yanmei even though everyone else knew it wasn't her fault. The last simulation had been rough on her, too. Her ancestor had shot the arrow that had ruined Owen's knee. Or his ancestor's knee. Sometimes it was hard to keep that straight.

Grace and David sat across from them, next to Monroe, and Victoria stood at the front of the room before the desk, clutching her tablet to her chest.

"I doubt we'll receive another visit like that for at least a week," she said. "Perhaps two. I think it's safe to resume our work in earnest."

"What'd they say?" Monroe asked, leaning forward, his hands joined by interlocking fingers.

"They are focusing the majority of their tactical efforts on finding Isaiah, and they have a few leads. In the meantime, they want me to continue searching for the third prong of the Trident in the Animus. With all of you."

"Will they be sending more agents here?" Griffin asked.

"They're trying to keep this situation contained," she said. "The fewer Templars who know that one of our own has turned, the better. For the time being, the Aerie is ours."

"What about our parents?" Grace asked.

"They remain unaware of what has happened. If they want to visit you as they usually do, they are welcome." Victoria closed her eyes and rubbed her temples with her fingertips. "Which brings me to something I feel I must say."

"What's that?" David asked.

"I will not force you to remain here. After what has happened, here and in Mongolia, I cannot in good conscience keep you against your will. If you wish to leave, I will call your parents to come get you, and you have my word that Abstergo and the Templars will leave you alone."

The silence that followed led Owen to think that some of them might actually be considering her offer. And why wouldn't they? Their lives were in danger if they stayed. But so was the rest of the world, now that Isaiah had two-thirds of a weapon of mass destruction. Owen could leave the Aerie, and he might even be safe from the Templars, but that didn't mean he was safe. It didn't mean his mom and his grandparents were safe. The only way to protect them would be to stop Isaiah, and to do that, Owen had to work with Victoria.

"I'm still in," he said.

"Me too," Javier said.

Grace and David looked at each other, communicating in that wordless brother-sister way. Ever since Mongolia, something had changed in their sibling rivalry, and Owen had noticed that they seemed to be more in tune with each other.

"We're in," Grace said.

Victoria nodded. "That leaves you, Natalya."

Natalya stared at the floor a moment longer, and then looked up. "Where is Sean?"

"Security footage shows that he left with Isaiah," Victoria said. "I assume he is working with Isaiah to locate the third Piece of Eden."

"Willingly?" Javier asked.

"I'm not sure that word applies anymore," Monroe said. "Not when Isaiah has two prongs of the Trident."

"I'm staying," Natalya said, and everyone turned to look at her. "I'm staying for Sean. We have to save him from Isaiah."

"I understand," Victoria said.

"What if he doesn't want to be saved?" David asked. "He already chose to stay behind once before."

"We have to give him the chance," Natalya said.

"I agree." Victoria stepped away from the desk toward them. "And if we're going to help Sean and stop Isaiah, we don't have any time to lose."

"What's the plan?" Griffin asked.

Victoria swiped and tapped her tablet, and a holographic display appeared over her desk. It showed the double helix sequences of all their DNA, with sections of concordance marked, the places where their genetic memories intersected and overlapped. In the beginning of all of this, it had seemed an almost impossible coincidence that Owen and the others had ancestors present at so many of the same historical events, but Monroe's research had revealed there wasn't anything coincidental or accidental about it.

Something had bound their ancestors to the history of the Trident. That same influence, or force, had brought the six of them together at this moment in time. Monroe had learned that each of them carried in their DNA a piece of the collective unconscious, mankind's deepest and oldest memories and myths. Monroe had called that phenomenon an Ascendance Event, but he still didn't understand what caused it, or what it meant.

"We believe Sean and Isaiah have a lead on the third prong

of the Trident," Victoria said. She tapped the screen of her tablet, and the display switched to an image of the earth, with an area circled that included Sweden. "Sean's last simulation took place in the memories of Styrbjörn the Strong, a Viking warrior who fought his uncle for control of the Swedish throne in the late tenth century. Based on my analysis, some of you had ancestors present at their final battle in the year 985."

"Some of us?" Owen said.

"Yes," Victoria said. "Javier, Grace, and David."

"What?" Grace said. "Vikings? Really?"

"That's unexpected," Javier said, his tone dry.

"Perhaps." Victoria switched the image back to their DNA. "But it shouldn't be surprising, really. The Vikings were some of the most widely traveled people in the world during the Middle Ages. They left their mark, from the Middle East to Canada."

"What about us?" Owen nodded toward Natalya. "We don't have ancestors there?"

"No," Victoria said.

Natalya sighed, and Owen realized she was probably grateful for the break. But he wasn't. He didn't like the idea of waiting around outside the Animus. He wanted to go back in with the others.

"You two can always help me," Monroe said. "I've got a lot more work to do."

"Okay," Natalya said.

Owen nodded. At least that was something. And if he couldn't be in the Animus trying to stop Isaiah, maybe he could at least use the time to find out the truth about his father.

"The Viking simulation is almost ready," Victoria said.

"David and Grace, you'll be in your usual Animus rooms. Javier can use one of the spares. Why don't you all go downstairs and find something to eat before we begin."

"I'm not really hungry," Javier said.

"Then go downstairs to rest," she said. "The simulation will be taxing."

Her directive had a clear purpose. Victoria had things she wanted to discuss with Monroe and Griffin alone, and Owen didn't like that. It meant they were still keeping secrets, and he was tired of secrets. But it didn't seem like the right time to push it, so he left the office with the others, and they made their way toward the elevator.

"It's strange to see this place so empty," Grace said.

"I don't know what we'll find to eat," David said. "There's no one left to cook the food."

"There are always snacks down there," Grace said.

Owen pushed the button to call the elevator, and a moment later the doors opened. He watched Natalya as they got inside, wishing he could do something to make her feel better. She kept her head down during the elevator ride, and then lagged behind Grace and David as they led Javier toward the Animus wing of the Aerie facility.

Owen decided to stop and wait for her. "You okay?"

"I'm fine," she said.

"Really? Doesn't seem like you're—"

She stopped and turned to face him. "Are you okay?" she asked, and he felt a spark of anger in her voice. "Are you? With everything that's happening, tell me how you would answer a question like that."

"I—I guess . . . I don't know."

"I'm not okay, Owen. But if I say I'm not okay, you're going to want to talk about it, and I don't want to talk about it."

"We don't have to talk about it."

"Good."

"I guess I just want you to know I'm worried about you."

"Then just say that."

"Okay. I'm worried about you."

"I appreciate that," Natalya said. "I'm worried about you, too. I'm worried about Sean. I'm worried about all of us."

"You don't have to worry about me."

"No? I shot you in the knee with an arrow."

"No, you didn't. That was my ancestor. And your ancestor."

"So? I experienced it. Like it happened to me. But I couldn't change it. I didn't have a choice, and that almost makes it worse. You and Sean and the others, you think the Animus gives you freedom, but to me it's a prison. The past is a prison, where you have no choices, and I don't want to live there."

She walked away from him, and he followed after her. They entered a warm glass corridor that stretched through the woods until it reached another building, and before Owen could think of anything to say to her, they entered the common room, where the others had already found some food, mostly bagged chips and granola bars, but the fridge still held quite a bit of yogurt, milk, and juice. After they had each found what they wanted, they sat down at the same table to eat.

"Do you guys trust Victoria?" Javier asked.

Grace peeled the top off her pink strawberry yogurt. "Do you trust Griffin?"

"I don't think we can really trust either of them." Owen opened up a granola bar and broke off a bite. Javier had spent time with Assassins, and Grace had spent time with the Templars. Loyalties had already begun to form, but not for Owen. "They're both hiding things from us," he said.

David took his glasses off and used his shirt to clean them. "Victoria could have turned us over to the Templars, but she didn't. Griffin could have done his Assassin thing and killed us if he wanted to, but he hasn't. Just because they have secrets doesn't mean we can't trust them."

"That's true," Grace said.

"I still think we need to be careful of Victoria," Javier said. "Try not to tell her anything—"

"I tried that," Natalya said. She hadn't brought any food to the table. She just sat there, looking around at each of them. "I tried not to tell them what I knew. And Yanmei ended up dead because of it."

"That wasn't your fault." David put his glasses back on and looked directly at Natalya. "Remember what Griffin told you? This is war, and Isaiah is the enemy."

"It's actually not that easy for me to just blame Isaiah for my mistakes," Natalya said.

Javier folded his arms and leaned back in his chair. "All I'm saying is, with Victoria, we need to be careful."

"And I agree with you," Natalya said. "I'm still worried about what happens after we find the third piece. Even if we can stop Isaiah, what happens after that? The Templars and the Assassins will just go back to fighting over the Trident, and I don't think either of them should have it."

"So what are you saying?" Grace asked.

"I don't know," Natalya said. "I don't know what to do. For now, we need to save Sean. Or at least give him the chance. After that, I just hope we can figure something out."

A few minutes later, Victoria entered the common room with Monroe and Griffin.

"The simulation is complete," she said. "It's time to begin."

CHAPTER THREE

David wondered how this time in the Animus would work. He and Grace would have the same ancestor, but they couldn't both be in those memories at the same time. During the Draft Riots simulation, he had only experienced an indirect memory, a reconstruction from extrapolated data, while Grace got the full dose. It was the only way they could be in the simulation together, but it also meant David could die at the hands of racist thugs, or at least his ancestor could, a frightening experience he never wanted to think about, let alone repeat.

"Javier," Victoria said.

Next to David, Javier sat upright. "Yes, ma'am?"

"We've prepared your Animus. Monroe will take you there and get you situated."

"Are we all going into the same simulation?" Javier asked.

"No." Victoria looked down at her tablet. "You'll be in separate simulations, though you might interact with the other's ancestor."

"Why keep us separate?" David asked.

"To reduce the risk of desynchronization," Victoria said. "Shared simulations are less stable, and we don't have time to troubleshoot problems. We'll run this operation as cleanly as we can."

"Okay, then." Javier rose to his feet, and he and Monroe left the common room.

"How will that work with us?" Grace asked, nodding toward David. She'd apparently already wondered the same thing he had. "We have the same ancestor."

"You will take turns," Victoria said. "Each of you will get to experience your genetic memories. If it becomes clear that one of you is better suited to this simulation, we might stop switching you out."

David looked at Grace. There was a time that they might've turned this into a competition, because of course he wanted to be the one to go into the Animus. Not that long ago, he'd almost looked at this whole situation like a virtual reality game, back when his ancestor flew planes in World War II. But things had changed since then, and he knew now how important it was that they find the last Piece of Eden. If that meant Grace got to be a Viking instead of him, he was all right with that.

"You can go first," Grace said.

"I was about to say the same thing."

"Sure you were."

He gave her a smile, and then Victoria asked them to follow her.

They left Owen and Natalya in the common room with Griffin and walked with Victoria down the glass Aerie hallways to the Animus room where David had spent a lot of time in the last few weeks. The coppery scent of electricity and the subtle but insistent hum of machinery charged the air, while several computer monitors blinked from the sterile white walls. David crossed to the Animus and stepped inside the waist-high metal ring. He clipped his feet into their mobile platforms, giving his legs almost complete freedom of movement, and then Victoria helped him climb into the full body framework that supported every joint, allowing even the slightest motions. Within that ring, David could walk, run, jump, and climb as the simulation demanded, all without going anywhere.

Victoria tightened the last of the clamps and straps. "Secure?"

"Secure," David said.

"Let me double-check the calibration before we put the helmet on." Victoria stepped away to one of the nearby computer consoles.

"You're going to look pretty stupid in those horns," Grace said.

"Vikings didn't really have horns on their helmets," David said. "In a real battle horns would—"

"I know that." Grace shook her head. "Just be careful, okay?"

Her voice had the same tone as when she used to tell him not to talk to the gangbangers, and which streets to avoid on the way home from school. But he wasn't that kid anymore. "You don't have to take care of me. I'm good."

"Tell that to Dad. Maybe then he'll leave me alone about you."

"I'll be careful."

Victoria returned to the Animus. "Everything looks optimal. Are you ready?"

David nodded, and Grace stepped back and away.

Victoria brought the helmet down from its nest of wires above. "Okay, here we go." She placed the helmet over David's head, and the whole world went black. No sights. No sounds. Like getting smothered with nothing.

Can you hear me? Victoria asked through the helmet.

"Yes."

Good. We're all set out here.

"Whenever you're ready."

Loading the Memory Corridor in three, two, one . . .

A flash of light shredded the black nothing inside David's helmet, and he closed his eyes. When he opened them, he saw gray. A shifting, billowing void of shadow and haze surrounded him. The Memory Corridor was supposed to make the transition to the full simulation smoother, and David thought it probably accomplished that, except nothing could make the next part easier.

Parietal insertion in three, two, one . . .

David took a deep breath, and then his head took an electromagnetic beating. The energy pulses were supposed to quiet the part of his brain that kept him grounded in time and space, but for several moments he couldn't think of anything else except the hammer inside his skull.

Loading genetic identity in three, two, one . . .

The pain receded. David gave it a moment, then opened his eyes and looked down at himself, blinking away the last of his disorientation, only to feel a new type of confusion set in.

He was a giant.

Or as close to a giant as a man could get.

David raised his ancestor's hands and studied them, fascinated. It wasn't their white skin, although that was weird, but the sheer size of them. They were somehow more than just hands, as if David were wearing leather baseball mitts. His arms and his legs were huge, too, but not like he'd been going to the gym. He didn't look like a bodybuilder. He was just big. Tall and wide and strong.

David? Victoria asked. *How are you doing?*

"Good," David said. "But it feels weird for you to call me that when I feel like Goliath."

Victoria laughed in his ear. *Written records from this time period are scarce, and extremely unreliable. We know very little about who your ancestor is, or how he will be involved with the Piece of Eden. I can't even tell you his name.*

"I should be able to figure all that out once I settle into his memories."

Good. But it might be a bit of a rough transition until you do.

"If I can't get it to work, Grace can try."

That's the idea. Are you ready for me to load the full simulation?

"Give me a second."

Of course.

David turned his thoughts inward, searching for the mind of his ancestor within his own, digging deep for a voice that wasn't his, listening closely. When he finally heard it, he engaged that voice in a conversation. Not of words, but the thoughts and memories of his ancestor, a farmer and warrior named Östen Jorundsson.

Östen owned his own land, a modest holding at the base of

a round hill not far from a lake, with pastures, a small woodland of spruce and oak, and a spring that bubbled water cold enough to crack teeth. Östen took far more pride in his land than he did his many victories in battle. He fought when called upon by his king, or when honor demanded it, but would rather be at home, sharing a warm fire next to his wife, or fishing with his son, or singing with his daughters. It was a life David could want for himself.

"I think I'm ready," he said.

Excellent. Loading the full simulation in three, two, one . . .

The Memory Corridor shattered into a blinding, crystalline dust, which ebbed and swirled, then gradually massed together into sturdier forms, assuming the vague shapes of buildings, trees, and ships. David's eyes adjusted to this new reality forcing its way into his mind. But it wasn't really a new reality. It was an old reality and an old voice speaking for the first time in centuries, and soon David stood fully in Östen's world.

Before him, rich green grass covered the main pasture, grazed by his twenty-six head of cattle. They were sturdy mountain stock, mostly white with black spots, and he hadn't polled them, because horns made bears and wolves doubt themselves. The sun had begun to dip low, spreading a golden patina over his farm and the land below, all the way to the shores of Mälaren to the south.

David knew, through Östen, that it was time to bring the herd in. So he gave Östen his voice, and then cupped his hands to his mouth. The cows looked up at his call, but went back to grazing, more interested in the summer grass at their hooves than anything he had to offer. Östen glanced down at Stone

Dog, who lay at his feet, perfectly still, eager, waiting for a nod from his master to shoot him out into the field.

David hadn't seen Stone Dog's breed before. He was like a cross between a stubby-legged corgi and a wolf, but he could run, and he knew just how to round up the herd, circling, barking, pressing the cattle together, and driving them toward Östen. They came mooing and bellowing, and with Stone Dog's help, Östen pushed the herd into its fenced enclosure for the night, a small paddock near enough to keep watch against predators.

"Well done," Östen said once the cows had been secured.

Stone Dog's tongue flapped from one side of his mouth, and his eyes shone.

"Let's go see how Tørgils is getting on, eh?"

Östen turned from the cattle in the paddock toward the large byre that stood next to the stable, near the hall, and on the far side of it he found his son chopping wood. At fifteen, Tørgils stood as tall as Östen had at his age, but he had his mother's almost-black hair, the color of wet soil. Arne the Dane labored next to him in his breeches and loose-hanging tunic, and as Östen surveyed the results of their splitting work, an ugly awareness crept over David and then seized him by the neck.

Arne was a slave.

Östen used a different word in his thoughts and memories. He called Arne a *thrall*. But the word didn't matter. What mattered was that David's ancestor owned a *slave*.

"Father?" Tørgils had stopped swinging his axe. "Are you well?"

David didn't know what to say. He felt too shocked and angry to listen to Östen's voice. He didn't want to hear it. To think of what slavery had done to African Americans, and to the world, only to find out that his own ancestor had enslaved someone else . . . David wanted to shout back at Östen, but he couldn't, because he was supposed to *be* Östen.

At his side, Stone Dog growled at him suddenly, his hackles high and head low as he backed away from the strange boy wearing his master's body.

"Father?" Tørgils asked again.

Arne the Dane, slender and hard as a nail, looked at David now. "Östen?"

David shook his head. No, he was *not* Östen.

The simulation trembled, distorting the farm with ripples and seams, and the quake only worsened with each moment that David refused to synchronize.

What's going on? Victoria asked. *You were doing great, but now we're losing stability. Are you okay?*

"No," David said.

The simulation is about to collapse.

"I know!"

David, whatever is happening, you need to rein it in.

His anger did not feel like something he could control.

I can pull you out and put Grace in—

"No." David didn't want that. He didn't need Grace to protect him or rescue him anymore. Besides, she'd probably have a harder time with their slave-owning ancestor than he did. "Just hang on," he said and took a deep breath.

Tørgils, Arne the Dane, and Stone Dog had all been caught in the glitch storm, frozen in place. David focused on the dog first, and listened to Östen's memory of how Stone Dog had been trampled by a two-year-old cow when he was a pup, but jumped up and shook it off as if nothing had happened. "That dog's head must be made of stone," Arne had said, and the name planted itself.

David smiled at that memory, and the simulation jolted back to life, still uneven and jerky, but moving again.

Excellent, David. Keep doing what you're doing.

David turned to Östen's son next, remembering a time from his toddling when he had lost a perfectly good axe trying to hunt fish with it. The water had claimed the weapon, and Tørgils had splashed and shouted at the fish, enraged. Östen had laughed and taught his son how to use a hook and handline, and Tørgils had taken to it like an heir to the god Njörðr. Not long ago, at the age of fourteen winters, he had pulled in a salmon the length of Östen's leg, and the pride of that moment still lingered.

These were memories David could listen to. These were moments he could want to be a part of, and they made synchronization possible.

You're almost there. Simulation stabilizing . . .

But when David looked at Arne, his anger flared again, and his grip on synchronization slipped. This wasn't something he could reconcile. It wasn't possible to identify with this. It went against everything David knew to be right.

He remembered how many winters ago, before Tørgils was born, Östen had joined a raid against the Danes, from which he'd brought Arne back in chains as his prisoner and thrall. It didn't matter that Östen had since removed those chains, or that he wasn't a cruel master.

It was still wrong.

When David tried to convince himself it was right, or tried to see slavery how Östen saw it, his anger sent the simulation reeling again.

We're wasting time, Victoria said. *I need to know if you can do this.*

David didn't want to admit that he couldn't. He just needed time and perspective to figure out a way to get his mind in agreement with Östen's. He didn't need Grace.

David, the simulation is—

"I know." He could see for himself that he was desynchronizing. "Just wait."

For what?

He didn't know. He took one more look at Arne, and tried to force himself to believe it was right to enslave the Dane. But no amount of will could ram something into his head that wouldn't fit.

David—

The world fell into a blender, taking his mind and body with it. For several moments, he felt only pain that radiated from every point in his body, all at once, as though layers of him were being sliced away, exposing nerves, until the last shred of him vanished, and only his mind remained, spinning around and around in a maelstrom, detached from any place or point in time, or even a sense of who he was.

David.

He heard the voice, but it wasn't holding still, and he didn't know where it was coming from.

David, I'm going to take your helmet off.

The voice sounded familiar, but before he could figure out

who was speaking to him, a white-hot light burned his eyes back into his head, and then the fire raged from his mind down his spine, into his stomach and his arms and legs.

"David, can you hear me?" the first voice asked.

"David?" came another.

He knew the second voice better than the first, and he opened his eyes. Grace stood in front of him. Grace, his sister. David blinked, and it all rushed back at once. Who he was. Where he was. Why he was there. Like someone had opened the floodgates, and it was enough to drown him. A swell of nausea climbed up his throat.

"I'm gonna throw up," he said.

Victoria lifted a small bucket to his mouth just in time. His stomach convulsed, painfully, and he lost the food he'd eaten. Grace stood by until he was finished, and then she helped him out of the harness, and the Animus, onto his wobbly legs.

"And that's why you don't desynchronize," she said.

"Now you tell me."

She put her arm around him. "What happened in there?"

David shook his head. "Give me a minute."

Grace helped him over to a swivel chair, and he fell into it, hard enough to send it rolling backward a couple of feet. Victoria walked over to him, jabbing at her tablet.

"Your neurovitals looked good during the simulation," she said. "Elevated blood pressure, though."

"I was angry."

"Angry at what?" Grace asked.

"Angry at him. Our ancestor."

Grace frowned. "Why?"

"He—" David's head still throbbed, making it hard to form a sentence longer than a few words, and it would take a lot of words to explain. "Can we . . . talk about this later?"

Grace looked at Victoria. "Yes."

Victoria paused a moment, and then offered an abrupt nod. "Fine. We'll take a break. Then we can debrief and plan the next step. Perhaps you can help prepare your sister for her attempt. In the meantime, I'm going to go check on Javier."

She left the room, seeming irritated, and Grace looked hard at David, not saying anything.

"What?" he finally asked.

"Are you okay?"

"You don't need to take care of me. I'm okay. I just need to rest."

"Fine." Now she was the one who seemed irritated. "But then I want an explanation."

David nodded, hoping that Javier's ancestor would turn out to be the one with access to the Piece of Eden. That way, it wouldn't matter who David's ancestor had been, or what he had done.

CHAPTER FOUR

Javier waited, suspended in a structural body harness as Monroe initiated the machine's core. He had never been in an Animus like this. The previous two had kept him reclined, but this one allowed complete stationary mobility, and it felt good to think about getting back in a simulation. Javier had tried to make himself useful while Owen explored the memories of his Chinese ancestor. He'd even broken into a police warehouse and stolen the evidence used at the trial of Owen's father. But that wasn't the same as chasing a Piece of Eden through history. Nothing was as important as finding the rest of the Trident before Isaiah did.

"They've made some upgrades to the Parietal Suppressor," Monroe said.

"The what?"

"The Parietal—never mind. It'll take too long to explain. The point is, this will feel different than my Animus, or Griffin's."

"Different how?"

"Hard to describe."

"You can run it, though, right?"

"Of course I can." Monroe stood. "Are you ready?"

Javier nodded. "Yes."

Monroe checked each of the straps, clips, and buckles one more time, making sure Javier was secure. "So are you an Assassin now, or what?" he asked almost casually as he pulled the Animus helmet down from the nest of wires overhead.

Javier hesitated before answering. "No."

"You sure about that?"

"Why?"

Monroe shrugged. "Just try to remember what I've told you."

Javier may not have become a member of the Brotherhood, but he had definitely thought about it. "I believe in free will."

"So do I. That's why I don't want to see any of you giving it over to the Templars. Or the Assassins." He lifted the helmet. "Here we go."

Javier let him place the helmet over his head, surprised at the totality of the barrier it created between him and the outside world. He heard nothing and saw nothing. But then something buzzed in his ear, and Monroe spoke.

You reading me?

Monroe's voice had guided him through Mexico in the sixteenth century, and New York City during the Draft Riots of 1863. "Just like old times."

This part won't feel like old times. I'm going to engage the Parietal Suppressor. You'll notice it, but it will pass quickly. Okay?

That didn't sound pleasant. "Okay . . ."

This is it. In three, two, one . . .

The Animus shoved an ice pick down through the top of Javier's head. At least, that was how it felt. He gasped and clenched his teeth against the shock and the pain, which only got worse when someone stirred the ice pick. Javier lost track of everything except that agony.

Hang on. Almost there.

Another excruciating moment passed, and then the pain vanished as quickly as it had come. Javier opened his eyes and saw the undulating void of the Memory Corridor.

You all right? Monroe asked.

"Yeah." Javier took a deep breath. "Does it do that every time?"

They say it gets easier.

"I can't imagine it getting worse."

I'm about to load your ancestor's identity. This will feel more like what you're used to. Are you ready?

"Sure."

I'll count you down again. Three, two, one . . .

Javier felt an invader in his mind, an occupying force marching through his thoughts, trying to replace them. Monroe was right. This felt familiar. Javier would soon have to surrender his own mind to synchronize with the simulation. He looked down at who he would become and saw a lean frame, perhaps early twenties, with white, pale skin, and freckles on the backs of his hands. He wore close-fitting wool and leather armor, with a short beard and a shaved head.

We don't have any information on this guy. You'll have to get to know him.

"Then let's do this."

You got it. Loading full simulation in three, two, one . . .

The Memory Corridor darkened, turning to night. Black shadows emerged, and stars sparked to life overhead. A moment later, Javier stood on a narrow forest path, listening to the wind shake the trees to either side. He smelled wood smoke on the air, coming from the east, which meant the camp lay nearby.

But what camp, Javier didn't know. That thought had come unbidden, an advance scout ahead of the main force. Javier let down his guard to admit an army of thoughts like that, surrendering his mind to that of his ancestor, and Thorvald Hjaltason took the field. The Svear crouched and slipped away into the cover of the trees, following the trail of smoke, creeping toward the camp, and Javier became aware of the completely silent way in which Thorvald moved. The way his ancestor extended his senses into the almost total darkness of the woods. The hidden blade strapped to his wrist.

"He's an Assassin," Javier said.

So it would seem.

That wasn't Monroe. That was Victoria.

"So you're watching me now?"

Yes. Monroe has important work to do.

Javier felt uneasy with the idea of a Templar managing his simulation, even though his ancestor in New York City had been an Assassin hunter, Cudgel Cormac, the grandson of the Templar Shay Cormac.

It seems you have both Assassin and Templar ancestors.

But Javier knew which one he preferred and settled back into formation behind Thorvald, allowing the Assassin freedom to pursue his objective, whatever that might be. Though summer had come, winter still had its sword drawn, and the night air carried its cold edge. The aroma of wood smoke grew stronger, and Thorvald kept to the thick of it, downwind, in case his targets had dogs that might scent his approach, while the wind covered the sounds of an owl he disturbed with his passing.

Soon, he saw the distant flicker of firelight through the trees, and at that point, he went up. The canopy of the trees concealed his approach as he climbed, leapt, and swung his way toward the encampment, free-running through the branches and trunks in the same way Javier's Templar ancestor had traversed the rooftops of Manhattan.

When he reached the camp, he came to a stop, high in the shadows, and settled down to listen. The fire popped below him, sending up sparks and smoke nearby. Five men sat around a stone ring, sucking on the heads of the fish they'd had for dinner. They were bondsmen who had fled their masters before settling their debts, and had been living in the wilds, which their faces and clothing spoke plainly. Thorvald supported their freedom, but something had brought them back to the Uppland, something worth risking capture over, and he needed to discover what it was.

For a long while, the bondsmen said little.

But Thorvald knew patience. And he waited.

When the fire burned low and needed more wood, one of the men, with a nose like a raven's beak, ordered another to fetch it.

"Fetch it yourself," the other said. "For the last time, I don't take orders from you, Heine."

"And you best mind your tongue, Boe Björnsson," Heine said. "My memory is as long and sharp as my spear."

"And yet, you forget that I broke your nose." Boe stared at the first man from across the red coals. The other three hadn't moved, but seemed to be watching the exchange with mild amusement.

"I haven't forgotten." Heine paused. "You'll know that, before the end."

"So you've told me," Boe said. "Many times."

"You doubt me?"

Boe laughed. "Have I fetched the wood?"

"No. But you'll wish you had when I gut you—"

"That's enough, Heine," one of the other men finally said, having apparently grown impatient. "Save it for the real battle. After that, you can kill each other at your leisure."

The real battle? Thorvald didn't know what that meant, but it seemed that these bondsmen had come back to Uppland expecting a fight. But over what? And against which enemy? These questions needed answers before Thorvald could leave.

Heine rose to his feet, glowered at Boe with a look Thorvald knew well, and then stormed away from the camp into the woods. The others settled down to sleep, and Thorvald watched and waited some more.

The fire turned to embers, filling the camp with the red light of Muspelheim, and the men began to snore. Then Thorvald saw Heine returning, but not as a comrade. He came slinking through the shadows, staying just over the firelight's border, until he stood near Boe. Thorvald knew what he intended before the bondsman had even pulled out his knife.

A breath later, Boe's eyes shot open as Heine pounced on him, smothering the man's mouth with one hand as he drove the blade into Boe's throat with the other.

"You see now, don't you?" Heine whispered like a snake.

Boe thrashed weakly, silently, but he was already a dead man, and Heine held him down until the life went out of his still-open eyes. The murderer pulled his knife free, wiped its blade and his hands on Boe's cloak, then snatched up his pack. The other three men slept on as Heine vanished into the woods.

Thorvald left them with the corpse and pursued Heine, but without overtaking him right away. Instead, he simply kept pace until Heine had put enough distance between himself and the camp to avoid rousing the others. Then Thorvald surged ahead through the branches to lie in wait, and as Heine scurried below, Thorvald fell upon him, driving him hard into the ground.

Heine buckled with a crack and a whimper, and before he could make another sound or fight back, Thorvald touched his hidden blade to Heine's throat.

"Struggle and you'll drown in your own blood," he said, crouching over him.

Heine swallowed and the apple of his throat moved the tip of the blade. "Who are you?"

"You haven't realized it yet, but your back is broken. You think you're in a position to question me?"

A moment of night-silence passed in which Heine looked down at his legs, but they didn't move. His face paled against the darkness.

"You see now, don't you?" Thorvald said. "Answer my questions, and I might give you a swift death."

Heine's nod was slight and full of fear.

"You're an escaped bondsman, but you've come back. Why?"

"I heard I could earn my freedom. My own land."

"How?"

"By fighting the king."

Thorvald had not expected that answer. Eric had enemies, but none who would be foolish enough to rise in rebellion. "Why?"

"Because he is a usurper," Heine said, almost spitting the last word.

"So it is for Styrbjörn that you fight?"

Heine shook his head. "I don't know. We were simply told to be battle ready."

"Your fighting days are over."

"Then finish me."

Thorvald held the hidden blade to Heine's throat for a moment longer, but then he pulled it away, and with a flick it disappeared, back inside his leather gauntlet. "No," he said, still crouching. "I need you to give the other bondsmen a message."

"What message?"

"That I will be hunting them. I stand for their freedom, but if they return to the Uppland in treachery, I will find them and kill them. If they are already in the Uppland, or pretending loyalty, I will root them out. If Styrbjörn is returning, there will be war, and if the bondsmen will not fight for their king, they will fight for no one. Do you understand?"

"How—how do you expect me to deliver this message?"

Thorvald rose to his feet and looked down at the wreck of a man, his useless legs bent at wrong angles. "In the morning, when your former companions discover your treachery against Boe, they will come looking for you."

Heine's mouth opened. "No. Please—"

"You will tell them exactly what I have just told you, and in that act perhaps you will reclaim a small amount of honor. Then I expect you'll plead with them for mercy."

"They will show me none."

"As you showed none to Boe."

Thorvald turned his back on the murderer and strode away, back down the forest paths along which he had come. He wondered if Heine would call after him to beg, but he didn't. Thorvald didn't know whether the man would convey the message, but the words didn't actually matter. Heine's body would be message enough. His fellow bondsmen would want to know what had happened to him, and even if he told them nothing, they would know they were in danger. For their cowardly lot, perhaps that would be enough to send them back into hiding. The larger problem would be Styrbjörn, if he was indeed preparing to attack.

Thorvald needed to return to the Lawspeaker with this, and he didn't think it could wait until morning.

He hurried through the forest, back to the clearing where he had tied his horse, Gyllir. The brown stallion, like the rest of his northern brethren, stood only fifteen hands tall, but he was agile, and strong, and never tired. Thorvald mounted and spurred him toward Uppsala, where the king of Svealand had his hall and the gods had their temple, galloping through the night along lonely roads.

Toward dawn, as the sun reached over the hillocks to the east, Thorvald reached the line of posts that led to the holy place. Each stood twenty feet tall, hewn from the straightest pine, placed upright every fifteen feet in beds of stone. He followed this line of pillars, each carved with images honoring the gods and the heroes who had risen to live with the gods, past the mounded barrows and graves of kings, until he came to the temple itself.

The morning light glinted off the shields that adorned its walls and roof and the golden paint that gilded its pillars. The temple's size also distinguished it from other noble halls, standing twice as long and half again as wide as that of King Eric. But that was as it should be. This place housed the gods.

Thorvald dismounted before its great doors and led Gyllir around to one of the outbuildings near the temple, a small hut with walls of clay and a turf roof. He tied his horse outside it and pounded on the door.

"The gods aren't awake yet, and neither am I!" came a shout from within.

"It's me," Thorvald said.

Footsteps approached, and then the door opened. "Thorvald, come in. I didn't expect you back so soon."

Torgny the Lawspeaker waved him inside. From behind Thorvald's mind, Javier studied the old man, who might have been the most ancient human being he had ever seen, and certainly the closest thing to a wizard. Torgny wore a long tunic, belted loosely at his waist, that gave the impression of a robe, and his hair and beard were both flowing and white. His milky eyes, and the way he held his head up without fixing his gaze on anything, let Javier know the Lawspeaker was blind.

Thorvald stepped into his hut and shut the door behind him. The single room contained little light, save the few slanted beams that cut their way in through cracks and gaps in the walls. Torgny also possessed few pieces of furniture, but the two men took seats on opposite sides of a wooden table near the old man's bed.

"Are you hungry?" the Lawspeaker asked.

"That can wait."

"When food can wait, the Valkyries ride." Torgny leaned

closer, over the table, and lowered his voice. "Tell me what you have learned."

"It's Styrbjörn."

"What about that upstart?"

"The bondsmen you sent me to find. They had come back for war."

"Styrbjörn means to make war against Eric?"

"I'm not certain, but I believe so."

Torgny pushed back from the table, rapping on its edge with the fingers of both hands. "I have heard rumors, of course. He took command of the Jomsvikings. But he's been raiding against the Danes. I thought he was the Bluetooth's problem."

"Perhaps he was."

"But perhaps not any longer."

"What would you have me do?"

Torgny looked down into his lap, his head bowed, a posture he adopted when deep in thought. Back when Thorvald had first met the Lawspeaker and had seen this habit, he'd thought that the old man might be dozing off. Though that might occasionally happen, in spite of Torgny's denials, Thorvald had nevertheless learned it was foolish to ever assume the Lawspeaker wasn't listening.

"Go east, to the sea," Torgny finally said. "If Styrbjörn is coming, he will bring his fleet through Mälaren."

"Yes, Lawspeaker."

Torgny looked up, and his eyes found Thorvald's, as if the old man could see him, and it felt as if he had more to say.

"Yes, Lawspeaker?"

"Why now?" the old man asked, almost to himself.

"Pardon me?"

Torgny spoke louder. "Our Brotherhood has so far been successful in keeping the Order from infecting this land, but our enemy is out there, and we must remain vigilant."

Javier realized then that both of these men were Assassins, one the mentor, one the student. It seemed that Thorvald did what Torgny no longer could.

"Why do you mention the Order?" Thorvald asked.

"I am worried about what Styrbjörn brings with him. His sister married the Bluetooth, who has had traffic with the Franks and with Rome. It is possible that Styrbjörn, whether he is aware of it or not, has become a tool of the Order. He must be stopped, Thorvald. Even if I am wrong and he does not serve the Order, he does not bring freedom to Svealand. We must keep Eric in power."

"I understand."

"Go," the Lawspeaker said. "Watch the seas. I believe you will see Styrbjörn's ships before long, and when you do, report back to me."

"Yes, Lawspeaker." Thorvald bowed his head. "And what will you do?"

"I will speak with the king," the old man said. "I will tell him that war may be upon us. Then I will eat my breakfast."

CHAPTER FIVE

N atalya sat in the common room with Owen, and things were still a bit tense between them after the confrontation they'd had in the corridor. For a long time, neither of them spoke.

She hadn't meant to unload on him like she had, but it was getting hard to feel so alone. It didn't seem like any of the others thought the way she did about any of this. It didn't seem like Yanmei's death upset them the way it should. The way it still upset her. It didn't seem like they worried about what would happen to the Trident after they found it, or more important, who would control it. Natalya found it exhausting to be the only one who seemed to really see what was going on.

"At least you don't have to worry about going into the Animus this time," Owen said, breaking the silence in the room.

Natalya nodded. "I guess."

"I thought you said the past was a prison."

"It is."

"Then why—"

"I don't *like* going into the Animus, but at least if I do, I can try to do something to stop the Assassins and the Templars from finding the Trident."

Owen looked at her for a moment. "I guess that's true."

Natalya knew that both times Owen had been in the Animus, he'd experienced the memories of Assassin ancestors. But he didn't seem to be committed to the Brotherhood like Javier already appeared to be. "Which side are you on?" she asked him.

He fumbled with the zipper on the Assassin-issued leather jacket he still wore. "I don't know. My own side, I guess. Like Monroe."

"Isaiah showed you a simulation of your father's memories, didn't he?"

"Yeah. Before he went all megalomaniac."

"Did you learn anything from it?"

"Nothing I can trust. Monroe is right. It would be pretty easy for the Templars to manipulate a simulation so I see what they want me to see." He paused. "But I don't trust the Assassins, either."

Maybe Owen did see some things the same way Natalya did. "So what are we going to do?"

"Like you said, we need to save Sean. So I'm planning to play along for now. Stopping Isaiah is what's most important. At least Griffin and Victoria both know that."

"Their truce won't last forever."

"No," Monroe said behind them, "it won't."

Natalya and Owen both spun around, and Monroe, standing in the doorway, held up his hands.

"Relax, I wasn't spying on you. I just got here. You two ready?"

Natalya nodded and rose to her feet. Owen joined her, and they followed Monroe from the common room and back down the glass corridor to the Aerie's main hub. From there, they crossed to a wing of the facility where Abstergo scientists had been doing research prior to Isaiah's defection. They passed several darkened laboratories filled with equipment and surrounded by glass walls. Natalya saw what looked like artificial arm and leg prosthetics, as well as different pieces and types of Animus technology.

"It's been a long time since I was here," Monroe said, leading them into one of the labs.

Automatic lights switched on at their presence, illuminating the long room and filling it with a barely audible buzzing. There were several wide workstations and cubicles along the walls and also down the middle of the room, each with its own white desk, a bank of computer monitors, and other tools and instruments. Natalya recognized the centrifuges, but didn't know what most of the other devices were.

Monroe walked to a computer terminal near a very large wall-mounted screen, and switched it on. Natalya and Owen waited as he navigated through the Aerie's database.

"Let's see what they've done with all my work," he said.

Several minutes went by, until Monroe seemed to find what he was looking for. He switched the image from his computer monitor over to the big screen.

"There it is," he said. "And they've added all the current data."

Natalya studied the images in front of her. On the left, she saw representations of DNA fragments, one next to her name and picture, and another next to Owen's. Each of the teens Monroe had brought together possessed a link in a larger chain displayed on the screen. To the right of that, Natalya saw a time-line of world history that traced the appearances of the Trident and its prongs.

"This is the Ascendance Event," Monroe said. "There are two dimensions to it. On the left, you see the results of my work studying the DNA from humanity's collective unconscious."

"The what?" Natalya asked.

"She wasn't there when you explained that," Owen said.

"Oh." Monroe looked in her direction. "Right. So, psychologists have theorized that human beings all have an ancient, shared collection of memories, which explains why so many people are automatically afraid of snakes and spiders, and why stories of heroes are so similar all over the world. We call it the collective unconscious."

Natalya looked at the screen again. "And you found DNA for it?"

"Yes," Monroe said. "You can think of it as an embedded signal in our genome. But in the present day, it only survives in fragments. I've been trying to put together the complete sequence for years, without success. Then I found you two and the others." He pointed at the screen. "Between the six of you, I now have all of it."

"Wait." Natalya looked again at the images, evaluating the meaning of what he was saying. "What are the chances of that?" she asked.

"Not tremendously unlikely." Monroe smiled. "But it doesn't

stop there." He pointed at the second half of the screen. "The six of you also happen to be connected to the history of the Trident through your ancestors, across time and even continents. And to answer your question, the odds of that, combined with the collective unconscious, are so low, it might as well be impossible. Yet here we are. Which means that all of this can't be due to chance."

"If it's not due to chance," Natalya said, "that means . . . are you saying it's intentional?" Even as she asked that question, she wondered who, or what, could bring something like this about.

"Intentional is a tricky word," Monroe said. "It implies consciousness, for one thing, which is not what I'm saying. I don't think anyone or anything is steering this ship. But it might be that the autopilot has kicked in."

"But that means someone had to program the autopilot in the first place, right?" Owen asked.

Monroe sighed. "Let's not overextend the metaphor. I'm a scientist. I stick to what is observable and measurable, and that's what you're going to do while you help me."

"What can we do?" Natalya asked.

"We have two questions." Monroe moved to a whiteboard and grabbed a dry-erase marker. He pulled the cap and started writing, the tip of the pen squeaking, and Natalya smelled the light fumes of the chemical ink. "First," Monroe said, "what is the nature of the collective unconscious DNA? Isaiah thought of it in terms of power and control. He wanted to know how he could use it as a weapon. But I don't think that's its purpose. Second, how does the collective unconscious relate to the Trident? As we've discussed, it can't be a coincidence that both of these dimensions have emerged at the same time. I believe they're part of a larger event. In fact, I think the collective unconscious might even hold the key to stopping the Trident."

"How?" Natalya said.

"I'm not sure," Monroe said. "But if you look at the history of this weapon with your ancestors, it's almost like the ascendance of the collective unconscious has taken place in *response* to the Trident. But we need to understand the collective unconscious before we can conclude that."

"Okay," Owen said, and took a seat at one of the workstations. "So how do we understand it?"

"That's where things get interesting," Monroe said.

"Interesting how?" Owen asked.

"Now that I have the complete sequence for the collective unconscious, I can use the Animus to create a simulation of it." Monroe snapped the cap back on the marker.

Owen leaned forward in his chair and looked over at Natalya. She took a seat of her own in an ergonomic chair made of white mesh and plastic. She was trying to imagine what a simulation of the collective unconscious would look like, but couldn't.

"How would that work?" she asked.

"Well, it's really just memory," Monroe said. "Old memory. The oldest memory, actually. This DNA goes back to the beginning of humanity. But it's still memory, which means the Animus can use it."

Owen pointed back and forth between himself and Natalya. "And you want us to go into this simulation?"

"Yes," Monroe said. "And to answer your next question, no, I don't have any idea what it will be like. It could make no sense at all, or it might be full of archetypes."

"Archetypes?" Natalya said. "Like from stories?"

"Basically," Monroe said. "Archetypes are images found around the world that have a shared meaning. Like the way most everyone can recognize the figure of the wise old mentor, or the fact that just about every culture in the world has its own version of a dragon. The collective unconscious is made up of archetypes and instincts."

"Will it be safe?" Natalya asked.

Owen frowned at her. "Why wouldn't it be?"

"No, she's right," Monroe said, and nodded for her to continue.

Natalya looked at Owen. "Think about synchronization. How is that even going to work with this simulation? What about desynchronization? And then there are the Bleeding Effects. What will those be in a simulation like this?"

"Exactly," Monroe said. "This simulation comes with risks because we don't know how your minds will receive it or cope with it. If I'm being candid with you, it could be extremely dangerous."

"Dangerous how?" Owen asked.

"You won't be going into this simulation in the memories of an ancestor. You'll be taking your own mind fully into it. If you get lost in the simulation, or too deeply traumatized by it, you could do irreparable damage to your psyche. Your mind could break."

Those were the very things Natalya feared, though she wouldn't have necessarily put it into those words. A broken mind sounded terrifying.

"And you want us to go in there anyway?" Owen asked.

"The decision is yours," Monroe said. "It always is. But no,

I don't *want* you to go in there. I don't want any of this. But our situation is dire, and this is the best way to understand what the collective unconscious really is. Maybe the only way."

"Why don't you go in?" Natalya asked.

"That's a fair question," Monroe said. "One answer is that I can't. You might have heard something about it from Isaiah and Victoria. When I was a kid, my father was . . ." He bowed his head, and the skin around his eyes tightened, as if he felt pain. "Well, let's just say he left marks. Deep scars. Physical and emotional. I tried to use the Animus as a way to go back and confront my father. All that did was open up old wounds. And it created new ones." He paused. "Bottom line, you can't change the past. Now a normal Animus simulation can be dangerous for my mind, but a simulation like this would be impossible."

In that moment, the way Natalya looked at Monroe changed. He had his own past and his own secret pains, which she had never deeply considered. But he had also said that was only one answer to why he couldn't go into the collective unconscious. "Is there another answer?" she asked.

"I also have very little of the collective unconscious DNA," he said. "They're not my memories. Same with Griffin and Victoria. For the simulation to remain stable and make synchronization possible, whoever goes in there needs to have as much of that DNA as possible. That means you six are the best candidates, and of the six, you happen to be the two here working with me."

"Lucky us," Owen said.

Natalya felt some pretty fierce apprehension about this, but she had also become intensely curious about what she would experience in the simulation. What would she see if it worked? This would be like going back in time to the beginning of mankind. These would be the memories that every person on earth shared, to some degree. Regardless of who you were or where you came from, these were the memories everyone had in common. Natalya wasn't going to pass up an opportunity to catch a glimpse of them. If she got in there, and things seemed dangerous or harmful, she could always quit. But until then, she planned to try.

"I'll go," she said.

Monroe nodded. "I admire your bravery."

"I'm in, too," Owen said. "But I want you to do something for me."

Natalya wasn't surprised by that, and Monroe didn't seem to be, either.

"I think I can guess what that might be," Monroe said.

Natalya could guess, too.

Owen stood up and folded his arms. "I want you to let me see the real simulation of my father's memories. You couldn't before, because you didn't have the right kind of Animus in your bus." He looked around. "Now you do. I don't trust what Isaiah showed me. But I trust you."

Monroe looked at Owen for a moment, and then nodded. "Okay. You do this for me, and I'll do that for you."

"Deal," Owen said.

Monroe turned back to the workstation, and the images vanished from the large screen. "I've got some more extraction and calculation to do, and then the Animus has to render the simulation. I don't need you here for that, so if you want to wander, you can. Just don't go far. We'll start the minute the simulation is ready."

Natalya and Owen looked at each other, and then both turned toward the lab door. Before they had exited, Monroe called to them.

"Thanks, you two," he said.

Natalya nodded, and they left.

Out in the hallway, Owen asked her, "Where do you want to go?"

They could always go back to the common room, but there wasn't much to do there, other than just sit and stare at each other. "Let's just walk around," she said. "Maybe get some fresh air."

He pointed in the direction of an outside door down the hallway.

They walked toward it, and found that it led to one of the Aerie's many patios and balconies. Two benches there formed an L and faced the forest that covered the mountain and surrounded the facility with the scent of pine. The tops of the oldest, tallest trees swayed back and forth in a breeze, their arthritic branches creaking.

Natalya took one of the benches, and Owen took the other. The warm sunlight felt good on her cheeks, and she lifted her face toward it, her eyes closed.

"Are you worried at all?" Owen asked. "If this simulation is as dangerous as Monroe made it sound . . ."

"I think we have to take the risk," Natalya said. "The stakes are too high."

"You're probably right." He paused. "What did the Piece of Eden show you?"

She opened her eyes and looked at him. He was asking about

the effect of the fear prong that Isaiah had used against them back in Mongolia. Each piece of the Trident had a different power and effect. The prong they had searched for in New York caused others to put blind faith in the person who wielded it. Natalya hadn't experienced the power of that first relic, but she had felt the fear caused by the second.

"You don't have to answer if it's too personal," Owen said, then paused and stared off into the trees. "I saw my dad. He confessed to everything. Even killing that guard. And he didn't feel guilty about it. He was smiling."

It made sense that would be his fear, and Natalya nodded. "I'm sorry."

"It's hard to get that out of my head, you know?" he said.

She did know. The Piece of Eden had shown her something, too. A nightmare she'd had for a few years now. Not every night, but often, and it always played out the same: she was walking to visit her grandparents after school.

Natalya loved their tidy, plain apartment with its old wooden floors, so full of her grandfather's jokes and her grandmother's cooking. After school, she was supposed to go straight there, but instead she stopped in a park to use a swing set. Laughing, she tucked her legs, then stretched out her toes as far as they would go, over and over, back and forth, trying to get as high on the swing as she could. After what felt like several minutes had passed, she got off the swing to be on her way, and that's when she noticed it. The sun had almost set. Somehow, she'd been swinging for hours, not minutes, and now she was very, very late. Her grandparents would be so worried about her. So she sprinted all the way from the park to her grandparents' apartment, but when she finally got there, ready to blurt out her rehearsed apology, lungs burning and out of breath, she noticed their door was ajar. But not by much.

That dark gap, only an inch wide, looked and felt all wrong.

She didn't want to open the door the rest of the way. But she had to. So she pushed on it, cold with fear, widening the utter silence beyond, and then stepped through.

The first thing she always noticed in her nightmare was the blood. It was everywhere, tracks of it splattered up the walls and even on the ceiling. Then she noticed the bodies of her murdered grandparents. She saw what the killer had done to them, and she wanted to look away, but she couldn't, and even if she did, the image would remain in her eyes.

The police and her parents always arrived shortly after that, with sirens and screaming. Her mom shouted at her, shaking her, asking her why she hadn't been there. Natalya *should* have been there. That's when she always woke up.

And that's what the Piece of Eden had shown her, though it had felt more real than her nightmare ever did.

"It's okay," Owen said, bringing her back to the mountain, the Aerie, and the patio. "You don't have to tell me. Sorry I asked."

"Don't be sorry," Natalya said. "I don't—"

The door opened behind them, and Monroe waved them inside. "It's ready," he said.

CHAPTER SIX

After he'd recovered from the effects of his desynchronization, Grace listened as David explained that his ancestor, Grace's ancestor, owned a slave. Grace wasn't surprised. Vikings enslaved other Vikings. Grace had known that, but she hadn't stopped to think their ancestor might have been a part of that system, and she could understand why it made David so angry.

"I don't know how to synchronize with that," he said, still sounding rattled.

Victoria lowered her tablet. "What do you mean?"

"For me—" David put both his hands out in front of him. "Okay, when I'm in the Animus, I have to find common ground with my ancestor so I can relate to them. If I can't see things the way they see them, I can't synchronize with them."

"Interesting." Victoria folded her arms and tapped her index finger against her lips. "So you need agreement with your ancestor. And this is something you can't see the way a Viking would see it."

David nodded.

That wasn't how synchronization felt to Grace. For her, it was like letting someone come into her house. She didn't have to accept everything about them to do that, but then, she hadn't ever tried inviting in a slave owner before.

Victoria turned to her. "Do you want to give it a try?"

Grace didn't think she had a choice if she wanted to find the Piece of Eden before Isaiah did. "I'll give it a try," she said.

David slumped down lower in the chair and sighed, and she couldn't tell if he felt relieved or annoyed. Maybe a bit of both. He'd made it pretty clear that he didn't need her to protect him anymore, or bail him out of trouble. But the piece of the Trident in Mongolia had shown her that he did. This needed to be done, regardless of how David felt about it.

"Stay out of trouble," she told him.

Then she walked over to the Animus, and Victoria helped her climb in and suit up. When Grace was strapped and secured, Victoria brought the helmet down and placed it over her head, plunging her into emptiness.

Are you ready? Victoria asked.

Grace took a deep breath, preparing herself for the hard part. "As ready as I can be."

Good. In three, two, one . . .

Grace endured the painful intrusion of the Parietal Suppression, traversed the momentary disorientation of the Memory Corridor, and emerged into the Viking world of Scandinavia.

She stood in the doorway of her home, watching a man approach, carrying some kind of thick staff across her land.

Grace sensed her ancestor waiting outside the walls of her mind, ready to inhabit her with his memories. She didn't find his presence aggressive, or combative, but rather patient and strong. She felt in him a gruff kindness that probably wasn't obvious to everyone who knew him, and in that way he reminded her of her father.

But then she thought about his thrall. His slave.

Sudden anger reinforced her walls against him. In the face of that evil, what did it matter how patient or kind he was? He wasn't anything like her father.

Grace? How are you doing?

"I'm okay."

You haven't locked in yet.

"I know."

The simulation won't stabilize until—

"I know."

Grace didn't need Victoria to tell her that. What Grace needed was to figure this out, and quickly, because this was for David. She faced this challenge so that he wouldn't have to, because that was what she'd always done. Like the times she'd hurried him out of the store before he noticed the security guard following them around, or the times she told him not to speak back to the gangbangers as she walked him past the corner where they hung out. She always placed herself between him and trouble.

One little push. That's all it would take to send David down the wrong road. Why should he have to reconcile himself to this if Grace could do it for him?

Her ancestor's name was Östen, and she tried to learn what she could about him from the other side of the wall. She felt his love for his wife and children. She felt the pride he took in his land, crops, and livestock, and because of that, she allowed herself to watch him laboring alongside Arne the Dane, ignoring her anger as best she could. She observed the two men sweating and laughing through the summer shearing of Östen's sheep, wool clinging to their forearms, tickling their noses, and drifting into their food as they took their midday meal together, eating the same cheese and thin barley bread.

Slavery this might be, both unjust and wrong, but at least Östen was not cruel. Perhaps that was enough for Grace to permit him entrance.

Though wary, she opened the gates of her mind, and Östen came in with the warm strength of a boulder that had been sitting in the sun. As Grace allowed him nearer, she realized she could not and would not justify him, but she didn't need to. She only needed to accept that this was who her ancestor was, instead of fighting it, for synchronization to happen.

We're looking better out here, Victoria said. *Excellent work. Continue doing what you're doing.*

That woman really had no idea what she was asking of Grace, or David. Victoria could acknowledge all she wanted how hard it must be, but she would never know. Neither had Monroe known when he'd sent them back to experience the atrocities of the Draft Riots. And for what she needed to do, Grace didn't need them to know. She wasn't doing it for them.

Almost there.

Grace allowed Östen to settle in, planting his feet as if her mind was his farm, and at last she felt fully synchronized with his memories.

The man approaching his home with the staff drew nearer, and Östen recognized him as his neighbor, Olof, whose fields and pastures bordered his, and with whom he had never had a disagreement. The staff he carried was the Bidding Stick, and Östen felt a heaviness in his arms at the sight of it. His son, Tørgils, came around from the cowshed.

"Father?" he asked, squinting into the distance.

"Go inside and tell your mother we have a guest."

Tørgils did as he was asked, and Östen waited until Olof drew near enough to greet.

"I wish I came to you bringing a fairer wind," his neighbor replied.

"Do you summon me to the Thing?" Östen asked, though he already knew the answer by the shape of the Bidding Stick.

Olof shook his head. "We are summoned under the *ledung*. Eric calls us not to counsel, but to war."

"Against?"

"Styrbjörn."

Östen nodded, unsurprised. Years ago, after the death of Styrbjörn's father, it had been decided by the Thing, under counsel from the Lawspeaker, that until the unruly Styrbjörn was of age, his uncle, Eric, should rule in his stead. That judgment had angered the prince, and he had departed his country with the fury of a storm. At the time, Östen had pitied those who might lie in the path of that storm, wherever it made landfall. Now it seemed the howling maelstrom had returned home, and there was to be a reckoning.

"Come inside," Östen said. "Eat with us."

With a shake of his head, Olof handed Östen the Bidding Stick. "I wish I could accept the honor, but time is scarce, and I need to make my own preparations."

Östen nodded, accepting the heavy summons. This Bidding Stick was a thick length of knotted oak, charred on one end with a cord tied to the other.

"Where?" Östen asked.

"Uppsala," he said. "We gather at Fyrisfield."

Östen nodded, and Olof bade him farewell, returning the way he had come toward his own land. Östen watched his neighbor's departure for a few moments, and then turned to go inside.

Within the central hall of his home, he found that Hilla had laid out cheese, smoked fish, bread, and ale. As Östen came inside, she looked past him, over his shoulder, as though for their guest.

"He could not stay," Östen said, setting the heavy Bidding Stick in the middle of the table.

Hilla and Tørgils stared at it without speaking. Östen's daughters, Agnes and Greta, drew closer to see what had brought such silence into the room.

"It's a piece of oak," Greta said, looking up at Östen.

She had been too young to remember the last time such a summons had taken place. "It's a Bidding Stick," Östen said. "The king has summoned me."

"What for?" Agnes asked.

Hilla turned away from the table and went to her loom in the corner, where she resumed her weaving. Östen watched her, but even without the help of his memories, Grace could read the angry way Hilla pulled and beat the thread. But there wasn't anything Östen could do or say to appease her. To refuse the Bidding Stick would mean death and the burning of their farm, but that was not what angered his wife. She knew that a part of him wanted to go, not for the sake of battle and bloodshed, but for his honor.

"Father?" Agnes asked.

"It summons all the men to war," Tørgils said, not yet considered a man by the Bidding Stick.

Östen laid a hand on his son's shoulder. "Carry it to the next farm. As quick as you can, so that you can return before nightfall."

Tørgils picked up the Bidding Stick. "Yes, Father." And he left with it.

After that, the rattle of the loom sounded even louder and more agitated in the small hall.

Östen turned to his daughters. "Agnes, why don't you take Greta outside for a little while."

"What should we do?" Greta asked.

"Go fetch Arne. I think he's milking the cows."

"Yes, Father," they said in unison.

A moment later, Östen and Hilla were alone, and he crossed the room to the corner where she attacked her weaving, saying nothing to her at first, simply watching the way her strong arms moved the shuttle and beater. He smiled at her careless braid, loose and uneven in places as it always was. As long as he had known her, she had never tried to lighten the color of her dark hair with lye as other women did, and he loved and admired that about her.

"What do you want, Östen?" she asked without turning around.

From within a corner of her mind, Grace smiled at her ancestor's predicament, wondering if he understood its precariousness, and how he would answer.

"I want a skein from you," he said.

Hilla ceased weaving and turned around to face him, frowning. "You want a piece of thread," she said, sounding unamused.

"Yes."

She raised an eyebrow at him, and then turned to pick up a skein of gray yarn. She stretched out a length of it, cut it off with her knife, and handed it to Östen. He shook his head, and extended his wrist.

"Tie it," he said.

Still frowning, but now also shaking her head in confusion, Hilla wrapped the thread around his wrist.

"Make it tight, and tie it fast," he said.

"What is this for?" she asked.

He nodded toward the loom. "Watching you just now with your weaving, I fell in love with you again."

She finished tying and shifted her stance, placing one hand on her hip. "Did you, now?"

"I did." He looked down at his wrist. "And now I will carry that moment with me into battle. This is the thread of my life, and only you can cut it off. When I return home."

His answer seemed to disarm her, and her posture lost some of its hardness. "You fight for yourself, Östen. For your own glory and—"

"Styrbjörn has returned," he said.

Her frown vanished.

"This isn't a petty squabble between Eric and a Geat chieftain," he continued. "Styrbjörn must not be king, or we will all suffer under his rule."

She reached down and touched the thread at his wrist. "I see."

"I don't like the thought of leaving you—"

"I know." She laid her other hand against his chest. "But don't worry about us. I have Tørgils and Arne. All will be well here until your return."

"Hilla, you are—"

"And you *will* return." She looked directly into his eyes. "Won't you?"

"Yes." It was the only vow Östen ever made knowing he might break it. "Only you," he said, holding up his wrist.

Just then a shadow fell across them as a figure stepped through the door, blocking the sunlight. It was Arne the Dane, reminding Grace that no matter how good a husband and father Östen was, no matter how honorable in the other aspects of his life, in this he would always be dishonorable. But she reminded herself she didn't need to justify him, and even though she felt some of her anger returning, the memory continued.

"You asked for me?" Arne said.

"Yes," Östen said. "Olof brought the Bidding Stick just now. Styrbjörn has returned."

"I see." Arne stepped farther into the small hall. "When do we leave?"

"I will leave tomorrow. You will stay here."

"Yes, Östen." The Dane bowed his head. "Then I am not to fight?"

"I need you to look after the farm with Hilla and Tørgils."

"Very well." Arne gave Hilla a nod. "We'll manage."

"I am relying on you," Östen said. Then he and Hilla glanced at each other, and she nodded her approval for what he was about to say. They had been discussing it for some weeks now. "When I return, if you have served my family well in my absence, we will talk about the terms of your freedom."

Arne bowed his head even lower. "Thank you, Östen."

"You have earned it," Hilla said.

With that, Arne the Dane left the hall to return to his work, and Östen set about gathering and packing what he would need for the journey to Uppsala. Throughout that process, Grace considered what had just occurred, searching through her ancestor's mind for a better understanding of it. Thralls, it seemed, could be freed, and while the promise made to Arne had the appearance of generosity, Grace couldn't forget the fact that the Dane should never have been enslaved in the first place.

Hilla helped Östen prepare his food stores of dried fish, cheese, and hard bread, along with some smoked mutton. He gathered his knives and other tools, extra clothing, and bundled it all into his cloak.

After the evening meal, surrounded by his family, he sharpened his spear, his sword, and his axe by the light of a sun that would set but little at this time of year. He accompanied the grinding of the whetstone with stories, some his, some those of other people, and some those of the gods. After Agnes and Greta had fallen asleep, he gave instructions to Tørgils for the managing of the farm. Even though Hilla and Arne would be there, it was time for his son to take on more responsibilities. After Tørgils had gone to bed, Hilla nestled up to Östen by the fire until it was time to sleep.

The next morning, Östen bade his family good-bye and departed while the ghost moon still haunted the sky. The journey to Uppsala would take several days by foot, and he set himself a hard pace, following the old roads to the great temple. Grace, almost a passenger on this journey, took in the countryside of lakes, rivers, forests, and hills, while her ancestor marched to war.

CHAPTER SEVEN

Sean lay in bed, and even though the sun hadn't risen yet, he had been awake for hours. He couldn't sleep with the room bobbing and swaying, as if he were still aboard the ship in Styrbjörn's mind. Even though Viking vessels were far more flexible than Sean would have thought, bending with the currents and waves to a frightening degree, they were still relatively small and easily tossed about by the sea. For a while now, that sensation had been following him from the Animus. Some kind of Bleeding Effect. Sean wondered if he would ever enjoy eating again. The only thing that brought relief was to get back into the simulation.

A bird chirped outside the high window in his room, signaling that morning wasn't far away. Isaiah would be coming for him soon. He knew he'd never get back to sleep, so he sat up, and then leveraged himself easily from his bed into his wheelchair. The strength in his upper body was one thing the accident hadn't taken from him.

Through his window he saw the yew tree that had been his view each morning for the past several days. They'd moved from the Aerie facility and flown here, an old monastery out in the middle of nowhere, surrounded by rugged green mountains crisscrossed by stone walls. It looked like England or Scotland to Sean, but when he'd asked about it, Isaiah had told him he didn't need to worry.

Sean was safe.

His parents knew where he was, and they were proud of the work he was doing.

Isaiah was proud of the work he was doing.

That was all he needed to know.

And Sean had faith in Isaiah. He believed in the mission. Sean's work in the simulation would lead them to the final piece of the Trident, and when they found it, they would have the power to end the war between the Templars and the Assassins forever. They would have the power to set things right for the whole world.

Sean looked around his small room, imagining the devout monks who had occupied this chamber through the centuries, and what they might have experienced before the modern world had brought in heat and electricity.

The bird sang again, sounding somewhat farther away, and then someone knocked at the door.

"Sean?" Isaiah asked. "Are you awake?"

"Yes, sir," Sean said.

"May I enter?"

"Yes, sir."

The door opened, and Isaiah ducked into the room, his presence seeming too large for its close walls. "I see you are ready. Excellent. We have much to do."

"Yes, sir."

Isaiah strode around to stand behind his wheelchair. Sean normally hated it when people pushed him, ever since he'd gotten the hang of wheeling himself. There was nothing wrong with his upper body, and it was important for him to know he could go where he wanted to go. But it didn't bother him to let Isaiah push him.

"Off we go, then," Isaiah said, reaching around to hand Sean an energy bar.

Sean accepted it, and the wheelchair moved.

They exited his room and moved down the monastery's silent corridors, past stained glass windows only dimly lit by the sunrise, and past a courtyard dotted with weedy flower beds.

"How are you feeling?" Isaiah asked.

"I'm tired," Sean said, taking a bite out of the bar. In fact, he had never felt tired in the way he did now. The exhaustion reached into the deepest recess of his mind, but left him upright, awake, but not quite himself.

"I know you're tired," Isaiah said. "But your efforts will be rewarded. I need you to be strong. I need you to tell me the moment you think the Piece of Eden might come into your ancestor's possession."

"Yes, sir."

They came to the monastery's front gate, where one of the Abstergo vehicles waited for them, idling. It was painted white, and looked a bit like a Humvee, if that Humvee had gone back to school for a double PhD in aerospace engineering and computer science. It was a prototype that Isaiah had commandeered, and Sean called it Poindexter, just to keep it from getting too full of itself. Since coming here, it had been his regular means of transportation, because the only space in the monastery complex large enough for the Animus was the chapel, which sat at the top of a hill. A very cumbersome climb with a wheelchair.

Isaiah rolled Sean up to Poindexter, and at his approach, a rear door opened and a ramp lowered to the ground automatically.

"Welcome, Sean," Poindexter said, with its precisely enunciated robot voice.

Isaiah wheeled Sean up the ramp and secured him inside the back of the vehicle. Then he hopped into the front passenger seat.

As always, no one sat in the driver's seat.

"Are we going to the chapel again this morning?" Poindexter asked.

"Yes," Isaiah said.

"Very well," the vehicle said. "We will arrive in approximately four minutes and thirty-two seconds."

"Thank you, Poindexter," Sean said.

"You are welcome, Sean."

The vehicle rolled out, moving along a course it had calculated to the inch.

Isaiah shook his head. "I can think of nothing more unnecessary than manners with a machine."

"Maybe," Sean said. "But when that machine is controlling the steering wheel, I'll play it safe."

As they reached the top of the hill and came to a gentle stop, several Abstergo agents greeted them and helped Sean out of the vehicle. Isaiah had brought dozens of men and women from the Aerie, and more had joined him since then. They acted as guards, technicians, and labor.

"Is everything ready?" Isaiah asked Cole as he pushed Sean toward the chapel.

"Yes, sir," she said, her manner somewhat severe. She had been head of security back at the Aerie. "I believe they finished calibrating a few minutes ago."

At the chapel entrance, one of the other agents opened and held its heavy wooden door, and Isaiah wheeled Sean through. Inside, the old pews had been stacked against one wall to make room for the Animus in the middle of the floor. The air smelled damp and earthy, but not unpleasant. Thick wooden rafters stretched overhead, much of the vaulted space beyond them kept in shadow. This church wasn't like the bright cathedrals Sean had seen in movies, with all their stained glass. This place felt more like a fortress, with narrow windows that let in little light, keeping the edges of the chapel in darkness.

Technicians circled the Animus beneath the only real source of light, a broad chandelier made of iron with bare bulbs, stepping over the wires and cables that snaked across the flagstones. Isaiah wheeled Sean up to the device and then helped him out of his chair and into the harness, strapping him to the frame. Then Isaiah brought the helmet down and placed it over Sean's head.

He'd almost grown accustomed to the trauma of the Parietal Suppressor and the transition into his ancestor's memories. Almost. But it was over quickly, and it had become both easy and natural for him to synchronize with the familiar currents of Styrbjörn's mind.

He sat in the hall of Harald Bluetooth, at a table with the Dane-king. Styrbjörn's sister, Gyrid, sat next to them, and it seemed she had settled well into her title as queen. But before she was Harald's wife, she was a princess of the Svear, as wise and cunning as Styrbjörn was strong.

"You must sail the fleet up the coast of Götaland," she said. "Then west through the lake of Mälaren. There are many who loved our father, and some of them silently oppose Eric, even now. If our allies see you sailing along the coast and through the very heart of Svealand, they will be emboldened to join the battle in the name of Styrbjörn the Strong."

"The Strong?" Styrbjörn asked.

"Have you not heard?" Gyrid looked from her brother to Harald, whose face had reddened. "Word of your battle with my husband has spread. They say you possess the strength of ten men—"

Harald slammed his mug of ale on the table. "This plan is too risky. My men and my ships are yours to command, but I won't let you send them to the bottom of the sea. Mälaren is a trap. There is only one way in and out of that lake, and if Eric orders it blocked—"

"You speak as if you are already planning your retreat," Styrbjörn said.

"I plan how I enter my battles," Harald said. "And I plan how I leave them."

"Perhaps that is why you lose," Gyrid said, and the Dane-king flushed even deeper.

"I like the queen's plan," Styrbjörn said. "We'll sail through Mälaren, then up the Fyriswater, and then march on Uppsala."

Harald shook his head, his jaw grinding hard enough, it

seemed, to crush rocks. But he said nothing in objection, for what could he say? He had lost the battle to Styrbjörn and surrendered in front of his men. But Styrbjörn saw fire in his brother-in-law's eyes, and noted the way his hand was never far from the curious dagger he wore at his side. Sean noted it, too, as the memory swept him along, but until that prong of the Trident came into Styrbjörn's possession, noting it was all Sean could do.

Harald's anger amused Styrbjörn, and he decided to blow across its embers. "Something vexes you, Harald?"

The Dane-king stared at Styrbjörn for a moment, and then smiled, revealing his rotten tooth. "To what god are you devoted?"

"To no god," Styrbjörn said. "They are all the same to me."

"Do you not fear them?"

"No."

"To what are you devoted, then? To a woman?"

"Not until I have my crown, for I would marry a queen."

"Have you found no woman worthy of you?" Harald asked. "There is a shield-maiden in my hall named Thyra. She is both beautiful and strong. Perhaps—"

"No," Styrbjörn said.

Harald pulled at a loose thread in the embroidery of his tunic. "You are devoted to your men, surely."

"I am glad to fight alongside the Jomsvikings, but I have not sworn to them, nor they to me. They follow Palnatoke, who met me at the crossroads in single combat, with honor, even in defeat." His statement was intended to shame Harald for his quick surrender.

"The old rituals are coming to an end," Harald said. "Their honor is fading."

Styrbjörn shrugged. "Among the Danes, perhaps. After all, it would seem your men remain devoted to you."

"There is much more to a king than his victories." Harald paused a moment, and then looked over at Gyrid. "You are devoted to your sister, perhaps?"

Styrbjörn had once been devoted to his sister, and she to him. But she had come into her power, and now possessed her own crown. Harald Bluetooth would never rule her, for she was the master of both her fate and her honor. Now it was Styrbjörn's time.

"I am devoted to myself," he said, "and none other."

Harald's eyebrows went up, and he nodded, as though he had just realized something. "I think I understand."

"I doubt that." Styrbjörn drained the last of the ale from his mug. "The matter is settled. We sail through Mälaren. Word will spread. Men will flock to my banner. Eric will fall." He spoke as if his words had the power to reshape the world by their utterance.

In memories like this, Sean felt almost overpowered by the strength of Styrbjörn's mind, and that to synchronize with his ancestor's fearlessness and force of will, he needed to become stronger himself. He had experienced something similar in New York City and London as he had followed the memories of another ancestor, Tommy Greyling.

"My ships are yours to command, Styrbjörn," Harald said. "As are my men. I will await news of your victory—"

"Await?" Styrbjörn glanced at Gyrid.

She looked hard at Harald. "Surely, husband, you will fight at my brother's side."

It was obvious to Styrbjörn, and likely to Gyrid, that Harald had not intended to sail to Svealand. In truth, Styrbjörn didn't want Harald to sail with him, but he knew the Danes would fight better if led by their king, even though their king took his orders from a Svear who had defeated him in battle.

Harald Bluetooth touched his dagger again, the Piece of Eden, fixing his stare upon Sean's ancestor for several moments. Then he looked away, appearing both frustrated and perplexed.

"I will sail with you," Harald said.

Styrbjörn nodded, but Sean had become aware of something. He was pretty sure that Harald had just tried to use the power of the dagger on Styrbjörn, and upon reflection, he realized this was the second time it had happened. Sean raised his head above the waterline of Styrbjörn's mind and spoke to Isaiah.

"Harald knows what he has."

That makes sense, Isaiah said. *Sources from this time period tell us that Harald managed to unite all of Denmark and Norway under his rule. He was a very powerful man.*

"If that's true, then why didn't the dagger work on Styrbjörn?" Sean asked.

Harald attempted to use it?

"Yeah."

Are you certain?

"I think so."

If your ancestor was able to resist the power of a Piece of Eden, it is essential that I understand how. Did Styrbjörn do something to shield himself?

"No. It seemed automatic. Like he was immune."

Stand by, Isaiah said. *I'm going to terminate the simulation so I can analyze the—*

"No."

Isaiah paused. *What did you say?*

"Do not terminate. Leave me in here." Sean sounded more forceful than he meant to, which surprised him, but he wasn't ready to return to his own body and mind yet.

I make those decisions, Sean. Isaiah spoke with a low and even voice. *You do not tell me what to do.*

"Then I'm asking. Leave me in the simulation. Please."

No. I have other priorities—

"What about my priorities?"

Your priorities?

"Yes." Sean didn't know where this confrontation was coming from.

Sean, my priorities are your priorities. You don't have priorities of your own.

"Yes, I do."

If that is the case, I would suggest you rid yourself of them quickly. Principles and priorities come at a price that I doubt you are prepared to pay.

"I think I can judge that for myself." Sean felt as if he were in a simulation of his own mind, listening to another person talk, wanting to shut them up. Almost as though Styrbjörn were speaking through him. "This is my simulation, and if I want to stay in it, then I—"

Something smashed through Sean's skull, seized his mind with its fist, and then wrenched it from his body. The simulation shredded around him, and he felt himself shredding, strips and layers of him torn away by the raking of claws until there was almost nothing left that he recognized as himself. He was but a single thought floating in an endless nothing. Then a blinding light replaced the nothing, and he opened his scorched eyes.

A tall man with green eyes stood in front of him. Sean blinked, and then recognized him.

Isaiah held a bucket up to Sean's face. "Vomit," he said.

Sean obeyed, hanging like a doll from the Animus framework, his mind still reeling.

"That was foolish of you."

"Which part?" Sean asked. He thought back to what he had said, and still couldn't explain where it had come from. He also wasn't sure he regretted it, in spite of the violent desynchronization.

"It is foolish to provoke me, Sean." Isaiah leaned in closer. "I know you want the Animus. You want it desperately, but I think you've forgotten that I control your access to the Animus, as I have just demonstrated."

"But you won't cut me off," Sean said, not quite as confidently as he had spoken in the Animus. "You need me to find the dagger."

Isaiah leaned away from him. "You still don't understand."

Sean noticed then that all the other Abstergo technicians had left the chapel. He and Isaiah were alone, their voices echoing against the stone.

"What don't I understand?" Sean asked.

Isaiah walked away from the light, into the dark recesses at the far end of the chapel. A few moments later, he returned, carrying something long and thin, like a spear.

No. Not a spear.

It was a trident with two prongs, its third prong missing. Until now, Sean had only seen the relics as daggers, but with their leather grips removed, they now looked like what they were: two parts of a larger deadly weapon. Isaiah had combined them and mounted them on the head of a staff.

The Trident of Eden.

He carried it toward Sean with authority. "Now," he said, "I will make you understand."

CHAPTER EIGHT

Owen followed Monroe and Natalya back down the hallway to the lab, and Monroe led them into an adjacent room with three different Animus rings that looked similar to what he'd seen elsewhere in the Aerie, but not as polished. They seemed more industrial and skeletal, with exposed wires and components.

"Will these do the job?" Owen asked.

"Of course." Monroe walked over to one of them and gave it a solid pat. "These are mostly used for research. They were built as workhorses. They're not as pretty as the others, but they'll perform."

Owen glanced at Natalya and shrugged. "If you say so."

Monroe looked at both of them, sighed, and nodded. "Let's get you situated."

"You seem nervous," Natalya said.

"I've been researching the collective unconscious for a long time," Monroe said, "hoping to one day get a look at it. But now that it's here, I . . . Just try to be safe in there, okay?"

Owen would have liked more reassurance than that. "Okay."

Monroe directed him and Natalya toward two of the Animus rings that he had networked together, allowing them to share the simulation. Owen stepped inside his ring and climbed up into the framework of his exosuit, which did feel more sturdy and solid than it looked. Monroe helped Natalya buckle in, then did the same for Owen, and they were ready to go inside.

"Another couple of notes," Monroe said. "First, I've been looking at the Animus code for this simulation, and it's significantly atypical. This isn't a memory of an experience in the way you're used to. It's not a sequence of events, with cause and effect. It's more holistic than that. More organized. Almost like it was written with the end in mind."

"That should make synchronization easier, right?" Owen asked. "We won't be tied to a certain memory. We don't have to worry about making the right choices."

"Maybe," Monroe said. "But that's the other thing. This simulation is old. The data is intact, but we're talking dawn of humanity here. This is actually an incredible moment. I mean, I know we're doing this to stop Isaiah, but it's so much more than that. You two are about to step inside a place that makes us who we are as human beings."

"We'll take notes," Owen said.

"You'd better." Monroe pulled Owen's helmet over his head, and after a few moments of complete silence, he heard Monroe's voice in his ear. *Are you both reading me?*

"Yes," Natalya said.

"Yes," Owen said.

Excellent. Are you ready to begin?

They both said yes.

Hold tight. Initiating Parietal Suppressor in three, two, one . . .

Owen grimaced through the intense pressure, the sensation of his skull bones grinding together, until the weight lifted away, and he opened his eyes upon the boundless gray. Natalya stood next to him, rubbing her temples, and she appeared as herself. He looked around, waiting for shapes to materialize out of the nothing.

How are you two doing?

"Good," Owen said. He was wearing his favorite jeans, the comfortable ones with holes in them that he pulled out on lazy Sundays, and a T-shirt. Somehow the Animus must have pulled that from his own memories. Natalya wore jeans and a loose, button-down navy blouse.

"I'm fine," Natalya said, her eyelids pinched shut.

You ready for the next step? This is the big one. Neil Armstrong big.

Owen watched Natalya and waited until she opened her eyes, blinked a few times, and then gave him a nod.

"I think we're ready," he said.

Okay. One giant leap for mankind in three, two, one . . .

Instead of resolving itself into shapes, the Memory Corridor darkened. It turned from gray to black, as black as the inside of the Animus helmet. For a moment, Owen wondered if something had gone wrong, and he was about to ask Monroe, but then a faint speck of light flickered ahead. At first, it only sparkled weakly, like a distant star, but gradually it grew brighter, and nearer, until it caused Owen to squint.

"What is that?" he asked Natalya. "Some kind of—"

LISTEN TO ME. A woman's voice rang in Owen's head like a bell, resonating through his whole mind. **THE WAY OF THE PATH IS THROUGH FEAR, DEVOTION, AND FAITH. FIND THE WAY THROUGH EACH OF THESE, AND I SHALL BE WAITING FOR YOU AT THE SUMMIT.**

Then the light slowly diminished, but as it shrank it also changed, gaining hard, square edges. When it finally settled firmly into place, Owen realized they were now standing in a tunnel, and the light had become an open doorway at the far end of it. Behind them lay only blackness, which left them one direction in which to go.

"Did you hear that?" Natalya asked.

"Yes," Owen said.

Is everything okay? Monroe asked. *The Animus is having a really hard time converting this data into an image on my end. You're going to have to tell me what you see.*

"There was a light," Natalya said.

"A talking light," Owen added. "Now we're in a tunnel."

A talking light? What did it say?

"The way of the path is through fear, devotion, and faith," Natalya said. "And something about waiting for us at the summit."

Well, that is certainly interesting. It means we're on the right track.

"How so?" Owen asked.

Because the prongs of the Trident each have a different effect on human minds. One causes fear, one causes devotion, and one causes faith. That can't be coincidence, which means the simulation you're in is connected to the Trident somehow, just like we'd hoped.

"I guess we keep going," Natalya said. "To the summit."

Owen nodded. "I guess so."

They set off toward the distant doorway, the echoes of their footsteps filling the tunnel. The walls to either side seemed to be made of dry stone, hewn rough and uneven, and the air smelled of dust. Eventually, they reached a point where the light coming in through the doorway no longer blinded Owen's view of what lay beyond, and he caught glimpses of huge tree trunks.

"It's a forest," Natalya said.

A forest? Monroe asked.

"We're almost there," Owen said.

They approached the end of the tunnel, but stopped and stood at the threshold for a moment, peering out into the deep, dark woodland, very different from the one that surrounded the Aerie. These trees were unlike any Owen knew of. They stood close together, with wide trunks, worm-eaten bark, expansive branches, and exposed roots that seemed ready to pull up so the trees could go walking. Very little sunlight made it down through the dense canopy of leaves and needles, but where it fell, fine grass grew like hair, and where the sunlight could not reach, a soft black soil covered the ground.

"You could get lost in there," Natalya said.

Owen agreed. Not too deep into the woods, a hazy and impenetrable shadow consumed everything. But more than that, just at the edge of that darkness, where the forest swallowed itself, the trees appeared to be distorted, or moving. Owen blinked and squinted, wondering if he only imagined it, along with the faint and distant sounds of wood cracking and groaning. It was almost like the simulation had glitches.

"Monroe?"

Yeah?

"Is the simulation stable?"

Yeah, it looks good.

"Are you sure?" Natalya asked, which meant that she had noticed it, too.

Hang on.

Owen and Natalya both breathed in at the same time.

"I don't want to go in there," she said.

"I don't, either."

But if they didn't enter the forest, where else were they supposed to go? They couldn't go back through the tunnel. Owen saw no light at the other end.

Okay. Monroe had returned. *I've checked everything. The simulation is stable, so whatever you're seeing, that's how it's supposed to be. That's the memory.*

"That's disconcerting," Natalya said.

Maybe not. I told you, this DNA is different. It's not going to behave like a normal simulation. It's more . . . primordial.

"It's the forest that's disconcerting," Owen said. "The only way forward is through it."

Maybe it—maybe it's not a normal forest.

Owen peered again at the shifting woods. "Uh, yeah, it's definitely not a normal forest."

No, I mean, maybe it's not just a forest. Maybe it's the *forest. The archetypal Forest.*

"The Forest is an archetype?" Natalya asked. "How does that work?"

Archetypes aren't just people. They can be places and objects, too. The Forest appears in numerous myths.

The air just outside the tunnel felt heavy and smelled of

something Owen couldn't quite identify, a scent that was green and rank. Something about it tensed his body and tingled his neck, but he couldn't recognize it, and didn't know why it unsettled him. Regardless, their situation hadn't changed. "So what you're saying is, we *do* have to go through the Forest."

"Unless we just stand here," Natalya said. "Or we leave the simulation."

Owen nodded and sighed. "Right."

I'll be right here, Monroe said. *I can pull you out if things go south. But remember why we're doing this. The collective unconscious DNA that you all carry is connected to the Trident.*

"Understood." Owen took a step forward, crossing the boundary. The soft, rich soil gave way a half an inch beneath his foot, and he noticed mushrooms growing all around. He took another step, and another. When he and Natalya stood some yards away from the tunnel, they turned to look back at it.

From this side, the opening through which they'd entered the Forest wasn't a tunnel, but a stone portal. Two rough and massive stone slabs had been set upright on their edges, parallel with each other, and a third slab had been laid on top of them, forming a doorway with nothing but forest on the other side. The gray rock from which the slabs were made bore weather scars and blooms of lichen. The lonely monument stood there among the trees of the Forest, silent and imposing, and Owen couldn't tell whether it or the woods had been there first.

"No going back that way," Natalya said. "The tunnel is gone."

"This memory isn't stable," Owen said. "I don't like this."

"Monroe said it's fine. Let's just keep going for a little while and see what happens."

Owen looked around them. The Forest in each direction appeared endless. "Which way?"

"I don't think it matters." Natalya looked to her left and her right, and then gestured to her right. "Let's keep going that way, I guess."

Owen resumed walking in that direction, and when he reached the first spot of sunlight and grass, he paused to look up. A seam of empty sky looked back at him, and from the perspective of the Forest, the break in the canopy was a wound full of blue blood. He and Natalya left that light behind and ventured deeper, trying to walk in as straight a line as they could, winding their way without a path through the trees. Their journey seemed to drive the distortion's edge before them, as if they traveled in a pocket of reality they created as they went.

Owen heard birds singing and knocking at the trees. He heard insects thrumming and chittering. He smelled leaves, and flowers, and dirt, and occasionally, that disturbing and rank odor, as on they walked.

It was impossible to say how far they traveled, and Owen had only a vague sense of the passage of time, but he eventually reached a point in the Forest that stopped him against his will. He looked down at his feet, and then his mind became aware of the terror his body already felt.

"We're not alone," he whispered, trembling.

Natalya froze and peered off into the trees. "We're not?"

"No." His eyes widened and his heart thumped. "Do you feel that?"

"Feel what?"

"There's something in the Forest with us." He couldn't see it, but he could feel it as surely as he felt the soil beneath his feet.

"What is it?"

"I don't know." But Owen knew that whatever it was, he had been smelling it all along. "Let's keep moving. Quietly."

So they resumed their journey, taking care with their steps to avoid twigs and roots, neither of them speaking. Tree after tree they rounded and passed. Hundreds of them. Thousands, perhaps. And then Owen glimpsed something up ahead. A difference in the unending pattern of the Forest. He couldn't see what it was, but it was large, and it lay on the ground.

He stopped and whispered to Natalya, "Should we go around?"

"No. Let's see what it is."

He nodded, and they crept closer, using the trees to hide behind, until they were near enough to see it wasn't a living thing, or even a moving thing. Owen stepped out into the open and approached it, still confused. It seemed to be made of some kind of translucent material, all folded and twisted, about six feet wide. But then Owen saw how long it was, stretching off in either direction through the trees.

"What is that?" Natalya asked.

"I don't kn—"

But then Owen noticed a subtle repeating pattern in the material. And he realized how he knew that foul odor. It was a smell from his third-grade teacher's classroom. She had a terrarium, and on the first day of school that year she had introduced the class to its occupant. Until then, Owen hadn't thought that snakes would smell, and most of the time they didn't. But sometimes they did, and so did the terrarium.

Natalya leaned closer. "Wait, is that skin?"

"Yeah," Owen said. "It's a shed skin."

Natalya turned to look at him. "From a snake?"

"Looks that way." Owen took in the size of it again, recalculating. "It's huge. Not just anaconda huge. It's *huge* huge." Owen wondered where the previous owner of the skin might have gone. "I want to see just how long it is. Should we find the head? Or the tail?"

"I guess."

Owen decided to turn to the left this time, and they followed the snakeskin as it curled and wound away into the Forest. They walked a few yards, and then a few more, expecting it to stop, but the skin kept going, and going, until they'd walked several hundred feet without reaching the end of it. The skin behind them seemed to vanish with the trees in the shadows, and Owen wondered if this was another distortion in the simulation that Monroe claimed was stable. An endless loop of snake.

"This has to be another archetype, right?" Natalya said.

Owen nodded. This was the presence he had sensed. "Let's try to get out of this Forest before it finds us."

But they still didn't know exactly how to get out, other than to just keep walking. So that's what they did, but much more cautiously now. Owen jumped at every rustle along the ground and every snap above him in the branches, and over time, his unrelenting dread burned off the edges of his senses so that he started hearing and seeing things that weren't there. Figures darted just out of view. Voices whispered unintelligible speech. The Forest had swallowed him.

How are you two doing? Monroe asked. *I'm showing spikes in your adrenaline and cortisol levels. Both of you. Increased blood pressure and heart rate, too.*

"Snakes will do that," Natalya said.

A snake?

"I think you would probably say *the* Snake," Owen said.

You found the Serpent.

"Just its skin," Owen said. "The Serpent is still out here."

"Maybe it's a good archetype," Natalya said. "Like the snakes on that medical staff."

The caduceus? Monroe said. I doubt that. The snake is almost always a symbol of fear and death. Exceptions to that usually mean we've tried to take control of that fear by inverting the meaning of the symbol. Even worshiping it.

"I'm sorry, are you trying to help?" Owen asked.

Yes, I am. Just remember, this is a memory. Probably from a time when our ancestors were smaller and the snakes were bigger. But this memory isn't literal. It's symbolic. Symbols can't hurt you.

"Are you sure about that?" Owen asked.

Yes. Just keep a firm grip on your fear and your mind.

"What if we can't?" Natalya's face looked pale in the dim light. "What if—?"

"Shh!" Owen said.

A sound had found its way into his mind. A quiet sound, a sinuous sigh along the ground, from somewhere in the Forest nearby. Owen held still and waited, listening, watching the trees.

Nothing made a noise.

Nothing stirred.

And then he saw the Serpent.

Its head emerged first from the woodland depths, the size of a leather sofa. Black and crimson scales gleamed around its mouth and nostrils, and framed its copper eyes, which seemed to shimmer. Its slender tongue whipped the air as it slithered directly toward them, bringing more and more of its endless body out of the shadows. The sight of it immobilized Owen, as if he were a panicked rodent.

"Run," he whispered, as much to himself as to Natalya.

CHAPTER NINE

avid sat deep in his chair, alone in the common room, facing the windows. He stared out into the trees, and thought about the Viking simulation. The fact that Östen owned a thrall hadn't stopped Grace from synchronizing with the memory, but the process was apparently different for her. So she had stepped in and taken over, rescuing him like she always did. But this time, it also kind of felt as though she'd left him behind, so David had left her in the Animus and come here to be by himself.

He wanted to call his dad. But he'd be at work right now, and as a welder, he couldn't exactly drop everything and answer his phone whenever his son called. Even if David could talk to his dad, he wasn't sure what he'd say or ask.

David had to deal with this on his own.

Back in Mongolia, he and Grace had come together in a way they never had before. She'd finally treated him like he was more than just a little child. She'd trusted him. But then Isaiah had used that dagger. The fear prong of the Trident. David would never forget the vision that had invaded his mind.

He was walking home from school and he was alone, even though Grace had told him not to do that. But Kemal and Oscar hadn't waited for him, so what else was he supposed to do? He'd made it about halfway to his house when he saw Damion standing on a corner up ahead. Everyone in the neighborhood knew Damion. Everyone knew to stay clear of him. So David ducked into a drugstore to wait it out for a bit.

He bought a Coke, and then he flipped through some magazines, until someone bumped into him from behind.

"Watch it," David said, turning around.

A huge white man stood over him. He wore a ball cap backward, and had a blond goatee on his chin. "What'd you say to me?"

David swallowed, but he wasn't about to back down. "I said watch it."

The man stepped closer, eyes narrowed, smelling like mildew and bad cologne. "You threatening me, boy?"

"No." David's heart beat hard enough to make his T-shirt quiver. "And don't call me boy."

"You threatened me." The man reached under his shirt. "Everyone in here will say you threatened me."

David ran, scrambling down the aisle, and then out the drugstore door, where he crashed right into Damion and dropped his Coke. The brown soda splashed all over Damion's shoes and pants. David didn't wait around to see what would happen next. He knew what Damion would do, so he kept running.

He heard shouting and swearing behind him, and he knew Damion was chasing him. But when he looked back, it was both of them. The white guy was chasing him, too, and both men had guns. If they caught him, they would kill him.

David had to get home. If he made it home, he'd be safe.

So he took every shortcut he knew, and ran faster than he ever had, but he couldn't escape his attackers, who were always there. Always behind him.

Somehow, it was dark by the time he reached his block, but when he got to his house, the lights were out. He leapt over the gate and raced up the porch steps, then frantically unlocked the door and burst inside.

"Grace!" He closed and bolted the door behind him. "Dad!"

No answer.

"Mom?"

Through the blurry window in the door, he could see the wavy figures of Damion and the white guy approaching his gate, the streetlight behind them turning their shadows into giants climbing David's front steps. There wasn't anywhere else he could go. No other place to hide.

"Grace!" he shouted. "Dad!"

The dark house ignored him. The two men stepped through the gate and walked toward the door.

David was alone. He wasn't safe. The door wouldn't stop them. The windows wouldn't stop them—

That was where the vision had ended. That was David's greatest fear. Not Damion and the white guy.

The empty house.

David was on his own.

But he didn't want to be afraid of that. He didn't need his older sister to come in and save him. Right now, the only thing he wanted was to get back inside the Animus, but he still had to figure out a way to synchronize with his ancestor. How was Grace able to do it? Why wasn't she as angry as he was? She'd probably say that she *was* just as angry as him. And yet she was in the Animus right now and he wasn't, because it was different for her, apparently.

Could it be different for him? It was all a mind game anyway. Did he need to agree with his ancestor on everything? He'd always assumed so. But maybe not. Maybe that assumption was actually the thing blocking him. Maybe it wasn't the anger, after all, but the belief that his anger had to be a barrier.

There was only one way to know.

He rose from his chair and left the common room, then returned to the Animus room, where he found Grace still harnessed inside the ring. He'd never really watched someone using the Animus from the outside. His sister looked a little goofy, walking in place with the helmet on her head. Victoria sat at the computer terminal nearby wearing a headset with a delicate microphone, monitoring multiple screens that displayed information on the simulation and Grace's biodata.

"How is she doing?" David asked.

Victoria glanced at him, and then went back to watching Grace. "She's good. Good physiological response. Strong synchronization."

David nodded. Then he pulled up a chair next to Victoria and sat down.

"How are you doing?" she asked.

"I'm fine," David said. "But I want to try again."

"You want to go back into the Animus?"

"Yes."

She looked at him and cocked her head. "To be candid, I don't think that's a good idea. We can't afford to waste time—"

"I can do it," David said.

"But why bother? Grace is in, and she's locked. We don't need anyone else."

"Maybe she needs a break. She'll need one eventually, right?"

Victoria gestured up at the screens. "She seems to be doing well."

"Could you ask her?"

Victoria leaned away from David, her elbow on the armrest of her rolling chair, and didn't answer for several moments. "I suppose," she finally said. Then she touched a button on the side of her headset. "Grace, how are you doing?"

Pause.

"Good to hear," Victoria said. "Do you need a break?"

Pause.

"Okay, then, let's keep you—"

"Can I talk to her?" David asked.

He received a sigh of apparent irritation, and then Victoria spoke into the microphone. "Grace, I have David here with me. He'd like to speak with you and . . . yes. Hang on a moment." She pulled the headset off and held it toward David, her eyebrows raised.

After he'd taken the headset and put it on, he adjusted the microphone and said, "Grace?"

Hey, she said. *You feeling better?*

"Yeah," he said. "But this is weird. You're right here, look-ing like an idiot with that helmet on, but you're also there. In Viking land."

Sweden, actually. Or Svealand. Östen would clarify.

"Right. Speaking of that guy, I think I want to try again. So if you ever need a break or anything—"

You want to try the simulation again?

"Yeah."

You don't have to. I got this.

"I know you do. But you don't need to do that for me. I want to do this."

You sure?

"I'm sure," he said. "It's okay. I'm good."

His sister went quiet.

"Grace?"

Put Victoria back on.

"Sure."

David handed the headset over, and then waited as Victoria put it back in place, tugging the microphone toward her lips.

"Grace, it's me," she said. "Yes, I—what's that?"

Pause.

"I see." Victoria looked over at David, and he caught a hint of a smile on her face. "You need a break, do you? Very well. Stand by."

David sat down and waited while Victoria took Grace through the extraction procedures and pulled her out of the sim-ulation. After the helmet came off, Grace blinked and shook her head, her hair a little wild, as Victoria undid some of the clamps and straps.

"Could you give us a hand?" Grace asked.

"Oh, sure." David jumped up and went over to help his sister out of the harness and the ring. Then it was his turn to climb in, and Grace worked with Victoria to secure him in the Animus framework.

"I need to switch over to your profile and biodata," Victoria said. "It'll just be a moment."

David watched Grace take the chair he'd been using. She sat down and wiped some sweat from her forehead with the heel of her palm. Then she pulled out her ponytail, and with the elastic held between her teeth, she ran her fingers through her hair, pulled it smooth and tight toward the back of her head, and then stretched the elastic back around it.

"So what's going on in Sweden?" David asked her.

"Östen is at Uppsala, where an army is gathering. They're expecting a battle."

David nodded. "Okay."

"What if you desynchronize?" she asked. "You want to go through that again?"

He was trying not to think about that. "I won't."

Grace rose from the chair and walked over to him. "Just remember, you don't have to justify him. You don't have to agree with him or make excuses for him. You don't have to explain him or apologize for him. You don't even need to accept what he did. All you need to do is accept that he did it."

"Okay," he said. "Thanks."

She nodded and backed away, and a moment later, Victoria stood up and said they were ready. She brought the helmet down and placed it over David's head, and then she spoke in his ear. David felt impatient, already looking past the process of entering the simulation, to the simulation itself. He just wanted to be inside the memory.

Minutes later, that's where he was, standing in a large encampment on a marshy plain, inhabiting the body of a giant. David immediately turned his mind inward, toward Östen's, facing his ancestor in all his human successes and failures. His family, his stubbornness, his hard work and honor, his stoniness, his victories in battle.

His thrall.

David felt his anger rising at the thought of Arne the Dane, but this time he didn't try to extinguish it or ignore it. He didn't try to force himself to agree with something that he never could. Instead, he reminded himself that he could still synchronize with his ancestor in spite of it. David could still converse with him. He could find other common ground with him. And he could stay angry with him.

Like Grace had said, it wasn't David's job to justify Östen as a man of his time and his people. David didn't have to excuse him at all.

You're doing well, Victoria said. *Much better than last time. You're almost there.*

David needed only to talk with his ancestor, and so he opened his mind to Östen's thoughts, and he listened, accepting what he heard not as truth, but as Östen's truth, however wrong it might be. Gradually, he felt himself synchronizing, not because he saw things the same way Östen did, but because he understood Östen without forcing himself to agree.

That's it. You have it.

David sighed and gave Östen his voice.

Before him in twilight lay the Fyrisfield, a great plain that followed the course of a marshy river from Uppsala south to the lake Mälaren. Hundreds of campfires burned across its breadth, like the sparks of Muspelheim fallen to the earth from the firmament. Large tracts of its sodden expanse never dried out during the year, and it was not a place Östen would have picked for a battle. But it lay in Styrbjörn's path to Eric's hall, and the army of the true king would make its stand here.

Östen turned back to the fire he shared with a dozen other men, including Olof, his neighbor back home. Most in this circle were farmers and herders who had likewise answered the call of the Bidding Stick. Some of them were seasoned fighters, others only barely come into their beards, but each of them knew they might not leave this place except in the winged company of Odin's warrior women.

As Östen took his place and sat down, a shadowy figure neared their camp.

"Who approaches?" called Alferth, a man whose right hand possessed only three fingers.

The figure came into the firelight, and Östen recognized Skarpe, a freeman from West Aros. Mud covered his legs from his boots to his thighs, the rest of his clothing wet through. It looked as though he'd suffered a mishap in the marsh, and some of the other men laughed at the sight of him.

"Skarpe, you fool," said Alferth. "There isn't any gold on this plain."

"So you've said." The soggy man took a seat close to the heat of the fire.

"Then why are you out there rooting around in the marsh like a pig after mast?" asked another.

"You know the story as well as I," Skarpe said. "The difference between us is that I believe it."

Alferth pointed off into the darkness. "You believe that Hrólf scattered his gold out there, and that Eadgils stopped to collect that gold instead of pursue his enemy?"

Skarpe shrugged. "Eadgils was a greedy king. And I think there's a good chance he didn't find every piece of gold on this plain."

"Bah!" Alferth said. "You know what I think? I think you're a raven starver, and one of these days you plan to run off—"

"I'm no coward," Skarpe said. His hand had gone to the knife at his side. "I'm certainly not afraid to fight you, Alferth. Nor any man here who—"

"There will be no fighting under the *ledung*," Östen said.

Every man around that fire turned to look at him.

He continued. "Or have you forgotten? Until Eric dismisses you, the only men you'll fight and kill will be Styrbjörn's men. When the battle is over, if the gods have kept you alive, then you can kill each other if that is how you wish to spend your good fortune. But not before. Am I understood?"

Östen wasn't in command of these men, but they nodded toward him nevertheless, and he looked each of them in the eye before returning his gaze to the thread tied around his wrist. He yearned for his wife and his bed. It had never bothered him before to sleep in a war camp and listen to the bluster of frightened men facing their deaths. He had never complained against the rough ground he lay upon or the biting flies that found his neck. Perhaps he was getting old, or a bit white in his liver.

Olof leaned in toward him. "That was well-spoken."

"But perhaps not well-heard." Östen nodded toward Skarpe,

who glowered at the fire in his sodden clothes, his eyes full of flames.

"Let every man wait for battle in his way," Olof said.

Östen nodded, and David nodded with him. Östen looked up into the sky and saw the Great Wagon in the stars. He was about to lie down to sleep under his cloak when a commotion rose up out on the plain. Men called and shouted in the distance, and some carrying torches ran between camps. Östen rose to his feet.

"What is this?" Olof asked.

Some moments later, one of the runners passed by them, but paused long enough to tell them that Styrbjörn's fleet had entered Mälaren, and he brought not only the Jomsvikings with him, but Dane ships as well.

"How many ships?" Östen asked.

"I don't know," the runner said. "You can count them when they land in two days' time." With that, he moved on toward the next camp.

"Two days," Olof said. "Two days until we fight."

Östen sat himself back down. He wasn't counting the days until the battle. He was counting the days until he went home.

CHAPTER TEN

Thorvald and Torgny approached Eric's long hall. Though not as impressive and imposing as the temple, it was large and fitting for a mortal king, ornamented with carvings of gods, warriors, and beasts that fought endlessly along its walls and pillars. At its wide doors, the marshal of Eric's personal war band met them and blocked their entrance with five of his men. Javier sensed within Thorvald that this was unusual, but not necessarily unexpected.

"Hail, Lawspeaker," the marshal said. "And to you, skald."

Thorvald nodded a reply, but remained poised and alert.

"Hail, *stallari*," Torgny said. "We would speak with the king."

"The king is in war council," the marshal said.

He offered no further answer, and neither he nor his men moved aside, making their full intention known. Thorvald then looked each of them over, assessing stance, size, arms, and armor. If necessary, he could mortally wound three of them before the remaining two had drawn their weapons.

"The council is why I have come," Torgny said.

"The king has counsel enough, Lawspeaker," the marshal said, without meeting Torgny's blind gaze. "Your time would be better spent at the temple, appealing to the gods on Eric's behalf."

"You should guard your words more carefully," Thorvald said, "lest the gods take a dark interest in you."

The marshal's jaw hardened. "And you should—"

"At all times the gods take interest in courage and honor," Torgny said. "Which they reward. Or punish when found lacking." He stepped closer to the marshal and looked up at him with his clouded eyes. "The king has never refused my counsel before, *stallari*. On whose order do you stand here before me?"

The marshal recoiled as far from Torgny as he could without physically giving ground, appearing unnerved by the Lawspeaker's words and gaze. "I take no orders from any but the king."

"But the king did not command you to bar me. We both know that." Torgny took another step toward him. "But someone did, so tell me, how much did your honor cost? Was it cheap? Perhaps I might wish to buy it at some point in the future."

"Watch yourself, Lawspeaker," the marshal said, but his voice had no strength behind it.

"I am watching *you*," Torgny said.

The marshal blanched, by a degree, and Thorvald seized the moment.

"The king awaits his Lawspeaker," he said. "We will keep him waiting no longer."

Then he led Torgny around the unmoving marshal and through his confused men, who looked to their leader for guidance. But the Lawspeaker had disarmed the marshal and rendered him harmless, all without Thorvald needing to lay a hand on him.

Inside the hall, dozens of members of Eric's court gathered in clusters at tables and along the two middle hearths that ran nearly the length of the room. Banners hung from the heavy beams above, and the air smelled of roasting pork and red wine. Some of the nobles looked up at the Lawspeaker's entrance, and some of them bowed their heads in deference as he passed. Some of them simply glared, for jealousy and rivalry could be stronger than a fear of the gods.

"Someone here does not want us influencing the king," Thorvald said in a low voice.

"Is that not always the case?" Torgny said.

"I worry the Order might have already found a way in."

"That is unlikely." But Torgny nodded. "Let me deal with it."

They strode the length of the hall to the king's throne at the far end, and behind it, they reached the king's private chambers, rooms appointed with Saxon silver and tapestries from Persia. This time, no one denied them entrance, and within the council room they found Eric leaning over a table, surrounded by his highest jarls and closest kinsmen. Thorvald studied their reactions upon seeing the Lawspeaker, hoping to discern which of them might be the enemy, but none of the faces betrayed their wearers.

Torgny bowed his head. "Greetings, my king. May the gods grant you victory."

"I look to you in that matter, Lawspeaker," Eric said. He wore a blue tunic embroidered with red and gold, his hair and beard in braids. Two wolves snarled at each other from the ends of a silver torc around his neck, and numerous finger rings from all corners of the world glinted on his hands. "Why are you late?"

"A delay that proved inconsequential," Torgny said, his response clearly designed to provoke their enemy. "I beg your forgiveness."

Again, Thorvald searched the reactions of those present, but their enemy remained hidden. He and Torgny drew closer to the king, and, upon his table, Thorvald saw a map of the country and its borders.

"We're discussing how best to make our stand." Eric pointed at the mouth of the Fyriswater, where it poured into Mälaren. "Some, like Jarl Frida, argue for a confrontation farther south, here."

Frida nodded. "Styrbjörn aims his spear at the heart of Svealand," she said. "I say we place our shield so that he cannot reach it."

Eric pointed at another place on the map. "Others believe we should wait for Styrbjörn here at Uppsala, where we are strongest."

Torgny nodded, but said nothing, and Thorvald waited. So did the rest of the room.

A moment later, Eric looked up, his brow creased. "Does the Lawspeaker wish to speak on this matter?"

"Not yet," Torgny said. "There is another matter I wish to speak of first."

"What matter?" the king asked.

"A dream," Torgny said. "A vision. For you alone, Eric."

That sent a rustle and grumble through the nobles, which the king silenced with a raise of his hand.

"Time is short, Lawspeaker."

Thorvald spoke up then. "All the reason to give each moment its due."

Eric frowned at Thorvald, tugging on his beard, but then nodded. "Out, all of you."

Now the faces of the nobles were indistinguishable from one another for their shared ire, each of them an enemy in that moment. But they obeyed their king and filed out of the chamber, and after they'd gone, Eric went to his chair and sat down.

Now Thorvald and Torgny stood alone before the king, the only other being in the room the king's house-bear, a brown sow he had raised from a cub and named Astrid. Unconcerned with the affairs of men, she slept chained in a corner of the room, against a wall, and the rumblings of her breathing sent tremors through the bones of the hall. The sight of her surprised Javier, but not Thorvald.

"We both know you've had no vision," Eric said. "So tell me what your blind eyes see. What would you see done?"

The Lawspeaker dropped his empty gaze to the floor, where it stayed until Thorvald could sense the king growing impatient. "May I speak freely?" Torgny asked.

"You are the Lawspeaker," Eric said. "Of all men, you may speak freely."

"I wish to bring something into the light," Torgny said. "You know of what I speak, though you have been content to pretend you do not see it moving in the shadows."

The king's guarded expression held its ground. "Go on."

"You have never asked the name of my Brotherhood, and I have never offered it. But we have watched and supported you, as you have ruled with wisdom and justice. We have advised you. As skalds, we have shaped the stories that are told, to inspire our people. We have fought and killed your enemies, at times with your knowledge, and other times without it."

Eric shifted in his chair. "There are some things better left unsaid, Lawspeaker."

"I agree," Torgny said.

"Then why bring this to me now? Why not leave your work and your Brotherhood in the shadows?"

"Because my Brotherhood has an enemy. We oppose an Order that has gained tremendous power among the Franks, and their influence is spreading. They have had dealings with Harald of Denmark, who sails with Styrbjörn."

"I see." Eric rose to his feet and paced around his chamber. "You believe my nephew, Styrbjörn, has brought your enemy Order to our lands?"

Torgny nodded. "I fear that is so."

Eric stopped pacing near Astrid the house-bear, who raised her great head to sniff his hand, her huge nostrils flaring with each powerful breath. "This is your fight," the king said. "Is it not?"

"It is," Torgny said. "But it is also your fight. If the Order establishes a foothold here, they will seek to control you, and failing that, they will seek your downfall."

That seemed to finally catch the king's ear. "Do you believe Styrbjörn has entered into a compact with this Order?"

"No," Torgny said. "Styrbjörn is far too willful and unpredictable to serve their purposes. But I assure you the Order is taking an interest in the outcome of this conflict."

Eric returned to his seat. "What does this mean for the battle?"

"Styrbjörn cannot simply be defeated. His army must be annihilated. We must destroy any agents of the Order who lurk among his or Harald's men. Not one seedling can take root."

Eric nodded. "Done."

"No," Torgny said. "Styrbjörn fights with his pride above all. He will seek to challenge you, as he did before you banished him."

"He was a boy then. If he seeks to challenge me now, my honor will demand that I accept."

"I know, my king. Which is why he must not be allowed to reach you. You must not meet his army on any open field of battle, either here or to the south. Not yet."

"Then what are you suggesting?"

Torgny turned to Thorvald. "Here I turn to my apprentice, Thorvald. You will find him to be even more cunning than I am."

Eric looked at Thorvald. "Speak," he commanded, and waited.

Astrid stirred in the corner, awakening. With a deep huffing, she rose and lumbered across the room on her heavy paws, dragging her chain, to stand beside Eric's throne. The king reached out and scratched her neck as if she were a hunting hound. Javier felt very small under the power of that moment. It was like staring a legend in the face. But Thorvald did not shrink.

"We must harry Styrbjörn relentlessly," he said. "He must pay dearly with the lives of his men for every foot of ground he gains on his way to Uppsala, so that when he arrives, his force will be small enough to crush."

"How?" Eric asked. "He will simply row his ships up the river, which will bring him almost to my doors."

"Jarl Frida's plan showed wisdom, but not cunning." Thorvald turned to the map, and Eric left his seat to join him. Astrid followed at her master's side, her head high enough to rest her chin upon the table. Thorvald pointed to the mouth of the Fyriswater. "We stop him here, as she suggested, but not with an army."

"With what, then?" the king asked.

"Let me take a company of men," Thorvald said. "Strong men, the strongest I can find. Fighting men. We will plant stakes in the river—"

"A palisade?" Eric asked.

"Yes. We will keep his ships from ever entering the river. Styrbjörn is impatient. He won't take the time to tear down the stakewall. He'll leave his ships and march overland."

"And then?"

"I use my company as an axe to cleave away his army's limbs."

The king narrowed his eyes, and then he grinned. "I like this plan. My kinsmen and the other jarls may not."

"They won't accept it if it comes from my apprentice," the Lawspeaker said.

"It must come from the Lawspeaker," Thorvald said. "It must come from the gods."

"Which god?" Eric asked.

Thorvald thought for a moment. He had no idea where Styrbjörn stood now in relation to Asgard, but in his younger days, he had always favored Thor. That made the choice a simple one.

"Odin," Thorvald said. "When an impudent son rebels, it must be the father who puts him down and punishes him."

Next to Thorvald, Torgny nodded his approval.

Eric grunted. "Very well." He reached under the left sleeve of his shirt and pulled a golden arm ring down over his wrist. He handed the band to Thorvald. "Go with my authority and choose your men well. The Lawspeaker and I will speak to the others."

Thorvald bowed to the king, and then turned to his mentor. "I shall not fail," he said.

"Bring them the judgment of the Norns," Torgny said.

Thorvald left the council chamber and returned to the great hall, where the nobles waited in a mass near the throne. He said nothing to them, and met none of their eyes as he stalked through the throng toward the doors. The marshal stood near them, and when he saw Thorvald, the anger on his face showed that his earlier befuddlement had turned into a shame that demanded a reckoning.

"I would have words with you, skald," the marshal said, stepping into Thorvald's path.

"And I would have words with you." Thorvald stepped to the side to go around him. "But not today."

The marshal reached out his arm to block him. In an instant Thorvald had him twisted around, shoulder and elbow joints straining painfully behind his back, with a dagger at his throat.

Not his hidden blade, but an ordinary knife. The marshal winced, eyes open wide in shock.

"I go on the king's errand," Thorvald said, right into the marshal's ear. "You will not delay me. But I swear I will return, and at that time, if you still have cause against me, then we shall have words. Understood?"

The marshal nodded. Thorvald released him, and the man staggered away, rubbing his arm. Thorvald gave him a glare of contempt and marched through the doors.

There were warriors enough among Eric's war band for Thorvald to assemble his company, but he didn't want professional fighting men from Uppsala, and he was no longer sure of their loyalties if the marshal had been corrupted. Instead, Thorvald wanted warriors from the countryside who knew the land well, who loved the land, and would therefore fight all the more viciously to protect it. That meant he would seek his company from among those summoned under the *ledung* by the Bidding Stick.

He mounted Gyllir and rode south onto the plain of Fyrisfield to scout among the encampments there. He trotted past dozens of farmers, craftsmen, and common laborers, and occasionally, when he caught a spark of courage in a countenance, or saw confidence in the holding of a weapon, he stopped to ask a single question.

"If I could grant you one wish, right now," he said, again and again, "what would it be?"

The answers came easily.

A woman.

Ale.

Victory.

An honorable death.

But none of them gave the right answer.

He did not have much time to give this selection, and as the day wore on, he wondered if he should simply draw men from among the war band, after all. But then he spied a giant in a camp not far away, who stood heads taller and wider than any man around him. The kind of man who called to mind the children of the jötnar and their stolen human brides. Thorvald rode toward him at a brisk trot and dismounted as he neared the stranger's circle.

"Greetings," he said. "I come to you with the king's authority."

"You have it backward, friend," said a man missing several fingers. "You see, we're all here by order of the Bidding Stick, so I believe we come to *you* with the king's authority."

He laughed, and so did some of the others. The giant did not.

"You there," Thorvald called to him. "What is your name?"

"Östen," the giant said. "What's yours?"

"Thorvald," he said. "How do you earn your livelihood?"

Östen frowned. "Sheep. Why is that business of yours?"

"It is not my business." Thorvald raised his sleeve to reveal Eric's arm ring, and the sight of it forced the gathering into silence. "As I told your finger-deficient friend, it is the king's business."

Östen's frown softened, and he nodded. "How may I be of service to the king?"

Thorvald surveyed the giant's hands, his scars, his bearing, and did not need to ask if he could fight. Östen could fight very well. Instead, Thorvald asked the question he had asked of all the others that morning.

"If I could grant you one wish, right now, what would it be?"

"To go home," Östen said, without hesitation, as he touched a single thread tied incongruously around his thick wrist.

Thorvald smiled. That was the answer he had been waiting to hear.

CHAPTER ELEVEN

Natalya ran.

Not toward.

Away.

Her body wasn't hers. It belonged to her fear, and it carried her through the Forest, leaping over roots and dodging around the trees. Her mind wondered where she could run or hide in a wood that was the same in every direction, but her body asked no questions. It took the icy fuel of her adrenaline and filled her every muscle with it. It whipped her heart into such a frenzy she couldn't tell its beats apart. It numbed her to the scrapes and bruises acquired in her flight. It told her mind not to interfere. Her body knew what to do.

Owen ran beside her, and she tried to stay aware of him, even though she couldn't tell if he was aware of her.

The Serpent chased them. Its speed seemed impossible, blinding, as if the trees and uneven ground offered no obstacle. As if the Forest and the Serpent shared intent.

The monster gained on them, and then, with a sudden lunge, it entered the corner of her right eye. She turned toward it just as it struck, its mouth opened wide to reveal white flesh and ivory fangs as long as her legs. But the strike missed her by inches, and one of those fangs stabbed deep into the tree nearest her, and became embedded. The Serpent coiled up and thrashed, trying to tear itself free.

Guys? Monroe said. *Talk to me. What's going on?*

"A little busy right now!" Owen said, and then he called to her, "Are you okay?"

Natalya nodded, still bewildered.

"Let's go that way," he said, pointing in a new direction.

Guys? Monroe said.

"Not now!" Owen shouted back, sprinting away.

Natalya ran after him.

With the Serpent's attack, her mind had taken back some control. The Forest to either side and in front of her presented nothing but endlessness, a desert of trees. They couldn't outrun the monster, but they also couldn't hide. They couldn't even climb the trees to escape, because she was pretty sure the Serpent could reach them. She felt she had to be missing something.

As a memory, and a simulation, this made no sense. There had to be more to the collective unconscious than these two archetypes. There had to be something beyond them. The voice had said something about a path, and also fear, devotion, and—

Fear.

And Monroe had said that the Serpent archetype repre-
sented death and fear.

A few feet ahead of her, Owen skidded to a stop, and she
almost ran into him.

"What are you—?"

"Shh!" he said.

She looked around him and saw the Serpent. Not its head.
Just its huge, never-ending body, slithering across their path with
the sound of a rushing river, disconcertingly unaware of them.

"Which way do we go?" Owen whispered.

They couldn't go back the way they'd come, unless they
wanted another encounter with the Serpent's head. And it
seemed foolish to turn to the left or right and follow its body if
they were trying to escape from it. That meant they had to
go over it.

"I don't get it," Owen said. "If this is all just a symbol,
shouldn't there be a magic sword around here? Something we
can use to kill it?"

"We have to climb over it," Natalya said.

"Wait, what?"

"It's the only way." She stepped forward, right up to the
nightmare express of skin and scales rolling by. The snake's
body was almost as tall as she was, and was smooth enough to
gleam, which meant that climbing it, especially while it was
moving, would be difficult.

"You're serious," Owen said, stepping up beside her.

"Can you think of another way around it?"

"No. But I also think this whole simulation is messed up."

Natalya couldn't argue with that. The Forest around them
still seemed to twist and contort itself in the darkness just outside

the edges of the dim light. The Serpent's body emerged from and disappeared into that same boundary. It felt as if they had become trapped in a moment, or a thought, that replayed itself on an infinite loop, and the only way to break the loop was to move ahead.

"So how do we do this?" she asked.

Owen looked around. "Maybe we climb one of the trees?"

She cast her gaze up with his, searching for a low enough branch to grab on to. None of the trees nearby offered one, so they walked along the path of the Serpent until they found a tree they could use.

From its side grew a branch just thick enough that Natalya could barely encircle it with her hands. She latched on to it, and with her feet against the trunk she pulled and heaved herself up until she rested in the branch's crook. Then she offered Owen her hand to help pull him up, and soon they were both safely above ground.

Natalya hugged the trunk of the tree and shimmied around it onto another, higher branch, and then another, until she reached one that stretched out far enough in the right direction and looked strong enough to support them.

"Here goes," she said.

Owen looked at her, looked down at the Serpent, and nodded.

Natalya lowered herself into a straddle over the branch and scooted out onto it several feet. Then she leaned forward to hug the branch, crossed her legs at the ankles, and allowed herself to swing over and around so that she was hanging by her arms and her legs. Then she inched along, hand over hand, making her way slowly outward until the branch sagged and complained, and she'd gone as far as she dared go. But when she looked down, she discovered she was suspended directly over the Serpent's body, not nearly far enough to make it to the other side.

"What now?" Owen asked, still clinging to the trunk of the tree.

"Um—" What else could she do? "I'm going to let my legs go. Then I'll hang on to the branch with my hands until I'm ready to drop onto the snake."

"Wait, onto the snake?"

"Yeah." She nodded toward the far side of the Serpent. "I'll try to fall off that way. You know, drop and roll."

"Yeah, good plan," he said with a shake of his head. "What if the snake doesn't want us to use it as a trampoline?"

The Serpent was so enormous, Natalya hoped that it might not even notice them. She reaffirmed her grip on the branch with her hands, took a deep breath, and muttered, "This better be worth it, Monroe." Then she let her legs uncross, and as they fell away from the branch, her body swung by her fingers and hands. But she didn't drop. Not yet.

It was hard to tell from her angle, but it seemed as if her toes now dangled about two or three feet above the Serpent's body. Not a problem at all, when she wasn't landing on a moving surface of reptile scales. But she felt her hands getting tired, and if she didn't go soon, she wouldn't be able to choose the moment for herself.

"Okay!" she called to Owen. "Wish me luck!"

He gave her a weak thumbs-up.

She let go.

A second later, her feet touched down, and she immediately dropped her body to all fours as the Serpent whisked her suddenly away, moving much faster than she had expected. She glanced back at Owen, up in the tree. His mouth hung open, and he grew distant until he disappeared into the woods.

She was supposed to fall off. Not go for a ride. But then she looked ahead and saw the trees careering by to either side, marking her passage through the Forest at exactly the speed of her terror. She felt the wind in her hair, and beneath her hands she felt smooth, hard scales, which were neither cold nor warm, but about the same temperature as the air.

She was riding a giant snake that had eyes like brass cymbals and fangs so large their venom wouldn't matter. A beast that had almost killed her only minutes before and probably wouldn't miss a second strike.

She was *riding* it. Keeping a grip on her fear, like Monroe had said to do.

She knew she should jump off, but she didn't want to. Not yet. This dangerous moment had captured her, and she wasn't quite ready to leave it. She and Owen could keep running from the Serpent, but for how long? This archetype seemed to fill the Forest, and it would find them eventually, but at least this way, she rode it by choice.

"Natalya!" It was Owen's panicked voice in her ear, in the same way as Monroe's. "Natalya, are you okay?"

"I'm okay," she said. "I'm here."

"You were supposed to fall off!" Owen said. "What happened?"

"I don't know. Where are you?"

"I'm on the snake with you! But now we can jump off together. Let's—"

"No," Natalya said. "Wait."

"Wait? What for, beverage service? Because I don't think they offer that on this thing."

Natalya didn't understand why she was hesitating.

"Natalya," Owen said. "We need to jump."

He was right.

"Okay," she said. "Get ready. We'll—"

But then it was there. The Serpent reared its head in front of her, looming out of the murk with its eyes upon her, flicking its forked tongue. Natalya felt the same all-consuming, mind-emptying panic she had when seeing the creature for the first time, and she lost the ability to move or speak. She could only watch as the Serpent eased into alignment with itself, bringing her directly toward its mouth.

She had to move. She had to fight it.

"Natalya?" Owen said. "Hello?"

"Jump," she whispered, straining and shaking.

"What?"

"Jump!" she shouted, and managed to tip herself to the side, rolling off the Serpent's back into a fall. She hit the ground hard, and her momentum tumbled her a few feet, slamming her back into a tree.

The Serpent's body continued to rush past her for a few moments, but she didn't spot Owen riding it, which hopefully meant he had listened to her and bailed out somewhere down-snake. She didn't dare call to him to find out, because even in that moment, the Serpent's body had slowed, and from every direction she heard the rasp and rattle of its scales against the trees. Then she saw one of its great looping coils slide into view. Then another, and another, until she was surrounded, and the whole Forest appeared to writhe with its impossible body.

Natalya cowered where she was, in pain, frozen in place as if already impaled against the tree by the Serpent's fang. At any moment, its silent head would slip around the tree she leaned against, and there would be nothing to do, and nowhere to run. Its mouth would open, and it would swallow her alive. The thought of it brought a scream to her throat, but she covered her mouth to trap it inside and stay hidden for just a few moments more. Just another moment or two of fear, fighting the inevitable.

Unless Monroe could pull her out before then. The simulation would end either way, with her death or with an evacuation. But she wouldn't have learned anything that could help stop Isaiah. He would still be unstoppable if he found the Trident.

Well, if she was going to fail, it might as well be on her terms, but it wouldn't be because she'd asked Monroe to save her. After all, the voice had said the path was *through* fear. So she accepted her fear, instead of fighting it. Against every instinct buried in the deepest corners of her mind, she stood up. Then she took several deep and even breaths, listening only to the sound of herself. When her hands stopped shaking, she closed her eyes for a moment, and then she stepped out from behind the tree.

The Serpent whipped its head toward her, tongue flicking, but she didn't run from it. In accepting her fear, she found it had actually vanished, for it no longer served a purpose. Now she stood her ground, calmly facing the enormous monster bearing down on her.

The Serpent closed the distance between them almost instantly, and Natalya closed her eyes, allowing it to happen when it happened. She felt the soft Forest floor beneath her feet, and high above the smell of snake she caught something light and fragrant. A blossom of some kind.

A shadow crossed her, blotting out even the meager light in the woods, and then she felt something flick the top her head, tossing her hair. The Serpent's tongue. After that came the monster's mouth, which pressed against her head and opened, sliding down over her face, soft and dry, smothering her. She remained aware of a painful squeezing at every point on her body that soon forced her mouth open to let the air out of her. She was in its mouth, about to enter its throat. She lost awareness then of where she was, and she felt herself slipping into nothing—

"Natalya!"

Her eyes shot open.

"There you are!" Owen called.

She looked down at her body, and discovered she was unharmed. The Serpent had vanished. She stood upon a path paved with red stone, a path that began at her feet, and the Forest around her had changed. Bright sunlight suffused it with a soft green glow that had banished the barrier of darkness. The path of red stone ran along the ground and around the trees in loops and whorls that made little sense, but away to the right it straightened out and proceeded confidently into the Forest.

"You found a path," Owen said, running up beside her. "Where did the Serpent go?"

Natalya looked again at the path, its regular stones laid close together like scales, much of its course a coiled knot. "I think . . . I think the Serpent *is* the path."

"What?" Owen looked down. "Really?"

"It ate me."

"What?" he blurted. "What do you mean it ate you?"

"I mean I felt it. I was inside its mouth. And then I was just . . . standing here."

Owen appeared to be tracing the path with his eyes, taking it in. Then he threw up his hands. "Sure. Why not? That makes about as much sense as anything else in this place so far."

"It does make sense. Sort of. When you think about what that light said." Natalya pointed to where the path straightened out. "I think we should follow it."

Owen agreed. "Maybe it leads out of the Forest."

"I think it does."

So they followed it, from the place where Natalya had accepted that her simulation would end, into a woodland still as thick and deep as it had been before, but which Natalya no longer found threatening. Instead, its vast distances called to her, enticing her to wander from the path and explore. But she resisted, fearing what it would mean for her mind if she became lost in this simulation.

"Monroe?" Natalya said.

Yeah?

"Just seeing if you were there," she said.

Oh, you mean you guys have time for me now?

"I don't think you realize how big that snake was," Owen said.

Big enough to turn into a path?

"So you are listening," Natalya said.

Of course I am. But like I said earlier, the Animus is having a hard time showing me what's going on. You guys are going to have to figure most of this out for yourselves. I'm actually starting to suspect that's the whole point.

"So what do we do now?" Owen asked.

Follow the yellow brick road.

"Right," Natalya said. "Maybe this path is *the* Path."

Man, I wish Joseph Campbell were here.

"Who?" Owen asked.

Joseph Campbell? Monroe sighed. *Let me put it this way. If you're on the Path, then Campbell has the map. But he's not here, so it looks like you're going to have to find your own way. So I'll leave you to it. Grace just walked in, and she needs to talk to me. But I'll be here if you need me.*

"Over and out," Owen said.

A large bird rose up from the trees to the right and flew over them, caressing the Path with its shadow, and a light breeze seemed to follow it. Natalya spied squirrels scampering up and down the trees, and smiled at the angry flip of their tails that accompanied their scolding chatter.

"If the last Forest had a giant snake," Owen said, "then this Forest definitely has elves."

Natalya agreed with him, but if there was an Elf or Fairy archetype inhabiting those woods, she never appeared, and after walking a distance that didn't seem measurable in miles, they glimpsed a break in the trees ahead. The edge of the Forest. As they drew closer, she saw a figure waiting in the road. It appeared to be quite large, but not human.

"What do you think?" Owen asked.

She shrugged. "I think we'll find out when we get there."

CHAPTER TWELVE

Grace waited until she was sure that David wasn't going to desynchronize, and then she left him in the Animus room to go for a walk so she could think.

It wasn't that she resented him for taking over the simulation. Even though she liked to tease him, she didn't feel the same level of personal rivalry that he did. He had to prove that he didn't need his older sister. Sometimes, it seemed as though he needed to prove it to her, and sometimes it seemed as though he just needed to prove it to himself. Either situation could be irritating. But watching him put that helmet on, and then knowing he'd left their world behind for a Viking one, had unsettled her and she wasn't sure why.

Maybe the vision had something to do with it.

The Piece of Eden in Mongolia had shown her the future

that most frightened her. The future she spent so much energy trying to prevent. It showed her a future in which David had done just about everything she had ever warned him not to do. He got older and ran with a bad crew, and got caught up in some really bad stuff. The vision showed her a David she didn't recognize, and it ended the night that he died. A night that began with two detectives knocking on the door, demolishing their family, and ended with the faces of her grief-stricken parents. A night of screaming and tears and anger so hot an inner part of Grace burned to ash.

After Isaiah had left with the dagger and the vision had ended, Grace had cried and hugged David so hard he probably wondered what was going on, but she hadn't told him then, and she still hadn't.

Now she needed some air, and some sky. She knew of a balcony next to the office that used to be Isaiah's, so she walked to the Aerie's main elevators and rode one of them to the top floor.

Outside, she found the day overcast with clouds that seemed the color and weight of cement. But even without the sunlight she'd hoped for, it felt good to stand in the open, surrounded by wind and mountains. For several peaceful minutes she just stood there, leaning against the balcony's railing, thinking of nothing.

But then she thought of David again, downstairs in the Animus.

That still bothered her. And it hadn't bothered her before. David had gone into simulations on his own, but something had changed since then, and the only thing she could point to was that vision. It scared her now to let him out of her sight, even into a virtual reality.

She had to get her mind off it somehow, so she went back inside, and, out of curiosity, she tried the door to Isaiah's office. It opened, which wasn't too surprising, since he had probably taken everything with him and there wasn't any reason for Victoria to lock the door. But she looked around anyway, and found the desk and its drawers empty.

There was a bookcase, however, and Grace thought reading might distract her and help her pass the time, if she could find something interesting. The titles she scanned dealt mostly with history, including a few biographies, most of it probably related to the Templars. There was a book on the Borgias, one about a guy named Jacques de Molay, and another called *The Journal of Haytham Kenway*, among many others. But she also noticed a couple of random books that didn't fit the pattern, one of them a book on Norse mythology.

Having just experienced the memories of Östen, she pulled that volume from the shelf, and then made herself comfortable in the big chair behind the desk. The first thing she decided to look for in the book was any mention of a magical dagger, because if the Vikings had a prong of the Trident, maybe there were legends about it. But after checking each of the mentions listed in the index, she concluded none of them fit. So she started just flipping through the pages, stopping to read anything that looked interesting, and realized pretty quickly the Norse gods were strange.

Especially Loki.

Here was a handsome half giant who could convince anyone to do just about anything, including getting Thor into a dress and a wedding veil, and he went and had three kids with a giantess. One of them was a half-dead girl they put in charge of the underworld, another one was a sea serpent, and the last one was the giant Fenris wolf. The gods kicked Loki's kids out of Asgard, which made the three of them into the mortal enemies of the gods.

That brought Grace to Ragnarök. The end of the world. Or at least the fate of the gods. In the final battle, Loki's wolf-son killed Odin, and the sea serpent killed Thor, which meant that, in a way, the gods had brought about their own demise. Grace turned the page to read on—

A folded sheet of paper fell out of the book onto the desk.

Grace set the book aside and picked up the paper, which contained a handwritten note. As she read it, she realized that it had been written by Isaiah, and her eyes widened in fear at his words. The situation was even worse than they had imagined. Much worse.

He didn't want to be a king. Isaiah wanted to destroy the world. He wanted Ragnarök.

Grace jumped up from the desk and ran from the office, back to the elevators, where she jabbed the button and fidgeted furiously until the elevator came, and she rode back down to the ground floor. She didn't trust Victoria or Griffin enough to go to them with this. That left Monroe, so she sprinted across the atrium toward the laboratories, and after searching several darkened rooms, she finally found Monroe seated at a computer terminal. Owen and Natalya walked in their Animus harnesses next to him, and he gave Grace a quick, perplexed nod as she came in.

"It looks like you're going to have to find your own way," he said into his headset, and she realized he was talking to Owen and Natalya. "So I'll leave you to it. Grace just walked in, and she needs to talk to me. But I'll be here if you need me." He touched a button on the display and then swiveled in his chair to face her. "Everything okay?"

She handed him the note without saying anything, and waited as long as she could to let him read it before speaking. "What is he talking about?" she asked. "Disasters? Cycles of death and renewal? Ragnarök?"

Monroe shook his head, then refolded the note and tapped it against his knee. "It seems that Isaiah has developed some peculiar ideas."

"Peculiar ideas?" Grace said. "He thinks the world needs to die!"

"To be reborn, yes. It's a common mythology around the world. First, a cataclysmic event occurs. It could be a great flood. It could be fire. But it wipes the slate clean, and, afterward, the survivors are left with a purified new world. That's a part of Ragnarök people sometimes forget. The cycle starts over. Apparently, Isaiah thinks we're long overdue."

"I—I thought he just wanted to conquer the world. Not kill everyone."

"Not everyone. I'm pretty sure Isaiah plans to survive. Then he can set himself up as humanity's next savior and ruler."

Grace remembered another detail from the note. "Who are the Instruments of the First Will?"

"Something I've only heard rumors about." Monroe held up the note. "Where did you find this?"

"In a book on Norse mythology. In Isaiah's old office."

"Have you shown it to anyone else?"

"Not yet. I don't trust Victoria, or Griffin."

Monroe gave her the note back. "You hang on to that, but let's keep it between us for now. I want to find out if Victoria knows about this. If she does, then I want to know why she's keeping us in the dark."

Grace nodded.

"Try not to worry. This doesn't change anything. No matter what Isaiah has planned, we're going to stop him."

She wished that reassured her, but it didn't. Grace now knew this was a doomsday scenario, and now that she knew that, she needed to do something about it that much more urgently. She looked at Owen and Natalya again, the hydraulics and machinery of their harnesses whispering as they strolled in place. Then she noticed a third, unoccupied Animus next to theirs.

"Could I go into their simulation?" she asked Monroe. "I want to help."

"What about your ancestor's simulation?"

"David's got it." And she couldn't let her fear for him stop her from doing what needed to be done. Besides, she told herself the dagger's vision wasn't real. He was safe, for now. "I can help Owen and Natalya."

Monroe looked over at the Animus machines and studied them for a moment. "It would be possible. But you should know it might be very dangerous in there. I'm worried about the risk to your mind."

"Owen and Natalya are in there," Grace said. "If I want to help them, it's my risk to take."

"True enough." Monroe rose from his chair. "I'll let them catch you up with everything once you're in there, if that's okay. It'll take me some time to tie this third Animus into the other two."

Grace found herself a chair of her own. "I can wait."

It did take some time, but eventually Monroe had the empty Animus ready to go. These three machines looked different from the others, more industrial, like they were stripped down to the bare hardware. Grace stepped inside the ring and climbed into the harness. Several minutes later, she stood blinking in the Memory Corridor, waiting to join the simulation. Monroe let Owen and Natalya know that she was coming in, and then he counted her down.

The world that appeared out of the gray void did not feel right, in a way that was hard for her to describe. It lacked a certain specificity. She stood on a path made of stone, but she couldn't say what kind of stone it was. A beautiful forest grew all around her, but she couldn't identify the types of trees. It wasn't that she lacked the knowledge. It was something about them that made them unidentifiable, like they were somehow *all* trees. They looked very real, as real as any rocks and trees she had ever seen, and yet, not real.

"Grace!"

It was Owen's voice.

She looked and saw him waving at her from farther down the path. Natalya stood next to him, and they waited as she jogged the distance to catch up. When she reached them, they seemed genuinely happy to see her.

"What is this place?" Grace asked.

Owen spread his arms. "This, my friend, is the Forest." Then he tapped his foot. "And this is the Path. With capital letters. You missed the Serpent." He pointed down the stone trail ahead of them, and Grace saw a distant figure in silhouette where it looked like the Forest ended. "We have something up there we're not sure about yet."

"This is a simulation of the collective unconscious," Natalya said.

"Oh, right." Grace remembered Monroe explaining that concept, back when they'd hitched a ride to Mongolia in an Abstergo shipping container. Now she took in her surroundings from a different angle, and its strangeness made more sense. "So these are archetypes."

"Yes," Natalya said, sounding a bit surprised.

Grace nodded down the path, toward the something. It looked like an animal of some kind. "So is that an archetype?"

"We don't know," Owen said. "We were on our way there when Monroe said you were coming in, so we decided to wait."

"And why exactly are we in here?" Grace asked. "Monroe didn't really explain the point."

"The collective unconscious and the Ascendance Event are connected to the Trident," Natalya said. "When we came in here, a talking light told us to follow the path through fear, devotion, and faith. We've already gone through fear, I think. We're supposed to go to the summit."

"With a capital *S*?" Grace asked.

Owen shrugged. "Probably."

"Then let's get to it," Grace said.

Owen and Natalya nodded, and the three of them set off down the stone Path. Gradually, the simulation seemed less strange to Grace, replaced by a vague familiarity, even though she had never been there before. It wasn't quite déjà vu, but it was similar to that. She assumed that's because archetypes were in some ways familiar to most people. That was one of their defining characteristics. As for the figure up ahead, it had begun to resolve itself, and it wasn't long before Grace could tell what it was.

"It's a dog," she said.

"A big dog," Natalya said.

"Maybe it's *the* Dog," Owen said.

The closer they got, the more likely that actually seemed. This dog was enormous, and had a wolfish appearance, with fur the color of dried blood, yellow eyes, and a thick mane around its neck. Grace had never been afraid of dogs, but this one was big enough to look her straight in the eyes while seated on its haunches. She felt a bit safer when it started wagging its tail, brushing it back and forth over the Path as the three of them approached.

"So what happens now?" Grace whispered.

"I don't know," Owen said.

"Well, what happened last time?"

"The Serpent attacked us—"

The Dog barked, startling Grace. She jumped, and so did Natalya and Owen. It had been single bark, very loud and very deep.

"Let's not talk about things attacking, okay?" Natalya whispered.

But then, with a soft whine, the Dog stood up on its four feet. Grace prepared to run, in case it charged at them. But it turned in the opposite direction from them and trotted away down the Path, past the edge of the forest, into the sunlight of the open countryside beyond. They watched it go, but the Dog soon stopped and turned back to look at them.

It barked again.

"What's it doing?" Owen asked.

"I'm not sure," Natalya said.

Another bark.

It looked to Grace as if the Dog might be waiting for them. "I think it wants us to follow it," she said.

Natalya looked again and nodded. "I think you're right."

So they left the Forest behind and ventured out onto a section of the Path that wound through a dry countryside of white rock, thick grass, and short, gnarled trees. The Dog led the way, quickly adopting a routine in which it barked and waited to see if they would follow, and when they did, it proceeded to the next spot, where it barked again. There was just no way of knowing where it was leading them or why.

Watching the Dog lope along made Grace think of the Fenris wolf, the monster she'd read about in the book on Norse mythology, which brought Isaiah's note to mind. She would not have thought that following a Dog would help in her in the mission to stop him, but this was important somehow, and she had to trust in that.

Just like she had to trust David.

Soon they'd traveled far enough into this new terrain that the Forest behind them disappeared over the uneven horizon. With each bark, the Dog sounded more desperate, and possibly even impatient with them.

"Let's try not to get lost in here," Owen said, looking over his shoulder. "I don't want my mind to be trapped in this place permanently."

That must've been one of the dangers Monroe had mentioned. Grace shuddered at the idea of her mind staying in this simulation while her body just kept walking forever like a zombie in the Animus.

"I think we'll be okay if we stick to the Path," Natalya said.

"I hope so," said Grace. So they continued following the Dog, trying to keep up with it, until it stopped and barked at something off the Path.

Grace looked for what it might be, and she spotted some kind of stone monument at the top of a green hillock nearby. When she and the others turned in that direction, the Dog barked one more time, and then shot away from them up the mound toward the structure, tearing a seam in the tall grass.

"I guess we go that way," Owen said.

"Didn't we just decide not to leave the Path?" Grace said.

"It's not that far," Owen said. "We'll be able to see the Path from up there. And we might even see more of the simulation."

"It still seems risky," Grace said.

The dog barked at them from the top of the hill.

"It also seems like that's where we're supposed to go," Natalya said. "But let's keep the Path in sight at all times."

They agreed, but Grace still didn't like the idea. As they left the Path and marched up the hill, the grass at Grace's knees, she looked back constantly to make sure the red stones were still there, charting a course through the collective unconscious.

The angle of the slope turned out to be steeper than it had appeared, and the three of them were soon breathing hard, while above them, the Dog continued to bark, distant and echoed. A few minutes later, they reached the top. The structure Grace had seen from below turned out to be a circle of high stones, each several feet taller than her and a few feet thick. They stood quite close together, with only a few inches between them, but the circle had an opening not far from them. The barking came from inside it.

They hurried through the opening, and within the circle Grace found the Dog sitting next to a man, whining and wagging its tail. The man sat on the ground, his back propped up against one of the stones, his rutted face turned heavenward, with his eyes closed. His gray beard and hair were long and unkempt, and he wore coarse clothing made of fur and animal skins. A long wooden staff lay across his lap.

Grace, Owen, and Natalya approached him cautiously. This situation, and this figure, seemed even less predictable than the Dog.

"Do you think he's dead?" Owen asked.

"I'm not dead," the stranger said, opening his eyes. "But I am dying. And I need you to do something for me after I am gone."

CHAPTER THIRTEEN

Restrained in the Animus, Sean could do nothing as Isaiah stalked toward him across the chapel, wielding the incomplete Trident of Eden.

"Until now I have only relied on your faith," Isaiah said. "But it seems I must also show you fear."

Sean didn't know what he meant by that, but before he could figure it out, an image tore through his mind, casting every other thought aside, more powerful than any simulation. It came from a time before the accident, a recurring fear he used to carry around before his life had become something completely unplanned and unimagined.

He was standing on the soccer field. His teammates had turned their backs on him to go congratulate their opponents on their win. A win that Sean had made possible by screwing up.

It didn't matter how he had screwed up. The fear came in all varieties. Not just soccer, but basketball and baseball, too. Whenever Sean had taken up a new sport, the image had changed to suit it. But the shame remained the same. The knowledge that the crowd and the team had watched him fail. That he had let them down. The fear of what they were thinking and saying about him when he wasn't around. The belief that they were right.

He wasn't talented.

He wasn't good.

In fact, he was terrible, and it wouldn't matter how long and hard he practiced. He should probably just quit and do everyone else a favor. He knew the coach and his teammates wanted him gone, but they were just too nice to say it. They only kept him on the team out of pity. His stomach hurt when he thought about having to go back into the locker room with everyone. They'd pat him on the back and tell him it was okay that he screwed up, but it wasn't. Rather than face that, he wanted the field to open up beneath him and suck him down where no one would find him and he could be forgotten.

He was worthless. More than worthless, he was the one holding other people back.

"Sean," a soothing voice said.

The image left, and Sean returned to the chapel. Isaiah stood before him. Sean's cheeks felt wet, and he realized he'd been crying.

"Whatever you just saw," Isaiah said, "I can free you from it. But only if you listen to me and do as I say. Your ancestor, Styrbjörn, was a stubborn individual, and I think perhaps that is rubbing off on you through the Bleeding Effects. But I need you to stay strong and resist him. I need you to remember why we're here, and how essential you are. I am very proud of you for what you've accomplished so far. You and I, we can do this together."

As Isaiah spoke, Sean felt the ground firming up beneath him. He realized there wasn't any reason for him to fear that he might fail. Not when he had Isaiah. It didn't matter what his teammates and his coaches had said or thought about him. However badly Sean had screwed up before, that didn't matter now, because he had Isaiah and he believed what Isaiah said.

"Are you ready to go back into your ancestor's memories?" Isaiah asked.

Sean nodded. "I'm ready."

"Excellent."

The chapel doors opened and several technicians swept into the room. They scurried over to the Animus, and very quickly had the simulation ready again. Isaiah placed the helmet back on Sean's head, and gave his shoulder a firm squeeze before throwing him back into the wild river of Styrbjörn's mind. Moments later, he stood between Palnatoke and Harald Bluetooth, shoulder to shoulder at the bow of his ship.

The calm waters of Lake Mälaren had granted his fleet easy passage, though the journey had not been as swift as he would have liked. They had stopped at several villages along the way to recruit men to his banner, but few had joined. It seemed that in his absence, honor had become a rarity among the Svear, but it was also said that cunning trolls had begun to stalk the forests, high in the trees, ready to slay anyone who supported Styrbjörn. Escaped bondsmen had been attacked, and the word had spread. But Styrbjörn didn't believe in trolls.

Superstition or not, it was no matter, for he had more than enough warriors and ships to defeat Eric, and would soon reach the mouth of the Fyriswater. From there, they would row up the river to Uppsala and to battle.

Palnatoke seemed as eager for that as Styrbjörn, as did all the Jomsvikings, whose covenant disposed them to war making. But to his other side, Harald's cowardice had become more pronounced with each passing league, and his hand never left the dagger he wore. It offended Styrbjörn that his sister had wed this Dane, no matter his power and the size of his kingdom.

"What is that?" he finally asked Harald, nodding to the dagger. "It is a strange blade. I can think of no use for it. And yet you hold to it as a suckling pig to its mother's teat."

An angry red entered the white of Harald's face. "It is nothing to you."

"If it was nothing to me, I would not ask."

"Then it is simply nothing."

"I doubt that very much. What is it to you?"

Harald shut his mouth and held it fast, the first sign of resolve he had yet shown, and in that moment Styrbjörn's curiosity about the dagger reached a point where it would not be denied. Sean had been waiting for a moment like this, for his ancestor to finally notice the Piece of Eden.

"I have a bargain I wish to make with you," Styrbjörn said.

Harald glowered at him. To his other side, Palnatoke listened and watched with a glint of amusement in his eye.

"Are you not going to ask about the terms of my bargain?" Styrbjörn said.

"I am not," Harald said.

"I shall tell you all the same." Styrbjörn turned to face Harald in full, with his arms folded. "I will release you, and your men, and your ships. Here. Now."

Harald looked at him then, as a fish eyes the bait on a hook.

"I swear it," Styrbjörn said. "If you pay my price, I will release you, and you are free to return to your wife, my sister, with your honor."

"And what is your price?" Harald asked with narrowed eyes. "I expect you want my dagger? But I shall not give it to you, not for—"

"No." Styrbjörn looked away, as if he momentarily found the distant shoreline more interesting than their conversation. "I do not want your dagger."

"Then what do you want?" Harald now sounded irritated, and Palnatoke leaned forward, as if he, too, were waiting for the answer.

"I want you to take up your dagger," Styrbjörn said, "and throw it into the waters of Mälaren."

Palnatoke laughed.

Harald did not.

Meanwhile, Sean felt a sudden panic at the possibility that the dagger might at that moment be lost somewhere at the bottom of a very deep lake, depending on how this memory played out. That would also mean the end of the simulation, but it couldn't be. He couldn't fail Isaiah.

"As I told you"—Styrbjörn smiled at the Dane-king—"it is a small price. Your freedom and your fleet in exchange for throwing away a simple, useless dagger that you claim means nothing. What do you say to my bargain?"

Harald's anger finally showed itself in full. The Dane actually quivered with it. "To your bargain, I say no. And to you, I say may the gods curse you."

"But you no longer believe in the gods," Styrbjörn said. "You have your White Christ. And now I know your dagger is much more than nothing, which is all I wanted you to admit. I am satisfied."

Palnatoke laughed again. "You gamble like a dying man, Styrbjörn."

"It was a ruse?" Harald shook his head. "A game? You made false promises—?"

"Not false," Styrbjörn said. "If you had thrown that dagger away, I would have kept my word. But I knew you wouldn't part with it. Now, tell me why."

"Why?" Harald blinked, appearing somewhat befuddled. "The dagger is a holy relic. A gift from the emperor, the Saxon Otto, delivered to me by the cleric who baptized me a Christian. It came to Otto from the Father of the Church in Rome."

"It is a relic of the Christ?" Styrbjörn said. "And for that you would trade your freedom and that of your men?"

"I would," Harald said.

Though this confused and even impressed Styrbjörn, Sean knew it to be a lie, or at least a partial truth. Harald may have received the dagger in the way he'd just explained, but Sean still believed that he also understood its true nature, which accounted for his refusal to throw it away.

"Perhaps you do have a kind of honor," Styrbjörn said, though he doubted it was the kind of honor that would keep Harald from betraying him, if given the chance.

After that, the fleet sailed on and soon reached the mouth of the Fyriswater, but the ships came to a swift halt when Styrbjörn discovered his route entirely blocked by a man-made stakewall. Tree trunks had been felled and driven into the riverbed, jutting from the water at all angles, thick as bramble and lashed together. There could be no doubt as to its purpose, and Styrbjörn's disbelief quickly turned to rage when he realized what Eric had done.

"Row the fleet ashore," he ordered, and that night some of the men made camp on land, while others slept on their ships. Styrbjörn held a council around his fire to discuss the next course for his army. In light of the barricade, the Bluetooth argued for a retreat, the mere suggestion of which confirmed to Styrbjörn that the man was a coward.

"This was supposed to be a surprise attack," Harald said. "But it is obvious that Eric is prepared for you. More prepared than perhaps you realized."

"It doesn't matter how prepared he is," Styrbjörn said. "I will not retreat, and he will be no more successful than you in standing against me."

Harald ignored the slight, and Styrbjörn wondered what it would take to finally provoke the Dane, who simply replied, "He outnumbers you."

"As did you," Styrbjörn said. "But his numbers will mean nothing when I slay him in front of his men."

"Your strategy is too single-minded," Harald said. "Listen to me. I have won many, many battles, and in some I claimed victory without ever needing to draw my sword, but do not listen to me as a king. I speak to you now as my brother, for you are the brother of my wife, and I would not see her grieve your death. There is cunning in those stakes—"

"There is cunning in *me*!" Styrbjörn roared.

Harald shook his head. "Not as much cunning as I think you will need."

Styrbjörn restrained himself, and Sean could feel just how difficult that was. "If you had married anyone but my sister, Harald Bluetooth, you would die in this moment, by my hand. You call me a fool?"

"No," Harald said very calmly. "I think you are quite cunning, in your way. But I think you are impatient. You will need more than your axe and your shield to take back your crown, Styrbjörn the Strong. You will also need time and opportunity, but I do not think you will wait for either."

"I will not," Styrbjörn said. "I have waited too long already."

He hurled a log into the fire, and it kicked up a cloud of glowing ash and ember. All the men except old Palnatoke backed away from the stone ring. Styrbjörn regarded him, hesitant to seek his counsel, for he respected the Jomsviking, and if Palnatoke should agree with Harald, then Styrbjörn might be forced to yield. But to ignore Palnatoke would be the greater mistake.

"What do you say?" Styrbjörn asked, looking at his friend.

Palnatoke glanced at Styrbjörn, and then Harald. "I think we should not underestimate Eric. I agree there is cunning in that stakewall, but I do not agree that we should retreat."

Styrbjörn nodded, encouraged. "Go on."

"The question we must answer is how we deal with the impasse. Do we leave our ships and march to Uppsala? Or do we clear the river and go by oar and sail as planned?"

"Clearing the river will take too much time," Styrbjörn said.

"It will take time." Palnatoke nodded. "But perhaps that is what Eric wants. To delay you."

"Or perhaps Eric is trying to force you into an overland march," Harald said, "in which you will be more vulnerable."

Styrbjörn found both strategies believable of his uncle, but one of them more so than the other, because he knew Eric to be a coward. Eric had poisoned Styrbjörn's father. It had never been proven, but Styrbjörn knew it to be true, just as he knew that poison was a coward's weapon. Eric had staked the waterway for the same reason. He was afraid. He knew that Styrbjörn was coming, and wanted to slow him down any way that he could. That made Styrbjörn's choice a simple one.

"We march," he said. "We march hard and swift. Pass word among the men. Make ready to leave at dawn."

The Jomsviking captains left to spread the order, but Palnatoke and Harald lingered.

"You have more to say?" Styrbjörn asked them.

"Only that we should prepare for further treachery," Palnatoke said. "It is a long march to Uppsala."

"We will be ready," Styrbjörn said. "I do not expect it to be easy. But nothing will stop us."

"Then I bid you good night, brother-in-arms." And Palnatoke withdrew to his own bed, among his men.

Then it was Harald's turn to speak. "I believe you are marching to your death, Styrbjörn. But since I can see that you won't be dissuaded, I will bid you good night as well."

"It will take more than a few sticks in the river to frighten me into retreating," Styrbjörn said. "I fight my battles differently than you."

Harald nodded and turned away, but just a bit too quickly, and something in his demeanor raised suspicion.

"Where are you sleeping tonight, Harald?" Styrbjörn asked.

Harald hesitated, and Styrbjörn heard treachery in the silence. "I will sleep on my ship, with my men," Harald said.

"So that you can sail away before dawn?" Styrbjörn asked. "Leaving behind what little honor you possess?"

Harald returned to the fire and faced Styrbjörn from across the flames. "Out of respect for my wife, and allowing for your youth, I have borne your insults. But I will not do so endlessly."

Styrbjörn rose to his feet and walked around the stone ring to stand over the Dane. "You wish to defend your honor?" Though posed as a question, Styrbjörn intended it as a threat, and Harald's step backward suggested he understood it as such.

"I will defend my honor in my time and in the manner of my choosing. Good night, Styrbjörn." Then he turned away again, but Styrbjörn grabbed him by the arm and spun him around.

"You will sleep here tonight," he said. "Next to my fire."

Harald shook his head. "No, Styrbjörn. I will sleep on my ship."

"I don't trust you to sleep on your ship. But I know your men won't leave without you, which means you will not leave my side until we're well into our march."

Harald sighed. "What assurance can I give you? Since it is apparently not enough that I am married to your sister."

Styrbjörn did not need to think long for an answer, and within his thoughts, Sean's anticipation grew. "Leave your dagger with me," Styrbjörn said.

Harald balked. "Never."

"If you don't leave your dagger with me," Styrbjörn said, "you don't leave."

Harald scowled and tried to push past him, but Styrbjörn grabbed him by the shoulders, lifted him off the ground, and hurled him against a tree. Not hard enough to kill him, but hard enough for him to know how easily he could be killed. Harald staggered to his feet, wincing, and wiped at the blood now running from a gash on his head. Styrbjörn could see the hatred burning inside him, and knew that one day Harald would try to kill him. But not today.

Instead, Harald reached down and unbuckled the dagger from his waist. Then he trudged up to Styrbjörn and shoved the weapon into his hands.

"When your sister mourns you, I will be there to comfort her," he said. "Know that." Then he stalked away from the fire and disappeared.

Styrbjörn looked down at the dagger. It truly was a strange weapon, with a curve to its barbed blade, and an unusual grip wrapped in leather. For a Christ relic, it certainly didn't impress, especially when compared to the hammer of Thor or Odin's spear. But it wasn't important what Styrbjörn thought of the dagger. It only mattered that he could control the Bluetooth with it. As he buckled it around his waist, Styrbjörn smiled, but within his memory, Sean laughed.

"Isaiah!" he said "I have it!"

Excellent work, Sean. We're almost there, but let's not get ahead of ourselves. We still need to find out what your ancestor did with the prong.

"Right." Sean worked to calm himself. "Of course."

I see that Styrbjörn is about to sleep. Let's accelerate the memory a bit, shall we?

"Okay," Sean said, and the simulation sped past him in a blur of fragmented dream images, trolls and dogs and chopped wood and floods, then darkness, but that panoply ended abruptly when Palnatoke awoke Styrbjörn, dragging Sean back into the depths of his ancestor's mind.

"What hour is it?" Styrbjörn asked, sitting upright. He felt for the dagger, and found it still at his waist.

"A few hours before dawn," Palnatoke said.

Styrbjörn growled. "Then why do you wake me?"

"It's the Bluetooth," Palnatoke said. "He and all his ships are gone."

CHAPTER FOURTEEN

The dying caveman looked up at them with dull, watery eyes. Owen didn't know if he was technically a caveman, but that was what he looked like. He wore leather and fur, and no fabrics of any kind that Owen could see. His dark brown skin appeared almost corrugated, with black dirt deep in the folds and wrinkles, and he had pieces of straw in his long gray hair and beard.

"Can we help you?" Owen asked. "Are you hurt? Or sick?"

"You ask complicated questions," the man said.

They didn't seem complicated to Owen. He looked at Grace, and she gave a little shrug.

"You cannot prevent my death, if that is what you are asking," the man said. "After all this time, I have come to the end of my wanderings."

"What is your name?" Natalya asked.

"My name? I left that behind me on the Path many years ago. I had no use for it, and it only weighed me down."

His Dog seemed to have relaxed now that it had brought help to its master. It lay down next to him with a sigh and placed its heavy head in his lap, its yellow eyes rolling upward every few moments to look at its master's face.

"Does your dog have a name?" Owen asked.

"Oh, she is not mine."

Owen frowned. "But I thought—"

"She is not mine any more, nor any less, than I am hers." The stranger looked down and smiled, revealing a mouth of gray and missing teeth. He smoothed the fur over the Dog's broad head and scratched behind one of her ears. The Dog closed her eyes. "I suppose you could call her something if you like," the stranger said. "I just call her Dog. We've been together down the darkest of roads, and the most beautiful of roads, too."

"You're a traveler?" Natalya said.

The stranger seemed to think about that for a moment. "I think a traveler has a destination in mind. A place to arrive. I have had neither."

"So you just, like, wander around?" Owen said.

"I do." The stranger nodded, and then he wagged his finger at Owen, smiling again. "Yes, I am a Wanderer." He looked down at his Dog again, still scratching her ear, and his smile faded away. "Soon I shall wander where she cannot go."

"Are you sure you're dying?" Grace asked. "Maybe you—"

"I can't feel my legs," he said. Then he held up his right hand and flexed his fingers in and out of a fist. "I'm cold most everywhere else. I feel the life going out of me into the ground. Into this stone behind me. Into this hill."

"I'm sorry," Grace said.

"What for?" he asked. "I have beheld wonders and horrors and beautiful, everyday things. I have spent my life asking questions. Sometimes I found the answers, and sometimes I found more questions, and every so often, when I was very fortunate, I found the truth." He looked down at his Dog again. "There is only one question left for me to ask. But before that, a favor."

"A favor of us?" Owen said. "Is that why your Dog brought us here?"

"No. She is a Dog. She brought you here because she's worried about me. She knows that something is wrong, and she hopes you'll fix it. But now that you are here, yes, I have a favor to ask you."

"What can we do for you?" Grace said.

The Wanderer cleared his throat, and he paused. "After I am gone, will you find her a new companion?"

Owen had almost expected that, and he looked down at the Dog. One of her paws twitched, and her lip rippled, and he realized she had already fallen asleep, completely oblivious to what the Wanderer was saying about her. She was with him in that moment, which was all that mattered, and she was content. Owen smiled at her, but it was a sad smile. After her companion was gone, she wouldn't understand. She would be confused and all alone. In pain. And that wasn't fair.

"We'd really like to help," Natalya said. "But we don't . . . um, know anyone here."

"I see." The Wanderer scratched at his eyebrow with one of his thumbs, the nail chipped and worn down. "I . . . I worry what will happen to her."

A tightness gathered in Owen's throat, but he swallowed it down and said, "We'll take her."

Natalya and Grace looked over at him.

Owen knew this was only a simulation, and Monroe would say the Dog was a symbol, not a pet, but it didn't feel that way to him. He knew what she was about to face, and he couldn't leave her to do it alone. "We'll take her with us," he said. "We'll look after her until we find her a home."

"Thank you." The Wanderer closed his eyes again, and leaned his head back against the stone. "Thank you."

"You're welcome," Owen said.

"Not far from here," the Wanderer said, "there is a Crossroads. I think you will find someone for my Dog there, if you wait long enough."

"We'll go there," Owen said. "We'll find someone."

Grace and Natalya hadn't objected to this plan, but Owen could tell they felt unsure about it. They didn't smile and they didn't nod. Truthfully, Owen felt unsure about it, too. If they took this Dog and spent time waiting at the Crossroads, wherever that was, that would mean less time spent searching for the Summit and the key to this simulation. Less time figuring out how it could help them stop Isaiah.

The Wanderer leaned forward and laid his chest over the Dog in his lap, embracing her huge head. She woke suddenly and sat up, alert. Then she reached her nose toward his face, sniffing, and lapped his chin once with her tongue. She whined.

"You know," he said, exhaling. "You can smell it."

She rose to her four feet and stepped closer, licking his face again, insistently, urgently, his cheeks, his forehead, his nose, his lips. He closed his eyes and let her. Then he dug the fingers of both hands into the scruff around her neck and pulled her close, touching his forehead to hers.

"I know," he whispered. Then he leaned back against the stone, and looked up into the sky. "It is snowing. I will ask my question now."

But it wasn't snowing. It wasn't even cold. Owen looked up.

And then it was snowing.

Delicate white flecks found their easy way down from an ashen sky, and some of them touched Owen's face with their icy edges. The Dog whined again. Owen looked down, and he could tell the Wanderer had died. His body was empty. The Dog licked his lifeless face, waited and whined, and licked, and whined. She looked up at Owen, as if desperate for him to do something, and then she looked back at the Wanderer, who had left her. The snow gathered on her coat, white against her dark fur, and now she barked, sounding frantic, but not at anything, or anyone. Out of confusion and fear.

Grace looked at the Wanderer's body. "I know he's not real, and he didn't really die. But it's still hard."

"I'm not sure I know what real means anymore," Natalya said. "When the—"

The Dog let out a sound like a moan as she lay down next to her dead companion, placing her head in his lap as she had been doing only moments before.

"Poor thing," Grace said.

"Now you see why I couldn't leave her behind," Owen said. "You want to talk about what's real? For me, if it feels real, it's real. And I feel for that Dog."

"So do we," Natalya said.

The snow now fell heavily, and within moments white drifts

had gathered around the body of the Wanderer, slowly burying him with the Dog mourning at his side. Owen looked through the opening of the stone ring, and noticed that it didn't seem to be snowing elsewhere. Just the top of the hill, where the temperature had fallen quickly and suddenly.

"I think we should get back to the Path," Natalya said.

Owen agreed, and he called to the Dog, "Come, girl."

She didn't move. Didn't even look up.

Owen stepped closer to her, and tapped his leg. "Girl, come."

He saw her ears move, angling toward him, so he knew she was listening to him and just choosing to ignore him. With her size, he was still afraid to approach her, but he realized he would have to if he wanted to convince her to come with him. So he moved closer, one step at a time, watching her reaction to his presence.

"Be careful," Grace said. "I was just reading about a Norse god who got his hand bitten off by a wolf."

"Thanks, Grace, that's a great story," Owen said, taking another step.

"I'm just saying—"

The Dog growled, and if Owen had heard that sound while he was on a hike, he would have assumed it was a bear or a wolf. He would have taken off running, and he wouldn't have had a choice about it. That growl shook his bones. But instead of running from that hilltop, he stopped where he was and held his ground. The Dog turned her head slightly toward him, watching him with one eye, but she wasn't showing her teeth and the growling had stopped as he had halted. He slowly lowered himself to the snow where he was and sat down.

"What are you doing?" Natalya whisper-shouted. "Owen, come away."

"You guys go ahead," Owen said without taking his eyes from the Dog. "We'll catch up."

"Are you for real right now?" Grace asked. "You want us to leave you alone? In this simulation? With that thing?"

"She's just scared," Owen said. The Dog had started to pant, even though she was lying in the snow. "I'm just going to sit here for a while and see if she'll calm down."

"We don't have time for that," Natalya said with a bit of chatter in her teeth from the cold. "And I think that Dog can take care of itself just fine."

"That's not the point," Owen said. "And I told you guys to go ahead without me."

"I guess it's a good thing I came in here," Grace said. "Natalya needs someone with sense in their head."

"Owen," Natalya said, "stop and think about this. Think about where you are. Think about the risks."

Owen knew the risks, and knew he sounded ridiculous, but it didn't feel that way. This seemed important, and real, and he wasn't ready to give up. The snow had nearly buried the Wanderer's legs, with just the tops of his leather leggings poking through. The snow collecting on the Dog's fur had turned clear and icy around the edges.

"I'm serious, you guys," Owen said. "Just go. I'll be fine."

"It's freezing," Grace said.

"I'll be fine. I'm not leaving her."

Natalya shook her head, and then shrugged. "Whatever. Okay, fine." She turned to Grace. "Let's go, I guess."

"Guess so," Grace said.

They turned to leave, but Owen kept his eyes on the Dog, waiting. He wasn't sure what he was waiting for, but he waited.

The snow beneath him started to melt and soak into his clothes, and the cold finally got to him. He brought his arms in close to his chest, and pulled his legs up so that he was almost sitting in a fetal position. Over time, the falling snow clung to his eyelashes, and he felt its weight on his head and shoulders. When he shook like a dog to throw it off, the actual Dog raised her head and watched him. He imagined her judging his technique.

"I'm not good at that, am I?" he said.

The Dog laid her head back down, and she whimpered.

"I'm sorry," Owen said. Then he looked over his shoulder to make sure Natalya and Grace were gone. "I lost someone, too. It didn't make any sense to me. It still doesn't. I didn't even get to say good-bye, so you're lucky you got to have that." He rocked his body to try to warm himself with some movement. "But you can't just lie down. You have to keep going. That's what he would have wanted you to do."

The Dog looked at him as he talked, and then she yawned with a little whine, showing all of her many sharp teeth.

"Come, girl." He patted the snow-covered ground next to him, leaving an impression behind.

She watched him, but didn't move.

"Will you come?" He patted it again. "Come."

The Dog looked at the spot Owen had indicated, and he felt certain she understood exactly what he wanted. But still she stayed where she was. He'd begun to doubt whether she would ever voluntarily leave the Wanderer's side. He certainly couldn't pull her away, even if she decided not to hurt him as he tried. She was just too big.

Owen shivered now in a way he couldn't control. Violent convulsions seized his muscles and held them tight. It would still be easy enough for him to walk, or crawl, out of the stone ring, to escape the snow into the warm sunlight. But he refused to do that. Even if it meant he froze to death right here in this spot and desynchronized, he wouldn't leave the Dog. She had to know. She had to know that you can lose someone who means everything to you, and still keep going.

Besides, if she was devoted enough to stay by her companion, he could stay by her. So he stayed and stayed, hoping that if he did freeze to death in this simulation, it wouldn't do any permanent damage to his mind.

By now the snow had covered the Wanderer's legs and reached his waist. As for the Dog, Owen could still see the ridgeline of her back, as well as her neck and her head, but everything else lay buried.

He didn't know how long he had been there. He was trying to figure it out by watching the rate of the falling snow as it piled up, but before he got there his thoughts collapsed in a jumble and he lost track. He grew sleepy, and he'd read enough books and watched enough TV to know that was a sign of hypothermia. But he didn't care. He had made up his mind about staying until the end, and maybe going to sleep would make desynchronization easier.

That thought felt appealing. Simple.

Sleep.

"I . . . admire your . . . devotion," he said to the Dog. Then he flopped onto his back in the snow, staring up into the dancing sky. "Devotion," he said again, thinking that word was important, but he couldn't remember how or why. He closed his eyes, and he felt himself drifting up into the sky like a snowflake that gravity couldn't catch.

Higher he went.

Farther.

He could get lost up here in all the nothing. Just a speck floating away and—

Something hot branded his cheek. Something molten in the icy cold that burned him back into his body. He felt a gentle prodding, from his head to his knees. He felt something tugging on him, and heard a tearing sound, and then something jerked his whole body under his armpits, dragging him through and over the snow. He felt it sliding beneath him, its divots and swells, and he heard rough breathing in his ear.

It was the Dog.

As his mind came back down from the sky, he became aware of light falling against his eyelids, a warm wind across his skin, and the whisper of grass beneath him. When his body came to rest, he opened his eyes, squinting, and saw the head of the Dog directly above him. She looked down at him, panting, and then bent closer to lick his face.

"Okay, okay," he said, raising his hands to keep her at bay. "Good girl."

She backed away and stood there wagging her tail. Then she barked.

"I'm getting up," Owen said. But every part of him hurt as it thawed out, and it took him a while just to sit up, and even longer to struggle to his feet. His hair and clothing were soaking wet, and his favorite T-shirt hung loose and torn over his shoulder where the Dog had apparently used her teeth to pull him.

She had seen him collapse, and she had saved him.

And there he was on the hillside, a little unsteady, looking down at the Path below, while a dense bank of fog smothered the stone circle just above him. The Dog sat beside him, and Owen reached over to scratch behind her ear in the way he had seen the Wanderer do. Her fur was wet and cold with melted snow, and she smelled like any dog would, except maybe worse.

"Thank you," he said. "I want you to know that wasn't my plan. But if someone asks, I'm going to say that it was."

From his vantage, he could see the course of the Path as it wound away through the white rock bluffs and green hills. He scanned along it, but couldn't see any sign of Grace or Natalya. Off in the distance, he wasn't sure how far, it appeared that another road intersected with the Path, forming a crossroads.

"That must be it," he said, looking over at the Dog. "That's where we'll find you a new companion. Come, girl." He took a few slow and heavy steps down the hillside.

But she didn't follow him.

He looked back, and so did she, staring at the shroud of fog. She had saved Owen, but that didn't mean she was ready to leave her Wanderer behind. She whined and shifted weight on her paws, almost taking a few steps in place.

Owen sighed. He had nearly frozen to death for her. If that wasn't enough for the Dog to follow him, he didn't know what else he could do. Natalya and Grace were up ahead somewhere, and it might be possible to catch up to them. He still didn't want to leave the Dog, but now that she seemed to have broken out of her grief, at least enough to leave the Wanderer's side, he felt better about it than he had before.

"Come!" he called, one more time, putting as much command into his voice as he could, and then he turned away from her. He decided he would not look back. He would simply walk down the hill. She would either follow him or she wouldn't.

He was halfway down the hill before she barked. He kept going, slow and steady, without looking back. A few paces on, she barked again, and still he kept walking. But her next bark sounded closer. A few moments later, she barked directly behind him, and then she loped up alongside him, panting.

He looked over at her. "Good Dog."

She still appeared uneasy, walking with her head down, occasionally glancing back at the hill, but she kept pace with him until he reached the safety of the Path and set off in the direction they'd been traveling before. Hopefully, Grace and Natalya hadn't made it too far ahead of him.

CHAPTER FIFTEEN

t was difficult to be certain in the darkness, but it appeared that every Dane ship had broken away from Styrbjörn's fleet and now rowed back the way they had come. David and Östen marveled at how well Thorvald's strategy had worked. All the labor hewing and placing stakes in the Fyriswater had been rewarded, and Styrbjörn's army had now been greatly reduced before the fighting had even begun.

"Now our work begins in earnest," Thorvald said to his company. "But from this night it will be bladework."

There were thirty of them gathered around the skald, men he had chosen from among those gathered under the *ledung*. Östen had been the first, followed by Alferth and Olof, and from there they had moved from camp to camp across the Fyrisfield, taking with them only the strongest and fiercest they could find.

It had also been important to Thorvald that all of them were Svear and men of the land.

"In the coming days and weeks," Thorvald now said, "you may find your sense of honor challenged, for we will not meet Styrbjörn in the open. Not yet. We will strike, and then we will vanish, and then we will strike again. I have kept our number few, because we are not the axe and shield. We will be the knife in Styrbjörn's back, and it is very likely that many of us will not return to our homes. If you want no part of that, you may leave now and return to Uppsala. I will not hold it against any of you."

None moved to leave, but that did not surprise Östen.

Thorvald had proven to be a strange man, but a capable one. He was not large, but he was incredibly strong, and though he was a skald, he possessed a warrior's spirit. He also possessed a cunning mind the like of which Östen had never encountered.

"Rest for an hour," Thorvald said. "Styrbjörn marches tomorrow, and we must be well ahead of him."

"What if he orders the Jomsvikings to clear the river instead?" Alferth asked.

"He won't," Thorvald said. "Especially now that the Bluetooth has abandoned him. His rage will not sit still long enough to clear the river."

The skald had been right about Styrbjörn up to now. Östen trusted him in this, and moved to find a bed place and take what sleep he could. They had made no fire, and would leave no sign behind, nothing to betray their presence to the Jomsvikings. Olof and Alferth followed him, the three of them having formed a loose bond, and as they settled into their cloaks, Alferth spoke with a voice as low to the ground as a shadow.

"I don't like this."

"I'd prefer a fire as well," Olof said.

"No," Alferth said. "I don't like all this sneaking about. I'm not a thief or a murderer. When I kill, it is in plain view of the gods."

"You could have left just now," Olof said. "Why didn't you?"

"Because then I would have looked like a coward."

"Then you made your choice," Östen said. "The greater dishonor now would be to fail in it."

"Why are you here?" Alferth asked Östen. "We've all heard your name. This work does not seem fitting of your reputation."

The thread tied around Östen's wrist had somehow survived the previous day's labor in the water and mud, and though it was now crusty and soiled, it held fast. "And what reputation do I have?" Östen asked.

Alferth said nothing. He seemed caught in a net that Östen had not meant to cast, afraid to answer in a way that would offend.

Östen decided to let his friend escape. "I once fought for my glory and honor," he said. "But now I fight for my family and my farm, and I will defend them in whatever way brings victory to Eric."

"I respect you for that," Alferth said. "But Odin calls up the slain from the battlefield, not from the darkness and obscurity of ambush."

"My farm is not large," Östen said. "But it is mine, and Eric has never envied it. He has been fair in all his dealings with the landowners. Olof's land sits next to mine, and he also knows this to be true."

Olof nodded.

Östen continued. "Eric's brother was not so honorable. The assassin who poisoned him did a service to the Svear. If Styrbjörn returns, I fear he will take after his father, and we will return to the old ways." He paused. "If bladework in Thorvald's company means I give up my seat in Valhalla, it is so my family will keep our land when I am gone."

Alferth said nothing, but he nodded deeply.

In the quiet that followed, David felt pride in his ancestor, but also confusion. How could Östen stand so strongly for freedom, but have a thrall at home working on the same farm he fought to defend? It was a confusion that could desynchronize David if left unchecked, so he went back to what he had decided earlier. He didn't need to justify or agree with Östen to understand him.

"What is that?" Olof asked, a new, reddish glow against his face.

Östen looked southward toward its source, where great flames had erupted along the shore of Mälaren. From this vantage and distance, it was difficult to see what burned, but that close to the water's edge there was only one thing it could be.

"By Odin's beard," Alferth said.

"He burns his ships," Olof said.

Alferth sounded ready to laugh in disbelief. "He's a madman."

"No," Östen said. "The Jomsvikings covenant never to retreat from a battle. With this act, Styrbjörn has insured they keep their oath better than Harald Bluetooth kept his."

Olof nodded in agreement. "They will be more determined now."

Alferth grunted. "And I won't sleep now."

But Östen lay back down and closed his eyes. This changed nothing for Thorvald's company. The Jomsvikings would be a fearsome enemy whether Styrbjörn burned their ships or not.

Better to take what rest could be had, while it could be had. He closed his eyes, and not long after that, David entered a fragmented dream space within the simulation.

You are doing well, Victoria said.

"Thanks," he said. "How's Grace doing?"

She's fine. Monroe actually just let me know she's in the simulation with Natalya and Owen.

"Oh." David had imagined Grace waiting outside the Animus this whole time, watching for him to mess up in case she needed to step in again. He didn't know if he felt better or worse knowing she wasn't there. Maybe both.

I also heard from Griffin and Javier. You might be interested to know that Thorvald is Javier's ancestor.

"That's Javier?"

No, remember? Javier is in a separate simulation. But he is experiencing some of the same events you are from a difference perspective.

"We'll have to compare notes later."

Yes. In the meantime, I believe your ancestor is waking up.

David returned to Östen's conscious mind as Thorvald roused him, and even though David looked at the skald a bit differently now, he did nothing different about it. Östen sat up, wishing for another hour of sleep before they marched, but in the next moment he discovered it wasn't yet time for the company to depart, and that everyone else still rested.

"What is it?" he asked Thorvald.

"There is a task I must complete," he said. "I am leaving you in command."

"Is your task a solitary one?"

"It is."

"And you're going now?"

"I am."

Östen nodded. He did not want to ask what the task might be, preferring not to enter that far into Thorvald's purposes. But there were other, necessary questions. "What should we do in your absence?"

"Take the company north," he said. "When you reach the Mirkwood, I want you to lay traps."

"We can't trap an entire army," Östen said.

"Of course not. You will simply lay enough traps, in enough places, to slow the army down. If Styrbjörn's men are searching the trees for signs of danger, they're taking their mind from their march."

"I see." Östen thought about his own experience fighting. "If we injure one man in two dozen, that should—"

"Kill," Thorvald said. "Not injure. You must kill one man in twenty."

"That will be difficult."

"Not with this." Thorvald pulled a small bundle of oilskin out of his pouch, which he carefully unwrapped to reveal a fine bottle of glass filled with a viscous pale liquid. "This poison is extremely potent. A few drops will kill a man." Thorvald looked up at Östen. "Though perhaps not a man of your size."

"How should I administer this poison?"

"It will kill quickly if eaten or it gets into a wound. So lay your traps to injure, and this will do the rest. It can still kill if it touches the skin, but more slowly. Also, water won't destroy it, but whatever you apply it to must be dry." He rewrapped the bundle and handed it to Östen. "I suggest you wear gloves when you handle it, and then take care with those gloves."

"I understand," Östen said, tucking the bundle away.

"If your task is well done, the Jomsvikings will make camp for the night in the forest, to tend their poisoned brothers. You and the company will use the cover of darkness to harry them in their sleep. Strike from the trees, deliver a blow—a killing blow if you can—and then vanish. Offer them no respite."

This plan was not only cunning, but merciless.

"I'll find you when my task is complete," Thorvald said. "But if I should fail, continue north to the Fyrisfield with as many as yet live."

Östen nodded.

"Farewell." Thorvald pulled a hood over his head, concealing much of his face, and he turned to leave. But he had only an axe at his belt and nothing else.

"Where are your weapons and shield?" Östen asked.

"I have all that I need for my task," Thorvald said, and then he was gone.

Östen woke Olof and Alferth, and the three of them got the company under way, racing north much faster than Styrbjörn's army could march. Not long after sunrise, they reached the southern edge of the Mirkwood that lay between them and the Fyrisfield. Its expanse of towering spruce and pine stretched east and west far enough that Styrbjörn would have no choice but to march through it.

Olof organized their company into smaller parties, and then sent them off in all directions to lay snares and traps among the ferns, brush, and moss-covered stones. They armed their traps with thorns and splinters of wood. Östen went around to each of them and applied a few drops of the poison to the barbs and sharp points, and when he had finished, the company hurried on a good distance and did the same again. In this way they proceeded north, turning the forest as they went into a place where death might be waiting around every tree and at every step.

Östen worried about the many farms and villages the Mirkwood touched. The poison would kill a Svear out gathering wood or berries as easily as a Jomsviking. But the people of the countryside knew of Styrbjörn's coming, and Östen could only hope they had already sought refuge elsewhere.

Toward afternoon, the company stopped to take some food and rest near a marshy meadow on the Fyriswater. The flowers growing there reminded Östen of his daughters, who would plait each other's hair with them.

"Styrbjörn must have entered the Mirkwood by now," Olof said. "Which means the unluckiest of his men are already dying."

"Let us hope," Östen said. But he realized they needed to know for certain if, and how well, their strategy had succeeded, especially if they were to attack the enemy camp that night as Thorvald had ordered. "I will go back to see where they are," Östen said. "The rest of you remain here."

"Be careful you don't get poisoned by one of our own traps," Alferth said.

Östen nodded, and then he left the company, heading south into the woods. He traveled as quickly as he could, leaping over fallen trees and streams, using the brush and terrain as cover to keep himself hidden. The traps he had just poisoned were still held in his mind, so he was able to avoid them easily enough. But the farther he went, the slower he had to go, to make sure he didn't end up a casualty of Thorvald's cunning.

As evening approached, Östen finally heard something up ahead. He ducked behind the wide trunk of a tree, listening and waiting.

They were men's voices. The Jomsvikings. They called to one another through the trees as they moved through the forest, sometimes shouting that they'd found another snare and rendered it harmless, and the way was clear. But sometimes one of them would cry out in alarm and pain, and Östen counted each of those as a death.

The enemy's ranks moved slowly, as Thorvald had predicted they would, allowing Östen to stay ahead of them, and hidden. But he prayed to the gods that the Jomsvikings would at least reach the end of the snares and traps before making their camp. It would not be wise for Östen and the company to go raiding at night through poisoned woods. A short while later, the gods answered him, and the Jomsvikings halted their march in safe territory.

Östen returned to the meadow where he had left the other men, and after reporting the location of the enemy encampment and what he had observed, Olof again assisted by dividing the company. Then, when night had fallen completely in the Mirkwood, Östen gathered them all to give them their orders.

"Let none of you think you fight for your honor," he said. "In this night's bladework, you are nameless. You are an apparition. You appear from the forest, you strike, and then you vanish. Our purpose is to leave confusion and fear behind us. This is what Thorvald ordered."

"Thorvald isn't here," said Alferth. "And I am not a thief in the night."

Östen marked him with a nod, but continued. "If you tarry, if you think to stay and look your enemy in the eye to watch the life go out of him, I hope your honor will comfort you in your death."

Alferth folded his arms, appearing unsatisfied, but Östen

could not force him to understand. Each man had to fight in his own way.

"Return here while the sky is still black," Olof said, at Östen's side. "We leave at the first sign of blue."

"Pray to the god you favor," Östen said. "Then do the work of trolls."

The company disbanded, and each party stalked away into the night. Östen led three men, including Alferth, along the Fyriswater toward the western side of the Jomsviking camp. The night gave them little guidance, save the stars reflected in the water, but soon they smelled wood smoke and spied the yellow flicker of firelight off in the trees. They crept forward, slowly and silently, and chose the nearest of the fire rings. Each man drew his weapon, whether axe, sword, or knife, and at Östen's whispered command, they charged.

The trees flew by, nothing more than black stripes as the fire grew nearer and brighter. Östen kept his eyes from looking directly at the light, and focused instead on his target, a man sitting on a small rock, his knees up near his chest.

When Östen burst from the trees, some of the Jomsvikings looked up in surprise. But that's all they had time to do. From the edge of his sight, he glimpsed Alferth and the other two men rush in behind him. Östen neared his target, caught him hard in the head with his axe, and continued running, quickly leaving the circle of light behind him. The first shout of alarm didn't rise up until he and his three men had regrouped some distance away, watching the results of their sortie from the darkness.

Östen's man lay dead or unconscious. So did another. Two more men staggered, while several of their companions rushed to give them aid, shouting and cursing. Two men ran from the fire, deeper into the encampment, no doubt to raise the wider alarm.

Then they heard similar, distant shouts from other points in the forest, and Östen could feel the chaos rising.

"Again," he whispered.

Then he and his men rushed the same fire ring. The Jomsvikings were better prepared for this attack, and they clashed with them, but only briefly. Östen struck one of the men already injured, and he went down. Then Östen returned to the forest.

His companions were slower to join him, but eventually freed themselves of the firelight. Östen now saw three Jomsvikings on the ground, with two more wounded.

"Let's move on," Östen said.

They crept back toward the river and followed it a little farther south, until a different campfire came within view. Most of the men around it looked to be wounded already, lying on the ground or leaning against the trees.

"Poisoned," Alferth said.

Östen nodded. "Focus your attacks on the men tending them."

Then he led the first charge, and the second, until the fire ring held more dying men than it had but moments before.

The sounds that echoed throughout the forest spoke of disarray in the Jomsviking encampment. But that tide would turn soon. Order would be restored. Östen sensed they only had one more raid before their enemy would be too prepared, and he selected another campfire farther south than the last.

They charged, and Östen's axe bit hard to both sides as he

tore through the enemy ring. He had crossed the border, back into darkness, when a towering figure burst into the red light. He was a young man, a strong man, and he exceeded even Östen in height.

"Styrbjörn!" someone roared.

On the other side of the camp, Alferth leapt out of the forest, and Östen could do nothing to stop him.

The fight lasted only a few moments. Styrbjörn laid waste to Alferth's body. Östen had never seen such ferocity and power, and he could only hope that a passing Valkyrie had witnessed the end of his friend. The other two warriors in Östen's party then rushed from the shadows, apparently thinking to attack Styrbjörn simultaneously. An arrow struck one of them in the neck, shot by an archer just emerging into the light. Styrbjörn dealt with the second man as easily as he had Alferth.

As Östen watched this, his rage grew into something almost unstoppable. He tightened his grip on his axe and prepared to charge. But then he felt the gentle tug of the thread around his wrist. He could barely see it in the darkness, but it was still there. His talisman calling him home. He thought of his wife and his children, and he lowered his axe, even as Styrbjörn stood over the bodies of three good men of Thorvald's company. Men who—

"You out there!" Styrbjörn bellowed. "I know you can hear me! I demand safe passage to Uppsala! If these attacks continue, I will burn this forest to the ground! If you set any more snares, I will burn this forest to the ground! If I cannot rule this land, know that I will surely destroy it!"

It wasn't a ruse. Östen knew he spoke the truth, and thought again of the farms that touched the Mirkwood, the fields and pastures that grew near it, and the lives that depended on it. What would a victory over Styrbjörn matter if the Svear lost the very land they were trying to protect?

They would have to let Styrbjörn pass.

But Östen vowed in that moment that one day he would exact revenge on Styrbjörn. One day, he would show Styrbjörn the true meaning of ferocity.

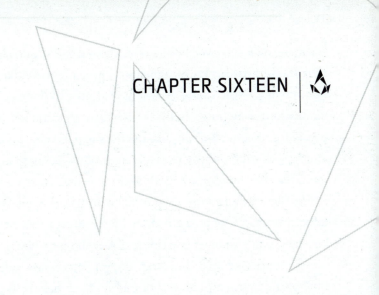

CHAPTER SIXTEEN

Javier knew the giant was David and Grace's ancestor. But they weren't sharing the simulation, so it wasn't David or Grace that he spoke to as he gave his orders and left the company in Östen's very large hands.

Styrbjörn's ships burned in the distance, even as those of Harald Bluetooth retreated back to Jutland. Thorvald could guess what had happened to bring both events about, but he needed to know for certain, if he was to plan his next moves. It would be easy enough to sneak into the Jomsviking camp and kill Styrbjörn, but that might be a mistake if the Jomsvikings felt honor bound to exact revenge, to say nothing of the nobles who secretly supported Styrbjörn's return. Before Thorvald acted, he had to know more.

He raced through the night, using his Odin-sight to leap

through trees and over boulders in the darkness, until he drew near the Jomsviking encampment on the shores of Mälaren. He became one of the shadows and moved inward undetected, listening and watching, until he reached the council ring of Styrbjörn. Then Thorvald became as silent as a burial mound, and he observed the discussion from a position near enough to smell the salt cod on the breath of the Jomsvikings.

Styrbjörn had grown mighty since his banishment, standing taller now than Östen or any man Thorvald had seen before. At his right hand, an older warrior spoke to those gathered.

"I supported the burning. It was necessary after the Bluetooth's betrayal, lest any of our number believe we might also retreat."

"And what of the oaths we swore to you, Palnatoke?" one of the Jomsvikings said. "Years ago, when we entered Jomsborg. Do you remember? Were those not enough? Are the years we have fought for you not enough to convince you of our honor?"

Thorvald knew the name and reputation of Palnatoke, but had never seen the man. Though gray-haired and battle worn, he remained straight-backed and broad shouldered, plainly still a deadly fighter, and able to command.

"I don't doubt the honor of anyone standing here, Gorm," Palnatoke said. "But our numbers have grown, and the youngest among us are not so steadfast—"

"Then name the men you doubt." The man Gorm spread his arms. "Let this be in the open."

"I will not," Palnatoke said. "Now is a time for unity."

Gorm looked hard at Styrbjörn. "And yet you divide us by allowing this Svear to burn our ships."

"This Svear?" Styrbjörn smiled, but it held no amusement. "Have you forgotten my name?"

"No," Gorm said. "But I do not honor your name, and that is no secret. We follow Palnatoke."

"Then cease talk of this matter," Palnatoke said. "It is done. We were sworn to this before the burning of the ships, and we are sworn to it now. We march for Uppsala, and—"

"Palnatoke!"

All of them turned as two warriors approached the council ring, a woman marching between them. She wore ring armor, and carried a sword at her side, marking her a shield-maiden. Though not a beauty, she was closer to pretty than she was to plain, with blond hair braided tight across her head, and a fine nose. Javier smiled inwardly at Thorvald's attraction to her.

"Who is this?" Styrbjörn asked.

"A Dane woman," said one of the men escorting her. "Her countrymen left her be—"

"I was not left behind," the woman said, her voice steady and clear. "I chose to stay."

Styrbjörn stepped toward her, slowly, until he stood almost directly over her. "Why?"

The shield-maiden kept her eyes forward, and if Styrbjörn's presence intimidated her, she did not show it. "Because I will no longer fight for a raven starver. My devotion to Harald has broken."

"And your oaths?" Styrbjörn asked.

Now she looked up at him. "I swore no oath to him."

"No oath?" Palnatoke said.

"He never asked it of me," she said. "He assumed my loyalty."

"That was his mistake, it seems," Styrbjörn said. "Will you swear yourself to me?"

She cocked her head and looked Styrbjörn over, from his boots to his brow. "If you are an honorable man, I will swear to you when you are king, and not before."

Styrbjörn laughed. "What is your name?"

"Thyra," she said.

"Harald mentioned you," Styrbjörn said. "He offered you to me when—"

"I was not his to offer," she said. "As you would have learned had you accepted."

Styrbjörn laughed again. "Of that, I have no doubt. But now we must discuss what is to become of you. You stayed when your king and countrymen left. Do you intend to fight with us?"

"I intend to fulfill the oath Harald swore to you." She looked around the council ring. "I want it known that there is honor among the Danes."

"No," Palnatoke said. "The Jomsvikings permit no women."

"You permit no women into Jomsborg," Styrbjörn said. "We are not in Jomsborg. Besides which, you permitted my sister."

"Your sister was the daughter of a king," Palnatoke said.

"So am I," Thyra said.

Her declaration surprised Thorvald, which Javier knew to be an unusual experience for his ancestor. The others in the council ring appeared equally stunned, and for several breaths no one spoke except for the fire.

"Who?" Styrbjörn finally asked. "Whose daughter are you?"

"I am Harald's daughter," she said. "My mother was a shield-maiden."

"Has he claimed you?" Styrbjörn asked.

"No," she said. "And I have never desired it."

"Why not?" Palnatoke asked.

She turned to him and scowled. "Would you?"

Now Palnatoke joined Styrbjörn in laughing, and both men agreed that Thyra would join their ranks, and as a member of the council ring, which soon resumed its discussions of their coming march. Thorvald listened until the council separated, and then he crept out of the encampment to a distance from which he could observe the army's movements and plan his own.

It seemed that while Styrbjörn did not have the loyalty of the Jomsvikings, he had Palnatoke's sworn support. That meant Thorvald had to consider what Palnatoke would do if Styrbjörn were assassinated. Given the reputation of the Jomsvikings, their honor-bound answer would be swift and brutal. Thorvald decided that killing Styrbjörn was not yet an option, and turned his strategies instead to robbing Styrbjörn of support, to weaken him.

When the sun appeared, the Jomsvikings massed into ranks and marched. Thorvald stayed ahead of them, and later in the day, when they reached the Mirkwood, he went up into the trees.

Östen had already led the company through, and Thorvald could see the hidden snares they'd left behind. He waited to see if the first of the Jomsvikings would detect the traps, but they didn't, and when those traps sprang, men took injuries. If Östen had used the poison as ordered, those men would die later that day, but until then, the Jomsvikings felt no significant threat, and even laughed at the Svear and their harmless snares.

Thorvald leapt and climbed from tree to tree, staying high above the ground, following the army, and it was some time before the injured Jomsvikings noticed the first effects of the poison. By that time, many more of them had been tainted, and upon realizing the danger surrounding them, Styrbjörn ordered his force to a halt.

His roaring reached Thorvald high in the trees. He assailed the cowardice of his enemies for using poison, his immense anger entirely by Thorvald's design. It was poison that had slain Styrbjörn's father, after all, and the memory of that would infect Styrbjörn's judgment as surely as this new poison infected his men.

The simplicity and effectiveness of his ancestor's plan awed Javier. One cunning Assassin with thirty men had managed to halt an army. Perhaps not for long, but the Jomsvikings had lost all momentum.

After that, they slowed their advance through the Mirkwood, pausing to check for traps and disarm them, but they didn't find them all, and each subsequent injury only increased Styrbjörn's rage. Eventually, some of the men who had already been poisoned volunteered to lead the way through the forest, to spare their companions. Their deaths already assured, they felt no fear, and Thorvald admired their sacrifice and loyalty.

By evening, the number of dying men, and the danger of moving through the poisoned woods in the darkness, forced the Jomsvikings to halt their march and make camp for the night. Thorvald watched them settle down among the trees, the smoke from their dozens of fires blooming from the ground like fog. He climbed along the branches and trunks until he found Styrbjörn's fire. Thyra sat with him, while Palnatoke went through the camp to check on his men and bid farewell to those soon to die.

Thorvald settled to wait for nightfall, which fell with suddenness in the Mirkwood. He heard no laughter from around the campfires. The Jomsvikings seemed to have been hardened by their casualties, and they didn't know what to do with an enemy they couldn't see. They would be looking for a place to lay their anger.

Thorvald planned to give them one, and Javier found himself marveling once again.

A few hours went by, and after midnight, when those who could sleep had done so, and those who couldn't sat lost in their fears, a distant cry of alarm went up to the north. Östen and the company had begun their raiding.

Styrbjörn and Palnatoke leapt to their feet.

A second cry sounded from a different direction, and then a third. After the fourth and fifth, it seemed the entire camp had fallen under attack, and Thorvald smiled from his hidden perch.

"Fall back and form ranks!" Palnatoke shouted to those who could hear him. But many could not.

Styrbjörn's anger had reached the point of madness. Thyra tried to steady him, and warn him against rashness, but he ignored her and took up his sword and his axe. Then he charged away into the darkness, blindly seeking an enemy.

"That fool will get himself poisoned," Palnatoke said.

"Should I go after him?" Thyra asked.

"No," Palnatoke said. "He won't listen to you. It falls to me."

He gave a few last orders, and then ran after Styrbjörn. Thorvald left his position and gave pursuit, free-running through the trees in a gradual descent to the ground, waiting for the right moment.

Palnatoke ran in and out of firelight, asking the men in each camp which way Styrbjörn had gone. When he entered a place thick enough with darkness, between campfires, Thorvald fell upon him from above.

But somehow, the old Jomsviking deflected his hidden blade and threw him off. Thorvald rolled away and jumped to his feet, his axe and blade ready.

Palnatoke strode toward him, his sword drawn. "A hood to hide your face? Are you ashamed of what you do?"

"I bring the judgment of the Norns," Thorvald said. "You've reached the end of your skein."

"Try and cut it, then."

Palnatoke seized the first strike, but Thorvald ducked the blow and came around with his axe. Palnatoke leapt clear, more agile than he seemed, and the two men circled each other. Palnatoke could easily have called for help from one of the nearby camps, but he didn't. He couldn't. Not without risking loss of respect from his men.

The Jomsviking lunged, but it was a feint, and it almost threw Thorvald off-balance. He blocked Palnatoke's sword with his hidden blade, barely, taking some of the impact with his forearm, and managed a swing of his axe while Palnatoke had come in close.

The older man grunted, but the wound was shallow. It may have broken a rib, but not likely. "What is that little knife you wear?" he asked.

"You will find out soon enough," Thorvald said.

Palnatoke came again, harder, and without deception, trusting in his strength. Thorvald dodged and parried, waiting for an opening, but his opponent offered none. It was time for him to seize the attack. He ran for a tree, and then sped up its trunk, using his weight to launch himself over the Jomsviking, catching his enemy's shoulder with the beard of his axe.

The metal bit hard, and pulled Palnatoke backward. The Jomsviking planted his feet and spun, tearing his shoulder free of the axe, but Thorvald was ready with his hidden blade, and with a lightning thrust, the old man died, almost instantly.

Now Thorvald ran west through the forest, toward the river, using the sounds of battle and his Odin-sight to guide him. He heard a man shout Styrbjörn's name, and he raced toward it, arriving in time to see Alferth fall. Two more of his company followed and died. It would take a dozen of the finest warriors to stop Styrbjörn in his rage.

Another figure moved nearby, and Thorvald saw Östen not far from him in the trees. For a moment, he worried the giant would also charge Styrbjörn, but he didn't, and Thorvald crept toward him.

"You out there!" Styrbjörn shouted. "I know you can hear me! I demand safe passage to Uppsala! If these attacks continue, I will burn this forest to the ground! If you set any more snares or traps, I will burn this forest to the ground! If I cannot rule this land, know that I will surely destroy it!"

Thorvald considered attacking Styrbjörn then. But in the moment he took to plan his approach, he noticed a strange weapon at his enemy's side. A dagger. Its shape seemed familiar, but also sinister, and it stopped him. He heard Torgny's words counseling wisdom, and patience, and cunning.

Javier saw the dagger for what it was, the first glimpse they'd had of it in this simulation. Their race against Isaiah and Sean had now begun in a way it hadn't a moment before. The urgency had changed.

Östen moved toward the river, and Thorvald decided to follow him, leaving Styrbjörn for another day. When they had reached a distant enough point from the encampment, he called out, and Östen turned.

"Thorvald?"

"Follow me," he said, and led Östen to the Fyriswater. "Is anyone else with you?"

"They fell against Styrbjörn."

"Their fate is theirs. Where is the rest of the company?"

Östen pointed north, and Thorvald let him lead the way along the cold boiling of the river. Gradually, the sounds of chaos in the encampment faded until they couldn't be heard. They traveled then through the tranquility of a night forest, accompanied by the scent of pine and the lonely call of an owl.

Eventually, they reached a meadow on the river, where they found eleven men waiting. Thorvald had hoped to find more, but Östen informed him they had given the company until blue light to return. So they waited.

"Did you complete your task?" Östen asked him.

Thorvald nodded. "I completed a task."

"What task?" asked one of the others.

Thorvald considered how to answer, and decided to give these warriors the truth. Their labor over the last days had earned his trust. "I slew Palnatoke, leader of the Jomsvikings."

The men went quiet.

"Why him?" Östen asked. "Why not Styrbjörn?"

"Have my strategies failed?" Thorvald asked. "Have I led you astray?"

"No."

"Then let that be your answer."

"That is not enough," Östen said. "Good men are dead."

Thorvald sighed. He knew Östen meant no challenge, nor dishonor, and he did not want to return either to him. "Styrbjörn has no army without the Jomsvikings," he said. "But they are not sworn to him. They follow Palnatoke. So in killing Palnatoke, I have severed what bond they had to Styrbjörn. Come morning, they will blame him for the death of their captain, and we shall see if he has an army after that."

Östen nodded. "And what of Styrbjörn's threat to burn down the forest?"

"We must take him at his word," Thorvald said. "We must—"

A group of five warriors emerged into the meadow. Among them was Olof, who reported that the Jomsvikings had rallied and killed or captured many of their company. He did not believe that any more would come, and as the sky had finally turned, it was time to march. Thorvald ordered the men north, to Fyrisfield, their number reduced by half.

"So we'll let Styrbjörn pass through the forest?" Östen asked.

"We will," Thorvald said. "If the Jomsvikings follow him, we will let them pass through the forest as well."

"Have we reduced their number by enough?" Olof asked.

"No," Thorvald said. "But do not lose heart. I left designs for a war machine with the Lawspeaker. If Styrbjörn brings the Jomsvikings to Fyrisfield, death awaits them there."

CHAPTER SEVENTEEN

Natalya kept looking back down the Path as she and Grace walked slowly away from the hill. She expected to see Owen running up behind them at any moment, possibly with the enormous and frightening Dog. But she saw nothing, even after walking for quite some time, and she began to worry that they had made a mistake leaving him behind.

"I thought he would be right behind us," she said.

Grace looked back. "He was smitten with that Dog."

"I don't think it was about the Dog," Natalya said. "And I think maybe the Dog is a part of what we're supposed to be doing in here."

Grace stopped walking. "You think we should've stayed with him?"

"I don't know. I think that was something he had to do. Or

something he thought he had to do. He wasn't going to leave, I know that, and I'm not sure he wanted us there."

"So what should we do now? We could stop and wait for him, I guess."

"We could." Natalya looked forward down the Path, and she glimpsed a small boulder directly ahead. "Let's keep going for now. I want to see what's up there."

Grace nodded, and they resumed their slow walk through a countryside of white rock ledges and green turf. The landscape felt both old and new at the same time, like a deep layer of earth that had only recently risen to the surface. The Path remained very much the same as it had been, and the wind smelled faintly of sage.

As they got closer to the stone, which turned out to be about the size and shape of a pig, Natalya saw that it sat by a crossroads where a dirt trail intersected their Path. Carvings covered the stone with geometric shapes, spirals, and figures of men and extinct animals. This was the Crossroads the Wanderer had mentioned, where Owen could find a new owner for the Dog.

"Maybe we should wait here," Grace said.

"I was just thinking the same thing," Natalya said, and they sat down on the boulder back-to-back.

Even though this part of the simulation felt more open than the Forest had, it had its own kind of boundary. The endless rolling hills closed them in and kept the horizon from view. It still felt to Natalya that if she left the Path she could get lost here, maybe forever, just on a larger scale.

But in another way, this simulation didn't bother her like the others had. Here she was herself, and she could make her choices. She wasn't trapped by the past and what her ancestors had done.

She didn't have to shoot anyone with a bow or fight anyone. She was glad to be here instead of the Viking memories.

"How is David doing?" she asked Grace.

"He had a hard time synchronizing, but he's got it now."

"Is that why you came in here?"

"Well, I wasn't going to sit around doing nothing," she said. "After I read—" She stopped and looked away.

Natalya wondered what she had just left unsaid, and she was about to ask when Grace pointed down the road.

"Is that Owen?"

Natalya looked, and it was. He trudged along the Path with the Dog trotting next to him.

"Looks like he's brought man's best friend with him," Grace said.

"I'd rather have that Dog as a friend than an enemy," Natalya said.

She got up from the stone and walked a few steps toward Owen to wait for him on the Path. As he got closer, she noticed his shirt was torn at his shoulder, but she saw no blood, and he didn't seem to be injured. He smiled at them.

"You okay?" she called.

He nodded. "I'm good." Then he pointed behind Natalya. "You guys found the Crossroads."

"We did," Grace said, rising from the stone.

Owen reached them, and the Dog stepped forward, wagging her tail, looking back and forth between Natalya and Grace. She was panting a little, with her tongue hanging out, and except for her size, she seemed like any other dog. But her size was enough to keep Natalya uncomfortable.

"You got her to come with you," Grace said.

"Yeah." Owen looked over at her. "I had to trick her into saving my life, but she came. Thanks for waiting for us, by the way."

"Saving your life?" Natalya asked.

"It's a long story," he said. "Between me and her."

"So what happens with her now?" Grace said.

Owen looked in each of the Crossroads' four directions and then he shrugged. "I guess we wait here for someone to come along?"

Grace sighed and took her seat back on the stone.

"You guys can go on if you want," Owen said. "Really."

"No," Natalya said. "We'll wait. I think this is a part of what we're supposed to do."

"It is," Owen said. "I realized this is the devotion part of the Path."

That made sense to Natalya. She took a seat on the stone next to Grace, and Owen sat down on the grass next to them. The Dog lay down on the warm red stones of the Path and went to sleep; while they waited, the three of them talked. Not about the simulation, or about the Trident, or about the Templars and Assassins. They talked about stuff that was unimportant, but still mattered, like the shows they liked to watch, and the music they hated, and stupid things they'd seen online. They talked about home, and their pets, and what they had been doing before all this started. But then at once they all fell silent.

Owen pulled up a handful of grass and threw it into the breeze. "It seems kind of ridiculous to think about going back to regular life, doesn't it?"

Grace nodded. "Yes, it does."

"But I hope we can," Natalya said. "I'll take my ridiculous, regular life any day."

"Sure," Grace said. "But regular life for some people is—"

"There's someone coming," Owen said, rising to his feet.

Natalya turned. A figure approached them, following the dirt trail as it rose and fell with the swells of grass and land. The three of them said nothing as they waited, all previous conversation lost. The stranger appeared tall and broad, and more details took shape with each of his steps. Unlike the Wanderer, he wore wool and woven fabrics studded with beads and shells, but like the Wanderer, he had dark bronze skin. His black hair and beard were long, but trimmed and clean and free of gray. He walked with a spear tipped with black iron, and when he reached them his eyes went straight to the Dog.

"That is a fine creature," he said without any greeting, his firm voice an imposing wall that kept others back. "Is she yours?"

Natalya wasn't sure what to think of this man, any more than she had known what to think of the Wanderer. Did these archetypes represent people? Actual people who had lived? Or were they ideas of people, just symbols in the same way the Serpent had been a symbol?

"She is mine," Owen said.

The stranger nodded. "I would have use for a Dog like that."

"Use?" Owen asked, stepping between the stranger and the Dog.

"Yes, of course," the stranger said. "To watch my tower. It stands on the other side of that hill. No one would dare steal my gold or my silver with that Dog standing guard. I assure you, she will be treated well. I'll feed her the finest meat from my table, and I'll give her a bed of clean straw."

Owen studied the man for several moments. Then he shook his head. "I don't think so."

"Perhaps you misunderstand me," the stranger said. "I will buy her from you. I will pay you handsomely—"

"No," Owen said. "She's not for sale."

The stranger scowled, and Natalya noted his spear again as he stared hard at the Dog. It almost seemed that he was thinking about taking her by force, but Natalya hoped he wasn't that stupid. Who would try to steal a Dog big enough to think of the thief as dinner? In the end, he lifted his glare from the Dog to Owen, and then he went on his way down the trail, presumably toward his tower, without saying another word.

"What happens now?" Grace asked after he was gone.

Owen sat down next to the Dog, and she rolled over to show him her belly, which he gave a rub. "We keep waiting," he said.

So that's what they did, talking very little now. Natalya wasn't sure how long they waited, because the time of day didn't seem to change here. They might have even sat there for hours, but the sun stayed where it was overhead, just a bit off center. An afternoon sun. But eventually, another stranger did approach, this time coming from the direction the previous man had left. As this new traveler drew near, Natalya saw that he was a short, round man with a balding head, wearing woolen clothes, and walking with one of those shepherd's staffs that had a crook at the end of it.

"Greetings!" he called, smiling, his voice creaking with the softness of an old leather coat. "It is a fine day to be on the Path, is it not?"

"Yeah," Owen said. "A fine day."

Natalya already liked this man more than the last, but it was Owen who had to like him enough to give him the Dog as a companion.

"But it's always a fine day on the Path, isn't it?" the man said as he came to a halt near them. Then he leaned on his staff, and he puffed air out of his red cheeks. "What are you three doing here at the Crossroads?"

"Waiting," Owen said.

"Waiting?" the man asked. "What for?"

"Just waiting," Owen said.

"Nonsense. We're always waiting for something." He looked at Natalya with strange blue-and-gold eyes. "Perhaps you have all been waiting for me, and I've been waiting for you."

"Why would we be waiting for you?" Grace asked.

"I wouldn't know," he said. "You haven't told me."

"That's because we're not waiting for you," Owen said.

"And yet there you are, and here I am." The stranger then looked down at the Dog, and his eyes opened wide, as if he hadn't noticed her until that moment. "What a magnificent animal," he said. "A breathtaking piece of creation." He looked up. "Does she belong to one of you?"

Owen nodded. "She is mine."

"That is wonderful." The man gave Owen a tight-lipped, knowing smile, as if Owen had done something he should be very proud of. "Wonderful, indeed." He looked down at the Dog again, and his smile loosened. "How very fortunate you are. I am not so fortunate, for I am in need of a dog."

"Need?" Owen said.

Natalya thought that was an improvement on having a "use" for the Dog.

"I need a dog to guard my herds and my flocks," the man said. "There are dangers at the borders of my pastures, and I can't protect my animals every moment of every day."

"What dangers?" Grace asked.

"Great dangers," the man said. "Unspeakable dangers."

"So you need a guard dog?" Owen said.

"Yes," the man said. "But not only a guard dog. There are times when a lamb or a calf goes missing. They might get frightened by a storm, or they might fall into a ravine. I need a dog to herd them. To keep them together and safe." He looked down. "A dog such as this."

Owen scratched his chin without taking his eyes off the man, and seemed to be giving this offer more thought than he'd given the first, which surprised Natalya. If they were looking for someone to take the place of the Wanderer, a shepherd and a rich guy were both the wrong choice. Neither life would be like the one the Dog had known.

But Owen turned to Natalya and Grace and asked, "What do you guys think?"

Not only had Natalya thought this was Owen's thing to decide, the decision seemed fairly obvious.

"I don't think this is the guy we're waiting for," Grace said.

"But what about my herds?" the man asked. "My flocks are in danger. Why are you taking away the very thing they need for their safety?"

"He's not taking anything away," Grace said. "To take something away from you, it has to be yours to begin with."

The man's eyes narrowed at Grace for a moment, and with a *tsk* he turned toward Owen. "My need is true and just. I believe you surely see that."

"Maybe I do," Owen said. "But I'm still not giving you my Dog."

"I see." The man turned away from them, shaking his head.

He took a few steps, and then he looked back. "I do hope you will not be punished for this choice."

"Punished how?" Grace asked.

"When the Path brings you misfortune, you will know." Then he continued walking and was soon lost over the rise of a hill.

Grace snorted. "I'm pretty sure this Path is guaranteed to bring misfortune at some point, but it won't be because of that guy."

Owen sat down next to the Dog, and she inched closer to him and placed her huge head in his lap, just as she had done with the Wanderer. Owen scratched behind her ears, and then he looked at the rip in his shirt. "I think you guys better make the decision the next time, though."

"Why?" Grace asked.

"I don't think I can choose." He stroked the top of the Dog's head, and she closed her eyes. "I don't want her to go to anyone, really. But she has to. I know we're supposed to find her a new companion."

If the Dog had really saved Owen's life, at least inside the simulation, Natalya could understand why he would find it hard to part with her. But Natalya had also come to believe he was right. This was something they were supposed to do. An objective in the collective unconscious.

"Sure," she said. "We can decide."

Grace agreed, and they both sat down near Owen in the grass while the Dog slept, and more time passed without any way to mark it. Natalya found herself growing drowsy in the endless afternoon as she listened to the slow and easy breathing of the Dog.

"This feels like . . ." Natalya tried to find the words. "I don't know. Like we're in a story. A folktale or something."

"Maybe we kind of are," Owen said.

When a third figure appeared in the distance, Natalya almost didn't notice, but Grace did, and then Natalya stood up too fast. She shook her head to clear the rush and focused on the newcomer, who she could already tell was a woman.

The stranger strode with slow purpose on the Path ahead of them, and the narrow foot of her plain walking staff echoed against the stones. She was young, of the same dark complexion as the other travelers they had met, with curly bronze hair pulled back into several braids. She wore leather clothing, and as she walked, her gaze roamed the land and the sky.

"Hello!" Natalya called to her.

"Hello," the woman said. But she stopped short of them, near the stone, and she walked around it. She seemed to be studying the carvings that covered its surface, perhaps reading them, and Natalya wondered if the rock was some kind of signpost.

"Are you lost?" Natalya asked.

The woman paused as though she had to think about the meaning of the word. "No. I'm where I want to be. Why do you ask?"

"I saw you looking at the rock, and I just thought . . ." But Natalya didn't know how to finish that sentence.

The woman looked at the stone again, appearing confused. Then she asked Natalya, "Are *you* lost?"

Next to Owen, the Dog had woken up and taken note of the new stranger, her ears perked forward as she sniffed the air.

"We know where we are," Natalya said. "But we don't know where we're going."

"If that's what it means to be lost," the woman said, "then I think we all are."

"Where are you traveling?" Owen asked.

"Where?" The woman frowned, as if once again she didn't understand the question. "I'm just walking the Path."

"So you're wandering," Grace said, eyeing Owen, and Natalya knew in that moment they were all thinking the same thing.

"Yes, wandering," the woman said. "That's a fair word for it, I suppose."

That was when Owen finally got to his feet, the Dog at his side, as if he meant to say something. But he didn't, and several silent moments went by. The woman's gaze traveled from the three of them to the Path beyond the Crossroads, and she seemed ready to move on. But she hadn't even asked about the Dog, and it seemed as though Owen was just going to let her walk away.

"We, uh—we met a Wanderer, like you," Natalya said. "This Dog was his."

The woman regarded the Dog then and smiled. "She's beautiful."

And that was all she said.

Owen just nodded.

"Have you ever traveled with a dog?" Grace asked.

The woman shook her head. "No. I don't have a use for a dog. Or a need for one."

Natalya had no idea where to go from that.

"I'll be moving along now," the woman said.

But she couldn't leave yet. Not without the Dog, unless Owen planned to bring her with them for the rest of the simulation. He might actually want that, but Natalya still believed they had to do this before they could move on. She just didn't know how.

The stranger walked between Natalya and Grace, bowing her head, and then passed very close to the Dog, who looked up and wagged her tail for the woman.

She smiled at the Dog, and then said, "Safe journey to you—"

"Wait," Owen said.

The woman turned toward him.

"Do you—do you want my Dog?"

The woman craned her neck toward Owen. "Do I want her?"

"I can't keep her," he said, and cleared his throat. "She was really only mine until I could find a companion for her. And you're the only person we've met who I think should have her. She belongs with you."

The woman stood there for a moment, frowning, and it definitely seemed as if she wanted to say no. But then her frown relaxed, and she took a step toward the Dog with her hand outstretched, braver than Natalya had been. She first let the Dog smell her fist, and then her fingers and palm, and then she scratched the Dog's fur under her chin. That's when the Dog sat down and leaned against her with a contented sigh, thumping her tail, and the woman raised an eyebrow.

"She really is beautiful," the stranger said.

"Will you have her?" Owen asked. "I want to give her to you."

The woman paused, and then replied, "Yes. I think I want to have her with me."

Owen let out a very long sigh. "Thank you."

Natalya believed that to be the right decision, and the right end to this story they had just played out. But it meant that Owen now had to say good-bye.

He did so by digging his fingers into her scruff, and scratching behind her ears. The Dog seemed to be smiling at him, and she licked his face until it was time for her to leave with the new Wanderer, who had already started down the Path.

"Come!" she called.

The Dog glanced at her, and then looked at Owen.

"Go on," he said. "It's okay."

The Dog cocked her head almost sideways.

"It's okay." Owen waved his hand. "Go."

"Come!" the Wanderer called again.

This time, the Dog took a few hesitant steps toward her new companion, yellow eyes still fixed on Owen, and she whined.

"You're a good girl," he said. "Keep going."

"Come!"

The Dog took a few more steps, and a few more, until she finally broke into a trot that caught her up to the Wanderer, who reached out and gave her neck a pat. After that, the two of them grew smaller together on the Path, until they were gone.

Owen just stood there, watching, even after there wasn't anything more to see. He didn't say anything. He kept his face blank, and his eyes stayed dry. Natalya didn't know what to do for him, because she still didn't understand what had happened with the Dog, probably in the same way Owen didn't understand what had happened with the Serpent.

"You ready to go?" Grace finally asked.

He nodded. "Sure."

"You okay?" Natalya asked.

He shrugged. "The important thing is we just took care of devotion. If that voice at the beginning of all of this was right, that just leaves faith."

Grace walked up to him and gave him a hug. He seemed surprised for a moment, but then he hugged her back and said, "Thanks."

Then the three of them faced the Path ahead, but as they took their first steps beyond the Crossroads, the sky darkened, diving from gloaming to cold midnight with a suddenness that made Natalya gasp. It was as if someone had doused the sun.

"What is it with this place?" Grace asked.

"Maybe that guy was right," Owen said. "Maybe we're being punished."

CHAPTER EIGHTEEN

Grace shivered as they walked, the sky bright with stars that looked wrong, even though she couldn't say how. She didn't know a lot about the night sky, but she could identify a few constellations her dad used to point out when she was younger, and here in the simulation, those shapes seemed askew. The moon shone with a cold radiance, like a flashlight through ice, illuminating the Path ahead of them.

Their surroundings had changed, too. The easy rolling hills had steepened and sharpened, and the white stone bluffs had become gray rock cliffs. The Path found its way by staying low, changing course with the basins and the bottoms of the ravines.

Owen hadn't said much since giving the Dog to the new Wanderer, but that didn't surprise Grace.

"I had a cat when I was about three," she said. "His name was Brando."

"Brando?" Natalya asked.

"After Marlon Brando," Grace said. "My dad picked it. He said the cat walked around like the Godfather, which he did. But I loved that cat." She could still remember the way his nose tickled her ears when he was purring.

"What happened to him?" Owen asked.

"We found out David was allergic. So Brando had to go."

"Oh," Owen said.

"My parents got this older couple to take him. The day they came to pick him up, I locked myself in the bathroom. My parents were trying to get me to say good-bye, but I thought if I refused to say good-bye then Brando couldn't leave. When I came out of the bathroom, he was gone."

She hadn't thought about that cat or the day he'd left in years. But watching Owen say good-bye to the Dog had brought it all back, and she was surprised that it still hurt.

"I'm sorry," Owen said.

"Thanks," Grace said. "And just so you know, that Dog didn't even compare to Brando."

Natalya chuckled and Owen laughed.

"Since I never met Brando, I'll have to take your word for it," he said.

"Trust me," she said.

A moment later, Natalya shivered and looked up at the sky. "It's so clear. You can see the Milky Way."

The three of them walked in silence after that, staring up at the stars. The Path stretched on and on, without any branches, forks, or crossroads. It had only two directions: forward and backward, and they had already seen what lay behind them. Unless they wanted to hold still and do nothing, they had only one choice, so they kept moving.

The night seemed as timeless as the day had felt. The moon and stars held fixed positions, and they looked closer to the ground than they were supposed to be, as if they could dress themselves in clouds. The three of them walked and walked and gradually the high hills closed in, becoming a canyon with sheer walls to either side that pinched off their view of the sky near the horizon. But something up there caught Grace's eye.

She thought it was a star at first, but it was very bright, and she realized it was too bright. It sat in the wedge formed by the canyon, and as they walked closer to it, the light brightened, and Grace realized it wasn't in the sky at all. It sat at the top of a mountain.

"Is that the light you guys saw at the beginning?" she asked them.

"Maybe," Natalya said.

"I'd say that's probably the Summit, though," Owen added.

Grace glanced up at the rims of the canyon, projecting forward ahead of them, and assumed that was where the Path led.

"It's a long way away," Owen said.

But it turned out it wasn't. Their journey brought the mountain and its summit closer much more quickly than Grace had expected. Either the distance wasn't as great as it seemed, or they walked faster than she thought they did, or maybe it was just the odd way time ran here, because they soon reached the end of the canyon, where an enormous human figure loomed over them.

It had been painted or burned against a sheer rock face on the mountainside, a giant's simple shadow, without detail or gender. It stood at least a hundred feet tall, but maybe more. It was hard for Grace to gauge the distance from where she stood, and the darkness hid most of the mountain above. She also couldn't see the light at the Summit anymore.

"I hope that's not a self-portrait," Owen said.

Grace looked over her shoulder at the moon. "It seems like in this place, it could be."

"Where do we go?" Natalya asked. "The Path ends here."

Grace looked and saw that she was right. The Path stopped at the giant's feet. But to the figure's right, she noticed a narrow channel cut into the rock. It zigzagged up the mountain as high as she could see, and she guessed even higher than that.

"Hey, there's a rope over there." Natalya walked in a different direction than Grace was looking, toward the figure's left.

She and Owen followed her, and they did find a rope descending from the darkness. Next to it, someone had chiseled a very narrow, steep staircase. It climbed vertically, straight up the mountain, each stair no more than a few inches deep. It was practically a ladder. Grace felt queasy just looking at it.

"Do we have to climb this?" Owen asked.

"I think we do," Natalya said.

"Uh, there's a path over there." Grace pointed to the figure's right. "Not *the* Path, but a path. It might be safer than this way."

They crossed to the giant's other side and looked more closely at the path Grace had seen. It didn't have stairs, and was just a little over a foot wide, but not nearly as steep as the rope climb, because it switched back and forth.

"I don't like either of these," Owen said.

Grace agreed with him.

"I think we have to pick one of them," Natalya said.

Grace did not want to agree with that. She didn't like heights. She had never labeled it a phobia, but it was definitely a fear, one she had always thought healthy.

"Maybe there's another way?" she said, even though she knew there wasn't. The canyon stopped where the mountain began, enclosing them on three sides, and the only way out was up, or back.

"I don't see another way," Natalya said. "If we want to get up there, and that's clearly where we're supposed to go, we have to climb one of these."

Owen looked at the path, and then stared off to the right toward the rope. "I think I'm leaning toward Staircase of Doom over Trail of Death."

"Why?" Natalya asked.

"Look at this thing," he said, gesturing toward the path. "It's barely wide enough, and there isn't anything to stop you from falling. You're just on your own. At least with the rope, you have something to hold on to."

Natalya nodded. The two of them returned to the staircase, and Grace followed them, unsure whether she agreed.

"See?" Owen grabbed the rope. "You just hold on to this."

Grace looked up. "Yeah, but we don't know where that goes. We don't know what it's attached to, or how old it is. What if it snaps? Without that rope, you fall."

Owen looked up, and then he let go of the rope. "Good point."

"So that's what we have to decide," Natalya said. "Use the ladder and pray the rope holds, or take the path and hope we don't need the rope."

Grace still didn't like either option. It didn't even help to tell herself it was only a simulation. But it was a simulation that held unknown dangers, and she wasn't sure what falling to her death would mean in here. There were apparently some ways her brain just refused to compromise, and looking up at the path and the rope, she felt herself falling already. What if her mind couldn't recover from that?

"I'm taking the rope," Owen said.

"I think I am, too," Natalya said.

Grace did not think so. If she had to choose, she would choose the option where she didn't have to trust a mystery rope. The path told her everything it could, which wasn't much, but she hoped it would be enough.

"I'm going to take the path," she said.

The other two looked at her.

"Don't you think we should stick together?" Owen said.

"Maybe," Grace said. "So come on the path with me."

"I think the rope is safer," Owen said. Then he looked up. "Maybe we should ask the giant which one is best."

Grace believed for a very brief moment that might be possible, because why not? This was a simulation of the collective unconscious. Who knew what the rules were? But when she glanced up, the massive figure didn't move, or speak, or seem to notice them at all.

"I don't think we should split up," Natalya said. "I don't think I can use that path. I need something to hold on to."

The three of them looked at one another.

"Okay," Grace said. "So we hold on to each other, if we need to."

Owen and Natalya looked at each other, and when it seemed

that they'd come to some unspoken agreement, they both inhaled and nodded.

"Okay," Natalya said. "Okay, let's do this."

Grace sighed, and then made herself walk to the path. She knew that once they started up it, there would be no going back. They wouldn't be able to turn around, or climb down backward. They would achieve the Summit, or they would fall.

"I think I can," she whispered to herself, and Owen chuckled.

"So who goes first?" Natalya asked.

"I will," Grace said.

Otherwise, she worried she would lose her nerve. So she took the first step, and felt the grit of the mountain's stone beneath her shoe. She took another step. And another. And another. She leaned a bit toward the mountain, so that she could reach out with one of her hands if she needed to steady herself.

Natalya came behind her, followed by Owen. After Grace had taken a few dozen steps, she reached the first switchback, and she pivoted with the path, an inch at a time, until the mountain had moved to her other side, and for a moment she could see Natalya's and Owen's faces. They both looked grim, focused, and determined.

Grace took more steps, dozens of them, to the next switchback, where she changed direction again. She repeated this several times, and, with each fold in the trail, the climb up the path seemed to be getting easier. Even routine. But then she looked down.

Vertigo seized her gut and her head, nearly tipped her into open air, but she threw herself against the mountainside, her hands splayed against the ice-cold rock.

"Are you okay?" Natalya asked.

They had climbed very high. As high as the giant's shoulders, Grace guessed. The ground seemed very far below, the path little more than a red ribbon. The wind had picked up, too, and it was a freezing wind, with gusts that whispered in her ear that she would die.

"I'm okay," she said, clenching her teeth against the chatter of the cold and her fear.

She took several deep breaths, and then resumed her climb. One step, then another, and another. One switchback, then another, and another. She kept her eyes rigidly straight ahead, but every so often, she risked a quick backward glance, just to make sure Natalya and Owen were still there. Together, they made steady progress up the mountain, leaving the giant far below.

"Hey, guys," Owen said. "Look down."

"Owen," Grace said, "whatever energy my feet aren't using, I'm spending it trying *not* to look down."

"But the ground is gone," he said.

A moment later, Natalya said, "He's right."

Grace stopped. Then she very carefully lowered her eyes, and this time when she looked down, she saw nothing. The view below them had turned darker than the sky, and Grace stared into an abyss. She wasn't sure what would happen if she fell into it, but it looked as if the plummet might never end, and she would be trapped in her terror.

"How much farther is it?" Owen asked. "Can you guys see the top?"

Now Grace steadied herself with her hand and looked up. The sheer rock wall faded into the night, the Summit still hidden somewhere above it. "I can't see it," she said.

"Me neither," Natalya said.

Owen sighed. "Just making sure."

Grace resumed her careful climb, but not long after that, she felt the first twinges of fatigue in her thighs. Each step after that kindled a slow fire in her muscles, until they burned hot and red. But the top of the mountain remained out of sight, and she wondered for the first time whether she could even reach it. Not because of falling, but because it was just too high, and she physically couldn't do it.

"Is anyone else getting tired?" she said, breathing hard.

"I am," Natalya said.

"I'm slowing down," Owen said.

"Should we stop for a rest?" Grace asked.

The other two agreed, so they halted their climb and very carefully sat down on the path. Grace wedged herself into a position as securely as she could and faced the night sky above, and the abyss below, with her feet hanging over the edge. She was too tired to talk, and since Natalya and Owen didn't say anything, she figured they felt the same way. The three of them just sat there, resting their legs and catching their breath.

At first, it felt good, and reassuring. Her legs stopped quivering, her heartbeat slowed, and her breath came easier. But then the wind found her as it rushed up the mountainside, and it turned her to ice where she'd been sweating only moments before. It whispered to her again, turning her mind toward doubt, and she began to wonder.

What if there wasn't anything up there? What if that light they had seen at the Summit was some kind of optical illusion, and they climbed toward an empty promise? What if it didn't matter if the light was real, because they would never reach it? It was too high, and the path was too narrow, and they would fall before they ever got close to it.

At first, it seemed these thoughts came from within Grace, but she soon realized they called to her from the abyss as she stared down into the heart of it. It promised her open arms, and told her how easy it would be for her to simply push off from the ledge. Not much effort, and then she would need no effort at all. If they would never reach the Summit, or if they did, and they found nothing there, why make the climb at all? Why cling to an indifferent mountain that kept silent in the face of her struggles? The abyss heard her, asked nothing of her, and waited to receive her.

One little push. That's all it would take. Just lean a little, and then a little push with her hands—

Grace gasped and looked up. Thoughts of her brother wrenched her sight and her mind away from the abyss. The stars and moon hung low and gleaming, almost closer now that they had climbed so far. Natalya and Owen seemed lost in their own thoughts.

"Guys," she said.

They didn't respond.

"Guys, listen to me." She reached out and touched Natalya's arm. "We have to keep moving. If we sit here, we won't make it."

Natalya swung her head toward Grace slowly, as if anchored to the abyss. "I'm beginning to think we never were going to make it. This is impossible."

"No," Grace said. "No, you're wrong. That's not what you think, Natalya. You're the one who beat that Serpent, remember? You helped Owen find the Dog a new companion. We can make it."

"How do you know?" Owen asked. He'd been listening to them, apparently. "How do you know we can make it?"

Grace didn't have an answer for that question. She didn't know they would make it in the way Owen asked the question. But she believed they would make it because she had confidence in herself and in them.

"I just know," she said to Owen.

Natalya sighed and shook her head. "I think I'm done with this."

Grace saw her lean forward, and in the second that she saw it and realized what Natalya was about to do, she reached out her hand and grabbed Natalya's wrist.

"No!" she shouted.

But Natalya pushed herself off the ledge, and Grace braced herself as she held on.

Natalya dropped as far as she could until her wrist and her arm yanked her back around and into the mountain, almost pulling Grace over the side. But she lay down flat on the path, one arm hanging over the edge, and held on.

"Owen, help!" Grace shouted. She looked down into Natalya's open eyes and saw terror. Whatever had prompted her to jump, that spell had broken.

"Don't let go!" Natalya screamed.

"I won't," Grace said. But she couldn't hold on forever. "Owen!"

"I'm here!" He scrambled up and reached one of his hands over the edge to grab Natalya. "Okay," he said. "We've got you. We're going to pull you up."

"Hurry," Natalya said.

Grace looked at Owen. He gave a nod, and they pulled at the same time, lifting Natalya closer.

"Give me your other hand," Owen said, and as soon as Natalya raised it high enough, he seized it.

After that, Grace and Owen hauled her up, each grasping one of her hands, until Natalya was able to get a knee up on the ledge. A few moments later, all three of them sat on the path with their backs against the mountain. Natalya had her eyes shut tight, chest heaving.

Grace looked past her and scowled at Owen, breathing hard. "What took you so long?"

"I don't know." Owen shook his head and looked downward. "I don't know."

But Grace knew, and she wasn't really mad at Owen. She was just scared at what had almost happened.

"I'm sorry," Natalya said.

"It's okay," Grace said. "But we have to keep moving."

"Okay." Natalya opened her eyes and nodded. "Okay."

They rested just a few minutes longer, until they had caught their breath, and then they resumed their climb. The abyss was still down there, calling for Grace's surrender, but she refused to listen to it. She also still had doubts about what they would find at the Summit, and she continued to fear that they might fall before they reached it. But instead of dwelling on those questions, she focused on the placement of each foot with every step she took.

Hundreds of steps.

Maybe thousands.

It became a kind of meditation in which she became lost, and up they went, until suddenly, without warning, there was no more cliff wall beneath her hand. Grace pried her gaze from the path and looked around, blinking. They weren't at the Summit of the mountain, but they had reached the top of its sheer face, and the path led them away from the abyss, along a glacier that glowed blue in the moonlight. Its ice filled a gap between two ridges, and atop the taller of them, Grace saw the light, though it wasn't as bright as it had looked from the canyon. But it was there.

It emanated from within a huge, shimmering dome that rose out of the mountain like half of a giant pearl. Beneath it, cut right into the rock, was a doorway, and their path led them directly toward it. Grace continued to lead the way, and they walked the glacier's edge until they stood beneath the entrance.

"I think this is the end," Owen said.

"It has to be," Grace said. "There's nowhere else to go."

With that, they went inside.

CHAPTER NINETEEN

Even though Sean held the Piece of Eden in his hand, it felt impossibly far away, separated from him by hundreds of years and who knew how many miles. And the hands weren't actually his. They were Styrbjörn's, and the Viking still didn't understand what he had. But he carried the dagger around, and he studied it, because he suspected it possessed some significance that went beyond its holiness as a relic of the Christ.

"You should destroy that dagger or throw it away," Gorm said. "It offends the gods."

"And how do you know what offends the gods?" Styrbjörn asked. "Do you speak for them? Are you now a seer?"

They sat in the morning light around the embers and ashes of the previous night's fire, still camped in the Mirkwood. Thyra kept to Styrbjörn's right hand, while Gorm and several other Jomsviking captains faced him angrily from across the ring. They had not yet spoken of retreat, but Styrbjörn knew he was in danger of losing his army. He could feel it. If but one of the captains suggested they abandon their purpose, the rest would follow.

"Palnatoke is dead," Gorm said. "I do not need to be a seer to know the gods are displeased."

Styrbjörn raised his voice. "Palnatoke knew the length of his skein was set. He faced the end of his life in battle, instead of hiding in Jomsborg. This dagger had nothing to do with it, and you take away the honor of his death by claiming otherwise."

Gorm said nothing in reply.

"I honor Palnatoke," Styrbjörn continued. "And so I will seek vengeance for his death. But I wonder what you will do."

"Do not pretend you fight Eric for Palnatoke's honor," Gorm said. "You fight for—"

"I do not think he pretends," Thyra said. "I think Styrbjörn is as angry as you are at Palnatoke's death, just as he is angry at his uncle. Can he not fight for both? For his crown and also the honor of his sworn brother? If you speak against Styrbjörn, you speak against Palnatoke."

She forged her words with the calm and steady assurance of a blacksmith's hammer, and Gorm said nothing against them. The Jomsviking lowered his head under Thyra's gaze, as though she were a queen, rather than a shield-maiden. Styrbjörn was surprised at how quickly he had come to admire Thyra and value her presence at his side. But now was not the time to weigh it.

He pressed Gorm further. "I am still wondering what you

will do to honor Palnatoke. How you will fulfill the oath you swore not to retreat."

Gorm looked up. "We will fight. But know this, Styrbjörn. We fight for vengeance. We fight for our oaths and our honor. We do not fight for your crown."

Styrbjörn nodded. In the end, it did not matter why the Jomsvikings went to battle. It only mattered that they fought. "Prepare your men. We march for the Fyrisfield."

Gorm bowed his head, but there was no love or respect in it. Then he and his captains left the fire ring, and when they had gone, Styrbjörn turned to Thyra.

"Thank you for your counsel."

"I spoke only the truth," she said.

"I think you changed the tide of Gorm's mind."

"But not my father's, or he would still be here as well." She looked at the dagger Styrbjörn wore at his waist. "I'm amazed Harald left that behind."

Styrbjörn looked down at it, and Sean focused more intently on the memory's current, as he always did when the dagger became the focus of the simulation. "It seemed to be more than just a relic to him," Styrbjörn said.

"It always did. I've thought many times there must be power in it."

"What kind of power?"

She tipped her head sideways, looking up into the trees, and her green eyes captured sunlight. "I would say that it drew others to him. Enemies would leave his presence devoted to him. But only when he wore that dagger."

Sean knew exactly what she had observed. That was the

power of this prong of the Trident. But Styrbjörn still looked at the weapon with suspicion, even as he kept it at his side.

A short while later, the Jomsvikings stood ready with their spears, swords, axes, and shields. Those too injured or weak from poison remained behind, while the rest marched that day toward Uppsala. Styrbjörn led them through the forest, at the head of their army, to show them that there were no more poisoned snares, and none of Eric's warriors to harry them. They came within sight of the Fyrisfield in the later afternoon, where Styrbjörn expected to see Eric's army mustered on the plain.

But it lay empty.

No warriors. No encampment. Just an open expanse of grass and marsh.

"Where are your countrymen?" Gorm asked. "Surely Eric sent out the Bidding Stick."

"He must have gathered them north of here, at Uppsala," Styrbjörn said.

"Near the temple?" Gorm asked. "Why would he risk a battle there?"

"Perhaps he thinks the gods will save him," Styrbjörn said.

Before they entered the plain, they fanned out and formed ranks, and then Styrbjörn marched the Jomsvikings forth at the spear point of their wedge. They emerged from the Mirkwood beating a steady rhythm on their shields with their axes, like drums. They chanted and marched, sweeping northward. To the west, the Fyriswater flowed down into Mälaren, and to the east, the marshes lay dank and reedy. Ahead of them, the green land swelled and dipped like the loosened sail of a ship billowing in the wind. It had been years since Styrbjörn last walked here, the land of his fathers, where he ran as a boy. Years spent in exile, waiting to avenge his father's murder and claim his crown. At last his time had come. He could feel his rage and thirst for battle rising.

"What is that?" Thyra asked.

Styrbjörn looked at her. "What?"

"Listen," she said.

At first, he heard nothing over the sounds of the Jomsviking march. But then he felt a rumbling in the ground beneath his feet, and he heard distant thunder, though the sky was clear.

"Something is coming," she said. "Eric's army?"

"No," he said, listening. "It's something else."

He searched the horizon as the sound grew louder, and nearer. The Jomsvikings ceased their chanting and shield-beating to listen. They halted in their march at the base of a low, broad rise, and they waited, weapons ready.

"You're right," Thyra said. "That is no army."

"Whatever it is," Styrbjörn said, "we will kill it, or destroy it."

Thyra didn't nod, or agree. She simply looked at him with a blank expression he didn't understand, and then returned her attention to the plain. Styrbjörn tightened his grip on his axe, Randgríð, and then he smiled at what was about to begin.

A moment later, a huge beast appeared over the distant rise. It charged down toward them, bellowing, and at first Styrbjörn didn't understand what he was seeing: a solid, many-legged mass bristling with horns, spears, and swords that spread almost the width of the Jomsviking line. Then Styrbjörn realized it wasn't a single thing, but many, a herd of cattle hundreds of animals long and three or four deep. They had been yoked and tied together so that they moved as one, studded with weapons, a living war machine, unstoppable, meant to trample, crush, cut, and impale. Styrbjörn had never seen anything like it.

It was an army breaker.

Any warrior caught in its path would be maimed or killed, and Styrbjörn knew what was about to happen to the Jomsvikings. They couldn't retreat southward, because the cattle would run them down. If they fled to the east, the marsh would simply mire them. That left but one route of escape.

"To the river!" Styrbjörn ordered, waving his axe over his head, then blowing on his war horn.

The Jomsvikings heard him, then turned and raced west to get clear of the behemoth. Thyra ran with them, and when Styrbjörn was sure she would make it to safety, he turned and sped directly toward the oncoming storm. The Jomsvikings' eastern flank would not have time to get clear before the cattle slammed into their line. Styrbjörn had to find some way to break up the beasts.

They stampeded toward him with wide, rolling eyes, and frantic bellows, mindless with fear. He returned Randgríð to his belt as the distance between him and the war machine closed. When the cattle were but yards away, he launched himself into the air using all his strength, sailing high enough to clear the first spears and horns.

But as he came back down, a sword slashed his thigh, and he tumbled sideways onto the heaving shoulders of a bull. The beast threw him, and he nearly slipped through a gap between two oxen. His legs dangled among the pounding hooves, and the rushing ground snagged his heels, trying to pull him down the rest of the way to his death.

Styrbjörn grabbed on to a heavy yoke and hauled himself up, using the rest of the wooden framework for support. His thigh bled heavily, and he had only moments to act.

He pulled Randgríð from his belt and went to work hewing, splitting, and sundering the ropes and wood around him that made this herd into a weapon. Soon the thundering line of cattle fractured, and then it broke in two.

But that wasn't enough. Styrbjörn balanced and jumped along the surging backs of the animals to another joining, where his axe work made a second break.

The war machine now charged in thirds, the gaps between them widening, the remaining tethers weakening. At least some of the Jomsvikings could now make for the openings that Styrbjörn had made.

He turned and leapt from the rear of the war machine, landing in a hard roll behind it. Then he got to his feet and watched the cattle charging away from him toward his men, and a moment after that, the air shattered with the sound of impact. Shields tore, and men screamed, and metal rang. Some of the Jomsvikings made it safely through the gaps, but far too many went under, and they were spat out from under the cattle, broken and dying, as the machine rolled mindlessly onward.

Styrbjörn raced through the muddy, shredded turf toward his men, but before he reached them, he heard a new sound coming from the north, this one familiar. He turned and saw Eric's army charging down, coming to slay those that had survived the stampede.

"To me!" Styrbjörn bellowed, raising Randgríð, and he blew the command on his war horn. Then he turned to face Eric's army, and moments later, ranks of Jomsvikings formed around and behind him, among them Thyra and Gorm.

"Shield wall!" Styrbjörn ordered, blowing again on his horn.

"They outnumber us at least four to one," Gorm said.

Styrbjörn pointed to the west. "The sun will set soon. All we have to do is last. Today we show them how hard they have to work to kill us. Tomorrow we show them how hard we will work to kill them."

Around Styrbjörn, and in other pockets across the plain, those Jomsvikings who could still lift a shield fell back together, shoulder to shoulder, shields and spears outward. Thyra stood next to Styrbjörn, and she noticed his thigh.

"Is it bad?" she asked.

Though he felt blood pooling inside his boot, he said, "It is nothing."

She gave him a fierce and eager smile that surprised him, and which he returned.

Then Eric's army fell upon them.

It was close bladework after that, thrusting with spears and swords, pushing back against the enemy with their shields. But Eric's men were farmers and freemen summoned under the *ledung*, many of them inexperienced in battle, while the Jomsvikings were men sworn to raiding and war. For every blow one of Styrbjörn's took, they returned five on Eric's. Thyra proved herself skilled and deadly, and as the day wore itself out, the shield walls held, and as evening fell, Eric's army withdrew across the Fyrisfield to their camp.

The Jomsvikings gathered their wounded and their dead,

and returned to the Mirkwood, along the boundary of which they found the remains of the cattle war machine. Many of the animals had died upon impact with the trees, and those that hadn't appeared to have run deep into the woods. The men butchered several cows and ate beef that night, as much meat as their bellies could hold, and afterward, Gorm came to Styrbjörn at his fire.

"I wish to swear to you, Styrbjörn," the Jomsviking said. "I and all my brothers. We saw all that you did. Forgive me for doubting your honor."

"You are forgiven," Styrbjörn said as Thyra sat by and stitched the wound in his thigh.

Gorm continued. "They will sing songs about your feats this day, and tomorrow the Jomsvikings will fight and die by your side, to the last man if the gods will it. This is the oath we will take."

As Sean observed this memory flowing along, it struck him that Styrbjörn had acquired the unwavering loyalty of the Jomsvikings without using the power of the dagger.

"Oaths tomorrow," Styrbjörn said. "For now, there are wounded and dying warriors who need their captain. Go to them, Gorm, and you and I will talk again."

Gorm bowed his head, this time in sincere devotion, and left Styrbjörn's fire ring. After he had gone, Styrbjörn stared into the flames, into the deepest, hottest hollow among the logs and coals. He would need a strategy for the next day's fighting. Eric still had superior numbers, and he had yet to send his personal war band into battle.

"This wound was far worse than you let on," Thyra said.

"I said it was nothing. And that's what it was."

She shook her head, frowning.

"What are you thinking?" Styrbjörn asked.

"I am thinking that I would have you for my husband," she said.

He whipped his gaze toward her. The fire cast its light against her red cheeks, and into her hair and eyes. "Are you mocking me?" he asked.

"No," she said. "Why would you think so?"

He looked away from her, flustered and unsure of himself.

"Do you plan to marry?" she asked.

"I will marry," he said. "When I have avenged my father and claimed what is mine, I will marry."

She nodded, but with a slight frown. "You are the first man I have met who I think worthy to be my husband. And I think I am the first woman you have met worthy to be your wife."

She spoke with plain confidence, and she was right about the way he saw her, but he had kept those thoughts apart from the rest of his mind until he could properly consider them. Because this was not the time for those thoughts. He had a war to win, and an uncle to kill.

"I think we should wait to discuss this," he said.

"I don't think we should wait," she said. "I would marry you tonight."

"Tonight?" He stared at her then, shocked by her boldness, but also admiring of it. "Why tonight?"

"Because after tomorrow, you will be a king, and I don't want you or anyone to think I marry your crown. I don't marry Styrbjörn the Strong. Years from now, when our grandchildren sit at your feet, I want you to tell them of this night. You will tell them that I wanted you even in your exile. I wanted to marry Bjorn."

Styrbjörn liked hearing her say his true name, and had no wish to correct her. He regarded her for a long while, and she said nothing more, apparently intent on giving him time and space to think. It was true that he wanted to marry one day, and it was also true that he would want to marry Thyra above any woman he had ever met. But tonight? Must it be tonight?

When looked at from a certain angle, there seemed to be madness in her words. Yet from a different angle, she made more sense than anything else he had encountered in this mad world.

"In what way would you wish to marry?" he asked.

"In the old way," she said. "Witnessed by the gods."

"And what of the bride price? The traditions?"

"I don't care about any of that."

He nodded, and he gave it more thought, until he reached a decision that in fact he had already made without knowing it. "I will marry you tonight," he said. "But I must ask something of you that you will not like."

She smiled, and when he looked at her then, he decided with finality that she was beautiful.

"What?" she asked.

"I ask you not to fight tomorrow," he said. "You must leave the battlefield."

"What?" Her smile vanished. "No husband of mine would ask me—"

"I may die tomorrow," he said. It was the first time he had spoken those words to anyone, including himself. The only reason he considered them now was out of love, not for Thyra, though he believed he would love her, but for Gyrid, his sister. "I do not want to die," he said. "But the Norns have already cut my skein, and if I am to reach the end of it tomorrow, then I would ask you to bring word of me to my sister. She will be your sister, too, and I ask you to comfort her, and take my place at her side."

Thyra looked at him with the same blank expression he had seen earlier that day, and he wondered if he would ever learn to read it, and if so, how many years it would take.

"I know that I can't make you go," he said. "And I would not try. But I do ask it of you. Will you grant me this?"

Thyra didn't answer him for a very long time, but he knew better than to press her.

"I will," she finally said. "Though I didn't think I would."

He laughed. "Neither did I." He nodded toward the forest. "And now I have a shrine to build."

So they walked away from the camp together deeper into the Mirkwood, and soon they came upon a great boulder twice as tall as Styrbjörn. It bore a crack right down the middle of it, as though it were a frost giant's head that Thor had struck with his hammer, and they decided they would make their vows before it. Styrbjörn gathered pale stones in the twilight and piled them up against the boulder to make a shrine, and though they had no honey or grain, he placed a golden ring upon it. When it was complete, Styrbjörn gave his Ingelrii sword to Thyra, and vowed to be her husband, and to honor her above all others, and to let no one speak against her. Then she gave her sword to him and swore the same oaths, and thus they sealed their marriage before the god Frey, who was the father of all the kings of the Svear.

"Now the blood sacrifice," Styrbjörn said. "I will find us an animal—"

"No." Thyra looked at his belt. "We already have an offering that will please the gods."

Styrbjörn looked down, and then he pulled the Bluetooth's dagger from its sheath. He studied it for a moment, and then he placed it on the shrine, and dedicated the offering of the Christ relic to Thor. He asked for aid from the sky god in the coming battle. Then he shoved the dagger within the split in the boulder and he piled the stones up higher against it, to hide it from the view of passersby.

When that was complete, Styrbjörn and Thyra returned to the camp as husband and wife, leaving the dagger in its resting place. If it was still there, then Sean could easily find it.

"Isaiah," Sean said. "Can you hear me? Did you see that?"

Yes, Isaiah said. *Excellent work, Sean. Excellent.*

"Do you have the location?"

We do. I can pull you out of the Animus now. Styrbjörn's memories are about to end, at any rate.

"They are?" Though Sean had fulfilled the purpose of the simulation, he wasn't quite ready to leave his ancestor behind. "Why?"

It seems that Styrbjörn will shortly pass on his genetic memories, when he conceives a child with Thyra. We don't have DNA of his memories after tonight.

"So he didn't have any more children?"

No, of course not.

"Why of course not?"

I—I thought you knew, Isaiah said. *It is a matter of history that Styrbjörn died during the battle of Fyrisfield.*

CHAPTER TWENTY

O wen stood in a corridor unlike anything he had encountered in the simulation thus far. Where the Forest and the Path had seemed old, or primitive, this place seemed advanced. The gray walls to either side appeared to be made of a metallic stone, veined with a network of thin, golden lines that spread like circuits. Ahead of them, the hallway ended at the entrance to what appeared to be a bright, cavernous room.

"I don't think this is an archetype," Owen said.

"There's still only one way for us to go," Grace said.

So the three of them listened and walked carefully down the corridor, which seemed to pulse and shimmer at the edges of Owen's vision, but not when he looked directly at the walls. Their footsteps made very little noise, even as a deep, resonant sound filled the space around them as constant and noticeable as a heartbeat.

When they reached the end of the corridor, they crept to one side and peered around the corner, into the chamber, and found they were now beneath the dome they had seen from outside. Its shimmering curvature spanned a vast vaulted space suffused with a pale blue light. Directly under the dome, several large platforms bore strange objects and equipment that Owen didn't recognize or understand. It might have been machinery, or computers, or simply sculptures. Crystalline walkways, staircases, and conduits linked the platforms together into a structure that looked almost molecular. It climbed up into the space beneath the dome, and descended into a silo that had been hollowed out of the mountain beneath them.

"What is this place?" Owen asked.

"Maybe it's an archetype for a mad scientist's lab," Grace said.

"Something like that," Natalya said. "I think this is the key Monroe is looking for. The Pieces of Eden came from an ancient civilization, right?" She nodded toward the middle of the chamber. "That looks like it was made by an ancient civilization to me."

YOU ARE CORRECT, said a strange voice.

Owen turned toward it as a figure walked up from below. She had long dark hair, and her pale skin seemed to glow from within. She wore a silver headdress that might have been a helmet, and her white robes nearly touched the ground. As the stranger approached them, she spoke with the same voice they had heard at the beginning of this simulation.

WHAT YOU ARE SEEING DOES BELONG TO AN ANCIENT CIVILIZATION. MY CIVILIZATION. She turned away from them. **COME.**

Owen, Grace, and Natalya followed the stranger to one of the crystal staircases, which they ascended, stepping out over the seemingly bottomless chasm below. Owen gripped the cold handrail tightly.

"Who are you?" Natalya asked the stranger as they climbed.

I AM A MEMORY OF ONE WHO CAME BEFORE, the stranger said, and that was all.

She guided them from staircase, to walkway, to staircase, up into the highest reaches of the dome, until they attained a platform near the peak of the structure. A kind of bed waited there, its contours shaped and molded from the same metallic stone. It reminded Owen of an Animus, and upon it lay a woman, with the same copper complexion as the archetypes they had encountered. A sheet covered her body from the shoulders down, and she appeared to be sleeping.

I AM KNOWN BY MANY NAMES, the stranger said. **BUT YOU MAY CALL ME MINERVA.**

"Like the goddess?" Grace asked.

MY PEOPLE ARE THE SOURCE OF YOUR MYTHS, AND I HAVE HAD MANY NAMES. The stranger spread her open hands to either side. **ATHENA. SULIS. VÖR. SARASWATI. WE WHO CAME BEFORE REIGNED OVER HUMANITY FOR THOUSANDS OF YEARS.**

The voice of the stranger, Minerva, entered Owen's mind with such power it blurred his vision, and the figure of her wavered, and grew large, and burned with light.

TO THAT END, WEAPONS AND DEVICES WERE FASHIONED. THE TRIDENT WAS MADE TO RULE WITH PERFECT

AUTHORITY. She waved her arm, and overhead the dome darkened. Then images filled it, and chased one another across its surface. Scenes of battles, and fields strewn with thousands and thousands of dead bodies. **MY PEOPLE. WE FOUGHT OURSELVES. WE FOUGHT YOU, OUR CREATIONS. WE DESTROYED OURSELVES, BECAUSE WE MADE A MISTAKE.**

She walked over to the contoured bed, and she touched a part of it that looked no different from the rest. But at her touch, pulses of light began to travel the golden veins within the substance of the platform, illuminating it, and this light flowed into the sleeping woman. Minerva then looked back at Owen and the others, and he waited, saying nothing.

Owen wondered if they were supposed to do something, or say something. He looked at Grace and Natalya, who both appeared equally confused.

YOU DO NOT ASK ME WHAT MISTAKE, Minerva finally said, sounding weary, and Owen got the feeling that they had just failed a test they didn't know they were taking. **MY PEOPLE BUILT A CIVILIZATION OF UNPARALLELED STRENGTH AND BEAUTY. WE BENT THE CHAOS OF NATURE TO OUR WILL. WE UNLOCKED THE CODE OF LIFE ITSELF, AND BECAME ITS MASTERS. WE DID ALL THAT AND MORE, AND YET WE, THE ISU, DESTROYED OURSELVES, AND YOU DO NOT THINK TO ASK ME HOW? ARE YOU SO SURE THAT HUMANITY CANNOT ALSO FALL?**

"How?" Natalya asked. "How did you destroy yourselves?"

Minerva now paced about the platform, shaking her head, periodically casting glares at them that seemed almost disappointed. **PERHAPS I HAVE FAILED. PERHAPS I HAVE MADE A SECOND MISTAKE.**

"Please," Grace said. "We've come a long way."

I KNOW YOU HAVE. Minerva stopped pacing. **I LAID THE PATH MYSELF. AFTER THE CATACLYSM OF THE FIRST DISASTER, AN EJECTION FROM THE SUN LEFT OUR CIVILIZATION IN RUINS. AS I SPEAK TO YOU NOW, FROM THE PAST, MY PEOPLE ARE ALMOST EXTINCT, AND I AM SHORTLY TO JOIN THEM. HUMANITY WILL SURVIVE US, AND WHEN WE ARE GONE, I FEAR YOU WILL BE LEFT WITH OUR LEGACY. OUR WEAPONS.**

"The Pieces of Eden," Owen said.

THAT IS WHAT HUMANS CALL THEM. Minerva stepped toward them. **IF I COULD DESTROY THE TRIDENT, I WOULD, BUT IT HAS DISAPPEARED. I KNOW IT WILL NOT STAY HIDDEN FOREVER, AND WHEN IT IS FOUND, HUMANITY WILL SUFFER. THAT IS WHY I HAVE BROUGHT YOU HERE.**

She returned to the contoured bed and stood beside it. Then she gestured with an open palm toward the woman lying upon it.

I FASHIONED THE WHOLE OF THIS COLLECTIVE MEMORY IN MY FORGES, AND I INSTALLED IT DEEP IN THE MINDS AND CELLS OF A FEW HUMAN

BEINGS. I READ THE BRANCHES AND POSSIBILITIES OF TIME, AND I PREDICTED AND INTENDED THAT THEIR ANCESTORS AND THE TRIDENT WOULD BE DRAWN TOGETHER, DOWN THROUGH THE CENTURIES, AND I FORESAW THE DAY THAT HUMANITY WOULD NEED MY HELP. AND HERE YOU ARE.

"But what does this mean?" Owen asked, still bewildered by everything Minerva had said. "How do we stop the Trident?"

IN COMING HERE, YOUR MIND HAS RECEIVED A SHIELD SO THAT YOU CAN DO WHAT I COULD NOT AND DESTROY THE TRIDENT.

"But how?" Natalya asked. "How does this collective memory help?"

THE WAY OF THE PATH IS THROUGH FEAR, DEVOTION, AND FAITH.

Owen thought about the Serpent, the Dog, and the third part, which had to be the cliff they had climbed. "But what does that mean?" he asked. "How is that supposed to help?"

YOU ARE ONLY HUMAN, AND WOULD NOT UNDERSTAND. BUT THIS MEMORY HAS UNLOCKED YOUR POTENTIAL, AND WHEN THE TIME COMES, YOU WILL HAVE WHAT YOU NEED.

Owen didn't feel any different, and he didn't know how this simulation could have possibly changed anything for him.

"You never did tell us how you destroyed yourselves," Grace said.

WE FORGOT, she said.

"Forgot what?" Owen asked.

WE FORGOT THAT WE WERE A PART OF THE UNIVERSE, RATHER THAN APART FROM IT. WE FORGOT THAT WE STOOD NEITHER AT THE CENTER OF CREATION, NOR OUTSIDE IT. WE FORGOT THAT DANGER AND FEAR ARE NOT THE SAME THING, AND WHILE WE FOUGHT AGAINST OUR FEARS, WE FAILED TO SEE THE TRUE DANGER. WE FORGOT ALL OF THIS UNTIL THE UNIVERSE PUNISHED US WITH OUR OWN SUN, REMINDING US OF OUR PLACE.

Minerva waved her hand in a wide arc over her head, and the dome opened like the widening pupil of an eye, revealing the night sky. **DO NOT REPEAT OUR MISTAKE. DO NOT FORGET.**

"We won't," Owen said.

Minerva nodded. **YOU HAVE REACHED THE END OF THE PATH I LAID FOR YOU. REMEMBER EVERY STEP YOU TOOK.** She waved her hand once more, and then she vanished.

The platform fell away from them, along with the rest of the structure and the dome around it, splintering and fragmenting into the pit at the heart of the mountain. Owen remained suspended in the night sky next to Grace and Natalya, surrounded by stars and facing a commanding moon. But those lights slowly faded and died, until he hung in total darkness, unable to even see his friends nearby.

Something tugged on his head. He flinched and reached up

to fight it off, but he felt human hands, and the Animus helmet, and then the helmet lifted away.

He stared, confused, and then squinted and blinked. He was back in the Aerie lab. Monroe stood in front of him, and then clapped him on the shoulder. Grace and Natalya hung in their Animus rings next to him.

"What happened?" Owen asked. "Did we desynchronize?" It didn't feel as though they had. It was the smoothest exit from a simulation he had ever experienced.

"No," Monroe said. "You didn't desynchronize. The memory just . . . let you go."

He helped the three of them disconnect from their harnesses, and then step out of their rings. Owen rubbed his head and his eyes, and went back through his memories to make sure the simulation was all there, and not fading like the dream it almost seemed to be. But the memories stayed, and in some ways, that made them even harder to understand. The earth apparently had an entire history that no one knew about. An ancient, mythical race had gone extinct. If anyone but Monroe had sent them into that simulation, Owen would have suspected the whole thing was fake.

But it was real.

"Everyone okay?" Monroe asked. "No adverse effects?"

Owen shook his head.

"I feel fine," Grace said.

"Me too," Natalya said.

"Good." Monroe sighed. "In that case, you can tell me exactly what you saw in there. Let's have Natalya start, and then you two can fill in any details she misses."

So they all took seats, and Natalya walked Monroe through

the entire simulation, beginning with the Forest and the Serpent, and ending with Minerva, and the shield she claimed to have given them. Owen filled in what had happened with the Dog while the other two had gone ahead, and Grace spoke more about their experience climbing the mountainside. Monroe said very little, only stopping them to ask brief questions. When they'd finished, he sat there with his arms folded across his belly, covering his mouth with one of his hands, apparently thinking through everything they'd told him.

"This is extraordinary," he finally said. "You three have just answered some of the biggest scientific questions that I have ever asked. And to top it off, you've had indirect contact with a Precursor."

"A Precursor?" Grace asked.

"The Isu. A member of the First Civ. Those Who Came Before. We have several names for them." He shook his head. "But that doesn't mean we can comprehend them. Think about what it would take to create a genetic time capsule meant to open at a specific time tens of thousands of years later."

"But Minerva didn't open it; you did," Grace said.

"It seems that way . . ." Monroe said, but left off the rest.

"Is what Minerva said true?" Natalya asked.

Monroe uncrossed his arms and leaned toward her. "Which part?"

"All of it," she said.

Monroe nodded. "More or less. It all happened tens of thousands of years ago, so we don't know exactly what happened. What we do know is that we have the Pieces of Eden. We have found some Precursor temples. Others before you have had contact with the Isu in different ways, including Minerva. Their civilization did exist, and it was incredibly advanced. We believe they were destroyed by a coronal mass ejection known as the Toba Catastrophe. So, yes, what Minerva told you is basically true." He turned to Grace. "There are even some who want to bring the Isu back."

"The Instruments of the First Will?" Grace asked.

Monroe nodded.

"Who're they?" Owen asked.

Monroe gestured to Grace in a way that gave her the floor, and she pulled a folded-up piece of paper out of her pocket.

"I found this in that book of Norse mythology," she said. "Isaiah wrote it."

"What does it say?" Natalya asked.

"It says he doesn't want to rule the world." Grace held up the paper. "He wants to destroy it."

"Wait, what?" Owen had assumed Isaiah wanted to be another Alexander the Great. "Why?"

"He thinks the earth needs to die to be reborn," Grace said. "It's a cycle. He says we've been preventing this cycle from happening, and there should have already been another great catastrophe. But there wasn't, because the Assassins and the Templars stopped it. So now Isaiah wants to make it happen another way."

Owen knew that could easily be accomplished with the Trident. Not only could Isaiah use it to create an army, but he could turn other countries against one another, with their nuclear weapons and bombs.

"So who are the Instruments of the First Will?" Grace asked.

"I've only heard rumors," Monroe said. "But within the Templar Order there is supposedly a secret faction trying to restore another Precursor named Juno to power. From Isaiah's writings, it sounds like he was aware of them. Maybe even a part of them for a time. But if he was, he isn't any longer. He's decided that *he* wants the power, not Juno." He rose from his chair. "I'm going to go check on the other two simulations and see how David and Javier are doing."

"What should we do?" Grace asked.

Monroe glanced around the lab. "You can hang out here, or you can go back to the common room and wait. Then I'll know where to find you."

"What about me?" Owen asked. Before he had agreed to go into the simulation of the collective unconscious, Monroe had promised to show him the real memories of his father's bank robbery.

"This isn't the time," Monroe said.

"You promised—"

"I promised I would help you, and I will. But I think you know there are more urgent matters we need to take care of first."

Owen's impatience turned to irritation. "But all we're doing right now is waiting around for Javier and David to find the dagger."

"Which might happen at any moment." Monroe strode toward the door. "Besides, I'd rather have your mind clear for what lies ahead."

"Why wouldn't my mind be clear?" Owen asked.

Monroe gripped the door handle and paused. "If you have to ask that question, I wonder if you're ready to get what you're asking for." With that, he exited the room, leaving the three of them alone.

CHAPTER TWENTY-ONE

Thorvald stood next to the Lawspeaker in the king's tent. Eric sat in a dark wooden saddle chair, with Astrid at his side, but they were otherwise alone. Javier still hadn't grown accustomed to the presence of the huge house-bear, and she startled him whenever his ancestor encountered her. A brazier offered orange light and white smoke, which gathered in the peak of the tent before escaping.

"The cattle killed a third of the Jomsvikings," Thorvald said. "Those that survived held their ground behind their shield walls. The battle ceased with the setting of the sun."

"Styrbjörn?" the king asked.

"He lives." Thorvald did not see a need to tell the king what Styrbjörn had done to stop the cattle. Not yet. Thorvald could hardly believe it himself, and for the first time since this engagement had begun, he wondered if their enemy could win. "His army pulled back to the Mirkwood."

Eric nodded. "Your strategies have been very effective. I commend you both, and I wish to reward you." He produced two small leather pouches from within his tunic and handed them to Thorvald, who tucked them away.

The Lawspeaker bowed his head. "We serve our people that all might live free."

"And how would you serve them now?" the king asked slowly, his question weighed down by the words he didn't say, but fully intended. "Has the time come?"

"Yes," Thorvald said. "As it came for your brother."

"I've told you." Eric turned and looked at Astrid. "I don't want to know anything about that."

Javier felt Thorvald's struggle to restrain his anger. The king wanted the bladework of the Brotherhood on his behalf, yet protected his own sense of honor by refusing to speak openly about it, as though he could convince himself it had nothing to do with him. But everyone in that tent except the house-bear knew what he meant and what he asked of them.

Even so, the Lawspeaker did not appear angered by the king's weakness. "Thorvald will go tonight, and tomorrow we shall see what the dawn brings."

"Do not wait until dawn to inform me," Eric said. "Wake me if you must."

"As you wish," the Lawspeaker said.

Eric nodded, and then Thorvald and the Lawspeaker left the king's tent.

Outside, they walked through the encampment surrounded by the sounds of steel against grindstone, and the ringing of blacksmiths' hammers. They heard laughter, and smelled meat cooking over fires, and the mood about the camp felt high and confident. Their numbers were greater than the Jomsvikings, and Eric's war band would join the battle the next day. Victory seemed inevitable.

"Take nothing for granted," the Lawspeaker said, seeing right into Thorvald's mind with his blind eyes. "Whatever these warriors believe, any battle can turn with the beat of a raven's wing. Think of the dagger you saw. If it is what you fear, we may have already lost this battle, regardless of our cunning or our strength."

"I understand," Thorvald said.

"The time has come to bring Styrbjörn the judgment of the Norns. He must not ever again take up his sword or his axe."

"He won't."

Torgny nodded. "If you find this dagger, bring it to me."

Thorvald grasped his mentor's hand. "I will."

With that, he left the Lawspeaker in the war camp and made his way southward over the Fyrisfield. The moon had not yet risen, which meant he could avoid being seen, but raced through darkness. He had to rely on his Odin-sight, sensing more than could be had by his ears and eyes alone, following the contours of the land and avoiding its pitfalls and marshes.

As he came upon a clutch of low boulders and leapt over them, his Odin-sight caught a glimmer near the ground, and he stopped to investigate it. A thick coat of moss covered part of the rock there, and as he peeled it away, he found a small piece of hack-gold encrusted with dirt. Thorvald stared at it for a few moments, puzzled, but then he remembered the story of Hrólf, who scattered his gold across the Fyrisfield to distract his enemies while he escaped. It seemed there might be truth to the legend, after all, and it gave Thorvald an idea. One final cunning strategy, perhaps the simplest of them all.

He pulled out the pouches the king had given them, and inside he found a small trove of silver Arab dirhams. Hrólf would not have scattered such coins as these all those generations ago, but Thorvald did not believe that detail would matter to the Jomsvikings. He arranged the coins over one of the boulders, and then he pulled out another vial of the same poison he had given Östen. Very carefully, he laced each piece of silver with death, and after the poison had dried, he scattered the coins as he traveled the rest of the way over the Fyrisfield.

When he reached the Mirkwood, he climbed up into the branches, and once again ran freely from tree to tree, passing unseen over the sentries, until he reached the heart of the camp. The cattle had done tremendous harm to the Jomsvikings. Many lay broken and dying, and though their brothers tended them, they would not live through the night. And yet the camp did not seem so different in spirit than Eric's. After all of their casualties, the courage and will of the Jomsvikings had not yet broken, and Thorvald admired them for it.

He eventually found Styrbjörn in council with a Jomsviking captain, while a shield-maiden dressed a wound in his thigh. The sight of the woman surprised Thorvald, because Jomsvikings allowed only men in their ranks.

"They will sing songs about your feats this day," the captain said, "and tomorrow, the Jomsvikings will fight and die by your side, to the last man if the gods will it. This is the oath we will take."

It seemed the courage and strength that Styrbjörn had shown now bound the Jomsvikings to him, with the loyalty that their code and their honor demanded. They truly would fight to the last man, which meant that Eric's army would be left with no choice but to destroy them all.

Thorvald watched as Styrbjörn dismissed the captain, and after some moments of silence, fell into conversation with the shield-maiden. The two of them spoke in low voices on the subject of marriage, surprising Thorvald once again. When they moved away from the encampment into the forest to make their vows, he followed them through the trees, observing from a distance.

Eventually, they came upon a large, sundered stone, and Styrbjörn built a shrine before it, and offered up a gold ring from his arm to Frey. As he and the shield-maiden exchanged their vows and their swords, Thorvald considered striking them both down. It would be a simple enough task, distracted as they were by each other. But the Tenets that Torgny had taught him held him back.

He did not know this shield-maiden. She could be no Jomsviking. Perhaps a Dane? She might even be an innocent, and if she was, the Creed of the Brotherhood forbade Thorvald from shedding her blood. Before he struck, he had to know who he would be killing.

"Now the blood sacrifice," Styrbjörn said below. "I will find us an animal—"

"No," the shield-maiden said. "We already have an offering that will please the gods."

Thorvald wondered what she meant, but then Styrbjörn pulled out his strange dagger and placed it on the shrine. In dedicating the offering to Thor, Styrbjörn called the weapon a relic of the Christ, which meant the dagger might be what Thorvald feared it was. But if that was true, why would Styrbjörn offer it up on the eve before a battle? Why would he give away the very thing that could secure his victory?

After Styrbjörn had finished at the shrine, he placed the dagger inside the crack in the stone, piled up a few more rocks, and then he and the shield-maiden left in the direction of their camp.

Thorvald waited a few moments to be certain they had gone, and then he descended from the trees to the boulder and the shrine. The golden arm ring held no interest for him, and he pushed it aside along with the smaller stones until he'd uncovered the large crack, and the hidden dagger within.

Javier felt a thrill. "I have it," he said to Griffin.

Good. Very good. Stay with Thorvald. Let's see where it goes from here. "Of course."

This is a whole branch of the Brotherhood I didn't know about, Griffin said. *It's incredible. With your heritage, your blood, I know you have it in you to become a truly great Assassin.*

Javier didn't know what to do with that. He liked hearing it, but he also fought against it within his mind as he dove back into the memory.

The dagger was not an ordinary weapon. Thorvald could see that plainly. But that didn't mean it was an ancient weapon of the gods. He had never held an Aesir blade before, so he couldn't say for certain whether this was divine or not. But he believed it was, which meant that he needed to get it safely into the hands of the Lawspeaker.

Styrbjörn's death would have to wait.

Thorvald ascended to the treetops once more, and he made his way back through the Mirkwood, and then over the Fyrisfield, where his silver glinted weakly in the starlight. The Lawspeaker had left his hovel near the temple and taken a tent within Eric's encampment, and as Thorvald approached it, he found Torgny sitting outside near the fire with his chin buried in his chest, snoring.

"Mentor," he said, touching the Lawspeaker on the shoulder.

Torgny looked up, inhaling deeply through his nose. "You have already returned? How long have I been in contemplation?"

"Only you would know the answer to that." He touched the dagger's pommel and grip against the Lawspeaker's hands. "I believe it is what I thought."

Torgny accepted the blade, and though he could not see, he turned it over and over in his hands, and Thorvald worried he would cut himself, but he didn't.

"I believe you are right," the Lawspeaker said.

"Can you tell what power it possesses?" Thorvald asks.

"No. What of Styrbjörn?"

"He lives," Thorvald said. "He married a shield-maiden in secret as I watched. To kill him would have required killing her, and I don't know her."

"You were wise to stay your blade," the Lawspeaker said. "Better that our enemies go unharmed than we risk doing harm to our Creed."

"Eric will not be pleased."

"But we have this." Torgny held up the dagger. "I think it will please the king."

"You're going to give it to him?"

"Not in the way you think. Let us go to him."

The Lawspeaker rose from the fire, and then Thorvald led him through the camp, which had grown much quieter as the warriors there labored at sleep, until they reached Eric's tent. Two guards posted at the door allowed them entrance, but immediately inside they faced a huffing, snorting Astrid.

"Steady," Thorvald said to the mass of brown fur shambling toward him. "You know us."

"Eric," Torgny said loudly and forcefully, and the king stirred with a snort.

"What is it?"

"Your house-bear," the Lawspeaker said.

"What? Oh." He first sat up, and then climbed to his feet, his furs and blankets falling away. "Astrid, to me," he said, tugging on her chain.

The bear stopped her approach, but not her noisemaking, and turned to lumber over to the king, where she sat herself down and leaned against him.

"Is it done?" the king asked.

"No," the Lawspeaker said.

"No?"

"We have something better." He extended the blade toward the king, and Eric took it, frowning.

"What is this?"

"That is a Christ relic," Torgny said. "Styrbjörn took it from Harald Bluetooth, who received it from the great Christian Father in Rome."

Now Eric's frown turned to a sneer of disgust. "And why would I want this?"

The Lawspeaker turned to Thorvald. "Tell him what you saw."

It became clear then that Torgny intended to wield the dagger as a symbol, so Thorvald said, "Styrbjörn thought he could obtain the favor of Thor by offering that relic to the sky god. But Styrbjörn was careless, and I have taken it from the shrine. If you were to offer this Christ relic to Odin, and dedicate tomorrow's battle to him—"

"I thought I was not to fight Styrbjörn," Eric said.

"That is still true," the Lawspeaker said. "You are not to

fight him. But your army will, and with Odin's favor, their victory will be assured."

"The Jomsvikings have now sworn to Styrbjörn," Thorvald said. "It will go better for your rule if Styrbjörn is defeated on the battlefield, in the open, rather than in the shadows. Let it be known among your army that you have Odin's favor."

"But will Thor not be angry?" the king asked.

"The offering was poorly done," Thorvald said. "Thor's displeasure will fall on Styrbjörn."

"And if Styrbjörn challenges me?" Eric said.

"He must not be given that chance," the Lawspeaker said. "You must stay away from the battle."

"No." Eric shook his head, his cheeks glowing red. "I am no raven starver. I will not cower in my tent. I will fight with my people, even if it means my death."

"That speaks well of your honor," Torgny said. "No one doubts your courage. But the people of this land need you to rule for many years hence."

And Thorvald knew that the Brotherhood had spent too many years establishing Eric's rule for him to die the next day on the battlefield. And die, he would. Thorvald had seen Styrbjörn fight. The king would be no match for his nephew's size, strength, and youth. There were few men who would be. But Thorvald thought of one.

"The people of Svealand need me to lead them," the king said. "On this, I swear your counsel will not sway me."

Thorvald could see that was true. "Then lead them," he said, "but choose a champion. One who will fight Styrbjörn for you if it comes down to single combat. There is no dishonor in that."

"Perhaps no dishonor," Eric said. "But neither is there honor."

"It must be this way," the Lawspeaker said.

"There is a giant in your army," Thorvald said. "His name is Östen—"

"By tradition, my marshal is my champion."

Javier remembered the way the marshal had tried to prevent the Assassins from entering the king's war council, and so did Thorvald, who shook his head. "I know him, and he will surely fall. There is only one man among all the Svear I would send against Styrbjörn."

Eric laid a hand on Astrid's head and scratched her fur as he studied the dagger. "A strange blade for a relic," he said. "I will never understand these Christians. They offend me."

"They offend the gods," the Lawspeaker said.

"Then let us appease them," the king said. "Let us offer this thing to Odin."

So they left his tent, and the three of them walked through the encampment at the midnight hour, with Astrid tethered by her chain to the king. Then they left the camp and traveled to the temple at Uppsala, where they entered that hall by the light of a single torch. Astrid came into the temple with them, and she sniffed the air, peering into the darkness outside the torch's reach, where gods and heroes stood as sentinels, in silence.

Torgny knew this place without torches, and without sight. He brought them before the wooden pillar of Odin, which had been carved into the trunk of an ancient ash tree and raised at one end of the hall. The Allfather stared out with his one eye, armed with his spear, Gungnir, which he would wield in battle against the Fenris wolf at Ragnarök.

By torchlight, the Lawspeaker took the king through the blót ritual. They called on Odin to listen to their plea, and they asked for his favor in battle, but instead of offering up the life and blood of a horse, or a pig, they gave the dagger, and in doing so they pledged their worship to the Aesir over any other false god. The king took oaths, and swore his life to Odin, vowing to enter Valhalla ten years from that day. He dedicated the next day's battle and all its dead to the Allfather. The mute figure of Odin towered over them in the quiet, darkened hall, half in shadow, and gave no sign that they had been heard.

At the end of the ritual, Torgny guided the king from the temple without speaking, and behind them, Thorvald secretly recovered the dagger. After the three of them had returned to the king's tent, Eric said to Thorvald, "Bring Östen to me. I would meet this champion." Then he and Astrid went inside.

"I'll wait here with Eric," Torgny said, moving toward the tent's entrance.

Thorvald left the Lawspeaker and went in search of his company. The men he had chosen to thwart and harry the Jomsvikings had remained together, even upon rejoining the rest of the army. He found their fire a short time later and easily spotted Östen's sleeping bulk among them. Thorvald approached him loudly enough to wake him, and then called his name.

Östen rolled toward Thorvald, his eyes only half open. "What is it, skald?"

"Come with me," Thorvald said. "You are needed by the king."

Östen's eyes opened the rest of the way and he rushed to his feet, again surprising Thorvald with his speed, given his size. "The king asked for me?"

"Yes," Thorvald said. "And I can think of no one better. Bring your weapons and your shield."

They returned to Eric's tent, and Thorvald led Östen inside. The Lawspeaker waited there with the king and his house-bear, and Östen bowed his head upon entering.

"You have need of me, my king?" he asked.

"Yes," Eric said. "Though it is not by my choice. I've summoned you according to the counsel of others." He turned to Torgny. "Skald?" he said, suggesting that the Lawspeaker should explain, and then he sat himself in his saddle chair.

Torgny smiled. "Though I cannot see you, Östen, I can tell that you are a man of uncommon honor."

Östen bowed his head again. "I thank you for that."

"And a man of renown," Torgny added.

"Perhaps when I was younger," Östen said.

Thorvald stepped toward him. "Tomorrow we battle Styrbjörn to the end. It is likely that he will seek out his uncle, the king, on the battlefield."

"To challenge him," Östen said.

"Indeed." Torgny placed his hands together behind his back. "As another man of uncommon honor, the king would of course accept such a challenge—"

"He should not," Östen said.

The king leaned forward in his chair. "And why is that?"

It must have seemed a dangerous question, for Östen bowed his head low, and dropped his shoulders, but still he seemed to brush the roof of the tent with his hair. "You would die, my king," he said. "Forgive me for saying it, but I have seen Styrbjörn fight. You would not leave the battlefield, and Svealand would be lost."

Eric narrowed his eyes, and then leaned back in his chair. As Thorvald watched and listened to the exchange, he felt grateful that Östen had confirmed all the reasons for choosing him.

"And you?" Torgny asked. "Would you fight Styrbjörn?"

Östen turned toward him, and for the first time since Thorvald had met the giant, he saw fear at the tightened edges of his eyes. Östen didn't answer the question at first. Instead, he looked down at the skein still tied around his wrist. Thorvald didn't know what that thread might mean, but it clearly held significance.

"I would fight him," Östen said, firmly, but quietly.

"If you stood beside your king in battle," the Lawspeaker said, "and Styrbjörn rushed toward him, what would you do?"

"I would engage Styrbjörn in bladework," Östen said, "before he could reach the king to challenge him."

Torgny nodded. "It is as I said. A man of uncommon honor."

Thorvald clapped Östen on the back, glad to have judged him rightly. "From this moment forward, you will be the king's spear and shield. You will remain at his side until this storm has passed. Do you accept this honor?"

Östen took a deep, rumbling breath, sounding much like Astrid. "I accept."

"Odin will be with you," Torgny said. "So let the morning come."

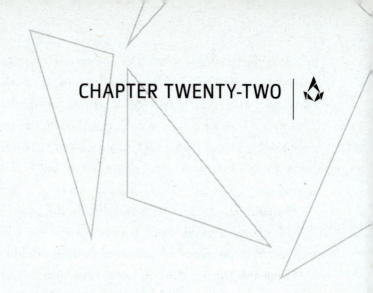

CHAPTER TWENTY-TWO

A low fog lay in wisps over the Fyrisfield in the hours before dawn, gathering more thickly in the folds and dips, and covering the grass with dew. Östen followed the king, who led his house-bear by her chain until he reached a stone enclosure. Someone had planted a heavy stake in the middle of it, and the king fixed Astrid's chain to that stake. As they left the house-bear there, and closed the gate behind them, Östen grew curious enough to ask a question, one that David had wondered about also.

"Would she fight in battle?"

"Astrid?" The king looked back over his shoulder, toward the enclosure. "Yes, if I commanded it, she would."

"But you don't want her to?"

"I captured her as a cub," the king said. "I raised her up, and

I trained her. I've had her for ten years now. So, no, I would not command her to fight. Every warrior on the battlefield would want to kill her, and she means too much to me to let that happen."

"She seems to have grown accustomed to her chains."

"They are there for her sake. Without them, she might wander and kill livestock, or a hunter might take her."

Östen had killed bears. In the summer, their fat tasted of the berries they foraged. They gave fierce competition to the wolves, and a strong pack could sometimes bring a bear down. But it was hard for Östen to decide which animal lived a better life. Astrid safe in her chains, or the wild bear risking death.

"When we left my tent this morning," the king said, "did you notice that large raven in the yew tree?"

"I didn't."

"Then it was a sign for my eyes alone." He smiled as they walked back through the encampment, which had fully awoken to arm itself for battle. "Odin is watching over us. My offering was accepted. The Lawspeaker was right."

"He is very wise," Östen said. "And Thorvald is very cunning."

"Both offer me valuable counsel," the king said.

At his tent, they gathered their weapons and shields. In addition to his ring mail, the king donned the golden-scale armor of a defeated Grikklander, and then they were joined outside by the elite housecarls and the captains of the king's war band. Some of those seasoned warriors looked at Östen with suspicion, especially the king's marshal, who cast him glances sidelong, but none dared voice their misgivings.

The king gave his captains their orders. The strategy was simple, because the king knew exactly what Styrbjörn would do.

The Svear would offer the Jomsvikings a solid front to attack, and Styrbjörn, ever defiant, would attempt to break their line with a wedge to reach the king. But then the center of Eric's front would feint backward, to draw the Jomsvikings farther in, while at the same time, the Svear clans at the flanks would extend and entirely surround the enemy. Now that the size of Styrbjörn's army had been reduced, the Svear could trap and crush them.

"Also spread word of this," the king said. "Last night I made an offering to Odin, and this morning I have been given a sign. The Allfather is with us, and victory will be ours."

The captains left to take those words and the king's command to the clans they would lead into battle. Östen and the king found a vantage to watch the sun rise over the plain, first a spark, then an ember, then a flame. Its warmth thawed the rime and banished the mist.

Not long after that, Östen glimpsed the Jomsvikings coming over the horizon, and almost in that same moment, the Svear horns sounded. He and the king left their vantage and raced from the camp out onto the open field, joined by the marshal and a company of one hundred housecarls.

The clans massed their ranks along the Fyrisfield, thorny with spears and flapping banners, roaring their battle cries and banging on their shields, drowning out whatever howling the Jomsvikings already sent their way. The king raised his own spear and gave the order to march.

Horns blared down the line, and the front advanced. Östen kept pace with the king at his right hand, while the marshal kept to Eric's left, and the housecarls and standard-bearers marched before and after them, their pace disciplined and unwavering.

The smell of turf in the air, and the dew of the Fyrisfield that wet Östen's boots, reminded him of his fields back home, and he wished he could wash his face in the cold spring as he did most mornings. He looked down at the thread tied around his wrist, and then he kissed it.

Before long, the Jomsvikings broke over a hill ahead of them, like a wave crashing over the bow of a ship, and on they came.

The king gave his next command, and the horns sounded. The housecarls prepared to fall back while fighting, and Östen readied his axe and shield.

The Jomsvikings launched their charge, boots all a-thunder, as though they truly had the favor of the sky god. Östen could see fury in their eyes and their teeth as he searched their line, finding Styrbjörn near the front, at the point of the wedge. The sight of him, and the memory of Alferth, fanned the embers of his own anger into flames.

The enemy stormed closer, devouring the ground before them until very little distance remained. At the final moment, the king then gave the third command, and the horns sounded.

The housecarls formed a shield wall, and when the Jomsviking wedge rammed into it, the Svear gave ground like a willow branch, bending without breaking. The maneuver gave no signal of retreat, but incited the Jomsvikings to press harder. Swords and axes fell hard on shields, and spears stabbed into the gaps.

Östen stayed at the king's side, behind the line, watching Styrbjörn, who tore through all in his path as housecarl after housecarl stepped forward to bar him.

"Your men die for you," the marshal said.

"I know it," the king said, his voice strained.

"You could end this with single combat," the marshal said. "Surely you could defeat your nephew."

Östen looked hard at the man, who had voiced no objections to the strategy until now, waiting until this moment of battle rage to press the king. There seemed to be something sinister in that.

"The king has already decided what he will do," Östen said.

The marshal smiled. "I would never presume to speak for the king."

"Peace, *stallari*," the king said. "Östen is right, though I loathe it. He is here at my call, to fight for me when the time comes."

The marshal lost his smile then, and he glowered at Östen with open hatred. "So you are now the king's champion?"

"I am," Östen said.

In that moment, the Jomsvikings managed a sudden, renewed surge, and the housecarl shield wall nearly broke, sending warriors backward into Östen and the king. Östen managed to keep his footing, and after a quick glance found Styrbjörn a safe distance away. But the marshal had moved, and as Östen turned to look for him, he found him at his side and glimpsed the flicker of a blade thrusting toward his ribs.

He spun to block it, knowing he couldn't.

But the blade never reached him. It fell to the ground from the marshal's limp hand, and Östen saw shock on the marshal's face.

The man stood with an arched back, staring just over Östen's head, eyes wide and mouth open. Thorvald stepped out from behind him as the marshal's whole body collapsed, and Östen noticed a strange and bloody blade on the skald's wrist.

Thorvald gave him a nod, and Östen nodded back. From a few yards away, the king looked down at the body of his former marshal as though it were a pile of dung, and then returned his attention to the battle.

The feint continued for several hundred yards, until Östen heard the distant horns of the flank clans signaling that they had executed the pincer maneuver and begun their rear assault.

The king blew on his own horn, and the housecarls dug in, their shield wall first holding fast against the press of the Jomsviking line, then pushing back against it, driving the Jomsvikings before them.

The faces of the enemy showed surprise, and anger, and finally realization as their own horns bellowed from behind.

Östen stepped over the wounded and dying, both Svear and Jomsviking, and as warriors fell, others leapt into their place. He had to restrain his own urge to join the fray, and it appeared the king did as well, judging by the way he held his spear. Thorvald and his wrist-blade had vanished.

"Where is the skald?" he asked the king.

"He goes where he will," Eric said.

A housecarl next to Östen cried out and looked down, where a wounded Jomsviking on the ground had stabbed his calf through with a long knife. Before Östen could act, the king leapt past him and thrust his spear into the enemy's throat. The wounded housecarl pulled the knife from his leg, wincing, and stabbed the dead Jomsviking with it.

"Can you still fight?" Östen asked him.

He nodded and pulled off one of his belts, which he used to bind his leg tightly to stanch the bleeding. After that, the rear housecarls finished off any wounded Jomsviking yet living.

For hours they clashed. The Jomsvikings refused to die eas-ily, but the housecarls pressed inward, their bladework slow, steady, and hard-won. The invaders' horns continued to sound from the rear, calling for reinforcements, but there were none to be had. Östen maintained his watch on Styrbjörn, who fought ferociously and raged, unable to stop this tide from turning.

"The day is ours," Eric said.

"Not yet, my king," Östen said.

The Jomsvikings had sworn to fight to the last man, and it seemed they would fulfill that oath, but at what price? How many Svear lay dying or dead? How many families waited at home for someone who would never return?

"Eric!" Styrbjörn shouted, loud enough to be heard over all the other sounds of war.

Östen readied himself and waited.

Styrbjörn threw his shield aside and grabbed the top of the housecarl's shield in front of him, but rather than pushing against him, he yanked on it, pulling the man off-balance, and threw him to the ground. Then he stepped on the man's back and used it to leap into the air, right over the heads of the housecarl line.

He landed swinging his axe, and the Svear fell away from him in shock. "Eric!" he shouted again. "I challenge y—"

"I challenge you, Styrbjörn!" Östen stepped in front of the king. "Single combat!"

As the battle continued behind him, Styrbjörn pointed his axe toward Östen. "My quarrel is with my uncle! Who are you?"

"I am the friend of a man you killed, and I seek retribution!"

Styrbjörn strode toward him, and Östen could see a wound in his thigh bleeding through his leather and ring mail. "You would fight me?"

Östen readied his own weapon. "Yes."

"Then let us not delay!" Styrbjörn rushed him, almost faster than Östen could raise his shield, and landed a blow that rattled the marrow in the bones of his arm.

Östen fell back, but was ready for the next attack, deflecting it deftly. He tried to counter, but Styrbjörn leapt aside easily and swung again, almost striking Östen's head. Never had he fought a man so quick, or so strong. Having seen what Styrbjörn did to Alferth, Östen had expected a fearsome opponent, but had trusted in the gods that he would prevail. Now, facing this enemy, Östen believed he may have reached the end of his skein.

Styrbjörn struck again, and again, and the second blow shattered Östen's shield. He tossed the splintered wood and twisted metal aside, and now both men fought with axes alone.

"Is this what you want, Uncle?" Styrbjörn asked.

The king stood by with his spear, watching the duel.

Styrbjörn waved his arm toward the ongoing battle. "All these men fighting me in your place?" He laughed. "Where is your honor?"

"His honor is his own," Östen said. If this was to be the end of his skein, he would meet it fighting, without fear. "My honor claimed you first."

"So be it," Styrbjörn said. "But you die for nothing."

He swung his axe, and as Östen ducked the strike, Styrbjörn bashed his face with the side of his metal armguard. Östen staggered away, blood filling his mouth, but had no time to recover before Styrbjörn was on him again.

Östen used his axe to fight off three blows, as though he fought with a sword. After the third, he seized an opening and rammed Styrbjörn hard in the chest with his shoulder, sending the other man sprawling backward.

Östen didn't wait for his enemy to hit the ground before leaping after him, and his axe bit deep into Styrbjörn's arm, right in the elbow joint of his armor. Blood poured instantly from the wound at a pace that might soon be fatal, but Styrbjörn ignored it and attacked again.

After several repeated slashes that Östen managed to dodge and block, the tip of Styrbjörn's axe caught him in the side, opening a gash through armor and flesh. Östen struck Styrbjörn in the throat with his fist and fell back to check his wound, relieved to find the blade had cut through his skin but not all the way through his muscle.

Styrbjörn choked and took a shambling step toward Östen, wobbling on his feet. It seemed the loss of blood had begun to weaken him. He blinked and took another step, but then dropped to one knee, his head drooping.

"The silver," he said, shaking his head. Then he spat. "Coward."

Östen stepped toward him. "You name me coward? Now? After I have—"

"Not you." He looked at the king. "My uncle. He has poisoned me, just as he did my father."

Eric stepped forward. "I did not poison my brother, and I have not poisoned you."

Östen knew who had done it, even if he didn't know how, and he wondered how Thorvald had accomplished it.

"Eric the Coward." Styrbjörn laughed. "Whether you did it or you ordered it done, it is the same." He looked up at Östen. "Let's finish this."

"You cannot fight. I won't—"

"Finish this!" Styrbjörn shouted, and then grunted and growled his way to his feet, his arm and axe hanging loose at his side. He nodded toward the Jomsvikings still fighting for their lives. "I will die on my feet with them. Now finish this."

Östen did not know which would be more honorable. To let Styrbjörn leave the battlefield and suffer until his death by poison, or strike him down now in his weakness.

"Östen!" the king shouted. "Kill him!"

But even then, Östen hesitated. He couldn't kill a man this way, and within his memories, David felt himself in perfect agreement with his ancestor.

Styrbjörn took a step toward him. "I will decide this for you."

"Stop," Östen said.

But Styrbjörn took another step and very slowly hoisted his axe over his head. "If you do not finish this, I will finish you."

Östen took a step backward, but raised his axe. "I didn't want this."

"I know that," Styrbjörn said. "You have more honor than a king." He staggered forward another step. "I've lost too much blood anyway. If the poison didn't kill me, your blow would have. I would rather my death be yours. Not Eric's."

Östen looked Styrbjörn in the eyes and saw his pupils quivering, going in and out of focus. The former prince took another step, and came within striking distance of Östen. Then his axe moved, and Östen reluctantly raised his own with hands that wanted no part of this. That was when he noticed that the skein was gone from his wrist. That delicate, blood- and mud-soaked thread had finally broken away, lost somewhere in the chaos of the battle. In that moment, the only thing Östen wanted was to have it back. He would have traded a golden arm ring as thick as his thumb to have back that ordinary, filthy piece of string from Hilla's loom.

"Styrbjörn!" a woman shouted.

Östen turned as a shield-maiden charged at him, sword drawn. But before she could reach him, three housecarls set upon her. Her blade flashed, and her shield rang as she fought them, holding her ground, returning blow for blow with blinding speed and agility. But no warrior could last forever, and even now, several more housecarls closed in.

"Thyra," Styrbjörn whispered, and dropped once again to his knees. "No."

"Who is she?" Östen asked. "Tell me quickly."

"My queen," he said.

"She's your wife?"

"Yes."

Östen sprinted toward the melee. "Halt!" he shouted. "Halt!" But they ignored him.

He grabbed one of the housecarls from behind and hurled him away. When the other two turned toward him, the shield-maiden tried to seize the opportunity to kill one of them, but Östen blocked her with his axe.

"Halt, Thyra!" he bellowed.

At the sound of her name, she stopped, shoulders heaving.

Östen pointed. "Go to him. While you can."

She looked from Östen to Styrbjörn, and then she raced to her husband's side. Östen held out his hands to make certain the housecarls would stay back, and then went to stand near her. He couldn't hear what they said to each other over the sounds of the Jomsvikings' destruction, but he could tell the moment Styrbjörn died by the way Thyra bowed her head low, though Styrbjörn remained upright on his knees, hunched over, his lifeless body leaning against her.

In that moment, Eric raised his spear, and he strode toward what was left of the Jomsviking army.

"I sacrifice you!" he shouted. "The dead! The dying! And

the yet-to-die! I dedicate your blood to Odin! The Allfather, who granted me victory!" With that, he hurled his spear into the heart of the Jomsvikings.

Not one of them fled the Fyrisfield.

To a man, they stayed and died.

At the end of the battle, Eric bound Thyra, and summoned Östen to walk with them. They left the Fyrisfield, where the housecarls and captains sought out the living among the fallen of their clans, and they walked through the war camp. Then they left this behind also, and eventually reached the stone enclosure where Astrid waited on her chain. The house-bear rumbled and got to her feet at the sight of Eric, and Östen could see deep scratch marks in the dirt around the stake.

Thyra stared at Astrid with her jaw set and her chin high, but her hands shook.

Eric said nothing.

"Why have you brought this woman here, my king?" Östen asked.

"I have not yet fed Astrid," Eric said.

Thyra's lips parted, but she didn't gasp, and she didn't look away from the house-bear.

"My king," Östen said, "you cannot mean to do this."

"Why not? She is the wife of my traitorous nephew. He who would have murdered me for my crown and taken Svealand for himself. He who threatened to destroy this land if he could not rule it."

"That was Styrbjörn," Östen said. "Not her."

"But if I let her live, will she not seek to avenge him?"

"I will not," Thyra said. They were the first words she had spoken since the death of Styrbjörn. "I wish only to go home."

"To Jutland?" Eric asked. "You are a Dane?"

She nodded.

"You would return here with the Bluetooth," Eric said. "Or perhaps you would go to Jomsborg, and bring more Jomsvikings—"

"I will not," she said again.

"You are a shield-maiden!" Eric shouted. "You fight as well as three of my housecarls together. I cannot believe that you will leave me in peace—"

"You must not feed her to your house-bear, Eric," said the Lawspeaker, appearing suddenly beside them with Thorvald. Östen hadn't heard them or seen them approach. "There are some who will secretly mourn Styrbjörn among your own nobles. If you do this thing to Styrbjörn's wife, you will make bitter enemies of them."

"Then what am I to do?" the king asked.

The Lawspeaker regarded Östen with his milky eyes. "Give her as a thrall to your champion. The man who slew her husband."

That suggestion angered Östen, who had not slain Styrbjörn, and did not want his widow as a thrall, and it angered David, who still hated that his ancestor owned slaves.

"That would be seen as both fitting and just," Thorvald said.

Eric looked at Östen. "Even though you faltered at the end," he said, "you fought well." Then he turned back to Thorvald. "What of my marshal?"

Thorvald bowed his head. "Forgive me for not warning you, but I had no time. He was about to kill Östen."

Again, Östen bowed his head in gratitude toward the skald.

"Why?" Eric asked.

"So that Styrbjörn might kill you," the Lawspeaker said. "The marshal sought your downfall, and we believe he was not alone. In time, we will find the den of these vipers. Until then, do what you can to avoid turning anyone else against you."

Eric looked at Astrid for a few moments, and then he handed Thyra's tether to Östen, who accepted it without offering any thanks. The king entered the stone enclosure, where he separated his house-bear's chain from the stake, and then he led her outside, past the others, and set off in the direction of his hall.

"I will go with him," the Lawspeaker said. "He will need my counsel in the coming days."

The old man shuffled away, calling to Eric, who stopped and waited for him to catch up before he and Astrid lumbered on. Östen watched them go, the house-bear chained to a king, and the king chained to a man far wiser and more cunning by links he couldn't see.

Thorvald turned to Östen. "How bad is your side?"

Östen looked down. "It will need attention, but it didn't open my gut."

"Then you should leave at once. Get her out of here before there is more trouble." He gave Östen a handful of hack-silver, a small fortune. "Leave your things, and pay for what you need on the road."

"I do not want her," Östen said.

Thorvald took his arm and led him a short distance away. "Then do not keep her," he whispered. "Only get her to safety first." He then pulled out a strange dagger, and even though Östen didn't recognize it, David did. "I want you to take this blade and hide it well," Thorvald said. "Far from here."

"Why?" Östen asked.

"It may not look it, but this dagger is dangerous," Thorvald said. "It must never be used, not even by me. For that reason, it cannot stay in Uppsala, and you are perhaps the only man in Svealand with whom I would trust it. Do not show it to that Dane woman."

Östen accepted the dagger, and tucked it away out of sight within his tunic.

"You are an uncommon man," Thorvald said loudly. "I doubt our paths shall cross again, but I am honored to have known you."

"The same to you, skald," Östen said. "You will write a song about today?"

"Of course," Thorvald said. "Too many heard Styrbjörn call him 'Eric the Coward.' That cannot stand. He will be Eric the Victorious, because that is what Svealand needs him to be."

Östen shook his head. "I will leave you to your word craft," he said, preferring that to Thorvald's poison craft, or the narrow blade concealed at his wrist, and they bade farewell.

Östen led Thyra from Uppsala, to a ford over the Fyriswater, which they crossed, and then traveled slightly south of east, along the empty market roads. Along the way, they used the silver Thorvald had given them to buy what they needed from villages and farms, but rarely did they speak at all. Östen kept her bound, not because he wanted to, or because he feared her, but because word of them might spread, and they were not yet far enough from the king.

It was not until days later, when they crossed the border of his land, that he cut her binding completely. When they reached his farm, his family rushed to greet him. First, he gathered Hilla up in his arms, and he kissed her and squeezed her until she complained about his smell, and then he embraced Tørgils and Agnes and Greta. Arne the Dane then came with Stone Dog, who reached up to lick Östen's fingertips.

"The farm looks well, Arne," Östen said. "I haven't forgotten my promise." Then he introduced Thyra to his family, and he called her a guest, rather than a thrall.

That night they ate well, and afterward Östen walked by moonlight with Stone Dog up to the spring, where he took an icy bath in the only water that could make him feel clean after the battle he had fought. Then, with Stone Dog as his only witness, he wrapped Thorvald's strange dagger in an oilskin and buried it next to the spring, afterward covering the spot with a small cairn of stones.

Alongside Östen's mind, David took note of the location, the features that wouldn't change as much, even after centuries. "That's it," he said. "We've got it."

We've got it, Victoria said. *Good work, David. If you're ready, I'll bring you out—*

"Not yet," David said. "If—if that's okay. I just need to see something."

There was a pause.

All right, a few more minutes.

David rejoined Östen's mind and memories, and as his ancestor returned to his hall, he found Thyra standing outside, gazing up at the moon. Östen tried to walk past without disturbing her, but she called to him and asked him to join her, which he did.

"You are a fortunate man," she said, "to have a life such as this."

"I would die to protect it," he said.

She looked down at the ground, no doubt thinking of her dead husband, and he realized he'd chosen his words poorly, but didn't know how to repair them.

"I thought he would surely do it," Thyra said. "At Uppsala, I thought Eric would feed me to his bear, no matter what the Lawspeaker said."

"Why?"

"The power of symbols," she said, "and the meaning of my husband's name. Styrbjörn, the wild and unruly bear, and I, his widow, eaten by a bear on a chain."

Östen fell silent. "I hadn't thought of it."

Their exchange recalled to Östen's mind his own question on the subject of bears, and whether it was better to live on the king's chain, or to live free and risk death at the hands of hunters or the cruelties of the savage winter. Eric had made his choice, just as Styrbjörn had made his. For his own part, Östen knew what he would choose, and what every man deserved.

"My thrall is one of your countrymen," Östen said.

"Yes, I know his village."

"I intend to free him. You may stay or go as you wish, of course. But there is still plenty of Thorvald's silver left. I thought you might take it and go with Arne back to Jutland."

This was the moment David had stayed to see. Not because he needed to. Because he hoped to.

Thyra turned toward Östen, her pale face as blank and unreadable as the moon above. "Thorvald was right. You are an uncommon man." Then she looked back up into the sky. "I will speak with Arne, but I am not of a mind to leave just yet."

Östen frowned. "It will be dangerous for you to stay. Why would you risk it?"

She looked down at her right hand. "When Eric had me bound, one of the housecarls took Styrbjörn's Ingelrii sword from me. It was the blade he gave me with his wedding vows."

Östen began to understand, but now he worried even more. "You seek to recover it?"

"I do." She laid her sword hand against her stomach. "I will have need of it one day."

David? Victoria said. *It's time.*

But he didn't want to leave. He wanted to know what happened to these people, to Östen, and his children, and their children. He wanted to know if Thyra got Styrbjörn's sword back, and if Arne the Dane went home, and—

I need to pull you out, David. Remember why you're in there. Think about Isaiah.

He didn't want to think about Isaiah. But he knew he had to. "Okay," he said, and sighed. "Okay, I'm ready to leave. Let's go save the world."

CHAPTER TWENTY-THREE

Natalya waited with Owen and Grace in the common room. It was nighttime outside, turning all the Aerie's windows into mirrors, and she'd just eaten a second bag of barbecue potato chips, not because she was hungry, even though she was, and not because she liked barbecue potato chips, because she didn't, but because she was anxious and had nothing else to do. The two empty bags stared at her, asking *now what?*

"So how do you think the shield is supposed to work?" Grace asked.

Owen slumped low in his chair, his feet up on the table. "I've been wondering that, too. I don't feel any different."

Natalya sat forward, her elbows and forearms flat on the

table. "Well, we followed the Path through the simulation, right? The first thing we met was the Serpent in the Forest. I'm guessing that's the fear part. The next thing was the Dog, which was probably devotion."

"And climbing that mountain was faith," Grace said.

"Exactly."

"Right," Owen said. "We know all that. But I hope Minerva's big message wasn't just a summary of what we had already done. How is that a shield?"

Natalya had no idea. But since the prong Isaiah had used in Mongolia caused fear, and the other two caused devotion and faith, it had to mean something that they lined up with the archetypes in the simulation. But that insight still didn't explain where the shield would come from, or how they could use it to resist the power of the Trident.

"Maybe the collective unconscious is broken," Grace said. "Monroe said it's really old, right? What if Minerva's genetic time capsule went bad before it got to us?"

Owen closed his eyes, as though he was aiming for a nap. "I don't think that's how it—"

The door opened and Javier walked in, followed by David. Then Monroe, Griffin, and Victoria entered the room. Owen's eyes popped open as he got his feet off the table and sat up in his chair.

"Everyone staying hydrated after their simulations?" Victoria asked.

"Yeah," Grace said, restraining an eye roll, and looked at David. "Did you find it?"

He gave her a nod and a smile.

"We found it," Victoria said. "The Piece of Eden changed hands several times, but we now have our best estimate for its final location."

"So let's go get it," Owen said. "And then we figure out how to take the other two from Isaiah."

"I'm afraid it's not as simple as that," Victoria said. She took a seat at the long conference table. "The Templars have been trying to find Isaiah using more conventional means. They tracked him to an old Abstergo facility that was never completed, on the Isle of Skye near Scotland. They lost contact with the first strike team they sent in, and the second team found the site abandoned."

"What happened to the first team?" Grace asked.

"It seems they joined him," Victoria said. "That's the power of the Trident. Any force we send after Isaiah will only build his army and make him that much stronger."

"Isaiah is like a black hole," Monroe said. "If we get too close, he'll suck us in, and we'll become one of his followers."

"You mean slaves," David said.

Javier tipped his head toward him. "I was thinking zombies."

"Whatever you call them," Monroe said, "let me ask you, do you like the idea of Griffin fighting on Isaiah's side? Against us?"

Natalya did not like that idea at all. She had seen what Griffin could do to those he considered his enemies. But beyond that, she didn't like the thought of any of them losing themselves to the power of the Trident. They had already lost Sean to it, and Natalya still planned to get him out, somehow.

"That's why we can't just charge off to Scandinavia to find the Piece of Eden," Griffin said, standing near the table.

"Do we know where Isaiah is now?" Grace asked.

"Somewhere in Sweden," Victoria said. "That's as close as we can get."

"No, it's not," Javier said. "We know Sean was in the memories of Styrbjörn, right? And the last time he saw the dagger, it was hidden in a shrine in the middle of the forest. I was there. We know where that is. And even if Isaiah realizes it's not there, the only other place he'll look will be Uppsala. We know where that is, too." He glanced at David. "Isaiah will never guess that my ancestor gave the dagger to a giant farmer."

Griffin nodded. "Javier is right. And that gives us at least some idea of the perimeter we're talking about."

Victoria nodded, and then she tapped and swiped at her tablet. "The location from David's simulation is over forty miles from either Uppsala or the forest."

"Is that enough of a buffer?" Monroe asked. "If Isaiah realizes you're there, he'll be within striking distance."

"I think it's as good as we're going to get," Victoria said. "I'll arrange an Abstergo jet to fly us—"

"Wait a minute." Monroe held up his hand, looking at the table. "Before you do that, how do we know you can trust anyone from Abstergo at this point? Or the Templars?"

"What are you—" Victoria wrinkled her brow. "I'm not sure what you're suggesting. I told you, you're all perfectly safe here."

"That's not what I mean." Monroe pressed his index finger against the table. "How do we know Isaiah doesn't already have zombies, or slaves, or whatever you want to call them, *inside* the Order?"

"That's impossible," Victoria said.

"Impossible is a pretty big word," Monroe said. "Are you sure it applies? Are you sure the Order doesn't have some house-keeping to take care of?"

Natalya knew he was talking about the Instruments of the First Will, and Isaiah's connection to them. The question was whether Victoria knew about them. But instead of answering his question, she set her tablet on the table, frowning, and said nothing.

"It sounds like you know something, Monroe," Griffin said.

"I do." Monroe hadn't taken his eyes from Victoria. "The question is, does she?"

Victoria still said nothing, her face unsettlingly serene. Griffin took a step toward her, and the tension in the room escalated to feeling almost dangerous. Natalya knew Monroe wasn't going to budge, and it didn't look as if Victoria would break. Someone else would have to end the stalemate, and quickly, before they wasted any more time.

"We know about the Instruments of the First Will," Natalya said.

Monroe swung a disbelieving glare in her direction, trying to silence her from across the table, while confusion cracked the veneer of Victoria's serenity. Little creases appeared at the corners of her lips and between her eyebrows.

"What do they have to do with this?" she asked. "And how do you know about them?"

Natalya turned to Grace, and she pulled the paper out of her pocket.

Monroe threw up his hands and swore. "So much for keeping any of this between us."

"I found this in a book," Grace said, ignoring him. "Isaiah

wrote it. It seems like he was a part of the Instruments of the First Will."

"May I see it?" Victoria asked.

Grace hesitated for a few seconds, but then shrugged, and passed Victoria the paper. As she read it, the creases on her face seemed to deepen with her confusion. When she finished reading it, she passed the paper to Griffin.

"I had no idea Isaiah had ever been connected with the Instruments," she said. "I suppose he shares some of their objectives. But I can assure you, they are being dealt with. Internally."

"So you didn't know about any of that?" Natalya asked, nodding toward the paper in Griffin's hands.

"I knew about Isaiah's motives," Victoria said. "He sent me a similar document before he left for Mongolia. I honestly didn't think his reasons would make a difference to us and our plans. But he made no mention of the Instruments of the First Will to me."

"Now do you see why I was suspicious?" Monroe asked.

Victoria nodded. "If Isaiah was once allied with them, it's possible he would have spies and followers even without the power of the Trident. But *with* the Trident . . ."

"Now you see why we can't go to the Order." Monroe looked at Griffin. "Or the Brotherhood. We're on our own. The only people we can trust are in this room."

"That's better anyway," David said. "You already said that agents and strike teams won't help us here. In fact, they'll make it worse."

"Right," Victoria said. "Then I guess I need to arrange for a plane to Sweden."

Natalya looked around the room. "All of us?"

"Why not?" Owen asked.

"Because if something goes wrong," she said, "and Isaiah takes over our minds, there won't be anyone left to stop him."

"A smaller team will also stand a better chance of going undetected," Griffin said.

"Right." Victoria picked up her tablet. "So who's going?"

"This is in my wheelhouse," Griffin said. "I'll go."

"I'll go," said Javier.

"Nope." Monroe shook his head. "I don't think we should send any of you kids."

"Kids?" Grace said.

"But we're the ones with the shield," Owen said. "We're actually the best ones to send." And then he added, "As long as it works."

"I actually agree with Owen," Victoria said. "But Javier and David haven't been through the collective unconscious simulation, so they'll stay here. Monroe can run them through it while Griffin takes a team to Sweden."

"I'll go to Sweden," Owen said.

Natalya weighed her choices, but made up her mind when it occurred to her that Sean might also be in Sweden. "I'll go," she said.

Griffin nodded.

"I'll stay here, if that's okay," Grace said, and looked over at David.

"I need all hands on deck," Griffin said. "Your brother will be fine."

Grace bit her bottom lip, and then she nodded.

"I'll buy four tickets on the next available commercial

flight," Victoria said. "I can't charter an Abstergo plane without drawing attention, but I can use a corporate credit card."

"Commercial," Griffin said. "That means no weapons."

"I'm afraid so." Victoria focused on her tablet. "Isaiah left no weapons behind anyway. The only thing left here at the Aerie are some tools and devices used for pest control. At any rate, it's highly unlikely that Isaiah has the ability to monitor commercial air travel, so this is the safest option to avoid detection. To be on the safe side, you'll be traveling with fake passports."

"We will?" Owen said.

"Of course." Victoria smirked, then tapped the screen. "You can't land in Stockholm. That would create unnecessary ground travel, and depending on which route you take around the lake, it could put you too close to Uppsala." She tapped again. "Ah, this will work. There's a flight leaving for Västerås in eighteen hours. The airport there is only fifteen miles from the prong's location."

"No sooner flight?" Griffin asked.

"No," Victoria said. "But everyone needs rest anyway, after their simulations." She looked at David, and then the others. "The Animus keeps your mind stimulated, but your body is active and it still feels the effects of fatigue, even if it hasn't set in yet."

It occurred to Natalya that she didn't even know what time it was, just that it was late, and she suddenly felt exhausted, as if Victoria had just flipped a switch by mentioning it.

Monroe pushed himself up out of his chair. "I'll go see what I can cook for everyone. Then you can all get a good, long rest. You've earned it. I'm proud of you."

"So am I," Victoria said. "It's too late at night to call your parents, but you should all make a point of doing that in the morning."

As soon as she mentioned that, it was like she flipped another switch, and Natalya suddenly felt very, very homesick. She wanted her own bed, or better yet, her grandparents' sofa, where she sometimes slept better than anywhere else, and woke up to the noxious smell of buckwheat porridge on the stove, which she would gladly eat right now if her grandmother put it in front of her.

Monroe headed for the door. "Meet back here in twenty or thirty minutes if you're hungry."

Natalya decided to just stay put and wait.

"My mom still thinks I ran away," Owen said.

"Mine too," Javier said.

"Why?" Natalya asked.

"Because that's what I told her," Owen said. "I couldn't make up a story about being at a special Abstergo school. We were with Griffin."

Javier hung one arm over the back of his chair. "It's closer to the truth than what you guys tell your parents."

Natalya was too exhausted to argue with him; besides which, he had a point.

"So what's this Instruments group that you were all talking about?" Javier asked.

"Oh, right," Grace said. "You guys weren't there. It's kind of hard to explain, but basically, the Instruments of the First Will is a group of Templars who want to bring back the civilization that created the Pieces of Eden."

"And that would be a bad thing?" Javier said.

"Probably," Owen said, "since they destroyed themselves."

"Why do they want to bring them back?" David asked.

"Because they're Templars," Griffin said.

"I object to that statement," Victoria said. "The Instruments seek to restore Juno as their master. They believe humans should be *slaves* to the Precursors."

"Slaves?" David asked.

"Yes," Victoria said. "The Instruments are *not* true Templars."

"Or are they the truest Templars?" Griffin asked. "Maybe they're just the logical result of what the Templars started. The whole reason we have the Animus is because the Templars wanted to find Pieces of Eden. Your Order went digging for Precursors, and once you start down that road, where does it end?"

Victoria's lips thinned, and she offered no response.

"Sounds like it ends with the Instruments," Javier said.

Victoria rose from her chair. "I'm not hungry, and I have to arrange your flights. I'll see you all in the morning." With that, she swept from the room.

Griffin's argument echoed much of what Natalya had been thinking since this ordeal had begun. She didn't think anyone should have the Trident. Yanmei was dead because Natalya had tried to keep the others from finding the second piece of it. Once you allow yourself to use a power like that, where does it end?

How does it end?

Natalya shook her head. Griffin was wrong. "I don't think it ends with the Instruments," she said. "I think it ends with Isaiah. He doesn't want to bring Juno back. He wants to be the master. He wants to destroy and enslave the world."

The room went quiet after that, and it stayed quiet until Monroe wheeled a cart into the common room carrying plates and a big pot.

"Isaiah took most of the nonperishable provisions with him," he said. "The perishables have all gone bad. So for dinner we have buttered noodles with some garlic and thyme." He looked around the table. "Where's Victoria?"

"She doesn't like where things have ended up," Griffin said. "I think she's feeling a bit defensive of her Order."

Monroe nodded. "Can't say I blame her for that." Then he stuck a serving fork into the pot and dropped a pile of noodles onto one of the plates. "Who's hungry?"

Owen raised his hand. "Me."

Monroe passed him the plate, and then dished up noodles for everyone else. They all ate, and Natalya thought it actually tasted pretty good. Several minutes went by without anyone speaking, but then Monroe put his fork down.

"Of course, to be fair, the Assassins have been guilty of their own excesses. Haven't they, Griffin?"

Griffin stopped chewing.

"What excesses?" David asked.

Monroe picked his fork back up. "It's hard to say for sure, since the Brotherhood likes to keep everything in the dark. Especially their mistakes. Abstergo historians blame the burning of Constantinople on a man named Ezio Auditore, one of the most revered Assassins in history. Countless innocent deaths during that disaster. And then of course, one of Javier's ancestors, Shay Cormac, became a Templar after he caused an earthquake, and blamed the Brotherhood for it. And then there was Jack the Ripper."

"He was an Assassin?" Grace asked.

"No, he wasn't," Griffin said, his hands in fists on either side of his plate. "Not a true Assassin."

"Or was he the truest?" Natalya asked. "Assassins kill people. Once you start down that road, where does it end?"

"And who gets to say who's true and who's not?" Monroe asked.

"No one does." Griffin now rose to his feet. "Our Creed speaks for itself. Anyone who violates it is not an Assassin." He turned away and stalked toward the door, but before he left the room, he turned back and said, "Assassins *stopped* Jack the Ripper. We clean our house."

Then he was gone, and after he'd left, everyone finished dinner quickly. Natalya had pretty much lost her appetite with the mention of a serial killer, and only took another couple of bites.

"You all head to bed," Monroe said. "I'll clean up."

Natalya felt very heavy as she tried to get out of her chair, and her feet dragged a bit as they all walked to the Aerie's dormitory wing. She found her room and fell into her bed still dressed, and when she opened her eyes again, it was light outside, and she hadn't moved at all during the night.

She climbed out of bed, feeling sore everywhere, and trudged from her bedroom to the common room. David and Javier were there, and they seemed a lot more alert than she felt. Grace sat in an armchair, staring blankly, and Owen hadn't appeared yet.

Natalya shuffled over to Grace, and winced as she lowered herself into the armchair next to her.

"You too?" Grace asked.

"Yeah, what's the deal?" The Animus sometimes took a toll, but mostly in the form of headaches. A simulation had never left her feeling this beaten-up the next day.

"I don't know." Grace pointed her chin at her brother. "He was in for a lot longer than me, and he was practically skipping this morning."

"Javier looks fine, too." Natalya decided that the difference must have something to do with the collective unconscious, and she hoped that meant the simulation had worked after all.

A few minutes later, Monroe strolled in carrying a tray of biscuits he'd managed to bake up, along with some peanut butter and jelly to spread over them. The biscuits smelled like butter, and Natalya finished three of them before she stopped to wonder how many she should eat.

"Save some for Owen," she said.

The others all looked down at their plates, and then at the tray. There was one biscuit left.

"He'll be fine," Javier said.

That biscuit was cold by the time Owen stumbled into the room, and not long after that, Victoria appeared with their passports and plane tickets. Natalya went back to her room and took a shower, which helped soothe her sore muscles, and then she changed into a fresh set of Aerie-issued sweats and hoodie. By the time they left for the airport in an Abstergo van, she felt slightly closer to normal.

Monroe drove them down the mountain, with Griffin in the front passenger seat. Neither man spoke to the other for almost the entire drive, but as they pulled up to the airport curb, Monroe lifted the gear into park and twisted in his seat to face the Assassin.

"Listen, what I said yesterday about the Brotherhood . . . I was talking about it as a whole. Not about you."

Griffin nodded. "I appreciate that."

"And you do keep a pretty clean house," Monroe added. "Considering."

"Considering what?" Owen asked with a grin.

Monroe shook his head. "Get out of the van, you little punk. And stay safe. All of you. Don't take any unnecessary risks."

"We won't," Grace said.

They all piled out, and Monroe pulled away. Griffin led them through security without setting off any alarms, which meant he had either left his hidden blade back at the Aerie, or he had found a way to make it truly hidden, and they boarded their flight. Victoria had bought them first-class tickets, something Natalya had never experienced before, and probably never would again. But as she took her wider, softer seat, her sore body felt deeply grateful for Abstergo's corporate card.

She sat by a window, next to Griffin, and as the plane lifted off, he leaned back and closed his eyes. "See you in Sweden," he said.

Natalya looked out the window at the shrinking buildings and roads. "See you in Sweden," she whispered.

CHAPTER TWENTY-FOUR

They landed in the early afternoon. Grace had slept for part of the flight, but she'd also watched a couple of movies, and that had been a weird experience. With everything going on, movies seemed completely trivial, and even worthless, but what else was she going to do while she was stuck on a plane? One was a superhero flick, and the other was a comedy, and both had actually done a pretty good job distracting her from the reason she was stuck on that plane to begin with. Maybe that's all movies needed to do.

The city of Västerås looked lovely from the air, situated on Lake Mälaren, with a river running through it and a few small islands offshore. Once they'd landed at the small airport outside of town, Griffin rented an SUV, and then drove to a hardware store. He went in alone, and came back out with two shovels, which he threw in the back of the car. Then he drove them into the countryside, passing numerous farms, with barns and silos, ponds, grain fields, and pastures. They traveled through small stands of trees as well, but it wasn't until they were several miles from the city that they reached true forest.

When Grace thought of Hansel and Gretel getting lost in the woods, she imagined it to be a place like this. Huge pine trees and oak trees kept much of the forest floor in shadow, which felt oppressive in one moment and comforting in the next. Its depths both beckoned and threatened her.

"It's like the Forest," Natalya said.

"Without the giant snake," Owen said.

Grace rolled her window down, and cool, pine-scented air blew across her forehead. Above the car's engine, she heard a variety of birdsong coming from the trees, and then suddenly, as they came around a bend, she glimpsed a moose just off the road. The back half of its huge body stood in the shadows under the trees, while its head and broad antlers caught the sun. She'd never seen a moose in person before, and whipped around in her seat to get a second look, but it had already disappeared into the woods, probably startled by their SUV.

"The location David identified is on private property," Griffin said. "We don't have time to get permission from the owners, so we're just going to not be seen. Owen and Natalya are fairly proficient at not being seen." Grace could see his eyes in the rearview mirror looking at her. "What about you? You had an Assassin ancestor in New York, right?"

Grace nodded. "Eliza."

"Did you pick up anything from that experience?"

"Some," she said. Owen's ancestor, the Assassin Varius, had

trained Eliza, and the Bleeding Effects had given Grace some of her ancestor's hand-to-hand combat skills, and some free-running ability. "I'll try to keep up," she said.

Griffin drove them another few miles, and then turned the SUV onto a rutted forest access road, where a short distance in he stopped and killed the engine. "We'll walk from here."

They all climbed out, and Grace looked up into the trees and the filtered green sunlight, breathing the air in deeply. This place felt right to her, familiar, and she realized that she had been here before. Not this spot, specifically, but this land that her ancestor knew so well. She hadn't spent much time in Östen's memories, but it had apparently been enough to leave an impression.

"It's weird to do this without any weapons," Owen said. "No crossbow. No grenades."

"What about your hidden blade?" Natalya asked Griffin.

He held up his right forearm and tapped it with his other hand. "Ceramic. You guys get these." He handed Owen and Natalya one of the shovels each, and then he pulled out a phone. "Hang on while I pull up the location on GPS."

But Grace didn't need GPS. Östen always knew his way home. "It's that direction," she said, pointing off into the woods.

Griffin looked at her, then at the forest, then at his phone. "You're right. How did you know that?"

"Bleeding Effect," she said. "You're in my house now."

"Your Viking house," Owen said.

Griffin slipped the phone back in his pocket. "Lead the way."

So that's what Grace did, guiding them through the woods past boulders she recognized, though the streams they crossed flowed differently than she remembered. They didn't come across another moose, but they did see a small boar that bolted away, and through Östen, Grace knew that it was a young sow, and shy, and normally hard to spot.

They came at Östen's old farmstead from behind, walking up the backside of his hill where a cell tower now stood. The sight of it bothered Grace, but she knew it would probably bother her more to see what had become of Östen's land on the other side. There wasn't anything she could do to change it, though. It was just the passage of time.

"Let's be as quick as we can about this," Griffin said as they came over the top of the hill.

But Grace knew instantly there wouldn't be anything quick about it.

Below them, what looked like a small factory occupied the space where Östen's farmstead had once stood. A chain-link fence surrounded it, enclosing the spot that should have been Östen's spring. But instead of the spring, Grace saw a small brick building with a thick pipe running from inside it down the hill to the factory.

"It looks like they're bottling the water," Natalya said.

"That's exactly what they're doing." Griffin pulled his phone back out. "I don't understand. This wasn't listed."

"Look at all the dirt." Owen pointed at several places around the site of the factory where the turf and the trees had been cleared. "That's all fresh. I think they just built this."

Griffin pointed at the brick building. "That springhouse is sitting right on top of the Piece of Eden."

"So what do we do?" Owen asked.

"I'm thinking," Griffin said. "You do the same."

Grace tried hard to see the place through her ancestor's eyes, hoping it might give her an idea. She remembered Östen digging out a pool around the spring, to collect more of the water before it ran away to join the streams and the lakes. The rock had been hard, and the labor difficult. To build that new brick springhouse, they would have dug out even more, which meant they might have disturbed the dagger.

"When they were building this place," Grace said, "what do you think they did with any historical stuff they found?"

Griffin raised an eyebrow. "Now there's an idea."

Grace looked down at the factory. "I think we should ask if they give tours."

"Right," Griffin said. "Owen, Natalya, you stay here and keep out of sight. Grace and I will go down and check things out."

They set off down the hill, walking around the chain-link fence to the plant's front entrance, where Grace saw the company name and logo.

"You gotta be kidding me," Griffin said.

The logo bore the unmistakable image of one of the Trident's prongs in simplified silhouette, with the word *dolkkälla* written over it. "Can you translate the name?" Grace asked.

"Dagger Spring," he said. "I'm pretty sure that's what it means."

Grace almost laughed. "Hide in plain sight, right?"

Griffin shook his head. "Let's go see what's inside."

They hurried past the sign, up the driveway, to the plant's main entrance, its name and logo everywhere they looked. Through the front doors, they entered a modest lobby that smelled of fresh paint and carpet. A receptionist looked up from his desk, smiled, and said something in what Grace assumed was Swedish.

Griffin shook his head, and in that instant he lost all the casual menace he normally projected, and became a mild and embarrassed tourist. "I'm sorry," he said. "We're from the U.S."

The receptionist's smile changed, very subtly, taking on a shade of impatience and condescension. "Of course. What can I do for you?" he asked with only a slight accent.

"We were just driving and saw your plant," Griffin said. "Do you offer tours?"

"Not at the moment," the receptionist said. "We opened very recently. Perhaps one day."

"Where does your name come from?" Grace asked.

"That, I am happy to say, I can show you." He rose from his chair and came around from behind the desk, and then led them across the lobby to a glass door. The room on the other side of it was dimly lit, with glowing display cases. Some held fragments and small objects Grace couldn't identify from this far away. Some cases were empty. But at the far end of the room, by itself under a warm spotlight, the Piece of Eden sat on display.

"There have been several farms on this site going back many hundreds of years," the receptionist said. "We worked with scientists to preserve what we found. Most went to a museum, but we arranged to display these. That is the dagger. They found it buried next to the spring. Very strange, yes?"

"Unbelievable," Griffin said. "Can we go in?"

"No, I am sorry, the museum isn't ready. They are still adding to it." The receptionist then folded his hands in front of his waist and gazed through the glass door as if he never got tired of the view. "You are the second American to see this today," he said.

Grace looked at Griffin, the back of her neck prickling. Griffin looked at the receptionist.

"Is that right?" he said. "Where was he from?"

"She," the receptionist said. "I didn't ask where she was from. She read about us in the paper yesterday, and came from

Uppsala to see." He pointed toward his desk. "I have the article if you want to read it."

Grace tried to convince herself it was just a coincidence, but did a poor job of it. It was possible that the woman who came to see the dagger had nothing to do with Isaiah, but why take the risk? It would be smarter to simply hurry and get out of there.

"This was interesting," Griffin said. "But we better get going. Thank you for your time."

"You're welcome," the receptionist said. "Please come back when the museum is open."

"I wish we could," Griffin said. "But we aren't here for very long."

"Then you have a reason to come back to Sweden." The receptionist gave them a broad smile.

"That's true," Griffin said, nodding. Then he looked toward the front doors. "Well, have a nice day."

"You as well," the receptionist said.

Griffin waved a good-bye, and guided Grace through the lobby, then back outside. They walked as fast as they dared down the driveway, trying to avoid drawing attention, but once they reached the fence, they veered to the side and raced back up the hill. At the top, they found Owen and Natalya waiting where they'd left them.

"Well?" Owen asked.

"You're not going to believe this," Grace said. "They have the prong in there."

"How do you know?" Natalya asked.

"Because I saw it," Grace said. "It's just sitting there. On display."

"This plant is called Dagger Spring," Griffin said, and

Grace noted that his usual menace had returned. "They dug up the prong when they were excavating."

"So what's the problem?" Owen asked. "We just break in tonight and grab it."

Griffin stared down at the plant. "The problem is Isaiah. Someone else was here today asking about the dagger. He might already be on his way."

"Then maybe we shouldn't wait," Natalya said. "Could you steal it right now?"

"There aren't any guards," Griffin said. "I could easily force my way in and walk out of there with it. But they think it's a national antiquity. They'll be looking for it, and for me, which will make it harder for us to get it out of the country."

"So what do we do?" Grace asked. The prong was right there, within reach. But any option for taking it came with risks.

Griffin looked down at the ground and rubbed his shaved head. "We wait until this evening. As soon as that place shuts down, I go in, grab the dagger, and then we get the hell out of here." He looked up at them. "Agreed?"

Grace nodded, and so did Owen and Natalya.

"Okay." Griffin lowered himself to the ground and sat down. "Might as well get comfortable."

Grace did the same, and the four of them soon sat in a circle on the hilltop, surrounded by forest, waiting for evening to come. The fluffy clouds overhead shuffled along in their slow tumble, threaded by the occasional bird, and in the stillness, Grace thought of David. She hoped he was doing okay in the collective unconscious simulation, reminding herself that he would be safer there than she was here. No one said much, but the silence didn't feel awkward or empty. At least not to her.

Maybe it did to Owen. After they'd been there for a while, he cleared his throat. "If I get cancer from this cell tower, I'm holding all of you responsible."

"Cell phones don't give you cancer," Natalya said.

"Oh, really?" Owen said. "Do you hear that buzzing?"

"I think it's relaxing," Griffin said. "When I was a kid, I lived near a busy railroad track. You get used to having noise in the background."

"You were a kid?" Owen said.

Griffin nodded, smiling. "Believe it or not."

"Do they make onesies with little Assassin hoods?" Grace asked. "What was your first toy?"

"A switchblade," Griffin said, his voice flat.

For a few seconds, Grace couldn't tell if he was joking, and she looked over at Owen and Natalya, who had both stopped smiling. But then Griffin cracked, and he chuckled. "You guys almost believed that."

"No, we didn't," Owen said.

"Sure you did." Griffin leaned toward them. "Listen, I have to be honest with you guys about something. I didn't think you'd make it this far."

Again, silence followed, and Grace wondered if this was another joke. "Um. Thanks?"

"No, just listen," he said. "When I found out Monroe had dragged a bunch of kids into this, I assumed it would come to a quick, bad end for everyone. But here you are. It's impressive, that's all I'm saying. You've impressed me."

"Thanks," Owen said. "You're pretty nice for a ruthless killer."

Griffin fake-lunged at him.

"Smart-ass," the Assassin said.

"What time is it?" Natalya asked. "It feels late, but it doesn't look late."

"We're practically in the land of the midnight sun," Griffin said. "This far north, at this time of year, the sun stays up for a lot longer." He checked his phone, and then got to his feet. "But they'll probably be closing up shop soon. At least in the lobby."

Grace, Owen, and Natalya all stood up, too. Grace peered down at the plant and saw that the parking lot was mostly empty.

"Okay," Owen said. "So how are we doing this?"

"We aren't," Griffin said. "I am."

"Why?" Owen asked. "You just said we impressed you. We can help."

"This is a one-person job. More than that will just complicate it." He looked at Grace. "Tell him how simple this is."

"It's basically right there when you walk through the front doors," Grace said.

"The only hitch might be a security system, but I can deal with it." Griffin set off down the hill, but pointed back at them. "Stay there, Owen."

Owen scowled and folded his arms.

Grace kept her eyes on the Assassin the entire way as he skirted along the fence, seeming to move much more quickly than he had when she'd gone with him. A couple of times she even lost sight of him, as if he'd just vanished in the daylight. But then he appeared again, some distance on from where she'd last seen him. Her heart was pounding, even though Griffin had appeared perfectly calm and confident. When he reached the edge of the fence, he ran up the drive, and was lost to Grace's view.

"Now we just wait," Natalya said.

A few minutes went by. Then a few more minutes. Grace almost expected alarms to start going off at any moment, but realized that was stupid. This wasn't a government facility. It was a bottled water plant with a one-room museum. So no alarms went off. But Griffin didn't come out, either.

"It's taking longer than I thought it would," Natalya said.

"Maybe the security system is tougher than he thought," Owen said.

Grace watched, and listened. More minutes passed.

The she heard something. A distant, familiar whumping sound. She looked over at Natalya and Owen, and from their wide eyes, she knew they could hear it, too.

"Helicopters," Owen said.

"Hide!" Grace said.

They ran from the open hilltop back to the tree line, where they hid in the shadows, watching as two helicopters swung into view. They were large and black, emblazoned with the Abstergo logo, and similar to the ones Isaiah had escaped in from Mongolia.

"What about Griffin?" Natalya whispered.

The helicopters hovered low over the plant for a few moments, and then doors opened up suddenly in their sides, spilling coils of black rope. Abstergo agents in paramilitary gear then emerged from inside, and one by one they slid down the ropes.

"What do we do?" Natalya asked.

Grace didn't know. She felt helpless. They had no weapons, other than the two shovels.

"We've gotta do something," Owen said. "We can't just—"

Gunshots echoed up the hill, sounding distant and muffled, as if they came from inside the plant. Grace knew that sound, and it pierced her stomach.

"Seriously, what do we do?" Natalya asked.

Owen took a step forward. "I'm going in—"

"No, you're not." Grace grabbed him and held him back. "That's suicide."

"Well, I can't just stand here," he said.

"I'm not letting you go in there," Grace said. "I don't care how good you think you are. You aren't—"

More gunshots, these sounding louder and clearer, and Grace ducked her head involuntarily. Those had come from out-side, and much closer.

"Look!" Natalya said, pointing.

Down below, Grace spotted Griffin sprinting behind the plant, then up the hill along the main pipe. Three agents chased him, pausing to aim and shoot. But Griffin kept moving, errati-cally, and managed to avoid getting hit. As he reached the springhouse, one of the helicopters dove at him, and three more agents leapt to the ground, on the side of the fence near Grace and the others.

"He's trapped," Natalya whispered.

"Screw this," Owen said. He snatched up one of the shovels and charged away before Grace could stop him.

CHAPTER TWENTY-FIVE

G race watched Owen as he raced to help Griffin. A second later, she grabbed the other shovel and did the same, and before she really stopped to think about it, she was closing in on the first agent. They were focused on Griffin, so they didn't see the attack coming. Owen reached them first, swinging hard. Grace heard the metal impact of the shovel against the agent's helmet, and she spun almost 180 degrees before collapsing.

The other two turned toward Owen, but then Grace was there. She jabbed the shovel two-handed, like a spear, at the nearest agent's knee, and his leg buckled. Then she spun the shovel and brought it down on the agent's head, driving him to the ground.

From the corner of her eye, she saw the third agent raise his gun in her direction, and she raised the shovel reflexively, like a shield. A shot, a *clang*, and the shovel flew from her hands. But then Owen hit the agent from behind, hard.

With that, all three were down.

Grace looked and saw that Griffin had reached the fence, but he was struggling to climb it, and at the top, he simply rolled his way onto the other side, falling hard to the ground.

"He's hit," Owen said, sprinting toward him.

Grace ran, too, feeling like Östen, and Eliza, and herself, all at once.

The agents were still shooting, and bullets struck the ground around her as she and Owen helped Griffin to his feet.

He pressed something into Grace's hand, and she realized it was the prong, wrapped in a towel. She shoved it into one of her pockets.

"Get to the forest," Griffin said. "Go deep. The helicopters can't land. You'll lose them."

"You're coming with us," Owen said.

"No!" Griffin said, wincing. "Listen to me. I'm not going to make it. You have to move. Now."

But he couldn't stop them from staying at his side, and he kept limping along as they helped him up the hill. Grace looked back and saw six agents rushing after them, but they reached the trees first, where Natalya waited for them.

"What now?" she asked.

"We have to lose them," Owen said. "And get back to the car."

"Which way?" Natalya asked.

Grace paused, and let Östen step more fully into her head. She thought about the forest, which she knew well, and found a way. "There's a wash over there." She pointed to their right. "It'll keep us out of sight. We can follow it out of here."

"Sounds good to me."

Griffin grunted, like he meant to say something, but didn't.

They stumbled and raced through the woods, trying to hide behind the trees, until they reached the wash and clambered down its grassy embankment into a shallow, icy stream. Shouts echoed behind them from the Abstergo agents searching the woods.

"Let's go," Grace whispered.

She led them down the gully, Owen and Natalya on either side of Griffin, splashing through the water as the helicopters circled above. But Grace could barely see them through the trees, which meant that they would not be seen. Soon, the shouts grew more distant, as did the drone of the helicopters.

"Do you think they're giving up?" Owen asked.

"No," Grace said. "They know we have the prong. There's no way they're giving up. They're just looking for us in the wrong place, but they'll figure it out eventually. We have to keep moving."

"Griffin is bleeding pretty bad," Natalya said.

Grace looked over, and saw the Assassin's side was covered in red, and so was Natalya where she leaned up against him for support. His head wobbled, and his eyelids fluttered, even as he somehow managed to stay on his feet. Even with her very limited knowledge, Grace could see he needed urgent medical attention, but she had no idea how he could get it.

"Let's get him to the car," she said.

So they pressed ahead, staying low, listening. The frigid water turned painful, and she walked up on the mud and rocks when she could, knowing that eventually they would have to leave the wash to get to the car, and that would be the most dangerous leg of their escape.

"What?" Owen said.

Grace turned toward him, and saw him leaning his head toward Griffin.

"Hang on," Owen said to Natalya. "He's trying to tell me something." So they halted, and the stream gathered around their ankles. "What's that, Griffin?"

"Give—give my . . ." The Assassin's voice was a ragged, wheezy gasp. "Give my blades to Javier."

"No, man," he said. "No, those have to come from you. So you gotta stay with us."

Griffin shook his head. "Tell . . . tell him he—he earned them."

"You tell him," Owen said. "He's not going to believe me if I tell him that."

Griffin's mouth formed a thin smile. "Owen," he said. "Owen . . ."

"Yeah, Griffin, I'm right here."

"It doesn't matter," the Assassin said.

"What doesn't matter?"

"It doesn't . . . matter," Griffin repeated.

Owen looked at Grace, and said in a hushed voice, "I don't know what that means."

"Let's just keep moving," Grace said.

They resumed walking, and they made it another hundred feet before Griffin's legs gave out and he slumped into the stream. Water gurgled over his face, and they rushed to lift him up.

"Griffin," Grace said. "Griffin, stay with us."

But he didn't move.

Owen knelt down in the stream, his face right in front of the Assassin's. "Griffin," he said, shaking him. "Griffin."

Still no response.

"Help me," Owen said, grabbing Griffin by one of his arms. Grace and Natalya took the other, and together they pulled the Assassin's heavy body out of the stream. Then Owen dropped to his knees again and started CPR, counting off chest compressions and offering mouth-to-mouth.

Grace could see it wasn't working. Nothing could work, because Griffin was already gone, and there wasn't anything anyone could do. But Owen kept at it for several minutes, and Grace let him go for a while before she knelt down beside him and put a hand on his back.

"I'm sorry," she said.

Owen kept counting and pushing.

"Owen, he's gone."

"No," he said. "It would take more than that to kill him."

Grace looked up at Natalya, and she knelt down on his other side. They both put their arms around him, and gradually the compressions ceased, and he just leaned over Griffin with his hands pressing against the middle of the Assassin's chest. They stayed that way for several moments, saying nothing as the water behind them warbled on, which seemed wrong, as if the stream should have stopped.

Grace couldn't make sense of this.

It was a matter of minutes.

Only minutes.

Minutes ago, they were sitting on the hill, talking about Griffin as an Assassin baby. Now, minutes later, they were kneeling in a stream, with Griffin's blood on their clothes, and he was dead. She couldn't figure out how this had happened.

Owen sat up straighter, and Grace and Natalya lowered their arms from his back. Then he reached across Griffin to his right arm, and he pulled up his sleeve. There on his wrist was his hidden blade, this one ceramic. Owen undid the straps and slid it over Griffin's hand. Then he placed it on his own wrist.

"Just until I can give it to Javier," he said.

"His phone!" Natalya said, and she searched his pockets until she found it. But the stream had found it first, and the phone wouldn't do them any good now.

Grace didn't want to be the one to mention his wallet, but they were going to need money. They were stuck in a foreign country with fake passports, no cell phone, and a Piece of Eden. Without saying a word, she reached under him, found his back pocket, and then she pulled his wallet out. Owen and Natalya saw what she did, but they didn't say anything, either, and the three of them sat in silence.

Silence.

Something was missing.

"Do you hear the helicopters?" Grace asked.

Owen craned his neck. "No."

"I don't, either," Natalya said.

Grace didn't believe Isaiah had called off the search. Not when he knew someone else had taken the final prong of the Trident. But the helicopters weren't in the air anymore, and she couldn't hear anything in the forest except for what was supposed to be there.

"I don't want to leave him here," Owen said, looking at Griffin's body.

Grace didn't like the idea, either. But they'd left the shovels behind during the chaos at the bottled water plant, so they had no way to dig him a grave. And they also had to keep moving. They had to find a way to get the prong away from here, and away from Isaiah.

"He wouldn't want you to worry about him anymore," Natalya said. "You know that. He'd want you to escape, and get the dagger away from Isaiah."

Owen nodded, looking down at the hidden blade he now wore on his wrist. "Let's get moving. It's not going to get any easier by sitting here."

Grace and Natalya looked at each other and gently nodded. Then the three of them got up, and Grace led them forward down the wash, and it was suddenly a harder journey. Physically harder, as if she felt the weight of Griffin's lifeless body on her shoulders. But she persisted, refusing to look back, hoping that burden would lessen with distance.

It didn't.

But eventually they reached that place in the wash where they would need to climb out of it and cross through a stretch of woods if they wanted to get to the SUV. Grace listened for the helicopters, and still heard nothing. She couldn't hear any agents moving through the forest. But she didn't trust that silence.

"I think we should wait here for a while," she whispered.

"What for?" Natalya asked.

"Something doesn't seem right," she said.

"Something isn't right." Owen picked up a stick from the ground. "Griffin just died."

"No," Grace said. "Not that."

"Then what is it?" Natalya asked.

"Where did Isaiah go?" She looked up into the trees. "I don't like not knowing where he is, and I think we should wait here, just in case, until it gets dark. Then we go to the car."

Owen shook his head and snapped the stick. "Fine," he said.

Natalya just reached out and laid her hand on Grace's arm.

So they stayed there in the wash, wet and shivering, listening for any sound that might indicate Isaiah's return. After Grace had been sitting in the same position for a while, she moved her legs, and felt the dagger in her pocket, which she'd almost forgotten about. She pulled it out, wondering where Griffin had found the towel he'd wrapped around it, and as she unwrapped it, she noticed his blood on the fabric. The red-brown spot trapped her eyes and held them until she broke free of it and brought out the dagger.

The prong of the Trident. The Piece of Eden.

"So that's it," Owen said. "That's what this is all about."

Her ancestor, Eliza, had carried one of the daggers from New York City to General Grant on the battlefield. But Grace had never held one before. Its edge was still sharp after thousands and thousands of years, and even without its power, it would be deadly. Isaiah had demonstrated that when he used one to kill Yanmei.

"Put it away," Natalya said. "Please."

Grace wrapped it back up in its towel and slipped it into her pocket. Not long after that, she noticed that the forest had grown darker, and the blue in the sky had deepened. Evening had come, and soon that turned into twilight without any sign of Isaiah. If they were going to try for the SUV, now would be the time.

"Let's go," she said.

They climbed up out of the wash, over the embankment, and darted into the trees. In the gloom, Grace found that Östen's memories gave her an advantage. She knew this land, and that allowed her to run swiftly, which allowed Owen and Natalya to follow her.

They encountered no Abstergo agents as they made their way, and Grace heard no helicopters. The closer they got to the SUV, the more she thought she had been worried over nothing.

"I think I see it," Owen said.

He was right. Up ahead lay the forest access road, and the SUV was still there, its windows black and empty. They had made it.

"I'll drive," Grace said as they rushed up to the car. She reached into her pocket, and then she stopped, and almost didn't want to ask. "Who has the keys?"

Neither of them answered, and Grace felt her breath grow heavy in her lungs, pressing down. They had left the keys with Griffin's body. She tried the driver's side door, hoping that maybe it was unlocked, and that maybe Griffin had left the keys inside. But it wasn't unlocked.

"We have to go back?" Owen asked.

It had been hard enough for him to leave the first time. Grace didn't want him to relive it in the dark. "I'll go," she said. "I know my way. You guys stay here."

"I don't think we should separate," Natalya said.

Grace didn't like the idea, either, but if they all went, it would take more time than she felt they had. "I'll be fine," she said. "Just stay here and—"

A blinding beam of light smacked Grace in the face, and she held up a hand to shield her eyes. Then another light switched on, and another, and another, coming from all sides and closing in.

"I must say," said a familiar voice, "you kept me waiting so long, I had begun to wonder if this was even your car."

It was Isaiah.

Grace almost bolted, in panic and reflex. But her mind kept her feet in check, because she knew they were surrounded, and she wouldn't get far. It wouldn't have mattered if they had remembered the keys.

"Where is the Assassin?" Isaiah asked, a tall silhouette in the spotlights.

No one answered him.

"It was a fatal shot, then," Isaiah said. "So which one of you has the dagger?"

Still no one answered him.

"Let's dim those lights," he said. "Perhaps that will help them see this situation more clearly."

The spotlights swung their beams toward the ground, and Grace could now see the agents holding them, and between them, an even greater number of agents silently aiming their guns. Isaiah stepped closer, wearing Abstergo paramilitary gear, his green eyes somewhat paled by the artificial glare.

"You notice I don't have the Trident with me," Isaiah said. "You don't have to die tonight. I certainly don't wish it."

"You want your own Ragnarök," Owen said. "You want everyone to die."

"No," Isaiah said. "No, I don't want that at all. But many people must die for the world to be reborn in a better form. Do you mourn for the dead flakes of skin shed by the snake? Do you grieve the loss of the caterpillar after it has become a butterfly?"

"I think my history teacher would call those false analogies," Grace said. "The earth doesn't shed, and humans aren't its skin. And the caterpillar doesn't die to become a butterfly."

Isaiah nodded, almost approvingly. "I'm reminded of how exceptional you all are. More reason to spare you, because I don't actually wish for specific people to die any more than an exterminator wishes death on specific ants." He stared at Grace. "Does that analogy meet with your approval?"

"Where is Sean?" Natalya asked.

Isaiah smiled. "Your loyalty and devotion are admirable."

"Where is he?" Natalya asked again, but it was clear to Grace that Isaiah wasn't going to answer.

"What are you going to do with us?" Grace asked.

Isaiah snapped his fingers, and a group of the Abstergo agents closed in tighter, guns still raised.

"I had planned to simply leave you here," Isaiah said. "After I recover the dagger, of course. But I believe I may take you with me. You might be useful, given your lineages. But if you fight back on either score, I will have you killed, and while I do not wish for your deaths, believe me when I say I will not regret them."

Grace's legs had begun to tremble, from the cold and from her fear, but she hoped Isaiah couldn't see that. This was the closest she had ever come to death, and it was right here, just minutes or seconds away, like it had been with Griffin, and it was staring at her down the barrel of a dozen guns. The agents aiming their weapons looked at her as though she was nothing but a target. She might as well have been made of cardboard, and whatever shield Minerva had given her, it would be useless against bullets.

"You have the dagger, don't you, Grace?" Isaiah said.

She couldn't feel her body. She thought of David, and her parents.

"Cole, check her pockets."

One of the agents approached Grace, and she recognized the woman by her codename, Rothenberg, a Templar mole who had helped her escape from the Aerie with Monroe. But when the woman looked at Grace now, she didn't seem to care about any of that.

Javier was right. More zombie than slave.

"Don't move," Cole said, and even though Grace didn't want to obey, the part of her mind most driven to survive held her still. Cole reached into Grace's pocket and pulled out the dagger, which she handed immediately to Isaiah.

He shook the dagger from the towel, into his open hand, and closed his fist around the grip. "Were you as amused as I was by this prong's location?" he asked.

They had lost.

They had lost *everything*.

Isaiah had all three pieces of the Trident now, the very thing Minerva had feared all those thousands of years ago.

"You're forgetting about something," Owen said.

"Highly unlikely," Isaiah said. "But tell me."

"The Ascendance Event." Owen actually smirked, and made it convincing. "Monroe figured it out, and it can stop the Trident. Your superweapon is worthless."

What was Owen doing? Trying to intimidate Isaiah? Bluff their way out of this somehow? Or just showing the only card they had?

"The Ascendance Event?" Isaiah cocked his head and bent

down to look Owen in his eyes, their faces very close together. "You're lying."

"No," Owen said, returning Isaiah's stare, "I'm not."

A few seconds passed, and then Isaiah leaned away. "So Monroe finally did it. After all these years."

"Yes, he did," Owen said. "So like I said, your Trident—"

"Not to worry," Isaiah said. "I've taken care of that. Without Sean, you have no Ascendance Event." Then he nodded to himself. "You've changed my mind, Owen. You're not useful at all. In fact, I think you might be a danger to me." He turned away from them. "Cole, line them up."

"Yes, sir."

The woman waved over a few more agents. Two of them took Grace by the arms, high up near her shoulders, and they half dragged, half lifted her along and placed her in the middle of the main road. They brought Natalya and Owen over the same way to stand next to her, and then Isaiah asked for a gun.

"You're going to do it yourself?" Owen asked. "I'm surprised."

"That's because you still don't understand what I am." Isaiah strode toward them, now armed with a pistol. "I am the Fenris wolf. I have come to swallow the sun, and the moon, and I do not turn away from the task before me."

"I think there's probably a name for what's wrong with you," Owen said.

Grace wondered where he found the will to be defiant. She wondered where her will had gone as she felt the seconds ticking by, like her life was a thread, and she had come to its end.

CHAPTER TWENTY-SIX

You disappoint me, Sean," Isaiah said.

"I'm sorry," Sean said. "So sorry." He wanted desperately to please Isaiah, and he had been trying, spending endless hours in the Animus, reliving the same memories again and again, searching for any detail, or hidden clue that might reveal what had happened to the dagger after Styrbjörn left it at the shrine.

"There must be something you are missing," Isaiah said. "We have searched every inch of ground within three hundred meters of that rock, and the dagger isn't there."

"It must be," Sean said. "That's the only place it could be."

"Obviously not," Isaiah said. He turned to the technicians. "Prepare the simulation. We'll run it again—"

"No," Sean said. "Please. Let me out."

"I believe I have shown you what happens when you tell me no," Isaiah said.

"I know, I know, but please. I can't."

The inside of his skull felt scraped and raw. He'd been hanging in the Animus for what seemed like days, but he couldn't be sure because so much of that time had been spent in the simulation, where time flowed differently. Even during those moments when Isaiah let him out of the simulation, Sean experienced uncontrollable Bleeding Effects that terrified him. Viking warriors appeared out of nowhere and charged at him with their axes and spears. Giants and gods strode over him, threatening to crush him under their feet. A giant wolf lunged at his throat with its mouth full of teeth. Crashing waves filled the room, and the water level rose by inches until it covered his mouth and touched his nose, soon to drown him. Each of these and many other visions felt utterly real, and Sean found it more and more difficult to maintain his grip on what was him and what was not. Clarity rolled in and out like fog.

"When you find the dagger, you will be free," Isaiah said. "I want that for you. I do. But that is not mine to give. It is yours to earn."

Sean raised his head, and Isaiah was smiling, revealing a huge, rotten tooth that worms had eaten through and blackened. Sean blinked, and Isaiah was Isaiah again.

"The simulation is ready," one of the technicians said.

"Good." Isaiah reached for the helmet. "Don't fight this, Sean. You know it goes worse for you when you fight it."

He couldn't. Sean couldn't do it again. His mind had been reduced to cobwebs, its structure long gone, barely recognizable for what it once was. He felt certain another round in the Animus would wipe him away completely like a broom.

"Please," he said, whimpering.

"Try to relax," Isaiah said, lowering the helmet. "You will—"

"Sir!" A shield-maiden burst into the room carrying a dead raven, which she threw at Sean, and he screamed as the dead bird clawed and pecked at his face.

"Is he okay?" the shield-maiden asked.

"Pay him no mind," Isaiah said. "Where have you been, Cole?"

"I went to Västerås," she said.

The bird suddenly flew out a window, and Sean recognized the shield-maiden now.

"Västerås?" Isaiah said. "Why?"

"I read an article in the newspaper about a new company selling bottled spring water. Apparently, when they dug up the area during construction for their plant, they uncovered a unique dagger. The article had a photo."

"And?" Isaiah replaced the Animus helmet on its hook, which meant that he might not put Sean back in the simulation, after all, and for that, Sean sighed with relief.

"I wanted to be sure before I brought it to your attention," she said. "So I went to the plant. Look at this." She held up her phone for Isaiah to see. "They have it on display."

"This is extraordinary. You've done well, Cole. Very well."

"Thank you, sir. There's something else. I've been using Abstergo's network to monitor CCTV feeds. Mostly airports, for security. Earlier today I believe I saw Owen, Natalya, and Grace arrive in the country in the company of an Assassin."

"Prepare two helicopters and a strike team. They might catch up with us at any moment, and I will take no chances. We leave as soon as possible."

"Yes, sir." Cole turned and left the room.

"She found the dagger?" Sean asked.

Isaiah was smiling to himself, and that lasted for a few moments. Then he looked over at Sean, a bit suddenly, as though he had just heard him. "Did you say something?"

"Cole found the dagger?" Sean asked again.

"Yes. She did."

"So I don't need to go into the simulation anymore?"

"No, Sean. You don't."

"Thank you," Sean said, his whole body sagging with relief, and he waited for Isaiah to undo the clasps and straps that held him in the Animus armature. Since it wasn't powered up yet, the framework couldn't move, locking Sean in place. But Isaiah made no move to free him.

"Can you help me?" Sean asked.

"Help you?" Isaiah said.

Sean felt his mind returning as the fog receded. The old barn where he had spent so much time the past few days had grown warm around him, coaxing the aroma of wood smoke from the timber walls, which meant it was now afternoon. He still found this an uncomfortable place for the Animus, but there hadn't been time to make a dedicated structure near the location site of the dagger, and Isaiah had utilized an existing building instead.

"Help me out?" Sean said.

Isaiah acted as though he hadn't heard Sean, and turned to leave.

"Wait," Sean said, jostling his arms against the restraints. "Please."

But Isaiah continued to ignore him as he strode toward the barn door, and Sean didn't know what to say. Everything had stopped feeling completely real a long time ago. The last time he had really been himself, without any fog or pain or fear, was back at the Aerie. But ever since leaving that place, he had entered into a strange, parallel-feeling existence, as if the real him might still be out there, but somewhere else.

As Isaiah reached for the doorknob, Sean panicked and raised his voice. "You can't just leave me here like this!"

That stopped Isaiah. "Yes, I can," he said. "That is what one does with broken things for which there is no longer any use."

His answer rendered Sean speechless for a moment, but in that moment Isaiah left the barn without saying another word, and the technicians followed silently after him, leaving Sean alone.

Even then, he struggled to decide if this was really happening or not, or if this was all part of a Bleeding Effect hallucination. Those tended to come in waves and clusters, so he inventoried everything else around him: his wheelchair; the huge bale of rusted wire in the corner; the horse stalls, one empty, one containing a small pile of rags; the pitchfork hanging on two nails on the nearest wooden post; the old-fashioned bicycle with the ridiculously huge front wheel.

It all checked out, the same as it had been for days.

So that meant this was happening. Isaiah had just abandoned him here, still hanging in the Animus, his arms outstretched like a bird. Forever. But that couldn't be. Isaiah wouldn't do that. Sean had faith in him.

The minutes passed. Quite a few of them.

He heard the whine of two helicopter rotors gearing up outside, and then the full-throttle beating of the air as they took off. He caught sight of one of them through the gaps in the barn's roof, and a little while after that, he couldn't hear them anymore.

Silence gathered around him, and the shadows drifted out of the corners of the barn like smoke. He tested the Animus restraints a few times but knew it would be impossible to free himself.

After he'd hung there for an hour or so, the longest he'd spent in the Animus without being able to move, his shoulders and elbows began to itch. Then they began to ache. After another hour had gone by, they demanded that he move them, but he couldn't. He tried, straining against the straps and buckles, but nothing brought relief. All he could do to escape the claustrophobia pinning his body down was move his fingers, which he did constantly, making his hands into tight fists and pumping them like he'd done for the nurses who drew his blood in the hospital.

Time passed.

More time.

Hours.

Hours that Isaiah had left him there, and as that time passed, his faith in Isaiah faded until he knew that no one would ever come back for him. It felt as though Sean's worst fear had come true. He had failed. He was worthless, after all.

He hung there, his head throbbing, and his body screaming and shivering, robbed of the ability to do what bodies were made to do. He had never known torture like this, and he realized he needed to distract his mind from it, or he would either burst into flames or twist himself into a knot he'd never get out of.

He tried thinking of home and his parents. He wondered what they knew, if anything, about where he was, and vaguely remembered talking to them on the phone, on more than one occasion, with Isaiah sitting right next to him.

Next, he tried singing songs to himself. Then he tried shouting and screaming songs to himself. Then he heard shouting and screaming, as if it was on a loop. He decided to recite the alphabet. He recited the alphabet again. And again. The letters took on meaning that had nothing to do with their sounds, as though he wove a spell, summoning a fog that settled over his eyes and his mind, carrying him away.

Black and swollen *draugr* clustered at his feet, listening to his magic as he hung from the goalpost. The stands were empty, and a vicious wind swept across the field, stretching the yards into miles.

But in the distance, a figure approached, drawing closer, and closer, seeming undisturbed by the wind, or by the undead warriors who would suck on his bones if they could. He came up through their midst until he stood below Sean, and Sean recognized him.

It was Styrbjörn.

"That is a strange tree you are hanging from," his ancestor said. "Why do you not come down?"

"I can't. I'm tied up."

"Break the cords, then."

"They're too strong."

"But you are strong, are you not?"

"Not as strong as you," Sean said. "Nobody calls me Sean the Strong."

"Perhaps they should," Styrbjörn said. "This tree is as nothing if you command it to be so. Break the bonds! Go on, break them!"

"I can't."

"Break them! Now!"

Sean closed his eyes and pulled against the restraints, every muscle and cord in his neck, arms, back, shoulders, and chest strained close to tearing.

"That's it!" Styrbjörn said.

Sean roared, and Styrbjörn roared with him, and the wind howled, until Sean heard a loud groaning, and a snapping, and the goalpost began to buckle and bend.

Styrbjörn nodded his approval, and without bidding farewell, he returned across the field the way he had come, and then the wind began to shear away pieces of the *draugr*, taking limbs, and teeth, and eyes, until they had been stripped away, and Sean raged alone. He pulled and pulled and pulled—

Something hit him.

Or he hit it. And when he opened his eyes, he was lying at the foot of the Animus, under the safety ring. He was free. Parts of the armature were still strapped to him, but most of it hung above him, dangling, twisted, and broken. He didn't know exactly what had happened, or how he had done that, but he was free.

After pulling off all the Animus parts still strapped to him, he crawled across the floor of the barn to his wheelchair, which he lifted himself into, and then rolled himself to the barn door. Outside, he saw the massive stone where Styrbjörn had married Thyra, and the grid of rope all around it on the ground that Isaiah had ordered to aid in the excavation. A few agents, technicians, and guards still patrolled the site, and Sean wheeled himself through the camp as quickly and quietly as he could, trying to avoid being seen.

When he reached the parking area at the edge of the camp, he smiled. Isaiah had left in the helicopters, and hadn't taken any of the vehicles.

There was Poindexter. Sean wheeled toward the SUV, and at his approach, the door opened and the ramp descended.

"Hello, Sean," the car said.

Sean heaved himself up the ramp, and then maneuvered his chair into the back of the vehicle. "Hello, Poindexter."

The ramp lifted back into place, and the door closed. "Where would you like to go?" Poindexter asked.

Sean didn't know. He just knew he needed to get away, while his head was still clear. He was in Sweden, he knew that much. Isaiah had gone to a place called Västerås to get the dagger, and he worried that Victoria might catch up to him at any moment. That probably meant that one of the others, Owen or Javier, or someone, must have had a Viking ancestor as well. Maybe Isaiah was right, and they were in Sweden, too, and if they were, it might be possible to contact them.

"Poindexter," Sean said. "Are you still connected to Abstergo?"

"No," the vehicle said. "Communications systems are off-line."

"Can you bring them back online?" Sean asked.

"Yes," Poindexter said. "One moment . . ."

Sean waited, periodically glancing out the windows to make sure no one had spotted him, hoping he could figure this out before another wave of Bleeding Effects disoriented him.

"Communications systems online," the vehicle said. "Is there someone you would like to contact?"

"Can you reach the Aerie facility?" Sean asked. "Or Victoria Bibeau?"

"Yes. Connecting to the Aerie Facility . . ."

Sean looked at the small monitor in the console in front of him, where simple icons showed a dashed line traveling between a car, a satellite, and a phone. A moment later, Sean heard a dial tone, and then a few moments after that, the screen switched to an image of Victoria. He almost couldn't believe it. She was right there, staring at him through the monitor. She was the first real thing he felt like he'd seen in weeks.

"Sean?" she said. "How—?"

"Victoria," Sean said. "Thank God. Listen, I've escaped from Isaiah, but I don't know exactly where I am, or where I need to go. I need you to tell me what to do."

"Sean?" she said again. "I—I can't believe this. Okay. Are— are you hurt? Are you okay?"

"My head's not right," he said. "Too much time in the Animus, I think. But it comes and goes."

"Okay, we'll take care of that. You're going to be okay. I—I can't believe you called me. Griffin is there in Sweden with Owen, Grace, and Natalya, but I've lost contact with them. No one is answering the phone. I see you're in a vehicle. Would you be able to go to their last location? You can't . . . can you drive?"

"I have a car that can drive," Sean said. "Just say where you want me to go. Poindexter, listen up."

Victoria read out some coordinates, and the vehicle locked them in. "Estimated arrival time in forty-seven minutes, thirteen seconds," Poindexter said, shifting into gear.

With that, Sean was on the road, leaving Isaiah's camp behind, driving through a dense forest. The sunlight flashed repeatedly through the leaves and branches, strobing his eyes, and Sean covered his face to shut it out. But when he did that, he saw another forest, this one full of poisoned thorns, and rampaging bulls among the trees, and when he opened his eyes, the animals were still there, charging down the road after him.

"Victoria?" he said. "Are you still there?"

"I am," she said. "I'm not going anywhere until I get all of you back safely."

"You're a psychiatrist, right?" he said.

She paused. "I am."

Without warning, Sean felt his voice crack. "I think I need help."

CHAPTER TWENTY-SEVEN

Owen felt as if he was going to throw up. But he kept going, because there wasn't anything else he could do, and he wasn't going to do nothing. Natalya and Grace had fallen silent, and he thought they might be in shock. He wanted to wake them up. He wanted them to fight, even if they couldn't win.

"Seriously?" he said, even though Isaiah now stood in front of him with a gun. "You just compared yourself to a Norse myth? Hey, Grace, what happens to that wolf in the end?"

Grace looked over at him, but she didn't say anything. Owen waited, suddenly feeling alone and exposed. But then she cleared her throat.

"One of Odin's sons kills him," she said. "Rips his jaws apart."

"Right." Owen gave Grace a little nod. Then he turned back to Isaiah. "So if you're really that wolf, I guess you have that to look forward to."

Isaiah didn't react, either with anger or amusement. Instead, he placed a hand on Owen's shoulder in a paternal gesture, and Owen recoiled and shrugged him off.

"Don't touch me," he said, even though he knew how ridiculous that sounded when Isaiah held the gun. But Owen did have the hidden blade. The only problem was, as soon as he used it on Isaiah, all those agents would open fire, killing Grace and Natalya, and him.

"Do you remember the simulation I showed you of your father?" Isaiah asked.

After just losing Griffin, the question about Owen's dad landed an emotional blow to his gut, and his confidence doubled over. In spite of the way he'd been mouthing off, he was barely keeping it together. He couldn't deal with Isaiah bringing up his dad. Not right now.

"Surely you've figured out that I manipulated that memory, yes?" Isaiah said.

Owen refused to say anything back. He couldn't lose control.

"Would you like to know what I saw in the real memory?" Isaiah bent down again and looked Owen in the eyes, but this time, Owen refused to look back. Whatever Isaiah was about to say, he didn't want to see it, and he didn't want to hear it. But he couldn't stop it. "There was no Assassin there," Isaiah said. "Your father—"

"Shut up!" Natalya said, the first thing she had uttered since Isaiah had captured them. "Just shut up and leave him alone."

"Why are you picking on him like that?" Grace added. "You already got the gun. Whatever you were about to say just makes you pathetic."

Isaiah took a few steps backward from the three of them, tapping the barrel of the pistol against his thigh. Owen was glad to have Grace and Natalya back, even if this was it.

But Isaiah didn't point the gun at them like Owen expected him to. Instead, he just paced in front of them for a few moments, looking down at the road.

"Back in Mongolia," he finally said, "I saw it all. What the Trident showed you, it showed me also." He pivoted to face them. "Before I killed that Assassin with the prong, I saw what she feared more than anything else. Would you like to know what it was?"

"No," Natalya said, a guttural sound of rage.

"She feared her own father," Isaiah said. "The things he did to her. She relived them all. She died with that in her mind—"

Natalya made a choking sound, and Owen looked over. She was crying softly.

"Shut your mouth," he said. "Just do what you're going to do."

But Isaiah ignored him and walked up close to Natalya, his back straight, looking down at her. She didn't look up.

"Yes," he said. "Her death is your fault, just like that nightmare in which your grandparents are murdered. There will always be something you could have done differently."

Natalya's shoulders heaved once, twice, with her crying.

"Don't listen to him," Owen said. "Natalya, it's not real." But even as he said it, he realized it was the wrong thing to say. Yanmei's death had been very real.

Isaiah turned toward Grace, and strolled down to stand

before her. "And you. Know this: you can't save your brother, no matter how hard you try. After this, I'm going to go to the Aerie to find him."

Grace lunged at him, but Isaiah stopped her by raising the pistol to her forehead. She held up her hands and backed off, but the rage-glare didn't leave her eyes.

"If you hurt him . . ." she said.

"Oh, do finish that thought," Isaiah said. Then he waited.

But Grace said nothing more, and Isaiah turned away to face Owen, who knew exactly what was coming. He tried to prepare himself for it as Isaiah came closer. He tried to tell himself it wasn't real, and it wasn't true.

"As for you, Owen," Isaiah said. "What can I tell you that you don't already know? You just won't admit it to yourself. But your father did it all. Alone. In cold blood." He leaned in closer. "I'm talking about your father's own memories of what he did, of course. He actually sat and watched that security guard bleed out. He was surprised at how quickly it was over."

Owen bit down so hard he thought his teeth would shatter. But he offered Isaiah no other reaction. No other satisfaction. Isaiah was lying about his dad. His dad was innocent.

He was innocent.

He was innocent.

He was innocent.

But even as Owen told himself that once again, for the millionth millionth time, his mantra, it felt empty. He realized he didn't know who he was trying to convince. He realized he didn't know if he believed it anymore. He wasn't sure he had ever believed it, and thought that maybe this whole time, he had been angry at the wrong people, and blamed them for his own mistakes.

His mother wasn't weak.

He was.

His grandparents weren't wrongheaded and stubborn.

He was the fool who had lied to himself, and now he didn't know what to do with the truth.

Isaiah stepped away again, backing up to look the three of them over, a surveyor measuring impact craters. Then he raised the pistol, and Owen knew this was his last moment, but Isaiah stopped partway, and Owen heard the sound of a vehicle coming.

The sound of it stirred him up.

He looked to his left as two bright headlights sliced around a bend in the road, and then a large white SUV came barreling right for them. He reached out with both hands, grabbing Natalya's arm with one, and Grace's arm with the other, and dragged them backward so the vehicle would pass between them and Isaiah. Owen had thought maybe they could use the distraction to escape into the forest on the other side of the road.

But instead, the SUV screeched and stopped right in front of them. The side door opened, and there was Sean.

"Get in!" he said.

Natalya's mouth gaped. "Sean?"

"Hurry!" he said.

Owen jumped into the front passenger seat, and Grace and Natalya climbed over Sean into the back. Then Owen saw the empty driver seat.

"What the hell?"

Gunshots exploded, rocking the SUV with their pinpoint strikes. But apparently the car was bulletproof.

"Poindexter," Sean said. "Drive. Fast."

"Yes, Sean," said a computerized voice. The SUV floored its own gas, and the car gunned it down the road, pulling Owen deeper into his seat as the forest became a blur of black and gray in the darkness.

"A self-driving car," Grace said, sitting next to Sean.

"Yeah," Sean said. Then he raised his voice slightly and said, "Victoria? Are you still there?"

"I'm here," Victoria said, her voice coming through the car's speakers.

"I have them," Sean said.

"Oh, thank God," she said. "Is everyone okay? Can I speak to Griffin?"

Sean glanced around the vehicle, as if he had only just then realized that Griffin was missing. He looked at Grace.

She raised her voice a bit and said, "Victoria, Griffin is dead."

The line went quiet. "How?"

"Isaiah's agents," Owen said. He looked down at his wrist. "They shot him."

Saying it out loud like that made it real in a way it hadn't been just moments before. The SUV speeding them away from Isaiah was also speeding them away from Griffin's body, which was back there in the woods next to the stream, where it would stay.

Owen had learned a lot from Griffin. They had disagreed on things, but he respected Griffin, and even admired him. Griffin had put his own life on the line to save Owen's several times, and he'd given up the most important thing in his life— the Brotherhood—to stop Isaiah.

"I'm sorry," Victoria said. "How are you all holding up? Are any of you hurt?"

"We're fine," Grace said. "Just . . . shaken."

"I can only imagine."

"Isaiah has the third prong," Natalya said from the far back seat.

The line went silent again. "I've chartered a jet," Victoria said. "You're heading there now, and it will bring you back here. We need to hang up so you can take the car off-line. Otherwise, Isaiah can track you. So stay together, stay safe, and I'll see you soon. All right?"

"All right," Grace said.

"There's one more thing," Owen added. "I, uh, I told Isaiah that Monroe had figured out the Ascendance Event. I told him it could stop the Trident. I think Isaiah may be heading to the Aerie. I'm sorry."

"Then we have work to do," Victoria said. "I'll see you all soon. Don't forget to go off-line. Good-bye." The call ended.

"Poindexter," Sean said.

"Yes, Sean."

"Take communications systems off-line."

The car responded to the command, and then Natalya leaned forward from the back.

"Okay," she said. "Now you can tell us what happened to you, and what you're doing in this car."

Owen twisted around in his seat to listen.

"Well," Sean said, scratching his temple, "the thing is, I don't really know. I mean, I know, but I don't know if I can trust what I think I know, you know—?" He cut himself off and shook his head. "Okay, that sounded confusing."

He was behaving differently than he had back at the Aerie. He was twitchy, and seemed disoriented.

"I spent way too much time in the Animus," he said. "Isaiah made me do the same thing, over and over. The Bleeding Effects are bad." He paused, nodding his head. "Really bad. And Isaiah used the Trident on me, which . . . made me not feel like myself."

"Oh, Sean." Natalya leaned forward and put a hand on his shoulder.

Owen tried to imagine going through something like that, but he couldn't. "How did you escape?"

"Isaiah left me in the Animus to go look for the third prong. Somehow I—I broke out. Then I got in Poindexter and called Victoria. She basically took care of everything after that."

"Well, you're safe now," Grace said. "You're back."

"I'm coming back," Sean said. "But I still don't feel right. Victoria says it'll take time, but she'll help me."

Natalya gave his shoulder another squeeze from behind, and Sean smiled. The vehicle got quiet after that, and as the surprise and excitement settled, echoes of everything Isaiah had said came back and found Owen just as vulnerable to them as he was before. It was possible Isaiah had lied again. In fact, that was probably likely. But there was a doubt in Owen's mind now that had never been there before, or at least, he'd never openly acknowledged, even to himself. But now that he knew it was there, he couldn't ignore it. More than anything now, he wanted to get back to the Aerie. It was time for Monroe to let him learn the truth, whatever that truth might be.

A short while later, the car pulled onto a private airfield. Owen scanned their surroundings, and saw no sign of Isaiah, or any Abstergo agents. Instead, three planes waited on the tarmac, two small propeller planes, and one larger jet. The pilot, a middle-aged woman with golden-blond hair, waited for them with two flight attendants at the foot of a mobile staircase.

"Is it just me," Grace said, "or are you guys suspicious of everyone now?"

"It's not just you," Owen said. One of the flight attendants wore a fitted scarlet shirt with a black tie, while the woman next to him had on a navy blue skirt with a white blouse. Either of them, or even the pilot, might have been compromised by Isaiah. That was possible, and that's all it had to be for Owen to worry.

The car pulled up near the jet, and after it stopped to let them out, the side door opened and a ramp descended.

"Good-bye, Sean," the car said.

"Good—good-bye, Poindexter," Sean said, then quickly rolled himself down the ramp, toward the plane.

The pilot and flight attendants greeted them, and then helped everyone on board. The cabin looked almost exactly like the private jets Owen had seen in the movies. Plush seats with plenty of room ran down each side, with a wide aisle between them. Owen wondered how much this flight had cost Abstergo, but decided he didn't want to know. He was just grateful Victoria had arranged it. They all found seats, and a flight attendant pushed Sean's wheelchair to the rear of the plane for storage.

The crew brought them all Abstergo-issued changes of clothes, and shortly after that, they were airborne. Not long after that, Sean was asleep. It took longer for Owen to get to that place. His mind kept jumping back and forth between his dad and Griffin. But eventually, he grew drowsy, and he let himself close his eyes.

Victoria was waiting for them when they landed, and Owen was glad to see her. Grace and Natalya seemed to feel the same way, and Victoria even gave Sean a brief hug. Owen guessed she probably felt a different kind of guilt over what had happened to him than she felt toward the others.

At the bottom of the stairs, they all climbed onto a shuttle cart that rolled them across the tarmac, and soon they arrived at a helicopter pad, where a large helicopter waited for them. That was another first for Owen, and between the noise and the tighter space, he much preferred the private jet. Not that he would ever in his life have to make that choice.

The helicopter carried them toward, and then over, the mountains, and as they came in for their landing, Owen got to see the Aerie complex from above. It sprawled over the peak, but not in an aggressive way. Instead, it seemed to have insinuated itself very subtly into the surrounding forest, its glass corridors snaking through the trees, and much of its structure in shade. Upon landing, they pushed through the strong wind stirred up by the helicopter's blades, and entered the Aerie's main atrium.

Owen was surprised at how good it felt to be back, and next to him, Sean grinned as he wheeled himself across the open space. They went to the common room and were soon joined there by Monroe, Javier, and David, but Griffin's absence kept the room somber.

Javier and David had completed the simulation of the collective unconscious, and as far as Monroe could tell, it was basically the same simulation Owen, Grace, and Natalya had experienced. The same genetic time capsule. But Owen still didn't see how it would help them or shield them from the Trident or anything else.

"It didn't protect us in Sweden," he said.

"Did Isaiah use the pieces of the Trident on you?" Victoria asked.

Owen shook his head. "Not directly. But he tapped into the fears we all experienced in Mongolia. He even knew what they were, and he used them against us. I didn't feel like I had any protection from it at all. No shield."

Monroe turned to Grace and Natalya. "What about you two?"

"Same," Natalya said.

"Pretty much," Grace said.

Monroe frowned, and rubbed the heel of his palm against the whiskers on his chin. "Let me take Sean through, and then we can work on figuring this out."

"I don't think I can recommend that," Victoria said. "Sean has been through a tremendous amount of psychic trauma."

"Then I think it's even more important that we leave the decision to Sean," Monroe said.

Sean looked back and forth between them. "If it's something everyone else has done, then I'll do it. I'm already feeling better."

"Good man. I think it's important that you experience it. All of you. It seems that's how it was designed."

"Watch him closely," Victoria said.

Monroe gave her a thumbs-up, and then he and Sean left the common room.

"As for the rest of you," Victoria said. "You have a decision to make. It is very likely Isaiah is on his way here right now. The

Ascendance Event was always an obsession of his, and now we know why. He will come for Monroe's work, because he knows it poses a threat to him. The choice you have to make is whether you wish to be here when he arrives." She set her tablet on the table and folded her hands together next to it. "Griffin's death is a reminder of what we are dealing with. I have said this to you before, but I will say it this one last time. If any of you wish to leave, you may. I won't force any of you to stay."

Owen only had to give that a moment of thought. "I think we know what we're dealing with," he said. "Isaiah made that pretty clear back in Sweden when he pointed a gun at us and told us he was going to eat the sun and the moon. Now that he has the complete Trident, he can call himself Fenris wolf or whatever he wants, because he'll be unstoppable. I'm not sure what good it would do to go anywhere else. So I'm going to stay to fight him."

"Me too," Natalya said.

Grace and David looked at each other, and they seemed to be going through that same wordless tug-of-war they'd gone through since Owen had first met them. David wanted to stay and fight, and Grace wanted to protect her little brother. David refused to leave, so Grace decided she had to stay, and that was that.

"It looks like we're all in," Javier said. "This is for Griffin."

Owen turned to his best friend. He didn't know if now was the right time, but he also didn't know if there ever would be a right time, with Isaiah on the way. He pulled up the sleeve of his hoodie, and he undid the straps on the hidden blade.

"Is that what I think it is?" Javier asked.

Owen nodded. "He wanted you to have it. He said to tell you that you've earned it."

"He did?"

Owen slid the blade off his arm and handed it to Javier. "Those were his words."

Javier took it and looked hard at it, his brow deeply creased. "But I haven't earned it. I'm not an Assassin."

"I'm just telling you what he said, and I'm giving you what he wanted you to have. I guess you have to decide what you're going to do with that."

Javier nodded and set the blade on the table.

Victoria raised an eyebrow at it. "I'm going to pretend I don't see that. Instead, we need to come up with a plan."

CHAPTER TWENTY-EIGHT

saiah will come at us with every weapon at his disposal," Victoria said. "Not just the Trident. He'll bring every Templar agent he has managed to gain control over, because he'll assume the Aerie is guarded."

"When, really, we're on our own," David said.

Victoria sighed. "Yes, precisely."

"So how do we do this?" Natalya said. "We don't really stand a chance, do we?"

"The odds are not in our favor," Victoria said.

"Then let's even the odds," Javier said. "It's like the battle in the Viking simulation."

"Right." David had begun to nod along with him. "We just need to slow them down and take as many out as we can. Like Östen and Thorvald."

"How?" Grace asked.

Javier turned to Victoria. "We already know the Aerie has some defenses. We broke in once before. So the question is, how do you think Isaiah will attack?"

"By helicopter," she said.

"Then the first thing we have to do is make sure the helicopters can't land," Javier said.

"Some of Isaiah's forces will be driving up the mountain," Victoria said.

"Then we close the roads," David said. "We force them to climb the mountain on foot."

"And we lay traps in the forest," Javier said. "We keep as many of them as we can from reaching the top."

Victoria nodded, grinning. "It worked for your ancestors, I suppose."

"So we have a lot of work to do," Javier said.

The first thing they did was open up the Aerie storage and drag every heavy box and crate they could find out onto the helicopter pad. Then they stacked them up at random intervals, covering the surface with enough debris to make it impossible for any helicopter to land there. The trees that covered the rest of the mountain left no other openings large enough, which meant that if the helicopters wanted to land, they would have to do it pretty far from the facility.

Next, they drove with Monroe down to the base of the mountain, and he used a chain saw from the Aerie's tool supply to cut down several large trees, aiming them to fall across the road. As its deafening motor bellowed, and fragrant woodchips flew, Owen worried they wouldn't be able to hear any approaching helicopters. But before long, they'd downed three modest trees, enough to keep any vehicle except for maybe a tank from climbing to the Aerie by road.

That left the traps they planned to lay in the forest.

The Aerie still had its sentry system, which had been easy enough for Griffin to bypass that Owen didn't think it would slow down Isaiah and his team much at all. But Javier had another idea, something else he'd drawn from his experience in the memories of his Viking ancestor.

The Aerie still had a supply of pest control devices, including M-44 cyanide bombs. When Owen saw one, he realized it wasn't really a bomb as much as sprinkler head. Abstergo used the devices to cut down on predatory animals like coyotes and foxes around their facility. Isaiah had likely left the M-44s behind because he didn't consider them a useful weapon. But cyanide could be very effective at slowing down or even stopping any agents trying to climb the mountain. So the last thing needed to prepare for Isaiah's arrival was to plant the M-44s at periodic intervals in the forest, ready to poison anyone who passed by with a cloud of toxic gas.

After that, they could do nothing but wait.

Sean completed his time in the collective unconscious, and it actually seemed to help him recover somewhat from the abuse Isaiah had inflicted on him. But Owen assumed it would be a long time before he was really back to normal.

With preparations complete, they all gathered in the common room to discuss additional strategies. Monroe stood at the head of the table.

"When the helicopters aren't able to land," he said, "there's a good chance any agents on board will rappel down. Those are the ones we have to worry about first. The blocked roads and the traps we set will keep the ground troops occupied."

"So what do we do about the ones dropping down on us like spiders?" Natalya asked.

"We fight," Owen said.

"Griffin had a few weapons in his gear," Javier said. "Some grenades. EMP devices and some sleep bombs. If we use them effectively, we could do some damage."

"We need to pick a central location as our fortress," Victoria said. "I would recommend the garage below ground. There are a limited number of entrances, and no windows. With our smaller numbers, I think we need to force the enemy into a bottleneck."

"Agreed," Monroe said. "Everyone get what you'll need, and let's load it down there."

Owen didn't have much, but upon scrounging around the Aerie, mostly in the tools, he did find some objects that he could use as weapons even more effectively than he'd wielded a shovel back in Sweden. Then he loaded it all into the garage with everything else they'd found, and they worked at barricading the doors.

The last thing Monroe brought down was the Animus core containing all the data for the Ascendance Event. That was what Isaiah wanted, and he would have to fight for it if he hoped to claim it. After that, they gathered together once again in the common room to wait, and this time, no one spoke. Instead, everyone listened for the sounds of helicopters.

They had done everything they could. Owen doubted it would

be enough. But he was ready to face the enemy, just the same, still unsure of how Minerva's secret package would help them.

They waited.

And waited.

And eventually, they heard exactly what they had expected to hear. The distant thrum of helicopters. Isaiah had come for them.

"Battle stations," Monroe said.

Without speaking, they all rose from the table and marched from the common room, out to the main atrium. A few minutes later, helicopters circled overhead, having apparently taken note of the compromised landing pad.

"Get ready," Victoria said.

Owen pulled out the one EMP grenade he had, and then he remembered the first time he had encountered an Abstergo helicopter, outside Ulysses Grant's home at Mount McGregor.

Owen looked up at the aircraft overhead, examined the device in his hand, and glanced at Javier. "I'm going up to the roof," he said.

Javier looked at him a moment, and then nodded, realizing what Owen meant. "Let's do it."

They took off at a run, and Monroe shouted after them, but they ignored him. They skipped the elevators and went right for the stairs, bounding up them three and four at a time, climbing each floor of the Aerie until they reached the highest balcony.

They paused at the door before charging outside. The moment they appeared, they might get shot at.

"Are you ready?" Javier asked.

Owen armed the grenade. "Count me down."

"In three, two, one—"

Javier shouldered the door open, and Owen leapt through in a roll. As he came up, he found the nearest helicopter, hoping it would be the one carrying Isaiah, and he hurled the EMP grenade at it.

The second it left his hand, he heard the first shots, and dove back inside with Javier as bullets struck the cement balcony with sparks and chips and dust.

"Did you hit it?" Javier asked.

Owen didn't know, but he turned to look, and saw the blades slowing on the helicopter he had targeted. "I hit it," he said.

The EMP pulse had knocked out the helicopter's electrical systems, and the aircraft was going down in an uncontrolled spin, forcing the other helicopter to dodge away from it.

"Nice job," Javier said.

The disabled aircraft careened overhead, its tail swinging dangerously close to the Aerie's windows, and it occurred to Owen that the helicopter could very well crash into the building, which was something he hadn't considered.

"We better get back to the others," he said.

So they raced back downstairs, flying down the steps much faster than they had climbed, and found Monroe still furious. But the rest of them had also noticed the helicopter, and they watched it through the atrium's glass ceiling as it came closer, and closer, until it became clear how it would finally lose its tug-of-war with the ground.

"Run!" Victoria shouted.

They all sprinted toward her, and toward the garage, where they'd planned to hole up, just as the ceiling above them exploded in a glittering shower of glass, and the building shrieked from torn girders. Then an entire helicopter dove right into the atrium, nose first, its blades tearing up the building as it fell.

The others managed to get out of the way before it made an impact with the floor of the atrium, but they were on the other side of it from Owen and Javier.

The helicopter's blades struck the floor, causing an explosion of tile and subflooring, and a huge piece of one blade snapped off and went flying, slicing the air above Owen's head. He and Javier dove, and then dove again to get out of the way as the body of the helicopter smashed into the ground and rolled through the glass walls of the conference room, the lobby, and lodged itself in the front doors.

"Go!" Javier shouted.

He pushed Owen, and the two of them ran to join the others just as the first ropes from the remaining helicopter uncoiled through the now-opened ceiling. A moment later, agents descended through the breach, guns already firing.

Owen and Javier reached the rest of their team as they fled from the atrium, racing down the corridors until they reached the glass tunnel that would take them partway down the side of the mountain to the entrance of the garage.

"That was incredibly stupid!" Monroe shouted.

"But I took out a helicopter!" Owen yelled.

"You took out most of the building!" he said. "And you almost took us with it!"

Inside the tunnel, Owen had a better glimpse of the forest, and through the glass he could faintly hear shouting and gunfire from the Aerie's sentries. Whether the M-44s were doing their job, he had no idea, but he wasn't about to go out in that mess to find out.

A few moments later, they reached the garage, and they took up their positions guarding the doors in groups with the few weapons they had. Owen had one more EMP, and Javier had a sleep grenade. The others had their own weapons, also taken from Griffin's equipment.

"Get ready!" Victoria shouted.

Owen listened to the distant sound of what had to be the first helicopter exploding. Any moment now, the first agents would find them. His body had gone numb with the adrenaline of it all, but he kept himself alert and ready.

"If they come to your door, you know what to do," Monroe said, Sean in his wheelchair nearby, Natalya standing at his side.

Several moments later, he heard the sound of footsteps approaching, and voices over radio sets. He and Javier prepared themselves, and when the enemy came into view wearing Abstergo's enhanced paramilitary gear, they both attacked. Owen threw his last EMP grenade, knocking out the systems in their helmets for communication and visual enhancement.

Then he and Javier threw themselves into hand-to-hand combat. Owen drew on every experience, every Bleeding Effect, and laid into his enemies with his fists, his feet, and a length of a steel bar he had found among the tools, laying out as many of them as he could before retreating back through the hallway into the garage.

Across the large, open room, Monroe and Natalya had taken on a group of agents, and Owen wanted to go help them, but that would leave his door unguarded. A few seconds later, he was glad he hadn't given in to that temptation, because another wave of Templars came at him and Javier.

Without an EMP grenade, the only tool they had was Javier's

sleep grenade, which he tossed into the hallway. But its effects weren't immediate enough, and some of the agents made it through. Owen knew they weren't going to be able to hold out as long as they would need to.

Another group of agents ripped through the door Victoria, David, and Grace had been guarding, and now Owen went into defense, using every twist and dodge to try and disarm the agents of their guns.

"Fall back to me!" Monroe shouted.

This battle had turned to a losing one faster than Owen had expected. He and Javier first joined up with Victoria, David, and Grace. Victoria held her own well against her former allies, and David and Grace had both clearly gained their own Bleeding Effects from their simulations.

But it was hopeless.

Even if they beat them all, Isaiah hadn't even appeared yet.

And with that thought, as if summoned, Isaiah stalked into the room, wielding the complete Trident.

"Finish them!" he shouted.

"No!" Sean screamed, loud enough that Isaiah could hear. "I want you! I challenge you, Isaiah!"

"Halt!" Isaiah bellowed, and his agents ceased all their aggression and attacks within seconds. "After all your failures, you would challenge me, Sean?"

"I do challenge you!" Sean replied, wheeling himself forward.

"Do you still think you're Styrbjörn?" Isaiah asked.

"No," Sean said. "But I don't need to be to stop you. And I know that's what you're afraid of. That's why you're here."

Isaiah scoffed. He wore a sleek, white armored suit, and the Trident of Eden bore all three of its prongs in wicked formation atop a long metal staff. Owen now saw it not only as a source of power, but as a weapon capable of inflicting injury and death.

"The earth's renewal begins now," Isaiah said. "It begins with your deaths. You have brought this on yourselves."

"Actually," Owen said, taking a step toward him to stand beside Sean. "It begins with—"

Isaiah slammed the base of the Trident into the floor, as if planting it there. It cracked the cement floor beneath it, and the metal sang, filling the garage.

Then *fear*.

Owen closed his eyes, holding his head against the storm. He had been here before. He had seen this before. The worst of everything ever said about his father all made true. He knew the others now experienced their own versions of this hell. But for Owen, it had become something else since the last time he'd seen it. Monroe had always questioned whether he was ready to see his father's memories, and Owen hadn't ever understood what he meant.

But now he did.

Before, Owen had never considered the possibility that his father's memories would reveal anything other than his innocence. But Monroe was able to ask what would happen if the memories showed something different. Something Owen wasn't prepared to see. To be ready in the way Monroe asked, Owen had to accept that his greatest fear might be confirmed. He had to accept that his father might be a murderer. He had to accept that his grandparents were right.

He had to *accept* it.

That was the true opposite of fear. It wasn't courage, or bravery. He could be brave and afraid at the same time. But if he stopped fighting his fear, and accepted it, the fear lost its power. The way Natalya had accepted that the Serpent would eat her.

Was that what Minerva had given them? Not an immunity, but a way to deal with the effects of the Trident?

Owen looked directly at the vision the Piece of Eden showed him.

And he accepted that it might be true.

He accepted that he didn't know what his dad had done, and that he might never know, and maybe he didn't even need to know. He could move on, and live his own life.

With that, the vision fled, taking the fear, and Owen opened his eyes.

The others staggered under the weight of their visions, and Owen called out to them.

"You need to accept your fear!" he shouted. "Remember the Serpent, and step into its mouth!"

One by one, his friends opened their eyes as they escaped their own terrors, standing up straighter, blinking away tears, finally understanding the shield the ancient Minerva had given them.

"Listen up!" Javier said. "We charge him at once. Use everything you have. Every Bleeding Effect and every skill."

"No!" Isaiah shouted, and he struck the floor again.

This time, Owen felt his mind bombarded by wave after wave of awe, emanating from Isaiah.

"I offer you a better world!" Isaiah said. "Don't you understand? Don't you see? The earth is weak and diseased, kept alive for too long. It must be allowed to die to be reborn. I offer you this. The new earth will be your inheritance, if you but join me!"

Isaiah burned with radiance, drawing Owen toward him, and Owen wanted to serve that light. He wanted only to be near it, to feel its warmth. But he forced himself to close his eyes and shut out that brightness. He returned to their next stop on the Path, the Wanderer they had met, and the Dog who had traveled with him in complete devotion. And when Owen had to find a new companion for that devotion, he did not choose the rich man in his tower, or the shepherd with his flocks. He chose another Wanderer and seeker of truth.

Isaiah deserved no devotion, because his light was a lie.

Owen opened his eyes, and the glow around Isaiah tarnished and went cold. Then Owen took another step toward him. The others did as well, finding their own answers in Minerva's gift.

Isaiah's face now showed his rage, and he struck the ground a third time with the Trident. The cold flood that now poured over Owen's mind was a tide of despair, pushing him toward an abyss that beckoned him to embrace its oblivion.

Over its siren call, he heard Isaiah saying, "None of you can see what I see. None of you understand what I understand. But I can lead you from this fallen earth. I can carry you into a world of hope and rebirth."

Owen felt the abyss pulling on his mind, and there he was, back on the mountain, the wind clawing at his face, the Summit impossibly distant. On one path, Isaiah offered him a rope to hold on to. The promise of safety. But on the other path, Owen would instead rely on himself. No rope. Just his own strength. His own hands. His own will.

He turned away from the abyss, and he turned away from the rope that Isaiah offered. He would instead place hope and faith in himself.

With that, the torrent of despair washed away, and when Owen opened his eyes a third time, he stood only a few yards from Isaiah. The others had almost reached him as well, as they climbed their own mountains, but Owen decided not to wait.

He charged, letting his Assassin ancestors rise up through him. Varius, and Zhi, two different warriors from different times and different parts of the world. Both of them working in the darkness to serve the light. But Isaiah was prepared, and even though the Trident no longer had any power over Owen's mind, its deadly edges now sought his flesh.

Isaiah leapt away, spinning the Trident around his body, making it difficult for Owen to get close. But gradually the others joined him. Javier, and David, Natalya, and Grace.

The rage Owen had seen on Isaiah's face had become fear, and that made Owen laugh. Now Isaiah finally understood the Ascendance Event.

Isaiah flipped the Trident around and leapt at Owen, but the others joined in the battle and defended him, without weapons, instead fighting hand-to-hand. Isaiah proved to be a more formidable fighter than Owen would have expected. He spun and leapt and thrust and slashed, but Owen and the others countered his every move, and he began to slow.

Monroe and Victoria stood by, waiting and watching, as did Isaiah's agents, as if they understood that the challenge had to play out.

But the end had almost come. The battle was almost over. Owen and the others pressed Isaiah, throwing punches and kicks, until they finally began to land. Isaiah grunted, and flinched, and staggered as they launched assault after assault, until they disarmed him at last and flung the Trident away.

Isaiah watched it abandon him, and as he reached for it, Javier was there with Griffin's hidden blade.

One thrust, and it was over.

Isaiah slumped to the ground, and no one moved or said a word for a long time. They all stood around his body, breathing heavily.

Gradually, the hold he had over the Templar agents seemed to fade, and they looked at one another in confusion. Victoria ordered them all from the garage, while they were still dazed and off-balance, and then hurried toward the Trident.

But Natalya beat her to it.

She picked up the weapon, and gripped it tightly, with purpose.

"Natalya," Victoria said. "Please. Give me the Trident."

"No," Natalya said, her voice both calm and strong.

"Natalya," Victoria said. "I will not ask again. Give me the—"

"You know as well as I do you can't take it from her," Monroe said. "Though it would be interesting to see you try."

Victoria raised her voice. "You have no stake in this, Monroe. You walked away from the Order. From everything. But I didn't. I am still committed to making this world what it ought to be."

"Like Isaiah?" Natalya said. "Where does it end, Victoria?" She looked down at the weapon in her hands, and then she looked at Owen. "Minerva wanted us to do something else. Something only the six of us can do." She held out the Trident, and they all came together to grasp it.

Upon touching it, Owen felt an exhilarating surge of power that rippled the muscles in his arms and reached his heart, which began to race. But that power seemed to summon something else from deep inside him. He felt a presence ascending within his mind as though he were in the Animus, a consciousness so unknowable and vast he couldn't find the edges of it, or even make sense of it.

Then he heard Minerva's voice tolling loudly. **THE TIME HAS COME. YOU HAVE ALL BROUGHT ME HERE, AND NOW I WILL DO WHAT I SHOULD HAVE DONE EONS AGO.**

The power within Owen moved back out from his chest, down his arms, and into the Trident. Its staff and blades began to vibrate, mildly at first, but soon grew stronger, and stronger, until Owen didn't think he could hold on to it anymore. He looked at the others, and they were all gritting their teeth, holding fast, the Trident almost a blur in their hands, until suddenly it felt as though something gave way inside it. A fault line finally cracked, releasing all the stored-up power and energy it contained, which radiated outward in a shock wave. In its wake, the Trident had been rendered nothing more than a simple piece of metal.

Exhausted, Owen let go. The others did, too, and the Trident clattered to the ground.

"What have you done?" Victoria asked.

Natalya turned toward her. "We saved the world," she said.

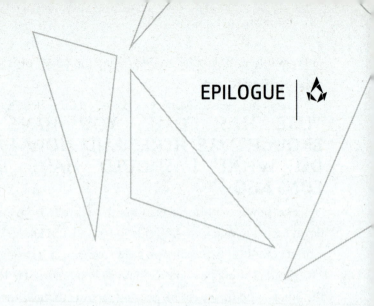

EPILOGUE

The town car turned onto Grace and David's street, and she felt a strange uneasiness about being home. In some ways, it was the same place it had always been, but in other ways it felt completely different. She knew things now that almost no one else knew. She had done things no one in her neighborhood had done. Victoria had told them all it would probably take some time to adjust to this new normal, but they would, eventually. She had also promised that the Templars would leave them in peace, so long as they did nothing to draw the Templars' attention. That promise felt a bit hollow to Grace, or even empty. It meant they were probably being watched. But she had no intention of entering the world of the Order and the Brotherhood ever again, so she told herself she had nothing to worry about.

The car pulled up in front of their house, and, next to her, David let out a sigh.

"Here we are," he said.

"Here we are," Grace said.

"I'm glad Victoria sent us in the car," he said. "Dad would have flipped out when he saw the crashed helicopter in the middle of the Aerie."

"Speaking of Dad," Grace said, "we agreed we're not telling him or Mom anything, right?"

"Right."

Grace looked hard at him.

"What?" he said. "I'm not going to tell them anything."

"Good," she said.

"You don't have to worry about me anymore," David said.

"I know I don't," she said. "But that doesn't mean that I won't. You're going to do what you're going to do, and I've accepted that. But that doesn't mean I won't black your eye if you step out of line."

"You won't always be there, Grace. That's what I've accepted. And that's okay."

She gave him a little shove. "Hop on out. Let's go inside and let them know we're here."

"Okay."

He opened the car door, and they got out and walked up to their porch together. Their mom opened the door for them before they'd hit the top step, and Grace could smell her banana bread baking inside.

Natalya opened the door to her grandparents' apartment and walked inside. She didn't smell anything cooking on the stove or in the oven, but that was okay, because the only thing she wanted was a hug, and when her grandmother met her at the door, Natalya reached her arms around her and squeezed a little too tightly. But her grandmother was a strong woman, and she could take it.

"It is good to see you, Natalya," she said. "So good to see you. We've missed you coming around. Are you home from that school now?"

"I am," Natalya said. "Home for good."

"You did well at this school?"

Natalya smiled. "I did."

"Then why did they send you home?"

"They sent everyone home," Natalya said. "They ended that program."

"That's too bad."

They walked into the living room, where her grandfather sat in his recliner reading the newspaper, his reading glasses sitting so low on the tip of his nose, Natalya wondered how they stayed on.

"Natalya!" he said, folding the newspaper to set it aside.

She walked over to him and leaned into a hug. "Hello, *dedulya*."

"What is wrong with this school that they send you home?" he asked.

"Nothing," she said. "It was only a temporary program. It's over now."

"Ah," he said, looking at her over the rim of his glasses. "Well, you're too good for them. You hear me? Don't you worry about it."

Natalya smiled. "I won't," she said, and she put her arm around her grandmother. "There are a lot of things I'm trying not to worry about anymore."

Owen had the car drop him off a couple of blocks away from his grandparents' house. He wanted a little extra time to think about what he would say when he walked in. They thought he had run away, and there would be lots of questions about that. There would be lots of doubt and suspicion at first, and Owen understood why. He accepted that.

His grandpa would probably want to take him for a drive to get ice cream, to see if Owen would tell him something he wouldn't tell his mom or his grandma. His mom would come into his room that night for the same reason. But Owen wouldn't tell them anything beyond what he had already decided, which was to be honest.

He had gone looking for information about his dad.

They would want to know where, and if he had found anything.

He would tell them he had been looking in the wrong place, and that he hadn't found anything. Monroe had made good on his promise, and offered Owen the simulation of his father's memories, but in the end, Owen had decided not to. If he needed so badly to know the answer to those questions, then the answers would have too much power over him, no matter what the answers were. Owen had decided he didn't want that.

He wanted to be okay not knowing. He wanted to accept that his father might have done those things Isaiah had talked about. But Owen also wanted to hope that his father hadn't. That was a strange place to be, sitting right in the middle, without answers. But it was the best place to be for Owen to move forward. Like his dad would have wanted him to.

Eventually, his slow walk brought him to his grandparents' door, and he tried the knob. It was locked. So he knocked on the door, and he took a deep breath.

He was home.

Javier sat in his bedroom with the door locked. Alone. Finally.

It had taken hours for his mom to calm down, but she had, and she accepted that he didn't want to talk about where he'd been for now. She wasn't going to let it go, and he knew that, but at least she allowed him some privacy for the moment. His brother wasn't going to let it go, either. His dad would just let his mom and brother do the work of hounding him, but he would want to know, too.

Mostly, they were all just glad to have him home safely. They worried about him more than they needed to, but Javier understood why. There were still places where it wasn't safe to be himself, openly. But that was getting better, too.

He sat on his bed and looked at two things. The first was the ceramic hidden blade that Griffin had given to him. The second was a phone number.

He hadn't asked Monroe for it. But Monroe had given it to him, and told him not to tell Victoria under any circumstances. Javier was to simply hold on to that number and use it when he knew what he wanted to do. Who he wanted to be.

He looked at the Assassin gauntlet for another moment, and then tucked it into a shoebox under his bed. Then he memorized the phone number, and tore up the piece of paper. Javier had always had the best memory of anyone he knew. Now that he had that number saved in his head, he'd never lose it. He didn't know exactly who would answer, but he had a pretty good idea. He could call it if he decided to.

But deep inside, he knew it wasn't actually a question of if.

It was when.

Sean sat in the waiting room, flipping through an uninteresting magazine he'd picked up without thinking about it. He and the receptionist had already finished their normal exchange. He'd told her school was going well. That he was feeling better. Then she had gone back to answering phones, and Sean had wheeled over to an open space between two of the chairs.

Before he reached the last advertising pages of the magazine, the door opened, and Victoria called his name.

"Good to see you," she said.

He let the magazine fall with a slap onto the chair next to him. "Good to see you, too."

She held the door open while he wheeled through, and then she led the way through the downtown Abstergo offices to another door with her name on it. She opened it, and Sean wheeled inside.

Victoria sat down in a white leather armchair, crossed her legs, and held her knee with interlaced fingers. "Any visual hallucinations this week?"

Sean wheeled his chair over to face her, parking himself about six feet away. "No."

"What about auditory?"

"I still hear some things. When I'm falling asleep. But I can't really make it out like I used to."

"That likely means they're fading, too."

"I hope so."

She pulled up her tablet and tapped at it a few times. "Your neurovitals have certainly improved. They've almost returned to normal parameters. You've been doing the meditation exercises?"

"Yup. Except when I forget."

She frowned, but it felt more like a smile. "And how often does that happen?"

"Oh. Just weekdays and weekends."

"Sean. You know how important they are."

"I know." Meditation was supposed to promote "mindfulness" and connect Sean to his body, but he didn't feel as though he needed to do that three times a day for twenty minutes. He was feeling better.

"As soon as you've fully recovered," Victoria said, "we can get back to the work Abstergo started on your prosthetics. You're almost there."

"I know."

She looked at him, tapping her lip with her stylus, and then put her tablet aside. "Do you not want a prosthetic that might help you to walk?"

"No, I do," he said. It would be great if he could walk again. How could it not be? That would certainly be more convenient than his wheelchair. There were still a lot of places that weren't accessible to him, like some stores and restaurants that weren't up to code.

"Then what is it?" Victoria asked.

"I'm . . ." Sean shrugged. "I'm just not in a hurry, I guess."

Victoria nodded. "Well. I'll take that as a good sign of your recovery. You'll be back to your old self soon."

"No," Sean said. "I'm going to be better."

Monroe had disappeared once before, and he could do so again. The Ascendance Event had shown him that his work wasn't done, but he wouldn't be able to pursue that work in cooperation with the Templars or the Assassins. They would never be able to see past their ideologies. He would have to find his way alone, just as he'd been doing when he found Owen and the others.

The headlights of the sleek Abstergo car he'd stolen reached ahead of him as he drove along the dark highway. His Animus core and what was left of the Trident sat in the back seat, also stolen. Natalya had insisted all the power had gone out of the Piece of Eden, but Monroe wasn't convinced the relic had given up all its secrets, and he planned to study it as soon as he found somewhere safe enough to proceed.

He also suspected that he wasn't quite finished yet with the teens. As with the Trident, their DNA held profound secrets that Monroe had only begun to unravel.

But for now, they deserved a long rest.

And, as always, their freedom.

YOUR FUTURE LIES IN THE PAST— EXPERIENCE THE EPIC ADVENTURE FROM THE BEGINNING!

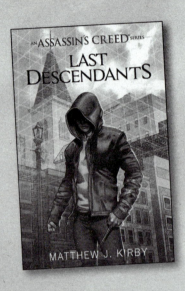

"THE FASCINATING, FREE-WHEELING BLEND OF SCIENCE, HISTORY, AND ACTION-ADVENTURE WILL MAKE THIS A SURE HIT, EVEN FOR THOSE WHO HAVEN'T PLAYED THE VIDEO GAMES."
—*KIRKUS REVIEWS*

"THE TARGET AUDIENCE WILL REJOICE THAT THERE IS FINALLY SOMETHING FOR THEM IN THIS THOUGHT-PROVOKING HISTORICAL FICTION SERIES."
—*SCHOOL LIBRARY JOURNAL*

UBISOFT®

© 2016 Ubisoft Entertainment. All Rights Reserved. Assassin's Creed, Ubisoft, and the Ubisoft logo are trademarks of Ubisoft Entertainment in the U.S. and/ or other countries.

scholastic.com

SCHOLASTIC and associated logos are trademarks and/or registered trademarks of Scholastic Inc.

ACLASTDESC

P9-DBY-706

Duck Duck Wally

···························

Gabe Rotter

Simon & Schuster Paperbacks

New York
London
Toronto
Sydney

Simon & Schuster Paperbacks
A Division of Simon & Schuster, Inc.
1230 Avenue of the Americas
New York, NY 10020

This book is a work of fiction. Names, characters,
places, and incidents either are products of the
author's imagination or are used fictiously. Any
resemblance to actual events or locales or persons,
living or dead, is entirely coincidental.

Copyright © 2007 by Gabe Rotter

All rights reserved, including the right to reproduce
this book or portions thereof in any form whatsoever. For information
address Simon & Schuster Paperbacks Subsidiary Rights Department,
1230 Avenue of the Americas, New York, NY 10020

First Simon & Schuster trade paperback edition August 2008

SIMON & SCHUSTER PAPERBACKS and colophon are registered trademarks of Simon & Schuster, Inc.

For information about special discounts for bulk purchases,
please contact Simon & Schuster Special Sales at
1-800-456-6798 or business@simonandschuster.com

Book design by Ellen R. Sasahara

Manufactured in the United States of America

1   3   5   7   9   10   8   6   4   2

The Library of Congress has cataloged the hardcover as follows:

Rotter, Gabe.
Duck duck wally : a novel / Gabe Rotter.
p. cm.
1. Ghostwriters—Fiction. 2. Hip-hop—Fiction.
3. Los Angeles (Calif.)—Fiction. I. Title.
PS3618.O869D83 2007
813'.6—dc22   2006037101

ISBN-13: 978-1-4165-3786-1
ISBN-10:   1-4165-3786-4
ISBN-13: 978-1-4165-3787-8 (pbk)
ISBN-10:   1-4165-3787-2 (pbk)

I dedicate this book to my parents,
for making *all* things possible.

To my sisters,
for being the best friends I could ever imagine.

And, of course, to Bree, my muse,
for being *nothing* like the women in this book.

I love you all.

Duck Duck Wally

DON'T JOIN THE MAFIA, BOBBY
By Wally Moscowitz

Bobby Russo's daddy drives a fancy car,
It's a big yellow Cadillac—he looks like a movie star!

With his big gold chains, and his slicked-back hair,
Bobby's daddy is cool! Bobby's daddy's got flare!

But big Tony Russo is not what he seems.
His car's trunk makes strange noises,
It bangs, shakes, and screams!

Sometimes he comes home with dirt under his nails,
And when Bobby asks why he spins wild tales
About gardens and flowers and planting some trees.
But Bobby remembers that plants make Daddy sneeze.

So what's Tony doing on all those late nights,
When Bobby can't sleep, so he turns on his lights;
'Cuz he hears scary noises coming from Dad's "special room,"
They go "ba da bing!"
They go "ba da boom!"

And Daddy's best buddies kinda scare Bobby, too.
They have silly names:
Johnny V, Sammy Blue.

They smack Bobby's back when they're saying hello,
And it stings really bad, but he won't let them know.
'Cuz Daddy tells Bobby that he's gotta be tough,
If he wants to be like Daddy, and buy Mommy nice stuff.

But Daddy gets mad, and breaks Mommy's dishes,
And says weird things about sleepin' with fishes.
And he storms from the house, and stays gone till next day,
But then he comes back, and Mom begs him to stay.

So Bobby starts to wonder just what's Daddy's job?
And he hears people whisper, "Tony Russo . . . the Mob."
Bobby finally asked Mommy, "Mom, what does 'mob' mean?"
Then under her breath, she mumbled something obscene.

She said, "they're dangerous people, who make others sad!
Don't join the Mafia, Bobby, it's bad, bad, bad, <u>bad</u>!"

—From *The Adult Children's Books Collection*

chizapter 1

I'm concerned that you might not like me.

Really concerned. And nervous, really. Really nervous and concerned. I'm frumpy, you know? I'm just like this frumpy, kinda chubby little boring man. Why would you have any interest in my story? It's not riveting—I'll tell you that right now. This isn't beautiful, elegant prose. Oprah would *not* dig me. I mean, I'm not a geisha or a boy wizard or anything. I'm not a renowned symbologist or, say, floating on a raft in the middle of the ocean with a tiger. I'm definitely not a thirtysomething single chick living in the city and having sex and buying shoes and being totally fucking cooler than you'll ever be.

I'm just this frumpy putz with a story to tell.

I'm not quite sure how to begin, exactly. I mean, because, how did it begin? I figure I should start off with some sort of a bang. Bangs are good—particularly when you start off with them. I could start by telling you that early in the day when my downfall began, I sat on the beach in Santa Monica and I was cold. Fine, it's not quite the throat-grabbing *whomp* that you might have been hoping for, but, hey, it is what it is. So anyway, I sat on the beach, and IT EXPLODED! The whole beach! *Kaboom!* Up in glorious, slow-motion flames for no apparent reason. There's your bang, okay? I hope it was exhilarating.

So, after the whole beach *blew up* and stuff, and it was all crazy and inexplicable and wild, the excitement subsided and I just sat there. And I was cold. This went on for many minutes. It was December, I should have told you, when it actually gets quite chilly in Los Angeles. I mean, it's not Antarctica or New Jersey or anything, but still, it was too cold to be on the beach. Why was I there? I don't know. I had nowhere else to be (par for the crappy course of my life) and I felt like the beach. The beach gets my brain working. Even if every other part of my body under my brain's jurisdiction is freezing its individual figurative ass off.

So I sat there that morning, pensive, alone, and cold, bundled up in a cable-knit sweater, wooly jacket, and jeans. With no concern for the wintry weather, a harried gang of seagulls dutifully provided their obligatory *caw-caw-caw*ing. The waves continued to melt ashore indifferently, despite the chill and the resulting lack of a significant audience. The salty air smelled nice, occasionally stinging my face with wind-thrown specks even smaller and somehow angrier than droplets. I stared at the choppy green-ish water, and in one smart, unbroken thought, thought: *The Pacific Ocean—a vast, pitiless, bewitching monster, full of sharks and urchins and other assorted creatures both beautiful and revolting—* And then, with a quick glance at the city behind me, I finished: *just like Los Angeles.*

And then, in my best Cali patois, I was all, *Dude! Awesome analogy, brah!* And then I went home because my ass was numb on the cold sand, my cheeks (both sets) were red, and I felt like a winner having escaped a seemingly inevitable shit-bombing from the noisy, swooping birds.

But I didn't leave my analogizing skills on the beach that day to be washed away by the icy waves like a plastic bucket torn from the hands of an industrious little tot in the throes of sand castle–building delight. (See?!) No. I took them home with me and began to build my own little sand—no—*analogy* castle (God, I'm good). After the first wonderful and profoundly poetic correlation I'd made 'twixt city and sea, I felt a sudden deep and desperate desire to craftily and succinctly sum up my life. I needed to paint a tidy picture for myself that might help me better understand the crazy game in which I was so hopelessly entangled. And it got me thinking about games. And life. Games. Life. Games . . .

And I finally realized: My life is a great big endless game of Duck Duck Goose. I wait anxiously for the metaphorical tap on the head, and when it comes, I spring into action! I chase and chase and chase with all of my might, but I never seem to grasp that quick little bastard called Success. Then it's back to wandering in frustrating circles, agonizing over what to choose next. It's a vicious, never-ending cycle. A game that I just can't win.

No, no, no. That's not it.

Maybe it's: My life is a great big endless game of Duck Duck Goose. I wait anxiously for the metaphorical tap on the head, but it never comes. Everyone around me gets chosen, and they take off running! Look at 'em go! But there I am. Always sitting there. A duck. A sitting duck. Never to be picked. Never the goose.

Okay, fine. I'm not very good at analogies. The Pacific Ocean thing was a fluke.

Let's start over. I shouldn't have begun with the beach thing. Didn't make sense. You don't even know who I am, for Christ's sake, why would you care that I was on the beach making up questionable analogies? Okay. Square one: My name is Wally. Wally Moscowitz. I am thirty-one years old. I am five-foot-six when wearing tall shoes. My hair has just recently decided to start falling out and, I guess, unlike myself, when my hair makes a decision it actually follows through with it. I am a tad bit overweight, always have been. I love bacon cheeseburgers with the same unbridled passion that most people reserve for their first love. That is, I think about them constantly, and if I'm away from them for too long, I'm likely to grow withdrawn and despondent. It's a sad commentary when one of the very first things you mention in describing yourself is a love affair with cheeseburgers. But I truly cherish them. And bacon. My old, dear friend bacon—been there for me since day one. *God,* how I adore him so. If I had any *real* friends, I'd tell them that if I were ever to lapse into unconsciousness, they should spare me the mouth-to-mouth resuscitation. Instead, they should quickly cook up some bacon in my vicinity so that the magical scent could tempt my feeble nostrils, and I would surely stir. I can't believe I've wasted this much time talking about bacon. Oh, what am I saying? Any time with bacon is time well spent. But let's move on.

My clothes are a bit baggy, but in a hip, shlumpy-cool sort of way. I try to buy all of my T-shirts at thrift stores. I like the really old (circa 1986, ideally), worn ones that assert delightful slogans like "Teachers are Terrific!" or "Jogging for Jesus!" I wear glasses. (Cool ones. Seriously. They are.) I look intelligent, and I am. That came out wrong. I'm not conceited. Just the opposite—I'm painfully insecure. In fact, just about the *only* thing I'm completely secure about is my insecurity.

I am simply trying to give you the facts: I have chubby fingers. I don't do well on boats. I'm not built for speed or quickness. I rarely floss. Okay, I *never* floss. But if I did, I imagine that I'd use one of those cool sword-like toothpicks with the little bow-shaped floss device on the end rather than traditional, old-school, run-of-the-mill dental floss. I'm just that kind of guy. I'm gadgety.

I live in Los Angeles, but you would never know that from looking at me. I spend too much time indoors. I'm not happy and/or healthy looking. I'm not well tanned or physically fit. My skin usually takes the greenish pallor of a poorly peeled cucumber; a very charming shade for your living room walls or your Ikea couch, but not so much for your face.

I love words. I try to use big ones whenever possible, though, admittedly, I'm not very good at recalling them when they're apropos. (Or am I?) I keep a dictionary next to my bed and I learn a new word each day. My father instilled that habit early on in my life. Then when I was eleven he taught me the meaning of the word "ironic" when he *died* in our *living* room. He was a very committed teacher.

You probably know someone like me. I have an uncanny, perhaps unhealthy, arsenal of movie quotes in my head. I love music. I read books sometimes, usually when the movie version is about to come out, so I can say (with an air of pretension), "The book was *so* much better." I secretly prefer *Us Weekly* or *People* to *Sports Illustrated*. I suck at using chopsticks. I'd rather die than shit in a public bathroom. I have a girlfriend named Sue who loves me much less than I love her. I am very good at Trivial Pursuit, only partly because I've memorized most of the cards. I'm the guy you'd call as your phone-a-friend if you were on *Who Wants To Be A Millionaire,* but I'd never be on it myself, because, despite my cool clothes and glasses, I'm still a big loser and I'd probably humiliate myself somehow. Like, my first question would be: "It's the official nickname for New York City. Is it A) The Island City, B) The Biggest Little City, C) The Big Apple, or D) Bagel Town, USA?" And I'd panic and think, *The* official *name? It must be a trick question! Everyone calls it the Big Apple, but that's not necessarily the* official *nickname. That would be too easy. The Biggest Little City could be right. Hmmmm. Or . . . New Yorkers* do *love bagels . . . Shit!* "I'll go with A) The Island City please, Regis? I mean Meredith! Shit! I mean shoot! Fuck! Shucks!" And then they'd just cut to black 'cuz I'm such a loser-slash-idiot.

I apologize if my language offends you. I'm not eloquent or pretentious. I mean, I'm not a moron or anything, but let's face it, I'm no Ernest Hemingway or J. D. Salinger or Danielle Steele. Nor do I profess to be. Even though I sometimes use words like "nor" and "profess." If you can't get through my colloquial style, then I suggest you put this down now and forget about it. If, however, you don't know what "colloquial" means, then you're probably in the right place.

You might be wondering what I do for a living. My "career." I'll get to that. First I'd like to tell you what led to the end of said career. My bladder did me in. You see, my downfall began in a public bathroom. Now, I don't intend to imply that I was an important person in any way, as the word "downfall" might suggest. I didn't have very far to fall, but still I fell. Down. So, while perhaps a grandiose choice of words, still quite apropos (I suppose at this point I should admit to you that "apropos" was the word I learned today from the dictionary by the bed).

This story is true. It transpired over an absolute whirlwind few days of my life. I'll warn you one more time: This isn't high art. It probably won't keep you on the edge of your seat. There's no surprise twist, no gratifying denouement. It wasn't all a dream. This isn't Hollywood. Well, yeah, technically it *does* happen to take place in Hollywood, but what I mean is, it's not some silly, bullshit Hollywood ending designed to make your girlfriend all teary-eyed and grabby. This is *life—my* life—and although it is crazy and maybe even unbelievable, it's the truth. No cherry on top. But why am I talking about the ending? First, the beginning.

....

I was shocked when I entered the cavernous linoleum- and ceramic-tiled lavatory. This may have been the record for most urinals I'd ever seen in a public bathroom. Okay, maybe "shocked" is too strong a word. Anyway, I called the *Guinness Book of World Records* immediately and told them to get their people down there ASAP. There must have been eighty of them; porcelain soldiers lined up, stoic, unflinching. Ready for battle with a never-ending stream of pricks whose only mission is to piss all over them. It's a thankless war that they just can't win.

The restroom was located in a large, shiny stadium in downtown Los Angeles. Quite a facility, fairly new and top-of-the-line everything. But the bathroom still stunk like piss. Go figure. It reminded me of grade school—that noxious stench of cheap powdered cleanser fighting the eternal losing struggle against the mighty, indefatigable army force of urine, under the harsh glow of fluorescent lights.

Thankful that I was at least alone in this vast, stinky cavern, I made my way past the first seventy-nine urinals to the very last one in line, just in case somebody else happened to enter. I despise bathroom interaction of any sort. I am there strictly for business and I prefer to keep my business matters private. Nothing worse than a stranger who wants to chit-chat at the urinal. I would avoid public bathrooms completely if I didn't have the bladder of a six-year-old girl. I'm such a pussy. Everything about me screams *wimp!* Even my internal organs.

I acknowledge that I'm a little bit crazy, but I just hate urinating while other people are around. I become paranoid that anyone in earshot of me is judging the size of my penis based upon the depth of the sound that the pee makes when it hits the water. You know, a big penis will emit a larger stream of urine, thereby making a deeper sound, while a little penis (I can only imagine) would make a delicate little tinkling sound. Not that it matters. My penis is neither large nor small, it is rather normal-sized. But I wouldn't want anyone to think I had a little one, you know? The trick is to push really hard while peeing in earshot of someone else, as the added pressure will create a faux big-penis sound when the pee hits the water.

After a lengthy hike, I was sorry to see that the last urinal in the long line was filled almost to the brim with bright yellow urine. I don't like to pee on other people's pee, either. Just the thought of little speckles of some unknown (or known, really) person's urine stinging my bare skin (or even my jeans, really) freaks me out. People in Los Angeles have this bullshit ecological scapegoat excuse for why they don't flush the toilet after they take a leak: In California back in the '80s when there was a water shortage, in an effort to conserve, SoCal residents were pounded via TV and radio spots with the adage, "If it's yellow, let it mellow. If it's brown, flush it down." Yeah. I'm serious. Well, this ain't the '80s, people. So learn to flush the freakin' toilet after you take a piss, you lazy, excuse-makin', non-flushin', sun-tanned motherfucker.

Being that the urinal was chock full of piss and probably clogged, the logical thing would have been to just use the next one. Unfortunately, I do not operate on logic. Instead of simply shifting over to the adjacent urinal, I wrapped my sleeve around my hand and flushed #80 (as if urinal #79 was somehow less safe from prying eyes than #80). Sure enough, Soldier #80 belched and puked his golden holdings all over the floor, and even more unfortunately, all over my shoes. I flicked my feet in an utterly useless effort to get the water/piss mixture off of my black Converses and moved to urinal #79. Just as I unzipped and pulled my thing out, the bathroom door opened, letting in a waft of rap music and a big black man whom I could see only peripherally. I tried to remain focused on my penis, willing it to work as the man walked toward the throng of urinals, and consequently, toward me.

"Yoooo! Fat Head Wally Mosco! Wus happenin', homey?" he said.

I looked up. His large crooked afro swayed slightly with the weight of the small comb that protruded from it, combined with his I-doubt-that-his-leg-is-actually-injured limp. "Oh. H-hey, Deezy. How are ya?" Funk Deezy. That's what they call him. I don't know his real name nor why they call him that. Nor why he feels like we're close enough friends for him to precede my name with "Fat Head." He kept strutting toward me, passing what seemed like thousands of perfectly good urinals. Alarm bells began to sound in my head.

"Pretty dope show they got goin' on out there, huh? You peep it?"

Twenty urinals away now, and still walking. "Y-Yeah. I peeped it. It's awesome. Uh, dope."

Ten urinals. No sign of slowing. "Ha haaa. Yeah. I bet you wrote most a dem lyrics he spittin', too!"

"Uhhhhh, yeah. Some. Yeah." Okay. So there you have it. That's what I do. I write rap lyrics. But this guy *absolutely* should not have known that. It's a major secret. More on that later. Deezy was five urinals away now, and still no sign of stoppage. I held my breath. Stage fright was putting the kibosh on my urination efforts.

"Word, dawg. You got skills, Mosco!" he said, as he saddled up at the urinal *right next to mine.* I shifted my body ever so slightly away from him. "Maybe one day I'll let you write some shit for *me,* dawg." I was panicking now, for several reasons. Mainly because he was seriously violating the most fundamental rule of men's bathroom etiquette (Rule: If possible, always leave *at least* one vacant urinal between urinators), but also because I just couldn't get my pee to flow.

What will he think!? What kind of man stands at a urinal for this long without even a drop of piss?! And what if he catches a glimpse of my schvantz? It's probably TINY compared to his!

What *should* have been my primary concern was how the heck this jerkoff knew that *I* was the one responsible for writing the lyrics that superstar rapper Oral B was onstage rapping at that very moment.

By some gift from God, I finally began to tinkle (in a big-penis sort of way—full pressure). With renewed confidence, I ignored Funk Deezy's attempt at conversation and blurted, "Yeah, hey, uh, Deezy? You mind not peeing—uh, pissin'—*right next to me*? There are like a hundred other urinals in here."

Deezy looked down at me crookedly, upping the uncomfortability factor a few notches, a feat that seemed impossible seconds earlier. "What'd you say, dawg?"

"I, uh, I said . . . I *asked* if you could maybe, you know, maybe move down a few urinals. There's plenty of room in here. No need to, uh, no need to be, to *pee,* so close. Ya know?" Oh, jeez. What a stuttering prick.

Deezy continued to look at me sideways, his eyebrows askew. "Whatsamatter, *fool*? You think I'm gay or somethin'?"

"Gay— Naw! No, Deezy. I know you ain't gay! Naw!" I don't know why I feel the need to talk like this when I'm around these rap guys. For some reason, as soon as they're nearby my grammar goes out the window. Like they'll think I'm cooler if I butcher the English language a bit.

I heard the deep bass of Deezy's pee hitting the water. *Black guys probably never worry about the sound of their piss stream.* With a sardonic, relieved smile he said, "Ahhhh, too late, Fat Head! I'm already flowin', nigga!" He put his head back, enjoying his piss, smiling big. And then: *"Pffff! Pfff-fff-fffff!"* Laughter. He was laughing at me.

"What?" I asked defensively.

"Pfff-fffff-ffff-ffff-ffff!!! Ha ha haaaaa!"

"*What?* What's so funny?" I asked, panicky.

"Ha *haa!* You scared I'm gon' see your lil hot dog! *Hahaaaa!*" He somehow managed to pee and laugh raucously at the same time.

"No!" I squeaked.

"*Hahahahaaaaaa!* Wally got a lil willy! *Hahahahaha!*"

"No! I don't! That's not—! That's not it! No! That's not why!" I was shouting now. Shouting and pissing.

"*Hahahahahahaaaaaa!* I heard dat you did! *Haaa!*"

"Deezy—!"

"Woooo! Wally Mosco got a tiny cocksco!"

"NO!" I yelled, thinking, *That didn't even make sense, you big asshole!*

"*Hahahahaaa!* Don't worry, Mosco! I won't tell tha crew you got a itsy-bitsy teenie-weenie! *Hahahahaaaaa!*"

"I don't!"

"Yeah, right! *Haaahaaaaaaa!*"

"*Nooo!*" I shouted, and everything happened so quickly after that. And yet, so slowly.

Some strange, uncontrollable defense mechanism kicked in in my body. As I screamed, *"Nooo!,"* I watched myself whip around toward Deezy in slow motion, like a fireman wrestling with a renegade fire hose, spraying my piss onto the leg of his orange velour jumpsuit. And like a swordsman reacting by pure instinct to a weapon slashing in his direction, Deezy whipped around in a defensive-block move, pissing right back on me in return.

Time returned to normal speed.

"WHAT THE FUCK, MAN?!" he screamed.

"Whoa! *Oh!* Sorry! Deezy! Oh my G—Sorry! That was such an accide—"

"What the fuck man?! Nawwww, dawg! Nawwww!"

Pants around our ankles and dicks swinging in the stale breeze, Deezy and I shared the most awkward dance of our lives (even more awkward than when I tried to do "the running man" at Joshua Finkel's Bar Mitzvah, and I fell on my ass right in front of Ashley Weintraub).

"Deezy, I'm *sorr*—" I didn't even have the chance to finish my sentence. The last thing I recall is Deezy's big, black, gold ring–encrusted fist heading toward my face. I think he hit me twice, but I only felt the first one.

chizapter 2

I'm sorry, did you say you write *rap music*?" inquired the uninvited little old Asian gentleman standing beside me at the Laundromat. Small and bony, dressed in a fascinating medley of corduroy-meets-cotton-meets-flannel-meets-nylon-meets-denim, bald, and bespectacled, this man looked remarkably like Mr. Miyagi from *The Karate Kid*. In fact, the only thing that separated him from being Miyagi-san himself was his hat—a neon green trucker hat with bright red Chinese writing across the front—in clear discord, yet strangely appropriate, with the rest of his mismatched ensemble. I wondered why he was standing here.

"Yes. Rap." I wasn't much in the mood for conversation with a stranger (and this guy certainly put the "strange" in stranger), what with my urine-soaked clothes, swollen black eye, cracked glasses, and bloody little bruises on the bridge of my nose where my glasses had stabbed me. Not to mention the fact that I'd had to sit on a garbage bag over the seat in my car on the way over here, so I wouldn't get Deezy-pee all over it, and I was presently sitting on a washing machine in my boxers and socks and an Oral B T-shirt that I'd bought at the stadium gift shop before I'd scrambled the hell out of there, stinking like a bedpan. I stopped at the first Laundromat I could find, and the last thing I wanted at this moment was to make small talk with Pat Fucking Morita.

"Hmmmm . . ." He scratched his thin-whiskered chin. "Mmmmmmoskowit was it?"

"Yes."

"Rap music."

"Yes."

"Like da black people."

"*Yes.*"

"Rap music."

I looked away, out the window. It was all I could do to stop myself from grabbing the little guy by his throat. I tried to ignore him and watch the bravest or homelessest dregs of the neighborhood sloshing through the rain outside. The window was covered in intricate etched-in graffiti, and I could only see blurry half-images of the outside world. Some hooligan must have had a shitload of laundry to do in order to work on this particular ghetto fresco.

"Moskowit . . . No, doesn't sound like a rapper name," he said, puzzled. I wanted to tell him to shut the fuck up and go away with his stupid neon hat.

"I'm not a rapper . . . sir. Okay? I'm a writer. A *ghost*writer." My finger traced the carved graffiti. It either said "Newton" or "Mamfor." Tough to tell.

"Ghooooostwriter . . ." He stretched out the word, relishing it like the first bite of a favorite dish he hadn't tasted in years.

"Yeah. You know? Like . . . ghost. You know? Ghost? As in . . . invisible . . . you don't see me." It doesn't escape me that my job is such a perfect metaphor for my life.

"Oh, yes. I understand it. Yes, yes. I do. Just trying to *fully* get it."

"Okay . . . You got it now?" I don't know why I was indulging him.

"Wellllll, you don't look so rich . . . I just thought—"

"What?"

"Well, I just thought . . . who do you write da rappings for?"

I let out a big exasperated breath. I wasn't getting out of this conversation. Some people just don't pick up on the not-so-subtleties of rhetoric. "I write for a very famous rapper—are you familiar with the genre?"

"Da Jon-Ra? Dat's his name?" He took off his hat and scratched his bald head.

"No, no, no. I meant, are you familiar with rap music? Do you know any artists?"

"Artists . . . Nooooo, nooo. I don't know dem."

"Then, dude, does it really matter who I write for?" I barked. He looked slightly offended. I had a sudden pang of sympathy for the little guy.

"Okay. Alright. I just thought dat maybe I'd reck-uh-nize a name." He turned his head. Then, after a few seconds, "I know about da LL Cool Beans."

"Cool J," I snapped.

"What?"

"LL—Nothing."

"My point is, I thought dey make a lot a lot a lot of money, dese rappers. I see dem on da TV." He folded his arms out in front of him in a lame interpretation of a rap pose. "They always say, 'Nigga, nigga, nigga, hey my nigga, I got all da women. Hey! Hey! Hey!' Right?"

I couldn't help but smile. The little guy managed to win me over.

"Yeah. Exactly. That was good, Mr.—"

"Chow. Mr. Ling-Ling Chow." He thrust his hand out for me to shake, and I did.

"Nice to meet you, Mr. Chow."

"So why don't you make da big monies like dem, Moskowit? I don't understand. Too fat?"

Easy there, squirt. "Nah. I just . . . I prefer to be behind the scenes."

"Isn't it violent back dere?"

"Violent? Nooooooo. That's all theatrics. It's all for show. I've never seen any violence, and I've been in the business for almost ten years now."

"Oh? What happened to your eye?"

I smiled. He got me again. "A rapper punched me in the face."

"See?! Violent!" He yelled and pointed at me.

"I pissed on him."

"Piss?"

"Yeah. Forget it." I looked out the window. We didn't say anything for a minute.

"What's his name?"

"The guy I pissed on?"

"Da guy you write rappings for."

"Ah, I shouldn't say, Mr. Chow."

"Call me Ling-Ling. Why shouldn't you say it?"

"Ehhh, well, you know. It's a big secret. If anyone found out, you know . . ." I drew a line across my neck with one finger.

He looked at me for a few seconds, computing. Then he slowly nodded his head. "Ohhhhhh . . . I see. He don't want people to know dat a little white boy named Moscowit is writing his rappings for him."

"Bingo."

"Ohhhhh, I understand." He bobbed his head a few times, and then: "You can tell me, Moscowit! I don't know him!"

I considered for a moment, and then for some reason that will forever escape me, I leaned over to him and lowered my voice. "His name is Oral B."

"Oral B?!" he said too loudly.

"Shhh. Yeah," I said, looking around.

"Dat's stupid! Dat's my toothbrush name!"

"He's very successful, Ling-Ling. One of the best-selling rappers in the world."

"Well den *you're* stupid, Moscowit! Why don't you make da money?!" I shrugged and looked back to the window, at the buzzing, red neon sign hanging there on a dusty chain. I wanted to say, "Because I'm a fuckin' loser, okay? Is that what you wanna hear, you little Asian prick? I'm a fuckin' loser-pussy, and I'm scared of everything and everyone." But instead I just looked out the window for a really long time. I could feel Ling-Ling's eyes on me.

"You're a saaaaaad man, Wally Moscowit," said the little Asian man with the neon green trucker hat standing next to me at the Laundromat. I nodded absently and watched the rain droplets slip-slide gracefully down the window. In the mottled reflection, they looked like tears streaming down my cheeks.

The dryer buzzed, rudely telling me that my clothing was finally dry. I said good-bye to my new pal Ling-Ling Chow, who said only, "Remember this, Moscowit—a gem cannot be polished without friction, nor a man perfected without trials." We stared at each other for a moment, and then he bowed slightly and walked away.

I put on my piping-hot jeans, burning myself on the sizzling zipper of my fly. I yelped and then glanced around to see if anyone had seen my act of wimpiness.

My heart stopped when I saw him.

I experienced the same terrible, icy feeling you get in the car when a cop turns on his lights behind you. This time, however, it wasn't a cop that inspired my fear, but a young black man standing at a machine directly behind me. His hair was in tight cornrows. He wore all black. He rested both palms on the machine, facing me. It wasn't his appearance that scared me, though. It was his expression. His snarky grin made my blood run cold. He wasn't smiling because he'd seen me burn myself. There was something more behind his knowing little look. *Had he heard my conversation with Ling-Ling?* We held the briefest eye contact and he glanced away, smirking to himself. The look we shared may have been fleeting, but it was loaded.

It was raining even harder when I left the Laundromat. Almost instantly my clothes were soaked and heavy. *Terrific. So much for the dryer,* I thought. I made the wet jog to my car as quickly as I could. When I got to my crappy little 1979 Volvo 200 wagon, it didn't look quite right. It looked . . . cock-eyed. I staggered around to the driver's side, and sure enough: flat tire.

Perfect.

I stood there in the rain for a minute and looked at the tire. I wasn't thinking of anything in particular. It wasn't a big epiphanic movie moment where I suddenly resolved that I needed to change my life. It was simply another shitty moment in my shitty existence, and it just flowed seamlessly with the rest of them.

chizapter 3

I wasn't *that* far from home, so I just said, "Fuck it," and drove with the flat. As I slowly *thump-thump-kathump*ed my way home in the pouring rain at about twenty miles per hour, I was thinking that if this were a movie, a dreadfully morose, piano-and-violin-laden song would be the musical accompaniment. All in all, the soundtrack to my life would be wholly melancholy and a real fucking bummer to listen to. As I approached my building, I hoped that Sue would be home when I got there.

The only reason I'd bothered to stop at the Laundromat was *just in case* she happened to be there when I got home—I didn't want her to see me drenched in urine. But I was kidding myself, because the truth was, she was never there anymore. Our relationship was strained nowadays. We used to be so in love—all over each other. Sex every night. The mornings too! We were ravenous! One thing about Sue, she is *good* with her hands. She makes her living off of those hands, so she'd *better* be good. Sue is a dog masseuse by trade. Go ahead, laugh if you want, but she's carved out quite a living for herself here in Los Angeles. She massages the fur of some of the most powerful dogs in Hollywood. I used to joke with her about giving a Shih Tzu a Shiatsu, and she would throw her head back and give a hearty, toothy laugh. Not anymore.

God, how different it was now. I practically had to beg for affection, let alone sex. Most of the time I felt like I was just

19

annoying her. We acted like a miserable old married couple. No touching. No kissing. No hugging. No hand-holding. No sucking on any body parts whatsoever. Just fighting and barely tolerating each other's presence.

I bounded up the four-floors'-worth of stairs as quickly as my chubby little legs would allow. The staircase in my building almost always stinks of curry, thanks to good old Pardeep Vishvatma in 2-C. Nice enough guy—overly nice, really—but he reeks.

My apartment door is painted a hideous, institutional shade of blue, and no longer has actual numbers on it, only the crusty silhouette of where "4-D" used to hang. No peephole either. Correction: It has the hole, just no lens. When I look through it the wind from the hallway blows through the hole and makes my eye tear. As I slipped the key into the old worn doorknob, which always makes my hand smell like I've been holding a fistful of pennies, I smelled the musty odor of old lady that always emanates from Mrs. Horowitz's apartment next door. She reeks too. My life just stinks in so many wonderfully varied ways.

The door creaked open and my dark apartment waited patiently for me to light her up. My best friend in the world, a pudgy little bulldog by the name of Dr. Barry Schwartzman, scudded up to me and stepped on my foot. He always does that. He stops with one paw resting on my foot, and looks up at me expectantly. What a face! I'm not exactly sure what kind of doctor he is, but I suspect that he may be a podiatrist. I could feel his hot breath through my pants leg, and in a strange way, it lifted my spirits. The Doctor, as Sue and I affectionately refer to him, is white and brown and chunky and cute as a fat little button. There is no one on this earth that I like more than Dr. Schwartzman, and I would guess that if he could talk and you asked him, he'd say the same about me. He loves me unconditionally, and the only condition I have is that he not shit on my couch. I think that's fair, and he's working on it.

Sue was definitely not there. I suppose that somewhere in

the recesses of my mind, I was half hoping that the lights were going to suddenly flick on and Sue would be there with a chicken potpie (with bacon) in one hand and some sort of delectable homemade dessert in the other hand, yelling, "Surprise!" That, of course, did not happen.

I didn't bother to turn on the lights. I was feeling blue, and the darkness seemed appropriate. Plus, I didn't want to have to see how disgusting the place was. It always looks best in the dark—just like me. My apartment is a hodgepodge of crappy half-broken Ikea goods and Salvation Army rescues. I have movie posters on my walls (Cool ones. Seriously. They are.) and empty beer and liquor bottle trophies lining the exposed space above my kitchen cabinets. It looks like a room in a frat house, and it smells like a room in a frat house for dogs. There is truly no place like home, and I don't mean that in a good way.

I dragged my feet heavily across the hardwood floor of the living room, doing my best sad-guy shuffle. I passed by my phone, hoping to see the little red blinking light that indicates when I have messages on my voice mail. No light. No messages. Not only was Sue not there, but she didn't even care enough to call and say good night. *Bitch.*

I moped into my bedroom and flopped down on the unmade bed. Dr. Schwartzman followed me into the room and stopped at the side of the bed, snorting out of either frustration or exhaustion, or possibly a sprinkle of each. He's too fat to make the leap onto the bed, so when he wants to get up he does this devastatingly-pathetic-but-achingly-adorable little dance where he jumps with only his front two legs continuously until I help him up. I reached down and grabbed the Doctor's fat, furry little figure and hoisted him up on the bed next to me. He snuggled his wrinkled face into my belly as closely as he could. I rubbed his neck and stared at the ceiling.

What the hell happened tonight? The day had been going fine. Just that morning I had been sitting on the beach, my biggest worry being my inability to come up with a cool analogy about my life. Then Brandunn called around 2:00 P.M. to invite me to the concert. I didn't *really* want to go, but when Brandunn Bell, aka Oral B, asks you to do something, you do it. Simple as that. He's a scary dude. In his twenty-five years he's supposedly been shot three times, stabbed four times, incarcerated for a total of three years, and has kicked more peoples' asses than you can count on your whole family's fingers, toes, and any other protruding body parts. He's no joke. That's what they say, anyway. It could all be an act—just as fake as his lyrics, but I'd never test him. He's unpredictable, like a pit bull. Likely to compliment you on your nice shoes one minute and punch you in the gut a minute later for wearing nice shoes around him.

Brandunn is called Oral B because "Everything that comes outta my mouth is fresh and clean and oh so smoooooove." In theory, he's an excellent rapper. Hard-core as hell. Great faceman. One of the best-selling rappers of all time, in fact. Trouble is, he's dumb as a bag of Cheese Doodles. He's kind of like 50 Cent, except mildly retarded. B can't write a rhyme to save his life. It's actually a small miracle that he can even read the lines that I write for him, let alone memorize and recite them. It's like some weird ghetto autism. Every single line he's ever said on an album has come from my brain, my pen. For example: "I fuck yo bitch till she can't breave, I'll break her legs so she can't leave. I love da beaver more than Wally Cleaver. I keep comin' on back like a golden retriever. My dick's as long as your fuckin' arm, you don't believe me, just ask your fuckin' mom." *Horrible,* huh? I know. I can't even write halfway intelligent songs for him. I have to dumb it down to fit his very limited vernacular. I know that "arm" and "mom" don't rhyme, but they do when Oral B says them. Trust me. That brilliant little gem is from the song "Eatin' Pussy Like Some Ribs." I can't take credit for the titles, unfortunately. Oral B comes up with those himself.

I *wish* I could write for a more intelligent rapper. God knows there are plenty of brilliant ones out there. Trouble is, the smart ones don't need ghostwriters, so here I am writing rhymes for the black Rain Man.

Regardless, this is not what I want to be doing with my life, believe me. I did not intend to get into this as a career. Wally Moscowitz was not meant to be writing rap music. I'm just a little Jewish boy from Westchester, New York. When I told my old Jewish grandfather what I do for a living he said, "You ever take a doody in the ocean? It's *exhilarating!*" My grandpa has Alzheimer's so that didn't mean much. But when I told my mother what I do she said, "You work for the schvatzas?! Oysh gevalt! Good! Now you can pay the hospital bills from the ulcer that you're gonna give me!"

Like this is what I want to be doing? Godz-Illa Records pays me shit. You believe that? Well you shouldn't, because it isn't exactly true. That's the cover story. Truth is, I get paid pretty well—but there's a major stipulation. Officially, I'm an "office assistant." That's what everyone at work (and everyone I meet) thinks I do, and we have to keep up certain appearances, of course, because if anyone (even at our company) found out what I *really* do, well, you know *that* story. So, it's an interesting dichotomy, see. They have to pay me enough that I'll keep my mouth shut, *but* they pay me completely under the table so that no one finds out—and I've been given explicit instructions not to spend it on anything that will give my financial status away. How much does *that* suck?! I've got all this cash but I have to continue with the appearance that I make shitty money so no one will know that I have money! The worst part is, I'm too scared to even put the cash in the bank, so I've got thousands and thousands of dollars stuffed in a shoebox in a closet in my apartment. What's the point of even having money? I can't buy *shit!* And my boss, Abraham "Dandy" Lyons, is *watching* me like you would not believe. One time, Sue, tired of my ripped and schlubby clothing, absolutely insisted that I go shopping and buy myself some new gear. Sue is *always* bitching that I have all this loot but I never spend it (on her *or* me). So we went shopping, and I dropped a few hundred bucks on some nice new duds. I wore a brand new shirt, some nice new slacks, and some shiny new kicks to work the next day. Dandy called me into his office about ten minutes into the day and made me take it all off. Then he took a pair of scissors to my poor shirt until it looked like one of those paper snowflakes you make in kindergarten. "Who are you? P. Diddy?" he asked, throwing the snowflaked shirt at my face. "Look the part, Mr. Moscowitz, or the next part you'll be secretly playing will be in a ditch somewhere." Now I'm scared to even order extra bacon on my cheeseburger for fear that my boss or one of his henchmen is going to pop out of the bushes with a pair of scissors to turn *me* into a snowflake. Oral B owns three Bentleys, a Maybach, a Lamborghini, a Ferrari, an Aston Martin, a Porsche GT2, two Mercedes-Benz SL 600s, a Mercedes G SUV, a Range Rover, a Range Rover Sport, a veritable fleet of Hummers, a BMW Z8, two BMW X5s, a BMW 765i (V12), two BMW motorcycles, four Harleys, three Ducatis, two turtle doves, and a partridge in a chrome-dipped, diamond-studded pear tree. All because of me. And I take the fucking '79 Volvo home from work every damn day. He's got bling bling and all I've got is Ling-Ling. It's bullshit. But that's just *me*. Story of my life. I'm a loser. A doormat for everyone I know.

Just about the only person in this world (not including Dr. Schwartzman, of course, who is disqualified because of his canine-inity) who even gave a shit if I woke up in the morning or not was Sue. And I wasn't even so sure about *that* anymore. She'd been so distant lately. We've been dating for four years. *Four years*. She used to spend almost every night at my place. Now I'm lucky if I even get a phone call to see how my day went. Sex? Ha! I'm lucky I still recognize the word. Haven't heard it in a while. There are goddamned poodles and little purse-sized rat dogs running around Hollywood that get more poontang from my girlfriend than I do. *It must be my penis,* I figured. Her ex-boyfriend played small forward for the Los Angeles Clippers. He is six-foot-seven, and I'm guessing that his penis is in direct proportion to his colossal stature. In a completely feeble effort to assuage my insecurity, she'd always tell me that it was *too* big, that she didn't like it. *Yeah right.* That's like saying, "No, I don't want that Ferrari. It's *too* nice. I prefer your '79 Volvo." Before I met Sue I liked the Clippers, but now every time I hear that they lost a game I get this little internal burst of joy.

Am I such a downer? Is it so hard to talk to me? Am I so repulsive? No, I tell myself. She's a tough cookie, that Sue. A real pain in the ass. She comes from a family with six kids; she was the youngest, and the only girl. She's used to getting what she wants. You could say that Sue wears the pants in our relationship. Only, they're not pants, they're a Prada skirt.

We used to talk a lot though. We would call each other countless times a day just to gush about some inane thing or another. At one point in our relationship, if you eavesdropped on our phone calls, you might have even heard something like, "You hang up first. No, *you,* silly! You hang up! No, you! Okay, on the count of three . . . " Not anymore. These days, when we do speak, she's just *nasty* to me. Always curt or bothered. I try to be a good boyfriend and say things like "How was your day, honey? Tell me about it." Not like I even give a shit, but I'm following good boyfriend protocol. I keep telling myself: As soon as I make some real money, as soon as the project goes the way I plan and I can focus more on her, it'll get better.

The "project," as it came to be known between Sue and me—maybe the real cause of our rift.

You see, I wrote these books. I've *been* writing them, really. And, I guess you could say I've become rather . . . preoccupied by them. Some might call it an obsession. I have faith that they're going to make me rich. I even have an agent, and he's got faith too. He says, "No good idea goes unpublished," and I believe him.

Here's the pitch: I write dirty children's books for adults. They look and sound just like every illustrated, rhyming children's picture book you've ever seen, except they're naughty.

They're in the voice of an innocent child, but they're written for adults, about inappropriate topics like whores and drugs. They're kind of like Howard Stern raped Dr. Seuss and they had an illegitimate love child. Perfect for the coffee table in the frat house or next to the john. Everyone who reads them thinks they're very funny. Even the publishers! The rejection letters all say the same thing: "Funny! Talented author. Very well written. Not our thing." Well *fuck you guys!* Stupid cocksuckin' motherfuckin' piece of shit bitch asshole cocksuckin' shit fuckers. I hate their very guts. But I'm not bitter.

Sorry, I digress. We were discussing today. One second I'm taking an innocent piss by myself in a distant urinal, next thing I know I'm lying facedown in a pool of urine. Oh, man. Ain't that a bitch?

This guy Deezy is a nobody, I told myself, as I rubbed Dr. Schwartzman's chunk-rolled neck. *He's not a rapper.* Not yet, anyway. *He's not on Godz-Illa's payroll.* I didn't think so, at least. I mean, I'd see him around the office all the time, but as far as I could surmise, he was just one of many "peeps" in Oral B's entourage. I didn't believe there was any *actual* relation between him and Oral B or, even worse, between him and Lyons. I wasn't sure how Deezy got into the posse. I'm not quite sure how anybody gets into the posse. I think there's some sort of written test followed by an oral presentation. You may need letters of recommendation. I don't know. Actually, for this particular posse you may just have to look scary and be 99 percent unintelligible.

My main concern at *this* point was the fact that Deezy *knew* that I write lyrics for Oral B. That's a *big* secret. *No one* is supposed to know that. *No one.* Underline, underline, exclamation point, exclamation point, exclamation point. If the world found out that some fat little Jew-boy was writing all of this hard-core gangsta rapper's lyrics, Oral B's reputation would be destroyed. He has won awards for his lyrics! Even a Grammy nomination! He's touted as a ghetto scholar. A poet of the people. *The Source* magazine named him one of the ten greatest lyricists of all time! Rep is everything in his world. B would be a laughingstock, and his career would be *finished*. As would their three-hundred-million-dollar record label. And I'd be a dead man. Abraham Lyons and Oral B are *not men you want to cross*. I could only pray that Deezy wouldn't blow my cover.

On a much smaller scale, I also really hoped that word about the pissing incident wouldn't get out. I already felt like a big enough loser at Godz-Illa Records. I already had enough people sneering at me in the hallways, calling me "Tickle Me Wal-Mo" or the "Wal-nut" or "Fathead Wally." I definitely didn't want *this* to get out. I'd be laughed out of the building. I felt somewhat reassured knowing that Deezy wouldn't want anyone to know I pissed on him, either. That's *so* not gangsta. It could ruin his image, and hence, the career that he was apparently trying to build.

It always takes me forever to fall asleep, and tonight was no different. My brain raced wildly, prancing frenetically about the minutiae of my life, considering *every* conceivable thing. *Is Lyons gonna find out that Deezy knows our secret? Do my books suck? What's up with Sue? Does she love me anymore? Am I too fat? Should I go on Atkins? Who the hell was that guy sitting behind me at the laundromat? Did he hear me spill my secret to Ling-Ling? Why did I tell Ling-Ling anyway? Will that little Miyagi look-alike blow my cover? Is it weird that I had a bacon cheeseburger for both lunch and dinner today?*

Ahhh, my life. Each day more fun than the last. I lay in bed, fully clothed, trapped in my shitty apartment, in my shitty existence, and slowly—expertly—worried myself to sleep.

UNCLE WILLY EATS CATS
By Wally Moscowitz

My Uncle Willy seems very nice,
But I think he eats cats, just like cats eat mice.
I didn't want to believe, but I just can't deny
The things that I saw and I heard from that guy.
It's not very often that we see Uncle Willy,
He's my dad's little brother, and he's really quite silly;
He's big and he's fat and he loves to tell jokes,
But sometimes I think that he bothers my folks.
'Cuz my mom's always mad when my dad says he's coming,
He eats all our food and he clogs up the plumbing.
And he stays here for weeks and he's really a slob,
And my mom always says, "Can't that bum get a job?"
But when Willy's around I sure laugh a lot.
He calls me cool names, like "tough guy" or "big shot."
And he takes me fun places, with really cool names,
Like McFadden's or Maloney's, and they all look the same.
They've got these fun stools that I sit on and spin,
We play darts and shoot pool, and I usually win.
Sometimes Uncle Willy gives me sips from his can.
We talk to the ladies, he calls me his "wingman."
But on one of those nights he dropped me home early,
'Cuz he met this big fat girl who called herself Shirley.

And she kissed him and hugged him and rubbed on his thigh,
And told me my Uncle was such a hot guy.
They dropped me off quickly and sped right away,
I didn't see Willy till late the next day.
That's when I realized that something was weird.
When he hugged me hello I smelled fish on his beard.
He kept coughing and hacking, so I said, "What's wrong, Willy?"
He looked at me, smiling, and he said "Nuttin' really.
I got a hair in my throat, it's from somethin' I ate.
Somethin' really delicious, last night on my date."
Then he winked at my dad, and laughed louder than thunder.
And that's when I really started to wonder.
Why's he so happy about this thing that he ate?
What could you eat that would be SO great?
It must've been something that's real lucky to eat.
Like some special fish, or some special meat.
I decided to leave them, but as I walked away,
I couldn't believe what I heard Willy say.
"No chance!" I thought. He wouldn't do that!
Would Uncle Willy really eat a cat?
It couldn't be true; I wished it was wrong:
But he said he ate her pussy all night long.

—From *The Adult Children's Books Collection*

chizapter 4

I was pulled out of a wonderful dream too quickly by a ringing somewhere in my apartment. In my just-awakened disorientation, it took me a moment to pinpoint that it was my phone, and it was in the kitchen. I jumped out of bed and ran to try to grab it, but of course, the ringing stopped just as I snatched it off of the cradle.

I looked at the little sticker on the wall, on which was written my voice mail retrieval number. I called the number and listened to a message from the high-pitched, eager voice of Renee, a young female assistant at Godz-Illa Records. She informed me that the big boss, Abraham Dandy Lyons, wanted to see me. This forced a hoarsely whispered "oh, fuck" from my sleep-crusted lips. This was not good. I think I mentioned earlier that Dandy Lyons is one intimidating, badass motherfucker. *Not* someone you get excited to go see. He's probably the most baddest-ass motherfucker walking the earth right now. He makes Oral B look like Mickey—no—Minnie Mouse. The first time I met Lyons, I was sitting in the waiting room of his office when the door burst open and a big white dude ran out screaming and crying and wildly clutching at his head, pushing aside chunks of long hair as he gripped and clawed at his head like a maniac. I happened to catch a glimpse, under the guy's frenzied hands, of bald, raw pink patches of scalp. Lyons calmly followed him out not a moment later with a handful of long black hair clutched in each fist. He placed the piles of freshly yanked locks on his assistant's desk and simply said, "Dispose of that, Renee," before looking at me with nary a smile and saying, "You must be Mr. Moscowitz. Come on in." I'd hoped the previous guy wasn't interviewing for the same job as me.

Deezy must have gone to the boss, I thought, because it wasn't very often that I got called in to see him. The last time I was summoned to Lyons's office, it was so he could warn me for the umpteenth time that if I ever opened my mouth to anyone about whom I write for or what my *real* job is, he would be wearing my balls, dipped in gold, on a necklace the very next evening. He makes sure to remind me of that about once a year, each time painting a masterful image of the pain he is capable of causing me. Let me assure you that there is absolutely nothing "dandy" about Abraham Lyons. He gives new meaning to the word "misnomer."

Before I went to see Lyons though, I had to wait for AAA to come fix my tire, and then I had a meeting at 10:00 A.M. with my self-styled superagent, "Uncle" Jerry Silver. Jerry runs his own agency in Los Angeles. Kind of a dump if you ask me, but better than nothing, I suppose. It's ingeniously titled "The Silver Agency." Jerry claims to represent some actors and actresses and some screenwriters, though I've never met any of his other clients. His office is in an old, shitty-looking building in Beverly Hills, its only desirable trait being its Zip Code.

I could never quite tell how well Jerry does. He must make decent money—he drives a pretty nice car. Okay, maybe "nice" is too strong a word. It's nicer than *my* car, anyway. It's a silver 1996 Corvette. The license plate says SAYUNCL. I often wonder if Silver is his real name or if it was given to him on account of the amount of it he wears on and about his body.

I met Jerry about ten years ago through a friend of a friend I once had. We were at a birthday party, and I was a little bit drunk. I heard that he was an agent and, in a rare moment of boldness, I told him about my book idea. He loved it. He signed me the next day. That was a loooooong time ago (ten years), and I haven't sold a damn thing. But he believes in me, and there's something to be said for that, I guess.

I walked into his office, and the smell of his cologne hit me harder than Deezy's punch in the face. I almost went down, but his assistant, Beth, an adorable, breadstick-slender, young African-American girl, grabbed my arm and steadied me. She waved her other hand in front of her scrunched nose. "You never really get used to it, huh?" she said with a cute, crinkly nosed wink. I shook my head in agreement. Jerry was on the phone, so Beth eased me into one of the plush chairs on the opposite side of his desk.

The always-flamboyantly-colored-shirt-wearing Jerry Silver sat behind a massive, highly polished oak desk, his obese ass squished so tightly into a chair—which looked more like a throne snatched from a castle somewhere—that I could practically hear that poor chair screaming in agony. Several silver chains rested on the puff of dark hair that protruded from beneath the collar of his shirt. A wet, yet somehow-still-always-burning cigar perpetually hangs from the left side of his mouth, constantly threatening to ignite his alcohol-and-cologne-soaked shirt. He may be pungent, but Jerry Silver is also very possibly the nicest guy I know.

"Enough, Richie! Enough! Listen. *Listen!*" He shouted into the phone. "Your head is so far up his ass—*Listen!* Your head is so far up his ass he can taste your fuckin' hair! That's right, Richie! That's right! And you know what it tastes like, Richie? It tastes like fuckin' Pert Plus! That's—*Listen!* That's because you're too fuckin' poor to buy *real* shampoo, Richie. Yeah! 'Cuz you're too stupid to come up with a good idea that anyone can sell. Good! Good for you! Yeah right. I kill people like you *on the way* to fights, Richie. Lunch Friday at noon. Cheesecake Factory, yeah." *Click.* "Heyyyyyy! Wally Moscowitz! My favorite little gangsta Jew boy! Great to see you, bud! What's with the shiner?" He stood up and leaned his sizeable gut over the desk to plant a wet kiss on my cheek. I held my breath so I wouldn't be forced to inhale any more of his toxic fumes.

"Hey, Jerry. Long story. What was *that* all about?" Jerry Silver is in the wrong business. Well, the wrong *end* of the business, anyway. He should have been an actor. The guy is an absolute sweetheart, a true teddy bear, but you wouldn't know it unless you were very close to him like I am. He likes to play up the tough guy, loud-mouth, obnoxious agent role whenever he thinks it will serve him well. And he's damn good at it. He could give Jeremy Piven a good run for his money. It's a bit schizophrenic at times, but I love the guy. He's always straight with me.

"Ah, you know. Playin' to the crowd." He took a huge gulp from a very interesting-looking bottle. It was tall and thin like a baton, with a light blue tinted plastic wrapping, and bright red, almost illegible cursive letters wrapping around the circumference. Before I could answer him, he gurgled, "Mmm *mmm*! That is a tasty beverage. You heard of this stuff yet? Bet you haven't!"

"What is it? Looks like water."

"It *is* water, pal. It's called Glacialle. Everyone is talking about it. Deeee-lish."

"Water. Everyone's talking about this *water*?"

"Yeah. Purest stuff I've ever tasted," he said with a straight face.

"Yeah? Tastes really, uh, watery?"

"Makes Evian taste like diarrhea in a bottle."

I laughed. "You know Evian backward is 'Naïve,' right?" I said.

"Yeah, yeah," he said with a smile, after another big swig.

"Only in L.A., Jerry."

"*Uncle* Jerry—and give it six months, kid. Every putz in the Hamptons and his toothpick girlfriend will be washin' their blow down with it. Don't be so high and mighty."

"Right."

"You'll be drinkin' it soon too, bud. In fact, here." He handed me a bottle of my very own. "It's not even in the stores yet. Got a case of it from a friend in Cannes. Distributes it. This is the *only* case of this stuff in the whole state of Cali. I want all of my clients to have a bottle." He took another gulp. "Mmm *mmm*. That *is* a tasty beverage," he said again, quoting a line from a Quentin Tarantino movie. Jerry is perpetually quoting Tarantino movies, which would be fine—I *love* Tarantino—but he claims to never have seen any of the movies. It drives me nuts. He does it constantly.

"Now, what's the deal, pumpkin? You look like shit. What's wrong? Tell Uncle Jerry."

"I feel like shit, Jerry. I feel like shit. I hate my job, I'm a loser. Same ol'."

"Aww, c'mon. You're not a loser, Mosco. You're a winner! You hear me? Why the heck do you think you're here, huh? You think I deal with losers?"

"Naw, Jerry. I don't think you deal with lose—"

"*Bingo,* Mosco. I don't deal with losers. Jerry Silver *does not deal with losers!* So quit moping around. I wanna be in the Wally Moscowitz business. You hear me? Not the Mopey Moscowitz business. Not the, uh, not the Wally Mope-a-witz business. Okay?"

"All right, Jerry."

"*Uncle* Jerry. And don't 'all right, Jerry' me, Mosco. You've got more smarts in that mopey little brain of yours than half this town put together. You hear me?"

"Then why can't we sell my shit, Jerry? I'm getting very frustrated here. I can't keep doin—"

"Wally, it's only been two years since you finished them all! Two years! That's nothing! Let me ask you something. You think they built the Empire State Building in two years?"

"They built it in like a year and forty-five days, I believe." Thank you, Trivial Pursuit.

"Ohhhh, you New York Jews and your condescending pessimistic bullshit. Listen—lighten up! It'll happen, okay? I promise! Would I lie to you, Wally?"

"Jerry—"

"*C'monnnn*. Don't 'Jerry' me, Wally. The answer is, 'No, Uncle Jerry. No, you would never lie to me.'"

"Okay, Uncle Jerry." I couldn't help but smile. Jerry, always the character, had that effect on me.

"'Okay, Uncle Jerry,' what?"

"Okay, you would never lie to me."

"You're goddamned right. And another thing. Listen to me, and listen good, kid. Cheer up. Okay? Cheer up. I'm not your psychiatrist and I don't wanna have to keep giving you these little pep talks. You're too smart for this!"

"Okay. Sorry."

"Don't be sorry, bud. Sorry is for weaklings. Anyway, I got a ten-thirty."

"Why'd you want to see me?" I asked, suddenly feeling like I was being dismissed.

"Here." He handed me a manila folder with a sizable stack of papers sandwiched within. I opened the folder and skimmed through the pages quickly; all rejection letters from various publishers.

"That's great. Fuckin' great. Just what I needed."

"Get used to it, kid. There'll be more where that came from."

"Oh, I'm used to it, believe me."

He fed me his usual bullshit. "Mosco, for every success story there are ten billion rejectio—"

"Save it. I know."

"And uhhhh . . . one more thing . . . ," he said, looking down at his desk.

"What?" I asked, sensing already that I wouldn't like where this "one more thing" was going.

"I want to change your name."

"What? What do you mean?"

"I think your name is holding you back. I want to change it."

"What, like a . . . a pen name? A pseudonym?"

"Yeah. Bingo. Something like that. Yeah."

"No, Jerry. No. I like my name. It's fine. What's wrong with my name? No. I don't want to do that."

"Frankly, I think the Jew thing is hurting you, Wally. You know? *Moscowitz*. Too Jewwy. Sounds like a rabbi or like, uhhh, I don't know, my dentist or something. I'm just saying, it could turn readers off. I'm just saying."

"What?"

"I'm just saying!"

"No, Jerry! How can you—Jerry, your real name is Silverstein, isn't it?!"

"Yeah! And, helloooooo—I changed it! Think about it, Mosco! A snappy-whizzity-boom-bang name is *everything* in this town! Right? I mean, without the Zeta she's just Kathy Jones, right? Think about it!" I thought about it, and I thought it was stupid.

"No, Jerry. I'm not doing it."

"Wallace Q Moscow," he said, spreading his hands out in front of him and staring upward dreamily as if he were reading the marquee at the premiere of his first movie. I looked at him like he was speaking Chinese, which he might as well have been. "No period after the Q," he added with two raised eyebrows. "Huh? How cool is *that*? Just . . . Q," he repeated dramatically, with a look on his face like that would blow me away.

"No," I said simply.

"Oh yeah."

"No," I repeated.

"Uh-huh. Yes. Definitely. Wallace Q Moscow. Absofuckinlutely."

"No, Jerry. Please. I'm not changing my name. No. I won't do it. No. That's my final answer."

"Well, too late, pal. I already did it."

"*What?*"

"Yeah. I did it. I sent out the next round of submissions to publishers with your new name on them instead."

"Jerry—"

"Do you trust me, Mosco?"

"How could you have done that without askin—"

"Hey! Do you trust me?" he asked.

"Jerry—"

"Do . . . you . . . trust . . . me? Just answer me."

I gave an exasperated sigh. "Yes, Jerry, I trust you, but—"

"Okay then. It's done. What's done is done. What can be done?" He clapped his hands once. "That's your name now. Done deal. Congratulations, Q. That's what I'm gonna call you from now on, by the way. Q."

I put my hand to my forehead, closed my eyes, and shook my head slowly. "Oy oy oy," I said quietly.

"There you go again with the Jew thing. Jeez. Okay, whatever. Listen, one step at a time, okay? What's up with your day job over with the, uh, the gangstas? Everything good?" he asked, trying to change the subject. It worked.

"I have a meeting with the big man today," I said.

"Big man who? Abe Lyons?"

"Yup."

"Re:? A raise?"

"Re: The fact that I peed on one of his employees."

"You *what* on *who*?"

"I pissed on some guy by accident."

"You *pissed?* On a guy? What are you talking about?"

I told him the whole story. He stared at me bewilderedly, shaking his head, and then made a clicking noise with his tongue that was tough to interpret. "Jesus, Wally. This is bad. You could be in trouble! Lyons is a mushroom-cloud-layin' motherfucker." Another Tarantino line. "You ask for a raise yet?" he asked, successfully changing the subject again.

"No. And I'm not doin' it now!"

"Why don't you let me call over there and negotiate for you? Let me handle the big guy."

"Yeah—so I can give you fifteen percent of my salary? That's okay, Jerry. I got this."

"Oh, you got this, huh?"

"Yeah."

Jerry stared at me a moment and then flashed his too-big, too-white front teeth at me in the same patronizing grin he always gives me right before he kicks me out of his office. "Okay, Mosco. Now get yer ass outta here and go write me some more of that hilarious Wallace Q Moscow genius shit for me to peddle to the highest bidder. And tell that farbissenah girlfriend of yours that I send my love," he said with a smirk and a wink. His phone rang, and he snatched it up. "Jerry Silver. Talk to me. Heyyyyy! Vinny!!!"

And we were done.

chizapter 5

My cell phone rang too loudly as I walked to my car; a delightful little cacophony by the good bastards over at Verizon. It makes me want to kill myself every time it rings. It was Sue.

"Hi, honey!" I said in the sweetest tone I could muster.

"Hey," she replied dully.

"What's up, babe?!"

"Nothing. What's up?" I just love this game. It's like pulling teeth. Clearly Sue had nothing to bring to the old conversation table. I don't know why she even bothered calling in the first place.

"Nothing much, babe," I said. "Nothing much." Dead air.

"Where are you, it's so *loud,*" she said, annoyed. There it was. I managed to bother her just by virtue of where I was standing when *she called me!*

I tried to shield the phone from the traffic, tried to stall and walk away from the street. "I'm ahhhhh . . . I'm . . . I'm in Beverly Hills."

"Why?" she asked in this fucking obnoxious tone that made me want to reach through the phone and choke the life out of her.

"I just had a meeting with Jerry."

"Oh great, my favorite person." Sue and Jerry had a mutual hatred for each other. She hates him just because he's an agent, and he hates her just because she's an icy bitch. Both pretty fair

39

reasons. Jerry's always trying to talk me into leaving Sue. He thinks she stifles my creativity. "Any good news?" she asked.

"Nah. More rejection letters," I said.

"Awwwwwwww. Don't worry, honey. They'll sell eventually. I just know it. I love you so much, and I support you one hundred percent." *Yeah right.* She didn't say that.

She really said, "Oh. *Great.*"

"Yeah. What's up with you? Wanna have dinner tonight?"

"Ummm. Maybe. Not sure though. I'll let you know. I have a ton of work today." I detected something weird in her tone. She sounded . . . nervous?

"Me, too. Going to meet with Abraham Lyons now."

"How's the Doctor?" she asked with the first sign of genuine interest, completely ignoring the conversation I'd tried to start. Sue loves Dr. Schwartzman more than she loves me.

"Doctor's great. He misses you!" *And so do I.*

"I know. It's just been a hectic week."

"Okay."

"Okay. I'll call you later."

"'Kay. Love you."

"Awwww. I love you too, honey. *Soooo* much! I can't *wait* to see you tonight. I'm gonna rip your clothes off with my teeth!" *Yeah right.*

She actually just said, "Okay. Bye." She couldn't even say "I love you, too"? It made my stomach hurt and my heart ache.

. . . .

Godz-Illa Records. An angry, darkly-mirrored, angular edifice in Santa Monica, towering menacingly over everything in its vicinity, just like the man in charge there. Abraham Lyons owns the building. The first twenty-four floors are rented to various companies that Lyons has his hands in in one way or another. For example, Dandy Couture, his clothing line, resides on floors fifteen through eighteen. Hungry Lyons, the adult video company he owns with his younger brother, Darrell, takes up several lower floors. And so forth. The real breadwinner, Godz-Illa Records, occupies floors nineteen through twenty-four.

The main office lacks any of the bling-bling ostentation that one would imagine adorns the office of a company whose chief export is rap music. The offices have a hip, industrial feel. Cement floors, exposed ventilation shafts and wires above, lots of light from elevated windows. Tastefully framed platinum records hang on almost every wall—most of them belonging to Oral B. Very cool space. The most impressive part of the building, however, is the top floor—twenty-five.

Lyons's office alone fills the penthouse. While Jerry Silver's office is the picture of mediocrity, Abraham Lyons's is the contrary. The word that comes to mind is "fabulous." I know that sounds slightly homosexual, but the way this place inspires my appreciation for interior design makes me feel like a big old queen. The exterior office is stark white. So clean that I would not balk if someone told me that the walls were repainted at the end of each business day. The couches in the waiting area are whiter than a big white bag of clouds (another brilliant analogy). The floor is a bleached hardwood. The receptionist's desk is white wood. Even the woman who sits behind the desk seems like she was hand-dipped in a vat of bleach just to sit there. Her skin is the same cadaverously white shade as the couches, and her hair is so blonde that I always expect her to speak with some kind of Scandinavian accent. Turns out she's from Jersey. I might not have even been able to see her if it weren't for the black Kangol hat she wore slightly tilted to the side, ruining her camouflage. God, I wish I could be so cool.

You're probably wondering how I wound up here (as I often do), secretly writing rap lyrics for the most famous gangsta rapper in the world. Funny story. When I graduated from college I was single, unemployed, poor, and miserable. I lived alone and I spent most of every day working on my books. I didn't have a television yet, because I couldn't afford it. I had a mattress on the floor of a studio apartment and a computer. That was pretty much it. My mom was sending me cash every month to cover my rent, plus a couple of bucks for groceries. Along with the rent check each month, without fail, was a copy of this crappy little newspaper that she subscribed to called the *National Jewish Times,* which had a large classified section in the back that included an extensive Jewish Personals section, in which my mother was absolutely convinced I was going to meet the nice Jewish girl of my dreams. I, of course, was not interested in meeting the kind of girl who needs to place an advertisement in the back of a Jewish circular to find a date, and so each and every issue wound up in the recycling bin.

Until one day I had to take a shit. *Bad.* And I had no toilet paper.

I really did feel bad about wiping my ass with a religion-based periodical, but what can you do? Beggars can't be choosers, and I was sure that God would forgive me. I figured, if he didn't care enough to allow me to afford enough toilet paper, then he really couldn't hold a grudge. So, as I went about tearing long strips from what happened to be the Jewish Jobs section, I reached back to wipe, and just before I did, something caught my eye: a tiny ad that read

> SEEKING TALENTED WRITER. POETRY EXPERI-
> ENCE A PLUS. RHYMING SKILLS NECESSARY.
> WRITING SAMPLES MANDATORY. FULL TIME JOB,
> STARTING SALARY $20K. SERIOUS INQUIRIES ONLY.

Needless to say, I was intrigued. All I'd done for the past few months was write. Write *rhyming* books, to be exact. It certainly seemed that I had the necessary skills for this job. Not to mention the writing samples. Twenty grand sounded pretty good at that moment, as I wiped my ass with a strip of news-paper. I decided to give it a shot.

I called and set up an interview. I was shocked and bewil-dered to discover, upon arriving a few days later, that the address they'd given me was Godz-Illa Records.

After I sat in the waiting room and witnessed the tall white guy running out clutching his scalped head and Mr. Lyons with his handfuls of hair, my interview began. It was a surprisingly pleasant meeting. Lyons, although certainly intimidating by nature, was very nice, and very interested in my writing. We spoke for about half an hour, he took my writing samples, and, with very little information about what exactly the job was that I was applying for, Lyons told me he'd be in touch in the next few days.

The very next day, I got the call. I was summoned to the office again, where Lyons surprised me with the explanation of what this new job would entail: I'd be writing lyrics for an up-and-coming rap artist that Lyons was essentially creating from scratch. I liked rap music (kinda), I liked writing clever rhymes, and I didn't have a pot to piss in. The whole thing seemed serendipitous. I took the job.

When our meeting had concluded, I had only one question. "Mr. Lyons, if you don't mind my asking, why did you advertise in the *National Jewish Times* for this job?"

"A fair question, Mr. Moscowitz," he responded. "And I'll give you a very honest answer."

I nodded.

"It's like this: My doctor is Jewish. My two accountants are Jewish. My seven lawyers—Jewish. My architect, my dentist, my money manager, my four agents, my publicist, my stockbro-ker, my decorator, and my wife's gynecologist—all Jewish. Do you see the pattern? When I need someone smart, this is the quarry in which I mine. It has never failed me before. I hope for both our sakes that it doesn't fail me this time either."

I hoped so, too.

Almost ten years later, here I was. Inching scarily close to failing Mr. Lyons, and growing more and more nervous as the minutes ticked by.

A short while after I entered and hesitantly sat on the pristine couches, terrified that my jeans (which hadn't been washed in a while) would leave some unsightly stain on the spotless fabric, the ghostly receptionist told me that Mr. Lyons would, like, see me now. I rose and gave a discreet glance back at the couch cushions. Clean.

The inner office is tastefully decorated in what I would describe, in my patently ignorant way, as a sort of Japanese Minimalist style. Muted shades: blacks, grays, browns. Some bamboo thoughtfully placed here and there. A large, multitiered white orchid in a stone vase sat purposefully on the corner of his desk in a spot that I myself would not have chosen, but that I was fairly sure was some sort of feng-shui strategy. The room was cool, and I imagined that if I took my shoes off, my toes would instantly freeze on the cold gray cement floor. Not that I would ever consider taking my shoes off in there. I think I would be killed immediately by one or both of the ridiculously large, dark-suited men standing at either side of the door.

The office's understated elegance and quiet power characterize the man who does business there. Lyons sat behind a black bamboo desk in a matching chair, and he didn't rise when I entered. In fact, he didn't even look up to give me the benefit of a disdainful glance. I was glad though, because when Abraham Lyons looks at you, you feel that he is looking into your very soul. I think a rectal exam is more comfortable.

He wore a dark gray suit that must have been picked out and tailored by the same team that decorated the office, because it could not have been more flawlessly matched to his surroundings. The delicate pinstripes on his jacket were in perfect accord with the barely discernible lines etched into the dark wallpaper behind him and the natural scarring on his bamboo desk. His unblemished black skin was in scarily precise harmony with the rest of the color palette of this extraordinary tableau. Abraham Lyons is truly a stunning physical specimen in every conceivable way.

"Sit," he said in his rich baritone rumble. I sat. And sat. And sat. Lyons didn't speak again for what felt like several minutes. He looked down at a piece of paper on his desk. I couldn't tell if he was reading, or simply gathering his thoughts. Perhaps even meditating.

"You pissed off one of my people," he finally said, without looking up.

"Pissed on." I smiled. What the fuck is wrong with me? When did I grow a set of balls? It just sort of slipped out. I think that somewhere in my mind I actually believed I might be able to make him laugh, lighten up the moment a bit. He did not laugh. I doubt that laughter is in his emotional repertoire. He did look up at me though, and my heart skipped a few beats as his pitch-black eyes drilled into me like a Makita through a cantaloupe.

"Oh, you got jokes, huh?" My heart almost fell out of my asshole. The legs of either his chair or my chair chirped momentarily on the floor, and I flinched.

"No. N-no. S-sorry, Mr. Lyons," I stuttered. He nodded discreetly to the two goons standing at either side of the door. I was sure that it was the old "crush his skull" signal. Instead they simply left the office. I guessed he wanted to crush my skull himself, in private. That's how I always preferred to crush skulls, too, so I could relate.

"Mr. Moscowitz, this is no laughing matter, I certainly don't appreciate your flippancy. You *urinated* on one of my employees."

"I know. I can explain. Actually, I can't really exp—"

"Enough."

"Yes, sir."

"This puts me in a very uncomfortable position, Mr. Moscowitz. You see, Mr. Muskingum, or Funk Deezy, as you probably know him, was on the verge of being terminated."

"You were gonna k-kill him?" Lyons shot me a look so piercing that it made the last look seem like a peck on the cheek. He held my gaze.

"No, Mr. Moscowitz. No. He was about to be *fired*. Not murdered. I am a businessman, not a thug, and frankly I resent the implication that I would be capable of such an atrocity." *Yeah right,* I thought. *He probably killed more people today before breakfast than Ted Bundy on his best day.*

"Oh my gosh. I'm sorry, Mr. Lyons. I'm really s—"

"Enough."

"Yes, sir."

"My point is, Mr. Moscowitz, that Mr. Muskingum is not to be trusted. He is a crooked, devious character who I no longer care to be associated with. You, however, have now put me in quite an unpleasant position."

"I'm really sor—" He lifted a hand, palm out toward me in a gesture that surely would have made a charging rhino rethink its trajectory.

"E . . . nuff." He paused. "Now that you've managed to somehow micturate on Mr. Muskingum, I can no longer terminate his employment at this time without facing certain legal action. I am therefore forced to have someone for whom I have extreme distrust and dislike under my employ." I said nothing. I made a mental note to look up "micturate" when I got home. I was pretty sure it was from *The Big Lebowski*.

Lyons looked back down at his paper. He was silent for another excruciatingly long time. The wheels in my brain were spinning on overdrive: *So Deezy IS an employee after all. What does he do? Does Lyons know that Deezy knows about what I really do? He must know. Should I say something? Yes. I should tell him. I should definitely tell him.*

I was snapped out of my reverie by the resumption of our conversation, which was really more of a monologue at this point. "I had a big decision to make, Mr. Moscowitz." I looked up at him like I was a boy about to be spanked by his father. I figured that I was about to be fired. "A big decision, indeed. Understand that I value you very much. You are a gifted writer and a hard worker. I entrust you with our company's biggest secret." I held my breath, waiting for the guillotine to drop. "I am not prepared to terminate your employment at this time." *Whew.* "Particularly not because of an unfortunate run-in with such a despicable character as DeAndre Muskingum."

"Thank you, Mr. Ly—"

"I'm not finished," he said with a bothered facial twitch.

"Sor—"

"*How*ever. Since word of this unfortunate incident has begun to permeate the halls of our hallowed organization"—*Shit. Fuck. Damn. Crap. I'm gonna be laughed out of the building,* I thought—"I am forced to take some action. I've decided to suspend you for a few weeks. With half-pay. I don't think it would be productive for anyone, including yourself, for you to be around here for a while." I wasn't sure whether to be happy about a paid vacation (kind of) or angry that I was being suspended over such a bullshit incident. Either way, it was time to tell Lyons that Deezy knew our secret.

"Mr. Lyons—"

"Mr. Muskingum will also be suspended."

"Mr. Ly—"

"This is not up for debate."

"But—"

"At all."

"I need to tell you—"

"No."

"But—"

"No."

It wasn't going to happen. Lyons wouldn't give me the chance. *Fine with me,* I thought. *This way I'm certain to walk out of here in one piece.* "I want you to lay low, Mr. Moscowitz. Don't do anything . . . out of the ordinary for the next few weeks. I want you to just stay away. Stay quiet. Let this pass. We will contact you with your return date. Do not speak about this incident with anyone. Do not contact DeAndre Muskingum. Do not contact Oral B. As of this morning, I assigned him a trustworthy temp who can adequately assist him in his writing in your brief absence. Do you remember our previous arrangement?"

"The one where my balls end up on a necklace?"

He didn't smile. Instead he leaned over the desk and looked me straight in the eye for the third and final time that day. "They wouldn't be the first. Are we clear?"

"Yes, sir."

He nodded and did something under his desk, which alerted the two skull-crushing giants that it was okay to come back in. They did. I didn't require any formal farewell ceremony to know that this was my cue to leave. I did so promptly without asking for a raise.

chizapter 6

No sooner than I walked out of the building onto the quiet Santa Monica sidewalk did the gentle vibration and courteous *ding!* of my cell phone alert me to some messages on my voice mail. I dialed the retrieval number, punched in my code, and heard the tinny-voiced computerized bitch who handles my messages for me say, "You/have/two/new/messages . . . First/message re/ceived/to/day at/twelve/twelve/P.M.:" "Yo Dubs, it's B. Hit me up on my ciz-ell, nigga. Aight? I got some shit to aks you about, aight?" *Great.* I got punished by the Boss, now it was time for the Underboss. Oral B wasn't going to be happy about this suspension thing. Brandunn (or B, as he called himself) was accustomed to being able to call me as many times a day as he wanted, *whenever* he wanted. Not only did I need to have lyrics ready for him at all times, but I had to be prepared to make up new ones on the spot if he happened to have some brilliant brainstorm about a subject for a song. Luckily for me, nine out of ten times his brilliant epiphany was about getting pussy, buying cars, or buying jewelry, so all I really needed to do was have an arsenal ready covering these topics.

I deleted the message.

"Next/message/re/ceived/to/day at/twelve/thirty-two/P.M.:""Wallace Q Moscow! Hey, bud. Uncle Jerry. I got big news, kiddo! *Big news!* I just made a follow-up call to one of the publishers we submitted to. They want to meet with you. *Today!* They love the books. They're psyched! Get your shit together and call me back ASAP. Way to go, bud!" *Click.*

Wow! What? Could this be true? Someone was interested! Jerry sounded very excited! I did a little hop-skip-booty-shake dance move on the sidewalk. Halle-freakin'-lujah!

I dialed Jerry's number as quickly as I could. Beth picked up on the second ring. "The Silver Agency."

"Hi, Beth. Wally Moscowitz," I said, feeling suddenly important.

"Oh, hey, Wally. Hold on a sec. I'll get Jerry." I waited, toe-tapping, with bated breath. Beth, not Jerry, came back on a moment later.

"Wally?"

"Yes?"

"Can he call you back?"

"Wh-what?" *Buzzkill.* "I thought, I mean, I think he needs to speak to me."

"Oh . . . well, uh, do you want me to, um . . . " *Yeah, bitch!* Get his ass on the phone!

"No, no. That's . . . that's okay. Just ask him to call me. P-please."

"Okay, Wally."

"As soon as he can."

"Okay, Wally."

Despite the buzzkill, I was still very excited and feeling the need to share the good news with someone. I dialed Sue's number. I paced on the sidewalk as her phone rang and rang. After about ten rings it went to voice mail. This is offensive. It means that Sue was standing there watching the phone ring because she didn't want to speak to me. I happen to know that when her phone is off or in a spot where she has no service, it goes *directly* to voice mail. No ringing whatsoever. So she was clearly screening my call. Sue knows that I know this call-screening secret, so that makes it even more hurtful when she does this to me. *Bitch!* I left a message informing Sue that—

good news—I had a big meeting with a publisher this afternoon, and that I might not be home until five or so. Maybe she'd be excited enough to call and congratulate me. Maybe even excited enough to stop by for a little congratulatory sex. *Yeah right.*

I took a deep breath and dialed Oral B's cell phone number. He picked up on the fifth ring, just as I was rehearsing a message to leave on his voice mail.

"Jeeeeyah?" he answered.

"B-Brandunn? B? It's Wally."

"Yeah yeah! Sup, Dubs?" That's what he called me all the time. Dubs. I think it's short for W, for Wally. I think.

"Hey."

"Sup, pimp? S'appenin? Yo lady was jes up in here."

"What?"

"Yo lady. Whatsername. My girl, Wandeesha, calls her over here to take care a da dogs. *Ruff! Ruff!*" He barked in a deep impersonation of or communication to his dogs.

"Sue? Was *there?*"

"Yeah, foo! She was rubbin' on my dogs and shit. Calms they punkasses down. Know what I'm sayin'?"

"Um, yeah, I just didn't know that she was—"

"Where you at, Dubs?"

"I just left Abraham's office."

"Oh, word? What dat nigga want?" he said, referring endearingly to his boss.

"He suspended me for a few weeks."

"Word? Jes for pissin' on dat foo Deezy?" *Shit. He knows.*

"Yeah. How'd you know?"

"Deezy was jes up in here, too. Told me da whole story. That shit is funny as a muhfucka, Dubs! Ha haaaa!" Glad *somebody* thought so.

"I got suspended. I'm not supposed to be talking to you."

"Yeahhhh, whateva, dawg. Look, I had a idea this mornin'. I need you to write up some shit fo me."

"Uh, didn't he, uh . . . didn't Abraham assign someone else to help you?"

"Whateva, nigga. Look, you my *dawg*, Dubs. Ya heard me? Dis homeboy ain't shit. You got a pen? Write dis shit down, nigga. I had a stroke a brilliance. Look, I wanna call dis one 'Fuck a Bitch Good Wit My Bling Bling Bizalls.' It's a bangin' ghetto luhh story bout a ill nigga who gets his ice chains diznipped in chrizzome right b'fo fuckin' dis hoe doggy steezy in the backseazzy of a fo fitty dot trizzy. Aight? But dey jes gettin' started, right? The ice ain't even cool b'fo some punkass nigga try to break him, right? Stick him for his cream, like nigga *what*. So dis cat jes mopes a nigga out, right? Chokes him wit da ice while he still up in dat twizzat!"

I think that's what he said. I'm usually pretty good at deciphering his dialect, but I have to say, this time I really couldn't be sure what the hell he was talking about. "Gimme sumthin' by tomorra, aight, God?"

"B, I'm really not supposed to be—"

"Yo, holla back, Dubs, I'm out." And he was gone.

chizapter 7

Tuck your shirt in, Mosco. You look like a schlub." Two hours later Jerry and I were waiting for the elevator on our way up to meet the folks at Bionic Books, a small publishing company out of Santa Monica.

"It's not like I had time to go home and change into something nice, Jerry."

He tilted his head downward and peered at me over his silver-framed sunglasses, one eyebrow raised in doubt. "Wally, my boy, no offense, but you don't really *have* anything nice."

"That's not true, Jerry . . . Yeah. Yeah. I guess it is kinda true." Like he was one to talk. Jerry looked like a used car salesman from the Valley, but I didn't say anything. I needed him to be in his best form. "This is crazy, Jerry. I can't believe we're here!"

"Let's not start suckin' each other's dicks quite yet," Jerry responded.

"Ha ha. *Reservoir Dogs*. Right?"

"What?"

"*Reservoir Dogs*." He looked at me like I was speaking Portuguese. "That line you just said is from the movie *Reservoir Dogs*. Right? Or was it *Pulp Fiction*?"

The elevator *pinged!* The shiny chrome-mirrored doors slid open. Several tired faces in business suits exited the car. "What are you talkin' about, Mosco?"

"'Let's not start suckin' each other's dicks quite yet.'" A serious-looking woman wearing short blond hair and a business suit threw me a disgusted look as she brushed past. "Tarantino. Right?" I realized he wasn't listening to me anymore. He was focused on some notes he'd taken on a yellow legal pad. There were only five buttons on the elevator panel. Each one had a different company name adjacent to it. I pushed the one that said Bionic Books.

"Listen, Mosco, we go in there, and *I* run the show. Okay? You with me?"

"Jerry, these are my stories, I want to pitch—"

"No. Listen, Mosco. You let me do the talking in there. You're there just to let them know you're serious about this. You're not some uppity jerkoff who sent his agent to handle his matters for him."

"But, Jerry, I'm passionate about these, don't you think that comes throu—"

"No. Listen. You done this before, Mosco?"

"No, but don't you think I shoul—"

He reached into his pocket and handed me his business card. He extended his hand for me to shake, and I did. "Hi. Jerry Silver. *Agent*." He pointed under his name on the card where it said "agent" in puffy, silver italic letters. "Let me handle everything. Okay?"

The elevator *pinged!* and the doors slid open again. I gave Jerry a defeated look, and we stepped into the cheerful, well-lit lobby of Bionic Books. Large, multicolored, goofy cartoon letters spelled out the company name on the wall behind the receptionist's desk. Horrible Muzac filled the room; I'm pretty sure it was a clarinet-only version of the '90s hit "I Saw the Sign" by Swedish pop foursome Ace of Base. The ebullient receptionist was all smiles from the moment we cleared the threshold.

"Hiiiiiii! Welcome to Bioniiiiic!" she sang, way too excited to see us. She looked like a woman who spent most of her time socializing with the ten or twelve cats she most certainly had running about her small apartment.

"Hi—" I blurted.

"Hello, sweetheart," Jerry interrupted. "We're here to see . . ." He looked down at a little notebook in his hand. "Gary Carter and Howard Johnson." I wondered if I was the only one who found it amusing that Gary Carter and Howard Johnson were both names of guys who played on the 1986 World Series Champion New York Mets.

"Greeeaat, grrreat. What are your names please, hon? Well, *hons!*" She giggled at her own swell joke.

"Jerry Silver and Wallace Q Moscow, honey."

"Okeee pokeee! Here y'are! I'll let the guys know you're here. Have a seat, *hons.*" Giggle giggle. I was tempted to punch her in the nose.

Jerry and I moved to the red-leather-and-chrome chairs and took a seat. The reception area was adorned with large framed posters on each wall. Each poster illustrated what I assumed to be the books that Bionic had published. There was one called *Timmy Loves Berries,* featuring a happy little purple octopus with blue spots who had a different kind of berry in each of his eight tentacles. Another, called *Bo Bo the Bronco Goes to Kindergarten,* featured a frightened little pony wearing a white sailor's cap, blue shorts, and a white T-shirt with a blue anchor on it, standing in a classroom full of smirking human children. And finally, what seemed to be their flagship enterprise (based solely on the size of the poster), a story about a lion and a monkey called *The Wild Adventures of Lie-Lie and Monk-Monk.* Lie-Lie had a safari cap barely containing his unruly mane and Monk-Monk wore khaki from head to toe and held a treasure map in his prehensile tail.

I was about to comment to Jerry that my books didn't seem to fit into the Bionic Books repertoire when the door to the waiting area was suddenly flung open. Two pudgy, red-faced, bald, strawberry-shaped guys *boing-boing-boinged* into the room like a middle-aged Tweedle Dee and Tweedle Dum. The first one, dressed in a hideous light green suit, thrust his hand out toward Jerry. The second one, in hideous blue, followed so closely behind the first that it appeared like he was riding piggy-back. They looked like they'd purchased their suits together back in 1975 at a garage sale at the home of a used car salesman.

"He-he-heyyyyyy! You must be Jerry Silver!"

Jerry seemed to want to match this guy's lively spirit. Playing to the crowd, as usual. "Yessiree, Bob! And you are?"

"I'm Gary Carter! This is my PIC—my partner in crime—Howard Johnson." They all exchanged enthusiastic handshakes.

"Call me HoJo, if you like," chimed Howard helpfully. HoJo's stupid smile was eclipsed only by his oversized round glasses for domination of his chubby face.

"Pleasure to meet you, gentlemen. This is my client, Mr. Wallace Q Moscow."

"Well, well! Nice ta meetcha, Mr. Moscow! Big fans!"

"Nice to meet you, Mr. Carter, HoJo. All we need here is Mookie Wilson and Daryl Strawberry and we got the whole '86 Miracle Mets squad!" Apparently they weren't aware of the coincidental nature of their names, because my joke was met with silence. "Heh. Keith Hernandez? No?" We all looked at each other and I smiled and waited for a mercy laugh. None came.

Gary Carter finally clapped his hands together. "So! Shall we?" He extended his hand down the hallway for us to follow. "HoJo will show you gents the way." We followed the fruit-shaped Howard Johnson down a short hallway and into a drab office, which looked like a page out of an Office Depot catalogue. Faux wood everything.

Jerry and I sat in uncomfortable chairs on one side of a large desk. Gary Carter took the chair opposite us, and Howard Johnson stood beside him, bent over, arms spread with both palms flat on the desk. I noticed a paperweight on the far side of the desk that read something along the lines of "Mean People Suck." That was when the minor worry that had been itching at me since we entered the place developed into a full-blown itchy-as-a-motherfucker rash.

"Well, gosh. Let me just first say that we just *loved* these," said Howard. He picked up a folder on the desk that must have contained my stories and shook it in his hand. "What a hoot!" I quickly realized that *both* of these guys were major blinkers. Meaning: They didn't stop blinking their fucking eyes. They *both* had serious blinking problems and it was making me feel very, very nervous, like I was gonna develop some kind of blinking issue or nervous tick myself just by virtue of being around them.

I thought I was supposed to remain quiet, so I said nothing until I felt Jerry looking at me. "Oh. Th-thank you. Thank you very much."

"Yeaaahhh! Yeah! Very clever! A real treat!"

"Thank you," I repeated. I looked at Jerry and smiled uncomfortably, unsure of how much I was allowed to speak.

"We think that these could be quite a fun project. Might fit in quite nicely here at Bionic," said a very blinky Gary. My heart rate picked up.

"Great!" said Jerry.

"Yeahhhh. Yeah. Hoot and a half," said Howard. "Why don't we talk to you guys a little bit about our vision."

"Twenty-twenty, I hope!" quipped Jerry. *Oh man,* I thought. *No jokes, Jerry.* But the guys laughed boisterously.

"*Haaaa!* Touché, Jerry! Tooooou-ché," gasped Howard, finishing up his laugh.

"We see a lot of potential here in these books," said Gary.

"Indeed," agreed Howard with a thumbs-up.

"Terrific, gentlemen. Do tell." I could tell that Jerry didn't like these two jolly fucks, but he kept his cool and indulged them.

"We see them as very valuable learning tools," said Howard.

"Yesss!" agreed Gary.

"These are subjects that have never been broached before in the children's book arena," Howard explained. "They could be a *wonderful* facilitator for parents who are having trouble initiating those tough conversations that no one wants to have with their youngins."

"Yessss!" agreed Gary. I didn't like where this was going.

"Picture this," said HoJo, his hands waving in front of him, wiping an imaginary canvas. "Little Duckies and Chickies."

"Wow," said Gary.

"Love it," said Jerry.

"Bear with me now . . . Duckies and Chickies," continued HoJo, "with a knack, if you will, a *penchant*"—he said this with a French accent—"for stumbling into situations that no chicky or ducky should *ever* have to stumble into! And how they rationalize these little sitches in an intelligent, patently chicky-ducky sort of way." He smiled, looking for our approval. "Huh?" he asked, palms up in the air. "Huh?"

I was on the verge of tears. Apparently, Jerry was okay with all of this. "Bingo! Wow, you guys clearly get it. That's exactly what Wallace here is trying to do . . . here." I looked at Jerry. He didn't acknowledge me. "Wow. You guys *nailed* it!"

"All righty! Then we're on the same page-ola!" Blink blink blink blink blink.

"Absolutely . . . ola," said Jerry.

"Swell! Then, what we need from you, Mr. Moscow . . . can I call you Wallace?"

"Uh . . ." *Can I call you Blinky?* I thought. I was too dumbfounded to respond. I think I may have nodded.

"Wallace. What we need from you, Wallace, is for you to just clean 'em up a bit. Okay, a *lot*." *Fuck.* "Sanitize the language. We might have to just start over completely with a few of 'em. Maybe all of 'em. Who knows? Same concept. Cleaner language. Chicky-ducky style. You smell what I'm cookin', Wallace?"

"Uh, I'm not sure . . ."

"Welllll, they're pretty risqué right now. I don't think any parent would feel real comfortable giving these to a child at this point. You know."

This was not good. Not good at all. *Time to speak up.* "They're not *supposed* to be for chil—"

"Yes!" Jerry cut me off. "Yessss. We completely hear what you guys are saying. In fact, you're preachin' to the choir. We were *just* discussing that on our way up here. Right, Q?" He glared at me. The Mets just looked on with dumb smiles on their plump faces.

"Well, no—" I blubbered.

"It's *my* fault really. I kept telling Wallace, 'Push the envelope, Q. Push it, push it, aaand push it. Be controversial.' When all along he was just saying, 'I gotta tone this down, Jerry. I just gotta. Gotta clean it up, you know? For the kids.'"

I wanted to protest. I really did. But I didn't say another word. I swallowed my pride and choked back some vomit.

"Great! Super! So we *are* on the same page!" Howard said with an enthusiastic clap.

"Oh, absolutely! Absolutely," said Jerry. "So? Are we in bed together here, gentlemen?"

"Whoa! Jerry! We just met!" said Gary. They all laughed stupidly. I was numb.

"Let's see some reworking. Maybe in a few days you can show us some good clean, fun stuff, and then we can talk about what it's gonna take to make you guys official members of the Bionic family," said Gary, as he rubbed his finger and thumb together making the international sign for "moolah."

"Sounds terrific, guys," said Jerry, as he rose. "It has been a pleasure."

"More than a pleasure," said HoJo. "It's been just ducky!"

They all laughed.

. . . .

"What the *fuck,* Jerry?" I whispered angrily as the elevator doors slid shut.

"Bye, sweetheart!" He waved merrily to the receptionist until the doors cut them off. "What the fuck, my boy, is that *we just sold your books!*" He held up a hand requesting a high-five. I left him hanging and stared at him dumbly. The elevator began descending. Jerry put his arm around me and squeezed me too tightly. The combination of his cologne and his suffocating grip almost made me pass out. "Whatsamatter, buddy? Huh? We did it!"

"Did it? What the fff—Jerry, we just totally sold out!"

"Sold out, shmold out. What are you talkin' about, Mosco? The only thing we're sellin' is your books! Finally! Be happy!"

"No, Jerry!" I slapped my own thigh in childish frustration. "No. This is *not* what I wanted. This is not what I wanted, Jerry!"

"Mosco. What are you *talkin'* about? You're gonna get paid, bud! Dinero! Finally!"

"Jerry . . . " I put my hand to my forehead as if to read my temperature. I tried to remain calm. "You don't get it, Jerry."

The elevator doors slid open, depositing us safely back on the ground floor. The late afternoon sun shone through a high window in the lobby, hitting me right in my eyes. I followed Jerry toward the parking lot blindly, seeing sunspots.

Without turning around to look at me, Jerry said, "What I *do* get is that you, Wally, are gonna be a wealthy man, and that *we* are gonna go celebrate tonight."

"Cele—? Jerry—you don't—"

"Oh, I get it, Wally. Believe me, I get it. But you're gonna have to push your tragic little artist's integrity out of your sad little brain if you wanna make some cash in this lifetime. Okay? I'm here to help you do that." We made it to his silver Vette. He pushed a button on his keychain and the car made a repugnant *beep-boop-beep!* sound, and we got in.

On the fifteen-minute drive to my house, Jerry talked the

entire time. I tuned him out. I think he was explaining to me how *not* to be such a wimp or something along those lines. To me it sounded like the *wah wah wah wah* sound that Charlie Brown's teacher makes when she speaks. We pulled up in front of my building, and Jerry let me out.

"I'll call you a little later, okay? I'm meeting some people for drinks around eight. You'll come meet us. We'll celebrate and drink all your concerns away, all right, bud?"

"Ahh, we'll see, Jerry." I closed the car door and moped away. I heard his window roll down. As I pulled open the door to my building, Jerry shouted, "Congratulations, Q! Cheer up! We're gonna be *rich!*" I let the door close behind me without giving him the benefit of a response.

The jarring stench of curry assaulted my nostrils as soon as I stepped foot into the stairway. As I approached the second-floor landing, the sound of East Indian pop music filled the stairwell, completing the sensation that I was walking through a street market in Bangladesh. As I sulked past Pardeep's door, my superfriendly, curry-cooking neighbor popped out to have a chat. Just what I was in the mood for.

"Eyyy. Id is Wally Moscowitz! Ow are you doink, my good frient?" he yelled over the music in his thick Indian accent.

"Oh, hey, Pardeep. How are you?" I tried to keep walking but old Pardy wanted to party.

"Ohhh, Wally. I tell you and I tell you and I tell you to call me 'Deep.' "

"Sorry . . . Deep."

"Ohhh, dat is quite all right, my good frient. I must ask you, Mr. Wally, why is your face so long?"

"Ahh, it's nothing, Deep. Don't worry about it. I just had a rough day is all."

"Ohhh, Wally. Dat is too too bad. Would you like some dinner to cheer you up? Dare is enough food in dare to fill maybe sixteen armies of donkeys!"

"No thanks, I just ate."

"Ohhh. Dat is too too bad. Okay, Wally. I will be seeing you soon, my good frient. And remember to cheer up! Tomorrow will be better."

"Yeah. I'm sure you're right." That's what I said, but inside I was really wondering if I would ever be truly happy in my entire life.

"Just tink of what dat man Forrest Gump says. 'Life is like a box of chocolates. You never know what you are goink to get.' Remember dat all of de time and you will feel ooookay."

"Okay. All right. Thanks, Deep." I wasn't sure that his choice of trite maxims was *quite* appropriate, but hey, it was the thought that counted. We parted ways, and I kept on huffing my way up toward my apartment.

As I trudged up the last two flights of stairs I thought, *Life is NOT like a box of chocolates, Pardeep. It is NOT always sweet and delicious and wonderful. Moreover, unless you are from Outer Mongolia or the South Pole or Upstate New York or some other remote part of the world where boxes of chocolate do not exist and thrive, somewhere where you've somehow managed to get through your ENTIRE life never having seen or sampled a single box of chocolates, you do know EXACTLY what you're gonna get in every single box. Especially since there's a little map on the inside of the lid that diagrams exactly which chocolate resides where! Why do we buy into this crap? What are we, retarded? Fuck you, Forrest, for inserting your corny saccharine bullshit into the public lexicon to be eaten up and regurgitated over and over again in perpetuity by silly schmucks like Pardeep Vishvatma. No, I take that back. Fuck your mother, Forrest. She's the imbecile who imparted her horseshit wannabe-sage philosophy into your half-wit brain, so that you could sit on that bench and pontificate to any poor lonely schmuck with the misfortune— not only to be taking the bus home—but to get stuck sitting next to you while waiting for it to pick their broke ass up. As if their lives aren't pathetic enough? Jeez! And now I have to listen to this happy horseshit from some blithe foreigner jerk-off whose biggest worry in the world is how much cumin to add to his curry? God my life sucks.*

As I approached my front door, I realized that I was being an asshole and I apologized internally to both Pardeep and the Gump family. My life was so dismal that I had taken to destroying the innocent advice of a kindly retarded man in a feeble attempt to make myself feel better. I couldn't even find a *real* retarded guy to pick on, I had to choose a fictional one. *Pathetic.*

When I entered my apartment, it took a few minutes before I realized that something was very, *very* wrong.

chizapter 8

I was bullshitting around for a minute or two before I realized that Dr. Schwartzman was not in the apartment.

I was in such a daze when I got home that I hadn't even noticed right away. I gave the room a panicked quick-scan. "Doctor?" I beckoned, with no reply. I gave a loud whistle. He didn't appear. I juked this way and that like a running back trying to avoid a tackle. I didn't know what to do first.

The bedroom: "Doc . . . ? You here, buddy?" Nothing. I moved to the bathroom: "Doctor . . . ?" Nope. The living room again, with another whistle: "Dr. Schwartzman?" No Doctor. Bedroom again: under the bed? No. Every closet: no, no, no.

Doctor Schwartzman was most definitely *not* there. I started to freak.

Maybe Sue came over, and they're out on a walk! Duh! I ran and grabbed the phone, punched in Sue's cell phone number. It went straight to voice mail. I left the calmest, most succinct message I could manage. "Hey, babe, it's me. Just got home, wondering if by any chance you stopped by and took the Doctor for a walk. He's not here, so . . . I just figured that's the only thing that could've, uh . . . there's no sign of forced entry, so, uhhh, you probably, you guys are probably just out on a walk or something. Which is cool. Call me, or I'll just see you, hopefully in a few minutes when you guys get back from your walk, if that's where you are and hopefully you are, so, uh . . . you know, see yaaaa, uh, soon. In a few. Hopefully. Bye." I hung up quickly when I noticed that the voice mail message light on the phone was blinking. *That must be Sue letting me know she has him,* I thought. I called the retrieval number. I heard Sue's voice on the message, and I was flooded with relief. But only for a moment. "Hi, Wally, it's Sue. It's like, ummmm, two o'clock or something. I'm not gonna be able to come over tonight. I'm really sorry. I just got a call from Bill Cosby's wife, Camille. Their Chihuahuas, Trinidad and Tobago, are having some serious stress issues—they got scared in the park by a bigger dog—and soooo, I need to go over there and treat them. They're waaaay out in the Valley, soooo, I'll be back late. But, I'll talk to you later, 'kay? Or tomorrow." *Click.*

There it was. Sue didn't have the Doctor. *Holy shit.* My heart started to really pound. I ran and checked the lock on my front door to make sure I didn't miss some indiscernible disfigurement caused by an intruder. The doorknob and lock both looked fine. *Even the most amateur burglar can get past a shitty old lock like that with no problem,* I reasoned. *Fuck! Fuck Fuck FUCK!* I ran around like a chicken with his balls cut off. My head was spinning and my brain was moving even faster than my chubby legs could move me in aimless circles around my apartment. *Think, Wally, think. There must be a reasonable explanation for this. Where could the Doctor be? Okay . . . Sue is out. Any friends? No, not really. My mom? She lives in New York. That's out. Maybe the dog walker has him!* I thought, knowing damn well that I do not have a dog walker. *Maybe that chick who walks that guy's dog on the second floor has him.* Clearly, all logic was gone from the equation at this point.

Deep down I knew what was going on. I was avoiding it but I knew.

Dr. Schwartzman had been dognapped.

I had a sudden inspiration. I threw open my front door and dashed down the stairs. I practically fell down the last five or six steps to the second-floor landing. The Indian pop music still echoed in the stairwell. "Pardeep!" I shouted over the music. I pounded on his already-open front door. "Pardeeeeep!" I yelled again into the cracked doorway. He popped his little hairy brown head around the corner.

"Eyyy! Id is Wally Moscowitz once agayne! Did you change your mind about dinn—"

"Pardeep, have you seen my dog in the last few hours?"

"Ohhhhhh, de Doctor? Nooooo. No. Unfortunately I have not seen my good good frient Doctor Barry Schwartzman. Is he missing?" His dumb, oblivious smile made me want to shake the life and the curry out of him.

"You didn't see anyone come down the steps in the last hour or two with the Doctor?"

Worry started to register on Pardeep's face as he realized something was very wrong. "Noooo. Is eberything okay, Wally?"

"Fuck! No. It's not, Pardeep. Someone took my dog."

"Ohhhh, *no! Wally! No! No! No!*" He looked genuinely devastated. "Dat is too too terrible!"

"Did you see *anyone,* Pardeep? Did *anyone* come or go from here besides me in the last few hours?"

"Noooo. No, Wally. I don't tink so. But I must tell you dat my music was berry berry loud. So it is berry berry possible dat someone could have slipped by without me ebber knowing!" he said sadly. Realization suddenly creeped its way into Pardeep's expression.

"What? What is it?" I asked him.

"Now dat I am tinking about dis, Wally? Come wit me!" He turned from the door and tore off into his apartment. He led me to the window and pointed down to the street and jumped up and down. "Ohhhhhhh. Ohhh goodness goodness me! Dat is it!"

I looked out the window but didn't see what he was talking about. "What is it?"

"Dat car! Dat black one right dare!" He pointed to a big shiny SUV parked across the street from our building. From above, it looked like a Cadillac Escalade, but it was hard to be sure. "Dat car has been parked dare aaaalllll day. Dare are men sitting in dare looking like dey are watching dis place aaaaalllll day. I am noticing dem two or three times since early dis morning!"

I was out the door before he even finished his sentence. I flew down the stairs, vaguely aware that Pardeep was following me. I bashed the front door of the building open and looked across the street. The SUV was still there.

The loud crash of the thick steel door smashing against the brick wall of the building alerted the driver of the SUV to my presence, and he started the engine immediately. I dashed across the street, Pardeep in tow.

The large tires screeched painfully and the truck took off in a brilliant black and chrome-rimmed blur before I could reach it. I'm not sure what I would have done had I actually caught up with the SUV. I can't really see myself tearing the door open and pulling the driver out, beating him until he told me who sent him.

The pitch-black tinted windows prevented me from seeing who was behind the wheel as the vehicle flew past us. I didn't get the plates. No distinguishing features. Pardeep and I stood in the street and watched helplessly as the SUV disappeared on the horizon.

"Ohhhh dat fuckermother!" yelled Pardeep, his fist thrust angrily in the air. He took the words right out of my mouth. Kind of.

Little did I know that the shit had just barely begun to hit the fan.

chizapter 9

I prefer to skip discussion of the following two days because they totally sucked in every conceivable way.

But I can't. They're sort of key to your understanding my mind frame when I made certain decisions or indiscretions that followed soon thereafter.

Here's what happened: I wallowed in sadness for Dr. Barry Schwartzman. I tirelessly, futilely searched the neighborhood over and over again. I knocked on every door in the building hoping to find a witness to this heinous crime. I went to the buildings on either side of mine, too. I even called the cops, who clearly thought I was a maniac. They told me that (*chuckle, chuckle*) they don't handle doggynappings. *Assholes.*

Jerry, like an angel from heaven, offered to put up a one-thousand-dollar reward for the Doctor's safe return. I plastered the neighborhood with hideously colored (all they had at Kinko's was pink and purple!) reward posters. I hung the posters on every corner, in every veterinarian's office, gas station, convenience store, pet store, toy store, music store, clothing store, liquor store, and porn store within three miles of my building.

I languished in my dirty little apartment, waiting to hear something—*anything*—that would indicate that the Doctor was okay. But there was nothing. No ransom notes. No phone calls. No *nothing*. Only despair and loneliness.

The *only* bright side of all this was that whomever it was that broke into my apartment and stole my dog hadn't known about my shoebox full of cash, and that was still there. *Slight* relief.

I relentlessly pondered the possibilities over the next painfully slow two days. Theories and suspects and motives ran through my muddled brain like looters in a riot; they came and went and came back again later to ravage some more.

Theory number one: Could the Doctor have simply gotten out of my apartment somehow and wandered away? Could my dognapping theory be completely paranoid and crazy?

No. I didn't think it was crazy. Not at all. It was crazier to think that that fat, lazy bastard (and I mean that in the most loving way), Dr. Schwartzman, would ever have the strength or the inclination to perform such a daring escape.

Theory number two: Abraham Lyons. Maybe he was trying to scare me or threaten me into silence, believing that my suspension—when piled upon my annoying money situation and general obvious misery—would make me want to go public about Oral B. If I *did* go public, it would certainly spell the end for Oral B and for Godz-Illa Records and would ensure me a terrific fifteen minutes of fame. Oral B would go the way of Milli Vanilli—a footnote in the Pop Culture Lexicon of Losers. However, the more I thought about it, the less I believed this theory. Lyons wouldn't have gone after my dog. It's not his style. He might go after my *dawgs* (translation: friends), if I had any, but not my pet. He knows I'm a terrified pussy who will keep my terrified pussy mouth shut. He's always counted on it. But could it have something to do with that kid in the Laundromat?

Theory number three: What about Funk Deezy? Could he have dognapped the Doctor in some twisted revenge plot? Did I wrong him *so* badly that it led him to *this*? I supposed that urinating all over him like a big, black, orange-velour-covered urinal cake was a pretty serious offense. Especially for a so-called gangsta such as himself. Yes, Deezy seemed a more likely suspect. Particularly since he knew I wrote for Oral B. *He probably knows I have money and he wants to extort me!* This worried me a great deal, because in my mind Deezy was capable of dogslaughter. He had nothing to lose. *But what could I DO?*

The terrible reality was, there was nothing I *could* do, except wait and pray that I would receive some word on the Doc's whereabouts. Fortunately, if I did receive a ransom note, I had about twenty-five grand stuffed in a shoebox in my bedroom closet that I could use for ransom.

Peppered among the whodunit thoughts and conspiracy theories were painful memories of all the good times the Doctor and I had spent together over the years. I fondly recalled the time when I came home from work to find that the almost tailless Doctor had suddenly grown a long black tail. I couldn't believe it! I soon discovered upon closer examination that he had eaten and fully passed one of my black dress socks, which was halfway out his asshole, masquerading as a tail. He gave a little yelp as I pulled the sock out and he bolted into the closet, where he spent the next few hours convalescing. Ahh, good times. I even went and put on that sock, just for old times' sake.

Just kidding.

Sue called around noon the day after the Doctor disappeared. She sounded pretty surprised and upset about the whole thing. She just didn't care as much about how *I* was doing as I desperately wished she would have. I needed her support. Badly. And it wasn't there. She was clearly preoccupied. Apparently, Barbra Streisand's papillon, Yenta, needed a dog sitter/masseuse for the next few stressful days while Babs played a couple of shows over in Vegas. It turned out that Sue was leaving for Vegas on a private jet later that same evening and could therefore not assist me in the search for my beloved pet. Yeah, she loved the Doctor and all—but Babs comes first.

Like I said, these two days *totally sucked.*

By the end of the second day, I was nearly out of my mind. When Jerry called me at around 7:00 P.M. I was a real mess. I was sprawled on my back on the cold hardwood floor wearing nothing but boxers and socks, singing a sad sad version of "Who Let the Dogs Out." I had a framed picture of the Doctor resting on my chest. I looked like a guy who had been floating in a lifeboat for months. My facial hair was overgrown, and my hair was mussed and greasy. I had barely eaten in days.

Jerry had called several times, never with any good news. I hadn't even bothered to answer his last three calls. I finally answered, because the thought of hearing the fucking phone ringing one more fucking time might well have pushed me over the fucking edge of fucking sanity. Jerry asked if I'd heard anything yet, and I told him—in a gravelly, underused voice—that no, I hadn't. He sounded concerned. He begged me to come out and have a drink with him, take my mind off things. A small part of me wanted to go. Mainly because I wanted to tell Jerry once and for all that the whole Bionic Books thing did not interest me. Yes, I wanted to sell my books (more than anything!), but I would *not* turn them into sanitized, precious, cutesy little Sesame Street handbooks for Mommy and Daddy to teach their kids about the evils of man.

Instead I just declined Jerry's invitation outright, preferring the quiet solace of my apartment to the cacophony of a Hollywood bar. He told me he'd be at the Kissing Room on Sunset if I changed my mind.

Two hours later, soaked to the bone in misery, I decided that I needed a drink and I needed it now.

What a life-changing decision that turned out to be.

....

I called Jerry for directions. "Heyyyyy, Wally! Terrific! This'll be great! Some liquor will make you feel better, Mosco. Maybe a little poontang too. I'm sure the ice princess ain't giving you any. Probably out somewhere giving a Dalmatian a hand job, right? Am I right?" I could tell Jerry was a little drunk. Already, I was starting to regret my decision. Unfortunately, he was correct; that's exactly where Sue was.

Twenty minutes later, a disheveled me walked into the Kissing Room. It looked like a place that was definitely cool once. Not so much anymore. It was mostly empty. The room was low and long and poorly lit, filled with dark-red, stressed leather furniture. Little hanging lights with opaque, amber-colored glass shades were suspended from the black stucco ceiling. Despite the laws in Los Angeles, the smallish room was filled with cigarette smoke.

I spotted Jerry sitting at the bar with a pretty young blond girl on each side of him. As soon as I saw him, I tuned into his voice loudly telling the bartender, "Three more of these apple martinis, Captain. And don't be such a cheapskate with the vodka this time, bucko. Make 'em stiffies." He was *definitely* drunk. I could tell he was showing off to his two female admirers. Playing to the crowd as usual. I watched the handsome bartender roll his eyes as he turned away from Jerry to pour the drinks. Jerry's blond companions, one pixie-cut and one long-haired, smiled approvingly at each other and then at him, apparently impressed with his braggadocio as they flirtingly spun back and forth on their stools.

I told myself I'd have a drink or two, give Jerry the news that we were going to decline the happy schmucks at Bionic Books, and go home. I walked up behind Jerry and put my hand on his shoulder. He turned to me at full volume. "Heyyyyyyyy! Wallace Q Moscow! Alive and well!"

I smiled weakly. "Hey, Jerry. Hi."

"Ladies, meet my most brilliant client, Mr. Wallace Q Moscow. No period after the Q."

The girls looked me up and down in that discreet (yeah, right) Los Angeles way, each finishing with expressions dancing oh-so-delicately between distaste or disgust and just plain old disinterest.

"Have a drink, Q." He turned to the bartender. "Hey! Sam Malone—two shots of tequila." The annoyed bartender, who had clearly had his fill of Jerry, slid two large golden shots in our direction. "Don't these come with limes and salt there, Sammy?" The bartender placed the limes and salt in front of us gently, teeth grinding, doing his very best not to fly over the bar and do bodily harm to Jerry.

We held up our shots. "To Bionic Books!" shouted Jerry. "And their newest, most successful author!" He grinned from ear to ear.

I hesitated a moment. "Uh, Jerry, about that . . ."

He threw his shot of tequila down his throat with some serious force, and sucked on the lime. "Woooooooo! That is goooood shiiiiiiiiiit! Drink your ta-kill-ya, Mosco!"

"But Jerry—"

"Take it!"

I took it. And a few minutes later, another. And another and another and another.

Next thing I knew I was about eight shots deep, elbows on the bar, resting my heavy head in my hands, droopy eyed, absolutely positively fucking drunk. A graveyard of empty shot glasses and sucked limes dotted the mahogany landscape before me. I looked to my right and watched Jerry flirting animatedly with the two blond bitches on either side of him, who sat riveted by his bullshit. I remember thinking, *Bitches. You can't beat 'em. And I mean that in EVERY sense of the word.* And then I recall thinking how brilliant I thought that was and wishing that I had a pen to write it down on the handy napkin that happened to be resting conveniently under the almost-empty drink in front of me, just waiting to be written on.

It was with the intention of finding said pen that I turned my head to the left and caught a glimpse of her, sitting only two stools away:

The Most Beautiful Girl in the Universe.

I stared. Maybe for too long, although I don't think she was aware. If she *was* aware, then she was cool as ice. Cool and *hot* all at once like a fistful of Bengay. This girl was probably used to being stared at. She was fucking *radiant.* Her hair was shoulder length but choppy. Jet black with a few streaks of glowing neon pink. She had roving green eyes, pouty pink perfect lips, red star-shaped earrings, and an adorable little curvy black leather–clad body like a motorcycle seat that I wanted desperately to sit on. She was the most stunning woman I had ever seen in my life. And from that very first glance she looked *achingly* familiar.

As she sat there stirring her drink, I felt an empty yearning within. A desperate loneliness. I wanted to talk to this girl, but I couldn't. I had a girlfriend who loved me . . . right?

You know what? Fuck Sue, I thought. *Where is she when I need her?*

I looked back at Jerry, who was watching *me* watch her, with just a bit too much interest. He winked and nodded his head toward her, encouraging me to make my move. The tequila gave me the courage to slide over to the empty stool that stood between us. She smelled like the first bite of a peach.

"Hi. I'm uh . . . I'm Wally." I did my very best to sound cool and suave and to not slur my words. "I really like your hairs . . . cut. And stuff."

She looked at me with pink-lidded, greener-than-grass eyes. My heart stopped. She said nothing, and for a moment I wondered if my heart was going to start up again. I also thought, *God, I KNOW this chick from SOMEWHERE.* Then she leaned over and whispered in my ear, "Hi, Wally. I'm bored." I got a boner.

"Ha. Oh . . . I'm ah, I'm so, I'm sorry to hear that."

"Take me home."

"Whaaat?" I smiled stupidly.

She pulled back just a bit, still boner-inducingly close to my face. "Take me home, Wally. I'm bored."

"Home? Well, I, uh, who, the uh, the thing is . . . that I umm, I—"

"Wally, you can sit here and stutter like a fucking moron by yourself"—back to the whisper in my ear—"or you can take me home and *fuck* me."

I was out the door.

There was a cab idling right outside the bar, and we hopped in. We didn't say a word the entire way home, because we were making out frantically like two high school kids parked at some idyllic make-out point.

We burst into my apartment, kissing intensely, hungrily. We were already undressed by the time we hit the bed. She smelled like a peach but she tasted like tequila. I can't say that I remember *all* the wonderful details, but I can say that it was fan-fuckin'-tastic. Stuff like this never happened to me. What a night! Just when I needed it most. Thankfully, I was drunk and distracted enough to forget aaaaaaall about my disastrous life for a while.

MY BROTHER PETE SMELLS FUNNY
~~By Wally Moscowitz~~
BY : WALLACE Q MOSCOW

I love my brother Pete, he's the coolest guy I know.
He goes to college and has long hair. I'm so glad he's my bro.
He's always smiling and laughing. He's never mad, or mean.
And Pete can sleep later and eat more snacks than anyone I've seen!
My friends say that he's scary, 'cuz his eyes are always red;
And he wears these shirts with skeletons on 'em, and talks about "the dead."
But I tell my friends they're crazy; how can they think Pete is scary?
Scary people don't sit for hours watching Tom and Jerry.
We always watch cartoons together—our favorite one is Scooby.
Pete says he likes it better after he visits his friend "Doobie."
Pete always hangs with Doobie, but I've still never met this guy.
When I ask Pete why, he simply smiles and tells me "Doobie's shy."
The other thing that bugs me is that Pete smells kinda weird.
When I told him that, he looked at me and a bigger smile appeared.
I asked him, "What's so funny? Why're you smiling at me like that?"
He just kept grinning at me, and then he gave my head a pat.
He said "Lil bro, I love ya, one day you'll have a 'Doobie' of your own.
But till that day, all that I'll say's that smell's my new cologne."

—From *The Adult Children's Books Collection*

chizapter 10

The sun blazed through my window like a searchlight on a police helicopter, brutalizing my eyes with painful, lid-penetrating brilliance. My still-sleeping eyes took a minute to adjust and communicate to my brain that there *wasn't* a police helicopter shining its spotlight directly into my window; there was, however, a big empty space carved into the sheets beside me where a woman had slept a short time ago. It took a whole few more seconds to comprehend that the phone was ringing (probably the thing that stirred me from sleep in the first place). I cleared my throat and practiced aloud, "Ahem, hello? Hello?" My sandpaper voice seemed to pass the awake-enough-to-answer-the-phone test. I grabbed the receiver. "Hello?" I half-croaked in the awakest voice I could muster.

"We have your dog," said a deep, computer-disguised voice. I glanced at the white clock on my nightstand; it read 10:04 A.M.

"What?"

"We . . . have . . . Doctor . . . Barry . . . Schwartzman," said the robot again. Even in my sleepy confusion I doubted that a robot was behind all of this. The guy was using some kind of voice-changing device.

"W-what? Where is—*Who is this?*"

"Blockbuster Video. Beverly and La Cienega. Comedy section. Look inside *Turner and Hooch* for further instructions." *Click.*

What? I held the phone away from my bed-creased face and looked at the receiver as if it was going to provide some visual explanation for what I'd just heard. *Was this a fucking joke?!* Turner and Hooch? *The '80s buddy cop movie starring Tom Hanks and that big drooling dog?*

We . . . have . . . Doctor . . . Barry . . . Schwartzman . . .

I flew out of bed and threw on the nearest clothes I could find: a pair of rumpled, torn-at-the-knees jeans, and a totally sweet blue T-shirt that reads "I ♥ Aunt Shirley's Magical Muffins, Davis, California." I put on my old gray New Balance running shoes, sans socks, and bolted for the door.

As I reached for the knob, I screeched to an immediate halt.

A pair of pink lace panties hung from the doorknob.

What . . . is . . . this? I thought, as I unhooked the delicate undergarment from the knob and slowly raised the underwear to eye level. They dangled daintily from my index finger, a sexy little mystery. I examined them with wonder in my eyes, a smile creeping into the corners of my mouth, and a pleasant stirring in my nether regions. Stuffed inside the crotch of the pretty undies was a small, balled-up piece of paper. I liked where this was going. I removed the paper and uncrumpled it. In bubbly, girlish handwriting it read:

> *Dear Wally,*
> *Thanks for the workout. Do me a favor—rub a few out before we meet tonight. It was fun but way too brief. Same time, same place.*
> *XOXO,*
> *Jem*

The smile that had been creeping up on me spread into a full-fledged grin. *Jem.* In my rush to leave the house I had almost forgotten about my night. *Wow. Jem! She has a name!* Pretty, pretty Jem, who smells like a peach and tastes like tequila and fucks like a porn star.

What an evening we'd had! Ideal, really. No talking, no inane getting-to-know-you bullshit. All business. We did our thing and she was gone in the morning. *Incredible.* And now this charming little communiqué assuring me that there was more wonderfulness in my very near future. I was looking at the panties, overjoyed at this special little token of Jem's appreciation, this perfect souvenir of my vacation in Awesome Town, when the unthinkable happened.

The front door opened, and Sue stepped in.

I thrust the panties from my face down into the pocket of my jeans, startling her.

"Hi. W-what was *that*?" she asked, puzzled by my sudden rapid movement.

"Sue! Hi! That was nothing! You scared me!"

"Oh—!" She stood there awkwardly, framed by the doorway, tottering between in and out. I could see the wheels of suspicion turning in Sue's brain. I stared at her innocently, nervously. Despite all the shit that Sue puts me through, all the agony of late, I'm still unbelievably, undeniably attracted to her. I don't know why—she's so clearly an unconscionable bitch. It's not her looks. I mean, she's *not* a hot chick in the traditional sort of way. Sort of smallish and thickish, really. Not at all curvy or voluptuous or *Maxim* magazine sexy. She's slightly shorter than I am, with long blondish hair the color of matzah, and a face just as flat. Her sleepy blue eyes glow like they're plugged into an electrical outlet. It's not the eyes that get me though, either—it's the full ensemble. There's just something . . . *cool* about her. Sue's got her own style. She's funky. She's original. She's got this nonchalant way of putting herself together in the nicest things—the most expensive labels—without looking haughty or ostentatious. The girl has just got something special. People instantly like her from the first time they meet her.

"What are you *doing* here?" I said. "I thought you were in Veg—"

"Yeah, I came back." She seemed nervous, brushing an invisible strand of hair from her face repeatedly. I know *I* certainly was nervous, but I had a good reason—some other girl's panties in my pocket. It hadn't fully occurred to me until that very moment that I was now officially cheating on Sue.

"Oh. Wow! What, uh, what happened? Show get cancelled?"

"Wellll, I . . . she didn't really need me, and I . . . I wanted to talk to you, and, uh, see how you were doing with the whole Doctor thing, and . . . " She trailed off. Put her hands in her pockets and kicked a dust bunny on the broken linoleum floor.

"Well, thank you," I said. She gave me an odd look that fell somewhere between pity and sympathy. Could've been disgust.

"Any word on the Doctor?" she asked, after more uncomfortable silence. Although I wasn't so sure that Sue loved *me* anymore, one thing was absolutely certain: She *definitely* loved the Doctor. She always had, always would. It's a sad state of affairs, really, that I can only guarantee my girlfriend's love of my pet. I guess the Doctor, although certainly pudgy and unathletic like myself, isn't balding and neurotic and always wanting to have sex with her. So it makes *some* sense.

"I just got a ransom note!" I blurted, still thrown by her sudden appearance.

Sue was taken aback. She cocked her head slightly to the side. "You got . . . a *what*?"

"A ransom note. From whoever took the Doctor!"

"That?" she asked, pointing to the crumpled-up note from Jem that I still held in my hand. I had shoved the panties in my pocket but neglected to hide the note. Fucking retard I am.

"This? No! No! This is, ahhhh, this is something else. This is, uh, this is nuh-nothing." I stammered.

"Oh . . ."

"Just a note from my, uh, from from my lagent." I shoved the crumpled note deep into my pocket.

"Your what?"

"Agent! My agent. You know, Jerry. My agent. It's Jerry. The note."

"Ooookayyy . . ."

"Yeah . . . No. That's uh . . . The ransom note I got is waiting for me down at Blockbuster Video. *Turner and Hooch* aisle. Comedy."

"Wally, what the *hell* are you talking about? You're being weird."

"I'm sorry, I'm just shaken up. I just got this phone call . . . " I explained the phone call to Sue, and she was mystified. "Wait— they said they had the Doctor? Like, *your dog,* the Doctor?"

"Yeah! Is there some other missing Doctor that I should be aware of? Did uhhh, did like, did my dentist, Dr. Levey, get abducted too?"

"So—someone is claiming to have *kidnapped* the Doctor?"

"Dognapped! Yes!"

"And you're . . . on your way to go get the *ransom note*? For the Doctor."

"Yes! You want to come with me?"

"Um, yeah. I mean . . . yeah. This is too weird." It occurred to me that we hadn't even kissed hello. One day earlier this would have *devastated* me. I would have been crushed. But not today! Nooooo! Not today. Now there was *Jem!* Woo hooooo! Jem! Gimme a J! J! Gimme an E! E! Gimme an M! M! What's that spell? *Jem!* Who'd I bang last night? *Jem!* Who was I gonna bang again tonight? *Jem! Woo hoooo!*

Last night was pretty frickin' *awesome* by Wally Moscowitz standards. I wanted to get up in Sue's face and yell, "How ya like me *now,* beeyatch?!" But I didn't.

Part of me felt very guilty about cheating on her, while another part of me wanted to take the panties out and rub them in her face and dance around the room singing songs about banging girls named Jem. Interesting dilemma. And still a third part of me was absolutely terrified that she would find out. So, no singing or dancing or panty/face rubbing.

"Let's go to Blockbuster," I said.

....

Sue had her car, which was excellent, because my car was at the bar where I'd left it last night, and I was dying to just get to Blockbuster already and find out what the hell was going on. The downside was that the car ride was terribly awkward. The radio was off, and the silence was deafening. Sue appeared to be deep in thought the entire time. She probably wasn't aware of it, but her eyebrows were arched harshly, her forehead crinkled neatly—the telltale sign that something was seriously troubling her. I had a feeling that maybe Sue had seen the panties after all, and knew that something untoward was going on. Or maybe it wasn't that. Maybe it was just because our relationship was weird these days and she wasn't sure how to act around me. Or maybe it was just a simple case of Sue's a bitch. Whatever it was, we didn't speak for the first several minutes of the ride. I sat in the fuzzy, cloth-covered seat with my legs fully extended and crossed out in front of me. Sue's car smelled like one of those yellow, vanilla-flavored hanging trees.

I finally broke the ice. "You okay?"

Clearly I was interrupting some involved inner monologue. She seemed surprised to hear a voice. "What?" she said, her reverie broken.

"You okay? You seem, uh . . . troubled."

"Yeah, I don't know. I'm just . . . this whole thing is weird."

"You're telling me."

"Yeah, but you don't seem . . . aren't you totally freaked out about Dr. Schwartzman? I mean, I figured you'd be a mess!"

I shot a laugh out of my nose. "You should've seen me yesterday. I've been an *absolute* mess since he disappeared. Today is the first day that I'm feeling a little bit . . . better."

"You seem . . . I don't know . . . not that concerned."

"Not that concerned?! Sue, believe me, I'm *that* concerned. Trust me, I love that dog more than *anything*. I've been to hell and back the last few days. Seriously. I'm just . . . I don't know,

I'm feeling somehow better about things today. Like he's gonna be okay."

"Okay, okay. That's *good*. That's really good. I'm really relieved. I'm really glad and relieved and just really glad to hear that." She gave me a tight-lipped smile, which I returned. It was nice to know that maybe she actually *did* care. At least a little bit. It also gave me another pang of guilt that I'd cheated on her. *And* that I planned to do it again. ASAP.

When we pulled into the gated parking lot at Blockbuster my nerves were revving with anticipation. I was out of the car before Sue had even come to a complete stop in the parking space. I heard her say my name in an aggravated way as I slammed the door and jetted for the entrance to the video store. It was about a quarter to eleven and the store was almost empty. I ripped the jingle-belled glass door open by its blue plastic handle and forty-yard-dashed it over to the comedy section. I immediately regretted my zeal and slowed to a more casual pace when I realized that the dognappers might've been watching me. I didn't want to look like a *total* pussy. Then I thought, *Maybe if I do run and go all crazy emotional, they'll be moved by my desperation, and they'll decide to just give the Doctor back to me immediately on account of how devastated I clearly am.* I broke back into a fat-jiggling sprint figuring, *Fuck it, I already showed them my cards.* I craned my neck over the aisles, trying to spot the comedy section, but I was too short to get the bird's-eye view I needed, so I ended up running the labyrinth of shelves like a dumb little fat balding Jew-mouse looking for a piece of cheese. I finally found the comedy aisle and jogged through the entire alphabet, scanning the titles as I went. I finally reached the T's and in the blur of titles I glimpsed *This Is Spinal Tap, The Truman Show,* and *Troop Beverly Hills* before finally landing on *Turner and Hooch.* I cracked open the plastic case. An envelope was taped inside.

As I tore open the envelope, I had a brief moment of panic, thinking, *The police might need to fingerprint this stuff for evidence! Shit!* But I quickly dismissed the thought when a second thought replaced it—I wouldn't be one of those foolish people in the movies who called the cops even though the kidnappers told me not to. That always led to surefire disaster. So fuck the fingerprints.

The note looked the way all ransom notes look in every movie I've ever seen:

> YoU Know wHo wE are . Do NOt coNTact us .
>
> kEeP YOuR MOuTH SHuT aND youp WILL gET YoUR
>
> doG BaCK WHeN tHiS IS aLL oveR . IF YOU DO
>
> Try TO CoNtaCt Us   or oPeN youR mouTH
>
> to anyone   THe DOctOR Dies . JuSt keep quiEt !
>
> wE WILL coNTaCT You sOON wiTH FurthEr
>
> inSTrUcTiONs .

I read it and then reread it. *You know who we are . . .* That was the part that freaked me out the most. *Who the fuck are you?* I didn't have any clue.

Sue finally approached and read the note over my shoulder. "'You know who we are'?" she read aloud.

"No fucking clue," I said. Actually, a few ideas I'd pondered over the past few days began to bubble to the surface. I needed to go home and give this some serious thought.

"This sounds like a bunch of BS, Wally," she said, back to her usual attitude.

"Frederick, will you *please* help me with rewinds? We're

falling *so* behind!" said a geeky voice somewhere nearby. I turned to see a skinny, twentysomething kid with the beginning stages of a greasy comb-over wearing a blue-and-yellow Blockbuster shirt hastily tucked into his puffy-at-the-waist khakis, shouting at his underling. I could just tell somehow—perhaps it was the combination of his thick, amberish lenses in the out-of-style, oversized frames, and his goofy-yet-still-somehow-empowered walk—that this guy was the manager, and not the brightest bulb on the marquee.

I strutted up to him with a plan formulating. I glimpsed at the name tag on his shirt. "Hi . . . Clifford? My name is Wally." I always feel my most confident around guys like this. It's one of the rare occurrences when I feel like a finer specimen.

"Yeah?"

"Are you the manager here, Clifford?"

"Assistant. Yeah."

"Great. Have you been here since the store opened today?" I was having trouble looking directly at him, because his face was severely acne-crusted and his lips were so dry that skin was peeling off of them in tragic sheets. His teeth were askew and painted with a gooey, yellowish-brown film. He was making me feel slightly ill. I had a feeling that his breath was probably horrendous and would've pushed me over the edge of the vomit cliff, so I stayed out of range.

"Yeah?"

"Have you had any customers today, uh, so far?"

"Wulll . . . yeah?"

"Okay. A lot of people? Been busy?"

"Um, no. Wull, yeah. Not really, no."

"No? Do you think you could tell me who you might've seen?" I asked.

"Ummmmmm. Not really. No," he said, his flaky lips cracking like the ground in a desert earthquake.

"No?"

"I saw a girl. A guy. Two guys. A lady. Some kids." He shrugged.

"Okay. Great, do you—"

"Why are you asking me all these questions? Are you like, with the police or something? Is the place like, surrounded by undercov—"

"Shhhhhh!" I looked around covertly and lowered my voice to a whisper. "Yes, Clifford. Yes. This is an undercover op. Case number eight-six-seven-five-three-oh-nine . . . dash two-two-seven. Please keep your voice down and don't ask any more questions. Just answer mine and we won't have a problem here, Clifford." Clifford looked at me wide-eyed, nervous but kind of excited.

"You don't really look like a cop—"

"Clifford! Shhhh. That's the point. I'm und—" I lowered my voice to a gentler whisper again. "I'm undercover, Clifford. Listen, help me. Please. The force *needs* you right now, Clifford." He gulped and nodded solemnly. "Can you describe any of the people who were here this morning?"

"N-no. No. Not really. I told you—there was . . . some guys, and . . . We're really behind on the rewinds, so I was d-doing that, and Frederick was suppo—"

"Clifford. Stay with me. Did you see anyone in particular lingering in the comedy aisle—over there?" I gestured toward the comedy aisle.

"N-no. No."

"Are you sure?"

"Ummm, I don't . . . um, not really."

"Did anyone ask you where to find *Turner and Hooch* today?"

"Uhh, noooo, but . . . well, no, no one asked me."

"No? But what?"

"Uh-uh. No. Nothing."

"Okay. All right. Thank you, Clifford. This is the longest conversation I've ever had. Take care." I walked away. Sue waited by the door with her arms crossed on her chest.

"Can we go now?" she asked, apparently annoyed at the inordinate amount of time I'd spent talking to Clifford. "I mean . . . this is silly."

"Yeah. We can go," I said. She turned and pushed the heavy exit door.

"Wait!" someone yelled behind us. It was Clifford. I ran back to him.

"What is it, Clifford?"

He leaned over the greasy formica counter and looked both ways, making sure no one was eavesdropping. "I just remembered something."

"What is it?"

"Last night. A guy. He asked me if I knew about any dog movies."

"What?"

"He asked me if I knew of any movies about dogs."

"'Kay, yeah? And what'd you say?"

"Oh—I said that, yeah. Yeah I know about movies about dogs."

"Okay . . . ? And?"

"And then he said, 'What movies?'" said Clifford, remembering the conversation just a little bit slower than I would've liked.

"Right. Okay? And what'd you tell him?"

"I told him that I could think of like, three!" I moved my hand in a circular motion, urging him on. "Oh, there's *All Dogs Go to Heaven,* which he wanted *really* bad, but it was out."

"Yeah?"

"There's *Dog Day Afternoon,* which I never seen, and he, um, I don't think he had ever seen it, either. So he asked me what else, and *I* said . . . *Turner and Hooch!*"

"Yes! Clifford, you're the man!" I could've kissed him on his crusty peeling lips at that moment. Ehh, definitely not, actually. "Okay! Now—the most important question of all . . . what did the guy *look* like?"

"Um, oh, that's easy. He was black. He had a, uhhhhh, an afro with a, um, whatchamacallit, a *comb* stuck in it."

"Reeeeeeally," I said, my mind reeling back to the last black man I'd seen with an afro and a comb stuck into it.

"Oh! And he had an orange jacket on."

Bingo.

Funk Deezy.

chizapter 11

Holy shit, holy shit," I mumbled to myself as Sue pulled out of the Blockbuster parking lot.

"*What,* Wally? What the fuck?" Sue asked, annoyed that I had done nothing but mumble incoherently since we'd left the store.

"Holy fucking shit."

"*What?* What did that man tell you?"

"That mother*fucker.* It's Deezy."

"What?"

"Deezy! Frickin' Funk Deezy took my frickin' dog."

"What? Noooo. Why would he *do* that? He wouldn't do that. Just because you accidentally peed on him? Noooo. No way."

"Well, yeah! He's—wait—how did you know about that? I didn't tell you about that."

"Oh, no, I heard it, uh—"

"You heard it when? How'd you hear it?"

"I heard it . . ."

"You heard it when you were at Oral B's house the other day massaging his dogs, which you didn't tell me about." She looked momentarily stunned but quickly reformed her cool expression. She didn't think I'd find out about that, and she wasn't accustomed to me being confrontational about anything. However, after my evening with Jem and my performance in the video store with old Clifford, I was feeling rather confident. She said nothing, so I stayed on the offensive. "Huh? Why didn't you tell me about that, Sue?"

"I don't know, I just . . ."

"You just *what,* Sue? You just . . . fucking forgot?"

Now she looked truly stunned. "Yeah, okay? Yeah. I *fucking* forgot. All right?"

"No. It's not all right . . . all right? I don't believe you."

"Well, that's really too bad."

"Sue, why wouldn't you tell me about that? You think I'd be pissed or something? Why would I be pissed if you just *told* me? And how can you say that Deezy didn't do it? You don't even know—I mean, you met the guy *once.*" Sue had met Deezy at the Godz-Illa Christmas party that year and they ended up chatting for a while because he was an acquaintance of her ex-boyfriend the Clipper.

"Wally, you're . . . you're so . . . uchhhhhhhh—" From her throat came the most annoyed sound her body had to offer.

"What, Sue? *What?* I think this is a very, uh, a very reasonable question, er, response! You were at *my boss's house.* How did that even come about?"

"Wally, I didn't do anything wrong! God! I really don't like the way you're fucking *attacking* me!"

"I'm not attacking you, I'm just asking."

"Yes, you are attacking me!"

"Well, it's . . . I'm sorry! It seems weird, Sue! It seems sort of . . ."

"What?"

"It seems sort of . . . it's just, it seems shady. I just don't understand . . . is all."

"Uccchhh."

"Uch what?"

"Uch you, Wally. Okay? Uch you. It really sucks of you to do this." We pulled up to my apartment and the car jerked to a sudden stop.

"What—? I didn't . . . You know what, Sue? No. You know

what? Uch you, too. Okay? Uch you, too. I didn't *do* anything wrong. I'm not attacking you. I'm just asking why you went behind my back and did something at my boss's house without telling me, and you're getting all defensive and irrational. I don't think—"

"Yeah—I get it, Wally. But you're being a real *dick,* okay? I don't know what's gotten into you—maybe you're just, like, super-stressed about the Doctor being missing or something, and I feel bad about *that,* but you know what? It *sucks* the way you're attacking me."

"Sue—"

"I'm gonna go."

I stared at her for a prolonged moment while she focused all of her attention straight ahead, out the windshield. Her teeth were so tightly clenched that her cheekbones looked like they might pop out of her skin. Finally, I opened the door and stepped out of the car, turning and bending back in to look at her. She didn't return my look, only stared blankly out the windshield.

"Sue—"

"I'll call you," she said tersely.

"Fine," I responded, slamming the door. I heard her drive off as I marched to my front door in a huff. If I had been paying attention I might have noticed the black Cadillac Escalade parked right across the street from my apartment and the two men sitting in the front seats, watching my every move.

....

Winded from climbing the many cement stairs, I feebly tried to fish my keys from the pocket of my jeans as quietly as possible. I was exhausted, but relieved that I'd gotten up here without having to talk to Pardeep. I didn't want to make any sounds now that might alert him to my presence. He'd been ringing my doorbell for the past few days trying to check up on me. I'd ignored his persistent knocking, trying my best not to feel too badly when I would hear him standing outside my door muttering sadly to himself, "Ohhh, Mister Wally Moscowitz. Ohhhh, poor poor frient. I am hoping dat he is oooo-o-o-kay. Ohhhh poor Dr. Barry Schwartzman." Again, he's a terribly sweet guy, but I just wasn't in the mood.

The joyful buzz from the prior evening was all but *gone* by now. Sue had an uncanny way of doing that to me. My only consolation was that I'd be seeing Jem again this evening. All I had to do now was get through the rest of the day. When I got into my apartment, I plopped down heavily on my tough old futon couch. I suddenly realized that I hadn't eaten much at all in the past three days. I ordered a large thin-crust pepperoni pizza from Domino's, and then, noticing the blinking light on my phone, checked my voice mail messages.

There were three. One from Jerry: "Heyyyyyyy—what's up, stud? My little Don Juan! That was one sexy mama you left with last night, huh? Call me. I want details. Sue, if you're listening— I'm just kidding." *Beeep.*

The second message was just a mess of rustling noises, and I knew right away who it was from. Me. I do this is *all* the friggin' time. My crappy cell phone isn't one of the ones that you can fold closed, it's one of those candy bar models where the keys are all exposed. My home number is one of my speed dial buttons, and so when my phone is floating around in my pocket, it always manages to make accidental pocket calls. Usually it just calls me at home and leaves a ten-minute message on my voice mail consisting mostly of rustling sounds and whatever very limited conversations I might happen to have with other human beings during the day. One time, I left a four-minute-long message on Sue's machine singing my heart out to the '80s hit "Let's Hear it For the Boy," as I was walking around cleaning my apartment.

I deleted it.

The last message was from Oral B: "Yo—sup, Duuuubs? Where you at, nigga? Your celly ain't workin'. I hope you ain't avoidin' me, foo! You got that lil rizhyme I aksed you to write fo me? Don't fuhget—I'm callin' dat shit 'Fuck a Bitch Good Wit My Bling Bling Bizalls.' Haaa! It best be a fuckin' banger, too, yo ass is takin' so damn long! I'm waitin', nigga. Holla atcha, boooy!" *Beeep.*

I mouthed the word "fuck" silently and hung my head. With all the drama, I'd completely forgotten about the song he'd asked me to write. I paced nervously for a minute before realizing that I could write some stupid Oral B lyrics by the time my pizza arrived. I grabbed a pen and pad and returned to the couch.

I decided to begin with the one, seemingly nonsensical line that Oral B had given me: "Fuck a bitch good wit my bling bling bizalls." The rest just flowed. I sat there for the next forty minutes, pen in hand, scribbling madly, barely stopping to think.

When the doorbell rang, I tore the page of lyrics out of my spiral notepad, folded it in quarters, and put it in the back pocket of my jeans. My mouth was watering at the very thought of food. It smelled so good that I didn't even wait for the delivery guy to give me my change. I handed him a twenty, told him to keep it, and hurriedly closed the door. I tore open the hot white cardboard box and chowed down. They say you can remove up to 20 percent of the fat just by dabbing the extra oil off the pizza, but I was too hungry. I stuffed my face like this was the last pizza in SoCal.

I ruminated on my situation as it stood. It was looking like Funk Deezy dognapped Dr. Barry Schwartzman. *That motherfucker.* I wondered what the hell he hoped to gain by dognapping the Doctor. *Maybe he thinks I'm super rich,* I thought. It was possible—he didn't know me. Didn't know about my shitty little apartment or my '79 Volvo with 300,000 miles on it. I had no real choice but to just wait it out. Maybe Jerry would have some good advice. When I was finished eating I returned his call.

"The Silver Agency," answered Beth.

"Hi, Beth. Wally Moscowitz."

"Wally! Heyyy! Hold on just a sec, okay?"

"Sure. Thanks."

Jerry came on a few moments later, saying good-bye to someone in his office. "Okay, honey. Good work. You're a peach. Talk to you later. Beth will validate your parking, sweetie. Okay, bye now. Hey—Wally?"

"Hey, Jerry."

"Yeah-heah-heah-heah, there he is!"

"Heh. Hi." I couldn't help but smile. Jerry was clearly very proud of me, and I was pretty happy that someone was there to witness my victorious exploit.

"Look at you, Mr. Big Stuff! That chick was smokin', Mosco!"

"Yeah. Not bad, huh?"

"Not bad? Incredible! Did you, uhhh, you know, do the Humpty Dance?"

I cleared my throat modestly.

"You did! You son of a bitch! I love it! *Love it, love it, love it!* Her ass taste like French vanilla ice cream?" I was pretty sure this was another Quentin Tarantino quote, but I knew Jerry would deny it so I let it slide.

"Peaches, actually," I responded.

"Ohhh, fuckin' A! You get her number?"

"Yeah, kinda. I'm meeting her again tonight. Same time, same place."

"Beautiful. Beautiful! Look at you! Love it."

"Yeah. Feeling good about it. Still real upset about the dog, though. I got a rans—"

"But poontang helps, huh?"

"Yeah, the ultimate panacea. But listen—I got a ransom note today."

"You're kidding. Tell me."

I told him the whole story, starting with Sue's surprise appearance at my place. "So? Whaddaya think?"

"I think I wish she woulda caught you so she would dump your ass already. Lord knows you aren't gonna leave *her!* Look at the quality of woman you're capable of, Mosco!"

"Jerry, what do you think about the ransom note?"

"Oh. It's obvious, isn't it? It's that scumbag that you work for. He's trying to keep you quiet!"

"What? Abraham Lyons? Noooo. You think?"

"Yeah I think! What do *you* think?"

"I think it's this guy Deezy that I pissed on! The kid in Blockbuster told me the guy who planted the note had a comb in his 'fro and an orange jacket on."

"So? Sounds like every schvatz and his homeboy."

"No, but think about it, Jerry. When I pissed on his leg, Deezy had on an orange jumpsuit. Now this guy in Blockbuster has on just an orange jacket—possibly the top half of a jumpsuit—minus the orange pants that are at the dry cleaners covered in my piss!"

"Ehh. You're pushin' it, kid. Coulda been anyone. I'd bet the farm it was one of Lyons's boys. He's scared you're gonna go public now after this whole pissing/knocked unconscious/suspension fiasco. I guarantee it. He's trying to shush you."

"I don't know, Jerry. I thought of that, but why would Lyons wait three days to give me a ran—"

"I'm *telling* you, Wally. Believe me. He's just shuttin' you up. It's insurance. Trust me on this."

"Okay. Let's just say you're right. Now what? What do I do?"

"Now what? Now you keep your fuckin' mouth shut if you want to see that pooch again. You don't call them, you don't talk about this. I'm serious, Mosco. They'll call you when they're good and ready. He's not gonna hurt your dog. He can't. Meantime, you only have two things to worry about at this point."

"What's that?"

"Number one: meeting this broad again tonight."

"And?"

"Number two: four P.M. meeting today at Bionic Books."

"*What?*"

"That's right, pal! They just called!"

"No! Jerry, no!"

"Yeah, bud! Round two!"

"Jerrrrry. No. Listen. I'm really just not—"

"Blah, blah, blah, blah, blah. I don't wanna hear it now, Mosco. Just listen to me—get your shit together, and meet me here at the office at three thirty."

"No, Jerry. I really don't wan—I mean, I just don't think that this is the righ—"

"*Wally*. What did I just say? None of that. Okay? This is a *wonderful* opportunity. I am *not* gonna let you blow it because of some pussy, artist integrity, whiny bullshit excuse. Okay? So get your shit together, and be here by three thirty."

"Jerry . . ." I audibly exhaled every ounce of energy and pride in my wimpy little body. Jerry took it as a sign that I was defeated. Maybe I was.

"That's my boy!" he said victoriously. "Talk later."

"Jer—" I started to say. But like always, he was already gone.

chizapter 12

I never made it to the four o'clock meeting.

I walked out of my apartment building around three o'clock, intending to grab a cab to go pick up my car at the Kissing Room, where it was still parked. As I walked, an enormous yellow Hummer slowly crawled up next to me, keeping pace with my slow strides. The deep boom of a large bass speaker thumped within the behemoth, rattling the windows and other loose parts on the vehicle. I was immediately scared. I didn't want to look up at the Hummer, but I couldn't help it. I glanced up briefly—unable to see through the darkly tinted windows— and then quickly back down at my feet, wondering who was watching me on the other side of that darkened pane. I picked up my pace. There was a bus stop about a hundred yards from where I was and several people waiting there for the bus, ensuring my safety—or at the very least they'd witness the heinous crime that was surely about to take place. The window on the passenger side of the Hummer rolled down, and very loud rap music spilled forth from the truck. I closed my eyes and took a deep breath, tempted to break into a run.

The music lowered slightly in volume. *"Ey!"* yelled a voice from the Hummer that sounded very much like an angry black man. I didn't look up. *"Ey!* Look, beeyatch!" I didn't. I kept walking, head down, ignoring the voice beckoning to me. "Ey! You heard me, beeyatch! *Ey! Lookit me, muhfucka!"* I was almost to the bus stop. Just a few more feet. "Ey! You wanna get shot, muhfucka! Huh? You want some holes in yo ass, muhfucka?"

Oh my fucking God I'm about to get shot, I thought.

"What crew you claiming, bitch? Ey!"

I am going to die in a fucking drive-by shooting. I was suddenly sure of it. *Why me?* I thought. *Oh my God, am I wearing gang colors? Do I have on all blue? Holy shit, I do.* I was wearing all blue, the uniform of the Crips. Or was it the Bloods? *Shit shit shit shit.* I was in full panic mode, when the voice said, "You about to die, honky! Hahahahaha."

I recognized the laugh.

I looked up and saw the big, gold-toothed grin of Oral B shining at me through the open window. He wore a camouflage bandanna around his head covered by a tilted black sports cap. He had his hand pointed at me in the shape of a pistol. "Ha haaaa! Sup, Duuuubs! Scared you, huh, nigga?" said Oral B, giddy now. Smoke billowed out of the car all around him, and I suddenly smelled skunk.

I broke into a relieved smile. "You scared the shit outta me, dude!"

I couldn't tell how many people were in the car, but however many it was went crazy with laughter; a lot of rocking and knee-slapping and howling. "Bahhh! He said, 'You scared the shit out of me, dude!' " repeated someone from the backseat, in a cartoonish imitation of a white person's voice. "Haaaaaaaa!" said Oral B. "Hey—git in, Mosco, we puffin' a fat blizzy right now."

I tried to keep the smile on my face. I wondered if Oral B knew that Deezy or possibly Lyons had dognapped Dr. Schwartzman. *I shouldn't be talking to him right now,* I thought. *Lyons told me to lay low.* I finally stuttered, "Oh, uh, thank, thanks B, but I can't. I have ay, uh, a meeting to get to."

"Hahahaaaa!" that voice mocked from the backseat again. "He said, 'I have a, um, meeting to get to, um, sir!' "

"Fuck you mean you got a meetin', dawg? You got somethin' more important than *me* to deal wit? Naw, dawg. Naw. Git in," said Oral B, suddenly serious. I wasn't about to argue. I stepped off the curb as the back door opened. I climbed in, and Oral B said, "The only meetin' yo ass has is wit this next blunt we about to spark, sucka!" I don't smoke pot—it makes me even more nervous and paranoid than I already am—but I wasn't about to argue that point either. I yanked the heavy door closed, and we pulled away from the curb. As I suspected, the two other passengers were Oral B's two parasitic brothers, who served as his "bodyguards" and almost never left his side. In life, these two buffoons had hit the jackpot. By virtue of being birthed from the same vagina as Oral B, they earned the right to "guard" him, which entails hanging out with him all day and doing nothing at all while earning exorbitant salaries. The driver, a grossly overweight, very dark-skinned, gold-toothed fella nicknamed Yo Yo Pa, always took the role of chauffeur. He's the fattest man I've ever known. I don't know why they call him Yo Yo Pa, but I'd be awfully shocked to find out that he plays the cello. I couldn't help but stare at his enormous gut pinned under the steering wheel. It looked like a fist squeezing a water balloon. B's other brother—the incredibly hilarious white-boy impersonator in the backseat—was a big, muscular, cocky jerkoff named Teddy Bizzle. This man, like his two brothers, had a mouth full of gold—a grill, as they call it—with diamonds pressed into the gold. A *T* on one side, and a *B* on the other. It's safe to say that his grill is worth more than most people make in six months. I wasn't real comfortable around these guys, but I was just glad that Funk Deezy wasn't in the car.

"What you got fo me, Mosco?" asked Oral B from the front seat, through the cloud of marijuana smoke that lingered from his last pull off the freshly lit blunt in his hand. I was distracted by Teddy Bizzle, who was snapping photos of his brothers with his cell phone camera and typing text messages to some unseen person out in the ether somewhere.

"Got?" I asked dumbly.

"Yeah, nigga! I aksed you to write sumfin, foo! Please don't tell me you ain't done nat shit!" he said, now twisted around, looking at me around the large seat with terrifyingly predatory eyes.

"Oh! Oh, yeah. I wrote it. Yeah. It's right . . . " I reached for my back pocket to retrieve the page of lyrics I'd written.

"Hold up, hold up," said Oral B. "We gotta get lifted first. Smoke this shit wit me." He handed me the blunt.

"I don't really . . . uhh . . . you know, oh. Okay. Thanks." I accepted the blunt and brought it to my mouth, too scared and embarrassed to say no. I felt like I was back in high school, and once again, couldn't handle the peer pressure. They all watched me manage the blunt awkwardly. Even Yo Yo Pa watched in the rearview mirror while he drove. This was great entertainment for them. I heard the imitation shutter-click sound that camera phones make when they snap a shot, and saw Teddy, out of the corner of my eye, taking pictures of me. *Great.*

I hadn't done this since college. I took a nice long pull, inhaling deeply. I lowered the blunt away from my lips and held in the hit until it began to hurt my chest. I tried my very best not to cough, not to look like an amateur, as, red-faced, I exhaled the large milky cloud. I coughed vigorously, wheezing violently, spittle shooting from my mouth and sticking to my chin. The entourage laughed hysterically again. Teddy Bizzle took more snapshots.

"He said, 'Pflphplhchl!' " said Teddy, imitating my spitting, coughing fit through his laughter.

"You (*cough*) have any (*cough*) water (*cough, cough, cough*)?" I managed to mutter between painful gasps.

"Naw, dawg. You be aight in a sec. Chillll," said Oral B, smiling sadistically.

"The more you cough, the more you get off," Yo Yo Pa said brilliantly from the driver's seat.

My fit finally ended, aside from intermittent little gasping coughs every minute or so. They all took huge, lazy, effortless drags off of the blunt as it went around. Oral B even blew a few perfect, undulating rings of thick smoke. He handed the blunt to me again.

"No. I'm cool. Thanks."

"No you ain't. You ain't coo till this thing is done, homey. Don't be a bitch."

I looked down at the blunt he was passing me, horrified to see that it wasn't even halfway done. "I really don't need anymo—"

"*Take it,* foo," said B forcefully.

I pinched it from his fingers into mine and took another tug. Much smaller this time. I baby-coughed and then passed it on to Teddy.

"There you go, dawg!" said Teddy. "See? You coo!"

But I wasn't "coo." My heart felt like it might burst out of my chest, and I was very stoned already. The music was back on, loud, and hitting me in waves that sounded like *wah wah wah wah wah.* I saw Teddy take another picture of me, laughing. I could feel my eyelids getting heavy and squinty. I couldn't keep a cohesive train of thought. This wasn't a *good* stoned. I was starting to panic at the thought of finishing the entire blunt.

When it finally got around to me again, I took a tiny, fake hit, without inhaling. Teddy called me out on it as I tried to pass it to him.

"Naw, man. Take anotha one."

I took another one, inhaling this time, and then passed it on. My heart continued to race. I was thinking, *I'm gonna have a fucking heart attack. This is it. Fucking cardiac arrest.* All the while doing my best not to show how panicked I was. I tried to keep a cool exterior, tried to feign normality as my eyes grew heavier and heavier and my world swam around me in heavy, rippling waves.

"Five-oh! Five-oh!" yelled Yo Yo Pa suddenly. My heart leapt, beating even faster and harder, if that's possible. I put my hand to my chest as if I could manually slow it down.

"Fuck," said Teddy to himself nervously, licking his thumb and forefinger and extinguishing the blunt between them. He opened his window, as did B and Yo Yo simultaneously.

I turned my head and peeked out the rear window. Sure enough, a police car crept up behind us. I quickly whipped back around, facing front, eyes wide in fear. The three of them all muttered their own personal versions of "Fuck, shit, dammit." I kept quiet, holding my breath, heart hammering in paranoid stonedness, thinking that I was surely going to jail. No, I was going to *prison* and I was going to live out the rest of my days dodging potential ass-rapists and neo-Nazis. I thought, *I know what I'll do. Once they get me in the prison yard with the other inmates, I'll just make pretend I'm absolutely out of my fucking mind to the point where no one will even want to go near me. Yeah! I'll walk around clucking and nodding and pecking and batting my wings like a chicken. All day and night. That'll keep 'em away,* I thought. *And the first guy who comes near me, I'll, I'll, I'll just go chicken fuckin' berserk like B'GOCK! B'GAAAAAAAHCK! And I'll cluck and peck and fuckin' claw his ugly eyes out and no one else will fuck with the crazy chicken-boy of cell block H . . .*

"Whew, he turned, man. He gone," said a very relieved Yo Yo Pa from the front seat, shaking me from my paranoid daydream. "Wooo! Had me shook for a quick sec, dawg!"

I turned and looked behind me, and the police car was in fact gone. *"Yeeeeeeah!"* I screamed, pumping my fist in the air like a rabid football fan whose team just scored a touchdown to win the game in overtime. The crew all looked at me in silence. I looked around at all of them, my eyes heavy and bloodshot. They erupted in laughter once again.

"Bahhhhhhhhahahahahahahaha! This nigga stoned as a muhhfucka, man! Hahaha!" said Teddy.

"Hahahahahha!" laughed Yo Yo Pa, slamming his hands on the steering wheel.

"Nigga said, *'Yeaaaaaaaah!'* Hahahahahahaha!" All three of

them laughed hysterically like a bunch of hyenas, shoving each other and bouncing around the car. I couldn't help but join in. In an instant, all of my paranoia had vanished, and now I was just happy and stoned, laughing along with the guys.

"Damn, nigga, you right, B, this cat is funny as a muhfucka!" said Teddy to Oral B.

"I told you, nigga. Dis nigga is hilarious. You is one funny lil muhfucka, Mosco."

"Hey, thanks, B. I really really appreciate it." And there was silence.

And then they all started cracking up again.

"*Ahhhh*ahahahahahahaaaaa! He said, 'I really really appreciate it, my brother,' " said Teddy, putting on his mock white-boy voice again and holding out a Black Power fist. "Hahahahahaha-hahaha!"

"Ahhhhhhhhhh shit. That is some funny-ass shit," said Yo Yo Pa.

"That is *so* not what white people sound like," I said to Teddy.

"Dat's what yo lil punkass sounds like, foo!" We all laughed together for a minute more, and then caught our breath.

"Aight, Dubs. Now dat you all lit up, time to bust some shit," said Oral B.

"You wanna hear some shit?" I asked. I was more stoned than I'd ever been in my entire life—but in a good way now.

"Yeah, man. Bust some shit fo us, Dubs," he replied.

I took the paper out of my pocket on which I'd written the rap lyrics earlier, and unfolded it. "You want me to read it? Or you want to?"

"Naw, man. Rap it. I want you to rap dat shit. C'mon. Bust it."

I smiled at him goofily. "Nahhh. I can't."

"Yeah, dawg. Bust it."

I gave in, stoned enough that my inhibitions were down. "Okay. Okay." I nodded my head. "I can do that. Okay. Here goes."

"You want a beat?" asked B.

"Nahhhh. I don't need a beat. Um, yeah. Okay. Gimme a beat." I looked down at the paper through squinty, heavy-lidded eyes and became concerned that I was too stoned to read. Oral B turned on the CD player and found a song that was just a beat with no vocals. I bobbed my head in a pretty uncool way (although I didn't think so at the time) for a minute, waiting for the right moment to begin. Finally, when I felt I had a good grip on the beat, I began.

"You know I fuck a bitch good wit my bling bling bizalls. Got sperm flowin' out me like Niagara fuckin' fizalls. I once had a thing wit this hoochie named Shiranda. Fucked her every Friday in her husband's hoopty Honda. Soon as he fell asleep I was over at their shack, fuckin' in the driveway, hittin' that shit from the back. Dis went on for months and months, and dat nigga didn't know, I was bangin' his Shiranda like a dirty lil hoe. But then she started buggin', askin' me to spend my loot, on some shoes and fuckin' dresses to make her chunky ass look cute. And then her mama started callin', too! Beggin' me to come and hit it! Her mama loved my dick more than Shiranda, so I let dem bitches split it. But then they callin' me ten times a day, blowin' up my spot, so I dug into my bag a tricks, and cooked up a new plot. I knew I had to tell her man, to get them off my back, so I watched the hoopty Honda parked outside their little shack. When her husband came outside the crib I knew that I'd be coo, 'cuz I saw dat fuckin' hoopty Honda belonged to fuckin' YOU (pussy!). So tell your girl and her mama to quit blowin' up my celly, 'cuz Shiranda's fuckin' ugly and her mama's cooch is smelly."

The boys went *crazy*. They were hysterical, laughing and slapping their knees, eyes and mouths wide in large O shapes, emitting various cries of "Ohhh shit!" and "Ahhh!" and other such whoops and excited sound effects. I finished up with a quick chorus. "You know I fuck a bitch good wit my bling bling bizalls, got sperms flowin' out me like Niagara fuckin' fizalls. Every label wanted B from coast to fuckin' coast, but I picked the Dandy Lyons cuz he paid the fuckin' most! You know I fuck a bitch good! Yeah Yeah! Beeyatch!" I ended with a big arm gesture, giving the middle finger, sideways, like some rappers tend to do. The crowd went wild.

"Yeah, Mosco!" said Teddy. "That was illlllllll, dawg!"

"Yeah, boy. Ill," said Yo Yo Pa.

"Aight, Dubs. Not bad, dawg. Not bad at all, man. Worth da wait, dawg. Word."

"You liked it?" I asked dumbly, stoned still, and feeling victorious.

"Yeah, man," said Oral B. "Word up. It's coo, dawg." He started boppin' his head to the beat. "I like dis beat too. It's makin' me feel like bustin' some freestyle. Watchoo think, dawg?" he asked Yo Yo Pa.

"Oh, fa sho," replied Yo Yo, bobbing his head along with the beat. Even in my extreme stonedness, I knew that Oral B definitely could *not* freestyle. That's why I write for him in the first place. He's a moron. I was excited to hear him try. I just hoped in my silly state I wouldn't laugh. That might get me killed. Not as funny.

He bobbed his head and licked his lips, getting ready to start freestyle rhyming. "Aight . . . You ready?" Bob, bob, bob, bob, "Aight? Aight? Aight? Look. Look." Bob, bob, lick lips, bob, "Aight, you ready? You ready? Aight look . . . " Bob, bob, "Aight my name is Oral B, you don't want to fuck wit me. Aight? Word. Bust it, Dubs." He was handing the mic over to me. He wasn't gonna do much freestyling after all. Both of his minions looked over at me, eyebrows raised, waiting for me to start rhyming now.

"You want *me* to freestyle?" Okay, give me a pen and a piece of paper and a rhyming dictionary and some time, and I can come up with some okay lyrics. But I am *not* the kind of guy who can think on the fly. Unfortunately for me, I was a little pussy in a truck with three huge badass motherfuckers, so there wasn't much room for debate.

"Yeah, dawg!" said B. "And make it good, Dubs. Show these cats where my loot is going!" *Your loot is going into a fucking shoebox in my closet,* I thought. But instead of voicing that objection, I gave it my best shot. As long as I live, I will never understand where it came from.

I started to bob my head to the beat. I closed my eyes. "Aight . . . Aight . . . ready? Ready?" (This is the customary warm-up procedure of a freestyler). "Aight, ready? Aight . . . aight . . . one , two, three . . . *Yo,* quit askin' me to fuckin' ghost write, just 'cuz I'm white like a motherfuckin' ghost, right?"

I was concentrating hard on coming up with rhymes, but was satisfied to hear them all go *"Ohhhh!"* excitedly in the background. Teddy Bizzle seemed to be shooting little video clips of me on his high-tech little cell phone.

"I'm stoned and I'm spinnin' and the chronic got me feelin' like I'm Lionel fuckin' Richie and I'm dancin' on the ceilin'."

"Ohhhhh!" and *"Yeeeeah!"* they all screamed again.

"I'm a fat little cracker from the suburbs of New York, and even though I'm fuckin' Jewish I still eat a lotta pork!"

"Hahahaha!"

"He said, 'Even though I'm Jewish.' Hahahahaaa!"

"I got a large circulation for my freestyle rhymes, plus I'm white and well-read like *The New York Times*!"

"Ohhhh!"

"I gotta be careful with the rhymes I recite, 'cuz y'all turn my words around like you was Vanna White."

"Ohhh!"

"No one flows like us, you fools write down our quotes, 'cuz you full a hot air like those Macy's floats!"

"Ohhh!"

"My words are worth more than Scrooge McDuck, and if y'all don't want to hear 'em then y'all *McSuck!*"

"Ohhhh!"

And at that point, luckily for me, the beat ended. I was glad, because I was almost spent. If the song had gone on any longer, I would have lost my flow. Somewhere in my stoned brain I'd been panicking, knowing that my lyrical well was about to run dry.

The guys applauded my effort with fist bumps and word-ups, and I was thoroughly proud of my performance. I'm telling you, I'll never know how I did it. Perhaps it was the weed.

"Yeeeeeeah," said Oral B stonily. "That shit was *fo* much, Dubs."

"Fo much?" I asked. I'd never heard that particular terminology before. "What's that?"

"You know *too* much? Fo much is *twice* as good, dawg!" he explained.

"Hahaaaa! Thanks, maaaaaaan," I responded, my eyes squinted in stoney glory. Oral B changed the song on the car's CD player, and Yo Yo Pa began to freestyle fluently from the driver's seat, although I was suddenly having trouble keeping my attention on him. My eyes were feeling so heavy now that I could barely manage to keep them open. I did my best to focus on the words that Yo Yo was rapping, but I soon lost the battle with consciousness.

The next thing I heard was, *"Dubs!"*

"Huh?" My head popped up from the headrest, in sleepy confusion, I'm not sure how much later. I'd passed out cold.

"You home, dawg. You aight?" asked Oral B.

"Uh, yah . . . oh, cool," I said, or something along those lines. I have only the most vague recollection of the following few minutes. I fuzzily recall exiting the Hummer, entering my building, gripping the railing and dragging myself up the stairs to my apartment in a burnt haze. It was four o'clock in the afternoon when I opened my door into a whole new world of shit.

WHO ARE THOSE LADIES?

~~By Wally Moscowitz~~
By: WALLACE Q MOSCOW

My Uncle Joey lives in the city,
And the block that he lives on is not very pretty.
There are hobos and weird people walking around.
There's litter and garbage all over the ground.
And right on his corner there's this whole group of ladies,
And sometimes their boss, too, who drives a Mercedes
And wears flashy clothing and walks with a limp.
I heard Uncle Joey once call him a "pimp."
So I asked Uncle Joey, "Hey, what does 'pimp' mean?"
He said, "I'll answer that question, when you turn eighteen."
So I'd sit at his window, and stare down below,
What those ladies were doing, I just didn't know.
They'd jump in a car but not go anywhere,
And all I would see was a head full of hair
Bobbing up and down in the front seat of the car,
I always thought it was pretty bizarre.
One day me and Joey walked by them real close,
And for the first time I noticed, these ladies were gross!

They had hair on their arms, and bumps on their faces!
Their teeth were all crooked!
They needed some braces!
They stood in a line, up against a brick wall,
They came in all sizes: short, fat, thin, and tall.
The first lady's dress was all diamonds and rubies,
And right through the dress I could see both her boobies!
The second lady was tall—like extremely big!
And her hair kinda looked like it might be a wig.
The third lady looked like her face had a beard!
The fourth and fifth ladies' makeup was all smeared!
They whistled and hollered weird things as we passed,
I could barely understand 'cuz Joey pulled me so fast!
I had so many questions, I just couldn't wait!
Like why they were so big!? And why they asked for a date?
Finally I spouted, "Her voice is so deep!
And why did she say we could have her for cheap?
And why'd that one lady call herself 'slutty'?"
Joey said, "Hard to explain, but those ain't ladies, buddy."

—From *The Adult Children's Books Collection*

chizapter 13

When I opened the door to my apartment, I certainly did not expect to see a shiny black handgun hanging on a piece of twine from the inside of the doorframe, twirling in front of my face like some demented mobile above the crib of a future criminal. But that's what I saw.

And it wasn't a stoned hallucination.

My first thought, of course, was, *Holy shit, a gun!* My second thought was, *Am I really that stoned?* And then, my third and most problematic thought was, *I should grab that gun!* I snatched the dangling firearm from the air, and as I pulled it toward my face to examine it more closely, the twine from which it had been hanging snapped crisply. I looked up and saw that someone had driven a small nail into the ceiling just above my door, tied one end of the twine to the nail and the other end to the trigger guard of the gun. *I just did exactly what I was set up to do—put my stupid fingerprints all over this thing,* I realized. The gun was cold, and much heavier than I would have imagined. I'd never held a gun before. It felt pretty sweet, actually. I ran my fingers down the cold, inky black barrel, figuring, *Shit, I already touched it, might as well check it out!* This scenario probably would have unfolded a bit less calmly had it not been for the goofy influence of the marijuana.

I stood there for a moment, gat in hand, wondering what the heck to do next. I figured I should put the thing down and wipe off the prints. Then what? Call the cops? I was way too stoned to deal with police. I decided that I'd wipe the gun down, maybe take a shower, sober up, and then call the cops and tell them what I'd found. En route to the kitchen, my plan was ruined when Homer Simpson emerged from the bedroom and charged right at me, full bore.

I'm telling you, this is what happened. Homer Simpson. And again, *not* a stoned hallucination. Homer, dressed in a light blue velour Sean John jumpsuit and smiling stupidly, continued to charge toward me, arms outstretched. *"Hey!"* I cried, my head and the gun swinging in Homer's direction in unison. *This is why I don't smoke weed.*

As Homer was almost upon me, my brain finally sorted out that it was a man in a Homer mask—not the *real* Homer—and that he was about to pummel me and that I wouldn't actually be harming my beloved Homer, and so I pulled the trigger and *blam!* The gun went off about half a second before the anti-Homer plowed into me, knocking me to the floor. I smashed the back of my head on the countertop on my way down and dropped the gun. When I hit the floor on my side, I watched Homer trip, scoop up the gun, and scutter away and out my front door. And then there was blackness.

....

A furious *POUND-POUND-POUNDING* pulled me out of the dark. I opened my eyes and saw my kitchen at a tilted, low angle from which I'd never seen it before. Dustier than I would have liked, but what can you do? I groaned and sat up onto my elbows, and there it was again, that *pounding*. "Police!" I heard now. *"Open up!"* Before I could even try to remember why I was lying on the kitchen floor, my door burst open and two tubby, uni-formed, generic cops came rushing in, weapons drawn. As soon as they spotted me, they began barking. *"Stay down! Down on the floor! On your belly!"*

"Wha—?"

"Down! Down! On your belly! Turn over!"

I did what they said, which wasn't difficult being that I was already down, and that seemed to relax them for a moment. They communicated to each other in cop-speak, which I didn't understand. I stole a glance upward and saw that one of the cops was covering me with weapon drawn, while the other surveyed the apartment to make sure that the threat had been eliminated.

"We're clear," said the cop, returning from doing recon in the other room. "Bedroom was tossed, and we're wet in here," he said, looking at the floor and tracing something with a pointed finger.

Bedroom was tossed? I thought. My mind went directly to my shoebox in the closet. *FUCK. And what the hell did "wet" mean?.* I wondered.

"Where?" said the cop guarding me.

"Right here," said the other cop, "and some by the door."

"Soaked?" asked the mustached cop who held the gun on me.

"Not very."

"Call it in." I could hear the other cop mumbling again in cop-speak, this time into his radio. Calling for backup, I supposed.

"What is going on here, sir?" shouted the cop, as if I were hearing impaired, prodding me with his boot as politely as is possible with the tip of a boot.

"I-I don't know. I just g-got . . . I mean, Homer . . . I was attacked!" I stammered. I wanted to tell him exactly what happened, but that was all I could manage to get out.

"You live here, son?" he ask-yelled.

"Y-yes, sir," I answered, my face pressed to the cold hardwood. It's not fun having a gun pointed at you. Even if the guy doing the pointing has a badge and a mustache and you're relatively sure he won't shoot you.

"Did you fire a gun in here, sir?"

"Y-yes, sir."

"Gun! Gun! We got a gun! Gun!" yelled the mustached, gun-pointing yeller. *"Where . . . is . . . the . . . weapon . . ."* he said, in what I guessed may very well have been his gentlest tone, as the other cop rushed back into the room, shaking the floor with each step.

"Where? Where? Where's the weapon? Where's the weapon? Now! Now! Gun!" they bellowed at me, unnecessarily. I wanted to say, *"There's really no need to yell, fellas."* I was thinking that these goofy schmucks must be rookies. They seemed nervous and overzealous and just generally . . . I don't know, *dorky*.

I looked around and realized that I no longer had the gun in my hand, and then, remembering that I'd dropped it, I looked to where it should have fallen, but it was nowhere to be seen. *Homer took it,* I recalled. "He-he t-took it," I stuttered.

"Your attacker?" ask-yelled mustache-cop.

"Y-yes, sir," I said.

The other cop boomed past me toward the kitchen, the floor vibrating against my face with every footfall. He tore open the first drawer he came to, ejecting its contents, before ripping open the second and third drawers. It was all so dramatic.

"It's not in there," I said. "He took it," I told the cop who had his gun on me.

"Okay. All right. Had a hunch," said the cop dejectedly, before his loud friend said, *"Do you need medical attention?"*

"No, I don't think so. I think I'm okay—"

"You just sit tight, sir. Detectives will be arriving in a moment."

I sat tight as I could with the hardwood floor imprinting lines onto my stoned face.

....

About fifteen minutes later, two plainclothes detectives arrived with several blue one-piece-suit-wearing CSIs in tow. I felt like I was on a television show. Like CSI, for instance. While we waited for the detectives, the dork-cops were kind enough to move me to the couch and ask again in only a slightly gentler tone if I needed any medical attention. I declined again. I was feeling uneasy about the whole situation. I wanted to say something cool like "I want my lawyer." But I didn't. I was still a little bit scared. And stoned. Although the events of the previous half hour had certainly done wonders to sober me up.

The first detective, a cranky, bespectacled man with male pattern baldness and a massive sandy-colored mustache and yellow skin and teeth that betrayed a long love affair with cigarettes, introduced himself as Detective Barnaby Schlage. His glasses were gold rimmed and aviator style, the lenses a light brown tint that gradually faded to clear from top to bottom. Mostly, though, he was all mustache. It was one of those 'staches that is composed of basically every hair color imaginable within the red/white/orange/brown spectrum.

His partner, a mousy black woman with slick hair pulled back painfully in the tightest bun I'd ever seen and a squarish gray business suit that looked like it had the ability to suck the friendliness out of any woman who dared put it on, didn't introduce herself. She slipped into the room behind her partner and surveyed the place with quick little darting glances. Her dark brown, beady eyes seemed to collect and store information at a very rapid pace. "That's Detective Karyn Strickland," said Detective Schlage. "She don't say much, but she sees it all. Stay put, son," he said, as he convened in the bedroom/bathroom area of the apartment with the officer who had searched the place earlier. Detective Strickland continued to explore the apartment with her eyes, occasionally pointing at one thing or another, directing the CSIs to take a closer look. I watched them rummage through my belongings with a mixture of interest and concern. I had nothing to hide, but that didn't mean they wouldn't find anything. After all, I certainly wasn't the one who'd hung the pistol from my doorframe. Homer had been in my apartment, and who knows what else he'd left behind.

Detective Schlage came back into the living room, frowning his bottom lip up into his bushy multicolored 'stache and shaking his head a little. He looked concerned. "Mr. . . . Markowitz, was it?"

"Moscowitz."

"Rrright. Sorry. I get those Jew names all mixed up. Why don't you explain to me just *exactly* what is going on here."

"Okay . . . well, I got home, and . . . there was this—should I have my lawyer here?" I looked up at him with innocent eyes.

"There was this . . . go on . . . " He sat down next to me, close enough so that I could smell most if not all of the cigarettes that he'd smoked in the last several hours. He took on a fatherly air suddenly, his hand on my shoulder, his scratchy voice sounding persuasive in a familiar, Wilford Brimley sort of way. "Mr. Mockenberg, why don't you just tell Ol' Barnaby what happened here. I'm here to help," he said. And I believed him.

"Okay . . . well, I came home . . ."

"Home from where, sir?"

"H-home from h-hanging out with some bud, some friends of mine."

"Okay . . . ?"

"Oh, and when I opened the door, there was a p-pistol. A gun—like, hanging from a string." He closed one eye behind his thick lenses and tilted his head slightly. He didn't follow. "There was, it was like, hanging. From my doorframe. By like, fishing line. The gun."

"Let me get this straight, Mr. Mockstein. After arriving home with some friends—"

"No friends."

"I thought you said you were . . . " He glanced at his notepad, which I hadn't even noticed before. "Hanging out with some friends of yours. No?"

"I *was*. Before. They didn't come home with me."

"Okay. So. You arrived home. Aaaaall alone. You entered the apartment to find a gun hanging from . . . *string* . . . from . . . *the ceiling?* And so . . . you . . . *grabbed it?*"

"Y-yes, sir."

"From the string."

"Yes, sir."

"Fishing line."

"Yes, sir."

"I see." He jotted some notes. His partner continued to scavenge. I noticed that they'd seemed to have discovered a bullet hole in my wall. "M'kay. Then what."

"Then . . . um, then I brought it over to the kitchen."

"The gun?"

"Y-yes, sir."

"With what intention?"

I thought about my answer before responding. Would I sound guilty if I told him the truth? That I'd brought it in the kitchen to wipe any fingerprints off of it? That sounded like a bad idea. *Definitely a bad idea.* Maybe I was being paranoid, but it felt from the very beginning that I was being treated as a suspect instead of a victim. "Ummm, I don't really know, sir."

"You don't know why you brought the gun that you'd just found hanging from a string from your ceiling into the kitchen?"

"It was hanging from the doorframe."

"And that makes a difference?"

"A . . . a difference?"

"Yes, Mr. Mockberg. Does it make a difference in the story? Whether it hung from the ceiling or the doorframe? Did that somehow dictate why you brought the weapon over to the kitchen?"

I didn't bother to correct the moron about my name. *Not good with Jew names. You anti-Semitic, big-mustached freak.* "Well, no. No, I guess not. I just wanted to get the story right."

Schlage looked at me right in the eyes. He was reading me. His mustache twitched like the ear of a horse being bugged by a fly, and then stretched into a smile. "Rrrright," he said, as he patted me on the knee. "Go 'head."

"Okay, so, I brought the gun into the kitchen, because . . . I just didn't know *what* to do. I'd never even *seen* a gun before. And while I was going to the kitchen—"

"Mr. Markstein, don't you think you should've called us the very minute you came home to discover a weapon hanging from your doorframe?"

"Yes, sir. Absolutely."

"So, why didn't you?"

"I was ston—uh, *s'totally* nervous. I was nervous. A-and, I never had the chance." I noticed that Detective Strickland and her lackeys had disappeared into the other room and that they'd been in there for quite a while. This began to worry me.

"And why was that?"

"Pardon?"

"Why didn't you have the chance to call us, Mr. Markowitz?"

"Oh, well, as I was walking to the kitchen th-this *guy* p-popped out of my bedroom."

"Describe this *guy*."

"He was wearing a m-mask. A Homer Simpson mask. And a sky-blue jumpsuit."

"Oooookay," he scribbled away on his pad. "This just gets wilder and wilder. But okay, and so, you shot this . . . Homer Simpson?"

"Well, yeah. I guess. I shot *at* him. H-he was charging at me and he startled me, and I-I just sorta p-pulled the trigger." Detective Schlage stood up. He towered over me, as if this was the big moment of revelation. Like he was about to solve a great mystery.

"Okay, Mr. Markowitz. I'm gonna pull out my trusty little tape recorder now, okay? Don't you worry, though. It don't mean a darned thing. Just keep talkin' like we was talkin'. M'kay?"

"Um, okay," I said, a bit confused. He hit the record button on his handheld, pocket-sized device.

"Go ahead, sir. Continue on with what you were saying."

"Umm, okay. Well, I pulled the tr-trigger. By accident."

"And? What . . . happened . . . then?" he asked very slowly, as if talking to a pre-schooler or a foreigner.

"I don't know. Like I said, I guess maybe I hit the guy in the Homer Simpson mask, but he knocked me out, so I'm not sure."

"I see," he said, ruffling his mustache with his pen.

"But it looks like maybe I didn't hit him 'cuz the bullet is in the wall over there." I pointed to where I'd seen them tinkering earlier. "See? They marked it already." Schlage frowned. He looked disappointed as he walked over to the wall and bent down to take a closer look. He rose and put his hand on his hip. "Where is the weapon, Mr. Markowitz?"

"He t-took it, I guess."

His mouth disappeared under his mustache again. "I see," he muttered. "Stay put," he said again, pointing at me as he exited the room, probably to go confer with his partner, the mouse.

I sat there, head pounding, hands in my lap, dazed. I let my head fall back onto the cushions of the couch, so that I was staring at the cracked ceiling. *Should I tell them about my dog? The SUV that had been parked outside of my building for the last few days, watching?* This all had to be related somehow.

The two detectives reentered the living room. "We got two phone calls from a witness who heard the gunshot," said Schlage, standing over me again, his arms folded in front of his chest. "The first call came at"—he untangled his arms and looked down at his notepad—"four-oh-two. Caller reported a gunshot, which sounded like it came from the apartment directly above his own. A black-and-white, car 9039, was dispatched to the scene. The second phone call came at . . . four-oh-nine. Caller reported seeing someone fleeing the building, but couldn't get a close look at the perp. Officers were en route and when they entered the apartment, they found you, sir, sitting on the floor, apparently injured and confused and/or distressed, bedroom ransacked. So tell me, Mr., uhhh, Markowitz, what is going on here?"

"I have no idea, s-sir. I told you. I found the gun hanging there when I got home. And then I was attacked and I fired it."

"Very very strange story, don't you think? What am I missing? What was this person doing here? What were they looking for?"

"I told you everything I know, sir. I know it all sounds crazy, but that's what happened. I swear."

Both cops sized me up. "This whole thing stinks," said Schlage. "I think it's about time to take a ride down to the station, Mr. Markstein."

"It's Moscowitz," I responded. "Wally Moscowitz."

He looked at his watch. "Twenty-one minutes and forty-three seconds. Took you *that* long to correct me. Not too sharp with the details, are ya . . . Mr. *Moscowitz,*" he said with a crocodile smile and a wink, as they picked me up and escorted me out of my apartment and into the backseat of a police car.

chizapter 14

They put me in that room that you've seen before in the movies. Cement floors, cement walls. One large black mirror/window. A small, metal-encased camera suspended in the upper corner angled down at the steel desk at which I sat. I couldn't help but stare at that big mirror and wonder who was staring back from the other side.

I sat there at the cold steel desk for what felt like forever, now stone sober, miserable, feeling like a bug trapped in a box. It dawned on me that I'd already missed my four o'clock meeting at Bionic Books, and that there was a damned good chance I was going to miss my meeting with Jem, which was the real bummer.

Eventually the door opened and Detective Schlage ambled into the room, Detective Strickland following quietly behind.

"Blood," he spat from behind his sandy mustache. I looked up at him.

"Pardon?" I asked.

"On your floor. Spots. A trail to the door. Some in the hallway, too. Buh-luhd."

"Oh, man."

"Yep. B-L-O-O-D. The red stuff."

"Do you think I . . . ? Do you think he's—"

He placed both of his hands on the steel table and bent down, face-to-face with me, an amused look on his mustached face. "Well, that's the Million Dollar Question, Mr. Moscowitz."

"Sir . . . I didn't want to hurt anyone. I told you exactly what happened. I was attacked!" I sounded whiny and pathetic, even to myself.

"You have any enemies, Mr. Moscowitz?"

That was a tough question. Only a few days ago, the answer would have been a resounding no. Now, the answer was complicated. *How much do I tell them?* I made a snap decision to say nothing. For now. "Um, no, sir. I don't have enemies."

Detective Schlage glanced over at his partner, who was raping me for information with her eyes. "You don't sound so sure." Schlage took a seat in the metal chair across the table from me and crossed one leg over the other. "Frankly, we're confused about your claim that the gun was hanging from a string upon entry to your apartment. Why would someone do that? And how did this person get into your apartment? There were no signs of forced entry."

"But d-didn't you find the nail above my door with the snapped piece of twine tied to it? Isn't that proof that I'm being set up?"

"Hmmmm. Could be, Mr. Moscowitz. Could be. We don't know quite *what* to make of it all. Why was only the bedroom ransacked? It's a very bizarre *sitch-e-ation.* Don't you agree?"

"Yeah, I do, of course! But I mean, I'm the victim here! Why do I feel like a suspect?"

"I don't know, Mr. Moscowitz. Why *do* you feel like a suspect?"

"I think I want a lawyer. And don't I get a phone call?" I wanted to call Jerry and ask him to get me a lawyer, since I certainly didn't have one, and also explain why I'd missed the big meeting. He was probably worried about me.

Detective Schlage rested an elbow on the steel table, his chin in hand. "What do you do, Mr. Moscowitz? For a living, I mean?"

"I work at a record label."

"Oh yeah? Great! I love music. What label do you work at?"

"Why is this relevant? I didn't do anything. I just want to go home."

"Oh, c'mon. Indulge me."

"Okay. Fine. I work at a label called Godz-Illa Records. It's a rap label." The name didn't seem to mean much to Detective Schlage, but Detective Strickland spun around and looked at me with newly interested eyes. I glanced at her, and the eye contact forced me to quickly look away, down at the table.

"Hmm. Godzzz-Iller. Sounds familiar . . . You heard of it, Karyn?"

I thought I saw her smile slightly, but maybe not. "Yeah. I've heard of it," she said in a deeper, sexier voice than I'd expected to come out of the tiny, somewhat homely woman. She looked at her partner in a loaded way, and said, "Abe Lyons."

Schlage nodded knowingly and stopped to think for a few seconds. "Rap, huh? That's a nasty business. Plenty of potential killers there, eh, Mr. Moscowitz?" I didn't dignify his remark with a response. "And what do you do over there at the Godzzz-Iller Records?"

I paused. Maybe for too long. This was the very critical moment. Decision time. *Do I come clean about the whole deal? Tell them that I ghostwrite for the most famous rapper in the world—and that my life may now be at risk because of it? Maybe they can help me.* "I . . . "

"Yes?"

"I . . . work . . . " *Or maybe they'd fuck it all up . . .*

"Yesssss?"

". . . in the office. I'm an assistant. Like, an office assistant." Schlage looked pleased. He reached over and smacked me on the bicep like an old chum.

"Great. Good for you, Mr. Moscowitz. Good for you."

Detective Strickland looked at her pager and signaled to Schlage that she needed a word with him. He got up and walked over to the corner where she stood. He bent down so she could whisper something to him without me hearing. He nodded curtly and she immediately turned and left. He was quiet for a minute. He paced around the room thoughtfully.

"So. Two calls from the neighbor. A few minutes apart. One gunshot. Blood on the floor. Bedroom tossed. No victim on the premises. What am I missing, Mr. Moscowitz?"

"I-I don't know, sir. I told you everything that happened."

"Well, let's just hypothesize for a minute. Give me your best theory."

"Well, I don't . . . I guess this guy was in the process of setting up some elaborate, I don't know, *thing* in my apartment. Some kind of setup. Maybe he was gonna frame me or something. I don't know. I must have interrupted him when I came home, and so he attacked me and took off."

Schlage made a face like he was sucking something through a straw, and then: "What was he looking for in your bedroom?"

"I have no idea." I opted not to tell him about my money. There is no way anyone could have known about it, and I was hoping that it would be there when I got home.

"Well! This is quite a story. Someone must want you in trouble real bad. Out of the way, I mean. Right? To try to pull off this elaborate setup? Pretty strange for a guy with no enemies."

"Well, I thin—" He *slammed* his hand down on the steel table, startling me.

"Quit bullshittin' me, Moscowitz. Cut the crap and tell me what the fuck is goin' on."

I was scared now. He was right. The story sounded ridiculous. But it *was* ridiculous. I wasn't lying. Sure, I wasn't telling him everything. But I wasn't lying. Maybe if he knew the *whole* story he'd see it my way. Time to come clean. I opened my mouth to speak—

The door swung open. Detective Strickland stuck her head back in, signaled for Schlage to go talk to her outside the room. Schlage gave me one long, hard stare, before pulling away.

"'Scuse us a minute," said Schlage, raising one finger to me as they exited the room.

Once they'd closed the door behind them, I took a deep breath and exhaled heavily. I hung my head, exhausted. I hunched over and rested my forehead on the edge of the cold steel table. I was mentally and physically drained. My watch read 7:40 P.M. It wasn't looking good for my date with Jem. I decided that when Schlage came back in, I would spill my guts. That was the best thing to do. I'd make them understand. Otherwise they'd keep me here all freakin' night until they figured out what the hell was going on. Maybe they'd find a dead Homer Simpson somewhere and then I'd be in some *real* deep shit.

The detectives were gone for much longer than the promised minute. When the door finally sprung back open, only Detective Schlage entered. He unlocked my cuffs. "You're free to go."

"Wha-what?" I asked, thrilled and puzzled.

"Free . . . to . . . go . . . We have three witnesses who corroborate your story, and there's no reason to keep you here. Like you said, you were attacked. Now get outta here, before my partner starts making up reasons to keep you."

"Th-thank you."

"Don't thank me—thank your Indian pal and those two Italian stallions."

Pardeep! I could kiss that hairy little bastard. And, *Italian stallions?* I had no idea who the heck he was talking about, but I really didn't give much of a shit at that point. It was time to get the fuck outta there. I quickly made my way through the crowded, buzzing building, toward the heavy front doors. It was almost eight o'clock. I figured I had just enough time to get home, take a quick shower, hop in the car, and get to the Kissing Room by about ten o'clock to meet Jem. I jogged down the steps onto the sidewalk. As I rounded the corner, just outside of the precinct's property, I felt a presence rapidly approaching from behind.

"Need a lift, Moscowitz?" said Detective Schlage as he sidled up beside me, keeping pace.

Fuck. "No. No, thank you, sir. I'll call a cab."

He grabbed my arm. *Tightly.* "No. I think you'll take that lift." He tugged me toward the parking lot, to his blue, unmarked Crown Victoria. He opened the passenger door and shoved me in as nonchalantly as he could, then rounded to the driver's side, scanning the lot for any witnesses to this little abduction.

He got in and fired the engine. "Time to take a nice ride, Moscowitz."

"Where are you taking me?"

"Oh, you'll see, my boy. You'll see."

....

We drove in silence for a while. I was silent, anyway. Johnny Cash was on the radio, singing something about having been "everywhere, man." Detective Schlage was trying to sing along, but couldn't quite keep up. That didn't stop him from trying. It would have been funny, really, if I hadn't been in the process of being abducted by a creepy police detective and on my way to who-knew-where. I kept thinking he was going to take me to a basement somewhere, tie me up, and make me do all sorts of weird sexual shit a la *The Silence of the Lambs* or *Pulp Fiction*. When the song finally ended, Schlage switched off the radio. "You are one lucky dude, Moscowitz. One lucky deed, indude."

I said nothing. I knew he wanted to tell me something, so I let him.

"Not just one witness. But *three*. Three! That never happens. Whew! One lucky dude."

"Are you taking me home?"

"This Indian fella who lives in your building—claims to know every tenant—called us as soon as he heard that gunshot. Few minutes later calls back to say he saw someone run from the building. Fine. That backed up your story, but I still had my doubts. But, here's the kicker: While we're interrogating you, two greasy guineas claiming to be private investigators that just *happened* to have been watching your building on a different case waltz into my station. Claim they saw a black guy come and go from your place in a hurry. They heard the gunshot, too. So, here we are."

"Wow. I guess I am lucky."

"Damn right you're fuckin' lucky."

"Weird, 'cuz I don't *feel* so lucky."

Schlage just raised an eyebrow and bobbed his head a bit back and forth, as if to say "yeah, I guess I see what you mean." We sat in silence for a minute. I could tell that he was gathering his thoughts. Finally he got to it: "Now. Tell me what you *really* do, Moscowitz."

Gulp. "Wha-what?"

"You heard me, son. Tell me what you *really* do over there at Godz-Illa Records."

Fuck. He's on to me. How the hell does he know? Internal panic set in. My heart started pounding. I heard Lyons's voice in my head saying, *Your balls, dipped in gold, on a necklace.* Now that I was outside the walls of the police station, I suddenly didn't feel like spilling my guts about the truth anymore. "I told you what I do, sir. I'm an off, an office assistant."

A few faint laugh-toots came from his nose, filtered through the heavy brush of his mustache. "Gimme a fuckin' break with that shit, will ya? You think I buy that horseshit? I know a lie when I hear one, bucko, and that is a bunch a poppycock. Just tell me what the fuck you do over there. Who you trying to protect?"

"I'm not! No, no protecting. I told you what I di—"

"Okay, okay," he said, not wanting to hear the rest of my stuttering bullshit. "What do you do then? S'far as 'assisting' goes?"

"What?" I asked, trying to stall for some time. I was trying to recall the semi-elaborate spiel I'd come up with a long time ago for use in this very situation.

"You heard me, Moscowitz. What . . . do . . . you . . . do . . . ? In the office? As an assistant? What do you do?"

"We, uh . . . I do all sorts of stuff. I . . . make copies . . . of stuff.

Answer phones. Get coffee. I uh, I hand out flyers, I post, uh, posters. Around. That's a big part of it. You know, posters. And stuff. Of rappers' new albums . . . uh, coming out. You know?"

"Yeah? And who gives you these posters? How does that work exactly?"

"The posters?" I asked.

"The posters."

"How do they work?"

"That's right."

"Well—"

"Who gives them to you? What is the person's name?"

"Who? Well, all different, you know, people. Higher, uh, higher-ups."

"Right."

"Right. So, uh, I get 'em, and then I go out and start hangin' 'em—"

"How many do you usually get?"

"How many . . . we, uh, you know, we usually get about five hundred. Or so. More or less."

"Five hundred?! Whew! That's a shitload a posters!"

"Yeah. Yeah, you know, we post 'em all over the city. So, yeah. Five hundred." Schlage pulled into the parking lot of what appeared to be a vacant, derelict strip mall. He drove around back behind the empty stores, parked the car, and shut the engine off. We were all alone. He turned to me.

"So that's all you do, huh? Assistant?"

"Yes, sir. That's all I do."

"Alllll you do. You sure about that?"

"Yes, sir."

"That's funny. What if I told you that I know something, Mr. Moscowitz?"

I was silent.

"That's right. I know about what you *really* do. And I can help you. But this is your last chance, Wally. I'm not kidding. Last chance. If you need my help, *I will help you.* I'm serious. We can get you out of whatever mess you're tangled up in. But this is *it*, Moscowitz. Right now. This moment. If there's more to this story, if you're lying about what you do just to protect someone else, now's the time to tell me. This is your get-out-of-shit-free card. Last chance. Right now. Out with it."

I considered it for a moment. But only for a moment. I didn't trust this guy. This was like a game of poker. If I waited too long to respond I'd be showing Schlage my cards. I looked him right in his tinted lenses. "I already told you, sir. *That is what I do.* There's nothing more to tell."

He looked at me, held my stare, tried to get a read on me, but I knew I had him. If it had been his mousy-eyed little partner I wouldn't have been able to hold the look. No way. She'd have seen right through me. But not this guy. A smile formed under his bushy 'stache. "Okee-doke." He turned and opened his car door and got out. *Oh shit. What is he gonna do?* He walked briskly around the front of the car, pulled open my door, and yanked me out. "C'mon," he said, as he pulled me toward the rear door of one of the stores.

"What's going on?" I asked, terrified.

He didn't respond. We arrived at the heavy steel door and he rapped on it, shave-and-a-haircut.

"Who is it?" asked a deep, muffled voice from the other side of the door.

"Porky Pig," answered Detective Schlage. The door opened.

The room was dark. The large plate-glass windows at the front of the store were covered with brown paper. Barely any light shone through around the edges of the paper. I couldn't see who'd opened the door, because my eyes were adjusting to deal with the change from the semi-lit parking lot to this very dark room. Detective Schlage ushered me to what felt like the middle of the room. My eyes began to adjust. Behind me, I could see the silhouettes of two enormous men by the door we had just come through.

"Mr. Moscowitz," said a very familiar voice from somewhere

in the dark. I spun around, trying to pinpoint the direction the voice had come from. I was still spinning like a moron when a desk lamp clicked on to my left. I turned to see Abraham Dandy Lyons sitting behind an ornate, antique-looking desk in the middle of the otherwise empty room. *Detective Schlage brought me to Lyons? What is going on here?*

"I thought I told you to lay low," said Lyons in his deep, no-nonsense rumble. The large, beautiful desk sat oddly in the middle of this dusty, concrete, scrap-filled room. The walls and ceiling were all exposed wiring and pink insulation strips. Plastic sheets hung from the cracked and broken drywall. I could feel the loose nails and sawdust on the floor beneath my sneakers. I was too confused to speak. I looked from Lyons to Schlage and back to Lyons. "That's right, Mr. Moscowitz. Detective Schlage is . . . a good friend of the company's. How did he do, Detective Schlage?"

"Kid passed with flying colors, Mr. Lyons. Couldn't get a *word* outta him," said the detective proudly, smacking me on the back. "And believe you me, I tried."

So Schlage worked for Lyons. The car ride interrogation was a test of my loyalty. Schlage did his best to try to get me to talk about my *real* job at Godz-Illa, but I'd kept quiet. Passed the test, as it were. I was proud of myself, vaguely insulted, and morbidly curious as to what would have happened to me if I'd told Schlage the truth . . .

"Y-you were testing me?" I asked Lyons.

He looked at me with the smallest trace of a smile on his lips. "Do you have a problem with that, Mr. Moscowitz?"

I hesitated not at all in saying "N-no. No problem, sir."

"That's what I hoped you'd say, Mr. Moscowitz. You can understand the magnitude of the situation, no? The importance of testing loyalties?"

"Y-yes, sir. I do. I completely understand."

"Just be happy that you passed the test. Now, I repeat myself, I thought I told you to *lay low*," said Lyons, shuffling around some papers on his desk. I wondered what kind of paperwork got done in this oddball office. And why were we here and not the main office? I hoped it was simply because Detective Schlage couldn't be seen at the Godz-Illa offices, and not because the enormous men by the doorway needed somewhere where they could crush my skull and not worry about ruining the décor.

I wasn't sure how to respond to Lyons. After all, I *would've* laid low, had all this crazy shit that was completely out of my control not gone down over the past few days. I thought about how Jerry was certain that Lyons was behind Dr. Schwartzman's dognapping. I didn't *think* Jerry was right, but I guess I wasn't *positive*. What harm could come from telling Lyons about the whole situation? If he *was* responsible, maybe I would be able to tell by his reaction. I decided to tell Lyons everything that had been going on. Including what I'd tried to tell him the day before—that Deezy knew the truth about me and Oral B.

"I have been, sir. I've been trying, anyway."

"But . . . ?"

"But, some things have happened in the past few days that were out of my control."

"What *things,* Mr. Moscowitz?" asked Lyons. I hoped he wasn't getting impatient with me already. I had a lot to tell him.

"Well . . . I—"

"Why don't you start by telling me how you ended up in the police station today?"

"I honestly don't know, Mr. Lyons. I think I'm being framed."

"Framed? For what?"

"I don't know, sir."

"C'mon, Mr. Moscowitz."

"Sir, I came home today—"

"Home from where?"

"Home from . . . hanging out. With some friends."

Lyons raised an eyebrow, as if he knew that I had no friends. "What friends?"

Uh oh. This was where I might get into some trouble. Lyons had explicitly told me—ordered me, really—to not communicate with Oral B. "I was with Oral B, sir," I said in a mumbly way, with my head down.

"Pardon?"

"I was with Oral B, sir. He picked me up on my way to a meeting with my agent. He gave me no choice. They made me get in the car with them."

"They *made* you, Mr. Moscowitz? Who's *they*?"

"B and his brothers."

"I seeeee," he said, scratching his finely manicured chin hair. He let that marinate in his brain for a few seconds. "Go on."

I told Lyons all the details of arriving home, finding the gun, et cetera. He listened without interrupting. When I finished he sat idle for well over a minute, stroking his chin and rotating almost imperceptibly in his chair. "Who are these Italian gentlemen?" he eventually asked.

"I have *no idea,*" I said. "The detective said they were observing my building on some PI case, or something. That's all I know."

Lyons turned back to face me. He stared at me for a while in an excruciating way, forcing my eyes down into my lap. "Tell me, Mr. Moscowitz, in your heart of hearts, what do you believe happened in your apartment today?"

"Frankly, sir? I don't know. But I suspect it might have been Funk Deezy. DeAndre Muskingum."

"And why do you say that? You believe that just because you urinated on him he tried to—I don't know—what was he trying to do? Set you up somehow? Doesn't quite compute with me. Why wouldn't he just have you beat down by some of his homeboys?"

"There's more," I said. "A lot more."

Lyons turned his head slightly and raised an eyebrow. He looked over at Schlage, who shrugged and said, "News to me."

"You've been busy, Mr. Moscowitz," said Lyons.

"Not in a good way, sir. It's been a rough coupla days."

"Go on," he said.

"Well, my dog was dognapped, for starters."

"Your *dog*?"

"Yes, sir. Stolen. From my apartment."

"Okay . . . ?"

"And I was devastated. And then, a few days later, I received a ransom note."

"For your dog." I could hear the slightest bit of mocking in his tone, and I didn't appreciate it.

"Yes, sir."

"And what were the demands of this . . . *ransom* note?" His broad shoulders bounced slightly in a silent chuckle.

"The note simply said to be quiet. Not to talk to anyone. That I would be contacted later if I kept my mouth shut."

"What were you supposed to stay quiet about?" Either Lyons was a superb actor, or this was the first time he'd heard about the ransom note.

"The note didn't specify. Can I be candid with you, sir?"

"By all means."

"The note sort of sounded like . . . well, with all due respect, sir, it sounded like it, uh, it sounded like it was meant to be from *you*."

Lyons leaned all the way back in his chair and took a deep breath through his great nostrils. "From me, huh?"

"Y-yes, sir."

"In other words, you took the meaning of the note to be that *I* wanted you to keep quiet about your job, and that I would hold your dog hostage in order to ensure that you did so?"

"Well, y-yes, sir. With all due respect."

He rocked gently in his chair for a moment, lips pursed. "Why would I do that? You've worked for me for many years. Why do this now?"

"I don't know, sir. Maybe . . . in light of the suspension. Or something."

"But you didn't *really* believe it was from me. You said you thought it was Deezy."

"Well, yes, sir. I didn't know. I wasn't sure. I didn't know *what* to think. I was confused. And sc-scared."

"But what would Deezy want you to remain quiet about?"

"I haven't figured that out yet, sir. Maybe he wanted me to *think* the note was from you."

Lyons nodded his head very slowly, digesting. Something seemed to click in his brain. He went rigid. "Here's my problem with that story, Mr. Moscowitz. If you didn't believe the note was actually from me, if you believed that it was DeAndre Muskingum trying to *make you think* it was from me, then that implies that DeAndre Muskingum knows the secret. Knows what you really do." *This guy is fucking good.*

I looked at him with terrified puppy dog eyes, and nodded slowly, seriously.

"I beg your pardon?"

"He *knows*."

"He knows *whhhat*?" He enunciated the word "what" so intensely that it came out as *"whhhooowhaT."* The *T* at the end of his "what" was sharper than a thumbtack.

"He knows our . . ." I instinctively looked both ways and over my shoulder. "He knows *the* secret. That I write B's lyrics," I whispered the last part. Lyons stared at me with such ferocious intensity that I would not have been at all surprised if laser beams suddenly shot out of his eyes and exploded my head.

"WhhooowhaT?" he asked in an even more urgent and terrifying whisper.

"Y-yeah. H-he knows." *Oh, shit.*

I kept quiet for fear of certain death. He slammed both hands down on the desk simultaneously. "How . . . the *FUCK* . . . does he *KNOW*?"

"I don't kn-know how, uh, he knows. I sure didn't, I mean, he mentioned it to me in the bathroom that night."

"Before or after you urinated on him?"

"Before." He inhaled so deeply through his nose that I held on to the arms of my chair so as to not be vacuumed up into his vast nostrils, then lapsed back into silence and closed his eyes. He finally exhaled and I swear the papers on his desk were flapping in the wind.

"You need to leave now, Mr. Moscowitz. Get him outta here," he said to the not-so-jolly white giants. They rushed over to me and grabbed me by both arms. I was scared out of my mind. "Take his ass home." They forcefully escorted me to the door. "Mr. Moscowitz?" Lyons beckoned, as I was being dragged across the threshold. We stopped before stepping outside. "This time, I mean it when I say *lay low*. I'm going to get to the bottom of this. Stay out of the way."

By the time I got home it was well after nine. My apartment was an absolute mess—the police had finished, but they hadn't done the best clean-up job, and my bedroom was upside-down. Every drawer had been pulled out, the mattress was off its box spring, and the contents of my closet had been emptied onto the floor. When I saw the closet, my stomach dropped. I walked slowly toward it. I looked up to the top shelf, in the corner where I kept the shoebox.

It was gone.

I took a deep breath, put my hands on my head, stood there, and stared for a minute.

I realized that if I wanted to get to the bar in time I was in a serious rush. There was nothing I could do about my money right now. I'd have to worry about it later.

I took the quickest, coldest shower I could manage and got dressed at lightning speed. I was in a cab by a quarter after ten.

I could only pray that Jem would still be there when I finally arrived.

....

She wasn't.

It was a quarter to eleven by the time I jogged into the smoke-filled Kissing Room. I looked around, trying to be as nonchalant as possible and failing miserably. I looked like a kid who'd lost his mom in the mall, my eyes wide and wandering hopefully, my head whipping this way and that.

Jem was definitely not there.

I took a seat on a stool at the bar and ordered a shot of tequila. I downed it immediately and ordered another. I patted my pants pockets, checking for my cell phone. I'd left it at home—not that it mattered; I didn't have Jem's number and she didn't have mine.

I thought about the day's events. Lyons had actually shed some light on the situation for me. If Deezy had indeed sent that ransom note, what was his point? What did he stand to gain from me believing that Lyons took my dog? This whole time I'd sort of been thinking that Deezy was just fucking with me, messing with my mind because I'd urinated all over him. But that didn't make much sense. Not with the ransom note. And how the hell could anyone have known about my money stash? *There's more to the puzzle,* I thought.

Four shots and twentysome-odd minutes later, I resigned myself to the fact that I'd missed the boat. The beautiful and mysterious Jem must have found some other poor lonely schmuck to go home with. *She probably does this kind of thing all the damn time.* She's a philanthropist. A wonderful, charitable soul who gives herself to people in need. Provides miserable putzes like me with a few good memories to whack off to for the rest of their pathetic fucking lives. *Oh well, I had a pretty good run.*

And then, at the very apex of my drunken despair, she floated into the bar. The sexy little enigma herself. *Goddamn!* I thought. She was even hotter than I remembered (and still utterly famil-iar). I wanted to tell everyone in the room, as they were all looking at her, too, that I banged that girl! Some guys smiled, others whispered to their drunken buddies and pointed as she passed. I felt like a stud.

She gracefully approached and then glided past me. We made eye contact. She bit her lower lip discreetly and gave only a small wink at me. *Sexy fucking wink* though, let me tell you. I didn't know a wink could be so sexy.

She sat two seats away. The handsome bartender, who I may or may not have seen half-naked on a billboard on my way to the bar, smiled at her in a familiar way and asked her, with raised eyebrows, what she needed. She said something that I couldn't quite hear, but I'm certain it was both clever and witty, because the bartender threw his handsome head back, not at all disturbing his stiff, spiky golden hair, and let out a raucous laugh. He reached up high for a bottle of Patrón Tequila—the good shit—and poured four shots. She immediately downed one, sans lime, without even the slightest disturbance on her stunning face. She pulled a second one over toward her chest, then pointed to the bartender, indicating that she wanted him to take one, and then pointed in my direction, designating the last shot for me. In one fluid motion, she turned the finger that was pointing at me and curled it up and around in a sexy little get-over-here gesture. I hopped to the next stool as smoothly as my drunkenness would allow, which, unfortunately, wasn't very. I stumbled, missed, recovered, and then mounted the stool. We all held up our shot glasses.

"To the lady," the handsome bartender said.

"Absolutely," I said, disappointed that this was the most clever remark I could summon. We all downed our shots. For the second time that day, I was *fucked up*.

I looked at Jem. "Djyou know—"

She held a finger up to my lips, effectively shushing me, and unnecessarily—but quite sexily—adding "shhhhh," for good measure. She bit her lower lip slightly again, and I wanted to rip her clothes off. She grabbed my hand, and I was stung by the utter softness of hers. Sue had rough hands. Small, rough, rather-ugly-despite-the-manicure, I've-been-rubbing-dogs-all-day hands. Not like these. These were incredible. These were the Kobe beef of hands.

Jem rose from her stool without another word, pulling me toward the bar's exit. I followed her quietly, eagerly, toward another evening of festivities.

chizapter 15

I swear that I woke up with a smile on my face. A big, sexually satisfied, I-am-man-hear-me-fuckin'-roar sort of smile. This girl was amazing. I wanted to write song lyrics about her, or at least sing "Wind Beneath My Wings" to her. I wanted to draw little doodle-hearts with our names in the middle, maybe carve it into a tree somewhere. I wanted to hold her tightly and smell her hair. Trouble was, I couldn't do that, because when I lifted my head off of the pillow and glanced in her direction, she was gone. All that remained was a slight indentation in the sheets where she'd slept. Again. The girl was like fucking Houdini.

I rose out of bed and made my way to the bathroom, head shaking in slightly amused disbelief. *I guess you can't get into the head of a girl like Jem,* I thought. For now I was just thrilled to get into her pants.

I took a leak and then turned to the sink to splash some water on my face and wash some of the sleep away. As was becoming standard routine with Jem, I was stopped dead in my tracks.

A note was stuck to the mirror above the sink.

I reached for it and discovered that it was glued to the mirror with a glob of toothpaste. "There's Scotch Tape in the kitchen, you sexy, amazing, adorable, lazy bitch," I said aloud.

Oh, I can't stay mad at you, darling! I thought with a smile, as I unfolded the note. I got a nervous pang in the pit of my stomach when I realized that this note might be her bon voyage.

> Dear Wally,
>   Great job, Tiger! More tonight.
> Same time, same place.

Then a little scribbled *XOXO,* and then *jem,* with another little scribble-heart dotting the lowercase *j*.

A smile spread across my face as I reread that first complimentary line. *"Yeah!"* I yelled. "Who's the *man!?*" I looked at myself in the mirror, all smiles. I pointed to my reflection. "You. You're *good,*" I said in my best Robert De Niro impression. This relationship was perhaps the coolest thing that had ever happened to me. I felt like some sort of smooth, 007 superspy, rendezvousing nightly with a secret seductress. I truly didn't mind the lack of an actual speaking relationship. This was mysterious and exciting. I smiled to myself and decided that I'd earned a serious breakfast with some serious bacon.

I strolled toward the kitchen with a new spring in my step. Two things occurred en route, which, in tandem, ended my breakfast before it even began. First: I passed by Dr. Schwartzman's doggy bed and stopped, staring down at it in all its emptiness. When I looked up I caught a glimpse of myself in the nearby hanging mirror. I didn't look quite as pale as usual. I had that post-coital glow, and it disgusted me almost as much as it delighted me. "How can you be happy at a time like this, you fucking bastard?" I said to my reflection. I looked down at the empty doggy bed. "I'm sorry, Dr. Schwartzman," I said to the bed. "I'll find you today, buddy. I promise."

At this point my breakfast wasn't ruined, it was just tainted. It would have been a sad breakfast, yes. I would have grudgingly eaten that perfectly crispy bacon. In silent protest I would have swallowed mouthfuls of cinnamon French toasty goodness. I would have raised my glass and toasted my pulp-filled orange juice to my missing comrade, the Doctor. It would have been a breakfast in his honor. That's how I'd been justifying it to myself anyway, when the phone rang. The voice on the line preemptively ended my breakfast once and for all.

I picked up on the third ring. "Hello?" I said/asked.

"Where have you been?" barked the deep, computerized voice of the dognapper.

"I've been, I've been *here*."

"I've been calling since yesterday," retorted the robotic voice. The robotic asshole was getting a little bit catty with me.

"I . . . uh, I'm sorry. I went—"

"Shut up," snapped Mr. Roboto.

"Y-yes, sir. I just want my dog back. Tell me what I ca—"

"Shut up!"

"Sorry."

"If you want to see your dog again, go to Blockbuster Video for further instructions," said the dognapper.

"But—" I heard a click. "Hello? Hello?" Mr. Roboto had hung up on me. I looked at the phone in my hand and wondered if I would ever be able to end a phone call like a normal human being.

....

Unshowered, extremely hungry, and disheveled, I pulled into the Blockbuster Video store parking lot after taking yet another taxi to go pick up my car, which had been parked outside the bar for the past few days. When I finally burst through the door, I was sweating profusely from nerves and because I'm fat and that's what I do. I moved toward the comedy section, intending to begin my search for *Turner and Hooch*. Out of the corner of my eye, I spotted Clifford in his ill-fitting blue-and-yellow collared shirt, working the rewinds. He happened to look up just as

I glanced his way, and we made eye contact. He did a double take as I passed.

"Hey!" he shouted, pointing at me.

I glanced back his way. "Yeah?" I asked, barely slowing my rush to the comedy aisle to hear what the moron had to say.

"You! You-you're that guy from the other day. The c—" He lowered his voice to a whisper. "The cop. Right?"

"Uh, yes. I am." I lowered my voice now. "I can't talk right now, Clifford. I'm on the job." I started to walk away.

"Umkay. I was just gonna say that that's so freakin' weird that you just came in. Some chick and her kid just came in and rented *Turner and Hooch* like one second ago! And also that same black dude with the afro was here first thing this morning . . . " He shook his crusty head in bewilderment. "So weird."

I stopped. "What'd you say, Clifford?"

He looked at me with his perpetually vacuous expression. "I said some lady and her kid just rented *Turner and Hooch* which was weird 'cuz that's the one you were askin' about the other day'n they had the same dog as that one in the movie, they said. I could see him tied up to the bike rack outside. Big ol' hairy dog just sittin' there—"

"Clifford—when did they leave? Quick!"

"They just left. Prolly still out there if you run."

I bolted out the door. If they got away with the ransom note stuffed inside their video I might never see my dog again. Just my luck.

I turned the corner of the building at full speed, but slowed to a neck-craning, investigative walk when the large parking lot came into view. It was a big lot, shared by several other stores in the same mini-mall that housed the Blockbuster. I saw several people getting into or out of cars. Doing a quick scan, I eliminated all the men and zeroed in on just two women in two separate cars who appeared to be leaving. One of them was strapping a child into a car seat in the back of an SUV. I saw a dog in the trunk. Bingo. I sprinted toward her. "Lady!" She didn't respond. "Hey!

Excuse me!" I shouted as I got closer. *"You! Lady!"* The woman turned and saw me sprinting toward her, full speed, eyes wild. She looked petrified. She reached into her purse and fumbled around for a moment before pulling out a can of pepper spray just as I arrived at her car.

"STOP!" she shrieked. *"Don't come any fucking closer!"* She leveled the pepper spray at my face.

I screeched to a halt and put my hands up in the air. "Lady, no! No! I'm not—"

"I will fucking mace the shit outta you, asshole!" she screamed. Her baby started wailing at the top of its small-but-ultra-powerful lungs. Her dog went ballistic, barking up a veritable tempest, adding to the madness of the moment. *"Don't you fucking move!"* the woman shrieked. And then: *"Helllllp! Helllllp!"* She screamed bloody murder, as did her baby and her dog.

"No! Lady! No! I'm not attacking you! I just wanted to ask you a question! Please! I swear! I'm completely harmless."

"I'm being muuuugged! Helllllp!" She continued to scream, as did her dog and her child.

"No! No! Lady! I'm not!" I backed up a step, my hands still in the air out in front of me, fingers splayed in a gesture of empty-handedness. "I'm harmless. I just have a question."

She looked at me sideways, trying to get a read on me. She began to slowly lower her can of pepper spray.

Encouraged, my hands still held out in front of me, I pleaded further. "Look at me! I'm a fat little harmless man. I just wanted to ask you something and I was in a rush." She lowered her weapon even further, finally believing my words. "I'm sorry," I said. "I didn't mean to scare y—" Before I could finish, I was absolutely bulldozed—*plowed*—to the ground by some unseen force.

I was disoriented for a second, the back of my head resting on the bumpy pavement. I looked up at the blue sky and the slowly moving clouds, thinking, *Clouds are fluffy*. I was spinning, unsure of what had happened. It was a relatively peaceful moment, shattered by a tremendous, horribly painful *whack* in my ribs. I doubled over in pain. Realization flooded my panicked brain. *Someone knocked me to the ground and now they're kicking me! And kicking me again!*

"You wanna take advantage of an innocent woman, huh, scumbag?" I managed to hear in between ruthless kicks. I was balled up in the fetal position and I couldn't even get a look at my beater. "Huh, tough guy?" *Kick.* "Huh? You're a big man, huh?" *Kick.*

I think I heard the woman saying, "No! Don't!" But that may have been my hopeful imagination. After I'm not sure how many kicks, the man finally stopped kicking the crap out of me. A few more and I would have been spitting up chunks of lung. I looked up when I finally felt it was safe and I saw Clifford and another young Blockbuster employee holding the man back. Clifford was saying, "He's a cop, man! He's an undercover cop! Quit it, man!"

"Oh, Christ. A cop? No kidding? Shoot," I heard the man say.

They helped me up. I was hurting badly. I hadn't taken a beating like that since high school. I could've sworn that every single one of my ribs was broken.

"You're a *cop?*" the woman asked. I looked at her, too injured and winded to respond.

"You don't look like a darned cop," said the man who'd just kicked my ass, in a dubious, deep Southern twang. I turned my gaze to him, and it was hateful.

"He's not gonna answer you," said Clifford. "He's deep undercover, man."

All eyes were on me. Clifford and his underling held me up, one of them under each of my arms. I finally caught my breath and looked directly into the eyes of the Southern douchebag who'd just kicked the living crap out of me. "Get . . . the fuck . . . outta here . . . ," I snarled venomously.

He looked at me, suddenly convinced that I was for real. He took a few steps backward. "I, uh, apologies, sir. Apologies," he said, and he took off jogging, glancing back nervously once or twice.

"Are you all right?" asked the woman.

I took a deep breath just to make sure that I still could. It hurt. "Yeah. I'll be fine."

"Oh my God, I'm *so* sorry about that. I get scared very easily."

"Oh, really?" I asked. *You dumb bitch.*

"Well . . . what did you want to ask me?"

"Ask you?"

"Yeah. Before that guy . . . beat the crap out of you. You said you wanted to ask me something, or something?"

"Oh. Yeah. I wanted to ask you if . . . did you just rent *Turner and Hooch*?"

"What?" she asked, puzzled by my seemingly ridiculous question.

"Did you . . . just rent . . . *Turner and Hoo—*"

"No, man! That ain't her," said Clifford with casual finality.

I looked at him. He shook his head. "Different lady, dude."

....

Clifford and his coworker walk-carried me back into Block-buster. "What's the big deal about the *Turner and Hooch* DVD?" Clifford asked.

I wasn't in the mood for talking. Each and every breath I took sent pain shooting throughout my entire body. "I really can't talk about it, Clifford." I leaned back in the chair, both hands on my ribcage, trying to breathe as painlessly as I could.

"It's not even a good movie," he said, shaking his oversized greasy head.

I realized that I'd glanced over something he'd said earlier, when I first entered the store. "Did you say that black guy was here this morning?" I asked.

"Yeah," said Clifford.

"Same afro? Same orange jacket?"

"Same guy from last time."

"And what'd he do?"

"Um, well, I was watching him. 'Cuz, um, I remembered him from last time."

"What'd he do, Clifford?" I asked again.

"He, um, he just went over to the comedy section again. Like last time. VHS."

Then it hit me. *What's the big deal about the* Turner and Hooch *DVD?*" Clifford had said a minute prior.

"Clifford!" I said, reenergized.

"Yeah?" he asked goofily in return.

"Did you say that that woman rented *Turner and Hooch* on DVD?"

"Yup," he said.

"So . . . that means you still have the VHS version in stock?"

"Uhhh, we *should*. No one ever rents that crap. Lemme check the computer." Clifford began to poke at his keyboard with one finger.

"Don't bother, Cliff," I said, rising slowly, achingly, from the chair. I hobbled to the comedy section, which, incidentally, I had been en route to before my ass-kicking. I passed by all the familiar comedy titles, and sure enough, a young Tom Hanks in a cheap suit and his big drooly dog were just sitting there on the shelf. I cracked open the case. The letter inside was in a style identical to the first ransom note's.

IF yOu wAnT tO sEE YOUr dOg AGAiN WiRe **$50.00O**

iNtO CAYMAN NATIONAL BANK ACCOUNT #476-899-6302487-WM3

WiThIn 48 HOurS. YouLL bE vEry SorRy iF YOu dOnT.

As I read the note, my heartbeat sped up, and a lump formed in my throat. *Fifty thousand dollars? Where the hell am I going to get that kind of money?* I might've had half of that before my shoebox was stolen, but now I had *no chance!*

My knees went weak, and I sat on the floor. I was suddenly overwhelmed. Dr. Schwartzman. My only friend in the world. Gone. *I'm so, so sorry, Doc.*

I brought my knees up toward my face and rested my elbows on them. I cradled my face in my hands, and, for the first time since all the chaos began, for the first time in years, I cried.

chizapter 16

I cried deeply and completely. I cried for Dr. Schwartz-man. I cried for Sue. I cried for my job and my stolen savings and my dead dad and my mom who was ashamed of her only son being a failure. I cried for everything that my life was and everything that it wasn't. I had to stop crying rather quickly though because it was absolutely *killing* my bruised and/or broken ribs. I also didn't want Clifford to see me like this. So I got it together and rose from the crusty blue-carpeted floor of the Blockbuster VHS comedy section.

I thanked Clifford for all of his help, and assured him that the force was with him, which he seemed pretty psyched about. I walked outside, unsure of my next move. I decided to call Jerry. Maybe he'd know what to do. Not to mention the fact that I'd completely flaked on him the day before with the meeting at Bionic and I was sure he was either real pissed or real worried. His assistant Beth picked up on the first ring with her usual greeting, "The Silver Agency."

"Hi, Beth. It's Wally Moscowitz."

"Wally! Oh my God! Jerry has been looking for you for, like, ever! Hold on!" She patched me right through.

Jerry came on like a tornado in Kansas. "Wally!?"

"Jerry—"

"Wally, where the *fuck* have you been? I've been calling you since yesterday! I've been worried sick!"

"Jerry—"

"You didn't show for the meeting! What the heck were you *thinking?* Are you hurt? Are you all right?" he yelled.

"Jerry—"

"You don't show up, and then I get another one of these stupid fuckin' messages from you where your cell phone calls me while it's in your pocket and all I can hear are ruffling noises and rap music and—"

"Jerry—"

"I thought the worst, Wally! I thought someone hurt you. Maybe kidnapped you like your dog! I've been going *nuts!*"

"*Jerry!*" I finally yelled back.

"What? Tell me. What? Where were you? Where *are* you? What? Tell me. I wanna hear this. What?"

"I was . . . " I hadn't thought it through. At once I realized that I couldn't tell him that the previous day when I should have been in a meeting with him, I had actually been out getting stoned with a bunch of rappers. "Some shit came up, Jerry."

He made a poofing sound. "Some *shit* came up? *What?*"

"Jerry—"

"Some shit. That's what you tell me. Some *shit* came up. I'm worried sick about you, and I'm supposed to buy that, Wally? What the fuck?"

"Jerry—"

"Ohhh, okay, Wally! Some shit came up! I know just what you mean. Don't worry about it, then! I hate when some shit just *comes* up. Just sneaks right up on ya sometimes, that shit does. Okay, then! No worries, pal. Forget I mentioned it!"

"Jerry—"

"No, Wally. You're gonna have to do better than that! You missed the big meeting! How could you do this? This better not be all because of your whiny artist's integrity wussy crap again. Tell me it's not about that, Wally. Please. Tell me. Please."

"No, Jerry. No. Of course not. I'm sorry I missed the meeting, Jerry. I really am."

"You should be!"

"I am, Jerry."

"Well you should be!"

"I am," I said, trying to pacify the unpacifiable.

"Okay! Now where were you?" He really wasn't going to let this one go.

"Jerry . . . I was with Oral B. Okay?" I don't know why I said *that* instead of telling him about the situation with the police. It just came out.

"What?! What are you, *crazy*? I told you to stay away from those guys! They're dangerous right now!"

"Oral B is not dangerous. Well, not to me, anyway."

"What the hell are you *talking* about, Wally? They're trying to keep you quiet! They may be the ones who dognapped Dr. Schwartzman!"

"No. It's not them, Jerry. And it wouldn't be Oral B, anyway. Even if it was Godz-Illa related. It would be Abraham Lyons. But it's not. It's not them. I *know* it's not now."

"Oh? How do you *know* it's not them all of a sudden?"

"Well, long story, buuuut, the shortest version is, I just got another ransom note. With demands." I felt the emotion rising back up in my chest now, but I couldn't cry. I think he could hear the pain in my voice, because he softened up.

"Oh, shit. Shit. I'm sorry, Mosco. I'm sorry. I shouldn't be yelling at you like this, with all this crap going on. What happened? What do these maniacs want from you? Tell Uncle Jerry."

I took a deep breath. "They want fifty grand."

"*Fifty grand?* Holy cow! For your *dog?* Jesus! Who do these maniacs think they are?"

"In forty-eight hours."

"Oh, Jesus Christ on a bike. You're right. What the hell is Lyons gonna do with fifty g's? That's a drop in the bucket for him. Fifty k! Jeez!"

"I know, Jerry. I know. It's crazy! What am I gonna do? Where the fuck am I gonna get fifty thousand bucks?!" There was silence and then Jerry laughed a little.

"You laughing, Jerry?"

He laughed again.

"Why the hell are you laughing, Jerry? This is serious shit!"

"Well, I'll tell you why I'm laughing, Mosco. I got good news and I got more good news and then I got a little bad news."

"Okay . . . ?" I asked, nervous. I couldn't imagine what Jerry could possibly say. I prayed he was about to offer me the money, but I doubted it.

"Well, the good news is, I went to the meeting without you yesterday."

"Yeah?"

"Yeah. And, the more good news is, they made an offer."

"Wh-what? Okayyyy . . . what kind of offer?"

"They want to pay you ten grand per book, up front. Six books. That's sixty grand. Plus you'll earn royalties, of course."

"Sixty— Oh my God, Jerry! Oh my God! That's . . . crazy! I mean, amazing! Right? I think!" I was excited, but torn. The *last* thing I wanted to do was sell my books to those morons at Bionic Books. They would ruin them. But now . . . *sixty thousand dollars*! I could get the Doctor back! My best buddy—back home! I realized that there was more. "What's the bad news, Jerry?"

"Well, I was in a bad mood, Wal. You stood me up."

"Yeah? And . . . ?"

"And it was a decent offer, and I was thinking, 'The kid doesn't want the deal? He wants to flake on me? Good. Fuck him. He ain't getting it then.' "

"And?" I asked in a glum way, knowing where he was headed.

"And . . . I, uh, I told them to shove it."

....

After hanging up with Jerry amid assurances that he would do whatever it took to get the deal back on over at Bionic, I limped back to my car, thinking all the way. Cayman National Bank, the note had said. I wondered if I should call Lyons and tell him about this. It would be risky. Who knew what this maniac dognapper would do to the Doctor if he found out. And frankly, I still wasn't completely positive that Lyons had *nothing* to do with it at all. Best to keep it to myself for now.

I got in the car, holding my sides and wincing with every movement. I was in bad, bad shape. There was only one thing that could soothe my pain at that very moment.

Cheeseburgers.

I stopped at a little burger stand that I frequent and ordered a bacon cheeseburger, chili fries, and a Coke. I got my food and I moved toward a table.

"Moscowit!" someone said in a whispered sort of shout, as they tugged on the tails of my shirt, yanking me down into a booth.

It was my old buddy Ling-Ling Chow. Day-glo green trucker hat, clothing collage, and all. "Hey, Mr. Chow."

"Sit here," he said, holding me down by my shirt a bit more firmly. I grimaced in pain as I took a seat across from him. "What now, Moscowit? You hurt again? Last time the eye. Now what? More rappers beating you up, neh?"

"Nah. No. I just, uh, I hurt my ribs."

"Suuuuure you did, Moscowit." I'd forgotten how much the little guy had annoyed me the last time we'd met, before I'd actually started to like him.

"Listen, Mr. Chow—"

"Ling-Ling."

"Right. Ling-Ling—I'm glad to run into you again. I, uh, I wanted to make sure we were clear about you not telling anyone about my secret. You know what I mean? My job?"

"Yes! Yes! I know, Moscowit. Biiiiiig secret. Safe with Ling-Ling. Don't worry. Flies never visit an egg that has no crack."

"Okay, good. Thanks. And, uh, I also wanted to ask if you happened to notice that guy sitting behind us that night at the laundromat. Black kid? Maybe he said something to you about our conversation after I left?"

Ling-Ling frowned and furrowed his brow. "No, no. I din't see any man. No."

"Okay. All right," I said. This was a relief. I'd been thinking about the look on that kid's face for the past few days and wondering if I was just being paranoid about the whole thing or if he could figure into this mess somehow. In retrospect, it didn't seem like such a big deal. Maybe he did just see me burn myself on the hot zipper after all.

"I hoped to see you again, too, Moscowit," Ling-Ling finally said.

I turned to him, surprised. "Oh yeah? Why's that?"

He turned to me. Looked into my eyes. "I was thinking about you after you left the laundromat. Made me feel very sad." He put his hand over his heart. "You have sorrow," he said sternly. I hoped I wasn't about to get a psychiatric session with the little Asian man in the green hat that I'd met at the laundromat. My head was pounding, my stomach was aching, and I just wanted to eat.

I didn't want to encourage Ling-Ling, so the only thing I could think to say to try to end the conversation was, "Oh. Okay."

"You are a good man, Moscowit. That is easy to see. But I can tell you are involved in some very bad things."

"Nah. Ling-Ling, I'm fine. Really. Don't you worry."

I smiled at him, but he didn't smile back. He looked at me the way Mr. Miyagi looked at the foolish young Daniel-san. He started to shake his head. "No, Moscowit. You are not fine. I saw deep sadness in you last time. Deep deep sadness. And pain. Not just in eye. Not just in ribs."

"Nah, really. I appreciate your concern, Ling-Ling. But I'm fine."

"Little man. Big heart."

"What?"

"Just like Ling-Ling."

I smiled. "Right."

"Moscowit, they can beat you here"—he pointed to my face—"and make bruise. And they can beat you here"—he pointed to my ribs—"make bruise. But don't ever, *ever* let them beat you *here*," he said with a sharp finger pointed at his heart. His finger thudded on his chest plate.

I stared at him. He stared at me. We had a moment.

"Sadness . . . is bruise of heart," he added quietly, poignantly.

We were silent as I digested Ling-Ling's words. I swallowed a lump in my throat. "Okay. I see. Thank you, Ling-Ling." He bowed his head without breaking eye contact.

Believe it or not I was genuinely touched. Or maybe I was simply feeling emotional after the good cry I'd had back in Blockbuster. More likely it just felt good to feel like someone might actually care about me, even if it was just some guy I met at the laundromat.

Ling-Ling was finished with his food and his sermon, and he rose. "You are stronger than you think, Moscowit. Trust Ling-Ling. I been around long time. Not until just before dawn do men sleep best; not until men become old, do they become wise."

He gave my shoulder a squeeze, and turned to walk away.

After a few steps, he turned back and said, "Oh, Moscowit. One more thing. Whenever Ling-Ling in difficult situation, I aaaaalways remember something my father told me: 'You can only go halfway into a dark forest; then you are coming out the other side.' " He nodded slightly, turned, and left.

I inhaled my food, got in my car, and drove home.

If I'd known what was waiting for me, I might have ordered another burger.

....

I tenderly pulled open the front door of my building and stepped into the staircase. Large hands grabbed me roughly from both sides. "Hey!" I yelped, but was silenced by a large, dry, cold hand clamped over my mouth. Four bulbous arms lifted me clear off the ground with brutish force and yanked me back out the door. I struggled fiercely, suddenly unbothered by the terrible pain that had been stabbing at my sides for the last hour, the hurt extinguished by fear and adrenaline. I couldn't get a good look at my captors, but as I was tossed into the backseat of a car, I did manage to catch a glimpse of its exterior. It looked like some kind of government or police vehicle. Upon landing awkwardly on my face in the backseat, my suspicions were confirmed by the thick, bulletproof divider between the front and back seats.

After unceremoniously tossing me in the back, one of the two brutes rounded the front of the vehicle in order to get into the driver's seat, and the other opened the passenger-side door. I recognized the two scary, well-dressed giants immediately: Abraham Lyons's skull crushers.

chizapter 17

I looked at the two ginormous men through the thick glass between the seats. This was the first time I'd had the chance to examine them up close. They were two of the biggest human beings I'd ever seen. Their heads were at least as large as watermelons, and equally hairless. Each of their shoulders measured about the wingspan of a pterodactyl. I leave out the description of their necks because they didn't appear to have any. I didn't know people could *be* that big. *They must be former football players or something,* I thought. *They're beasts!* Upon closer examination, the one in the passenger seat looked to be Samoan, while the driver was white. They both looked cramped in this midsized car. *They'd probably be a lot more comfortable in a bigger vehicle, like Oral B's Hummer,* I speculated. *Or a 747.* They must have taken this car in an effort to be less conspicuous. It's tough to be inconspicuous when you're eleven foot ten and your buddy is twelve foot four.

I was terrified. I really didn't need to ask, but I did anyway. "Where are you taking me?"

The big Samoan goon sitting shotgun turned his gargantuan body as much as he could (which wasn't much) and said, "Mr. Lyons wants to see you."

"Okay . . . He could've called." I said quietly. The big man gave a laugh and shook his ridiculously huge head, then turned back around to face front and muttered something under his breath to the tune of "Dumbass little cracker." *I am so fucking dead,* I thought. *Something terrible is about to happen. I just know it. He would've called if he just wanted to see me.* Lyons had never sent anybody to get me before. *He probably told these ruffians not to be gentle. He probably said, "Bring that little shit to me. Dead or alive." I'm fucked. Maybe that kid at the Laundromat DID hear me and he's talked to Lyons, threatened to go public.* I was suddenly certain that Lyons had decided I'd become too much of a risk, and that it was time to silence me forever.

....

We pulled up to a rear entrance to Lyons's building. This was the building that I'd worked in for years, and yet I'd never known that this luxuriously appointed back entrance existed. A skinny young black guy in a tuxedo—the valet—rushed out past the tuxedoed doorman and opened the car door for the White Giant. The Samoan Giant opened my car door for me. There was no roughhousing this time. I guess they trusted that I wouldn't try to get away, now that I'd seen their collective strength. They were absolutely correct. When the doorman politely opened the glass and gold-plated door, saying, "Welcome, gentlemen," I followed the giants obediently.

The door led directly to a small, finely decorated foyer and an elevator. One of the giants hit the button, and the doors instantly slid open. We entered the car, and they pushed the only button on the panel. The doors whisked closed, and the car began to rise swiftly. The sudden movement jarred me, tipping me into the wall. I winced and held my tender rib cage with both hands. One of the giants took notice. "We hurt you, there, lil man?"

I tried to play tough. "Nahhh. Got in a fight this morning."

Samoan Giant gave that same patronizing half-laugh he'd given me in the car earlier, and White Giant arched one eyebrow bemusedly as if to say, "This little fat fuck gets into fights?"

When the elevator dinged open, I was glad because my eyes had just wandered worriedly to the weight capacity sign, and I was concerned that the three of us were possibly pushing its limits.

We stepped out into some kind of small, gray, highly-polished cement holding room. There was a black, heavy-looking door opposite the elevator. White Giant pushed a small doorbell that made a buzzing sound, pushed the door open, and we stepped directly into Abraham Lyons's office.

I hadn't seen this entrance/exit door the last time I was here, and when the giant closed the door behind us, I realized that on the office side, the door isn't a door, but a bookcase. Completely hidden unless you knew where to look. Very Scooby-Doo.

Lyons sat regally behind his large, immaculate bamboo desk. As usual, he was flawlessly dressed in a finely tailored suit, which blended impeccably with the office's décor. And like the last time I was here, he didn't look up when we entered. He was engrossed with a piece of paper on his desk. Or maybe his eyes were closed. From my angle it was impossible to tell.

"Sit," he finally spat, without looking up. I sat in the chair directly across from him, only brave enough to look at him because he wasn't returning the look. "We have a problem, Mr. Moscowitz. A big, big, seven-point-oh-*Richter* fucking problem. And I think that *you* are at the epicenter."

My eyes widened slightly in fear and confusion. "Wh-what, whaddaya mean, Mr. Lyons?"

He looked up at me, his dark eyes lancing my skull. He stared at me for a painfully long time, and somehow, I held his gaze. I must have looked pathetic. Lyons finally broke the stare to nod at the two giants, who quickly exited through the main office door.

Lyons tilted his head back slightly but didn't take his eyes off me. His jaw was clenched and I could see the muscles pulsing in his face like alien worms swimming underneath his skin. I couldn't remain quiet, the silence was just too painful, and Lyons was just too scary. I blurted, "What, what happened, Mr. Lyons? Why am I, I mean why did—"

"Quiet," he said, interrupting my babble. He paused again, before saying, "There are some things we need to discuss."

"Okay," I said, swallowing hard.

"I just received *this*," he said, thrusting one finger down onto the paper on his desk with so much force that it made a thumping sound akin to a bird flying into a window. He slid the paper toward me. I lifted it up to my face, and gasped.

LYOnS — YOU shouLDnt HAVe fucked with me !

I KnoW A sECreT   YoUr biG **cash CO**w **ORAL B** ISnT

the gREat mind BeHind the MUSic   woULdnt the

worLd *love* To kNoW **about** THIs ! WiRE TEN miLLion

DOLLaRs INto CAYMAN NATIONAL BANK account

476-899-6302487-WM3 WiThiN 48 HoURS oR this

IS frONt PAgE nEws   DOnt TRy aNY funny sTUFf

ShOW this tO NobODy !   I'M nOt plaYing gaMEs

This is aS gooD As ITs gonNa get

aNd it wOnT ever GeT tHAt GOoD aGAiN

I WILL RUIN you !

I gasped again. I shook my head as I read it. I could feel Lyons's eyes on me as I perused the note. He was trying to gauge my reaction.

"This is . . . this is unbelievable!" I said.

"Why is it unbelievable, Mr. Moscowitz?"

"It's exactly like the notes I got. It's from the same person!" But that wasn't all. There was something else about this note that stuck in my craw. Some alarm was beeping frantically in the far reaches of my brain that I couldn't quite put my finger on . . .

"Notes?" he asked, emphasizing the *s*. "You got more than one?"

"I got another one this morning," I said. Luckily, I had the latest ransom note folded up in my back pocket. I pulled it out and dropped it on the desk. Lyons unfolded it and began to read with a furrowed brow. Of course, it took him much longer to respond than I would have preferred. After a veritable eternity, Lyons looked up, but not at me. His gaze wandered past me to some imaginary place millions of imaginary miles away.

Eventually, his gaze began to ooze slowly downward, back toward me. We locked eyes. "I am only going to ask you this once, Mr. Moscowitz. *Once*. And if you lie to me . . . " He made a clicking sound with his tongue and shook his head. "Don't lie to me. Did . . . you . . . have . . . *anything* . . . to do . . . with this letter?" he asked in the most terrifyingly deliberate manner. Lyons awaited my response like a dog awaiting table scraps—ready to pounce. He watched me very carefully, reading my every facial expression for signs of lying or faltering.

"Absolutely *not*, Mr. Lyons!" I said. He didn't need to hear my actual words. He would have *known* if I was bullshitting. His intense scrutiny was making me very self-conscious. *Do I sound guilty?* I thought. *Fuck. I totally sound guilty. I'm the worst non-lying liar of all time, and he's going to kill me. I'm fucking worthless anyway. No big loss to the world.*

Lyons stared at me for an eternity. I managed to stare back again. I knew that my life could very well depend on it. *Don't blink, Wally.* "I believe you, Mr. Moscowitz," he said at last.

"Well, good! You should!" I blurted without thinking.

He focused a hard, mean glare on me and leaned forward slightly. I leaned forward too, thinking that he wanted to say something quietly to make sure that no one else would hear, even though there was no one else in the room. Instead, he lashed out and grabbed my shirt like some sort of ninja or a striking snake. He stood and lifted me almost off my feet. "Don't you *ever*, *EVER* tell me what I should or should not do. You hear me?" One of his eyes was wide with anger, and one was squinted menacingly. I'll be honest, a little squirt of piss leaked out into my boxers.

"Y-yes, sir. S-sorry." Lyons dropped me, and I slumped back into the seat. He wiped the nonexistent wrinkles from his suit and sat back down in his throne, breathing deeply through his nostrils, regaining his composure. Although there is certainly no doubt that Abraham Lyons is one of the most intimidating men alive, this was uncharacteristic of him. He is notoriously cool and controlled, famous for never losing his temper. This minor outburst was significant. Lyons was stressed out.

"Now," he said, "as I was saying . . . I believe you. I don't think you have it in you to blackmail a man like myself, Mr. Moscowitz. And I don't mean that in an insulting respect. I mean to say that I think you are a good man. Straight up. And smart. Too smart for this idiotic bullshit. And I think—I *think*—that my secret is safe with you. You passed my test yesterday with Detective Schlage. Understand this though, Mr. Moscowitz: I don't trust *anyone* completely. I believe that my own mother would empty my bank accounts if given the opportunity. And that is why I am keeping an eye on you. In an Orwellian sense. Do you understand?"

"Yes, sir. I understand."

"Good. Now tell me more about your dog."

"My dog. My d-dog was dognapped. Abducted. From my apartment."

"And this dog is a thing of high value to you, I presume?"

"I love that dog like a brother." I realized how absolutely silly that sounded. "Like a son, I mean. I love him like he's my child," I stammered.

"And so the person or persons who are responsible for your dog's abduction must have known the depth of your feelings for this animal, correct?"

"Well . . . I hadn't considered that, but, yeah. I guess so." I really hadn't thought of it that way. I'd just figured that the dog-nappers took the Doctor because that was the only thing in my apartment worth taking, besides, of course, my shoebox.

"That said, whom do you believe is responsible for this abduction, and hence, the ransom notes which we both received?"

"After seeing your note, I'm pretty sure that Funk Deezy is responsible, sir."

"Explain how you came to this conclusion," Lyons said.

"Well, Deezy knows our secret. But he doesn't know that *you* know that he knows it. Does that make sense?"

"Continue."

"So, I figure that he's trying to blackmail both of us. He's after your money. He thinks he can use our secret to get it, and that *you'll* think that *I'm* the one blackmailing you, since I'm *supposedly* the only one who knows the secret. That ransom note you got sounds like it's *supposed* to be from me, just like the one I got sounds like it's supposed to be from you. He's trying to keep *me* quiet, keep me from contacting you, so his cover won't be blown, and we'll both simply cooperate."

Lyons nodded his head slowly. "I came to the same conclu-sion. It's too bad he's such an ignorant fool. It's a ridiculous plan."

"Yes, sir. It is." I was hoping that Lyons would offer to pay the ransom for the Doctor. But he didn't. He wouldn't do that until he was 110 percent certain that I was being straight with him. Maybe he *still* wouldn't do it at that point.

"Does Mr. Muskingum know the extent of your feelings for this animal?"

"No, sir. I don't see how he would. I don't really know him too well."

Lyons nodded slowly again, figuring something out. I could swear that I saw a slight smile hidden in the corners of his mouth. "And . . . tell me again . . . how did Mr. Muskingum find out our big secret, Mr. Moscowitz?"

"I told y—I have n-no idea, Mr. Lyons, sir. No idea."

He used that same penetrating stare on me. "Are you absolutely certain that you didn't *accidentally* tell him?"

"I *swear* on my own life, and the life of my mother, and my dog, that I did not tell him, neither intentionally nor accidentally. *Never.*"

Lyons continued to nod. "Hmm . . . I see. This is the key, Mr. Moscowitz. The key to this whole predicament. How did Mr. Muskingum find out?" He paused for a while to think, forming a steeple with his fingers. "Tell me then, Mr. Moscowitz, why and/or how did your conversation in the restroom with Mr. Muskingum a few days ago escalate to the point that you . . . *urinated* on him?"

I looked at Lyons blankly for a moment. "I just . . . it just, I don't really know, sir. It had nothing to do with the secret. He was jus—he kept, like, antagonizing me. It all happened so quickly."

Lyons nodded slowly again, squinty-eyed, back in pensive mode. He reached under the desk and pushed a button. I heard the door behind me open, and the two giants lumbered back into the room. "I'm missing an important piece here, Mr. Moscowitz. But I'll figure it out quickly enough. And you'll be hearing from me."

"Y-yes, sir."

"Do us both a favor, Mr. Moscowitz. Go home. And *stay there. In* your apartment. I'll be ringing you again real soon."

"Y-yes, sir."

"Now beat it. I've got work to do."

chizapter 18

About an hour later I recklessly flopped down onto my hard-as-a-rock futon couch. A shockwave of pain jolted through my body. *I'm gonna have to see a doctor about these ribs*, I thought. *What if I have internal bleeding? I definitely have broken ribs. Probably some serious internal injuries. I could be dying right this very moment, bleeding to death on the inside. It hurts. Ow.*

For no particular reason—maybe it was a conditioned association with pain—I thought about Sue for the first time in days. I wondered if I should call her. We hadn't spoken since she'd dropped me off in a huff two days ago. *How could she not call me?* If for no other reason than to find out if the Doctor was okay. *She's a heartless bitch.*

Fuck it. I'll call her, I thought. I reached for the cordless phone, held it in my hand, antenna in my mouth, and paused to think before I took the plunge. *Am I the biggest pussy in the world? That bitch should be calling me! I'm the one laying on my couch in the middle of the day, injured, jobless, and dogless.*

"*Don't do it!*" said a little devil on my shoulder. "*You're just gonna look like a whiny little pussy.*"

The little devilish prick was absolutely right. *Let Sue come crawling back to me. This antenna tastes like boogers*, I thought, as I placed the phone back on the table, realizing that I'd sometimes stick the antenna in my nose mindlessly as I watched TV.

163

My thoughts returned to the ransom note that Lyons had received. I recited it internally to the best of my memory, and there it was again—that unidentifiable *thing*. I put my hands to my head in a literal attempt to wrack my brain. *What is bothering me so much about that fucking note?* My brain was too cluttered with all the chaos of the past few days, and I just couldn't put my finger on it. I knew if I could just distract myself, take my mind off of it, it would hit me at some point when I least expected it.

I grabbed the remote control and flicked on the television, always a good distraction. *The Price Is Right* was on. *Nice,* I thought. *My first victory of the day.* I heard a harsh *buzzzz* and then Bob Barker, now just a white-haired, suntanned skeleton with a skinny little microphone gripped in his bony hand, said, "Sorry folks, you've alllll overbid." When old Bob finally revealed the actual retail price of the living room set, a blond, bouncy-breasted co-ed with a boob-hugging "Marry Me, Bob!" T-shirt on and a bid of one dollar jumped and screamed her way all the way up to Bob. I experienced a moment of panic when I thought she was going to jump into Bob's arms for a hug like the girls would do back in the '80s when Bob was more virile, and that he would fall to the ground and disintegrate in a chalky gray cloud of bone-dust. Luckily that didn't happen; the bimbo quickly lost the stupid game she was consigned to, and Bob sent us into a commercial with the dependable assurance that we'd see her again in the Showcase Showdown.

I never made it to the Showcase Showdown. The commercial break changed everything. I finally figured out why Jem looked so goddamned familiar.

....

I sprang upright on the futon like a domino in rewind. I rubbed my eyes the way they do in cartoons (insert: *wee-wo-wee-wo-wee* sound effect), expecting that when I pulled my hands away from my face the image would be gone.

It wasn't gone.

A slightly younger, shorter-haired Jem strolled across my tele-vision screen through a field of vibrant wildflowers. Her arms up in the air, doing a happy little twirl, she joyfully exclaimed, "Life is *wonderful* when you're feeling healthy!" Cut to Jem standing in the rain without an umbrella, soaked to the bone, shivering, and very sadly saying, "But sometimes it can be a real drag. Especially when you suffer from painful itching and burning down below. Sound familiar?" The camera jumped to a close-up of her face. She looked right at the camera, and in her most grim tone said, *"Genital herpes."* Cut back to long shot. "But now, there's help," she said, as a friendly passerby handed her an umbrella, which she opened, finally getting refuge from the brutal downpour. "Millions of Americans just like you and me carry some form of the herpes simplex two virus. But now we have a way to *stop* the pain and suffering *dead in its tracks.*" The rain suddenly halted, and the sun shined down on Jem. She smiled, lowering the umbrella, which I could now see had "Her-pegra" printed across the top of it in bold yellow letters. "It's called Herpegra!"

The screen changed to a graphic: a purple silhouette of a human body with an animated yellow pill moving down the esophagus and blossoming out toward the genital area once it landed in the illustrated stomach. "Herpegra is a pill you take orally, which penetrates *deep* to quickly relieve the terrible itch-ing and burning often associated with genital herpes." Cut to Jem hiking among towering, copper-colored rocks in a scenic, Grand Canyon–esque tableau. "Side effects are rare, but may include dizziness, restlessness, mild dementia, nausea, diarrhea, skin decay, hair loss, mild fever, rectal swelling, and bleeding all over. Ask your doctor if Herpegra is right for you." Jem approached another field of glorious wildflowers atop the copper cliffs. "Don't let genital herpes ruin *your* sunny day ever again."

She spun around and fell on her back onto a springy bed of flowers, and then, with a big grin of finality, "Herpegra!"

The commercial ended and another came on, but of course, I didn't catch it. I was in shock. My jaw had dropped at the very first sight of Jem, and hadn't yet risen back to its normal position. I managed to switch off the television as my mind reeled. *She's an actress? What the hell? This doesn't mean she HAS genital herpes, does it? She's an actress! Right? Did she say rectal swelling?* I suddenly felt very itchy. I clawed at my groin area through my jeans, unsure of how to go on from here. *So many questions!*

I always wonder about the people on those commercials. Are their careers *that* bad that they have to resort to such pathetic measures? I mean, I guess it probably pays well, but still! How do they expect to have a serious acting career after that? Once branded as that chick from the herpes commercials, or the guy with chronic diarrhea, could they be cast on, say, a TV show or a serious film? There are certain roles you just have to turn down!

But how could I possibly confront Jem about this? How could I possibly sleep with her after this? Every time I touched her I would be thinking about that itching and burning sensation. Every time we had sex I would obsess over the fact that she was rubbing herpes all over my penis with every plunge. This was it. The end! The magical mystery of this relationship was over. Jem wasn't the cool, composed femme fatale anymore. I knew her secret identity now. *No wonder she went for a schlub like me! She's probably just as desperate as I am!*

I needed answers. I picked up the phone to call Jem, but realized that I didn't have her number. I didn't even know her last name. Shit, I'd never even spoken to her! How could I be so emotionally invested in a girl I'd never even had a conversation with? I told myself to stop thinking with my dick and start thinking with my brain. I knew I wasn't supposed to leave my apartment. But I had to talk to her. I would go meet Jem tonight at the bar and straighten this out. Despite Lyons's orders. Nothing bad would happen. There had to be a perfectly logical, acceptable explanation.

....

I got to the bar early, around nine. I knew that I shouldn't expect Jem there for at least an hour, which was cool, because I wanted to do some research. The good-looking bartender recognized me when I walked in, acknowledging me with a knowing smile and what I thought might just be an approving nod. I sat at what had become my usual stool. The bar was just beginning to fill up, though the place never got too crowded anyway.

"Tequila shots?" asked Johnny Handsome, as I settled in.

"Uh, sure. Yeah. Please," I said. He held up two fingers. "Make it three," I responded to his sign language. I was glad that this guy was here—the same guy from the previous nights. He was the one I wanted to talk to. I'd already figured—because of his perfect tan, his flawlessly gelled porcupine haircut, and his current occupation—that, like Jem, this guy was a struggling actor. I had further deduced, through analyzing their interaction the previous evening, that he and Jem knew each other. At least in passing. He brought over the shots, and I downed one immediately.

"Can I get you some limes there, bud?" he asked, revealing his annoyingly good teeth.

"Uh, nah. Thanks. I'm okay."

"Okay, Boss," he said, turning around to the register to ring me up. "Let me know when you need more."

Oh, I'll let you know, BOSS, I thought. Nothing irks me more than being called Boss. That or Ace or Sport or Chief or Guy or Captain. It's the height of condescension. I knew that it would take a few tequila shots before I'd have the courage to ask this cocky schmuck what I wanted to ask him. I'm very intimidated by overly confident, overly beautiful people.

Sure enough, after three shots, I felt a little bit looser. I held up one finger, signaling to Johnny Abercrombie that I needed some assistance. He walked over. "What can I getcha? More tequila, Slim?" *Uuuuugh. Slim.* Add that to the list.

"Uhhhh, yeah. Two more. But, uhhh, I also wanted to ask you something." I smiled awkwardly and drew figure eights on the bar with my finger.

He looked suddenly worried. "Oh . . . sure. What's up, Guy?"

"Umm, I noticed that you're, uh, you know, you're a pretty good-looking guy and stuff, and—"

"Whoa, whoa, whoa," he said, his hands now up in front of him defensively. "Sorry, Chief. I don't swing that way."

"Oh! No! God! No no no! Sorry. Sorry. I didn't mean it to sound that way. I'm not gay or anything—"

"Whew! Yeah—I was gonna say. I saw you leave with whats-ername the past few nights, so I figured—"

"Yeah! Jem! I did. I left with her," I said, relieved now that he saw me leave with a hottie and probably thought I was a total stud. Maybe.

But he was smiling now. And it wasn't so much an approving, deferential smile as a mocking, derisive one. "Jem? *That's* her name?"

"Uh, yeah," I said.

He gave a little laugh that forced his head back a bit, as if someone blew air into his eyes through a straw. "I thought it was . . . eh, I don't know. Anyway, what'd you wanna ask me?"

"Well, I wanted to ask you about *her,* actually. If, uh, if you knew her. Know her. Because you're both actors, and stuff. But I guess you don't."

"Who said I was an actor?" he asked, suddenly miffed.

"Oh! No! I mean—"

"Just because I'm a bartender? What—you think every good-looking guy who tends bar or waits tables in L.A. is a fuckin' actor?"

"No! No! I'm sorry. I'm—I didn't mean—"

"That's so fucked, dude! *So* fucked!"

"No! Dude! I'm—I didn't mean to offend you, it's just—"

His face melted into a smile and he started laughing. "Just kiddin', buddy. Yeah. I'm an actor." He laughed again and reached over and smacked me on the bicep like we were old pals. "Gotcha!" he said, pointing at me with his gun-shaped hand. "Guess I'm a pretty good actor, too! Had you on the ropes!" He shadow boxed to illustrate what he'd meant by "on the ropes."

I gave him my best fake laugh. Why must people fuck with me? "Yeah! You're good! You had me!"

"I had you at hello!" he said, quoting *Jerry Maguire* and loving himself.

"Ha. Right!" I said, indulging him.

"But, uh, no. I don't really know her. No. All I know is . . . well, *you* know," he smiled. "The whole herpes girl thing."

"Oh. Right," I said, fake smiling. *Shiiiiit.*

"Hope you wore protection, bro!" he said with another laugh, smacking me too hard on my aching bicep again. "Rumor has it she's got *the herps!*"

"Nahhhh," I said, humoring him. "It's just a commercial, right?"

He laughed. "I don't knoooow! I hope so—for your sake!"

"No, but I mean, it's not like she really *has* genital herpes! It's just a commercial, dude!" I said, fishing for whatever actual insights this douche bag might provide.

"Keep telling yourself that, bro!" he said, cackling obnoxiously some more.

"Nah, I mean . . . you don't know something that I don't, right? Like, for real?" I asked.

"No. Alls I know is this—she comes in here sometimes—lives nearby I think—always looks hot, but you're the first guy I've seen her go home with. I mean—*everyone on earth* has seen that commercial! Been on forever, right? Runs during Leno for fuck's sake. Anyway, that scares 'em off, I guess. Everyone calls her the 'Herpes Girl,' or whatever."

"Oh, *man,*" I said.

"Yeah. I mean, she's cool though. Totally nice and stuff from what I've seen. I wouldn't worry about it, dude."

"Okay. All right. Thanks, man," I said, holding up a shot.

"Cheers, brah. Good luck with that," he said with that shiny, mocking smile.

My vision was slightly skewed and my concerns slightly growing by the time Jem made her grand entrance. When I saw her, my heart skipped a beat. Not in a nervous way, either—despite the fact that I knew that I had to confront her about perhaps the most awkward thing *ever.* No, my heart-skip was more like the the-girl-who-I-like-just-entered-the-high-school-cafeteria sort of thing. She wore a tight little black dress that appeared to be made of lycra or some other clingy thing. The dress, a necklace of polished red stones, and sandals that were the same color as the necklace. Nothing fancy, but *shit,* she looked hot. But, as soon as I thought about genital herpes and my crotch began to itch, those amorous feelings vanished pretty quickly.

Same routine as the previous nights. She floated in, took her seat a few stools down from me, and ordered her tequila shots. She gave me that sexy little wink—only this time, of course, it was made considerably less sexy by the thought that her nether regions might be itching and/or burning. I noticed that the guys around the room, who yesterday I'd thought were looking at her and pointing and smiling because she was so exceptionally beautiful, were indeed pointing and smiling still, but only because they were in the presence of a D-list Hollywood celeb. One that they had a venereal disease–bearing nickname for. When she finally grabbed my hand and pulled me toward the exit, I no longer felt like the envy of the room. I was back to being good old Wally Moscowitz. The big joke. The laughingstock.

She must arrive in a cab and have them wait, I thought, as we got into the taxi, which stood idling at the curb for the third night in a row. The meter read $14.47. I must have been too wasted the previous nights to have realized it. This time I noticed the details: The cab stunk like cigarettes, despite the seventeen green pine trees dangling from the rearview. The blue pleather seat was greasy and slippery underneath me. It was also patched in several spots with duct tape. I did my best to not touch the greasy spots with my clean hands. There was a half-ripped sticker on the thick plastic divider between the front and back seats, which read "Lick it!" The driver's name was Abdullah Abdullahman, or something. Jem gave the guy my address, and we took off. We looked at each other, and Jem leaned in for a kiss. I was drunk, and, despite my earlier reluctance, her kiss was wonderful. She still tasted like peaches and tequila. Her tongue darted expertly about, and I reasoned that even if she *did* have genital herpes, she couldn't transfer it to me just by kissing. Or could she? I pulled away. "Jem, I want to talk to yo—"

"Shhhhhh," she held her finger up to my lips.

"Shno," I said, my answer blocked by her finger. "No. Not this time. I want to talk."

She leaned over and whispered into my ear, biting the lobe slightly, "I didn't come here to talk, Wally."

"Ahhhhhhh I know," I said, almost defeated by her sexy advances. Her hand had wandered under the waistline of my jeans and into my boxers. This snapped me out of my moment of guardlessness, as she neared my disease-free genital area. I pulled her hand away, and she looked at me with a confused frown.

"What are you *doing?*" she asked.

"Jem, I, uh, I don't know how to say this, but . . . I saw your thing today."

"My what?"

"Your thing. Your commercial. I saw it. On TV." She looked like I'd stabbed her in the gut. She yanked her hand away from me, and said, *"So?"* with the most injured/offended look on her face.

"So, I don't know . . . I just . . . " She was looking out her window now. I tried to peek around her hair to get a glimpse of her face. "Jem . . . ?" No response. As we passed under a streetlight, I saw her reflection in the glass. Tears streamed down her cheeks. The cool façade had shattered. "Jem . . ."

"Stop the car, please!" she suddenly said to the driver. He pulled over without question. She jumped out and slammed the door behind her.

"Don't leave," I said to the driver, and jumped out behind Jem, my ass sliding easily along the greasy pleather. Jem was fast-walking in the direction from which we'd come. I gave chase. "Jem! Wait up!" She didn't even slow down. "Jem! Please! Hold on!" She didn't. I ran after her, not sure what I'd do or say once I'd caught her. I don't know if she slowed down or if I finally picked up enough speed to gain on her but, either way, I caught up. "Hey," I said, out of breath, grabbing as gently as I could for her shoulder.

"Get *away* from me!" she yelled, smacking my hand away.

"Jem! Please!"

"Go away!"

"Jem, I want to talk to you!"

"No!"

"Jem, please!"

"Fuck you!"

"Jem! What? Please! Where are you going? Listen! It's just a commercial!" Apparently, on the wrong-things-to-say-to-Jem scale, this particular comment rated very high. She stopped on a dime and spun around. I almost slammed into her.

"Just a commercial?" she asked, baiting me.

"Well, yeah. It's just a stupid commercial." *How dumb am I?*

"No, it's not *'just a stupid commercial,' you asshole!*" she screamed, the tears flowing freely. I thought for a second that she was going to hit me.

"O-okay. Okay."

"Okay? That 'stupid commercial' has ruined my fucking life! All right?" she said, somewhere very near Hysterical-ville, as she turned and stormed away again. I stood there for a moment wondering how the fuck we'd gotten to this point. One minute ago she was all super-sexy, and now *this*. I followed her.

"Jem, please. Talk to me."

She spun back around, startling me again. "Fine! You want to talk? Fine. Let's talk. I was nineteen years old, fresh off the bus from Mississippi, and my very first day here I met . . . " She paused for a second, took a breath and wiped her tears. "I met this *guy* who talked me into doing this commercial. Said it was how *every* big actress got their start and that I was perfect and blah blah blah blah blah. So I did it! And now, seven years later, it's still running! Eighty times a freakin' day! I can't walk into a fucking casting office or a fucking audition or a fucking *restaurant* without hearing the whispers, *'Hey, it's the herpes girl,'* or *'Hey, how's that skin decay treatin' ya?'* My life and my career are both a big fucking joke, and I'll never work in this town again! Okay? You happy? Now you know the *whole hilarious story.*" She sniffled and wiped her nose on her sleeve, leaving a trail of tears or snot or both on the stretchy black fabric.

I wanted to say "So you don't actually *have* genital herpes?" But I didn't. All at once, I completely understood this girl. Jem was a lot like me. A joke. An outcast. Shit, I was basically talking to the female, sexy Wally Moscowitz! I stood there like a moron, speechless, eyes down, thinking, as she waited for some response from me, and then she spun around and stalked off, still crying.

"I don't give a flying *fuck* about some stupid commercial!" I blurted to her back. I'd realized in my moment of silence that I *truly* didn't. Who the fuck was *I* to judge this girl? I am not that shallow. If there was a chance that I could have something special with Jem I was going to go for it. She made me feel good. Lord knows that Sue only made me feel bad about myself. Jem could understand me, and I her. She stopped and turned around. She had wet trails on her cheeks, and her eyes were red and puffy already. She looked fucking gorgeous.

"You don't?" she asked.

"Couldn't possibly care *less*," I said, smiling.

"Really?" she asked, still dubious.

"Swear to God." I said, still smiling, holding one hand up solemnly. "You know, I'm not exactly the most popular guy in the class, either." She stared at me. I thought I might be making some progress. "I've had a *blast* the past few nights, Jem. You know? This has been . . . amazing. I'd like to keep it up if you'll let me. Maybe even, I don't know, like, *talk to each other*?"

She sniffled. Looked down and then up at me. "I don't actually *have* genital herpes, you know," she said with the slightest trace of humor behind her sadness.

"I never thought you did." *Liar.* "And if you did, I *still* wouldn't care." *Liar.* "We could both just take Herpegra and be fine." Jem walked back to me slowly, and then landed in my arms in a relieved heap. She cried in my shirt for a minute more, her body wracking in my arms. I wanted to say, *"Get it all out, honey, Wally's here."* But I didn't want to be too nice, fall into the dreaded "friend zone." Soon she stopped crying, and we kissed. Deeply and passionately. Our best kiss yet, by far. Because now, after only about a minute of conversation, we knew each other. Something important had passed between us, and thankfully, it wasn't a venereal disease.

The lovely moment was broken by the sound of a car door slamming. The cab driver had gotten out of the car, slammed the rear door that I'd left open, and was rounding back to the driver's side, swearing furiously. He was red faced and spouting irately in a language that I did not recognize. He thought we were ditching the fare. "Hey . . . ! No!" I yelled, pulling Jem by the hand back toward the cab. "We're coming!"

The driver did not peel out and tear away down the street as I'd expected him to. He waited for us, and, despite the fact that he would be getting a huge tip, he continued to grumble unintelligibly all the way to my apartment. Jem and I kissed some more in the backseat. I wanted to talk to her. I wanted to ask her all about herself, but the kissing was good.

When we got back to my apartment, we continued the smoochfest at the bottom of the stairs for a full minute before Jem whispered, "Let's go up." I nodded, and we dashed up the stairs, tripping and laughing all the way. I think I saw Pardeep peeking at us through his slightly cracked door. I could imagine the big smile on his hairy brown face, and it made me happy. Somewhere in my brain I realized I hadn't yet thanked him for springing me from jail. I made a mental note to do that at some point real soon.

When we got into my apartment, I was overpowered by the need to know more about Jem. I wanted to know her whole story. I pulled away from our passionate kissing for a moment, and said, "So, is it Jem, as in *To Kill A Mockingbird*?"

She bit her lower lip and said, "I prefer to think of it as in *and the Holograms.*"

She was referring to the '80s Saturday morning cartoon about a pink-haired rock star chick named Jem and her band, the Holograms. "She's got beautiful hair that's truly outrageous, truly truly truly outrageous," I sang the theme song, holding an invisible mic.

"You watched it?" she yelled, laughing and smacking my chest playfully.

"Noooo. Total chick cartoon! It was on after GI Joe, so I always caught the beginning." Truth be told, it was on after an even girlier show called *Beverly Hills Teens,* and I watched that, too. "Tell me more," I said, changing the subject.

"More about what?" she said in a cutesy way, trying to peck at my lips.

"More about *you,* Jem. I want to know everything." I was drunk, but earnest.

Jem pulled her one-piece stretchy black dress off in one fluid swooping motion. She stood in front of me completely naked, her skin pure and white and amazing, like the smooth sparkling slopes of a freshly snowed-upon mountain. "I know you do. And

I want to tell you," she said seductively, stepping closer to me. She leaned in and nibbled at my ear again in that same exciting, teasing way. She whispered, "Later. I promise. Right now, I just want you. Really . . . *really* fucking bad."

It was the single greatest thing that anyone has ever said to me in my entire life.

chizapter 19

I woke up smiling for the third day in a row. I rolled over with the intention of placing the most tender kiss I could on the sweet spot where Jem's hair meets her forehead. But she was gone.

I sat up, staring down at the tell-tale indentation in the sheets where Jem had slept. *Fuck!* I slammed my hand down on the bed, sending a puff of little floaty things up into the air. We'd had the most incredible night of lovemaking! We did it like, *three* times! And we talked throughout the night, between lovemaking sessions. We talked a lot. Jem listened to me more intently than anyone had in a very long time. And I did the same for her. We tickled each other gently and hinted about how we were both feeling something special happening. And then I held her in my arms as we slept. It was wonderful. My ribs didn't even hurt anymore. I was cured.

But now she was gone. Pulled a Houdini on me again. I couldn't believe it.

But then I smelled it: bacon.

She hadn't disappeared again. She was here. And she was cooking bacon. And that was good. As I sat there, letting the wonderful scent wash over me, she nudged the door gently open with her foot. She entered the room wearing one of my soft, old T-shirts and carrying two plates of eggs and bacon and pancakes, and it was sexy. "Breakfast in bed?" she asked in a sweet morning whisper. *Life ain't so bad,* I thought.

"Oh my God, yeah," I said. "I thought you were gone!"

"Gone?"

"Like the last few days. Some sly little note posted somewhere."

"No, no, no. No more disappearing. The games are over."

"Good. I mean, it was fun and everything, but, you know . . ."

"Done. Promise. Eat." She set the plate down in my lap, complete with a napkin and a fork and a knife. "Wait! One sec." She bolted out of the room and reentered a moment later with a glass of OJ and a bottle of maple syrup. This was too good to be true. I felt a momentary stab of guilt about Sue. Not because I was cheating on her, but more so because I didn't want to hurt Jem. I really felt like we were starting something serious here.

"Jem, I uh, I need to tell you something."

"I need to tell you something too."

"I, uhhhh, I don't know how to say this, and . . . well, I sort of . . . well, I'll just say it. I have a girlfriend. Now, I kno—"

"I know."

"—that I shoulda told you this earli—you *know?*"

"Yeah."

"How, how do you know?"

"I mean, duh, you have pictures of her all over the place. Sue, is it?"

"Oh, uh, yeah. Sue."

"I'm guessing that she doesn't treat you too well?"

"Well . . . no. I think it's more of . . . well, yeah. She sucks. Huge bitch. How did you know that?"

"I just, I don't know—"

Boom! She was cut short by a loud sound from outside of the bedroom. We looked at each other, heads cocked.

Boom! Boom! Boom!

"What the hell is *that*?" I asked.

"Sounds like someone pounding on your door," Jem said perceptively.

"What the *fuck*?" I said, rising out of bed and quickly hopping into a pair of ripped jeans and a T-shirt from a crumpled pile on the floor. "What time is it, anyway?" I asked as I moved toward the bedroom door.

"Like, ten," said Jem, looking fearful.

Boom! Boom! Boom! Boom! Boom!

"Stay here," I said to her.

I did a tiptoe-run to the front door. I looked through the peephole, but whoever was on the other side of the door was covering it with a hand. "Who, who is it?" I asked. *Boom!* they answered, startling me back from the door a bit.

"I'm not gonna open the door until you tell me who it is!" I said to the pounder.

"Open the fuckin' door before I break it down," said a deep voice very quietly through the door, a rude remark that I would have expected to be shouted, not whispered. Foolishly, I opened the door. Big fucking mistake.

As I unlocked the bolt and twisted the knob slightly, the door was *bashed* violently open, and I was knocked to the floor. The two giants from the day before roared into the room like Hungry Hungry Hippos, and I was the little white marble they were trying to devour. White Giant was wearing a throwback Raiders jersey with matching hat and black jeans, and Samoan Giant was wearing a whole camouflage ensemble. They looked *pissed*.

They both glanced around the room predatorily for a moment, and then spotted me on the floor where I'd fallen. Samoan Giant lunged for me, grabbed one handful of my shirt and one handful of my jeans in each hand, and lifted me off of the ground. Next thing I knew I was airborne. My legs smashed into a lamp that sat on my side table, crashing it to the floor, while my body just hit the hardwood floor like a slab of meat.

"You dumbass mother*fucker*," said the Samoan Giant as he

boomed toward me like an elephant, landing a swift kick to my sore ribs. "You done fucked up now, isumu." I tried to roll away, and he kicked me in my lower back. I hoped that the giants weren't aware of Jem's presence. It didn't seem like they were, as White Giant just stood there motionless with his back to the bedroom door, watching his cohort beat the crap out of me with a look of hatred in his droopy eyes.

"What's 'isumu'?" he asked his Samoan counterpart.

"Means 'rat' in Samoan," said Samoan Giant as he bent down and grabbed another handful of my shirt, this time at my chest, and yanked me up. "Couldn't keep your motherfuckin' mouth closed, huh, rat?" he asked, right before punching me square in the face, which *hurt*. A fucking *lot*. Getting punched in the face was becoming a bad habit of mine. The pain shot through every inch of my body. My eyes filled up with tears. I immediately felt the blood pouring out of my nose. I fell back to the floor, a bleeding mess. I wanted to play dead so they'd leave me alone, but I was terrified that they'd find Jem. I couldn't even ask them why they were doing this. Everything was happening so quickly.

"Tie his ass up," said White Giant, his back still to the bedroom door.

"Why?" asked Samoan Giant.

"'Cuz that's what Dandy said to do, dawg."

"Naw, fool. He said, 'Beat his ass good and then bring him in bloody.'"

"Naw. He said, 'Bloody and tied up,' dawg. I'm tellin' you," pleaded White Giant.

"We ain't gotta tie this lil bitch up! Fuck he gon' do?"

"Ya neva know, bro. Ya neva know."

"You got a rope?"

"Naw, dawg," said White Giant. "I thought you were bringin' it."

"Naw man—I ain't bring it 'cuz Dandy ain't said to!"

"Shiiiit. Aight. Just fuck him up good so he won't cause us no trouble or nothin'."

"Yeah. Aight, bet," said Samoan Giant, with another casual but swift kick to my torso. I doubled over, coughing in agony. As if the shot to the stomach wasn't enough, he followed up by smashing his lunchbox-sized fist into my temple, which made me see black spots and little squigglies floating around. I landed propped up against the wall, my legs splayed out in front of me. I had a clear view of the room now. What I saw scared me worse than anything else I'd experienced so far. Jem was creeping up in the doorway behind White Giant, my big red fire extinguisher that I keep next to my bed hoisted up in her hands above her head. *She's gonna try to take him out!* I tried to yell at her, but I was too badly beaten. I helplessly watched it unfold.

The giants were both yelling at me now, though I couldn't make out a word they were saying. My head was swimming in pain and my ears were ringing. I watched in horror as Jem leaned back a bit and bravely swung the big dull metal cylinder down at White Giant's head in one semi-swift move.

She missed.

White Giant was too tall for Jem and the extinguisher was too heavy, and so it glanced painlessly off of his shoulders, barely scraping him. She might as well have hit him with a roll of paper towels. Both giants turned to Jem. She looked terrified, backstepping into the bedroom. The giants looked at each other and started to laugh. She dropped the extinguisher, turned, and bolted into the bedroom, swinging the door shut behind her. They tromped after her. I couldn't even budge, couldn't stand up. I heard a loud *crash* from the bedroom. So loud that it penetrated the pounding in my ears and found its way to my brain. I thought I heard Jem cry out in pain, though that may have been my imagination.

Suddenly Jem's body was thrown violently into the bedroom doorframe, her back cracking when it hit the hard edge. She flopped to the floor like a rag doll, unmoving. White Giant picked her up by gripping one of her arms and one of her legs, and he swung her back and forth like a log, tossing her into a messy pile in front of me. My senses were returning. I heard Jem cry softly as she hit the ground, her face toward me, away from them. She looked a lot better than I did. She had a scrape on her forehead that was bleeding slightly, but that appeared to be all. The only thing she wore was my T-shirt, which was bunched around her waist now, giving them an unobstructed view of her naked ass. She looked at me, eyes wide in fear.

"Oh, shit!" said one of the giants. "Look what we got here!" Referring to Jem's near naked, now fully exposed body. The giants looked at each other with eyebrows raised. She started to crawl away but couldn't get very far.

"Let's have some fun wit this bitch," said the White Giant.

"Hell yeah," said the other. "Dandy ain't said nothin' bout bringin' *her* in!" They both laughed. "We gon' tear yo ass up, Wonder Woman!" yelled the White Giant, chuckling. Jem closed her eyes. The giants laughed some more, enjoying the terror they knew they were most certainly inspiring in both of us. They crept toward us. This was the very worst moment of my life. It lasted way longer than I would have liked.

....

White Giant picked Jem up and threw her over his shoulder effortlessly. "In there?" he asked his sick buddy, gesturing to the bedroom.

"Naw, fool. Let's make the isumu watch," said Samoan Giant with a big grin. White Giant grinned back and then looked at me.

"You hear dat, ratboy? This is what you get! This is what you get when you fuck wit Abe Lyons and Oral B, muthafucka!"

"Front row seats, beeotch!" said Samoan Giant as they laid

Jem down on the futon couch, preparing to have their way with her. Jem began to wriggle toughly, making a futile attempt to get free. Samoan Giant pinned her arms down with ease, holding them both with one large hand, and White Giant parted her legs, sliding his enormous body as a wedge between them. He went down to his knees, clamping her legs under each of his armpits and unzipping his fly. I tried to push myself up. *I can't let this happen!* I managed to get my hands underneath me. I pushed with all of my strength.

"Bet dat lil coochie ain't never seen a dick like this—"

With impeccable timing, my front door burst open again, and more confusion rushed into my apartment, this time in the form of two relatively well-dressed men with medium-sized, polished chrome guns drawn. They looked like New York Mafia goombahs straight out of a *Sopranos* episode. One of the men was tall and thin with a ponytail, the other short and squat with slicked back, thinning hair, and they each wore nice slacks, turtlenecks with gold chains hanging around the necks, and blazers. *The Italians,* I thought. They aimed their weapons at the equally confused giants. I heard two short, muffled *whoosh-whoosh* sounds, like blow darts being shot from a tube, and both giants staggered a step or two and then fell to the ground within seconds. *They must have silencers on those things,* I thought, looking at the strangely shaped guns. The two men rushed over to the giants, kneeling down to check their pulses. My utter bewilderment was furthered by the appearance of a third man, wider and more important-looking than the other two, who strolled in regally in a pinstriped suit after all the shots had been fired and the threat eliminated. He said, "Leave the thugs. Help the kids." The two goombahs rose from the bodies of the giants and came to our aid. "We gotta get yous guys outta hea," whispered the short goombah urgently.

Ahem. I cleared my throat and tried to speak. "Who . . . who are you?" I managed to sputter hoarsely.

"We're your guardian angels," said the Capo, with a proud smile.

"Can you stand?" the short goombah was asking me. I shook my head no. He helped me up, slinging my arm over his shoulder.

Jem rose on her own, using the coffee table as a booster. "I need to put some clothes on," she said.

"Do it, and quick," said the Capo. Jem rushed off to the bedroom. The Capo and the tall goombah pulled the bodies of the two giants into the kitchen, behind the counter and out of sight. Jem came out a moment later, fully clothed, a mixture of fear and relief on her pretty face.

"You got keys?" asked the Capo.

"Bedroom," I said through clenched teeth. The Capo directed the tall goombah to go and get them with a jerky movement of his head. I grabbed my cell phone off the table by the door. We left my apartment, and the mobsters helped me gingerly make my way down the stairs. I was completely confused and shell-shocked and still quite terrified, but I had no choice but to go with these scary men who had just saved our lives.

They led us out of my building and across the street to their vehicle, which was parked at the curb. Another surprise.

It was the Cadillac Escalade that had been watching my apartment for the past few days.

As we approached the vehicle, there stood a muscular, swarthy, goateed meter man at the rear of the SUV, typing the license plate number into a little handheld, ticket-printing computer. His khaki-colored uniform had his name, Rico, pinned onto his chest.

"Ey! Tha fuck you doin', Tito?" asked the short goombah.

"I'm citing your vehicle, sir. You're parked at a yellow curb, which is a designated loading zone."

"Yeah! And we're fuckin' loadin'!" said the tall goombah.

"No, sir," said the smug meter man, "I've been watching this vehicle forrr . . . seven minutes. You are not loading."

"You print that ticket and we're gonna be loadin' your fuckin' corpse into our trunk, fucko!" said short goombah in a very grave, completely un-joking sort of way.

"Nope. Sorry. You're getting a citation."

"Eyyyy! C'mon. I'm asking you nicely," said the Capo goombah, really much more threatening than the advertised "nicely." "Please. My friend. With all due respect. I know you have a job to do, but we were only here for a short time. And we're leaving. Now. So please. No ticket, okay?"

"Nope," said the little self-righteous bastard with a popping sound on the *P.* I didn't like where this was going.

"Ey. *No . . . ticket,*" said the Capo. "I'm not askin' this time."

"Too late. I already punched it in the computer," said the meter man with a satisfied grin. The Capo turned and looked at the short goombah with a raised eyebrow.

"Oh, you already punched it into the computer?" asked the short goombah, off his leader's look. He stepped in Rico's direction. "Huh? You already punched it in?" he asked, as he stepped even closer to the meter man, who stood his ground, fully focused on the device in his hand.

"Yep! Too late! Once it's in the computer . . . ," said the oblivious meter moron, with his hand in the air in a smug, satisfied shrug.

The short goombah got within a few feet of him. "Too late, huh? You already punched it in, you low-life fuck?"

"Back off please, sir," said the meter man, noticing for the first time just how close this little Joe Pesci was, his hand creeping to his radio at his waist. He flexed his muscles under his well-tailored khaki uniform.

"You're a tough guy, huh? Feel like a big shot with that little doodad? Go around ruining people's days? Huh, tough guy?" He got right up in the guy's face. I thought the muscular meter man was going to deck him.

"Sir—"

He snatched the little computer out of Rico's hands and

smashed it on the street. It shattered in a mess of plastic and springs and microchips. Jem and I both jumped. The tall goombah just looked on with a smile on his face. The Capo showed not a drop of emotion. "Oh! Heyyy! Look at that! It's not in the computer anymore, fuckstick! Huh, Pepe? What happened? Huh? You dropped your weapon, macho man!"

The Meter man glanced at the license plate and closed his eyes. "E B R 5 1 2. E B R 5 1 2." He repeated the plate numbers to himself in an effort to commit them to memory.

"You fuck," said the little goombah, as he pummeled the guy—first in the face and then in the stomach and then in the stomach and then in the face. The guy went down and curled up in the fetal position, rocking back and forth in fear and pain. "I hope you go to church, you miserable fuck, 'cuz you're going to hell," said the goombah between kicks. When he finally stopped kicking, he hocked and spit on the wounded meter man's khaki-covered back.

"Let's go," said the Capo evenly.

The tall goombah pulled his Napoleonic companion away from the moaning meter man. We all got in the Escalade, the tall goombah driving, the Capo riding shotgun, and the short goombah in the back with Jem and me. We sat as far away from him as we could manage. The tall goombah started the car and pulled away from the curb. I turned around to catch a glimpse of the meter man, rocking back and forth in the middle of the street now. "Fuckin' prick had it coming!" said the short goombah. "Special place in hell for those pricks. Am I right?"

Jem and I made eye contact. The fear in her eyes broke my heart. I reached for her hand, and she gratefully returned my tight squeeze. She rubbed her face against my shoulder the way a cat might do. "Someone tell me what the *fuck* is going on?" I asked after a minute, feeling suddenly emboldened.

"Whoa! Take it easy, compadre!" said the Capo. He took a

deep breath and then pulled a prescription bottle out of his jacket and popped it open, swallowing an unseen amount of pills without any water.

My bravery continued, for Jem. "No! I won't! You just killed two men in my apartment! And, and then you whisk us away without calling the cops or telling us anything, and you beat up a parking guy in the middle of the street, and, shit! I *demand* that you tell me what's going on!" I didn't sound too tough.

"Eyyyy! Lower your voice, cucina!" he said as he massaged his throat with a free hand, trying to help the pills along. He made a sound like he had a hair stuck in his throat. "We was savin' your life, if you rememba correctly," he sputtered through his efforts at dislodging the pills from his esophagus. "And no one is dead in your apartment," he said. The other two goombahs smiled knowingly.

"Bullshit! I just saw you shoot them both!"

"We shot 'em with horse tranquilizers," said the tall goombah as he drove. "Show 'em, Lou."

"See?" said the short goombah sitting next to me, as he held the weird silvery gun up for my benefit. I wouldn't have been able to tell you if it was a gun for tranquilizing horses, shooting Vietcong, or blasting space aliens.

"We didn't want to kill anybody in your apartment. We're tryin' to keep ya *out* of trouble. That's the *last* thing you need—two dead Andre-the-Giant-lookin' fuckers in your kitchen. They'll wake up in a few hours not knowin' *what* the fuck hit 'em," said the Capo with a chuckle, twisting his oversized torso around to face me.

"Who *are* you?" I asked him.

He turned around and faced the windshield. He drummed a little beat on the armrest with his fingertips. "My friends call me Balsamic Vinny. This is Five-two Lou, and Six-seven Kevin."

Cute names, I thought. "Who *are* you, though? Why did you just save us?"

"You're welcome, by da way," said Vinny, gesturing toward my building. "Looks like we got there just in the nick a time, as dey say."

"Thank you. Thank you very much. All of you," I said, looking around the car at the mobsters. "Now *please,* tell me what the hell is going on. Why have you been watching me?"

"You noticed, huh? Well, let's just say that I owed a friend of yours a debt, and this is how he asked me to repay it."

"What? Who?"

"Your good friend Jerry Silver. He called me a few days ago. Told me about your involvement with certain . . . *gangstas,* if you will." The guys all chuckled a bit at this. "He was scared for your safety and he asked that I keep an eye on you for a coupla days, till this whole thing blows ova. You know what I mean?"

"J-Jerry did this?" *Oh man,* I thought. *I love you, Jerry.*

"Dat's what I said, pal. You're lucky to know him."

I took a deep breath and wiped a hand across my face. Silence filled the SUV as we sped along to who-knows-where. I was wondering why and/or how Jerry Silver had apparent Mafia connections. I was thankful that he did. Finally, I managed to sputter, "H-how did you guys kn-know to come in when, uh, when you did?"

"I told ya—we been watchin'," said Vinny.

I rubbed my face with both hands, exasperated. "I don't understand why those guys attacked us like that! I just spoke to Lyons yesterday! Everything was fine!" *He did tell me not to leave the apartment . . .*

"Guess you haven't seen the news yet today, hotshot," said Vinny, tossing me a copy of the *New York Post* from the front seat.

On the front page was a large picture of Oral B holding up a glass of champagne, with Abraham Lyons in the background. It looked like it was taken at some recent awards show. The headline, in bold black letters across the bottom of the page, said, in the *Post*'s patently silly way, "ORAL B-USTED!" Under the picture, in slightly smaller font, it said "Uber-producer and phenom rapper uncovered as Fraud-Zilla. Pg. 2."

"It's all over da news," said Balsamic Vinny. Mentions your name a buncha times in there, too. 'Wally dis and Wally dat.' Dat's all they know. 'Wally.' No last name. They sayin' you're da guy who leaked it."

I examined the cover with shaking hands and rapidly increasing heart rate. "Seems to me like you're pretty much fucked, my friend," said Vinny, with a chortle.

chizapter 20

The goombahs took us to a dirty little motel just east of High-land Avenue, on Sunset Boulevard. They booked a very repulsive room on the second floor. It smelled like condoms and vomit. I gagged reflexively upon entering. The good news was they had Free Cable! as advertised by the enormous Technicolor signage outside the motel. This was probably a big deal back in 1982 when the sign was erected and the place hadn't yet been slathered quite so thoroughly in puke. "You think we can get a different room?" I asked, pinching my nose. "It reeks in here."

"Oh, yeah! Don't worry. This is just temporary. We're moving over to the Four Seasons as soon as our room is ready ova there," said Balsamic Vinny. His two minions guffawed. What an absolute riot these mafioso types are.

The room had two double beds, a large flowery couch (some of the flowers were actual flowers, while others were blood-like stains that had flowered themselves cleverly into the muddled bouquet), and two dirty-green armchairs—enough space for the five of us to get comfortable, if the word "comfortable" can be applied in such vile surroundings. Five-two Lou and Six-seven Kevin sat in the armchairs. Vinny sat on the edge of one of the beds. Jem and I chose the couch. Jem hadn't loosened her grip on me since we'd left my apartment, and I was okay with that. I was feeling horribly responsible for the mess I'd gotten her into, and I planned to protect her with my life from here on out.

I looked around the hotel room, thinking about how this was not a portrait in which I would have ever imagined myself to be painted. However, as menacing as these brutes seemed, I had to keep in mind that they'd just saved our lives.

"Here—" Vinny tossed me a cell phone. "Call Jerry. He's waitin' to talk to you. He ain't none too happy, eitha," said Vinny with a smirk.

"Great," I said, dialing Jerry's number. Vinny stretched out his arms above him with balled fists and thrust out his great gut in a stretch/yawn combo that made me think of a sleepy cartoon bear. He removed his expensive pinstriped jacket, folded it neatly in half, and rested it at the end of the bed. He wriggled a prescription bottle out of the inside pocket, opened it, and popped another pill without any water. He walked around to the side of the bed, removed his gold watch, placed it on the nightstand, and flopped down on his back. As Jerry's phone rang in my ear, I watched Vinny and thought about how I surely would have stripped that top blanket off of the bed before lying on it.

"*What—,*" Jerry snapped when he finally answered.

"Jerry, it's m-me."

"Me who?"

"Me! W-Wally."

"Mosco? What the fuck?"

"What?"

"*What the fuck, Wally?*"

"What?"

"*What the fuck did you do?*"

"Wha-what?"

"*What the fuck did you do, Mosco? Huh? What'd you do?*" In all the years that I'd known Jerry, I'd never heard him like this. He was *furious,* and I didn't know why.

"Jerry—what the hell? What do you mean?"

"What do I mean? What the fuck do you mean, what do I mean?"

"I didn't *do anything!* Why are you screaming at me like this?"

"Why am I—what are you, kidd—Don't play dumb with me, Wally! What the fuck did you do? Who did you call? Why is your name all over the fucking news?"

"Jerry, I have no idea! I saw the newspaper, but I didn't tell anyone anything! I was sitting in my house and next thing I know these, these, these . . . enormous *freaks* are trying to kill me!" *Why is Jerry so livid?*

"Don't bullshit me, Mosco! You fucked everything up!"

"Jerry, I'm not! I didn't do anything! What are you saying?" I looked around. Jem stared at me, worry all over her face. Vinny's eyes were closed now, his belly slowly rising and falling, completing the earlier-conjured image of a sleeping cartoon bear. Lou and Kevin were now playing cards in the corner of the room at a small circular wooden block of a table that was wedged between their chairs, pretending to ignore me.

"Your name is all over the news! Not your whole name— thank God. They're just saying that Oral B and Lyons are frauds, and that they've got some white, thirties, balding, paunchy guy named Wally writing all their shit for them, and that you leaked to the press!"

"I saw! But I didn't do it!"

"What the fuck, Mosco? Now you got guys tryin' to rub you out?! I could fuckin' *kill* you myself! I told you to just keep quiet! I've been trying to protect you! Why'd you *do* this, Mosco?"

"Do *what*?"

"You called the press! You leaked this shit! What, did they offer you money?"

"Jerry—"

"What the fuck? You know how much effort I've put into pro- tecting you? Now look where we are! You're running for your fucking life!"

"Jerry—"

"What the fuck, Mosco?"

"Jerry, calm down! I didn't do this! Why would I do this?"

"I don't know why, Wally. 'Cuz you're a schmuck, maybe? I don't know! But I know it was you! Don't bullshit me! Who else knew?"

"Deezy!"

"Deezy? The guy you pissed on? We're back to that?"

"Yes, Jerry! He's the guy behind all of this! He's the one who took my dog, and, and, the one who sent me the ransom notes, and he, uh, he sent Lyons a ransom note, too!" Even as I said it I realized it made no sense. Why would Deezy send Lyons a ransom note threatening to go public, and then leak the news to the press immediately afterward? He'd be killing any chance he had at the ten mil he was trying to bilk out of Lyons. Jerry, apparently, didn't pick up on the little hole in my explanation.

"Wasn't him," he said simply.

"Wh-what? What do you mean it wasn't him?"

"Funk Deezy? Aka DeAndre Muskingum? It wasn't him!"

"How do you know?"

"DeAndre Muskingum didn't leak shit to the press, Mosco, because DeAndre Muskingum is fucking *dead*."

"*What?*" My head started whirling again.

"Dead, Mosco. D-E-A-fucking-D. They found his body last night in a ditch in Echo Park. One bullet in his brain." *One bullet* . . . I calculated the possibility that Deezy was the guy in the Homer Simpson mask, and that my gunshot was the one that killed him. *I didn't shoot Homer in the head. And anyway, they found the bullet in my wall.* Jerry went on. "*That's* how I know that *you* are the one who leaked this shit! Not Deezy. And that's how Lyons knows that you're the one who leaked this shit. And that's why Lyons has enormous fucking monsters coming to your fucking house to fucking kill you!"

"Oh, man . . . oh, man," I said, standing now, and pacing, one hand grabbing a fistful of hair.

"You're goddamn fuckin' right, 'oh, man'! You know how bad this is, Mosco? You know how bad you just fucked this up—"

"Fucked this up? I didn't *do* anything, Jerry! I swear! And if you keep accusing me I'm just gonna hang up! Okay? I'm the one being hunted for death here, Jerry! Okay? What the fuck?"

"Okay, okay. You're right. You're right. I'm sorry. I'm sorry, bud, okay? I'm just upset. I'm just worried about you."

"Worried? Jesus! You're fucking belligerent!"

"I'm sorry, Wally. I'm sorry. Fuck." He took a deep breath and exhaled into the phone. "I've just put a lot of effort into, you know . . . It's just, when one of my clients—especially one like you that, you know, means so much to me—gets in trouble, it hurts me. You're like a son to me!"

"Oh yeah, sure, Jerry. Don't bullshit me. C'mon, man! I appreciate your help. I really do. These guys saved my life. But please, don't fucking patronize me, okay? You're just pissed because I won't be making money for you now!"

"Hey! That hurts, Mosco. I'm your Uncle Jerry! Don't say shit like that. You know I love you like a son! Look at all I've done the last few days to protect you."

"I know! But I've never heard you like this, Jerry!"

"You're right. Listen. Please. I'm sorry, okay? It's not about money. I shouldn't have been so emotional. I'm just worked up about this whole thing. I just . . . I thought you went behind my back. I'm just worried about you! I'm relieved you're okay."

"Okay."

"And all's not lost. I just spoke to Bionic. The deal is back on. Everything's fine. I even got them to expedite and frontload your advance so you can get your dog back. Okay? They were very sympathetic when I told them what happened to you. I'm sorry. I'm just worried about you. Okay, bud?"

"It's on?" I asked.

"It's on, kid."

"I'm gonna get my dog back?"

"The Doc is comin' home. We'll pay these bastards and be on our way."

"Okay. Oh man. Good. Great. Okay. Good."

"Yeah. I straightened it all out. Uncle Jerry took care of business. Okay? I'm sorry. We'll have the money in the next day or so. I had the contracts all written up and ready to go. They have them now."

I was gonna get the Doctor back. *And lose my books.* I swished around some imaginary mouthwash. "Thank you, Jerry."

"Okay, kiddo. We good?"

"We're good."

"'Kay. Now stay put while I try to sort the rest of this shit out."

"Jerry—I really didn't leak this shit to the press. I swear. I had nothing to do with it."

"Okay. I know. I believe you, Mosco. I do. I just got worked up. I'm glad you're okay. I'm trying to figure it all out. Don't worry. You're safe with Vinny and his guys. I'm working on a plan. I'll call you back ASAP."

"Okay, Jerry."

He hung up. I was feeling the most acute sense of vertigo. This was all so perplexing. And it wasn't about to get easier.

....

A half hour later, Balsamic Vinny was still sound asleep, the two henchmen were still leaning over the small circular table by the window, engrossed in a card game, pistols on the table, and Jem was in the bathroom. I sat on the couch, pressing on various spots on my body, trying to locate where I was bruised the worst. Surprisingly, after the beating(s) I'd taken, I was feeling okay. I decided to switch on the television to see what news coverage I could catch about the story.

I didn't have to search very hard at all. Before the picture on the TV even came to life, I could hear a gruff, baritone voice saying, "—gangsta." The screen came alive to reveal a portly, distinguished-looking black man with a gray goatee and a dark purple pinstriped suit on CNN. He was identified at the bottom of the screen as Hiram Jones, professor of African-American Studies at the University of Southern California. "This man— *these men,* I should say—have perpetrated a bold-faced lie to the African-American community for *years,*" continued Professor Jones. "Years! A community that has honored and cherished them as role models and icons, only to be made fools of by their utter deceit. Don't you think that they should be held accountable?"

"Well, I disagree with much of your wording," responded a skinny, spiky-haired young Asian man with a goatee and cool square-lensed eyeglasses, in a T-shirt and sport coat. He was identified as Won Joon Hong, editor of *BANG BANG Magazine.* "First off, there is absolutely *no proof* at this time that the allegations made against Abraham Lyons and Oral B are true at all. In fact, no one seems to know exactly *who* is responsible for reporting them to the media in the first place. Many dismiss them as rumor—"

"They are verified by several sources!" interrupted the professor.

"What sources, Professor?" shouted the young man over his elder. "What sources? I keep hearing that but I still don't see any proof! You're condemning them before we even have all of the fac—"

"I am not condemning anyone to anything, young man. The fact is—"

"The fact is there *are no* facts!" said Hong. "Just hearsay and some imaginary guy named Wally!" My heart jumped and my eyes opened wide upon hearing my name.

"The fact is," continued the professor, rattled by his aggressive young co-guest, "if you'll let me finish, Mr. Hong."

"Of course," said Hong, smiling uncomfortably through his utter exasperation. He clearly wanted to throw himself over the imaginary line dividing their screens and smash the professor in his very distinguished nose, whilst trying to remain professional during what might be his first television appearance.

"Thank you, son. The fact is that these men—Mr. Lyons in particular—are pillars of the African-American community in this country. They must uphold a certain standard of decency and ethics!"

"As should you, Professor!"

"I beg your pardon!"

"You are the one condemning these men in their time of need before they've even had a chance to respond to these allegations! What happened to supporting your people?"

"Supporting—Young man, I think I know what's what in my community a bit better than *you*."

"What? Dude, I been doin' this (*BLEEP*) for years!" said Hong.

"Whoa! Whoa! Okay, gentlemen," said a voice we hadn't heard yet, the screen cutting to a middle-aged, WASPy white guy with a conservative navy blue suit and red, white, and blue tie. "I think this debate has gotten just about heated enough. Perfect display of just how polarizing this controversial story has been since it broke early this morning. We'll just have to wait to hear what Mr. Lyons and company have to say at their press conference this evening. Next we move on to—" *Press conference? What is that about?*

I turned to channel four. An Asian anchorwoman identified as Susan Hakatomi was saying, "—on the charts last year. His current album, entitled *Don't Make Me Kill You, Beeyatch*, has sold over three million copies, and his current single, the title of which I cannot say due to its wildly inappropriate nature, has been number one on the pop charts for *twenty-seven* consecutive weeks." A picture of Oral B appeared in the upper corner of the screen. "He also has an unprecedented three other singles in the Top Ten as of this week. A spokesperson for Godz-Illa Records had no comment, simply stating that all questions will be answered at the press conference this evening." I was momentarily pleased that there was no mention of me in the report, but continued to be troubled by the idea of this mysterious press conference. "Speculation continues to grow at this hour about the man at the center of these allegations." The picture of Oral B disappeared, replaced by the words "WHO IS WALLY?" in big, bold, red letters. *Oh fuck*, I thought. "The man who is purportedly responsible for writing *all* of Oral B's lyrics throughout his career. All that is known at this time is that he is a white male in his late thirties who goes by the name of Wally. It is widely believed at this hour that he is the one responsible for exposing this scandal to the media. We hope to bring you more information about this mystery ghostwriter as we receive it."

Channel two's crusty, salt and pepper–toupeed and –mustached, tweed-suit-wearing anchorman, Dennis Fitzpatrick, was saying, "—top hip-hop artists. His boss, notorious entrepreneur, music mogul, and fashion phenom, Mr. Abraham Dandy Lyons, stands to lose what pundits are estimating at *hundreds* of millions of dollars, if the reputation of his highly successful entertainment empire—said to be worth upward of four hundred million dollars—is tarnished beyond repair by these allegations of fraud. But the question everyone is chattering about today on the street and on the Web is, who is Wally? The mysterious man who is supposedly the brilliant mind behind the Oral B phenomenon. Could this man really be the creative force behind this so-called gangsta lyrical genius? They're calling him everything from the great white ghost to Casper the Gangsta Ghost, to—"

I flipped to channel seven. The reporter there, a too-happy, red-afroed field reporter named Lena Charleston, was standing in front of the Godz-Illa building, saying into a skinny handheld mic, "—is Wally. We don't know his last name at this time, only that he is a white male, said to be overweight, in his thirties, and supposedly single-handedly responsible for creating the gangsta persona that Brandunn Bell, aka Oral B, has been fraudulently perpetrating for the last several years. Again—we remind you— these are unconfirmed reports. Abraham Lyons has called a major news conference for later this evening where he is expected to address these allegations. Betsy?" The shot cut to a slightly younger, African-American anchorwoman named Betsy Robson sitting behind a news desk.

"Thank you, Lena. You know, it's absolutely *nuts* how quickly this story has taken on a life of its own. MTV has reportedly instituted a "Wally Watch," during which they will offer a cash reward for any sightings of the mysterious man, and this afternoon they plan to air all of Oral B's videos and specials, as well as a countdown until the news conference begins at six. Rumors also flew wildly about the World Wide Web this morning, already spawning a Web site dedicated to the circus surrounding the story, entitled www.whoiswally.com. The gentleman who created the Web site is also apparently offering a sizable cash reward to anyone who can produce pictures or valid information about the mysterious man. *Extra* and *Entertainment Tonight* are offering equally lucrative rewards." She smiled, amused by my misfortune, and then tutted. "Boy, I sure hope this doesn't bring down Dandy Lyons," said Betsy. "I just *love* him!"

"He is a handsome man," added a woman from offscreen, possibly Lena.

"Debonair!—"

I switched off the TV. Oh man. This was bad. This was really, *really* bad.

The cell phone I'd called Jerry on, which sat on the stained wooden table next to me, began to vibrate, snapping me out of my brooding. The caller ID said "JERRY SILVER." "Hello?" I answered.

"Mosco—bad news." My heart sank. "Abraham Lyons just announced that he's holding a press conference tonight at 6:00 P.M. All the major networks are covering it. Big to-do."

"Yeah, I heard. So, why is that such bad news?"

"Why? *Helloooo*? The conference is all about you, Mosco! Word on the street is, he's gonna find you before then, silence you for good, then vehemently deny the whole story at the press conference. Gonna claim that this big mystery man Wally is nothing but a former employee who tried to blackmail him. That you made up the whole story, and now you've disappeared. He's got people lined up to smear you. Not to mention a whole different group lined up to *kill* you."

"What? I didn't *do anything*, Jerry!"

"But you won't be anywhere to be found to plead your case, pal. Lyons has got every gangsta-ass nigga, thug, crackhead, migrant worker, hooker, hooligan, punk, drug dealer, runaway, and sewer rat out on the street lookin' for you right now. Big reward."

"Oh my God. You gotta help me, Jerry!"

"I am gonna help you, Mosco. 'Course I am. Whaddaya think I'm doin' right now? We're gonna get you outta here way before they have the chance to get their paws on you. But you gotta do what I say. He's got eyes *everywhere*."

"I can't believe this is all happening! How did you get all of this information, Jerry?"

"I'm Jerry Silver, lest you forget, Wally. I may not have the reach that Lyons has got, but I've got my sources. Just trust me."

"I trust you, Jerry. Just tell me what I need to do."

"All you need to do right now is be patient. I don't want you holed up at that shitbox for too long. Who knows who saw you go in there. But for now, just hang. I'll call you in a little to tell you what's next. Be ready."

"Okay. Hurry."

"Hang tight, Mosco. It's gonna be okay."

"Okay, Jerry."

"Hey—"

"Yeah?"

"Don't worry, bud. Okay? I'm gonna take care of you."

I managed a smile. "Okay, Jerry. Thank you."

"*Uncle* Jerry. Okay? Talk soon."

"Bye."

He hung up. I realized that this was the first time in days that someone had properly gotten off the phone with me. I should have known it was a bad omen.

....

Jem had been in the bathroom for a long time. I hoped she didn't have diarrhea, but it wouldn't turn me off if she *was* shitting her brains out in there. Really, nothing could turn me off to her at this point. I put my ear to the door—not to listen for diarrhea, just to make sure she was okay. I could hear the sink running full blast. I gave a tiny knock. "Jem? You okay?"

"Yeah. I'm fine. Just give me a few minutes," she said as if from the other side of a waterfall. I could barely hear her over the gushing sink. I turned and the two goombahs were looking at me expectantly. I shrugged.

"Probably takin' da Browns to da Super Bowl, know what I'm sayin'?" whispered Five-two Lou with a wink. They both chuckled. I didn't find it particularly amusing at that moment. I plopped down heavily on the end of the couch closest to their chairs.

"So why do they call him Balsamic Vinny?" I asked the guys.

They looked at each other. Six-seven Kevin smiled and put his hand out in a gesture of offering, inviting Lou to explain. "Well, we didn't name him dat. We only known him a few years, and he had dat name when we met him. He came from New York a while back to escape the—" They looked at each other. "To escape the *life*," Lou finished. Kevin gave a satisfied nod of agreement. "But, uh, rumor has it that they called him Balsamic Vinny over there because he's from Modena, and he gets very bitter if not handled properly."

"I see," I said, thinking how absolutely clever those Mafia folks were getting with nicknames these days. When I think of the Mafia, I think of names like Jimmy da Chin, Tony da Shark, or Joey Bananas. This was a whole new level of cleverness. Eat your heart out, Scorsese.

"I am fuckin' *starvin'*," said Lou.

"I could use some chow myself," added Kevin.

Jem exited the bathroom. Her eyes were all red, and her cheeks puffy. She'd been crying. "Jem!" I jumped up and ran to her. "Jeez! Are you okay?"

She sniffled and nodded her head. "I'm okay," she said. "Just overwhelmed."

"Oh man, Jem, I'm *so* sorry. I didn't mean for you to get involved like this."

"No. It's okay, Wally." She grabbed both of my hands, looked into my eyes. "I'm glad I'm with you. I'm just scared, and, we need to talk abou—"

"How's about I leave you twos alone," said Lou. "I'll just be in here," he said, stepping into the bathroom. He stuck his head and arm back out a moment later and grabbed the playing cards. "Sorry," he said, shutting the door behind him.

"Yeah, uhhh, hows about I go and get us some grub," Kevin said, quickly grabbing his coat and exiting the room before the awkward silence became too much for him to stand.

"Come here," I said, pulling her close to me, feeling the wet warmth of her recently tear-streamed face against mine. "It's gonna be okay. Don't worry. These guys will protect us."

"I know. I just . . . maybe this isn't the best time to tell you—"

"You can tell me anything, Jem. I want you to know that."

She looked like she was going to cry again. "That's just it, Wally. I'm not . . ." She took a deep breath, gathered her thoughts, but didn't continue. She looked down into her hands, which hung down in front of her, one gripping and rubbing the other.

"You're not what, Jem?"

"I'm not . . . I'm not *Jem*." I let that compute a sec. *Not Jem?* What the hell did *that* mean? I must have looked just as baffled as I felt, because she forged ahead before I could start stuttering a bunch of questions at her. "I mean, I *am*, but I'm not. I'm . . . I mean, my *name* isn't Jem."

"Oh . . . Okay," I said, thinking, *Big deal, so she lied about her name.* "What's your name?"

"My real name is Ramona. Ramona Maltratado."

"Okay . . . Ramona. That's fine. That's cool. Ramona. Don't worry! You think I care? A lot of actresses take fake names. Like, you know, pseudonyms, or whatever. Don't worry about it, Jeh—Ramona! I have a fake name too! Wallace Q Moscow!" I held my hands out in front of me and attempted my cutest Jew-shrug.

"No, you don't understand, it's not a pseudonym, Wally. I just made it up. For you. *I lied,* Wally. I'm not who you think I am."

Something began beeping or ringing in a high-pitched tone somewhere in the room. I dashed over to Vinny's phone, expecting it to be Jerry with further instructions. It wasn't his phone that was ringing. I stopped and listened. Jem/Ramona listened, too, a curious frown on her pretty, teary face. I recognized the ringtone. It was grating in a terribly familiar way. Then I realized where it was coming from.

My pocket.

I'd forgotten that I'd grabbed my cell phone in the rush to leave my apartment earlier. I snatched it out of my pocket, desperate to catch it before I missed the call. I looked at the little screen where it displayed the name of the incoming caller, and was surprised to see the name "SUE." I held up one finger to Ramona and hit the button to accept the call. "Hello? Hello?"

"*Waaallllllly!*" she wailed into my ear, crying hysterically.

"S-sue? Sue? What's wrong? Wh-what's goin—"

"*Wallllly! He's deaddd!* He's deeeeeead! They killed him!" She wailed and moaned, sounding as tortured and devastated as I'd ever heard her. *Oh God . . . the Doctor . . .* My heart seized at the thought that she could be talking about my dog.

"Sue! Who's dead? Who—what's going on? Sue?" She cried inconsolably, and I wondered if she could even hear me.

"Ohhhh my Gaaaaaaaaaaaaahhhhhd! Oh my Gaaaaaahhd! What am I gonna do? They killed him, Wally! I'm so sorry! I'm a horrible per-er-er-son. Oh my God, I'm sooooooo sor-or-ry." She spit out all of her words through terrible heaves and sobs.

"Sue! Talk to me! Please! What is going on? Please! Stop crying! Talk to me! Who did they kill? The Doctor?"

"Deeeee! He's deeeeaaaaaad!" She sobbed heavily. "And you're in troubuuuuuuuhlll! And it's all my fault, Wally! I saw the news! It's all my fauuuuult! I can't handle this! Oh my Gaa-a-a-ahd. I caaaan't!"

"Sue?"

"This whole thing is all my fault. Oh my Gaaa-ahh-aaaaahhhhhd."

"Sue? Who's Dee? What in the world is going on? Can you stop crying?"

"I'm a terrible person, Wally! Terrible!"

"Sue. *Please.* I don't know what you're saying. I can't understand you! Please tell me what's going on!"

"DeAndre is dead, Wally! He's dead! The love of my life! And it's my fa-aw-ault," she said with a *huh-huh-huh* ragged breath from crying.

"Whoa, whoa, whoa . . . *what?* DeAndre? Your *love?* What are you talking about, Sue?"

"Ohhhhhhhh, Wally. Yessss. I'm so sorry, Wally! I'm so so sorry. I'm ter—I, I don't know what to—I'm just a terrible person, and, like, now what? And the Doctor . . . Oh my G—"

Just as the relief began to sink in that she wasn't telling me that my dog was dead, a new realization hit: "Wait—you were *cheating* on me? With *Deezy?*"

"I'm sorry, Wally! I'm sorry! I was more in love with him than I've ever been with anyone in my life! We're soul mates, Wally! And now he's—" She began bawling again. "Oh my Gaaaaaahh-hhhhd!" *That's how Deezy knew my secret,* I thought.

"What? Why are you calling me? You were *cheating* on me? What the fuck, Sue?"

"We were soul mates, Wally! Can't you understand that? We were gonna run away together! This weekend! You weren't supposed to know! I didn't want to hurt you like this, Wally! We were gonna run away! Just the three of us! And start over! And now he's deh-eh-ehhhhhhd. They killed him!" she bawled.

"What do you mean, 'Just the three of us,' Sue?"

"Ohhhhh, Wally, I'm so sorry. I never meant to hurt you like this! I only gave them your first name! I just meant to get back at Lyons for doing this to Deeeee-hee-heee! I'm so, so sorry, Wally. I really did love you once."

"Sue, what are you saying? Gave who my first name?" I realized who she'd meant as soon as I spoke the words aloud. "The press, Sue? *You* called the press?"

"I'm *sorry,* Wally. I wanted to get back at Lyons. He killed Deezy!"

"What did you mean the 'three of us'?"

"I meant [*sniffle sniffle*] me . . . DeAndre . . . " She paused for a while, seeming to collect herself. But when she spoke the next name she completely lost it, breaking into hysterics before she could even finish the name. "Me, DeAndre . . . and . . . the Dah-ah-ah-oc-octor," she managed to sputter.

The Doctor.

chizapter 21

I couldn't believe what I'd heard. *Sue had had the Doctor the whole time.* It didn't seem possible. Taking my dog away from me was one thing—but the ransom notes? Trying to blackmail money out of me as well? And cheating on me with a scumbag like Funk Deezy? What kind of sick individual was she? I mean, I knew Sue was a bitch, but this was a different breed of bitch. This was sociopathic! *If she wanted money from me, why didn't she just take the shoebox when she came for the Doctor? It doesn't make sense!* I tried to work it all out in my head: Sue and Deezy took the Doctor right before they blackmailed Lyons, so that they could skip town with some serious coinage in their pockets and live happily ever after with my dog and Lyons's money. I guess it was feasible, but I just couldn't believe it. Suddenly I didn't feel so bad about my adulterous relationship with Jem/Ramona.

The phone was still to my ear. Sue was sobbing pathetically in the background. I was at a total loss for words. She got herself together. "I'm so sorry, Wally. I just love him so much, the Doctor. He was the only thing [*sniffle sniffle*], he was the only thing keeping me here." *Am I supposed to feel bad for her?* "And we, we were gonna leave town with nothing but the clothes on our backs [*sniffle*], so DeAndre told me I should just take him. Just take him! I knew it was wrong, but I just [*sniffle sniffle*], I'm sorry, Wally. I really am!"

"Is he okay? How could you *do* this, Sue? I just don't . . . ? You *know* that dog is all I have! And *what do you mean* you were leaving with just the clothes on your backs! What a crock of shit! You tried to blackmail me, Sue! And Lyons! What about *that*? You think that's okay?"

"What? No! Wally! We didn't do that!"

"*What?* Bullshit!"

"No! We didn't, Wally! I swear. I swear to God, Wally! DeAndre and I did not send you that ransom note!"

"Bullshit, Sue! Bullshit! You guys sent the same note to Lyons demanding ten million! I saw it with my own eyes, Sue!"

"Wally, no! I swear! I would never! Why do you think I went to Blockbuster with you that day? I was totally puzzled when you told me you got a ransom note for the Doctor! We didn't do that! And I don't even know what you're talking about with the ten million! What are you *talking* about?"

"Sue, why would I ever believe you? All you've done is fucking lie right to my face for the past . . . who knows how long!"

She began to cry again. "Wally, I know [*sniffle*]. I know. I'm *so* sorry. I am. But we didn't send you those notes! And he's fine, Wally. The Doctor is right here and he's fine. And my DeAndre is dead, Wally! My love is dead! Don't you care?"

"Care? *What? Are you retarded?* I'm gonna be dead, too, when these guys catch up with me, Sue! Because you leaked my secret! *Dead!* Does that mean anything to you? I am fucking *dead!* Because you and your dumb fucking boyfriend tried to blackmail the scariest motherfucker in America! And then you called the fucking press! And he thinks I did it!"

"No, Wally! Please! We didn't! I swear!"

"And don't think I won't send them over to your place when they come to kill me, Sue!"

"Wally—!"

"Get my dog ready, Sue! I'm coming to get him!" No response from the bitch. "Sue? You hear me? I'm coming to get my dog!"

Nothing.

Then: "What was that?" she asked, sounding farther away now, as if she'd dropped the phone.

"Sue? You hear me?"

"Wally!" she yelled from afar, and then: *click.*

"I'm coming for the Doctor, Sue!" No response. "Sue?" But she was already gone. "Fuck!" I yelled, tempted to smash my cell phone against the wall. Lou, out of the bathroom now, put his hands up and waved them like a soccer goalie with a ball zooming toward his head, trying to keep me quiet. He didn't want to wake his slumbering boss, who didn't even stir the slightest bit. He continued to breathe thickly and whistle through his nose like a cartoon character. I slumped down onto the couch and closed my eyes, put my hands on my forehead. This was too much to compute. My head felt like it was going to explode. Ramona sat down next to me and rubbed my thigh and whispered, "It's okay."

But it wasn't okay. Despite the fact that, in my mind, I had already moved on from Sue (to Jem) to Ramona, this hurt. Bad. This was the worst betrayal I'd ever experienced. I was in shock. My head was swimming with questions. *Was Sue telling the truth? Did someone else send the ransom notes after hearing about my missing dog?* After all, Sue *did* seem surprised when she found out about the note, and why would she go to Blockbuster with me if she already knew what we'd find there? And why would she have waited three days after she took him to give me the ransom note? It didn't add up. *And most importantly, if she was trying to get money out of me, she would have taken the shoebox herself when she took the Doctor.* Could Deezy have done the blackmailing behind Sue's back? That seemed like a legitimate possibility. But something still bothered me about that second ransom note—the one Lyons received—something that I still couldn't pinpoint . . .

And then there was Deezy being found dead with a bullet in his head. I knew why *that* bothered me. It was a little bit too coincidental that Deezy was found shot to death the day after (I suspected) he was the one I'd shot at in my apartment. What the hell was he *doing* in my apartment anyway? It would make sense if Sue had told him about the shoebox, and he came for the money, but what was the deal with the gun on the string? This didn't make any goddamned sense! I couldn't for the life of me figure out what the connection was—if there even was a connection.

....

I wanted to get the Doctor immediately. Unfortunately, Lou forbade me from either: A) waking up his boss to ask permission; or B) going to Sue's house on a solo rescue mission. So I waited as patiently as I could for Six-seven Kevin to return "home" with the food, and more importantly, for Jerry to call back and give us the go-ahead to get out of the stinky little shit-hole motel.

Ramona was a godsend. She massaged my shoulders while I whined and rationalized and explained my situation to her and Lou. I was absolutely heartbroken over the magnitude of Sue's betrayal. Sue—the only person in the world who *knew* me, I mean truly, truly *knew* me—had stabbed me in the back, and I never saw it coming. She knew the depth of my weakness, my utter dependency and absolute trust in her, and she stomped on it. How long had she been cheating on me? My mind went back through allllll of the phone calls. All of the voice mail messages. All of the excuses over the past months of why she wouldn't be coming over tonight, or where she was going that weekend, or whose dog she was massaging. When all along she was massaging Deezy's hog. That fucking scumbag *loser!*

At least I got to take a leak on his leg, I thought, realizing that this shed new light on the whole pissing situation in the bathroom that day. No wonder he was antagonizing me! He'd been banging my girl! But was there more to it than mere machismo? Was there something else behind the taunting? Maybe it wasn't a coincidence that we'd just *happened* to run into each other in that bathroom. Maybe by pissing on him, I'd disrupted some plan that was supposed to have been set in motion by that ostensibly coincidental run-in. Maybe Deezy was supposed to have said or done something to me in that bathroom to get his and Sue's plan in motion. I'd need to give more thought to how that event may or may not have set off a chain reaction of fucked-up dominoes that had led to that very point of shittiness—where I stood in that horrific crack den of a motel, on the run for my life. *But then*—if that merciless, heartless, evil, backstabbing act of infidelity wasn't enough—she'd taken her knife out of my back, and then thrust it *right back in* even deeper and more cruelly than the first torturous plunge. After slowly starving me of her love, while surreptitiously sharing it with someone else—she took from me the only other thing in this world that I'd cared about, and the only thing that cared for me in return. My dog. Sue single-handedly pushed me over the edge! Just a few days ago, I'd been lying on my floor like a dead man. It was one of the darkest moments of my life, and it was all because of Sue. It truly was a betrayal of epic proportions.

But then came Ramona. She made everything okay. She was there to lift my spirits in my bleakest hour, and she was here now. I'd spent a good deal of time telling her all about the Doctor the night before, and she was thrilled and relieved to hear that he was okay. "I can't wait to meet the little chubber!" she said, in an effort to make me smile, which was successful. She completely dropped the subject of her fake name—knowing that I didn't need any more bullshit on my plate to deal with at that moment.

Kevin arrived a few minutes later with two armfuls of food. He had a pizza box balanced on one hand and a white paper bag in the other. The white bag contained two aluminum containers of pasta. One was spaghetti and meatballs, the other was baked ziti. The room smelled like a wonderful Italian kitchen that someone had just recently vomited all over.

The two potbellied goombahs didn't seem to mind the smell.

They dug into the food with reckless abandon, telling us to help ourselves as they tore open containers and slurped up pasta. They didn't wake up their boss, which I found surprising and slightly disrespectful. "How can he sleep through all of this?" I asked the guys.

"It's his medicine. Makes him tired," said Kevin through a mouthful of ziti.

"And cranky," added Lou, before shoving a folded, oil-dripping slice of pizza into his mouth. *No oil dabbing for him,* I thought, deciding not to mention the twenty percent cut in fat he was missing out on.

Ramona and I each helped ourselves to a slice of pepperoni. I suppose it would have been delectable under normal circumstances, but my mind was—of course—elsewhere, and I was having trouble eating. When Wally Moscowitz does not fully enjoy a slice of pizza, you know there is some serious shit goin' down.

Jerry finally called with furthur instructions. He was very short with me. I couldn't get a word in. I wanted to tell him about the Doctor—that I needed to pick him up from Sue's house ASAP—but the way he spat out instructions in rapid fire made it impossible. It was also quite evident that Jerry would've nixed any deviation from his rigid game plan. "Speed is everything," he said, and the plan was simple. It was 12:45 P.M. at the time of his call. We were to leave the motel at precisely one o'clock. We were to drop "the girl," as he put it, referring to Ramona, at her home. We were to proceed immediately to the Santa Monica Pier ("easy freeway access"), where sometime thereafter—he wasn't sure yet of the exact time—we would rendezvous with a "small but deadly Colombian man" named Marco, who would drive me out of town to a secret destination that I would be informed of when the time came. "Marco is a nervous man and doesn't want to give an exact meeting time or place just yet," he'd said. We were to head toward the Santa Monica Pier and wait for another call. If we weren't there when

Marco called, he would leave immediately, at which point my best and only chance of protection would be gone. I'd be on my own. *How does Jerry know all of these dangerous characters?* I wondered, as I hung up the phone with the very curt and the apparently very well-connected Jerry Silver.

"What's the marchin' orders?" asked Kevin as I put the cell phone down on the table.

"We have to leave here in *exactly* fifteen minutes. One o'clock on the dot." The two thugs instinctively and simultaneously glanced at their hibernating honcho as they continued to shovel mouthfuls of pasta and pizza into their mouths. "We drop Ramona off immediately—and then head for Sue's house to pick up my dog—"

"No!" Ramona interrupted, jumping to her feet. "I'm going with you," she said bravely.

I looked at her, standing there, wobbly-kneed, wearing my oversized T-shirt and a pair of my ratty sweatpants, her hair a mussed pile. In that instant she reminded me of one of those macaroni necklaces you make in preschool, made of noodles and liable to fall apart at any second, but still an unquestionable work of art. My heart swelled with pride and joy and what I think may have been the egg of love in the incubator. I know it's hard to believe that our feelings could have developed so quickly, but they did, and it was undeniable. This gorgeous, amazing girl who I'd only *really* known for about fourteen hours now was ready to stand by me. No matter the danger. I knew in my heart, however, that it was a bad idea. There were nasty people after me, and I couldn't put Ramona in that kind of jeopardy. Not after the connection we'd made.

"No," I said. "You can't. Not yet. I need to disappear for a few days. There are some seriously malicious motherfuckers coming after me, and I don't want you involved anymore. You're going home. We'll meet up in a day or two when all of this is settled. Taken care of."

"Wally—"

"I'm sorry, Ramona. That's that. We're in good hands, and we just have to trust Jerry. He's a good man, and he's gone way above and beyond to make sure that nothing happens to me. I won't put you at risk."

She looked doubtful, but resigned herself with a small nod. She draped her arms around my shoulders and tucked her face into my neck. "You promise you'll come get me in a few days?"

"I promise," I said.

"If you leave town, I mean like, *leave*-leave, I wanna go with you."

I pulled her away from me and looked in her eyes. "I know. And I promise, you will."

She swallowed hard. "'Kay."

"We gotta hurry up and eat this shit and get the fuck outta here," said Five-two Lou. "It's twelve-fitty already."

"I'm eatin'!" said Six-seven Kevin through another mouthful of pasta. He swallowed the bite forcefully, and continued, "We gotta wait for Vinny to get up anyways. Will you relax for Christ's sakes?"

"Guys—we can't wait for Vinny to wake up—Jerry said we *have* to leave by exactly one o'clock. We're on a tight schedule here. This deadly little Colombian dude is waiting for me," I said. "And I don't like pissing off deadly little Colombian dudes."

"I'm surprised the fat-ass didn't wake up as soon as he smelled the food!" said Lou with a chuckle.

I was surprised to hear Lou talk about his boss that way.

"I ain't wakin' him up," said Kevin. "He's so fuckin' cranky after he naps."

"Go 'head, kid," Lou said to me. "You want him up—get him up. We're eatin'."

That didn't sound like a good idea. "B-but he's uhh . . . cranky?"

"I already told yas—they don't call him Balsamic Vinny 'cuz he's good wit a salad," said Kevin. He looked at Lou and winked.

"Nice one," said Lou.

"Maybe I shouldn't," I said.

"Kid, if you're in a rush, I suggest you get him up," offered Lou. "He'll sleep till next winter." I think he just wanted to watch me do it. Sadistic bastard.

I looked at Ramona. She looked scared. I looked at Balsamic Vinny, still snoring away peacefully. *Just do it, you pussy. Show your woman how brave you are.*

I stepped over to the bedside. I leaned over and gently touched Vinny's shoulder. "Vinny," I said softly, trying to sound as motherly and gentle as possible. I was terrified. "Hey. Vinny. C'mon, man. Vinny, wake up." He choked on a snore. I heard one of the guys chuckle. I shook harder. "Vinny! Hey! Wake up! Vinny!" I was shaking him now, but he still wasn't opening his heavy eyelids. "Vinny! C'mon! *Wake up!*"

Vinny suddenly *bolted* upright, grabbing his gun and staring wide-eyed and wild, right into my eyes. I held my breath.

Vinny's face twitched oddly, all the while holding his eerie lock on my eyes. His creepy gaze shifted around the unfamiliar room. He seemed to be figuring out exactly where he was.

"What time is it?" he finally asked.

"Ihh-it's juh almost wuh-one," I managed to stutter. "J-Jerry called. H-he said we have to leave immediately."

Vinny's crazy eyes finally landed on the pizza box, and they softened. "Heyyy, pizzaaaaa!" He swung his legs over the side of the bed, stretched his arms way above his head, and in a funny, mid-stretch voice said, "Why didn't you wake me? I'm friggin' starved." He hopped off of the bed like a hungry little boy, grabbed a slice out of the box, and said, "Okay! Let's *do* this!"

We left the motel.

chizapter 22

Vinny was in a cheerful mood as we drove toward Ramona's house, but his mood seemed to darken as we explained Jerry's instructions. It darkened even further when I explained the whole Sue situation to him. He removed his prescription bottle from his jacket pocket as I spoke and popped another pill. I couldn't help but wonder what they were. *Probably something for his heart, or maybe his stomach.* Whatever it was, he sure took a lot of it.

Ramona gave Kevin directions to her apartment. She lived in Silverlake, a hip little area northeast of our motel. She held my hand so tightly that I started to grow concerned about my circulation. But she was worried about me, and that felt good. Despite the fact that I might lose a few fingers to her steely grip.

We stopped in front of Ramona's building. It was old Hollywood: a confused mish-mosh of Spanish and Mediterranean mock opulence. It was painted an unfortunate shade of burnt orange, with lime green trim, white pillars, and a red door. The roof was cracked terra cotta. "Let me walk you up," I said, as the car pulled to a stop.

"No, that's okay, Wally. You're in a rush. Just go."

"No. I insist. Please. It'll make me feel better to know you're safe and sound."

The lobby of her building smelled like my grandma's house.

We entered a tiny, ancient elevator, which I definitely wasn't thrilled about. "Don't worry. It *rarely* gets stuck," she said with a coy smile. We smooched the whole way up, knowing that this could be the last time we'd be together for a while. Maybe ever.

Ramona lived on the fifth floor. We held hands as we approached her door, apartment number 504. "Oh crap," she said suddenly, as her door came into sight. "Do you have a credit card?"

"Huh?"

"My keys are at your apartment. I didn't grab *anything* when we left this morning. We were in such a rush."

"What, are you gonna call a locksmith?" I gave her a card.

"No. Here, gimme." She slid it in the crack of her door, and it popped right open. She spun around and smiled. "Taaa daaahhhh!" she said. If you'd told me at that very moment that in about one minute I'd be more devastated than ever before, I surely would have balked. But that's what happened.

Ramona and I entered her small apartment. She didn't have a lot of furniture, but she made it count: a big, pillowy, pinkish couch; a small, blue, artsy, kidney bean–shaped coffee table on wheels; and a black, tic-tac-toe-style bookcase. Some tchotchkes here and there, and some cool pictures hanging on the walls. That was pretty much *it*. Simple, but well done, I supposed. "This is home," she said.

"Nice." On any other day I would have loved to get a tour and make myself comfy. Now was not the time.

I grabbed Ramona's hands in mine. "I'll call you *as soon as I can*."

She stared at me and rubbed the back of my hand with her fingertips. "I don't want you to go," she said, pulling me in closer for a hug.

That's when everything changed. It wasn't much. A minor detail, really. Frankly, I'm surprised I even noticed it. "Just be careful, Wally," she was saying, though it sounded very far away, as if spoken to me while I was asleep. I was no longer present in the reality of the room, my entire focus engulfed by what I was seeing over her shoulder. "Wally?" I heard her ask.

I didn't answer. She pulled away. "What's wrong?" she asked. What was wrong was there was a bottle sitting there on the counter that looked very familiar. It was tall and narrow like a baton, with a light blue plastic wrapping. It had red cursive lettering on the front that read "Glacialle." I heard Jerry's voice echo in my head: *"This is the only case of this stuff in the whole state of Cali. I want all of my clients to have a bottle,"* he'd said. *"Mmm MMM. That is a tasty beverage."*

As I stared at the tall, skinny, blue bottle, something important happened within my congested mind. A shift. An important switch was flicked. Suddenly, things made a little bit more sense.

....

The only case in Cali. He wanted all of his clients to have one. One of these *tasty beverages.*

Fuck . . . me.

"Wally . . . ? What's wrong?" I was frozen, locked wide-eyed on the bottle. *What the hell did this mean?* "Wally?" I stumbled backward, bumped into a chair, fumbled toward the door, never taking my eyes off of the Glacialle. Ramona followed my line of sight. "Oh my God. Wally. It's not what you think. Wally, no. I tried to tell you—"

To avoid crying like a girl right in front of Ramona, I had to turn and flee. She gave chase, so I slammed the door behind me to slow her down, adding a few more valuable seconds to my lead. I jumped in the elevator, hit *L*, and hit the Close Doors button about six hundred times in rapid succession. I watched Ramona's panicked face appear and then disappear in the crack of the closing doors. With a worrisome groan, the elevator car lurched downward.

I did my best to come to some quick understanding of what the heck was going on. *Another lie.* Ramona knew Jerry. *How could that be? What does it mean?* One thing it meant—the thing at the forefront of my mind—was our ostensibly accidental meeting in the bar that first night was no accident. Jerry had set it up. He was there! Watching! The time Ramona and I spent together had been a lie. Yet another deception by a woman whom I'd thought had real feelings for me. This one would be tough to get over.

But there was something else. Something even more troubling than Ramona's deception had began to take shape upon seeing that bottle. It was the memory of Jerry's words that had spurred it. *That's a tasty beverage.* Some rays of sunlight began to shine through my clouded mind. Unfortunately, I didn't have much time to analyze all the information. It was too overwhelming to try to process on the short elevator ride to the ground floor. All I knew for sure was, I couldn't trust *anyone*. Not Sue, not Ramona, and now, maybe not even Jerry. Every instinct in my body was screaming the same thing: *Run.*

....

As I bolted from the elevator in Ramona's lobby, I could hear her bombing furiously down the creaky, old-style wooden steps in the building, calling out my name in desperation.

I couldn't go out the front door. The mobsters would certainly spot me. And the mobsters worked for Jerry. I was on my own now. I decided to make a run for the back door (if there even *was* a back door). I took off toward where I imagined the fire exit would be, hauling ass down a long hallway, past about eight or ten apartments on either side. Luckily, I spotted a rickety Exit sign suspended from the ceiling at the end of the hallway. As I neared the door, I noted that it was one of those dealies with an alarm contraption attached to it and stickers and signs warning that the door was for Emergency Only! and that Alarm Will Sound! While the latter was disappointing, I felt that this most certainly qualified as an emergency. I threw my weight against the thick steel door, slamming into the release bar with my hip. The door flew open, followed immediately by a high-pitched, ear-busting chirping sound.

I ran with all of my heart in the direction of the nearer street, which would provide the most cover and the best diversionary options. I was operating on pure survival instinct. Ducking behind Dumpsters, between cars, weaving between streets and alleyways, hurdling over trash cans and fire hydrants and children and whatever else stood in my way, all the while glancing around me for signs that someone was on my tail. Like Forrest Gump, I just kept on running.

Next thing I knew, I was somewhere else. Gone was the chic, hipster neighborhood I'd been in only minutes before. It looked more like . . . well, like Mexico. Everything was in Spanish, and everyone had a mustache. I was pretty sure I wasn't being followed anymore at this point, so I needed to make some moves. My car was a long way away, and it probably wasn't safe to go back to my apartment right now anyway, so I did the thing I'd hoped I'd never have to do in Los Angeles. I took a bus. Or, in this neighborhood, el autobus.

I had to get to Sue's house. I was sure that the gangsters and Ramona would know that this was where I would head, but I had a very important advantage: I knew where she lived. They would have to figure it out. I was confident that I'd have a decent enough lead on them to be gone way before they even arrived. I intended on picking up the Doctor, speaking as little as humanly possible to Sue, and taking off. To where, I wasn't sure yet. But I'd cross that bridge when I got to it.

Two buses later, I ended up a few blocks from Sue's house. I limp-jogged the few blocks from the bus stop to her building. There was a call box at the end of a long, gated walkway that led to her two-story, L-shaped building. I hadn't been over here in about a month, but I typed in *pound-oh-two-one-two,* the entry code I'd memorized long ago. It didn't work. I tried it again to no avail. I scrolled through all the names in the directory, until I landed on S. Shadenfreude, 105. I typed in the code next to her name, and the speaker came alive with the sound of a ringing phone. It rang and rang and rang some more. "C'mon, Suuuuu-uue," I said out loud, doing a nervous little dance. Her answering machine picked up. "Hi! You've reached Canine Ranch Doggy Spa! To leave a message for Sue, please wait for the woof! Wooooof."

"Sue, it's Wally. I'm outside. Let me in please, Sue. *Please.*" There was no response. No relieving buzzing sound from the gate. I tried again. Same result. Either she wasn't home, or she simply wasn't picking up. *Goddammit, Sue. I just want my dog back!* She didn't answer the third, fourth, or fifth calls, either. This was desperation time. I eyed the gate. It was about eight feet high, constructed of vertical black steel bars with medieval points at the top of each. *I'm gonna scale this bitch. My dog is in there.* I jogged around to the side of the building, behind some tall, scratchy-looking bushes, so I wouldn't be seen by anyone on the street. I stepped up to the gate, got a good grip, and pulled myself upward. I had a flashback of being the little fat kid in gym class trying to climb the rope while all the athletic little pricks snickered from the sidelines. This wouldn't be like that. I had some serious motivation now. I pulled myself upward with all of my strength. I was halfway up, red-faced and sweaty, gripping the warm black metal bar for dear life, when I heard the buzz of the gate door opening. I looked over and saw that a young Hispanic couple had just entered the gate from the sidewalk. I released my grip on the bar and managed to stumble and trip the approximately six feet over to the entrance, just as the door was about to close. I dove forward to prevent it from clicking shut, landing on the concrete and skinning my knees and elbows. The door did not click shut. I got up as quickly as I could manage and ran toward Sue's first-floor apartment, my knees and elbows burning as the wind hit the open scrapes.

I pounded on her door. No answer. I rang the bell. "Sue!" I shouted. "Are you there?"

Nothing.

No. No no no no! Please tell me she didn't take off with my dog! Please! "Doc!" I tried the door. It was locked. I knocked again more feverishly. "Sue! It's Wally! Open up!" Nothing. "Sue!" Sue wasn't going to answer my knocks. This was it. The moment of decision. The old Wally would have turned and left. Maybe called the manager. Figured out some other way to get in. Not today. This was the new Wally, and I wasn't there to fuck around.

I stepped back from the door, charged forward, and gave it my best kick. My entire leg collapsed wimpily, reverberating like a stop sign in Chicago. Pain shot up into my back. The door smiled back at me like, "Nice try, pussy." This was the first time I'd ever tried this—cut me some slack. The cops made it look so easy on TV. I stepped back again, determined, part of my brain thinking, *Your leg is going to shatter if you kick that door again, schmuck,* while the other part of my brain was thinking, *Kick closer to the doorknob this time—you have to break the locking mechanism.* Without thinking, and (I swear) not even trying to be funny, I instinctually raised both arms, stood on one leg, and slowly lifted my other leg in the crane position á la *The Karate Kid.* I took a deep breath. With my last bit of bravado, I went for it. I kicked that door with all of my being. The frame cracked with a *snap* and the door flew open.

I rushed in and charged around the apartment, smacking open every door and giving the place a quick visual sweep. No one was here. Sue was gone. The Doctor was gone. *What the fuck do I do now?* I sat on Sue's couch, bent over with my head in my hands.

And then I heard something. *A scratching sound.*

I hopped up off of the couch and followed the sound down a short hallway toward the kitchen. The sound got louder, and then disappeared. I passed by a small linen closet, and just as I passed it, I heard it again. *Scratch, scratch, scratch.* I yanked open the closet door, and there he was.

My boy. My only friend in the whole world. Dr. Barry Schwartzman. Alive and well and hidden in Sue's linen closet. "Doc!" I bent down and grabbed his chubby little frame as he happily bounced up and down, thrilled to see me. He actually vocalized his excitement upon seeing my face, yipping ecstatically, saying (I'm sure) "Dad! Where you been, man? I've missed you so much!" Tears actually welled up in my eyes as I bent down and kissed his fat, furry head. He licked me frantically, snorting and drooling with excitement at this grand reunion. He smelled great. Sue must have given him a bath. *That cunt sure knows how to wash a dog,* I thought. "Let's get out of here, pal," I said, patting his back and standing up.

As I went for the front door, I thought, *Why the hell was he in the closet? Sue may be a bitch, but she's an animal lover first and foremost. She would never put the Doctor in a closet. Unless . . .*

Unless she was trying to hide him. *Who would she need to hide him from?* I decided to give the apartment another once-over. I walked over to the bedroom and surveyed it from the doorway. At first, rapid glance, it had appeared perfectly normal. But now I started to notice some minor details I'd missed upon my initial, cursory glance: Some of the dresser drawers were half-open and half-emptied; both closet doors were open, and there was a large space on the shelf where I was pretty sure Sue's large, red suitcase usually sat; her makeup bags were not sitting on her vanity where she did herself up every morning; her blow dryer was gone. In fact, where there was usually a ridiculous array of makeup and perfume bottles and hair products, there was nothing at all. It appeared that Sue had skipped town.

I left the bedroom and went to the kitchen. A lone piece of paper sat on the small wooden breakfast table, under the salt and pepper shakers. I picked it up:

TO WHOEVER.
LEFT TOWN FOR A WHILE. COULDN'T HANDLE ALL THE
BULLSHIT ANYMORE. MAYBE BE BACK. MAYBE NOT.
    LOVE,
      SUE.

You chickenshit, coward, bitch, I thought. *You couldn't even wait until I picked up the Doctor to get out of here? Couldn't look me in the eyes, you heartless, gutless whore* . . . I dropped the note back onto the table. *Where the hell did she go?* I wondered. *Maybe to her mother's?* Her obnoxious mother lived in an obnoxious mansion in an obnoxious suburb outside of Miami. She hated her mother and her mansion and her suburb. She would never go there for solace. *But where else could she go?* I looked at the note again. *"To Whoever"? Why did she address it like that?* She knew I'd be coming over to pick up the Doctor. Why didn't she write "Dear Wally?" I lowered the note and cocked my head, thinking. *Sue was a hysterical mess when I'd spoken to her earlier. This neatly written note doesn't jive with her hysterics.* I doubted very much that she would suddenly get it together, pack her shit and take off in a matter of minutes. *Not to mention leave this weird note in all neat, capital letters.* I knew Sue's handwriting, and this wasn't it. This note was coerced. I thought back to the phone call and realized that Sue had gone all weird and faraway at the end, as if . . . *had someone been in her apartment?* I stood there for a moment and scanned the kitchen again. Something struck me and I ran back into the bedroom. There was one thing that I knew Sue would *never* leave here if she'd truly left town for a while—of her own accord. Before her father died when she was ten years old, he'd given her a teddy bear named Fookie.

It was her most prized possession. I burst back into the bedroom.

Fookie was propped up on her pillows on the bed. *Goddamn.*

The Doctor began to bark ferociously. I turned.

Balsamic Vinny and his two thugs stood in the doorway in front of me.

chizapter 23

Fight or flee. Those are the instinctual reactions one should have in any dangerous situation. It's primal.

I just wasn't feeling very primal at that moment.

My strength and motivation had been stripped and sucked away like the sweet outer layers of a Tootsie Roll Pop, leaving nothing but the dark and sticky center. As if Sue and Ramona's betrayals weren't painful enough. Now maybe Jerry, too.

Yes, surrender felt okay at that moment.

At least it did for *me*. The Doctor, apparently, felt differently about the situation. And I tend to trust his professional opinion. After all, he's a doctor. He growled deeply, from a place I'd never heard him growl before. *This* was a good example of primal. He took a few steps forward, placing himself between me and the thuggish posse in the doorway. *My hero.*

I looked at Vinny straight in the eyes.

"She here?" Vinny asked. I shook my head and said, "What the hell do you want?" The Doctor let out an angry *woof.*

"Ey. How's about calling your dog off so's I don't have to shoot him wit a horse tranq," said Five-two Lou, holding one side of his blazer open to reveal the silvery gun tucked into the waistline of his slacks.

"No," I said boldly, surprising even myself. "I won't. And if you guys come any closer, one of you is gonna have a painful flesh wound," I said. "He bites."

"Oh yeah?" said Lou, reaching for his weapon.

"Lou," said Vinny, "cut the shit." Lou gave him a lingering look of protest—it almost looked like a challenge—but finally closed his jacket. Vinny turned back to me. "Wally. We need to talk. This is not what you think."

"Bullshit," I said.

"No. Really. It's not. *We're* not."

"Why are you here then, huh? Why are you chasing me?"

Vinny cocked his head to the side. "Hey! Come on in, hon," he said to his shoulder.

Ramona stepped into the doorway behind Lou and Kevin. They parted like theater curtains, revealing her in all her stunning beauty. I admit that my heart fluttered, only this time it was with regret and utter sadness at her deception and the fully realized loss of what I'd thought we'd shared. I couldn't look at her.

"Wally," she said in a half-whisper. I didn't respond. "Wally, please." I looked at my dirty, poorly tied shoelaces. "Wally, look at me."

And I did. What a mistake.

I saw it all in her eyes: the connection. The depth of our feelings. The fear of losing this. It was all there, and it was *real*. No bullshit. But I knew there was nothing to be done now. Whatever bond we might have established had been squandered.

Her eyes were big and round as chestnuts, sorrowful and pleading. I realized that I was mirroring her expression, and so I hardened my stare. "What? Do you think I'm gonna run back to you? You're a liar like the rest of them. Get out. All of you."

"Wally, no."

"Get out!" I shouted, suddenly sickened and irritated by their mere presences. My anger agitated the Doctor, who started barking and snorting.

"Wally!" Ramona shouted over his barking, "you have to listen to us! We have something very important to tell you! This is not what you think!" *We're not what you think,* Vinny had said earlier. *What the hell were they saying?*

I bent down and touched the Doctor at the scruff of his neck, calming and quieting him. "What," I said, gruffly inviting their explanation.

"It's not what you think, Wally," she said.

"I heard you. So what is it? Talk."

"I'm saying—"

"May I?" interrupted Vinny. "I tink dat maybe I can illustrate dis best."

"Please," she said, a small smile playing on her lips now. I wondered what was so fucking amusing.

Vinny removed his pinstriped coat. Then his suspenders. Then his tie. He unbuttoned the top buttons of his shirt. Mussed up his stiff, slicked-back hair into a frizzy grayish mess. *What the hell is this guy doing?* I thought. The others watched him, each one of them with an inexplicably amused expression. Vinny turned and faced me. There was a new quality to his face now— a softness that hadn't been there before, as if he'd just removed a discreet mask. The slick mobster transformed into a bedraggled softy right before my eyes.

"What the fuck?" I asked, totally weirded out.

"It's like dis, my friend." Vinny rubbed his nose with the back of one of his fingers, which seemed to somehow wipe even more of his toughness away. He cleared his throat. "My name," he said softly, "is not Vinny." His accent was gone. He no longer sounded like a Mafia don. He was all soft and gentle and . . . *nice.*

"What?" I asked. The rest of them snickered politely at my understandable reaction to his transformation.

"My name is not Vinny, Wally. And I'm not Italian. My real name is Murray. Murray Steinberger." He reached into his shirt and pulled out a gold chain with a Star of David dangling from it.

"Whaaat?"

"Murray Steinberger. That's the name I was born with. I've

been Balsamic Vinny Consigliere for about ten years. I'm an actor, Wally."

"What?" Yes. That was consecutive "what" number four. I couldn't manage to say anything else.

"It goes like this: I moved out here from New York on my fiftieth birthday. I was fat, single, poor, and depressed. I wanted to start over. I wanted to be an actor. I was here for six months and I couldn't get any gigs. There were no parts for fat, middle-aged, Jewish men. I met a guy named Jerry Silver. He liked my look. Offered to represent me. But he had one condition: I was Italian. Not Jewish. Not a wimpy fat guy. A tough, Italian, Mafia guy. He swore up and down that this would get me work. And you know what? He was exactly right! I changed my look and my talk a little bit, put on some tough-guy clothes, and sure enough, I started getting jobs almost immediately. I was the go-to guy for a while in TV or commercials when they needed a Mafia guy. And I built a rep. And then the strangest thing started happening. I found myself surrounded by *real* Italian guys—even when I wasn't working. It's a very small community out here. I'm talking *real deal* tough guys. Guys like Louie and Kevin." He threw a thumb back at them. Kevin yanked his collar with both hands, while Lou just scratched his chin, looking dangerous.

"So Lou and Kevin are not . . . uh, actors?" I asked.

"Fuck no we ain't no fuckin' actors," said Kevin.

"We ain't no fake tough guys," said Lou. "No offense, Vin."

"No," continued Vinny/Murray. "These guys are the real deal. But that was my problem. I never spoke up. I created a whole new persona. Made up stories about what I was like back in New York, and everyone ate it up. And yeah, these guys knew I was getting film work, but that was okay. It's L.A. They respected me. They wanted a leader with some real "family" experience back in New York. And that's what I provided. Or so they thought. But I got tired of lying real quick. Especially to these guys. And frankly, I was scared. I didn't want to get in too deep. I didn't want the real Goodfellas back in New York to find out about me. I was content just being a tough guy on film. So about a year into it, I told Jerry, 'I'm done. I don't want to do this Italian thing anymore.' Well, Jerry wasn't havin' it. He said it would kill my career. Said I'd never work again. And I still wasn't making big money. I hadn't landed any *big* roles yet, but Jerry was doing okay off of my small roles. He said he had big plans for me. 'Murray's dead,' he said. 'Forget about him. Sit shivah, or whatever you have to do to un-Jew yourself.' So I tried to."

"When did they find out?" I asked, jerking my thumb to his two goombahs.

"Ahhh, they've known for years," he said with a dismissive wave.

"He's like a father to us," said Kevin.

"Truth is, I'd do anything for 'em, and they know that," said Murray.

"Don't matter to *us*," said Lou. "Long as people *believe* dat Vinny is scary, den Vinny is scary. Ya know? Dis is Hollywood."

"These guys are the best," said Murray, with a look of true appreciation for his partners in (fake) crime. "Anyhow, two years later, I still hadn't made it big. *But,* I was working fairly steadily, and Jerry and I were making okay money. Not only that, but he was using my connections with certain . . . *ruffians* to take care of a lot of his business. We were like his enforcers. We pushed deals through. Threatened people. Watched over people for him. Like you, for instance. But I was miserable. It was giving me panic attacks." He pulled his prescription bottle out of his inside jacket pocket. "I pop Xanax like they're goddamned orange Tic Tacs. Every two hours. I'm a wreck! So, I went to Jerry again. Told him I was just gonna come clean. I wasn't gonna do this anymore. And that's when he really tightened his leash. He blackmailed me, Wally. Told me if I did that, he'd use all of his contacts to ruin me in Hollywood forever. Not only that, but worse, he'd get the word out to the New York families that I was out here in Los Angeles, pretending to represent them. And you know what? If he'd done that, I'd be dead. Because that's *exactly* what I'd been doing. Playing make-believe John Gotti! So he had me by the balls. That was five years ago. And I've been doing this ever since. But I'm tired, Wally. And when I realized what Jerry was doing to you, and then Ramona, I don't know, something changed. I snapped. I want to help you. And help myself. We *need* to stop this guy. Together."

Stop this guy? What the heck was he talking about? *When he realized what Jerry was doing to me? What was that supposed to mean? What was he doi—*

And then it hit me.

Jerry.

How could I have been so blind? Jerry! He was the one pulling the strings! Seeing that bottle on the counter earlier had been the key. It was like pouring Drano into a clogged pipe in my brain—like Brain-o, if you will. Upon seeing the bottle, I'd remembered Jerry's words of a few days prior: *"Mmm MMM. That is a tasty beverage,"* he'd said. That was a Quentin Tarantino line. That jarred loose that other thing that had been blocking up my mind the most for the past few days: *Lyons's ransom note.* There was something familiar about that note that I just couldn't figure out.

Until now.

The last line of the note: *"This is as good as it's gonna get, and it won't ever get that good again."* That's what was stuck in my craw. Now I remembered where I'd heard it. Christopher Walken said it to Dennis Hopper in the movie *True Romance.*

Written by none other than Mr. Quentin Tarantino.

Jerry Silver wrote *both* ransom notes. Jerry fucking Silver. That lying, greedy, money-hungry prick! *How could he do this?* Uncle Jerry! I never saw it coming! The teddy bear Jerry I thought I knew so well wasn't the real Jerry at all.

This explained why Jerry was so mad when the media found out about my secret. He'd just lost that ten million bucks he was trying to extort from Lyons! I also realized something else. "You guys weren't taking me to some Colombian guy. You were gonna feed me to Lyons," I said, realizing the silly pun I'd inadvertently made and hoping nobody would notice. Murray nodded sadly in acknowledgment of my epiphany. Jerry must have made some sort of consolation deal. He didn't want it to be a *total* loss.

"That was what made me crack," said Murray sadly. "You're a good kid, Wally. It'd be obvious to anyone who spent five minutes with you. I couldn't hand you over to that thug. I knew it was a death sentence. I just couldn't do it."

The volcano of realization continued to erupt in my mind. The disappearance of my dog, paired with the fact that Lyons had just suspended me from work, was like the aligning of the planets for Jerry. It was the perfect time to take advantage of *both sides*. He could blame the dognapping on Lyons, and I'd believe it because Lyons was already pissed off at me, and Jerry knew it would keep me quiet. And he could make Lyons believe that *I* was the one trying to extort ten million dollars out of him!

But where did Ramona fit in? I looked at her, hopeful now that maybe she could tell me something wild enough that it would override the fact that our whole relationship thus far had been a farce. "Talk," I said to her, still doing my best to sound somewhat disgusted.

She swallowed heavily, brushed her licorice-black hair back with one hand. "I never meant to hurt you, Wally."

I gave a little *Pffff.*

"Seriously, Wally. I'm so sorry that it happened the way it did, but I really care about you now. I know you feel it too."

"It was all bullshit."

"No, Wally—Jerry made me do it all. I never in a million years expected that I would fall for you. I was acting at first. Playing a role. And I had no idea that these guys were supposed to take you to Lyons. You have to believe me! I would never let that happen!" Murray shook his head in support of Ramona's claim.

"How did he *make* you do it, Ramona? He *made* you sleep with me?"

"Remember I told you the story about my commercial? How when I first got here some *guy* talked me into doing it?"

"Yeah," I said, knowing just where this was going.

"Well, that *guy* was Jerry. He talked me into doing the commercial. He became my agent. *He* made me he Herpes Girl. The laughingstock of Los Angeles. Not only that, but he is single-handedly the reason that stupid commercial still runs so often so many years later. The company loves the ad—they don't want to dump it. 'It's a classic!' they say. And they'll continue to run it until we tell them we want to pull the plug. We're still making money off of it, so Jerry won't pull it! I've been *begging* him to end it for *years*. But he says we need the money! Personally, I would flush that money down the toilet if it would get me my anonymity back."

"Okay, what does this have to do with me?" I asked.

"So then, a few days ago, Jerry comes to me with this proposal: 'Go to this bar, flirt with this guy, show him a good time, distract him, make him think of nothing except you for a few days,' and he'd let me off the hook! He'd finally pull the plug on my commercial. That was all I had to do. I met you, and you were nice enough, and cute, so I did what it took to make you think of nothing but me."

"Didn't you ever consider that there might be feelings involved? Or did you not give a flying fuck about how it might hurt the poor loser?"

"I know. I was blind and selfish. But something happened, Wally! You know? We *connected*." She looked at me for some support. I gave her none, just stared at her blankly. "Whatever, I'm sorry, okay? I know I was wrong before. But that doesn't matter now! Because of *us,* Wally. Please. I know you know what I'm saying. We found each other! And I won't lose you." She paused for a long time, stared at the floor, and then looked at me. "You make me forget all about that other shit. You make me feel normal, Wally."

"How the hell do I know that you're not still in on this with Jerry somehow?"

She looked back up at me with those big green eyes. She swallowed hard. "What else can I say, Wally?" We stared at each other some more. I explored her face: the tiny peaks and valleys of her perfect little lips, her olive skin with its lovely lines and minuscule scars and sporadic dots, and finally, her eyes. Those incredible little orbs of jade. Stupid little jade orbs. That's what got me. They swelled with tears and those tears tugged on my wimpy little heartstrings like Quasimodo in the bell tower, and I made a decision: I believed her.

"Okay," was all I had to say. She pounced into my arms. I sunk my face into her hair and squeezed her until I was pretty sure it was starting to hurt.

"I guess I think I might love you, or whatever," she whispered into my ear.

"I guess I think I might love you or whatever, too," I whispered back. Again, I *know* this seems ridiculously crazy to be saying those words to each other already, but who said love wasn't ridiculously crazy?

I felt a heavy hand land on my shoulder. "Let's bring this asshole down," said Murray. For the first time in my life, I felt what it was like to have people on my side. People who really cared about me.

"Ahem," said Lou.

Ramona and I turned around, having almost forgotten about our mobster spectators.

"Yes, Lou?" I asked.

"I, uh, I want to help you guys nail Jerry Silver. I think he's a piece a dogshit."

"Fuckin' dogshit," said Kevin.

I smiled.

"Okay," said Murray, clapping his hands together, his Italian accent back. "Let's get this muthafucka."

WHERE DID DING COME FROM?
~~By Wally Moscowitz~~
By WALLACE Q MOSCOW

Out of nowhere one day I got a new baby brother.
"Where did he come from?" I questioned my mother.

She said, "The stork brought him to us, just like he brought you!"
But something about this was different, I knew.

First of all Mommy's belly never got big.
When Aunt Rhonda was pregnant, she got fat as a pig!

And she was fat for months, I think it was nine.
But here this baby was, and my mommy looked fine!

There's other odd stuff, too, besides that first thing.
What I thought was the strangest, the kid's name was Ding!

I said, "Ding? Mommy, don't you think that's a weird name?"
She said, "Honey, be nice. All names can't be the same."

Apparently all families can't look the same either.
'Cuz there's Mommy and Daddy, and Ding looks like neither.

His eyes are both slanted and closed very tight.
His hair is jet black, which doesn't look right.
'Cuz Mommy and Daddy both have really blond hair.
My friend told me Mom must've had an affair.

Then one day I overheard Mom on the phone.
If I hadn't listened I would never have known
The truth about Ding, and where he came from.
When I heard what she said, I felt kinda dumb.

'Cuz I didn't understand what she was talking about
When she said "the black market," but I figured it out.
I felt bad for Ding now, and I'd never forget.
Turned out Mom and Daddy bought Ding on the Net.

—From *The Adult Children's Books Collection*

chizapter 24

We left Sue's apartment, trying to appear ordinary as we strolled over to our SUV across the street. Just your average, everyday group of friends—a chubby guy and his chubby dog, that chick from the genital herpes commercials, and three apparent members of the Mafia—walking out to their black Escalade.

Just another day in Hollyweird.

As we made our way down the path from her apartment and out the front gate, I started to feel truly optimistic for the first time in days. I had the Doctor back, and I had my girl. I had friends on my side. Sure, I still had a very angry gangsta millionaire and his army of thugs, bangers, and assorted derelicts out to kill me, and the cops would probably want to have a word with me during the course of the murder investigation of DeAndre Muskingum, but somehow, a happy ending still seemed like a possibility.

We all packed into the SUV, and Lou fired the engine. "Where to?" he asked.

"Good question," said Murray. "Should I call and check in with Jerry?"

"Was he expecting you to?" I asked.

"Well, I guess not until after we gave you up to Lyons and got the money."

"What time was that supposed to happen?"

236

"Ehhh, we were supposed to drive around with you—in the vicinity of Santa Monica Pier—until Jerry called me on my cell." Murray pulled his cell phone out of his pocket and wiggled it in between his thumb and forefinger. "He was gonna tell me where exactly to meet Lyons to drop you and get the loot."

"Okay. Let's head toward Santa Monica then," I said. Lou pulled away from the curb. Dr. Schwartzman was on my lap, looking up at me. I kissed the side of his head and rubbed behind his ears. "Hey, buddy!" I said. "Are you so glad to be back with me? Yes! Yes, you are!" I pulled the chunky rolls on his face back and made him look Chinese. I was so elated to have him back that I wasn't even embarrassed to be talking baby-talk to him. "Ohhhhh, buddy." I scratched his back, digging my fingers into his soft folds. Deep down in a place I didn't want to acknowledge, I'd truly thought that I would never see him again. He cooed and drooled and snorted with pleasure.

As I rubbed him and he licked my arm and made lots more snorting sounds, my thoughts went to the situation at hand. *What now?* I knew I needed to step up. Take action. Be a man. No more pussy Wally Moscowitz.

I had to call Abraham Lyons and make a deal.

It wouldn't be easy. The man clearly wanted me dead. At that very moment I was the bane of his existence. A disease. A flame that needed to be snuffed. It seemed that deal-making time was over.

But I had an idea brewing in my head. A safety net that just might be my salvation if I only had the chance to plead my case. I wasn't sure I could sell it to Lyons, but it was my only shot.

"I'm calling Oral B," I said, taking my cell phone from my pocket. They all looked up at me, surprised by this sudden declaration. There was something else in their looks besides surprise, though. They were impressed. They didn't think I had it in me to make a bold move like this. I dialed Oral B's number.

"You sure?" asked Ramona, derailing the confidence train.

"This is our only choice," I said. "Right?" I stopped dialing.

"It *is* our only choice," agreed Murray. "We have to get to Lyons *ASAP.* Get him on our side, and then call Jerry and have Lyons call Jerry too and tell him the plan went smoothly. That we dropped you off to him, and that his money is on the way. Jerry needs to think everything is going fine if we're gonna nail him before he disappears."

"We have two options," I reasoned. "One, we can wait for Jerry's call and then go meet Lyons as planned. Explain it all to Lyons face-to-face and try to talk him out of killing me on the spot. Or, plan B, I can call Oral B and arrange a meeting on our terms. Maybe try to explain it all on the phone first."

"Plan B," Murray and Sue both said at the same time, as did Kevin from the front seat.

"I hear this Lyons guy is one scary son of a bitch," added Murray. "We don't want to have to explain to his face under pressure."

"I'll probably wet myself either way," I noted.

A cell phone started ringing somewhere. We all patted our jeans. Murray pulled out his phone. He held it up, dangling from its antenna.

"Here we go," he said, with a panicked look. "What should I do?"

"Answer it!" Ramona and I both said.

"Pretend everything is going smoothly," I added quickly, before he flipped it open.

"Yo—Vinny here. JS. What's the plan? Uh-huh. Yeah. Everything is smooth as, uh, feathers." He shrugged at us. "Yeah. Dropped her off. Yeah. Yeah? Okay. Okay, Jerry."

Ramona looked worried. I put my arm around her to comfort her.

"You got it, Boss. Okay. Hold on." Murray handed me the phone. I threw him a panicked expression, then relaxed when I realized that as far as I was supposed to know, Jerry was still on my side. Murray mouthed "It's okay," or something to that effect. I took the phone, trying my best to suppress my hatred for Jerry Silver.

"H-hey, Jerry."

"Mosco, hey kiddo. You ready?" I couldn't believe how normal he sounded. Like selling my life to Abraham Lyons was just another deal.

"Uh, yeah. I guess so. Ready as I'll ever be, I guess."

"Don't worry, bud. Marco will take care of you. This will all work out just fine. Listen. I gave Vinny all the details. There's just one more thing."

"What's that?"

"Marco wants you to be blindfolded when you pull up. He doesn't want you to see what he looks like. He's a paranoid guy." *You fucking scumbag piece of shitfucking asshole fuck,* I thought. *You don't want me to get spooked and try to run when I see that there IS no Marco.*

"Um, okay, Jerry. Whatever I have to do."

"'Kay, bud. That's it. Call me when you're safe."

"Okay, Jerry. Thanks for everything." *You are SO going down, fat man.* I clapped the phone closed.

....

I dialed Oral B's number from Murray's phone, thinking that this might be the most important phone call I'd ever make.

"Who dis?" he answered irritably. What with all the devastating news coverage of the past few hours, it was safe to say that Oral B must have been having a very shitty day.

"B," I said quietly. "It's Wally."

There was silence. I imagined that he was standing in a room with Abraham Lyons and wildly pointing to the phone at that moment, signaling to his crazed boss that it was me. "Mosco? W'tha fuck, man? Where you at, foo?"

"I'm, uh, I'm somewhere safe. Listen, B, I need to talk t—"

"Don't call me 'B,' muhfucka! What, you think we friends? Huh? Huh, homeboy? You think we boys still?"

"B, Brandunn, listen, it's not what you think!"

"Fuck dat, nigga! Fuck dat! You fucked us, Mosco! And now you release dis bullshit to da news media!? Is you crazy, nigga?"

"No—"

"Is you crazy?! You's a dead man, muhfucka! You heard me?" he screamed. I heard someone say something to him in the background, heard some crinkling sounds as he covered up the phone with his hand.

"Brandunn, it's not what you think! Listen. Please. Just let me talk." I knew he wasn't listening. I could still hear the crinkling sounds, and some muffled conversation behind it in the background.

"You there?" he asked.

"Yes. I'm here."

"Listen, dawg. I'm sorry. I'm jus' heated. It's coo. We should talk about dis. Face-to-face. I ain't mad atcha. Let's work dis shit out."

Boy, he sure was convincing. What a tempting offer. "Brandunn, listen. I do want to talk. But I need to speak to Lyons. On the phone. Before anything else happens."

"Naw, dawg. Jes come meet us, we'll all talk, homey. Face-ta-face."

"No! Listen to me! I *need* to talk to Lyons. Put him on the phone, Brandunn. *Now.*" I stared straight ahead intensely. Out of the corner of my eye, I saw Murray and Ramona glance at each other. I hoped it was an impressed kind of glance.

"Oh, you makin' demands now, huh, playboy? You a big man now, Mosco?" He was getting heated again.

"Brandunn, please. I mean no disrespect. I have *never* disrespected you *or* betrayed your trust. I need to prove to you all that I am still on your side. And in order to do that, I need to speak to Lyons *immediately.*"

I heard him cover up the phone again, and exchange some

more muffled words, and then, "Call back in five minutes—"

"No!" I screamed, trying to stop him from hanging up on me. I knew that if I let him go, Lyons would immediately call Jerry to find out why the fuck I was calling him when Jerry had just told him that I was about to be delivered to him on a silver platter. I couldn't let that happen.

I waited for a response, but none came.

Oral B hung up.

....

"Fuck!"

"He hung up?" Ramona yelled.

"He's gone!" I said.

"Call him back! Quick!" shouted Murray.

"Before he calls Jerry!" shouted Ramona.

I dialed Oral B's number again. It rang. And rang. "What," he finally said.

"I don't *have* five minutes," I yelped into the phone. "I need to speak to him *right now*. If he calls Jerry Silver, we're done. Put him on right this second, or I disappear forever."

Oral B made a defeated clicking sound and passed the phone off to someone else. They exchanged a few words that I could not hear.

"Mr. Moscowitz," came the deep, dangerous voice of Abraham Lyons.

"Mr. Lyons. I need to talk to you."

"Then you need to come and meet me."

"No. You'll kill me."

"Mr. Moscowitz, DeAndre Muskingum is dead. He was dead before the story was leaked. I have no other choice at this point than to believe that you are responsible for releasing our secret to the media. If you want to attempt to vindicate yourself, you'll come meet me. If not, I will gladly hang up the phone. You can keep running, and I will find you myself. Sooner than you think.

I won't be quite so willing to hear you out, should you choose the latter."

I thought about it. I didn't see any other option but to agree to meet him. "Two conditions," I said. "One, you *do not* call Jerry Silver. I know he promised to deliver me, but the plan has changed. Calling him now would complicate things greatly for both of us."

"Fine."

"Two—I'm bringing my friends. I'm not meeting you alone."

"No. Alone," he said simply, in a way that meant it was not even up for debate.

"I'm bringing my friends, Mr. Lyons, or I'm not coming. You can hunt me down if you want. We won't go down without a fight. It won't be clean or easy," I said coldly. This was the hardest stance I'd ever taken. Against the hardest man I'd ever known.

Lyons was silent awhile, then: "Fine."

"Where do I meet you?"

"You remember the store where we met last?"

"Yes, sir."

"I suggest you hurry the fuck up." He hung up.

I closed the cell phone and let out a huge, relieved breath.

I recounted the entire phone call for the rest of the car. "I had no choice," I said.

"We better hope he keeps his word," said Murray. "No joke. If he calls Jerry—I'm tellin' you—we're fucked. Jerry will know we've all turned, and he'll bullshit Lyons into believing that we're all to blame. It'll be a massacre as soon as we walk through his door."

"Might be one anyway," added Ramona. Glass half-smashed kind of gal.

"He won't call him," I said, trying to sound my most confident, though I most certainly was anything but.

chizapter 25

We pulled around to the back of the abandoned mini-mall. There were three vehicles parked there: a yellow Hummer, a black Bentley, and a black Navigator. Lou parked the Escalade at the very end, closest to the exit.

"Okay," said Murray, "How many guns we have?"

"I got mine, Kev's got his, you got yours, right?" asked Lou.

"Mine's fake," said Murray.

Lou snorted. "You shittin' me?"

"No. Sorry, guys."

"Aright, well, doesn't matta. We got the shotty in the back, and the two tranqs, too. And yours looks real, anyways."

"Yeah, it does," said Murray, handing the fake weapon to me. "You carry it," he said. "I'll take the shotgun."

I was okay with that. I tucked the gun into my waistband. I felt a bit tougher, despite the fact that it was firing blanks.

Murray continued laying out the plan. "We go in there, weapons holstered. Wally, you tell Lyons upfront that we're strapped. We go in first," he said, pointing to himself and Lou and Kevin. "You follow right behind. 'Kay?"

"'Kay," I agreed.

"Any problems, you hit the fuckin' floor. Find somethin' to crawl behind." His fake Italian accent had returned. He was getting into character. Balsamic Vinny was back.

"Got it," I said, nervous but ready.

"What about me?" asked Ramona.

"You stay here," Murray and I said at the exact same time.

"No, Wally! I'm coming with you!"

"No, you're not, Ramona!"

"Yes, I am!"

"Ramona—"

"Ramona, listen," Murray intervened. "If anything happens, we need you out here behind the wheel. You gotta get help or else we could all die in there."

"No. I'm going in. If anything happens to Wally, I want it to happen to me, too." Her eyes were full of tears again. This girl was the real deal.

"No," said Murray.

"Murray, I'm coming in. If you go without me, I'll just come in after you get inside. You're gonna have to shoot me with that fuckin' horse gun if you want to keep me in this car," she said.

Lou raised the tranq gun and looked at Murray with a raised eyebrow. Murray shook his head no. "Fine," he said. "But take this." He handed her a small knife.

"Fuck dat," said Kevin, bending down to reach for something by his feet. He pulled out a tiny .22 caliber pistol from an ankle holster. "Take that. Hold it in your hand, in your pocket. Safety is off." He smiled and winked at her.

"Thank you," she said, quietly admiring the shiny little weapon.

Ramona and I looked at each other. I held her hand. She leaned over and pecked me on the lips. "Go get 'em, you badass," she whispered.

I let Ramona out of the car, and then turned to give the Doctor a good rubbing before I left. I kissed his snout gently. I felt a pang of guilt for leaving him. "Be back in a few, bud. Lay low." I closed the car door.

The five of us approached the building as one cohesive unit. Lou knocked on the door. After a heart-pounding ten seconds, it creaked open a crack. Someone peered out and then the door closed again. The guard was no doubt giving his scouting report to the boss inside. A few moments later the door creaked open again. Oral B's big fat brother Yo Yo Pa looked at us with deadened eyes and grinding teeth as he motioned for us to come in with a quick cock of the head. He had a silver pistol in his hand, hanging down by his big fat hip. The room was completely dark, except for a spotlighted circle in the center. The silence was creepy. "Walk to the circle," said Yo Yo Pa. "All y'all."

We walked blindly toward the spotlighted area, trying to adjust our eyes to the dark regions, straining to see who else was in the room. The circle of light was just big enough for the five of us. "Stand wit your backs against each other, in a circle," said Yo Yo Pa. We did so, after some awkward maneuvering.

The lights suddenly went on. Brilliant whiteness filled the room, blinding us all. When we stopped seeing spots we were greeted by the sight of Oral B, his brothers, Teddy Bizzle and Yo Yo Pa, Abraham Lyons, and the two giants I'd come to know so well, standing in a half-circle around us, each with a weapon or two pointed at us. There were small pistols, large pistols, and sawed-off shotguns. Lyons was holding what appeared to be a micro-Uzi. Oh, the guns came in all sorts of wonderful shapes and sizes.

We all stood tough, our shoulders pressing a bit harder on each other than they'd been a moment ago. Even *without* the guns Lyons had a menacing effect on people; *with* the guns, it was like an instant enema. I observed in that tense moment that the giants stared at Kevin and Lou with particular hatred, having been shot by the two goombahs with the tranquilizer gun earlier in the day.

"You ever notice, Mr. Moscowitz," said Lyons matter-of-factly, "that sometimes, when you turn the radio off, you suddenly realize upon hearing the silence that the music had been way too loud?"

"Wh-what?"

"People are like that too, you know. Sometimes you don't

notice just how goddamned loud someone is until you manage to shut them up for good." He flicked the safety off on his Uzi and leveled it at my head. "Talk," he said.

Gulp. "O-okay. Well, Mih-Mr. Lyons. Ih-it's not what you think, a-all of this. I mean, it's all wrong. I-I didn't do any, I mean, I didn't d-do what, I mean, I *definitely* would neh-never do the things—anything—that, uh, that you think I-I-I would neh-never—"

"You better quit stuttering and get your shit together, Mr. Moscowitz. The press conference is in less than three hours. I'm 'bout ready to see your head splattered on the concrete wall behind you."

I hadn't had time to really think my explanation through in advance. I certainly wasn't expecting this level of pressure. I was blowing my chance, and *fast.* "O-okay. I'm sorry. Mr. Lyons." I took another deep breath, determined now to keep my cool and explain myself in a cogent way. "There is a lot going on here . . . that you are not . . . aware of. I *did not* release ow-our secret to the media. I did not tell *anyone* about it, in-in fact. I did *not* t-try to extort any money out of you, either. I would *n-never, ever, ever* do any of those things. I have been nothing but loyal and honest with you f-from from minute one. I do, however, know who is responsible f-for all of it."

"Oh? And who might that be, Mr. Honest and Loyal?" said Lyons. "I hope you're not going to try to tell me that it was DeAndre Muskingum again. Because I am quite certain that Mr. Muskingum was unable to make any phone calls to anyone as of yesterday morning. Certainly not the media. Unless, of course, he was calling from beyond the grave."

"Well, n-no. Not Deezy. He had something to do w-with it all, but, but he wasn't the one p-pulling the strings."

"No? Indulge me, Mr. Moscowitz. Who was the brilliant puppet master?"

"Jerry Silver," I said.

Lyons chuckled. "Jerry Silver," he repeated in a familiar way, as if they were old friends. One of the men holding the guns in the half-circle around us made an annoyed sound. "Jerrrrrrrrry Silver, huh?"

"Yes. S-sir," I said.

"Somehow I'm not surprised," he said. "*Mister* Jerry Silver. The mystery man who suddenly appeared to deliver you to me on a silver platter. How convenient."

"Y-yes, I know."

"Well, Detective Moscowitz. Tell me more. And you better hurry. I got itchy fingers."

"Okay, well, m-me and you aren't the only ones who Jerry Silver tried to blackmail. My friends here, too."

"This is a big posse you got here! Lot of scratchin' for my itchy trigger fingers."

"Sir, this . . . p-posse is exactly how I can prove to you that Jerry is the master manipulator behind all of this. He's been maneuvering, lying and ch-cheating these people just as he has you and me. And I'd be willing to bet that there are other people who Jerry has blackmailed over the years who could validate my story, too. *Our* story," I said, pointing to Lyons and myself.

"*Our* story, huh?" I detected from his tone that I might have his ear now. "Explain to me how this is *our* story."

"Well, I haven't worked out, uh, *all* of the details yet, sir, but it goes something like this: I had my run-in in the bathroom with Deezy, wh-which you know about. Somehow, and I'm not *exactly* sure how yet, but somehow that set everything in motion. Now, the *only people* in my life who knew what my actual job was were my agent, *Jerry,* whom I've known for years and I trusted implicitly, and my girlfriend, Sue Schadenfreude, whom I also trusted completely."

"Mistakes on *both* parts, from what I understand," said Lyons.

"What?" I asked, wondering what he knew about Sue.

"I found out how Mr. Muskingum discovered our little secret, Mr. Moscowitz. Turns out that your 'completely trusted' girlfriend was having a secret love affair with Mr. Muskingum. I understand it was quite serious between them."

"He been hittin' dat shit fo a long-ass time!" added Teddy Bizzle.

"Yes," I said sadly.

"Yes. I have quite a few questions for Ms. Schadenfreude."

"She's gone," I blurted. "Skipped town."

"Skipped town, huh? Oh, that's too bad!" he said with a tiny smirk of satisfaction. "Jeez, I wonder if we'll ever find her." He didn't sound too worried. I heard one of the giants chuckling.

"She's the one who called the media on us," I said coldly.

"Pardon?"

"She's the one who leaked the secret to the press. Because she believed that you killed her . . . her *lover* . . . D-Deezy."

Lyons said nothing. He pursed his lips and took in a slow deep breath through his nose. He was letting this information digest. Finally he said, "Let me say *this:* If what you say is true, Mr. Moscowitz, then mark my words"—he walked over to me and leaned down to my level—"the media will not be hearing from Ms. Schadenfreude ever, *ever* again. No one will." He stood up and walked away from me with slow, deliberate steps. *"However . . . ,"* he said, turning to me, "so far, Mr. Moscowitz, I don't see how you were . . . how did you put it? 'Nothing but loyal and honest' with me 'from minute one'? This is all your fault, as far as I can surmise."

"Lemme blast this fool!" said Oral B, taking a step closer and cocking his gun, putting it disturbingly close to my temple.

"No! B! Please! It's not my—Mr. Lyons! Please! None of this would have happened if it hadn't been for Jerry Silver!"

"You better start making a case, Mr. Moscowitz." He signaled for Oral B to back off. B slowly lowered his gun, clicking with dissatisfaction.

"Okay. So, I figure that Jerry's been waiting to do this for a very long time—extort money from you, I mean—and for whatever reason, chose now to do it. I had my run-in with

Deezy in the bathroom. You suspended me. And I don't think our meeting in the bathroom was an accident. I think he must have been in cahoots with Jerry somehow and they planned for something to happen—maybe with the intent of getting me into trouble with you. I don't know. I may be giving them too much credit. But then Dr. Schwartzman was dognapped. That turned out to be by Sue, who was going to skip town with Deezy and wanted to take my dog with her. Jerry used that to his advantage. He sent me a ransom note for my dog, instructing me to be quiet, and he planted the idea in my head that you were responsible for taking the dog and sending me the note. He knows me; he knew that I would keep my mouth shut. But, just to be absolutely sure, he sent in Ramona"—I pointed to her—"who he was also blackmailing—to distract me, and take my mind off my dog, you, et cetera. I believe that Sue didn't know of Deezy's involvement with Jerry or about the ransom notes, but that Deezy talked her into taking the dog and made her think it was her own idea."

I veered off from the story to explain all about Ramona and how Jerry had fucked with her for so long. Lyons asked a few pointed questions, seemingly intrigued by the whole tangled web that Jerry had woven.

"Then the incident with the gun happened in my apartment. I still haven't *quite* figured that out, to be honest, but I know it fits somehow, because while it was going down, Jerry used that time to extort some *more* money out of me." I briefly explained to him the situation with Bionic Books and how Jerry sold my books just so he could keep all the money, since I believed it was for ransom. Lyons was absorbing my tale, which I was spitting out a mile a minute. "The Italian guys who got me out of the police station? That's these guys. They work—*worked*—for Jerry, too. They're supposed to be bringing me to you right now. But Jerry was blackmailing them, too, believe it or not, and basically, we all just figured this out." I told Lyons about Vinny/Murray. Again, Lyons asked a few pointed questions, astonished at the levels of exploitation that Jerry was capable of. "And then, when all the pieces were properly in place—me scared into silence, Deezy set to take the fall—Jerry sent *you* the ransom note for the ten million dollars, I guess with the intent to make you think it was from me. And it all seemed to be working. But then, when Deezy ended up dead, Sue went public with the story and that fucked everything up. Jerry didn't plan on that. His ten million was *gone* once that happened. But he found out that you were offering a bounty on my head, and that became his consolation prize. And so here we are."

Lyons's face held his signature look, somehow pensive and vacant all at once. I was tempted to say more, but I didn't. I was pleased with my explanation. Eventually, he said, "Well . . . That is quite a yarn, Mr. Moscowitz. Now please, if you would, explain to me just one . . . more . . . thing."

"Yes?"

He switched off the safety on his micro-Uzi again, stepped to me, and leveled it at my eye. "Explain to me why I shouldn't blow your heads off." He brought the sights of the gun up to his eye, winking into it and slowly (so damn slowly) panning us all with its thin black nozzle.

"Wha-what?" Ramona grabbed my hand and squeezed.

"Was that too hard to follow?" he asked, still winking into the weapon and panning slowly. "Allow me to be more explicit. What I said was, explain to me, Mr. Moscowitz, why I should *not* blow . . . your fucking . . . *heads* . . . *off.*" He enunciated each word ever-so-painfully. "As in, pull this trigger, and spray many small bullets into your collective faces. Because, as I see it, Mr. Moscowitz, ultimately you are still the source of all of my problems. *And* the solution. It all goes back to *you*, and I've got a press conference in"—he removed his eye briefly from the gun and looked at his watch—"two hours and thirty-five minutes, at which time I have a lot of explaining to do. It would be very easy to end this right here. Right now."

In a way, Lyons was right. If it hadn't been for me, Jerry

never would have known about the true nature of my job and wouldn't have been able to target Lyons. And furthermore, Sue wouldn't have known about my job, and wouldn't have been able to spill the news to her boyfriend and then to the media. He was right. It did all go back to me. And he *could* solve his problems by killing us all right there. *And he would.* I was suddenly sure of it.

But then I remembered: I had a safety net. "You shouldn't kill me, Mr. Lyons. Definitely not."

"I asked you *why* I should not kill you, not *if.*"

"Because I have something to offer that will prove that these charges are bullshit."

"What proof could you possibly have to offer?"

"Me."

"Excuse me?"

"Me," I said. "I am the best proof you could ever have. I am much more valuable to you alive than dead. What would killing me accomplish? The media wants to know who I am. The whole world is talking about me. What good would it be if I were to disappear, or worse, turn up dead? That would be pretty suspicious, right? Rumors would fly forever, and, pardon my saying so, but most likely, you and Oral B would be kinda fuhh—uhh, you know, in trouble. There would *always* be questions. But the fact is, there's no *proof* that I wrote Oral B's lyrics. If I were to show up at that press conference *with* you, telling the world that the whole story was bullshit, that I was simply a Godz-Illa employee and that this was all a hoax perpetrated by Jerry Silver, you'd be in much better shape."

He considered that. I was astounded that Lyons hadn't come up with this idea himself. Maybe he couldn't see past his misguided anger toward me. "Hm," he said with a small, slow nod. He paused to deliberate. The rest of his guys looked agitated. I wanted to plead with my old friend Oral B, who looked so anxious to put a bullet in my face and end this nonsense that I couldn't even make eye contact, for fear that he would snap.

"But who's to say that the public and the media won't simply twist the story around, say that I *made* you say those things?"

"Well, the ace in the hole is that we can pin the entire thing on Jerry Silver and we have proof! We'll tell the whole world of his plan to extort ten million dollars out of you. We have actual evidence—the ransom notes! And, not only that, but we have the three of us"—I gestured to Ramona and Murray—"as further evidence that Jerry Silver is a devious, blackmailing son of a bitch. Maybe other clients of his will come forward with stories that jibe with ours."

Finally, Lyons said, "Prove it."

"Wh-what?" I asked.

"I said 'prove it,' Mr. Moscowitz."

"P-prove what . . . ?"

"The press conference is in approximately two and a half hours. You want off the hook? Bring Jerry Silver to me. *Quickly.* I want to hear it from the horse's mouth. My men will go with you, and they will execute you if you try to run. They will do the same if you fail to bring him to me in one hour. Bring me Jerry Silver on the platter that you were supposed to be on, or it's *your ass.*"

"But, Mr. Ly—"

"That's all." He turned and walked away, over to his desk. "Time ticks, Mr. Moscowitz."

chizapter 26

We hustled out of the dark, abandoned storeroom, past murderous looks from Oral B and his brothers. Oral B looked like he needed to be restrained. The two giants stopped briefly to get whispered orders from Lyons and then followed us outside—they would be accompanying us to go retrieve Jerry.

We piled back into the Escalade, the giants in their own big black SUV, and we were on our way.

"Now what?" I asked.

"Well," said Murray. "We can head for the hills, and keep on runnin', and hope we can get away from the long arm of the Lyons . . . or we can go get Jerry."

This one was a no-brainer.

"Call Jerry," I said. "Tell him you made the drop, everything is fine, and you're headed to him with the money."

"Right-o," said Murray, pulling out his phone.

"If we can't get him, we'll have to resort to some sort of escape plan, that's all." We all knew that escape was not a legitimate option. "Where were you supposed to meet him to make the money drop?" I asked.

"Don't know," he said, dialing and bringing the phone up to his ear. We all watched in silence. Murray gave us the thumbs up. "Jerry. Hey. Done deal . . . yeah. Went fine. Yep, got it.

Counted twice. Okay. Okay. You bet! We're on the way. Right."
He collapsed the phone closed.

"His house. Culver City," said Murray with a grin.

....

"I wanna punch him in the face," I said decisively, as we waited
at a traffic light on Venice Boulevard a few minutes later. "I
think I really need to do that. Ya know? Like, avenge myself, or
whatever." The new Wally Moscowitz could do stuff like punch
people. The old Wally Moscowitz could only get punched.

"Uhh, sure, pal," said Murray, clearly dubious of my face-
punching capabilities.

"Like, maybe we can ring the bell, door opens, and *wham!* I
wallop him right in his fat mouth. Then we move on from there.
Sound like a plan?"

"I think just me and the boys should go up first, though,
Wally. Just in case Jerry's watching out a window. Then once
we're in, you and Ramona and the two linebackers back there
can come in and do as much face punching as you please. Sound
good?"

"Deal," I said with a satisfied nod, as we turned onto a small,
not-too-rich-not-too-poor residential street in Culver City. In all
the years I'd known Jerry, I'd never been invited to his home.
That was fine with me, but I'd always wondered what it must be
like.

After making another turn onto another small, residential
street, Murray told Lou to pull over. I turned and watched the
giants pull up right behind us. "Lemme go tell the big guys the
plan. I want them to wait a few minutes to pull into the driveway
after we do," he said. "Maybe you two should ride with them
from here," Murray said to me and Ramona. I felt her grip
tighten on my hand.

"No!" I blurted, a little bit too loudly. "Sorry, no," I said. "I don't feel comfortable putting Ramona anywhere near them after what they tried to do to her this morning."

"Okay. Fair enough," agreed Murray, hopping out and waddling back toward the giants' SUV.

"Thank you," Ramona whispered to me, planting a tender little kiss on my neck, and a tender little woody in my shorts.

"Fuckin' scumbags," said Lou under his breath.

A few minutes later, we pulled into Jerry's driveway. His house was a one-story structure, circa 1960-something, with a flat roof with pebbles all over it. The white and brown paint covering the house was peeling and chipped, a few windows were cracked and unpatched, screens torn, and the front lawn was a mess of weeds and skeletons of plants that once were. The most impressive part of the house by far was the silver Vette sitting on the pocked and potholed driveway, and that's not saying much.

Despite the fact that the windows on the Escalade were darkly tinted, Ramona and I scrunched down in the backseat, just to ensure that there was no way Jerry could catch a glimpse of us, should he have been looking out a window. "Good luck, guys," I said quietly, just before the three car doors slammed shut around us. We sat on the floor between the front and back seats, hugging our knees to our chests, and waited.

....

Bang!

"Was that a gunshot?" I asked Ramona, my ears perked, my head cocked to the side alertly. Dr. Schwartzman held the same exact pose. We'd been sitting in the car for only a few minutes, but of course, it had felt like weeks.

"What? No. I don't *think* so," she responded, cocking her head in mirror image of the Doctor and me. "I didn't hear it." We all sat there on the backseat floor of the SUV, heads cocked, switching the angle and direction of our cockage from one side to the other—as if one ear might reveal the sound better than the other—looking like total idiots.

"You didn't hear that?"

Bang!

"There it is again!"

Ramona switched the angle of her head-cocking again. "I think it was just—"

Tap, tap, tap.

The giants were at our window. The *bangs* I'd heard had been their car doors closing. *Calm down, Wally.* I jumped out of the SUV, my nerves revving like a Hemi. I decided to bring the Doctor in with us this time. Maybe Jerry would feel worse about what he'd done upon seeing how devastatingly adorable the Doctor was.

The five of us—Ramona, Dr. Schwartzman, the two giants and I—strode up to the front door. "Don't ring the bell, jes' bust right on in," said the Samoan Giant. I was feeling tough with them at my back, and I'd intended to do just that. I stepped up to the front door and tested the knob discreetly—it was unlocked. I gave it a small push, just to make sure it would indeed open when I kicked it, and then I stepped back and kicked with all my might. The door flew inward and smashed against the wall behind it, ricocheting back toward me. I caught it smoothly with my left hand, removed my glasses with my right, and stepped inside like the badass superhero come to save the day, with my crew of superbadass sidekicks right behind me.

Jerry and Murray and the boys were standing in the living room, in full view of the front door. Jerry spun around upon hearing the sound and looked right at us. The series of emotions that played across his face was priceless: first he was startled by the sound, then came shock, then bewilderment, then fear (upon noticing the giants), then escape instinct, then anger and confusion upon being grabbed and held there by Lou and Kevin, and then complete realization of the situation, and comprehension of just how fucked he really was.

"Uh oh," said Jerry, his composure regained, a snide grin on his fat face now, "Johnny Loser and his posse of *suckers* have come to capture the bad guy." He was smiling big now. Somehow, the prick was fucking *smiling*. If I'd had a spear I would have thrown it through his chest at that moment. A samurai sword, I would have lopped his fat head off. A sickle, I would have . . . mmm, not quite sure what to do with a sickle.

"We know about everything you did, Jerry," I said, my eyes filled with as much revulsion as I could muster. "How could you have done this to me? After all these years?"

"Get over it, Mosco. You got played like a schmuck, and I'm glad I don't have to deal with your pussy bullshit anymore."

I looked at him, saddened that I could have been so taken in by this piece of shit in sheep's clothing. "We're taking you to Lyons," I said.

"Well whoopty-friggin'-doo," said Jerry. Somehow Jerry really didn't seem scared at all. "Take me to your leader," he said in a cartoony alien voice, chuckling at himself. "Suckers," he muttered under his breath. *How the hell isn't he shitting in his pants right now?* I thought.

"C'mon over, Wally," said Lou. "You wanna punch him?"

It wasn't quite how I'd imagined it, but yeah, I *did* want to punch him. I walked over. Lou and Kevin stood behind him, each one of them holding one of Jerry's arms tightly, adjusting their footing, bracing for my punch. "Go 'head," said Lou. I tightened my fist, cocked it back slightly, licked my lips.

Jerry looked down at me and laughed a *pfff-fff-fff* sort of laugh, his shoulders wracking mockingly.

"What?" I asked self-consciously, my fist loosening and lowering involuntarily.

"You. That's *what*," replied Jerry with a derisive smile.

"What's so funny about me getting ready to punch you? You don't think it's gonna hurt to get punched?"

"Uhhh, not by you, slugger."

"No?" I asked, readying myself, my fist tightening again, knowing that he was only fueling my hatred, making it easier for me to throw the punch. *Nail this fat fuck!* I thought. *Everyone is watching!* I cocked my fist back a little further, squeezing it tight as I could, feeling awkward but determined, my adrenaline pumping, all eyes in the room on me. I was about to swing when—

"*Haaa!* Look at this little shit!" Jerry blurted. "You gonna hit me or what, Mosco? C'mon! Today, Tyson!" Jerry laughed again and shook his head. *Hit him. Now.* I reared back. Then: "You're a fuckin' loser, Mosco. Always have been, always will be."

You would think that this would have been the straw that broke the camel's back, the thing that made me lose it and just punch him square in his fat face, George McFly–style, right? But instead, it took the wind right out of my sails.

I dropped my fist. "If I'm such a *loser*, why did you waste so many years on me, Jerry? Trying to sell my books? Huh? You must have had *some* faith in me."

"Please. I knew from our very first conversation that you were a loser, Mosco! You came to me at that party, a little tipsy, wanted to pitch your little book idea, and I thought, 'Fuck, that idea ain't half bad! I can probably make a buck off this kid!' So I signed you. Your ideas were good—I'll give you that. I knew I'd be able to take advantage of you at some point—I mean, you *completely* bought my bullshit. And then, lo and behold, after working with you for a little bit, I hit the jackpot of all jackpots. I find out you work for one of the richest guys in town! And that woulda been enough for me! But no! Turns out you've got a little secret that you haven't told anyone except your cunt-hole girl-friend, and now *me*, your trusty Uncle Jerry. And voilà—my bet paid off. It was only a matter of time before I took advantage, pal. You're a born loser, Mosco. Nothing more. A patsy. All of you are. Losers like you don't make it in this world. You don't have the *balls*. Trust me when I say, you will never amount to jack shi—"

He was cut off when my fist smashed into his mouth and nose, sending blood and one of his front teeth flying through the air.

chizapter 27

Fut the fuck! You knocked my fuckin' toof out!" screamed Jerry, hunched over, hands to his mouth. Kevin and Lou had dropped his arms when I hit him. I stood and watched him, in shock, slowly shaking my hand out.

"That was from all of us, you *piece of shit,*" I said proudly.

He slowly raised his eyes up at me. Next thing I knew, Jerry was charging right for me. He moved pretty quickly for a guy his size, like a rhino or some other big fat bloody-mouthed thing, and I froze up. He would have made it to me too, had he not been clotheslined by the White Giant, who'd sprung up between us with a rock-solid arm to Jerry's chin. Jerry went down. *Hard.* He landed on his back with an audible *splat,* his head banging back against the hardwood floor. He began to cough and wheeze.

I looked down at my stinging hand, which was cut and bleeding from Jerry's tooth. It felt *awesome.* At that moment I was the toughest motherfucker in the world. I glanced over at Ramona, who looked scared but quietly proud. I stepped over to Jerry and stood above him, menacing and triumphant. "How's it feel to get your teeth knocked out by a no-balls loser-schlub, Jerry?"

"Vuck you, Osco," he spat. I kicked him in his round, protruding belly. He doubled over and coughed some more. I heard Lou and Kevin laughing with appreciation.

"Get him up," said Murray. Lou and Kevin came over and helped Jerry up onto his feet. They both had to hold Jerry by his meaty arms in order for him to remain standing. Murray, Ramona, and I stood across from him. He looked up at us with beaten, bloodshot eyes, his breath coming in ragged gasps.

"Do what you want to me," Jerry said through his bloody, freshly swollen lips and missing teeth. "You guys are still *phucked* . . . Speshally you," he said, looking at me with hatred in his eyes and a half smile on his busted lips.

"Yeah? How do you figure?" I asked him, still feeling victorious.

"Turn on the TB," he said, urging me with his head toward the medium-sized flat-screen across the room. I looked at Murray, worried now. He shrugged. I crossed the poorly decorated room, with its white shag carpeting and poofy brownish-red leather couches, and switched on the television. "Put da dews on," said Jerry.

Uh oh. What else could *possibly* be happening that I didn't already know about? *Why does Jerry look so fucking pleased?* The news was just coming back on after a commercial break. "BREAKING NEWS" slashed across the bottom of the screen in dramatic red letters with a music sting added for further melodramatic effect. The anchorman, Dennis Fitzpatrick, started in: "Thanks again for joining us for this eight o'clock edition of Channel 2 News. Breaking news to report out of West Los Angeles in a case believed to be directly related to the ongoing story we've been reporting about the controversy surrounding rap star Oral B and his boss, Abraham Dandy Lyons. Police have issued an arrest warrant and an all points bulletin for a Caucasian male, age thirty-one, named Wally Moscowitz, who is now wanted for a murder that was committed yesterday right here in Los Angeles County. The victim of that apparent homicide, a DeAndre Muskingum, age twenty-nine, of Inglewood, an employee of Godz-Illa Records, was found shot to death yesterday in Echo Park. Authorities tell us that the weapon that was used in the murder—discovered at the crime scene—was found to have suspect Wally Moscowitz's fingerprints on it."

Now I understood why the gun was hanging in my doorway that day. Jerry killed Deezy. Not Lyons, as I'd been suspecting. He needed to get my prints on the gun in order to set me up. *But if it was Deezy in the Homer Simpson mask, why did he frame me for his own murder?*

The anchorman continued, "Now we go out to Julie Morgan, who is standing in front of the Godz-Illa Records building in Santa Monica. Julie?"

"Tension is running at a *fever pitch* here in Santa Monica, Dennis, as the confused, angry crowd continues to grow outside of Godz-Illa headquarters in anticipation of this evening's press conference. The people gathered here just want to know what the facts are in this *baffling* story."

The screen cut to some footage of interviews with fans and protesters that they'd recorded earlier outside of the Godz-Illa Records building. The first interviewee was a large black woman with breasts like oven mitts and the most horrendous black-and-purple curled wig I'd ever seen. "We want answers, man! It's crazy! They got some little murderin' white dude writin' they songs? That's crazy! But yo, we stand by them guys! Oral B and them? They make good songs, man. Like, personally? I don't really care, man."

Next they cut to a young white kid with a too-crooked hat. "It *sucks,* yo! If Oral B is frontin', and some lil sucka named Willy or whateva is writin' all his shiznit, that's just mad stupid, yo. It's whack! It ain't real, yo! They supposed to keep it real, man! Na mean?"

Back to Julie Morgan, field reporter extraordinaire. "That's just a taste of the sort of agitated hullabaloo on the sidewalks of Santa Monica at this hour. We're waiting for any more information that might calm this restless mob."

"Julie, I'm sorry, we're gonna have to break away from you as we receive some more breaking news here . . . I'm being told . . . we now have the first confirmed pictures of the suspect, Wally Moscowitz." A fuzzy image popped up in the corner of the screen. It was a very low-quality picture, but it was definitely me. It looked like Oral B was in the immediate background in the picture, and we seemed to be in a car together. The anchorman continued. "The man at the forefront of this image is said to be the suspect, Wally Moscowitz, the now infamous man put in place by uber-producer Abraham Dandy Lyons in what looks to be the ultimate act of show business fakery, and just behind him is embattled star Brandunn Bell, aka Oral B."

I looked at Jerry. "Did you get this picture on TV?" He winked proudly and made a clicking sound effect to go along with it.

Dennis Fitzpatrick continued, "Again, this is the first reported image of *blaaaaaaaahblahblahblahblahblah* . . ." Everything faded into murk and cloudiness as I stared at the picture in the corner.

How do I know this picture? Everything about it was familiar. The clothes I was wearing. The way I was sitting. The expression on my face.

The blunt in my hand.

I had to talk to Lyons.

....

"Call your boss," I said to the Samoan Giant.

"Hold up, hold up," he said, pointing at the TV. "Looks like there's more."

Dennis Fitzpatrick continued, "Channel 2 News has learned from police that a city employee, parking enforcement officer Rico Gomez, spotted the suspect earlier today traveling with a group of men in a black Cadillac Escalade. Officer Gomez reports that when he approached the men, he was assaulted and badly injured. Police are now on the lookout for a black Cadillac Escalade, license plate number E B R 5 1 2. Again, that's E B R 5 1 2."

I clicked off the television.

I was officially wanted by the cops. For murder. Little old me. Wally Moscowitz. Running from Johnny Law. The new Wally was in full motherfuckin' eff-iz-ect.

The novelty wore off real quick, though, and reality set in. *I was wanted by the cops. For murder.*

Yeah—not so cool.

Particularly uncool at this hour, with the press conference looming. In order to clear my name (as well as those of Oral B and Lyons), I needed to be *at* that press conference. *Onstage.* I couldn't do that if there was an arrest warrant for felony murder in my name. Besides the fact that the cops would probably snatch me before I even got to the mic, I wasn't such a valuable asset for Lyons anymore—not as a murder suspect. In fact, I was worthless. My whole pitch to him—the "safety net"—was now kaput. Things were not looking good.

Of course, I had a new little piece of info now that could possibly save my ass with Lyons. The picture. Actually, the photographer.

Teddy Bizzle.

He'd taken the picture with his camera phone as we smoked pot in the Hummer the previous day. That meant he was somehow in cahoots with Jerry. Oral B's brother. Was this big enough to get me off the hook with Lyons? I wasn't sure. It certainly wasn't going to get me out of trouble with the cops. I needed something more. Like, *now.*

I glanced over at the giants, wondering if they were bright enough to grasp the implications of this breaking news. *Will they shoot me if they realize that I'm no longer useful to Lyons?* I hoped that Lyons wouldn't hear the news of my warrant in his little secret office in the abandoned storefront.

It's only a matter of time before they get the orders to kill me, I thought, looking at the giants. *What the fuck am I gonna do?* This was desperation time. I began to pace. I put my hand in my pocket. It landed on my crappy old cell phone, and *bam!* I had an idea. A revelation.

A long shot.

But it was all I had.

I turned to Jerry. I shook my head in a show of defeat. I put my hand to my forehead, feigning despair. I sighed histrionically. I took a breather. I slapped my hand down on a side table and yelled, "Fuck!" All the while one hand fiddled around a bit in my pocket.

"Looks like you're right, Jerry. I guess I'm pretty fucked," I announced.

Jerry pounced. "You were fucked the very minute you tried to tangle wit the best, fucko," he said through his swollen lip. "I'm Jerry Fucking Silver. Don't you ever fucking forget it."

"I don't know *how* the hell you did it, Jerry. God! I gotta admit, it was kind of genius. I mean, *fuck!* You fooled *everybody!*"

"You're goddamned right I did," said Jerry proudly, struggling, as his arms were still held tightly by Kevin and Lou. "It's not too hard when everyone around you is a fucking idiot!"

"But how could I have not seen that it was you pulling the strings the whole time? You were blackmailing me and Ramona and Murray *and* Lyons all at the same time and none of us figured it out?! I wouldn't think you were smart enough to pull something of this magnitude off!"

"Oh please," he said. "I've got the media and the whole world eating out of the palm of my hand."

"Just tell me one thing, Jerry. Please. 'Cause I'm missing something. Did you actually kill DeAndre Muskingum? Set me up?"

Jerry looked around a second, and it seemed to me like he was deciding whether to out himself in front of all these people. His ego got the best of him. "You're goddamned right I killed that scumbag!" He laughed to himself, before saying, "But not before I used him to do all my dirty work for me! Dumbest schmuck of you all!"

"Jerry, how could you *kill* somebody?"

"Oh *please,* Mosco. C'mon, guy. We're talking about ten million bucks here, sport! He would have ruined my whole plan! One less worthless schvatza the world has to contend with. Big friggin' deal. You should be happy I killed him! He was bangin' your woman!"

I shook my head. It didn't take any great acting to express my disbelief at the temerity of this man I'd thought I'd known for so many years.

Jerry added, "That moron actually believed I was gonna split Lyons's money with him. *Haaaa!* Just another idiot who got played like a fiddle."

"You know what, genius?" I asked. "One problem in all your brilliant planning. It didn't work! You got *nothing.* Zero. And now we're gonna take you to Lyons. What you got to say about *that,* Mr. Fucking Brilliant?"

"I aaaaalways have a backup plan, Mosco. You'll see." And he smiled again.

A cell phone rang. The Samoan Giant patted his jacket, and reached for his pocket.

Lyons saw the news report. Oh shit. Here we go.

Jerry was grinning from ear-to-fucking-ear.

"Hey, Boss," said the Giant into his phone.

chizapter 28

Yeah, we there. Yeah, got him," Samoan Giant said to Lyons. I glanced as discreetly wide-eyed as I could at Murray, hoping he realized the severity of the situation. Murray returned my concerned look with a little nod. Both of our hands crept toward our pocketed weapons. I thought I saw Ramona doing the same, but maybe that was just wishful thinking. Lou and Kevin were occupied by holding Jerry, but I didn't think that they realized what was going on anyway. Jerry clearly *did* realize it, judging by his wicked grin. The White Giant seemed oblivious, too, tinkering with some small nicknack on Jerry's shelves. "Yeah. We just heard dat," Samoan Giant said into the phone to his boss. "Yeah. Oh, word? Yeah? Shit. Okay. Aight. Aight. Bet." He clicked his phone closed. I braced myself for whatever he might do next.

....

The giant put the cell phone into his pocket, but his hand lingered and searched there just a bit too long for my taste. *He's gonna pull his gun,* I thought. *Now or never!* I pulled out mine first.

"Don't move!" I said, swinging my weapon up at him. Murray was right with me, pulling his gun out and aiming it at the other giant. They both threw their hands up, palms toward us, bewildered.

"*Whoa!* The fuck, man?" said the Samoan Giant.

"What are you doing?" I asked.

"I'm not doing anything, man! I'm just puttin' my phone away, man!" he said, clearly scared of gun-totin' Wally Moscowitz.

"What were you just reaching for?" I asked him.

"What?"

"What . . . were . . . you . . . just . . . reaching . . . for?" I said slowly, sort of mimicking the cool, hard-core style of Abraham Lyons.

"Nothin' man! I was jes' putting my phone away, man! I swear!"

"What did Lyons just say to you? Did he tell you to kill us?"

"Kill you? What? No, man!"

I took a step closer and jutted my gun at him a little bit and said, "Don't fucking lie to me, man!"

"I ain't lyin', dude! I swear!"

"What'd he say, then?"

"He said that Detective Schlage just called him to tip him off that the po po connected Jerry Silver to you, and they're on their way here to look for you right now. He said to *get the fuck outta Dodge, man. Pronto.*"

"You serious?"

"Yeah, man! You think I use the word 'pronto' often? Look. I *swear.* I ain't lyin'! We gotta *go, fool!*"

"What about *him?*" I asked, gesturing to Jerry, feeling harried now.

"He said to bring him back wit us to the spot!"

I decided in that frantic moment that I believed him. I didn't think that he was capable of coming up with that elaborate story so quickly, and he looked genuinely scared—and it wasn't just because of my gun—he wasn't even looking at *that* anymore. He was throwing nervous glances toward the windows and the front door, like he expected SWAT to bust in at any moment.

"Okay . . ." I started to lower my gun. "Are we cool?"

"Yeah, man! We coo! Now let's be the fuck out, man!"

I tucked my gun back into my waistband. Murray, however, didn't lower his. "Give us your weapons," he said to the giants.

"What? Hell no, cuzzz! I ain't givin' you my piece! C'mon, man! We gotta go! They on the way!"

"How do we know you're not lying? Give us your guns, and we'll go! If Lyons verifies your story, we'll give them back! C'mon, man! We're just being safe!"

I guess if the decision was between giving up their weapons and getting arrested when the police arrived shortly, it wasn't a very difficult decision. They reluctantly held out their guns. I grabbed one and Murray the other.

"*Shit!* You hear that?" asked Ramona. We all froze.

I did hear it. It was distant, but still undeniable.

Sirens.

．．．．．．．．．．．．．．．．．．．．．．

We all bolted for the door. The giants were the first outside and to their SUV. Murray stopped and whispered to me, "What are we doing? You think it's safe to go back to Lyons still?"

I nodded. "I hope so. I've got a plan."

He raised his eyebrows worriedly. "You sure?"

"Sure I got one, not sure it'll work."

"Fuckin' A," he said, and shook his head.

"Yep," I agreed, as we rushed toward the exit. I scooped up the Doctor, because I can run much faster than he can. I glanced over my shoulder when I got to the door and caught a glimpse of Kevin and Lou dragging-shoving Jerry toward the exit.

"I'll go with the big guys," said Murray, following the giants to their SUV as the sirens drew closer. As soon as he was in their car, they screeched away.

"Who's driving?" I shouted as I backpedaled to the car.

Lou tossed me the keys, which slid through my fingers and hit the driveway with a clang, startling Doctor Schwartzman. I opened the door on the driver's side, handed the Doctor off to Ramona, who was already in her seat, and I climbed behind the wheel of the big vehicle. *No time to think. Just drive.* I started the engine and was about to reverse out of the driveway when I realized that Lou and Kevin and Jerry weren't in the back yet. I peered over Ramona and the Doctor, and what I saw was just no good.

Jerry was on the ground, on his belly. Arms and legs splayed out in an X. All three hundred and seventy-five pounds of him. Lou and Kevin were tugging on his arms, trying to drag him toward the Escalade. I jumped out and ran around to them. The sirens were terrifyingly close now.

"What happened?" I shouted frantically.

"He just hit the floor!" shouted Lou.

"You won't take me alive!" screamed Jerry from below.

"Fuck!" I said in a harsh whisper. I grabbed an arm with Lou. We pulled as hard as we could but we could barely move Jerry's flabby body. It was like trying to get a dead cow into an SUV. I don't know if you've ever tried that, but it's not easy. The sirens were so close now that we had to yell to hear each other. *"Drag him!"* I screamed.

We were ten feet from the car.

"I'm trying!" grunted Kevin through clenched teeth, his face crimson.

Eight feet, and moving too slowly.

"Pull!" yelled Lou, the sirens sounded like they were just about a block or two away.

Six feet . . .

Jerry was doing a great job of distributing his massive weight and dragging his heavy feet and just making it generally very fucking difficult to get his fat ass over to the car.

Four feet . . .

And then something bad happened.

As we made one final pull towards the SUV, my cell phone slipped out of my pocket, landing on the driveway with a crack, and then Lou's heavy heel came down on it as he tried to drag Jerry. My old phone shattered under his foot with an audible *crrrruuuunch*.

This didn't bode well for my plan. But I had bigger worries at the moment.

We got Jerry to the base of the vehicle, but it was clear that lifting him all the way up into the SUV was going to be nearly impossible. Especially now with the sirens practically upon us. *Fuck! Where are the fucking giants when you need them!?*

"Screw dis! We gotta go!" said Lou. "We're gonna get pinched!"

I agreed.

Time to abort. We left Jerry lying in the driveway.

I jumped behind the wheel again. Lou and Kevin got in the back. I threw the car in reverse and pulled out way too quickly with a screech, shifting it into drive before we had even come to a stop, and hitting the gas too hard again. The powerful truck shot forward. I kept the pedal to the proverbial metal as we sped off. The engine whined as the RPMs shot up into the red. I squeezed the steering wheel so tightly that I wouldn't have been surprised if juice came out of it. I busted a hard right at the first cross street we came to. I caught sight of the cop cars in the rearview just as I made the turn. I wasn't sure if they'd caught the same glimpse of me. *Stay on the smaller residential streets for now. We don't want to be spotted on a main road.*

"Anyone behind us?" I asked.

"Not sure," said Kevin.

We all held our breath as we moved farther and farther away from Jerry's house, expecting the cavalcade of lights and vehicles to pop up behind us at any moment.

After about thirty seconds, the sirens stopped.

They're at Jerry's, I realized.

"I think we're good," said Lou. I exhaled. *They've got Jerry now. Son of a bitch liked his chances better with the cops than with Lyons. Who knows what the hell he'll tell them.*

"Fuck!" shouted Lou, slapping the leather seat. "We fuckin' *blew* it! We're *fucked!* He gave us a chance and we *blew* it!"

"We can't go back to Lyons, Wally. You know that, right?" asked Kevin.

I glanced at Ramona, who looked terrified. "Is he gonna kill us?" she asked.

"Everybody calm down," I said. "Okay? He's *not* gonna kill us. And we have to go back. Murray's with them. But I've got a plan." Truth was, I wasn't sure if my little ploy had worked or not. My broken cell phone could complicate things greatly. I wouldn't know for a little while yet.

chizapter 29

When we arrived back at the storefront, we made our way inside with butterflies—no, that's too precious—*giant evil bats* flapping around in our bellies. Lyons was at his desk, his micro-Uzi resting to his immediate left. That was a bummer.

Oral B, his two brothers, and the giants were sitting around a cheap folding card table, watching the news on a smallish, silver television.

Murray was sitting by himself on a chair in a different part of the room, fingering the Star of David that dangled from one of his gold chains. Everyone except Lyons looked up when we came in. The expressions on their faces when they saw that we were Jerry-less ran the gamut from pissed off to surprised to quizzical to nervous to terrified.

It took everything I had not to look at Teddy Bizzle. I knew that once Lyons found out that Teddy took that picture, it was gonna get ugly. What he'd done was a grave offense in this courtroom.

Lyons looked up only after we were all in the room and the door was closed and locked behind us, and when he did, for the first time I could see how stressed he was. He had dark rings under his heavy-lidded eyes. He scanned the bunch of us. "Where is he?" he asked.

I realized that it was probably my job to speak, but I couldn't summon my voice.

"Where is Jerry Silver, Mr. Moscowitz?" he asked again, his voice filled to the brim with irritation.

"We lost him," I confessed.

"What do you mean, you lost him? Doesn't he weigh four hundred pounds? I was told you were on your way back with him."

"We were, sir, but he managed to slip away right as the cops were about to arrive. So we had to, you know, *go*."

I expected him to lose it right then and there. Instead, he was silent. It was even worse that way. The silence was like getting kicked in the balls over and over and over again.

He stared at me like he was asleep with his eyes open. I realized that if I didn't tell him about Teddy *now,* there was a good chance he was going to pick up the Uzi and kill us all.

"It was him!" I suddenly blurted, pointing at Teddy. I'm pretty smooth, I know. Teddy jumped up with hands out in front of him defensively. He looked like he was on the cover of *Deer in the Headlights Magazine.*

Everybody else in the room was completely confused by this sudden outburst. Heads whipped back and forth like a tennis match viewed in fast forward. "Teddy took that picture!" I yelled, pointing at the TV.

"What are you raving about, Mr. Moscowitz?" asked Lyons, looking uncomfortable for maybe the first time ever.

"The picture of me on the news! Jerry Silver sent it to the media, but Teddy took it. With his camera phone."

Teddy, in what I felt was a pretty inappropriate response, pulled out his gun and aimed it right at me. I threw my hands up and stumbled backward a bit. Confusion took over as everyone pulled out their respective pieces. Murray, Lyons, Lou, Kevin, and both giants aimed at Teddy. Yo Yo Pa and Oral B didn't seem to know where to aim. Their weapons tick-tocked in the air like the pointer on the *Wheel of Fortune* wheel. Everybody shouted at everybody else. I stood frozen, staring into the barrel of Teddy's gun, only about six feet from my face.

"Ey!" Teddy shouted, his gun wobbling a bit with the exertion of vocalization. Everyone around him continued to yell and panic. "*Ey!* Listen up! *Ey!*" he shouted over the racket. The chorus died down. "Y'all muhfuckas listen up, aight?"

Oral B and Yo Yo Pa had their guns pointed down at the floor now. They looked like lost children, confused and scared. Teddy just looked crazy.

"What the fuck is goin' on, nigga?" asked B, as worried as I'd ever heard him.

"Listen up, man! It ain't how it looks!" said Teddy.

"It better not be, nigga!" said B.

"It ain't, man!"

"Aight den! You best start talkin', dawg! B'fo Dandy lights yo ass up, man!"

"Yo—I'll put this shit down, aight?" said Teddy, lowering his pistol slowly to the table while looking directly at Lyons. Teddy suddenly looked more scared than crazy. "Aight?"

"Explain yourself, Teddy," said Lyons, his eyes as round and menacing as I'd ever seen them. *"Now."*

"Hey, man, evvybody put dey guns down, man. Lemme explain, man."

Lyons cocked his gun violently. Pointed it at Teddy's temple. *"Talk!"* he barked.

"Aight man, look," Teddy sputtered. "I took dem pics in the car dat day when we was puffin' down, yo, right? But I din't sell dem shits to the news and shit, dawg! I swear, man! Dat's my brotha, man!" He was on the verge of tears. Sweat dripped down his temples.

"Why did you take the pictures, and how did they end up on TV?" asked Lyons in a new, terrifyingly gentle tone that did not at all match the considerably vicious weapon in his hand.

"Aight look, man. I got some shit to come clean about, aight? Some shit went down the uvva day dat I ditn't say nuthin' about. Not to any of these cats, aight?"

"What . . . the fuck . . . went down?" asked Lyons again

through clenched teeth, this time squinting his right eye and adjusting his aim on Teddy's head.

"Yo, man! Chill, man!" Teddy waved his hands in front of his face. "I'll tell you, dawg! Look, nigga! My boy Funk Deezy called me up the uvva day, right? Before he got murked. Said, 'Yo, Bizzle, I need a favor, dawg. It ain't big, but I'll hook you up wit some serious chedda,' right? So alls my man wanted me to do was get Wally Mosco outta his crib for a lil while, right? At dat exact time. Said he'd pay me two g's, man! Jes for that, yo! So I was like, 'Shit, nigga! That's cake!' Two g's? I could do dat! And den my man was like, 'Yo, Bizzle, I'll pay you *three more g's* if you can catch a pic of Wally Mosco wit Oral B!' And I was like, 'Yo, *hells yeah, nigga!*' Five g's, yo! That's some serious ducks, man! Right? No harm, no foul! So I got my brothas to go pick him up at his crib at the time Deezy said. We smoked some trees, hung out, I snapped the pics, and that was it, yo! But now all *dis!*" He hung his head, shaking it back and forth histrionically. "I had no *idea,* dawg. I swear! I had no idea what he was up to, man! He musta gave those pics to Jerry Silver or somethin'! I feel real bad and shit now, man!" He looked at Oral B. "I'm sorry, bro, man!" He looked down again, and then the tough guy started to cry. His shoulders wracked. He put a hand up to his head. He mumbled something that sounded like, "I'm so sorry, man. I din know. I din know."

"Put the gun down, Dandy," said Oral B, breaking the near silence. Everyone turned to him now, except Lyons, who kept his Uzi trained on Teddy, his face a statue. "You heard me, Abe?" said Oral B a bit louder, his gun suddenly pointed at Lyons's head. "I said put that shit down, nigga!" Lyons didn't move. I swallowed hard. I was expecting Lyons to pull the trigger at any moment. If he did, Oral B would pull his too, and . . . *shit.*

I braced myself. I looked at Lyons's trigger finger and could swear I saw it start to tug.

"How could you take that picture, Teddy?" Lyons asked. Teddy just looked down and shook his head. "Why did DeAndre

Muskingum want Mr. Moscowitz out of the apartment at that exact time?" asked Lyons quietly, still fingering the trigger. Teddy Bizzle was drenched with sweat.

"I don't know, man! Please, man!"

"Didn't you find it odd? Didn't you think to ask? Didn't you see the problem with photographing your brother and Wally Moscowitz together?" asked Lyons with a sickened edge to his voice, growing louder.

"Yeah, man! It was, man! I did! But it was big loot, man!"

I could see the muscles in Lyons's jaw pulsating, the ones in his hand tensing. "Why did he want Mr. Moscowitz out of that apartment? Tell me! What did he have to gain from that?" I knew that Deezy snuck into my apartment and hung the gun on the string and stole my cash while I was out smoking with Oral B and his brothers, but I didn't think Lyons realized that. I figured that Jerry must have made Deezy believe he was framing me for something else, when in reality he was getting my fingerprints on the gun so that when Jerry killed him, it would look like I'd done it. *And,* once the news got out that Deezy had been banging my girlfriend it would be all the more believable. I'd have a motive. I wondered if he'd planned on killing Sue, too? That certainly would have tied up loose ends . . .

I didn't want to say anything aloud, because all it would have taken was the tiniest little slip of the finger and that Uzi would have sprayed. Teddy's head would've been all over the wall behind him, Lyons's head would've been splattered all over his paperwork, and it would have all been my fault.

"I don't know, man! I swear!" I believed him. But of course, it didn't matter what *I* believed.

"Put the gat down, Dandy!" said Oral B a bit louder, more nervous than before. I thought that even if Oral B were to pull the trigger, the bullets would simply bounce off of Lyons's bulletproof skull. "I luh you, dawg, but you ain't shootin' my brotha, nigga! I can't let you do that, dawg!" said B, his voice shaking in fear.

Lyons inhaled slowly and deeply through his nostrils, sucking a large portion of the oxygen out of the room. I actually felt lightheaded. He slowly turned his head to Oral B, his nose and upper lip quivering in utter disgust. He turned back slowly to Teddy, and that was when he pretty much *lost it*. In one swift, Incredible Hulk–like motion, he flipped over his enormous desk with one hand, startling everyone. He made an inhuman noise that sounded something like *"rahhhhh!"* He took two strides and *kicked* Teddy in the chest (yes—in the chest!), sending him careening across the sawdusty floor like a penguin on ice. He stood over Teddy and pointed the gun back at his head. Then he started screaming. "I should have fired DeAndre Muskingum *months* ago! But I *didn't!* I kept him on only because *he was your friend, Teddy! You begged me! And I listened!*" Spittle flew from his lips, and his face went cherry red. "You *motherfucker!*" He shifted his aim and fired the gun into the exposed pink fiberglass insulation strips behind Teddy. *Badabadabadabadabada*. It was an automatic weapon, so it continued to furiously spit bullets for as long as he held the trigger down. It sounded like a sound effect from a war movie that was being played much too loudly in a very small room. Pink fibers and dust exploded into the air, pieces floating and flying about in clouds of particulate. We all turned and ducked and hid our faces, covering our ears. I hoped a gunfight wasn't about to break out. We'd all be swiss cheese. "And now *this!?*" Lyons screamed. *"Now this fucking piece of shit comes back to bite me in the ass?* And he was connected to *Jerry Fucking Silver?!*" He fired again and again into the poor walls. *Badbadabada. Badabadabadabada.* *"What the fuck is going on with this shit?! Is everyone fucking incompetent?!"* he screamed maniacally. *Badbadabada. Badbadabada.* The Doctor barked frantically. I ducked down low, almost under Lyons's desk. I reached over and pulled the Doctor close to me. I figured it was only a matter of seconds before Lyons went totally cuckoo and shot the whole room up.

But the gun *click-click-clicked*. Empty. Lyons threw it violently onto the floor. I peeked over the edge of the desk. Lyons devoured Teddy with wild eyes, his chest heaving.

"It's all *fucked*," said Lyons quietly. And suddenly, it was like his plug had been pulled. Dejection took over. Lyons looked defeated. "The conference is in a half hour," he said quietly, "and we're *fucked*." A terrible silence filled the room.

"Actually, sir, no, we're not," I said, rising from my hiding spot. *Here goes nuthin'* . . .

All heads turned to me.

"What?" asked Lyons.

"We still have one shot."

"What does that mean?" asked Lyons unenthusiastically.

"A plan, sir. Something I did earlier. I don't know if it worked or not, but there's a good chan—"

"*Spit it out, Moscowitz,*" barked Lyons.

"Oh. 'Kay, see, I have this little problem with my cell phone." I pulled the cracked phone out of my pocket and held it up so everyone could see. "Besides the fact that it's crushed, I mean. It's a piece of shit. See? It's old. Doesn't flip closed, you know? And so what happens is, it always makes inadvertent phone calls while it's in my pocket. 'Cuz if you hold down any of the buttons, it calls the phone number programmed into the speed dial for that button. So like if the 2 button gets pushed, it calls my girlfriend. The 4 button, Jerry. The 5 button calls my house. I do that one all the time. Leaves long messages on my voice mail recording whatever happens to be going on in the room. It sucks. But that's what got me thinking."

I saw Ramona's mouth stretch into a smile.

"Yes?" asked Lyons hopefully, beginning to see where I was going.

"So at Jerry's house before, while Jerry was confessing to everything, I held down the 5 button. Phoned home. And hopefully, if it all worked out, Jerry Silver's full confession is waiting for us on my voice mail."

This glimmer of hope made Lyons rise to his full height. "Well, can you check?" he asked breathlessly.

"Well, that's the only problem," I said. "My cell phone got smashed in our tussle with Jerry, and I don't have the message retrieval number memorized. It was in the address book of my cell phone. The only way to check the message is to call that number, and the only way to get that number is off of a little sticker on the wall next to my phone in my apartment."

He turned to the giants. "Call Detective Schlage," he said. "Tell him to get his ass over to Mr. Moscowitz's apartment. We've got a press conference to get to."

chizapter 30

I was to ride to the press conference with Lyons in the back of a limo-tinted, bullet-proofed Ford Excursion, one of four that showed up outside the storefront a few minutes later to shepherd us all to the conference. As I was about to step into the vehicle, Oral B approached me.

He grabbed my shoulder and spun me around. He stared me right in the eyes, his head slightly tilted back and to the side, his eyes squinted a bit. At a loss for what to say or do to my old friend, I offered him a handshake. He looked down at my extended hand, and shook his head no. "C'mon, B! Let's end this. I've always had your back, and I always will." He slapped my hand down. "Ow!" I said girlishly, snapping my hand back and rubbing it with my other hand. I immediately regretted the femme reaction, but I couldn't help but wring my stinging hand out. He continued to stare at me with deadened eyes. Then, out of nowhere, he bear-hugged me. He squeezed me tighter and tighter.

"I'm sorry, dawg," he said to the side of my head. "I shoulda trusted you, playa."

"That's okay, B. I understand."

"Dat's 'cuz you coo like dat, Mosco. You a good man. *My nigga.*" He slapped my back several times in an effort to make the hug a touch more gangsta.

"Let's go," said Lyons from inside the SUV.

B gave me one last squeeze on the shoulder, and said, "Aight? Let's do da damn thang."

"Thanks, B," I said, and we bumped fists.

"We right behind you," he said, meaning he'd be in the next car, but I like to think he meant it in a deeper sense, too. I stepped into the truck.

Ramona and Murray and the Doctor joined Lyons and me in our vehicle, and they sat together in the row behind us. A few moments later, piled into several identical, chauffeur-driven SUVs and hearts thumping, we headed for Santa Monica.

....

Lyons called Detective Schlage to make sure he knew exactly what to do. He'd have to break into my apartment (apparently not a difficult feat), get the number, check the message, and then if my plan had worked, record the message onto a tape recorder or something. Their phone call was brief. When he was done with Schlage, he turned to me, a different man than the one I'd always known. This Abraham Lyons had lost his trademark unflappable coolness. This was an Abraham Lyons on borrowed time. "Goddamn, I hope this works, Moscowitz."

A minute later he started outlining our game plan for the conference. Lyons felt that once the world heard our story, all the other pieces would fall into place. We just needed to be confident. Act as if we had Jerry's confession on tape, even if we weren't sure that we did. He thought that if we could explain to the world what Jerry Silver had done, just as I'd explained it to him earlier, we'd be exonerated. Hopefully, the cops wouldn't arrest me before we had our chance to plead our case. "Am I going to be speaking? Or are you going to explain it all?" I asked.

"I'm going to explain everything, but it's very important that you be up there. I'll probably have you answer some questions at the end." His phone rang. He answered it, and looked out the window as he spoke to whoever was calling.

I hoped with all my heart that I wouldn't have to say a word at the conference. *The whole world will be watching,* I thought. *Everyone is depending on you,* and I started to bite my nails again.

Ramona leaned over the seat behind me, and, as if she'd read my mind, whispered into my ear. "You're gonna be *great.*"

I turned around to look her in the eyes. I gave her a kiss on the lips. I smiled and turned back around to resume working myself into a nervous frenzy.

....

Lyons had been silent for a minute, his eyes closed. I figured he was putting his game face on. Getting into character. We could've all used a little of the old Lyons right then. "Here we go," he suddenly said, as we pulled up to the makeshift staging area that had been constructed outside of the Godz-Illa Records building. The place was absolutely *swarmed.* Media vans lined the street for three blocks in both directions as we approached. Reporters and fans and curious bystanders and police officers covered the sidewalks, gawking at the caravan of SUVs that cut through the crowds. Cameras flashed and people behind blue police sawhorses banged on the SUVs as we passed. I was in awe—I'd never seen such a circus in my life. *What would every- one do if they knew that the mysterious Wally was in the car with Lyons right now?!* Lyons pulled out his cell phone and called Detective Schlage. "You there yet? Hurry. We're already late." He hung up. "Schlage isn't at your apartment yet," he said, the nerves gone from his voice now, his signature cool back in place. "Steve, how long can we wait before we start this thing?" Lyons asked a grim man in a suit and tie and sunglasses who was sit- ting in the last row of the SUV, looking at a hand-held computer.

"We were supposed to have started ten minutes ago, Mr. Lyons."

As we got closer, I could see the sizeable stage that was set up for us outside the building. I could see the wooden podium, the broccoli-like bunching of microphones, the large, roped-off pit of folding chairs. Just below the stage, hundreds of cameras were pointed upward, and a gang of reporters stood and sat and moved about like corralled sheep, ready to take notes and fire questions. *Holy crap,* I thought. *A few days ago I could have disappeared off the face of the earth and I doubt that anyone would have noticed. Now this . . .*

The screaming and banging of the fans was deafening as we pulled to a stop at our disembarking point. I looked out the window at the thousands of angry, curious, excited faces. *This is it,* I thought.

....

"Listen, when we get out, I need y'all to stay close and stay low," said the big, black, bald bodyguard sitting shotgun. "These crowds are incredibly strong. We'll have some very big dudes all around us, but stay tight and low until we reach the stage. Okay?"

"Yes, sir," I said. I was paralyzed with fear. I was sure I was going to vomit. I began to sweat. *There is a legitimate chance I'm going to have a heart attack right now,* I thought. Lyons must have sensed my terror, because he put his hand on my shoulder. "Don't be nervous. Don't worry about what happens with Schlage. You're going to be fine, okay? You're my ace in the hole. Remember that."

"Okay. Yes, sir."

Lyons checked his cell phone, probably to see if Schlage had called yet, and then turned to the guy in the backseat. "How much longer can we wait?" he asked.

The guy shook his head.

Lyons turned to us. "All right, ready?" he asked. "Good luck." He nodded and, before we could respond with a "You, too," he stepped out of the car to be swallowed up by a tidal wave of screams and shouts and flashbulbs. I took a deep breath, grabbed Ramona's hand, and dove in.

....

It was like being eaten alive by a whale. We moved through its digestive tract like bits of flotsam on a very loud, throbbing current and were spit out unharmed into the light of the stage just a few moments later. I saw Lyons, Oral B, Murray, and Ramona onstage, as well as a few suited lawyers and other assorted handlers. All I could think was, *Don't look at the crowd. Don't look at the crowd.* As soon as I sat down on my appointed chair, the first thing I did was look at the crowd. And all I can say about that is, *holy fucking shit.*

From this vantage point, it looked like the Staples Center had emptied out after a play-off game onto this very sidewalk. I couldn't believe all the media attention the story was getting. *Must be an otherwise slow news day,* I thought. *On the other hand, it's not like Oral B is just a local celebrity. He's an international superstar.*

I noticed that the Santa Monica Police had closed the street in front of the building on both sides of the block, but that hundreds of people had flooded in when they opened the barriers to allow our cars in. Now they had to get all of those people back outside the barriers before the conference would commence. This delay was good. Maybe Schlage could get back to us with some good news before we began.

What I hadn't immediately noticed, in my state of shock and fear, was that the crowd directly below us had quieted significantly upon my arrival on the stage. I scanned the stunned faces below us. They were looking, every last one of them, at *me.*

The deafening roar of the crowd soon turned to a quieter, urgent buzz, then to murmuring, then to whispers, and finally, as Lyons approached the pedestal with his lawyer, near silence. *I guess we're starting,* I thought, my foot tapping rapidly.

Lyons's attorney, a sharply dressed older gentleman who looked like a Jewish Kenny Rogers, stepped up to the podium. The crowd waited with bated breath. "Ladies and gentlemen, thank you all for coming today. My name is Marc Levine. I am the lead attorney for Godz-Illa Records. As you all know, my clients, Abraham Lyons and Brandunn Bell—whom you all may know better as Oral B"—a cheer went up from somewhere in the crowd, greeted immediately by some boos, followed by a whole bunch of shushes—"stand before you accused of some very serious allegations. We are here today to address these ridiculous claims to the public, to the media, and most important to my clients, to their fans. And so, without further delay, I give you Mr. Abraham Lyons." The crowd clapped politely—those who felt obligated to, anyway. Most did nothing but watch the magnetic, impeccably stylish, stone-faced icon make his way to the microphone. Cameras clicked and whirred and flashed and buzzed.

He stood at the podium, stoic, scrutinizing the crowd. "Ladies and gentlemen of the press, our loyal fans, and everybody watching around the world, good evening," he said with a small, dignified bow. "I am here tonight to speak on behalf of myself, on behalf of my organization, on behalf of the most talented rap artist in the game today—Mr. Brandunn Bell—and on behalf of several other people, whom I will have the great honor to introduce to you shortly. Let me start by saying that the allegations made against us in the past days are preposterous, patently offensive, blasphemous, and absolutely, positively, categorically *false*. Let me repeat that for the cameras." He looked down directly into the lenses below. "Any and all charges made against my company, myself, and specifically against the name and career of our most talented, successful artist, Oral B, are absolutely *false*. And you journalists can underline that and print it in bold capital letters." The cameras clicked and whirred. There were some shouts from somewhere in the crowd, but I couldn't hear what they were saying.

"Yesterday was a sad day for the hip-hop community. The integrity of one of our greatest achievers has been challenged. This story is wildly *absurd*. Oral B is the *real thing*. His music is rich with grit and anguish and a truth that comes only from experience. He writes about his rough childhood. Growing up in the ghetto. Conquering his many obstacles to become a rich, successful superstar. This sort of thing cannot be faked, my friends. You cannot *grow* this sort of talent in a lab. This is the genuine article. This is his *life*." Dramatic pause.

I wasn't one hundred percent sure, but I could've sworn I heard someone in the far reaches of the crowd yell out *"Bullshit!"* Lyons didn't seem to hear it.

"*But,* folks, as wild and ridiculous as these accusations are, you have yet to learn the most disturbing part of it all: These absurd claims are but a small piece of a greater story. A blackmailing scandal of epic proportions. All perpetrated by one gentleman—if you can call him that—a man whom I would confidently characterize as a criminal mastermind, if I didn't think that this label would please him so much. This . . . *snake* . . . has been planting and harvesting roots of evil and corruption, of coercion and blackmail, of manipulation and entrapment for *years* in this town. Unabated. And it all led up to this. This was to be his big payoff. His magnum opus." Dramatic pause. And there it was again. A faraway heckler shouting something that sounded an awful lot like *"Bullshit!"* Again, Lyons seemed unfazed. "The man I am speaking of goes by the name of Jerry Silver. Mr. Silver is a Hollywood agent who is relatively unknown throughout Los Angeles, but who has managed to carve out a semi-decent living for himself by blackmailing his poor, determined clientele. This man is a true puppeteer. Using some of his client pool as his marionettes, he attempted over the last week to extort me and my company out of *ten . . . million . . . dollars,* using the threat that he would go public with this fictitious scandal that he felt, true or not, would ruin the career of Oral B and bring down the fine reputation of Godz-Illa Records." Lyons shook his head, and the crowd buzzed as it digested this new information. Now I was certain I heard more than one person shouting from the crowd somewhere. I still couldn't tell what they were saying. Lyons continued. "Folks, Jerry Silver almost got away with this scandal. But we figured it out before it was too late." I couldn't tell if Lyons was winning the audience over, or if the heckler(s) had started to gain a foothold in the general consciousness of the crowd and it was beginning to get to him, but whatever it was, I could sense something stirring in the audience.

"This shyster orchestrated quite a tangled symphony of lies and threats and confusion," Lyons continued. "Frankly, the entire picture has not been fully formed for us yet. We don't know the full extent of this villain's plotting. But we know enough." He let it all sink in, pausing again to collect his thoughts. The crowd murmured.

"Ladies and gentlemen—it ends here. *Tonight*. Fortunately for me, I am not alone in this situation. There is a long list of Jerry Silver's clients-slash-victims who've been used and abused. Three of these victims are sitting right behind me here on this stage tonight." He made a small gesture toward me, Ramona, and Murray. "These people were played by Mr. Silver as mere instruments in his grand ensemble, designed to extort yours truly out of ten million dollars. And they were abused terribly in this process. One of the people sitting behind me is a man whose name has been dragged through the mud since it was released to the media just over twenty-four hours ago. A bright young man whose life has been altered irreversibly by no choice or fault of his own. He has been accused of being a ghostwriter for Oral B. A ridiculous lie! But far worse, he has been falsely accused of murder. The police are hunting him down for a crime he did not commit. I'm sure you are all quite surprised to see him up on this stage with us today. That's right, people: *He is on our side*. Despite what the media may have made you think, we are both victims here!" He paused again, and in his silence, a new sound arose, a sort of low chanting coming from somewhere far back in the huge crowd. Lyons paused, seemingly trying to hear what they were saying. *Are they saying my name? Oh man!* Heads at the front of the crowd started to turn toward the chanting, as it floated louder and closer to us. I leaned over slightly to try to hear more clearly. It sounded like: "Uuuuuuuuuhhhh-ihhhhhh." *Waaaaaaalllllllllllllllllly? Are they chanting 'Wally?'* "Uuuuuuu-uuuuuuuhhhhhhllll-iiiiiiiiiiiiihhhhhhhhhh, Uuuuuuuuuuuuuuuh-hhhhlllliiiiiiiiiiiiihhhhhhhhhh." *I think they're chanting my name!* I instinctively rose out of my seat.

But then, in one succinct gust, the chant floated to my ears, and the words were crystal clear. The crowd was united in one nasty concurrence.

They were chanting, "Bullshit."

....

All at once it was clear. Lyons was bombing.

The crowd seemed to have turned against him, as more and more people joined the "bullshit" chant now. It was growing louder and louder and clearer and clearer by the second. It sounded like we were at a ballgame and the ref just made a terrible call, igniting the ire of the crowd. Lyons no longer had command over the spectators. The calm and order of the conference was unraveling into turmoil. Reporters were suddenly shouting questions now at Lyons. People in the crowd were yelling all sorts of things. Some supportive, I thought, but it was difficult to distinguish exactly what anyone was saying over the commotion.

But worst of all, because I'd thought they'd been chanting my name, I'd risen from my seat. Now I was standing awkwardly on the stage, unsure of what to do next. Lyons couldn't help but be unsettled now by the crowd's reaction. He turned around and looked at me, his eyes pleading for me to rescue him. We locked eyes, and he nodded. *Oh my God oh my God oh my God. He wants me to speak.* He turned back to the crowd.

"People! People! Please!" Lyons yelled into the microphones. "It's time to introduce the man you've all been waiting to hear from!" The cacophony died down just a bit, just enough so that everyone could hear him say, *"Mr. Wally Moscowitz!"*

With the mention of my name, the crowd fell almost silent. There was no more chanting. No more yelling. There were only the cameras. Hundreds and hundreds of cameras. Shutters opening and closing. Whirring and clicking and flashing and buzzing. I was frozen where I stood. I couldn't will my legs to move. Every terrible thing that had happened in the past few days had led up to this very moment. It was going to be up to me to convince the entire world. I couldn't do it.

I swear I was going to turn around and just *go.* Run. Leave the stage. Face whatever music I had to face. I couldn't handle this mess anymore. And just at that moment, at the very second I was going to give up, something popped into my brain. Something a wise man once told me. "Whenever Ling-Ling in difficult situation, I aaaaalways remember something my father told me. 'You can only go halfway into a dark forest; then you are coming out the other side.' "

I took a step toward the podium.

....

Just as I took my first step, I noticed some movement near the right side of the stage. I turned to see approximately ten police officers shoving their way up to the front. They made it to the very edge of the stage, stopped, and spread out, lining the entire side of the platform. An identical line of officers covered the left side of the dais also, blocking my exit there as well. They all eyed me like hungry wolves. *They're here to arrest me,* I realized. *It's over.*

....

I kept moving forward. I stepped up to the mass of microphones and looked out at the layers of crowd before me: the security guards, the cameramen and -women, the photographers, the reporters with tape recorders and pads and pencils, the police, the fans, and finally the swarms and swarms of people flowing almost endlessly into the distance. All eyes on me. I took a deep breath and exhaled, which the microphones picked up as a loud burst of static. "Sorry," I said. "Sorry." I shook my head, embarrassed at my amateurish mistake. I glanced back at Ramona, and she smiled and winked. I turned back to the crowd. *Time to do da damn thang.*

I launched into it. I told my story. Exactly how Lyons wanted them to hear it. I told them all about how I was taken advantage of by Jerry Silver. How he'd done the same thing to Murray and Ramona and who knows who else. Told them about the ransom notes. About my dognapped dog. About Sue and how I was framed for Deezy's murder. I told them (almost) everything (no mention of the fact that I really *was* Oral B's ghostwriter, of course). I did my absolute best to make them care, make them feel my pain. Understand what I'd been through.

At some point during my speech, I realized that not only were the police allowing me to speak before they arrested me, but I seemed to have the rapt attention of the crowd. *It's working!* I thought. *They believe me!* And just as I was nearing the end of my speech, feeling victorious, I felt a hand on my shoulder.

I was pulled back slightly from the podium. I was sure it was the police and that I was about to be whisked off to jail somewhere. This was the end. I winced and prepared for the cuffs.

chizapter 31

It was Lyons. He whispered something to me. I smiled. "I'd like to introduce one more speaker, if you'll allow me," I said to the crowd. "The most important speaker of the night. Detective Barnaby Schlage of the Los Angeles Police Department." I turned to see Detective Schlage striding toward me from just off-stage, a small smile peeking out from his bushy mustache. My heart soared. He gave my shoulder a gracious squeeze and stepped to the microphone.

"Thank you," Detective Schlage said to us. He turned to the crowd and unfolded a piece of paper on the podium in front of him. "Ladies and gentlemen. At six thirty-six this evening, Mr. Jerry Silver was arrested and charged with the murder of Mr. DeAndre Muskingum of South Central Los Angeles."

A collective gasp rang out on the stage and in the crowd. There was even some cheering and applause.

He held up his tape recorder. "This tape recorder contains a full confession by Mr. Silver to the murder of DeAndre Muskingum, as well as a full confession in regards to the blackmailing attempt on Mr. Lyons and Godz-Illa Records, including Mr. Wally Moscowitz. Mr. Silver has signed an affidavit that states that the conversation recorded on this tape is indeed authentic, and he was escorted without protest to the Santa Monica Courthouse where he was arraigned on all charges. In light of Mr. Silver's full confession, the arrest warrant issued for Mr. Wally

Moscowitz has been terminated. I have nothing further. Thank you." Detective Schlage quickly backed away from the microphone and exited the staging area, escorted by uniformed officers. The media shouted at him hungrily as he departed.

The greatest press conference in the history of the world was over.

Lyons stepped back up to the microphone. "Thank you all for coming out. God bless!" he shouted over the rowdy buzzing below. He gave a quick wave to the frenzied crowd and moved toward the stairs. We all followed, feeling like liberated men.

....

As we all stepped off the stage, Lyons motioned for a few of us to follow him. I followed him, basically carrying Ramona, who couldn't stop hugging me. Murray and Oral B followed us, too. We entered the building, and he escorted us into a private office on the ground floor. When all of us were in the room, he turned and gently closed the door behind us. Part of me thought he was gonna turn around and whoop and jump for joy. But Lyons just doesn't do that. He finally turned and said, "Thank you all. You did a terrific job today. You saved my company out there, and probably B's career, and it won't be forgotten. I want to make it up to all of you. Call my office on Monday morning, each of you, and schedule appointments." He looked at me directly in the eyes. I wasn't scared anymore. "Especially you, Mr. Moscowitz." For the first time, he smiled. We all did. He bowed venerably, turned and opened the door, and he was gone.

And just like that, my ordeal was over.

epilogue

Wouldn't it be darling if I told you that two years later I'm happily married to Ramona and we have one-year-old twin boys and three bulldogs and we live happily-ever-after on a Caribbean island and all we do all day is drink icy, pineapple-flavored cocktails and frolic on the beach as the sun sets in a fiery orange ball behind us?

That *would* be just fucking adorable. I love a happy ending just as much as the next guy. But that's not what I'm going to tell you.

Over the next few weeks Jerry Silver became a household name. Unfortunately, his arrest didn't shut him up. He started yapping the minute he could get in front of a camera. He was in prison, but don't let that fool you. He was loving every minute of his newfound celebrity. He quickly became the guy Leno was cracking stupid jokes about every night—the most famous criminal in the country. He sold the rights to his story to a movie studio for a reported seven figures, and he got a book deal with one of the big publishing houses for an undisclosed amount said to be in the million-dollar range. As much as it pains me to say it, I can't blame them, really. It's a pretty wild story about a pretty compelling character.

The details, which he clarified to the authorities, were pretty much on point with all that I'd surmised. He'd been making a remarkable living for years and years by extorting and embezzling and blackmailing money out of his various clientele. Turned out that he and DeAndre "Funk Deezy" Muskingum had in fact been planning to go after Abraham Lyons for quite some time, they'd just been waiting for the ideal moment to strike.

Jerry described Deezy as a stupid, greedy man who wanted to get rich at any cost and had no qualms about taking out anyone who might have gotten in his way. In this regard their philosophies were perfectly in line. Jerry revealed how he used Deezy as a pawn throughout the whole implementation, making him do all the dirty work (e.g., planting the ransom notes at Blockbuster, rigging the gun at my house), so that any potential witnesses would point to Deezy as the perpetrator, should they get busted. Just as I'd thought, Jerry made Deezy believe that he was planting the gun in my house to protect himself. That when Deezy showed up missing (having actually just fled town with Sue and with Lyons's money—or so he thought), they would find a gun with my prints on it, and maybe some blood and signs of a struggle at Deezy's place. People would believe that I killed him, ensuring Deezy's safe escape with his share of Lyons's money and my woman. That was the story he sold to Deezy anyway. Jerry's actual plan was to kill Deezy and Sue and frame me for their murders and then escape with all of Lyons's money for himself. Sue never turned up after that day I'd gone to her apartment to find the Doctor, so maybe death by Jerry Silver would have been a better fate than whatever may have befallen her. I try not to think about it.

Jerry claims that he always foresaw the big moneymaking opportunities he'd have by selling his story from behind bars, and that this was his final brilliant backup plan. Honestly, I can't wait to see Jerry's movie. I wonder who they'll get to play me. I hope no one too fat.

The most shocking part of all of Jerry's incessant blabbing to the media was that after he'd taken such advantage of me over the years, after all that he'd tried to do to ruin my life, he actually threw me a bone at the very end. I'm not sure why, but he told the media that I had nothing to do with writing Oral B's lyrics, that he'd indeed fabricated the whole story. I'm sure Jerry had some ulterior motive—maybe it made him look like a more brilliantly devious architect—but regardless, in the end, he helped us bury our secret for good.

After the media frenzy that was set off by the press conference, Oral B became even more of a hot commodity than ever before. He was the most sought-after celebrity in the entire entertainment world. He and Lyons graced the cover of every magazine on the newsstands. They did the talk show circuit. Like Jerry Silver, Oral B went on to sign lucrative movie and book deals. His album *Don't Make Me Kill You, Beeyatch,* has become the highest-selling rap album of all time. When his new album, *I'll Still F Yo Ass Up, Sucka,* hit the stores a few months after the controversy, it was one of the most highly anticipated albums to come out in years. I didn't write a single word of it.

After meeting that Monday morning, Lyons hired Murray, Kevin, and Lou as full-time bodyguards. They enjoy their roles as tough guys, they get paid well, and Lyons says he enjoys having "goodfellas" around.

Ramona and I spent the next few months getting to know each other. It was wonderful for the first few weeks, really truly wonderful. But the honeymoon period wore off pretty quickly. Turns out, the girl is certifiably fucking nuts. Every day, everywhere we went, she thought that everyone was laughing at her, whispering about her when she passed, pointing and giggling when she entered the room. The truth is, that rarely happened. I lived every day just praying that nobody would call her "Herpes Girl" within her earshot. The one or two times it *did* actually happen were devastating for her. She was inconsolable for days. I tried to help her accept this immutable title and move on, but she just couldn't do it. It consumed her. Plus, I think after the first few weeks together, my cute-dork appeal wore off for her.

I soon realized that Ramona and I didn't even really know each other. The absolute craziness of the situation that we'd gone through together—the intensity—made us believe we were in love when we really weren't. I believe the French call it *folie à deux*. Exactly one month after the press conference, I found a Dear Wally note stuck to my bathroom mirror with a glob of toothpaste. That was the last I heard from Ramona "the Herpes Girl" Maltratado. Sometimes when I'm watching *The Price Is Right* I hope I'll see her strolling across my screen in a field of wildflowers, but I think they finally yanked that stupid commercial.

The day after the press conference, I contacted Bionic Books to sort out my book deal. Luckily for me, Gary Carter and Howard Johnson made it *utterly* clear that after the controversy, they wanted nothing to do with either myself or Jerry Silver. They were actually so desperate to hush us up about ever having been connected with them, that they told me to keep the almost sixty thousand dollars that they'd paid to Jerry for my advance. I've never seen a penny of that money—I'm sure Jerry had it in an offshore account somewhere with other money he'd scammed over the years—but I didn't care. I was just relieved to have my books back.

I met with Abraham Lyons late that Monday afternoon after he'd finished meeting with everyone else. He offered me a very generous severance deal, which included a retroactive royalty on every Oral B song I'd ever written. It was a package worth almost a million dollars.

"We have to end this affair once and for all," Lyons said.

And that's what we did.

I went back to my boring, jobless, womanless, now-slightly-less-mediocre existence. I spent most of the next few months hanging out with my dog, making up for lost time. We ate a lot of pizza and watched a lot of *The Price Is Right*. I bought myself a new car and some expensive electronics. Truth be told, there were moments when I missed my old life. I mean, despite the thankless nature of my job, the shitty money arrangement, and the constant disrespect, I guess I always took a certain private pride in what I did. I was the wizard behind the curtain, and even if almost no one knew it, this knowledge was sacred and invaluable to me. My meeting with Lyons marked the end of a major chapter in my life story. I decided the best thing to do was to accept it for what it was and move on.

Of course, life is never as simple as that.

A funny thing happened to Oral B and Godz-Illa Records in the months that followed the controversy. They flamed up real bright at first, with big sales and lots of media attention. But then began a slow, fateful fizzle. B's new album came out, and shockingly, it was met with less-than-stellar reviews. The sales were big the first week, purely because of the controversy, but plunged steadily from there. Only one song (out of twenty-one) on the entire album became a single, and even that was pretty weak (it was called "Suck Nizzuts, Fat Slizzuts"). I bought the album for loyalty's sake, and frankly, it was pitiful.

About six months after all the controversy had passed, on a Wednesday afternoon in June, I sat on my very plush, very comfortable new couch watching my very large new plasma television and sharing a very delicious bowl of popcorn with my very fat dog, Dr. Barry Schwartzman, when there was a knock on my door. *Fucking Pardeep,* I thought. *What the hell does he want now?* "Yeah? Hello?" I shouted, twisting my neck to look at the door, wanting *so* badly not to have to get up and wishing for the billionth time in my life that I could open the door using my mind and a simple wave of the hand, Jedi-style. There was no reply from the other side of the door, and as usual, the Jedi hand wave had no effect. "Helloooo?" I asked again.

Nothing.

I rose and hobbled over to the door. "Who is it?" I asked again. The visitor responded with another brief *rat-a-tat-tat.* "No speaky the Englase?" I asked as I yanked open the door, immediately regretting my mocking tone.

It was the two giants.

"Ohhh, hey, fellas! Long time no see! You're not going to beat the shit out of me this time, are you?" I asked, only half kidding.

"Naw, man," said the Samoan Giant with a sheepish smile. "Mr. Lyons wants to see you."

"R-really? Why?"

"Don't know, man," said the White Giant, as both men stole peeks into my messy apartment, probably roused by the sounds of my incredibly freakin' awesome new surround-sound system.

"Ummm, okay, I've just got some things to, uh . . . how 'bout I drive over there in about a half hour?" I had no idea what Lyons could want, but I wanted to shower up and look presentable.

"Coo," said the Samoan Giant. "Half hour. We'll tell him to expect you. Back entrance."

Exactly thirty-two minutes later, Dr. Schwartzman and I stepped out of our car and handed the keys to the eager young valet out in back of Godz-Illa Records. The whole way over, I pondered this summons. I was a much different Wally than the one who'd arrived at this very door six months ago. I had a little money, a little confidence, and, really, no major worries.

Until now.

I stepped into the elevator, those old familiar nerves revving, and up toward the scariest man in town. Again.

....

"Mr. Wally Moscowitz," said Lyons quietly from his desk in the corner of the cool, dark office. I thought I detected the tiniest trace of the tiniest smile beneath his tough exterior. "Welcome back. Have a seat." I shuffled over toward him and sat down in the waiting chair on the other side of his desk. He looked at me across the acres of oak and said nothing. Abraham Lyons doesn't waste time with such trivialities as "How's life?" or "What's been doin'?" He gets down to business. He's nothing if not pithy.

After a moment of hushed staring, he simply said, "We want you back."

....

"Wh-what?"

"We *need* you back, Wally." I noticed that he'd called me "Wally." He *never* calls me "Wally."

"Are you . . . ? You serious?" I asked. *What the fuck is going on here?*

"Have you ever heard me make a joke before?"

"But Mr. Lyons—"

"Wally, listen. Sales have been wretched. The magic is gone. We need you back. Simple as that."

I looked around the office. "I don't know, Mr. Lyons. What if—"

"No *what-ifs*. You and I will be the *only* ones who know this time. We won't even tell Oral B. You write the songs, you give them directly to me. I give them to B. *That's it.* Zero risk."

"I just don't know, Mr. Lyons—"

"I'll pay you *double* the normal rate."

"It's not about the money. I just don't think I want to *do* it anymore."

Lyons looked down into his lap and shook his head. "What *do* you want to do, Mr. Moscowitz?" *We're back to Mr. Moscowitz now.*

What do I want to do? A fair question. A reasonable question. I certainly didn't want to sit around in my apartment for the rest of my life. I wanted *something*. I'd always wanted something. And that wasn't gone. I still wanted it.

"I want to publish my books, sir."

"Tell me about these books."

I told Lyons all about them. I pitched my little bacon grease–soaked heart out. Pitched like I'd never pitched before. I was (I thought) concise, charming, funny, and passionate. When I was done, Lyons curled his purplish bottom lip over his top one and nodded slowly.

"So, they rhyme, these books?" he finally asked.

"Yes, sir."

"They sound familiar. Have I read them before?"

"Yes, sir. Some of them. I used them as my original writing sample when I applied for the job here over ten years ago."

"Yes, I thought so. You know, they sound like little rap songs to me."

"Well . . . kind of, sir, yeah. I guess so."

"But more like nursery rhymes," he said.

"Right."

"Like Mother Goose," he added.

"But naughty," I said.

"But naughty." He nodded a bit harder, smiling now. "And written by a man, not an old lady. That would make you . . . *Father* Goose, huh?" he said, enjoying himself.

I was enjoying myself now, too. It felt like he was genuinely interested. "Yeah! I like that! Father Goose."

"Or! Even better: The Goosefather!" he said, slapping his hand on the desk.

"Haha! The Goosefather!" I said.

"I like this, Mr. Moscowitz. You know, I've published books before under the Godz-Illa name."

"You have?"

"Oh yes. Godz-Illa Publishing has several books in print. Biographies of our artists and such."

"Oh, wow!" I said, heart thumping with anticipation.

"And now, it looks like we're about to have a few more," he said, looking me right in the eye and rising from his chair.

"Wait—really?" I asked incredulously.

"You scratch my back, I'll scratch yours," he said.

I was awestruck. Flabbergasted.

"Do we have a deal, Mr. Moscowitz?"

"You better believe it!" I said.

He extended his hand, and we shook. "Welcome to Godz-Illa Publishing, Goosefather," he said.

And just like that, I was officially an author.

Since that meeting, I've been working feverishly on every aspect of the books with a new fervor: illustrations, cover art, marketing, the whole nine yards. I have complete creative control in executing my vision. Mr. Lyons assures me the books will be published in time for Christmas, and he expects them to be a big hit.

Which brings me back to where I started at the very beginning of all of this: My life is a never-ending game of Duck Duck Goose. But now, at long last, I'm the Goose. I got my tap on the head. Now watch me run.

COCAINE IS BAD, JUST ASK DADDY
By Wally Moscowitz, aka THE GOOSEFATHER

Mommy's friend Charlene is a crazy lady.
I think she's funny, but Dad says she's shady.

In and out of the bathroom she goes,
And then she comes out, always rubbing her nose.

I got really curious where she kept goin',
So I peered through the door, and I thought it was snowin',
'Cuz Charlene had white powder all over the sink.
Up and down went her credit card, klink klink klink—klink klink klink.

I pushed open the door, gave her arm a lil poke,
She said, "Hey, little buddy, I didn't know you did coke!"

I said, "It looks like the powder that I put on my tush,"
She said, "This ain't baby powder, honey, just ask President Bush."

Then she leaned down with a straw and sucked a line up her nose!
I couldn't believe it!
She said "Ahhhh . . . up it goes!"

And I looked at the table and then back to her face,
I asked, could I try? She responded, "Sure, Ace!"
So I grabbed the little straw and got ready to snort,
But before I could, I was quickly cut short,

When in burst my dad, his eyes all aflame,
He grabbed Charlene by her wiry frame.
He screamed and he shook her and he threw her out,
And at that point I knew without any doubt:

Cocaine is bad, my dad's no chump.
But while he was screaming,
I still took a bump.

—From *The Adult Children's Books Collection*

acknowledgments

I don't own a desk. I wrote this entire book while sitting atop my bed, back against the headboard, taking the term "laptop computer" perhaps a bit too literally. I'd like to thank the good people at Simmons Beautyrest for making this as comfortable as possible and also my chiropractor for helping to mend the probably irreparable damage. Hopefully after this I'll be able to afford a desk.

So many people helped whip *Duck Duck Wally* into shape. I'd like to extend extraspecial gratitude to my initial readers: Bree Abel, Steve Rotter, Jordan Young, Coulter Mcabery, Greg Walter, Mike Davis, and Kristin Haines. Your notes may have made me cry myself to sleep at night, but they were always honest, keen, and on point, and they made the book oh-so-much better. Later, but no less valuable, note-givers were: Karyn Rotter, Emily Rotter, Julie Rotter, Lewis and Lynar Abel, Toby Levine, Marc Stenzler, Ben Lerer, Pete Sununu, Christine Alvarez, Jared Greenbaum, and Doug Finkel.

Thank you to my kick-ass agent, Jud Laghi at LJK Literary Management for believing in me and in Wally, and for restoring my belief that good agents *do* exist. Thank you to my amazing film agent, Shari Smiley at CAA, for confirming and augmenting this belief.

Simon & Schuster rocks my world. Before this process began, I could never have imagined that I'd have the good fortune to work with so many talented and supportive people. This has been an outstanding experience, and for that I owe thanks to Aileen Boyle, Victoria Meyer, Alexis Welby, Jackie Seow, Jonathan Evans, Tony Newfield, Ben Holmes, and Ellen Sasahara.

Many warm thanks to the oracle, Mr. David Rosenthal of Simon & Schuster, for being so much cooler and more down-to-earth than I ever would have expected a man of his prominence to be. He took a chance on Wally and has backed it 110 percent, and for that I am grateful.

Finally, thank you thank you thank you to the-woman-for-whom-there-are-not-enough-glowing-adjectives-to-describe, my editor, Ms. Kerri Kolen of Simon & Schuster. Kerri was a tireless advocate for Wally since the very first read, and I am blessed to have her on my side. Kerri, I was constantly blown away by your shrewd insight and editorial ingenuity. You are one smart cookie. I thank you, and Wally thanks you.